To Elsa
Merry

from

Mam + Dad

7

PALACE

Voyager

PALACE

A NOVEL OF THE PINCH

Katherine Kerr &
Mark Kreighbaum

HarperCollins*Publishers*

Voyager
An Imprint of HarperCollins*Publishers*
77–85 Fulham Palace Road,
Hammersmith, London W6 8JB

Published by HarperCollins*Publishers* 1996
1 3 5 7 9 8 6 4 2

A catalogue record for this book
is available from the British Library

ISBN 0 00 224642 2 HB
0 00 224643 0 TPB

Set in Janson by
Rowland Phototypesetting Limited
Bury St Edmunds, Suffolk

Printed and bound in Great Britain by
Caledonian International Book Manufacturing Ltd, Glasgow

For Tad Williams
for all kinds of reasons

AUTHORS' NOTE

We wanted to make clear that what you have in this book is a very old-fashioned collaboration. Trends in writing come and go, and these days the word 'collaboration' often means that one writer, usually the better known, writes a detailed outline, from which the second writer produces the book. Not so here – both of us worked on developing the concepts of the book, the world, the characters, the plot, and so on, and both of us did a share of the actual writing.

Katharine Kerr
Mark Kreighbaum

PROLOGUE

He stood where he liked standing, alone on the edge of the crowd and watching, above the crowd, too, on a ramp halfway up and curling round the dome of the Spaceport terminal. Checking tickets, carrying luggage, herding children, sapients rushed past in both directions, but no-one more than glanced his way. He was hidden in plain sight by his clothes, the finely tailored but utterly undistinguished suit of a merchant. Pale soft shirt, grey short-tunic, and a slashed kilt of the same grey – human trousers, graceless wear for a stub-ugly species, did you no good when you carried a tail, even a short stump of one like his. In one hand he held a sample case, splashed with colour and the name of an importing firm. Inside lay jewellery, artificial amber from the planet of Souk, opals from Kephalon, providing him with both a cover story and money to live while he got his real job done.

He leaned on the railing of the ramp and looked down at the swarming terminal, where sapients of half a dozen races milled around or squabbled over the scanty seating. He heard the crowd as a roar and babble, half a dozen languages mixed with the flat tones of Gen, the official trade-talk of that region of the galaxy known as the Pinch. Over it all a booming noise sounded, as if a thunderstorm were gathering under the forcedome far above. He could see the source of the booms: hundreds of saccules, the short and pouchy native race of Palace, scurried and dodged through the crowd. Dressed in simple shifts, as if they were children ready for bed, they carried luggage, offered refreshments, cleared paths for their human masters, while they boomed and squealed and did their best to mimic real speech with the throat sacs and pouches clustering round their eating mouths. Their odour reached him as well, even up as high as he stood. The saccules gave off a smell-babble of scents that had earned them their nickname, Stinkers.

In his mind, though, the real stench came from the humans who swarmed thick below, all soft and somehow pulpy with their pale tan or dark brown skins stretched over fat and flesh. His own race glittered with grey-green scales, smooth and hard and pure, not tufted with dirty hair or clotted with the stuff, hanging limp from round skulls. Unclean – he stopped himself from spitting on the ramp just in time. He was here for vengeance, after all. He could follow their ugly little customs and courtesies as part of the game.

He'd have his revenge, that is, provided he could get past the autogates that led from the terminal into the city. Although his view was partially obscured by a bank of vidscreens displaying a constant barrage of news footage, from his distance the gates looked deceptively simple, a pair of featureless vertical rods a few yards high and set about five feet apart, but each one contained a sophisticated array of scanners, all tuned to different frequencies, as well as password protected, encrypted, and monitored round the clock by highly trained customs agents. No-one but a fool would try and pass through them with contraband or weapons. His prospective employer had promised him safe passage so long as he carried the photonic token he'd been given, but he found it hard to believe, when you couldn't even to bribe your way through. The AI in charge kept the locking codes secret from the agents and changed them daily for good measure.

For a better look he leaned forward, frowning with a twist of his long mouth; then he felt, rather than heard, someone stop behind him. A slight pressure from a hand touching the case he held, a faint draught of moving air – no more than that. The thief was good, but Vi-Kata, the deadliest assassin in the Pinch, was better. In utter silence he spun, kicked low, saw a human face grimacing with pain, its mouth open for a scream – grabbed with his free hand and flung – the shriek rang shrill as the thief flipped over the railing and plunged down, still screaming, his scream drowned in other screams when he hit headfirst, splattering across the floor.

'Stop him!' Kata yelled in Gen. 'The murderer! That way! Police! Police!'

Yelling, pointing, Kata raced down the ramp. A few young human men followed him, calling for the police as they chased their imaginary murderer. Down below, chaos swirled around the corpse. Muttering weeping sapients shrank back from the bloody mess on the floor or else stared, frozen in horror, blocking the way of the security guards trying to cordon off the corpse. Everywhere clots of saccules clutched each other and boomed. Their fear smelled like old vomit. Police sirens sounded, shrill and urgent. Kata had no trouble losing his impromptu posse as the confusion spread and swelled. He slipped off to one side and strode for the gates. Up close, he could see that every exit stood guarded by not just one gate, but a series, a long tunnel of autogates stretching toward the grey light of outside and safety.

Behind him, he could hear a police loudspeaker shouting for order and commanding everyone to stay where they were. Now or never. One customs officer, a pale pinkish human, had stepped a few paces away from his gate to stare slack-jawed at the cluster of police around the corpse. A perfect chance, but Kata hesitated for the briefest of seconds. He was under sentence of death on more than one world, and the police of all of those worlds had encoded his DNA signature into their security systems. He stepped forward, hesitated again, then shrugged and walked through, strode through, swinging his sample case, his skull crest raised at a jaunty angle. Eight gates passed, nine, ten, and then the door ahead, opening with a hiss of air.

None of them gave an alarm.

Kata walked out into a cold, grey light. Overhead, clouds swirled with the perpetual fog of Palace, where a sunny day meant a celebration. He paused on the walkway to button his short-tunic.

'Hey! Watch it!' A voice, a human voice, snarled from behind him. 'Clumsy Lep bastard.'

Kata turned and considered the speaker, paunchy and red-faced. Here on the public walkway – no, too many other sapients around, too many witnesses.

'My apologies, Sé,' Kata said.

'Yeah?' The human pushed past him. 'Your kind should go back where you belong!' He trotted off, heading for the movebelt crawling along the far side of the street.

Kata turned on his heel and strode off down the walkway. Although he had, of course, carried luggage onboard the liner – the stewards would have noticed and wondered if he hadn't – it could rot in the claim area for all he cared now. Ja Vin Hepo the jewel importer was due for his bloodless death just as soon as Kata made a few purchases with his imaginary line of credit. He passed a vidscreen, glanced at it, then swore and stopped to watch. Looping on the six-foot-high screen was footage of the thief falling and hitting, the splash of blood and the panic in the crowd. When had that slimy filth of a pix started recording? Did they have frames of him on that holotape? He'd forgotten how intakes and pix swarmed over Palace like lice, working for the newsgrids that practically ruled the planet. Kata's luck had held – the pix had looked up just as the thief screamed, apparently, because the loop started with the man arching over the railing. At the top of the frame Kata could just make himself out, but he was so obscured that he could have been any Lep in a business suit.

He hurried on. Around a corner stood a rack of sleek black robocabs and a queue of passengers, waiting their turn under the officious eye of a blue-skinned saccule dispatcher. The entire queue had their heads tipped back, staring in fascination at that same wretched loop on the vidscreen hanging above. In the queue stood other members of Kata's own race, the Ty Onar Lep, but these wore clothes better fitted for humans. Long tunics with sleeves and high collars, heavily draped kilts – they all hid the unique patterns of iridescent scales that marked a Lep as the member of a family line. Kata noted with disgust that one fellow even wore a human-style headband with his gene-glyph displayed, just as if his own scales weren't enough for him. Imitation humans! he thought – then reminded himself that they had their reasons for blending in to a human world. Some fourteen years past, at the end of a long war, the homeworld Ty Onar Lep had tried to invade Palace; they'd failed, but the Lep on planet, whose families after all had been citizens of Palace for centuries, still felt the lash of old suspicions, old contempt, no matter how loyal to the government they truly were.

And he himself, for all his pride, for all that he wore the traditional Lep websling around his waist over the traditional slashed skirts – was he any better after what he'd done? He'd dyed and altered his own bright scalings, changed them to match the pattern of an obscure line, denied and spat upon his own heritage, his own ancestors, all because of his work, all because of his family's shame. His own brother had gone over to the enemy, his own brother had sworn a vow to someday bring him to justice – and his own brother lived on Palace. Under his kilt Kata's tail lashed, just once, an involuntary gesture that he stopped with a spasm of sheer will.

The job was too good to pass up, he reminded himself, despite the risk. Already, in that matter of the autogates, his employer had shown him how powerful he was. His contact on Souk, the Lep who had actually offered Kata the job, had given him proof that this mysterious employer had some ancient technology at his command, devices lost in the rest of the Pinch for hundreds of years. If Kata could trust this unbelievably rich sapient's promises, soon the Line of Tal would be raised high again; he would have his true name back, not this Vi-Kata which meant, at root, the Outcast One and nothing more. If he could trust his new employer's word about his plans, *if*, there would be no more humans in the Pinch, soon and forever.

Kata changed robocabs three times, then stopped at a store on the Street of Rags to buy himself second-hand clothes and a leather shoulder-sack for the contents of his sample case. The case and the business suit ended up in a public recycler. Wearing a shabby slashed kilt, a short-tunic, and a wrap jacket several sizes too large – he kept the shoulder-sack hidden under it – he hailed another cab, changed it again, and fetched up at last at the gates of the Lep quarter, Finance Sect.

Flecked gold with lamplit windows, tall white multi-levels rose from narrow streets, darkening in the fading grey light of afternoon. High above him, strung back and forth from the balconies and protrusions of the multi-levels, hung tattered rope webs, as grey as the sky, a shabby mockery of the great green webs that spanned entire cities on Ri, the homeworld. The smell of cooking grease hung thick in the air. Finance Sect, once so prosperous, had taken a flood of refugees when the Government had passed new laws limiting where Lep families could live.

On the ground the squalor hit him like a stink. Dirty, silver-coloured children ran wild in the alleys, yelling, shoving each other, playing incomprehensible human games instead of proper dance-fights. As Kata walked through, cursing and slapping them out of his way, he noticed their scale patterns, each different – so! things had sunk so low that children of separate nests played together. Where were the *mahtis*, the keepers of the children? How could they leave the future of their lines exposed to all kinds of dangers, here in streets littered with shed scales and garbage? With shit, too, he noticed – maybe from the children, maybe from the half-starved animals, jadewing lizards and dogs, that slunk out of his way as he passed, but most likely from both.

Talking among themselves, a gaggle of young males strutted toward him. They held their sleek heads high to let anyone who might want to look see their red throats. Vi-Kata stepped into a doorway to make sure they passed by without touching him. The shame of it! How could any decent female accept such a blatant mating-offer! Or were there any decent females around here? He walked on, glancing round. Where were the grandmothers, wearing their immense coils of knotted silk, each knot marking an event in their family's history? Back home the grandmothers crouched on the polished and inlaid porches of their homes, or sat up in the webs, taking the sun while they tested each knot and sang of things past. And where were the grandfathers, their necks hung with gold chains and medallions, the wealth of their lines? Someone needed to slash a little sense into these stinking children. Someone needed to slice open one of those shameless red throats to make an example for all the other younglings. He only wished it could be he.

In a few more blocks, the multi-levels gave way to a maze of small houses and shops. Not even an attempt at webbing here, and the walls oozed a mossy green, stippled here and there with mustard yellow. Under every window sill, up under the overhang of roofs, purple fungi hung in fleshy, trailing sprays. The city, named Palace just as the planet was, lay prey to a vast variety of moulds and spores. Kata had no idea why the humans had chosen to build their capital on the edge of the biggest swamp on this watery continent. The citizens never seemed to know, either, when you questioned them. They liked filth, humans – that was to Kata's mind the simplest answer.

Through twisting streets he followed the detailed and precise directions of his employer's agent until he came to a nondescript scale polishing studio. Carved into the frame of the door was a series of hieroglyphs, the equivalent of a grandmother's knots, each standing for a moment of crisis or triumph for the line who owned the shop. Even on the homeworld most Leps these days replaced the glyphs by datablocks and Map icons – human innovations. Few Leps could even read the old symbols. Kata, however, read off the glyphs to himself and then wondered why he'd bothered. This family of scale polishers had only one claim to fame: their eldest son had gone over to the invaders and died in the war. Still, it showed more patriotism and pride than he'd seen so far in this quarter of humanized Leps, human-sympathizing Leps.

Kata scratched politely at the door. After a few moments a tiny panel slid back, revealing a peephole and a slitted grey-gold eye.

'E-ya?' The voice rapped the question out, crisp and demanding.

Kata's crest rose in the Lep equivalent of a smile. Here was a youngling with a bit of the true arrogance.

'K' chaak ni-*ta*!' I demand your throat! Kata might admire the door warden, but damned if he'd be dominated by him.

The door swung open so hard it bounced back against the wall. With a growl the door warden strode out, slashed skirts swinging round his powerful thighs. Kata sized him up quickly: the warden was at least a foot taller and much younger than he. Red and pale green scales marched down his grey arms in diagonal lines. So, his line came from Palace, and he himself had most likely been hatched and raised here. The male looked Kata up and down, then spat.

Kata raised his crest, then began to circle the youngling. He could hear the sound of windows being thrown open, doors being flung back. Leps called out, Leps came running to form a circle in the street round this dance-fight. Off to one side stood a grandmother with a bevy of young females behind her. Kata took off his jacket and shoulder-sack, then with a bow of respect handed them to the old woman for safekeeping. She raised her crest slightly and nodded her approval. Kata turned to the men's side of the circle.

'Watch well, my brothers!' Kata called out. 'Watch and see how the old ways live!'

The youngling raised his own crest, a grin of agreement. In the sensible corner of his mind, Kata called himself a fool for engaging in a public display like this. The fewer people who knew that the Outcast was on planet, the better. But to turn down a dance challenge? Never!

At first, the two merely circled one another. As the challenged one, the door warden's turn came first. The younger Lep began to spin, to leap high in the air. With every leap he flung his muscled arms toward the sky. The crowd began to clap and stamp their feet, pounding out the rhythm of the dance. Next the youngling feinted powerful blows, side strikes and claw swipes at his adversary while he kept up the dance, leaping right, then left. Kata merely watched, never flinching even when a clawed hand swept within a few centimetres of his eyes. At last the youngling finished his set. His huge scaled chest heaved as he lifted his head to the crowd, right and left, calling upon them to judge his adversary against him. The crowd fell silent. Heads turned; crests raised; eyes, gold and green and black, studied Kata. He could practically hear what they must be thinking. The youngling was strong and fast, with some grace and a store of confidence that would be the joy of any grandmother. What would the scrawny middle-aged Lep with the undistinguished scalings do in answer?

Kata showed his throat to the crowd, first right, then left. Slowly, as slowly as he could manage, he spread out his arms and hands to the sky. The crowd gasped: to claim the slow fight, the silence, was the right only of a great dancer. No-one moved, no-one clapped while he forced each claw out of each fingertip, very slowly, one by one. With his hands raised against the sky, he began to sway, very slowly, right and left, over and over. At the last claw the crowd gasped.

'Zah!' Kata called out.

They began to clap and stamp in the sacred rhythm. Kata began to move, to turn in place, slowly at first, then faster. The clapping swelled to match his speed as he whirled in place, faster, faster. The pounding feet of the watchers struck the rhythm for his pounding heart, so fast that the alley seemed to blur around him, but even so, each time he faced his adversary he made, with icy precision, a swift stab of a finger claw that would have blinded a blood opponent.

Round and round – then all at once he stopped. The crowd roared as he leapt far into the air, above the heads of even the tallest of the watching Leps. He landed in a perfect crouch with his clawed hand thrust up in an underhand throat strike. The youngling yelped and stumbled back. Breathing slow and softly, Kata held the position for a moment, then stood to raise his head to the watchers and ask for their judgment.

The crowd sighed, long and hot, as if they had seen a ritual mating. The grandfathers among them looked at each other, then hissed.

The young door warden slumped, spreading his arms out to acknowledge the judging, then stood straight and strode over to Kata. Only his eyes betrayed his fear. He tilted his head backward to expose his neck, then waited.

Kata leapt forward, snaked his head round, and touched the male's soft throat with his teeth, merely touched points to skin. Let the boy tremble, and he would drink blood.

'E-ya?' The youngling spoke softly, politely, but there was no trace of a whine or a beg in his voice.

Kata released the folds of throat and stepped back, licking the taste of salty skin from his lips.

'Eh, sid cad ni-ya.' Ah, your throat tastes of piss! But he raised his crest as he said it and clasped the boy forearm to forearm.

All round the crowd applauded in the low rumbling that sounded like human laughter, a shaking of the heart. The grandfathers nodded to one another, then called out, telling the crowd to go home and clear the street.

Kata reclaimed his goods from the grandmother, who allowed

herself another slight crest-lift of approval, then followed the youngling inside a dim salon, smelling of scented oils and rubbing alcohol. All along one wall stood red couches, each flanked by a tray of implements and soft cloths. Along the facing wall ran mirrors. At the back stood an open door leading inward.

'Do you know who I am, now?' Kata said to the boy.

'With all submission, I need the password.'

'Good for you! Kel amin del Umin.' No honour with Humans.

'Amin kath voli.' None except dead ones.

The youngling raised his head.

'We are honoured to host you. My name is Sar Elen.'

'What? Sar and Elen? Only two names? Do you shun the name of your line?'

'My line has no name until our people have a Standing.'

Kata grinned. He never formed friendships, but he liked this youngling.

'We have a network,' Elen went on. 'There are a lot of places you can shelter.'

'Well, that's very good of you, but I don't dare. I'll find my own shelter, youngling. Knowing where I am could kill you. Do you realize that? We'll never regain our Standing if the faithful get pulled in by the Palace police.'

'True. I take it you've come to use the passage?'

'Just that.'

Elen led him into the shop's back room, stacked with boxes of cloths and big plastic jugs of oil. He opened what seemed to be a closet, empty except for a bright red robovac on the floor and a rack of brushes and attachments hanging on the back wall. The youngling stepped back and merely waited, but his crest kept raising despite his obvious efforts to keep it down.

'What is it?' Kata snapped.

'I think you're in for a surprise, that's all. About this door.'

'Well, I know it's hidden. Don't worry. I know how to unlock it.'

Elen's crest quivered from the effort of staying flat.

Kata opened the shoulder-sack and took out what appeared to be an amber pendant. Whispering the activation name made the yellow-brown transceiver crystal first glow, then send out an electronic pulse – not that Kata could hear it, of course, but the hologram of cleaning equipment disappeared, revealing another door.

'Fare you well, Elen,' Kata said. 'And always watch your back.'

Kata opened the door and stepped through. A sensation like a thousand cold fingers ran over his scales, making him shudder and twitch. For a moment he nearly retched; then the sensation stopped as suddenly as it had started. He staggered a few steps forward and found himself inside a grey room with a black door on the far side. When he spun round, he saw that the door into Sar Elen's shop had vanished.

'What?' A trap, was it?

Yet he remembered things, a casual remark from his contact on Souk, and bits of data he'd learned in school, too, about the old days in the Pinch, before the hypershunts had closed and sealed it off from the rest of civilization. They had marvellous technology in the old days.

'Transport gates.' He whispered the words aloud. 'It has to be!'

He walked back to the wall that once had been a door and ran his hand along it. Not a seam, not a welt, nothing. He must have been delivered inside this room by a technology everyone thought lost forever. He could be anywhere at all on Palace, anywhere! He had the feeling that he'd never know, because he was willing to bet high stakes that the door on the other side would drop him back into the Lep quarter at yet another location. He went still for a moment, listening to something he'd heard – or was it that he felt the sensation around him? A very low throbbing hum or a distant vibration, perhaps heavy machinery? The sound of whatever it was never seemed to vary its rhythm, a big pulse, two small fast pulses, over and over. Turning, he considered the black door. Should he try to open it? His instructions said otherwise: walk through the passage and wait for our leader to join you. Very well. He'd wait.

Kata knew this leader only by the code name Riva, an ancient word meaning 'unblemished scales'. He had to be another Lep, but Kata was only thinking of him as 'he' for convenience sake. Was he male, female, of what line, what off-world Standing? Kata hoped that he was about to find out. Riva had hidden behind third parties and coded packets from the beginning. Kata had taken other jobs from him, over the years: an assassination here, a smuggling job there. Always the work had harmed the human presence in the Pinch. Always Riva, through his underlings, had spoken of the grand day when the Ty Onar Lep would once again be the masters and all other races, their slaves. It was an old dream, this empire of domination, and one that most of the Ty Onar had repudiated, over the long years when they'd been trapped in the Pinch. These days even the warlords of Ri talked of cooperation and the pooling of resources. But a few, a grand faithful few, remembered the old ways. Riva led them, and Kata served them in any way he could. Soon, any moment, he would meet the Lep who inspired them all.

But Riva was still hiding. On the wall to Kata's right a spot of light appeared, then burst, spread, and reformed into a hologrammatic projection, a revenant as they were called. Riva himself or herself, as the case might be, sat somewhere else, somewhere far away, even, controlling the rev through the Map, seeing and hearing through sensors on the walls. The hologram was a good one, a beautifully detailed grandmother Lep, clutching her knotted silk. The scalings down her arms matched those of the Line of Tal, the markings that Kata had dyed away. Riva must be a cybermaster, Kata realized. Only a skilled master of the Map could create such a fluid and detailed hologram. But – Leps were barred from the Cyberguild on Palace. An interesting riddle? No, a useful clue.

'Well, you're punctual, I see.' The revenant's voice, speaking Gen, was female.

'Ki-ovi-ta y-ya-lo ni –' When will you let me see your –

'Gen, my friend! Speak Gen!'

'T-ka Gen, li-dua iyik't Lepir.' Gen stinks, in the mouth of the Hero of the Lep race.

The revenant laughed and ran her fingers over her silk, but she said nothing. After a moment, Kata surrendered.

'Oh, whatever you want,' he said in Gen. 'You didn't bring me here to talk, anyway. There's someone you want dead?'

'Most certainly, my friend, but you'll be more than just a hired killer. I have many other tasks for you here on Palace, and the language of the Leps won't be much help to you. Best that you get used to speaking Gen from now on.'

'So?'

'So, be patient, Vi-Kata. You'll understand everything soon enough. For now, I have a simple enough errand for you. Two humans in the Pleasure Sect must die.'

'The Pleasure Sect?' Kata clacked his snout in the Lep equivalent of a sneer. 'That's just a brothel and playground. The citizens there are prisoners. What danger could anyone there represent?'

'That isn't your concern, my friend. These deaths are both small matters, yes, but –'

'On this world they take deaths seriously,' Kata interrupted. 'We'd better have good reasons for causing them.'

'True. You'd best be very careful. Don't arrange anything spectacular, shall we say? Caution first, even if you need to take a little extra time. After all, we're building a revolution. We need patience.'

'A revolution?'

Grandmother Riva opened her fanged mouth in a hideous grimace. It took him a moment to realize that the revenant was meant to be smiling – but it was a human smile.

'We tried outright war, didn't we? And it failed. You've heard the War Council on the homeworld, snivelling about peace, snivelling about pacts and treaties! We can't count on them for help. If we are to better our lot here on Palace, we must hatch our own eggs.'

Kata said nothing, but he found himself staring at her parody of a human smile and wondering many things.

PART ONE

Vida should have been studying. She was coming to the end of her schooling with that big last round of exams to face, but history was something she hated, especially bloody and violent history like the Schism Wars. It was too completely *loath*, thinking of people killing each other over the names and images of God. The wars had been over so long now, a thousand years, and who *cared*? From the window of her tiny room in the private part of The Close, she could hear distant music and a vast susurrus of far-off talk and laughter. Outside in the streets of Pleasure Sect the festival of Calios had begun. She left her Map terminal running on the school linkage, grabbed a cloak, and slipped out of her room. No-one in the hall? Good. She left The Close by a back way. Outside, the sky swirled grey, and the wind blew cool. She put on the cloak and hurried through the alley to the Boulain, the boulevard that snaked through the most expensive part of the sector.

Down the centre and to either side of the Boulain, trees nodded in the rising wind. Spiky native frond-trees, pale green and tightly furled, alternated with tall flowering rhodons from Kephalon. In among the trees food vendors had set up red and white striped booths, mobbed by sapients of all sorts of different races, humans and Leps amiably among them. Here and there as well, Vida saw gridjockeys, mostly pix, marked by their unmistakably outsized right hands, where they carried their camera implants. Out on the actual street, festival goers strolled back and forth in an impromptu parade, humans from nearby Sects, like Power and Agriculture, but she saw men and women of the patron class from as far away as Imports, and even a handful of Centre people on holiday. These festivals were about the only time that residents of the various Sects gathered together and got a chance to meet one another.

You could always spot the patrons, that is, the heads of important families, because they wore shiny silver headbands, made of simtil and marked with the glyphs of their genotype-line. Each patron led a noisy retinue – bodyguards, disarmed for the festival, servants in their best clothes, and musicians playing electronic song-boxes.

They'd even dressed their saccules up for the festival; the servants wore shoulder-to-hip sashes, embroidered with their masters' gene-glyph, over their usual grey shifts. Booming and wheezing in sheer excitement, the Stinkers trotted after each entourage on short fat legs, carrying immense triangular umbrellas to shield their masters and mistresses from the mist. At rare occasions guild retinues strolled by, each led by its masters, dressed in flowing robes sashed, shoulder-to-hip, with the colours of their guilds.

Dancing down the street in their slashed kilts came Leps, a powerful line, Vida knew, because walking gravely at the head of the group were two grandmothers, wound round with coils of knotted silk, pale grey and green, and a grandfather, jingling with gold chains. Behind them came a crowd of children, rushing back and forth, flapping their crests like fans, shoving each other and hissing. The adults brought up the rear, spiky crests raised high at the fun of it all. Their saccules were wearing fancy paper hats, pleated more or less like Lep crests, and as they passed, the crowd broke out clapping. Or most of it did – somewhere at the back a few voices, human males they sounded, yelled out something so nasty-sounding that Vida was glad she couldn't quite understand it.

If they'd heard it, the Lep clan ignored it. When Vida joined the applause, one of the Lep males bowed to her. He raised his hand and made a pantomime gesture of stroking hair – of course, it was her coppery-red hair that had caught his eye, a hair colour rare on Palace, and everyone knew what russet-red meant to a Lep male. When she blew him a kiss, he raised his throat, a gesture that earned him a clout from a grandmother who had turned back to watch this exchange. She grabbed his arm and hauled him onward.

Vida found herself wishing she could follow the parade, join the Leps, maybe, or attach herself to one of the crowds round a patron, to see how they would spend the festival or even follow them home, find some way out of the locked gates of Pleasure Sect and be free for a while, even a little while, even an afternoon. Since she'd lived in Pleasure all her life, eighteen years, she knew every corner of it all too well. When she let herself dream, she even yearned to take a shuntjammer to other planets like icy Tableau or the towering stalk-cities of Souk.

Unfortunately for her dreams, she was only a girl without family, the ultimate outcast in Palace society, an unlicensed and unauthorized birth, a genetic cull. Soon she'd be through with school and gain her official Not-child status, though she'd be far from an adult on a world where most people lived well past a hundred and fifty years. Not-child meant freedom for most young people, but for her it meant the shutting of a trap, when she would become just another Marked courtesan of the Pleasure Sect and live out her life here. Only lurid holonovels, her secret addiction, would ever take her to the stars.

'Vida!' A high furious voice cut through the festival noise. 'You get over here!'

Vida spun round and headed for the voice. It was Aleen, splendid in an emerald shimmercloak, knifing her way through the crowd. Since she'd dyed her hair the same emerald for the festival, she was hard to miss. Vida waited, knowing from long experience that there was no use in running. The tracer bracelet on her left wrist flashed red, faster and faster as Aleen, and the finder that she was carrying, reached her.

Although Vida was tall, all long legs these days, the madam still towered over her. Aleen snatched Vida's wrist, tapped in a code on her tracer bracelet, and studied the readout.

'You've been out of The Close for half an hour!' Aleen sounded frightened more than angry.

'Yes, Madam.'

'Where's Tia? She was supposed to be helping you study.'

'She had a client and had to go.'

'Oh?' Aleen's left eye suddenly glowed. The iris turned crimson and the pupil contracted to a point while Aleen read off data from her cybereye's terminal. 'Well, all right – that client's on the reservation list, yes. But still. You were told to remain in The Close. True?'

'Yes, Madam.'

'These festivals aren't safe. Visitors sometimes get drunk and attack unMarked girls. Haven't I told you this before?'

'Yes, Madam.'

'The extra price for your virginity is going to give you the money for your first investment. True?'

'Yes, Madam.'

'If you lose your virginity, you lose the investment. True?'

'Of course, Madam.' If Aleen was going to talk about investments, then Vida had heard the lecture a hundred times.

A trio of saccules, their chest sacs puffed up blue with pride, were driving a fivewheel through the throng and blowing great bass blasts from their throat sacs to clear away pedestrians. A pair of patrons riding the fivewheel flung bubbleflares into the air. Although most of the flares exploded into coloured light and perfume, every now and then a shower of coins sent the crowds scrambling. Behind the fivewheel stalked a Hirrel, caped in black sunsilk. The fabric fluttered as the Hirrel breathed through the leathery slits along her skinny torso. The alien's four huge eyes, slightly faceted, rippled in their sockets as she attempted to ignore a pair of enthusiastic Lifegivers, wearing the golden gloves of Witnesses, who followed along preaching.

'Are you paying attention to me?'

Vida snapped her gaze back to Aleen. The madam's lips were white with anger.

'Yes, Madam.'

'Huh.' She paused for a moment, then spoke more calmly. 'You will return to The Close and stay there for the rest of the festival.'

'Oh no! Not the whole festival!'

'Are you arguing with me?'

'No, Madam.'

Aleen seemed to be about to add some sarcasm, but mercifully her modified left eye glowed. She swore under her breath.

'I've got a reception to attend, and your little stunt has made me late.'

Vida said nothing. Stuck inside The Close for the entire festival! It wasn't fair.

'Now, go back to The Close and finish your lessons. We'll discuss this tonight.'

'Yes, Madam.'

Aleen started to speak, but her left eye stuttered a series of red flashes. When Madam paused to read, Vida bowed to her, started toward the alley leading back to The Close, then ducked behind a pair of intakes who were jacked into a portable Map terminal and downloading their reports directly onto the newsgrid. Vida waited, briefly, to see if Aleen had noticed, then melted into the crowd beyond. With luck, Aleen wouldn't realize that she hadn't told Vida to go back to The Close *immediately*.

Weaving through the trees, glancing at her tracer bracelet to make sure it stayed dull, Vida jogged down the Boulain until she could be sure Aleen wasn't following. At a public square, crammed with red and white booths, she paused to fish in the pocket of her cloak. She had some coins, tips from clients at The Close when she'd opened the door for them or fetched them drinks. She was supposed to be saving them, of course, but coin spending couldn't be traced. She bought an iced klosh, a pastry filled with berries. At the first bite fruit juice dribbled down her chin. She wiped it off on the back of her hand, licked the hand clean, then nearly lost the klosh when someone joggled her elbow.

At a narrow flight of steps she took her chance to get above the street. She hurried up to a terrace that ran in front of a fancy-looking clothing shop, where other festival goers were standing to watch the fun below. Vida squeezed between them to a trefoil flying buttress, where she could climb out and sit, looking down. Hogging the terrace railing stood gridjockeys, Lep, Hirrel, and human. All the pix kept their camera hands busy, pointing and shooting, while the recording units in their headbands picked up background sound. The intakes walked back and forth subvocalizing, their lips moving as if they spoke, channelling data into the record implants prominent and shiny at the base of their skulls.

Vida looked down and saw what the pix were angling to capture. Just at the edge of the square, some patrons from Centre rode an immense tenwheel cart, ornately designed with a webwork of gleaming rails and fanciful scrollwork. Instead of an engine, two albino vakr with huge ruffs of ice-white skin drew it, or were, rather, attempting to move forward in the mobbed square. Garang bodyguards, dressed in grey uniforms and carrying stunsticks, marched round the tenwheel. The guards, seven feet of lithe muscle, with golden complexions and golden hair, superficially resembled humans, until you looked closely at the extra joints in their arms and legs and the bizarre angles and slopes of their skulls under their golden-furred skin. Vida noticed a slender human man with a dark-skinned face like a knife blade trotting back and forth among them, snapping orders, glancing this way and that into the crowd. From the way he moved, she could tell he was both furious and worried.

Every now and then he would come to the side of the open carriage and lean in to discuss something with the man sitting behind the saccule driver. Tall and powerfully built, with dark skin and the slash of old scars across his face, the man would answer, then shrug as if dismissing danger. He wore a plain black tunic belted with metal segments that, Vida was willing to guess, were generating a forceshield. Next to him sat a beautiful woman, her skin pale, her long hair streaked red and blue, dressed in a fancier version of the grey uniform; blue tattoos covered her face and hands. Behind them, in the back seat, sat two young men and a boy, all uniformed. They looked bored and the boy, miserable.

The bodyguards began chanting, the deadly low sound of angry Garang Japat. Suddenly the crowd in front of the cart found it could move, after all. As the two vakr lurched forward and plodded into the square, Vida realized that she was seeing Karlo Peronida and his family, close by and live, not on the vidscreens. The crowd recognized him, too, and began to call out, Karlo! Karlo! the saviour of Palace! This was the military genius who had beaten back the Lep invasion of fourteen years before. Karlo had ridden the popular wave to establish himself as Palace's First Citizen, the first time a sapient from off planet had ever held the post.

At an order from Karlo, the cart paused below the terrace to allow the gridjockeys their holo op. The woman by his side, Vanna Makeesa y Parrel, was his current marriage partner, whose position as the head of the ruling Council made Karlo's position doubly strong. Everyone knew that her clan wallowed in money, the richest family on Palace, especially so ever since Vanna had destroyed their only rivals, the L'Vars, some thirteen years past. Vida wondered how you could hate a family so much you'd get them all killed, even by legal means, even if they were all traitors, betraying Palace to the Leps like the L'Vars had done. Vanna had lived long enough to nurse enormous hatreds; at two hundred years old, she was the oldest woman, if not the oldest sapient, on Palace. The constant twitches of her head and fluttering motions of her hands showed that she'd pushed the life-extension process to its limit.

At another order from Karlo, the young men in the back seat stood up to smile and wave for the pix on the terrace. She recognized Wan, who would be his father's heir if Karlo got his way and made the office of First Citizen hereditary. One of the Not-children, about twenty-two, Vida remembered, he was an extremely handsome man with his deep green eyes and his light brown skin – his mother, Karlo's previous marriage partner, had been a holostar and a great beauty. The small boy – as pretty as a girl, slouched back in his seat, now, looking at no-one – was the youngest son, Damo, whom the grids had labelled a cyber genius.

The third man, well into his thirties and Karlo's son by some woman he'd never even married back on his homeworld, was tall and rangy, all rough angles and big homely grin. Vida stared, fascinated by his square face, too long in the jaw, and his mouth, too thin for its stretch. You rarely saw anyone ugly on Palace, where every birth had to be licensed and every genotype examined and corrected for such flaws. All at once he flexed his long, muscular arms, grinned, and jumped up to the carriage's frame, which swayed under his weight. He waved to the crowd, who shouted his name in delight. Pero! Daring Pero! He dug into a trouser pocket and pulled out something – a handful of small coins, which he flung to the crowd.

A mob of children rushed forward; the carriage swayed alarmingly. Pero tossed his head and laughed as the pix above leaned over dangerously far to capture every second. Chanting fast, two Garang charged up, swinging stunsticks. When the mob fell back, one of the Garang leapt onto the carriage so gracefully it seemed he floated. He laid one enormous hand on Pero's shoulder and forced him down into his seat. Pero took it with good humour, laughing, waggling a forefinger at the Garang as the guard leapt down again. Karlo gave the saccule driver an order; with a boom it lashed its whip, and the albino vakr jerked forward. This time the crowd fell back and let them pass.

With the excitement over, and her klosh finished as well, Vida climbed down from her perch and regained the street. The mob trailed after the Peronidas and cleared, at least temporarily, the public square. A procession of Lifegivers, mostly humans, took the space over, walking solemnly in twos. Their silver-speckled dark robes, symbolizing endless space, fluttered around them as they traced out the sacred spiral of the galaxy, which had come from the darkness of space and to which in the end it would return. Each held a small speaker, and the clash of electronic gongs and drums marked out their steps.

Once they'd finished their dance, Vida headed across the square. Shoving back their hoods, the Lifegivers were breaking their formation, and the younger ones among them were laughing, caught up in the spirit of the festival. A young fellow not much older than she hailed her as she passed and handed her an Eye of God, a carved wooden disk with a hole drilled in the top so that it could be worn around the neck on a chain.

'Blessings upon you, child,' he said. 'Blessings for the festival. In the name of Calios.'

'Thank you, Sé.' Vida touched her thumbs and forefingers together to form a triangular, more or less eye shape, a gesture of respect that she had seen Aleen use many times.

The Lifegiver's eyebrows shot up. He really was rather handsome, she decided. Pity he was a monk.

'Excuse me, Sé,' Vida started. 'What –'

'Brother Lennos!' called out one of the older monks. 'Get over here right now!'

The Lifegiver scurried off, leaving Vida smiling. Overhead, the sky was swirling and lightening in the promise of a few moments of sunshine and a glimpse of blue sky. The light that fell round her turned silver and cast faint flat shadows. Vida pulled off her cloak and let the fugitive warmth touch her skin. The sound of bells, notes of music so pure that they seemed to burn in the air like candles caught her and drew her on. She'd always wanted to see the famous Pleasure Sect Carillon when it was sounding, and today it would give a proper concert. A floating clock told her the time had just reached the fifteens. If she hitched a ride on a wiretrain heading for the Hub, and there was a stop right near the Carillon, she could easily get back to The Close before Aleen left her important reception.

A few blocks from the square stood the Crossroads, an intersection of multi-levels that led to pretty much every interesting place in Pleasure Sect. Vida climbed the helical stair, pausing at each landing for the view, each a different part of the Southern Quad. The topmost landing opened into a longtube, a flexible tunnel whose diameter was about four times her height, made of a metal that was smooth and warm to the touch. Why the Colonizers had built the longtubes no-one knew, but nowadays they functioned as conduits for supply shipments, emergency vehicles and the like. Vida knew where all the longtubes were, where they went, and who used them. Her memory had amazed the people around her all her life. To Vida herself, remembering anything she'd ever seen was effortless and obvious. She still couldn't really believe that no-one else could look at diagrams and spatial displays and remember them the way she could or even to do more than just remember – she could turn the images this way and that in her head, add or subtract data, and then remember the new diagram as easily as another might work with it on a Mapscreen.

When Vida walked into the tube, she hesitated, wondering if she should go on. Only half the longtube's strip lights glowed. Powerflucs were happening more and more often, according to Aleen, who seemed to spend most of her time these days dealing with what she called the 'deproving infrastructure'. Vida could smell the musk of ver, little slinkers with a nasty bite. She closed her eyes for a moment and called up her image of the holographic wireframe of the Pleasure Sect she'd hacked from Aleen's master files. Even for her, rotating the entire image in her mind wasn't easy, but she eventually found the sinusoidal wiggle of red that marked this particular longtube.

The tube ran short and snaky, though at the far end her map marked some kind of construction problem. If she could make it to the other side, the shortcut would save her a quarter hour of travel time. She started trotting through the longtube, keeping her eyes moving for any sign of vers. She had a canister of Protec clipped to her belt; a squirt of that particular chemical would stop anything short of an enraged Garang Japat. Her boots slapped against the bottom of the tube as she moved, setting up a silky echo.

She'd just seen a faint glow of light at the opposite end of the longtube when she first heard another echo behind her. When she stopped to listen, the other echo also stopped. Had she imagined it? At a quarter past fifteens, no-one from The Close would be thinking of looking for her, but when Vida glanced at her wrist-tel, she found the flashing red proximity warning flickering. Vida unhooked her Protec canister. Whoever was following her was in for a surprise – except she knew better. Aleen had drilled it into her, what to do if she ever got caught in a dangerous situation. Avoid a fight. Never engage an enemy whose resources are unknown. Someone who'd gone to the trouble to find out her proximity code was a dangerous enemy. She put the canister back, then began to run.

She trotted as silently as she could, keeping close to the curving wall of the longtube. She could hear the echoes behind her speeding up, too, and when she slowed, she heard the echo slowing – but a good heartbeat late. Someone followed, all right. She took off running flat out, raced for the open end of the tube. In the boom and slap of echoes she found it hard to hear, but she was sure that the person behind her was gaining. All at once she remembered that odd mark on her map, that indication of unfinished construction. Was she going to be trapped?

Ahead the circle of light grew bigger; the air grew fresher; the opening loomed. Vida raced across the tube, looking ahead and saw a pierced steel gantry standing between the tube and the nearest roof. She hopped up onto the arm and climbed up the catwalk ladder. The sudden light struck her like a flash of fire and made her eyes water, but she kept climbing, blinking back tears. Just as she swung over to the top of the tube, she heard a curse from below her. She went tense, listening for a shriek, a fall – nothing. Whoever was chasing her had stopped in time. The top of the longtube bridged over to the verdant roof park on top of the Carillon Tower. As she dashed across, she glanced back and saw a ripple of speckled black flap to the right side of the longtube. Her pursuer! She tried to think, but could only stare at the robe. A Lifegiver! A Lifegiver was chasing her. But why? She shook her head. No, it had to be someone wearing a Lifegiver's robes, an imposter. Pretending to be a Lifegiver was a capital offence. Vida's mouth went dry. Whoever was chasing her was a serious criminal. She jumped off the bridge into the garden.

Moving as quietly as she could, Vida angled through the roof park until she found temporary shelter. She crouched down under a crescent of grey vines dotted with black and orange flowers, oozing sweet perfume. Her wrist-tel kept flashing, a crimson warning and a betrayal, locked on her arm beyond her removing it. Looking round she saw fern trees, red flowering poles, drapes of blue vines, and sprays of orange flowers. Glancing up, she saw the bell tower, a lacy fold and wrap of sculptured metal. The bell sounds themselves were photonic, of course, though an old brass bell had been installed in the tower as an artistic gesture. Was there a way down from inside the tower? She could only hope so.

One step at a time, trying to keep the rustling to a minimum, Vida made her way through the vegetation. With the holiday, there would be no workers up here to help her, not even a mech, much less a saccule gardener. Gardeners – tools. Vida crouched and searched for the sprinkler lines, then followed them, trotting bent double, to a valve. Her wrist-tel gave off bloody flashes that beat almost as quickly as her heart. The false Lifegiver was closing in.

Vida found a valve, then let out a shaky sigh of relief. Just above hung a section panel, all powered up and set for automatic. She switched it to manual and ran the side of her hand down every button on the panel. Instantly, the roof park exploded with water jets from whirring sprinklers; light bars poured out a flood of high-cal amber light; sprays of insect repellent spewed out of fluted pipes. She heard a string of curses too foul for any real Lifegiver to know. With a laugh touched with terror, Vida ran for the bell tower.

The Carillon stood inside a tangled growth of vines and decorative grillwork. Vida scrambled up this makeshift ladder to the opening at the top of the tower; she clung there for a moment, panting for breath. She could just see the curve of brass of the Carillon's false bell and what might be a stairwell panel. When she looked down, she saw a figure wearing black and white starred robes, all stained and wet, who was mercifully looking in the other direction – at the moment. She froze, clinging with aching hands. Although he kept his cowl drawn around his face and his hands inside the wide sleeves, his broad build, wide-set hips and springy gait meant he had to be a Lep. When he drew something long, dark, and metallic out of his sleeve, Vida scrambled up the last metre of grillwork and hurled herself inside the bell tower.

She lay gasping on the floor. Up above her the roof gleamed and glistened as the rare sunlight filtered in from outside; cubes of the strange blue glass-metal of the Colonizers lined the ceiling and continued down the walls a way. She rose to her knees, glanced round, and her heart turned cold. There was no way out.

The shape she'd read as a stair panel was nothing of the sort, only an angled black slab, featureless, joined to the wall along its height – some kind of old-fashioned Map access panel. Maybe, just maybe, it would have a help icon or a transmit. When she touched it, she felt a flare of warmth under her palm as the station came to life and brought hope with it, but no icons appeared. When in frustration she ran her hand over the surface, a faint glow caught the corner of her eye. She turned to see a revenant, its ghostly form shimmering through a series of body-shapes, human and alien. You didn't see many revenants in Pleasure Sect, though some of the older stations did produce them. Since they weren't fully functional, they appeared randomly, rarely spoke, and vanished without warning.

This rev finally settled on a human shape, apparently solid though it glowed around the edges, a man with large black eyes and very long metallic silver hair, which undulated as if in a private breeze. He looked strange, his skin far darker than any she'd ever seen, even on Karlo Peronida and his family, and his face was ridged with knobs of smooth metal. He wore a glittering jewelled gown like the clothes in historical holonovels set in the early years of the Pinch. The revenant considered her, then raised one hand. A light flashed into her eyes. When she flinched back and yelped, he grinned.

'Je'nevrelevpadumindoroolasveel –' The revenant spoke very quickly, with a strange accent.

'Huh?'

'Je'ne padum las vyl –'

'I don't understand what you're saying.'

'Vas'i je!' The ghostly hologram flickered and turned dim. After a few seconds, he returned to full power. 'I have assimilated current lingua-bases. Building Gen heuristic. Complete. Beginning identity search. Search complete. Searching for gene-base. Gene-base found. Cross-checking gene-base for verification.' There was a moment's pause. 'Greetings, User. Your genotype is a recognized priority access deen. Enter meta.'

'What?'

'Enter meta.'

'What's a meta?'

'A meta is an unambiguous data string for unique access and development of coordinated routines for action.'

'Huh?'

'Wait. Heuristic counter-program activated. Adjusting levels. Lexicons active. A meta is a password, a means for individual encrypted interaction with an artificial intelligence. I require a meta to create your account.'

'A password?'

'Yes,' said the rev. 'Enter meta.'

Vida's wrist-tel was flashing red and fast now. The fake Lifegiver must be closing in, probably at the bottom of the tower.

'I don't know the password.'

'No, no, Veelivar, you give me the password! I record it, you use it. The password becomes my name to you.'

'Oh, well, then.' She thought, remembered Brother Lennos and the Eye. 'The password is Calios.'

'Done. I am Calios. Veelivar account active. All stations unlocked.'

'That won't help!'

'Help? Enter your request.'

'I'm being chased, so I don't suppose you know a way out of here?'

'Explain.'

Vida raised her left wrist and showed the rev her flashing wrist-tel.

'Someone wants to hurt me, and they're using this to find me.'

'Interesting.' The rev's expression blanked for less than a heartbeat. Abruptly, the wrist-tel ceased flashing. 'I have re-directed this matrix. Please confirm with visual input.'

Vida crawled to the tower window and flattened herself against the wall so that she could look out sideways. She saw the figure in Lifegiver's robes at the base of the tower, but he wasn't looking up. Instead, he was staring at his wrist-tel. When he shook his hand, as if trying to shake some life back into a suddenly dead tel, his sleeve slid back. His wrist was covered with scales in a pattern of red and green swirls. So, it *was* a Lep, and that pattern would identify his family line. He also held a weapon, judging from the slender barrel and the power pack clipped to the handle. Weapons were forbidden on Palace, punishable by death. Why would a Lep risk so much to chase an unMarked girl? It didn't make any sense.

All at once, the Lep's wrist-tel began flashing again. Cursing, he ran back across the garden with amazing speed and grace. She watched him hurry across the bridge, climb over to the gantry, and whip himself into the longtube.

She turned around. 'That worked. Thank you.'

The rev was paying her no attention.

'Warning, trackers activated. End meta.'

'What?'

'End meta. Speak your password, Veelivar.'

'Uh . . . Calios?'

The rev grinned one last time, nodded, and vanished before Vida could ask what a veelivar was. She had no time to mess around here, anyway, when her pursuer might return at any moment. And she had a hunch that the rev had been running from someone or something, too.

Uncle Hi had long legs and used them, striding so fast through the festival that Rico Hernanes y Jons was hard pressed to keep up. Thanks to the crowds, though, every now and then Hi had to pause, muttering under his breath about wasted time, and Rico would sneak a fast look around. Once, he saw the Countess of Motta in her silver litter, marked with the stylized sigil of her family's gene-glyph, bobbing through the crowd behind saccule footmen sashed in silver over a red shift. A little later they paused at a blocked intersection, where, hanging from the side of a building, a two-storey high vidscreen showed a collage of images from the festival. Out in the street sapients stood looking up, trying to catch a glimpse of themselves or someone they knew onscreen while the actual festival swarmed around them. Rico joined them, tipping his head back to look.

'Come on, kid!' Hi snapped.

'Yes, Sé!'

Rico ran to catch up. He'd been dodging Hi's foul mood all day, from the moment Hi had yelled at his Garang bodyguard for the crime of arguing with him about his plans. Rico didn't know why his uncle wanted to come to the festival without his staff, but he'd told all twenty members of it to find other business for the day. Even Hi's factor, Jevon, had received a lecture about her place for pointing out that the Master of the Cyberguild had no business running around Pleasure Sect without a bodyguard, a dressing down that had left her pale and shaking.

When they reached the Boulain, Uncle Hi paused long enough to buy himself and his nephew an iced klosh. Rico dribbled pink juice down his best white shirt, while Hi ate at an angle, leaning forward to munch without staining his ceremonial robes, the midnight blue of the Cyberguild.

'You're a mess, kid,' Hi said.

'Yeah, I know,' Rico took a napkin from the vendor and rubbed in vain. 'Sorry.'

For a moment Hi considered him, his dark eyes brimming sad, as if the sight of his nephew made him weary. He was getting on, Hi, over a hundred now, and his thick grey hair, touched with white at the temples, showed it.

'We better finish our business here before it gets too late,' Hi said at last. 'I'm due back in Tech Sect tomorrow. Remember, this is just between us, right?'

'Not a word, yeah.'

'Good. Now come on.' Hi winked. 'It never pays to keep Aleen waiting.'

Rico nodded, not trusting his voice. If Uncle Hi realized how nervous he was, he'd become a family joke – well, a joke to most of them, anyway. It was the Jons clan custom to let their youngsters, boys and girls both, learn about sex at the proper age from professionals, and Rico had just achieved his Not-child status. His mother, though, had her own ideas about such things, and a much stricter view of life, and he knew she'd hate it – if she ever found out. He wasn't too crazy about it himself. He would have rather stayed at the hotel and worked with their interface to the Map;

Pleasure Sect had some archaic access points, fascinating stuff to Rico's way of thinking.

They started across a public square only to find it filled with a procession of Lifegivers. Muttering something unreligious, Hi motioned for Rico to stop and wait with him off the side. Rico found the spiral dancing and the shrieking whistles and gongs profoundly uninspiring. He started looking over the crowd for Marked citizens, the ones his older cousins had told him about. They had the bright red sun glyph of the Pleasure Sect tattooed on their foreheads, his cousins said, so you could tell them apart from the boys and girls who weren't Not-children yet. UnMarked girls were off-limits. Marked girls had no limits. His cousins always smirked when they made that distinction.

Rico grimaced. He wished there was some way he could avoid this. Like most upper-class children on Palace, he'd been immersed in such an overwhelming education that sexual matters belonged only to the dark corners of the night, when cousins whispered together about what they'd been promised for 'later'. Well, 'later' was here now, with a vengeance. Maybe he could just ask to go home? But Uncle Hi was his family's chief patron, and when you were just barely a Not-child, disobeying a patron's orders was a good way to get into deep trouble.

As the Lifegivers ended their dance and began to clear the square, Rico saw a girl standing and watching the monks. She was younger than he was, and plainly unMarked, but he couldn't help thinking that she was the most beautiful girl he'd seen in the entire festival. She stood straight, her hands on her slender hips, frowning a little, her eyes wide – even from this distance, he could tell they were a startling deep green. Her hair, a rich reddish colour that he'd never seen before, tumbled down her back in waves. Rico frankly stared as she strode across the plaza, her walk lithe, graceful. If Aleen's girls were like her, he decided, this whole thing was going to be easier than he thought. Only half-consciously he moved after her, following her through the crowd. When she paused to speak with a young monk, he hesitated.

'Rico, hey, where are you going?' Hi was following him.

'Sorry. I'd just like to see some of the festival, that's all.'

'Yeah, so would I. But.'

Rico glanced back to find his uncle smiling, a rueful twist of his mouth.

'I hate to admit this,' Hi said. 'But that hairy bastard of a Garang was right, y'know. This isn't all that safe. Let's stick together, okay?'

'Okay.'

They headed down the Boulain, dodging clowns and street vendors, ducking through the trees and food booths. Every time Hi saw a gridjockey, he'd swear and steer Rico away fast, before they could end up on the newsfeed or in some special presentation. At one point they found themselves caught between a parked tenwheel, all covered with flowers and full of chanting priests, and a portable Map terminal where gridjockeys stood jacked in, their eyes vacant as they stared into space, waiting for their downloads to finish.

'Almost there, too,' Hi muttered. 'Damn it.'

Cowering behind the tenwheel, they waited for the pix and intakes to move on. Out on the Boulain itself a crowd of sapients drifted in a thick crush, ordinary citizens, most of them, with a sprinkling of drug addicts and drunks. Pleasure Sect sheltered a lot of trash sapients as well as hard-working citizens, or so Rico had always heard them called, trash and sapient garbage. They shambled along, begging shamelessly, Leps as well as humans, holding out trembling hands as the prosperous citizens passed them by or paused, glancing around in embarrassment, to drop a few coins into their palms.

One of the beggars weaving unsteadily across the Boulain had a face that glistened with metal – circuit plate embedded into his cheek and studding his forehead. Around one eye gleamed a web of tri-stil, the optical fibre used to connect cybers to primary access stations for the AI network. He was wearing a piss-stained pair of grey trousers, but instead of a shirt or tunic he wore the tattered remains of a blue robe, all greasy and cut off short. Rico took off running, dodging his way through the startled crowd. On the far kerb he caught him.

'Arno. Oh my God, Arno!'

The beggar stopped, swaying a little, and raised a gaunt hand to a stubbled face. Around his metal eye the web stalks opened and fluttered as his head jerked to one side. His hand spasmed and flew up, dragging a dirty arm with it.

'I know you.' His voice rasped and croaked. 'Son of the morning.'

'Arno, no, look, it's Rico. Your cousin.' His voice broke. 'Your friend. Arno, don't you remember me?'

Glittering in the sunlight the metal face turned his way. The mouth, flesh barely visible under the circuit plate, twitched in something like a smile.

'Yeah. Yeah. I knew you on the stations of our cross, eh? We jammed together in the morning light, all-meta.'

'All-meta?'

'All-meta, morning light. For the son of the morning. Child of the Gyre.' His head twitched, flopped nearly to his chest, raised itself again. Inside their cage of tri-stil the eyes peered out, suddenly steady. 'Rico? That really you, cuz?'

Arno held out a hand and held it steady, his mouth twisted tight from the effort of will. Rico knew what his cousin wanted him to do. He glanced at the back of his own hand, where the flat circle of cuproid, his first implant jack, glittered. If they tried to connect in this jostling crowd? Dangerous, yes, but worth a try.

'Rico!' Uncle Hi's voice, booming in rage. 'Rico! Where the hell are you?'

'Who's that?' Arno muttered. 'Knew that voice.'

'Yeah. I'll bet you did. Here!' Rico turned, waving. 'Uncle Hi, come here!'

Striding in a wave of authority, all blue robe and hard dark eyes, Uncle Hi parted the crowd and swept through. He grabbed Rico by the shoulder.

'Come on. There's no time to waste here.'

'But it's Arno. We've got to get him out of here.'

Uncle Hi glanced at Arno, a flick of his eyes, then away. 'He's where he wants to be,' Hi said, but for the briefest of moments his voice wavered.

'Shit!'

Arno staggered back, then broke into a shambling run.

Rico realized that a pair of Protectors, dressed in their semi-armoured crowd control uniforms, stiff and red, were trotting after his cousin. They had their stunsticks raised and ready. Rico stepped forward and blocked their way.

'What's the trouble, officer?'

The Protector stared at him in sheer disbelief, then turned to Hi, the obvious authority.

'Well?' Hi said. 'What's going on?'

'None, Sé. Just thought that fellow was bothering you.'

'Not in the least. Hey, it's festival, right? He's too far gone to hurt anybody.'

Rico could just see the Protector smile under the smoked black vizor that covered half his face.

'Well, true enough, Sé, but you never know what trouble they're going to get into, that kind.' With a wave to his partner, he stepped round Hi.

Hi grabbed Rico's shoulder and held onto him while the Protectors trotted off up the Boulain. Rico could only hope that Arno had enough of a head start to get away.

'There's nothing I can do for Arno,' Hi whispered. 'Nothing anyone can do.'

'Maybe so, but I want to try.' Rico squirmed free, but Hi grabbed him again, harder this time.

'Rico! I'm telling you to quit it! That's an order!'

A direct order from his patron – Rico hesitated long enough for Hi to settle his grip two-handed, a painful clamp on his shoulders.

'But why? How can you just –'

'This is no place to talk about it. Now come on.'

Rico shook his head no and twisted in Hi's grip to look in the direction that Arno had taken. All he could see now were crowds. Even the bright red helmets of the Protectors had vanished in the general sea of colour. Hi must have seen the same; with a sigh he let Rico go.

'I could do something for him,' Rico snapped. 'Even if you can't.'

'For God's sake! You are the most goddamn stubborn –'

'He's my friend. And your son.'

'Yeah, I know that. I'm aware of it every day. This is no time to discuss it.'

'But –'

Hi swung back-handed and cracked him across the face, then pulled him away. Hauled along like a saccule cart, Rico felt his eyes watering. No-one had ever hit him before, not that any one but his patron could have got away with such a thing. He made himself a promise that this would be the last time, too. Hi found a clear spot around a corner and stopped, letting Rico catch his breath and wipe his eyes off on his shirt-sleeve.

'Sorry, Rico. I'm telling you that as your uncle, okay?' Hi's voice shook. 'But never mention Arno again. And that I'm telling you as your guildmaster and your family's patron both.'

Rico swallowed hard, swallowed a thousand insults, a thousand questions. Arno is your own son, how could you, just how could you? He could say none of it to his patron and guildmaster, not one word. All he could do was nod a yes he hated.

'Good.' Hi forced out a smile. 'Now let's go and have a good time and forget about this. Okay?'

'Okay.' Rico paused just long enough. 'Sé.'

Hi winced, but he said nothing.

Although Hi, wrapped in a black mood of his own, never noticed, Rico fumed as they hurried on, dodging the gridjockeys. The Cyberguild made rivals of its apprentices, not friends. Out of all the apprentices and younger journeymen around him, Rico had known only one person he could trust: Arno – brilliant, gifted Arno, the hope and pride of the entire guild, a product of centuries of informal gene-type breeding, really, since the guild's masters, male and female both, tended to pick marriage partners with their own abilities. Everyone talked about Arno, everyone admired Arno, but Arno had sought Rico out and made him a friend – only to disappear, to drop out of the guild and out of sight just a few months past. Now Rico had found him only to lose him again.

'I can't,' Rico said. 'I can't just not say anything.'

Hi groaned under his breath.

'Well, I'm sorry,' Rico went on. 'I know you're my master and my patron, but I don't care if you kick me out of the goddamned guild. I don't see how you –'

'Then shut up and listen!' Hi let out his breath in a sharp puff. 'Do you think I like seeing Arno that way? It's the drugs, Rico. Listen to me. Listen hard and think about what you've just seen. We can't get full access without them, but some people fall in love with the damn cyberdrugs, and then their lives are over. They end up here, begging in the streets to buy more.'

Rico stopped walking and gaped. Drugs? Arno was a drug addict? He shook his head, an unconscious no.

'Being a genius isn't easy,' Hi said. 'He found something he needed in those drugs, Rico, something I couldn't give him.'

'I'm sorry,' Rico whispered. 'I didn't know.'

'Do you think I wanted anyone at the prentice level to know? But hell, maybe I was wrong. I owe it to the rest of you, all you apprentices, I mean, to tell the truth about this. I don't want this happening to anyone else, understand me? And especially not you.'

'It won't, I promise.'

But as they walked on, Rico could only wonder why he didn't believe his uncle. No, not drugs, not Arno. He *knew* Arno, knew him better than Hi ever had. He was too smart, too strong, to fall like this. Something was going on, something had to be going on. Maybe Hi didn't even know the truth of it; in fact, judging from what his uncle had just said, most likely he didn't. Bet I can find out, Rico thought. Son of the morning, Child of the Gyre, and morning light – Rico repeated the metas until he could be sure he'd remember them. If he could get a chance to try them out without Hi or another guildmaster catching him, he was going to take it.

By the time Vida got home, coloured light flooded The Close. From some blocks away she could see its spires, glowing against the foggy twilight with a hundred strip lights of pink, crimson, and indigo. Behind its synthistone wall, it rose three storeys high, the best, the most expensive brothel in all of Pleasure Sect. She lingered a moment, watching the lights change in a ripple pattern. She could take at least a little pride in her life knowing that she'd be working The Close, not some mouldy cheap whorehouse down by the river.

A clock floated past – sixteen of the seventeens – she was late, over an hour late for dinner. Aleen would be furious. Vida ran down the alley to the gated back door of The Close. At the speaker unit she gave her name.

'Voice confirmed,' it whined. 'Print?'

She laid her thumb on the ID plate.

'Confirmed.'

The gate snapped open, and she trotted into the service tunnel. Behind her, the gate slammed shut. Vida was planning on sneaking through the pantry and up to her room the back way, but when she opened the back door, she found Tia, waiting for her. Aleen's second-in-command looked as fierce as a Garang whose blood oath has been denied. She stood in front of Vida with her arms crossed, like one of the fortified Colossi whose pulse waves guarded the main gate out of Pleasure Sect. Vida had about as good a chance of getting by her.

'Where've you been?' Tia's usually pleasant voice was flat.

'Seeing the festival.'

'Oh?' Tia's expression became even grimmer. 'I told you to stay home, didn't I?'

'You said to wait for you. You didn't say I had to wait in The Close.'

'You stupid little cull! Of all the times to disobey, this is the worst. Half of the damned Peronida Fleet is on shore leave, drinking and roaming around the Sect during festival. You might have been killed, or worse, out there.'

Vida dodged back, but Tia snatched her arm with a strong hand and looked her up and down.

'You've got grass stains on your leggings, you smell of insecticide and daalenerry flowers, and your hands are full of scrapes. Where have you been?'

'I got chased into a roof park by a Lep disguised as a Lifegiver.'

'Don't lie to me!'

'I'm not. It's true. I swear . . . by the Eye of God.'

Tia's eyes widened, but before she could speak, another Marked girl trotted up to them in a clatter of high-heeled gold sandals – Lera, wearing a purple, nearly transparent smartgown programmed to cling. She was in her thirties, still a Not-child, and likely to remain one forever, too, since she never let ambition overrule her laziness.

'Tia, Aleen's not back yet, and we've got clients waiting. What'll we do?'

Vida felt a flare of hope. Maybe she'd escape Aleen's punishment after all.

'Send some of the girls to the receiving area to entertain them,' Tia said. 'If Aleen isn't back by the end of seventeens, I'll help them choose, I guess. How many are waiting?'

'A dozen. One of them's that Cyberguild master you told us to look out for. I put him in the special room, like you said we should. He's bringing his nephew for his first time. The boy's kinda cute.' Lera giggled and winked.

'Fine,' Tia said. 'I'll attend to Sé Hivel myself. Wait for me inside, Lera.'

Lera clattered off. Tia gave Vida's arm such a hard shake she whimpered.

'I don't have time for this right now, but you've got to tell Aleen everything when she gets back. Now, go clean up and change, then come back down here and help in the kitchen. You are *not* to leave the kitchen for the rest of the night. You got that?'

'Yes, Tia.'

'You didn't tell the Protectors about this, did you?'

'No, course not!'

'Good. Smart girl. Now, go!'

Rico and Hi had arrived at The Close just before sixteens, just as the sun was setting in earnest, turning the swirling fog red and bronze. In the brassy light the brothel's plastocrete spires looked like engraved and burnished metal. As they headed toward the front gate in the synthistone wall, Rico noticed what seemed to be writing, big ugly letters scrawled in black, up high on the wall. He paused, then pointed them out to Hi.

'Lep loving bitch,' they spelled out. 'Lep filth must die.'

Hi swore under his breath with a growl of pure venom.

'This kind of thing has got to be stopped,' Hi snapped. 'Well, I suppose you can understand why this racist crap would spread to Pleasure. Some of the people here really need someone else to look down on. That's who joins political groups like UJU.'

'UJU? I didn't think anyone really believed in them. It doesn't make any sense, hating Leps.'

'Yeah, I agree, but I'm afraid a lot of people don't. Look at that big rally they're advertising.'

'No-one's going to really go to that, are they?'

'I bet they get a decent crowd. Someone's got to write those lousy pamphlets, don't they? And someone's got to download them. Well, come on. I'll mention this to Aleen's staff, and they can come out and clean it off before she has to see it.'

Behind the lacy metal gates stood a pair of burly human men, wearing pale blue trousers and shirts cut like a military uniform. Rico felt profoundly squeamish when he realized that they recognized his uncle for a long-time regular customer.

'Come in, Sé,' one said, bowing. 'Good to see you. Madam's holding a little party out back in the gardens.' He glanced Rico's way. 'Good evening to you, Sé.'

Rico mumbled good evening with a dry mouth.

Across a narrow gravelled courtyard rose the façade of the brothel, covered with small windows like the front of a hotel. The front door of polished wood slid back at their approach. Inside stood a pretty young blonde wearing a purple smartgown, close enough to transparent for Rico to make out the shape of her breasts and thighs, and a shadow that had to be pubic hair. Seeing a woman's body in holos, as of course he had, turned out to be different than the real thing. He looked away fast, afraid of staring, but she was looking only at Hi.

'I'm Hivel Jons,' he was saying. 'Where's Aleen?'

'Sé, Madam sends her regrets and asked if you'd wait for her. She had to leave on an urgent errand.'

'Errand? What the hell – Well, I'll bet Aleen didn't tell you where she was going.'

'No, Sé. Won't you come in?'

She settled them in a little room of plush furniture and lush plants, heavy with scentless flowers. When Rico touched a petal, his finger went right through it. The flowers were all holos. On one wall hung a big vidscreen, windowed into four panels, each showing newsfeed from the festival outside. The blonde trotted away, only to return with a short woman dressed in what Rico thought of as real clothes; he couldn't see through her black and beaded dress, anyway. She had eyes the colour of a sunset.

'Sé Jons,' she said, smiling, holding out a hand. 'And this is?'

'My nephew, Rico.' Hi paused to catch her hand and kiss it. 'Good to see you, Tia. Where's Aleen?'

'I don't know. No, honestly, I don't. She got a message over a closed comm about twenty minutes ago and rushed off with a couple of bodyguards.'

Hi's lips tightened, then smoothed, and he forced a smile.

'Well, she'll get back when she does, huh? No matter. Now. We're here to celebrate my nephew's coming of age. He was certified Not-child yesterday. Any ideas?'

'Aleen left instructions.' Tia winked, then turned to Rico. 'Would you like to see some holos of our girls, young Sé? Or would you prefer to be surprised?'

Rico's heart was racing, and he clasped his trembling hands behind his back. Suddenly he remembered the girl he'd seen on the Boulain.

'Um. Well. Do you have any, uh, red-haired girls?'

'Not right now,' Tia said. 'Only a young ward who isn't Marked yet. What about a blonde? Or wait a minute. Darla has brown hair, but it's got a reddish tone in it.'

Hi laughed and clapped a hand on Rico's shoulder.

'I've seen Darla,' Hi said. 'You'll like her.' He glanced at Tia. 'I'll wait for Aleen. The doorman said something about a party out in the Pause?'

'Yes, Sé. Lera, take the guildmaster outside, will you?'

'Fine,' Hi said. 'Oh, and Tia, someone's written on the front wall with a pressure can, it looks like. More racist junk.'

Tia sighed with a shake of her head.

'I'll get a servant out there. Sé Rico, if you'll come with me?'

Rico followed Tia down a long hall. He could hear music dimly, coming from a long way away, and every now and again distant laughter. About halfway down Tia ushered him into a lift booth that levitated them to the third floor in a whoosh of compressed air. In this new hallway, the light gleamed dim and mysterious, shimmering on the carpets of handwoven mats that seemed to suck up all sounds. He smelled perfume, spicy but muted. All along the pale pink walls hung two-dee art work. With a shock, Rico recognized Bassi Ev's famous *Night of the Following Day*. He paused, studying it, seeing brush strokes and whorls of actual paint. This had to be the original, worth more than he was likely to make in a lifetime. His mother would love to see this. At the thought of Barra, Rico felt his cheeks flush.

'Something wrong, Rico?' Tia said. He liked her voice, soft and full of warmth. 'It's all right to be scared, you know. All first-timers are scared.'

'Really?'

'Really.' Tia shook her head in mock-sadness. 'You poor guild boys! They don't really give you a chance to grow up, do they?' She winked. 'Not in the fun ways.'

He grinned, suddenly eased.

At the next door Tia knocked, and in answer the door slid open with a whisper. From perfumed shadows a young woman came to meet them. Although she was delicate and small-boned, she had heavy breasts; he could see them clearly under her wrap of transparent black. Her hair, cut in an exotic fan around her heart-shaped face, did indeed gleam with reddish highlights among the brown. Between her dark eyes sat the tattooed red sun. She smiled and let her wrap fall open, just a little, so he could see pale skin, a soft curve of stomach and a tuft of dark hair just below. All at once he realized that he never should have worried about being able to go through with this.

'Darla, this is Sé Rico,' Tia said. 'Please show him every courtesy.'

Darla smiled and caught one of Rico's hands in hers to draw him inside. He managed to wait before the door behind them closed to kiss her, but only barely.

Since The Close was Aleen's personal home, and she demanded quality, its kitchen was the best in the entire sector. When Vida came downstairs again, washed and changed into a worn shirt and an old pair of shorts, she found its long tables spread with refreshments ready for the reception buffet out in the Pause: steaming platters of weidal topped with cinnamon, fruits and klosh with fancy icings, plates heaped with pastries stuffed with exotic meats from the swamps beyond the city walls. When the cook looked the other way, she stole a few cinnamon pasta wheels and crammed them into her mouth.

Sugar, the old saccule that Aleen had bought some fifty years ago, caught her theft and shook a floury fist at her, but it 'laughed', or rather, the little bladders clustered on its face let loose a delicate fruit-like scent. Vida laughed, too, then went to the work-table to help stuff pastries. As the saccule flipped pieces of raw pastry over fillings, the overhead light prismed through the fine web of membranes between its fingers so that Sugar seemed to be adding rainbows to each piece. When Vida nudged Sugar and made a low honking sound, the saccule reached out and gently squeezed her arm. In the bright light Vida could see the bulging veins and age-white tissue covering all the pouches and bladders around its neck. Fifty years was a very long time for a neuter saccule. Vida moved away fast before Sugar could smell how sad she was. At least Aleen refused to have her saccule servants put down when they got old the way some humans did.

Laughing and shoving each other, some of the Marked men who worked the brothel hurried into the kitchen to grab platters for the buffet. Lera drifted behind them, saw Vida and her chance to put off working for a few minutes.

'Was Tia real mad at you?'

'She got over it.' Vida shrugged. 'I just hope Aleen doesn't chain me to a post until Marking Day.'

'Once you're Marked, you'll be a full citizen and you can leave The Close any time you want. Then Aleen will stop treating you like a baby.'

'I sure hope so. What about that kid? The first-timer?'

'Oh yeah! His name's Rico, and he is so sweet. His uncle's outside in the Pause, making business contacts, or something. You know Hivel Jons. He hasn't even looked at any of the girls.'

'How about the boys?'

'Nah. He's a dull one. Rico's with Darla, now.'

Vida smiled. Darla made a specialty of virgins.

'Come on, Lera,' Jeri called out. 'It won't break your back to carry something, too.'

Lera pouted in his direction but picked up the smallest tub of klosh.

'Come back later and tell me how it went,' said Vida.

'Sure.' Lera leaned close and added in a whisper, 'Too bad you're not Marked, this Rico asked if we had any red-haired girls. He looked so cute! I took one look into those deep dark eyes and wished *I* had your red hair.'

Vida laughed. But after Lera left, she found it hard to concentrate on her work. If only she were Marked, she could have asked for Rico. But even if she had, he would only go away again afterwards, back to his life of freedom, and here she'd still be, trapped in Pleasure Sect forever. Loath. Just too utterly loath. Vida picked up a baking sheet and threw it hard against the wall.

Hivel Jons y Macconnel was not a man used to being kept waiting. With a frightened Lera muttering excuses at his side, he stalked through The Close and stepped out through double glass doors to the sheltered garden of the Pause. Hanging on poles among the tall ferns and frond-trees, coloured lanterns gleamed. Flowers, real ones this time, oozed perfume into the warm night air. Laughing and talking, clients stood round in groups or clustered near the buffet tables, although a small crowd had gathered in front of the vidscreen hanging from a garden wall. Hi edged through the crowd and got himself a skewer of spiced meat and a glass of wine so dark a red it seemed black in the lantern light. At least Aleen set a good table at these functions. But where was the damned woman?

'Sé?' Lera still hovered at his elbow. 'Is there anything else I can give you?'

He glanced at her face, as vacant as a flower if as pretty.

'No thanks.' He reached into a pocket of his robes and pulled out a couple of coins, then pressed them into her hand. 'Run along.'

She smiled, bowed, and darted away, as if she were afraid he'd change his mind.

Hi took a long good look at his fellow guests, guildspeople mostly, since only the rich could afford The Close. He spotted plenty of clients with the sashes of masters slantwise over their robes, talking together and smiling like the best of friends – not that any of them believed it of the others. Off to one side stood a woman who towered over the Palace citizens around her. Slender as a stalk, with jet black hair wound round her head in braids – she had to be from Souk, whose low gravity grew humans tall.

'The ambassador,' Tia's soft voice murmured at his elbow.

'Ah,' Hi said. 'Is Rico okay?'

'More than okay by now.' She paused, smiling. 'He took to Darla, shall we say.'

Hi forced a grin and wondered why he disliked this woman so much.

'Fine. Just let me know when Aleen gets back.'

With a nod Tia walked away, pausing now and then to speak to a guest before she disappeared inside. It occurred to Hi that maybe he disliked Tia so much because she disliked him. Under her little smiles he saw an edge – not that he particularly cared. She knew her job, he supposed, and that was all that mattered. Just like Jevon did. He winced, remembering his factor's pale face that morning, and the way she'd clamped her lower lip between her teeth, determined not to cry. He should never have taken his nerves out on her, never! She was due for a raise; he'd better make it a big one. In front of him a saccule servant, dressed in a lacy black apron, paused with a tray of used glasses and napkins. Hi dropped his empty skewer into the litter and made a little hissing noise out of the side of his mouth. The saccule released a good-humoured smell like candy and wandered on.

Off by a wall covered with gold flowers, the round little Countess of Motta was standing draped in silver, and talking with two masters wearing the dark green robes of Power Sect. Hi strolled over, sipping his glass of wine, the only drink he'd allow himself this evening, and joined them. One of the Power men excused himself and wandered off, but the other stayed, though he moved back several steps in deference to the leader of the all-important Cyberguild, who would expect to keep the attention of a countess all to himself.

'Hivel, darling,' the Countess said and extended a lazy hand.

'Olletta, lovely to see you.' Hi kissed her hand, which smelled of perfume and mushrooms in equal measure, briefly. 'How are things out on the estates?'

'Damp, cold and filthy, of course. They always are. Festivals mean so much to us poor farmers. It's so rare that a swamp girl like me gets into Palace.'

'Swamp girl.' Hi raised his eyes heavenward. 'Poor farmers.'

'Well, rich farmers, then.' She smiled, glancing slantwise at the man from Power Guild. 'But farmers nonetheless. You'd all starve without us.'

'Which is why you're rich, yeah. Did you just come in for the festival?'

'No, I've got a little scheme in mind.'

'Oh, really?'

'Yes, really.' She raised an arch eyebrow. 'And I can't help thinking, Hivel, that it might in some way interest you.'

She smiled, he smiled, and he was thinking of her hereditary vote on the Upper Council. The Cyberguild could always use another ally when the time came to appropriate public monies.

'You're always interesting, Olletta,' Hi said. 'We should meet while you're in town. A lunch, maybe.'

'Yes, indeed. I'll have my factor call yours. It's about the Magnus AI. I heard on the newsfeed that it's going to be reprogrammed.'

'That's only talk. He's too damn valuable to mess with. I know what you've heard. It's those new robopumps that Industrial thinks can run the drainage system instead of Magnus. They haven't been tested enough to suit me. If the pump system fails, this city drowns.'

'Well, that's true.' The Countess allowed herself to look disappointed. 'There's just so many other things that an AI could be doing.'

'And the Agricultural Guild can think of a few requests?'

'Let's have lunch.'

'Okay, sure. I'll look forward to it.'

Around them the party began falling silent; the laughter faded, the talk stopped, sapients turned away. On the vidscreen on the far wall, the evening newsfeed had begun. A few at a time, the guests drifted over to watch the crack presenter team of Grid TransPalace. Each presenter, three humans and a Hirrel, appeared in a corner window, commenting back and forth on the windowed images that shuttered open and closed at centre screen. Hi, who got his newsfeed direct through an implant, raided the buffet.

It was some while later that Tia finally appeared, smiling at his elbow to tell him that Aleen was back.

'Shall I escort you, Patron Jons?'

'No thanks. I know the way by now.'

Tia's smile barely hid her resentment. Hi strode down the long hall to the lift booth, then punched in a code that only a few of Aleen's clients knew. Up under the spires lay a hidden fourth floor to The Close. Stepping out of the booth brought him into a tiny room that held only a door. Hi punched still another code. When it slid back, Hi walked through a pair of autogates into Aleen's public bedroom, a suite, really – a bedroom, a washroom, a little bar for drinks.

The bedroom had dissolved its walls with holoscreen views – a wide prospect of snow and mist from Tableau, a dense jungle from the Equatorial States of Belie, and a view of a garden, planted with life-forms he didn't recognize; in its sky hung a double sun. When he glanced back, he saw a fourth screen powering on around the closing door – a view of deep space, a nebula gleaming behind a spangle of stars. The bed itself stood in the centre of the room, overhung by a canopied webbing, hand-knotted by Lep women from gold and silver threads. He heard movement and turned just in time to see Aleen walking through the garden holo. She wore a modest grey slithergown and a dark green cloak. Her emerald green hair hung loose, flowing down her back.

'Where the hell have you been?' Hi snapped.

'Out cleaning up your mess.' Aleen took off the cloak and dropped it onto a chair. 'Or your nephew's mess. You don't want anyone to hear this.'

Hi reached through the front slit of his robe to his shirt pocket and brought out a flat featureless black card that looked like nothing but a strip of packing plastic. When he whispered a code word, a strip of red light ran round the edge. A blackbox card, as they were called, would defeat any surveillance mechanism on Palace. They were expensive, hard to find, and highly illegal.

'Nice,' Aleen said. 'Where did you get that?'

'You don't want to know. I've got my reasons for carrying it. Now, what's this mess?'

The door to the washroom slid back, and Arno walked out, wiping his hands on a towel. Apparently Aleen had objected to his filthy trousers, because he now wore a blue pair that were a size too big for him. He gave his father a lopsided grin.

'Those Protectors caught me,' he said, and his voice was perfectly clear and steady. 'Threw me in deeplock.'

'Thanks to what's-his-name,' Aleen snapped. 'Making sure they noticed you.'

'Hey,' Arno said. 'Don't blame Rico. I've never known anyone more loyal.'

'I wasn't calling him a traitor. I was calling him stupid.' She turned to Hi. 'Don't you people teach your kids *anything*? It's cost me a long pass to my second best house to crack your son out, and it's just a damn good thing the officer on desk duty tonight owed me a few favours, or I'd never even have heard about it.'

'Tell him the worst, why not?' Arno glanced round, then headed for a pale blue datachair in front of the deep space holo. 'The arrest went to file before Aleen's goon could stop it.'

'So? You're supposed to be a trash addict. They get arrested all the time.'

'They get tested down at the station, too. My blood's clean. And that went into the file.'

Hi swore under his breath. Arno flopped into the chair and stretched his legs out in front of him.

'Nice to see you, Dad. Aren't you even going to say hello?'

'You idiot! What the *hell* were you doing on the street? You're supposed to be in hiding.'

'Aren't you going to sit down?' Aleen snapped. 'You make me nervous, pacing around like that.'

Hi hadn't realized that he was pacing. He sat down on the end of the bed, facing Arno, and Aleen perched on the edge of an overstuffed grey chair.

'It's a long story, Dad,' Arno said, 'and you aren't going to like any of it. The short answer is that I didn't have any choice. It started two days ago. I was backtracking some rips in the Map, looking for that cybermaster who crashed that Customs gate last week. Remember that? And I was tipped to a coded echo hidden in gigs of scratch stuff in some garbage base on the outskirts of the Map. I never would have found it without the tip.'

Hi held up one hand for silence, then turned to Aleen.

'Do you want to hear this stuff?' he said. 'Knowing it could be dangerous.'

'Life can be dangerous. Especially around you.'

'Yeah, so it seems. I guess I should apologize.'

Aleen let her eyes meet his, just briefly, but he was sure that he'd caught her smiling. He turned back to his son.

'Get to the point, Arno.'

'It was an audio dump of a revenant hiring an assassin.'

'Oh yeah? All right, that's a point.'

'It gets better. This assassin is Vi-Kata. Yeah, that's right, the Outcast himself. Somehow he got on planet.'

'Past the autogates? That's hard to believe.'

'Yeah. But he's here now with a couple of contracts.'

'A happy little addition to the festivities, huh? Did you send the tip and the record to the Protectors' hot drop on their access on the Map?'

'Sure did. Marked it urgent, too. But well, that's not quite enough, I think.'

'Yeah? What's it to us?'

'Dad, the contract came from our old friend Riva.'

Hi opened his mouth, then closed it, considering for a moment.

'Interesting,' Hi said.

'Yeah. I thought so. Especially, since I'm one of the targets.'

Aleen caught her breath, but the two men merely looked at each other for a long, cold moment.

'Bad news,' Hi said at last. 'Who did the tip come from?'

'I don't know.'

'You don't know? How can you not know? There had to be a route mark.'

'There was, yeah, but from a place that doesn't exist, at least not any more. When I went to look for it, the routing led me up against the Caliostro firewall. Right at the bombed-out area. That AI's been a mess for how long?'

'A thousand years,' Hi answered. 'At least. But that doesn't mean there aren't any daemons and rogue agents still operating in there.'

'You're the only person I know who could get any use out of wrecked circuits like those.'

'Yeah? Sounds like there are two of us.'

Hi paused, thinking. He'd been meaning to squeeze some time out of his impossible schedule to look over poor old Caliostro and see if anything could be salvaged from those particular ruins. Maybe he'd better find the time right away. He looked at Aleen and found her reading something off the cybereye he'd given her.

'I'll need details,' he said to Arno.

'Sure. You can see why I wanted to tell you in person, though. Can't leave this kind of data lying around the Map uncoded. Rico has a meta, by the way, that'll get you to the dump.'

'Rico? By the bloody damn weeping Eye! Why did you –'

'One, because no-one would figure I'd give it to him. Two, because I didn't know if I'd live to reach The Close, and if I didn't, this way you would have data to start hunting with. And three, because he's a good Mapwalker, Dad, real good. Look.' Arno leaned forward earnestly. 'Rico's going to be better than me some day, he really is. I could see it from the first time I helped him jack into the Map. Everyone's always underestimated him.' He paused for a twisted grin. 'Because of me.'

'Well, I can see that. You threw a lot of shade around for other people to stand in. Okay. I'll take your word for it. He's just so damn young.'

'And naive,' Aleen muttered.

'I should have known you'd be listening,' Hi said, grinning. 'Arno, who's the other contract on? Anyone we know?'

'No, that's the weirdest part of the whole thing. Kata was hired to kill me and an unMarked girl named Vida.'

'What?' Hi said.

Aleen had gone very still, leaning forward on her chair.

'Yeah. Just some unMarked girl.' Arno spread his hands. 'Can't figure it. But if Riva went to the trouble to hire the Outcast to kill her, she must be one hell of an important clue. That's why I took the risk of leaving my hole. I was trying to get to The Close to see Aleen, so she could get you over here, so I could check with you about this. Didn't know you'd be here already, so I – '

'Shut up a minute, kid.' Hi had never seen Aleen pale before. 'What's going on? You know this girl?'

'Oh yes.' Aleen's voice was perfectly steady. 'She's my ward.'

Hi frankly stared, his mouth half-open.

'Well, hey,' Arno said. 'Then you'd know if there was some reason she's important.'

'Oh yes. There's a very good reason.' Aleen rose smoothly, calmly, smiled at them both. 'Excuse me. I'll just get her up here.'

'Wait a minute,' Hi snapped. 'I don't want her seeing Arno.'

'I can hide in the washroom, Dad. I want to hear this.'

Hi considered – safe enough, really.

'Just keep the door shut.'

'Dad, I could have figured that out, okay?'

Aleen walked over and reached into the Belie jungle to pull out a comm unit. She punched a code, waited, then nodded at its tiny screen, that vague gesture of a person whose call has been answered.

'Tia? Where's Vida?' A pause. 'Well, tell her to wash her hands and come up here. No, not my office. My public room.' Another pause. 'She what? Why didn't you tell me – well, of course – yeah, that's true – fine, fine, just get her up here now.' She powered out and stood for a moment, cradling the unit in both hands, before she spoke. 'Someone tried to kill Vida today. Fancy that.'

'What?'

'During the festival. A Lep chased her, she said, a Lep in a Lifegiver's robes.'

'Vi-Kata's idea of a joke. Lifegiver, life taker. Really funny.' Hi got up and walked over to her. Much to his surprise she turned and leaned into his arms. He could feel her shaking – an even bigger surprise. Even though she stood taller than he, at that moment she seemed small to him, small and soft.

'But why?' Arno said, rising. 'I mean, who is this kid?'

Aleen twisted free of Hi's embrace and gave Arno a look that made him step back.

'You'll find out later,' she snapped. 'Vida deserves to hear it, too.'

'Sure, hey, calm down.' Hi was half expecting her to turn on him for that soothing tone of voice, but she merely took a deep breath, as if following orders. 'If the girl's in danger, let's get her some protection. Hand me that comm, will you? I need to call my bodyguard.'

By the middle of the evening, the kitchen stood piled high with pans and spattered with grease. Honking and hissing, Sugar wandered outside for a well-deserved breath of moist air, while Vida programmed the cleaning bot. Two little saccule scullery workers stood watching, sucking the webs between their fingers.

'There, all done,' Vida said. 'You can push the red button now.'

They stared up at her hopelessly. No matter how many times Vida explained about the on switch, they simply could not retain the information. She pressed the red button for them, and the bot whirred to life. Squealing with delight, the scullies followed as it slid toward the nearest pile of garbage. Vida straightened up and found Tia standing in the doorway.

'Aleen wants to see you. Now.'

'Oh God. How loath! She's not even going to wait till morning to yell at me.'

'I'm afraid not. Vida, be careful. Watch what you say. I've never heard Aleen sound so . . . so . . .'

'She's furious, I'll bet.'

'Well, yes, but that's not what I meant. Something's really wrong.'

Vida felt as if her stomach had dropped a long cold way. She pulled off her apron, tossed it on the floor for the saccules to pick up, and bolted from the kitchen. All the way up in the lift booth, she could feel herself shaking. At the door to the public bedroom, she laid her palm on the announce panel so the door could tell Aleen she'd arrived.

'Come in, Vida,' Aleen's voice sounded from the speaker. 'The Eye of God has finally found you.'

When Vida walked in and found Sé Hivel there, sitting in

a grey datachair, she was so startled she could barely speak.

'Vida, sit down.' Aleen pointed at an armless formfit chair that she must have dragged in from her office. 'You may trust Sé Hivel. He's trying to help us.'

When Vida sat, Aleen hesitated, then took her usual overstuffed chair, a little behind Sé Hivel.

'First, tell me about the Lep.' Aleen sounded neutral, indifferent even. 'The one who chased you.'

Vida thought she'd seen all of Aleen's moods, but this was a new one. While Vida talked, telling Aleen about her run through the longtube and the roof park, the Madam sat perfectly still. Sé Hivel, however, leaned forward, nodding now and again at some detail.

'And so I hid in the tower.' Vida hesitated; she should tell Aleen everything, but the revenant had saved her life, after all, and it had been afraid of something, too. 'I thought I was a goner, but some men, humans, got into the garden. They were drunk, I think, and yelling and stuff. So the Lep ran away.'

'You're sure about that scaling on his wrist?'

'Yeah. I looked really carefully.'

'Well, we all know about your memory. Green and red spirals with a blue counter stroke?' She glanced at Sé Hivel. 'That's a very minor line that died out some years ago. Obviously a false design. The Lep must have dyed his scales. Clever.'

'Why was he chasing me, Madam?'

Aleen ignored the question and read from her flashing cybereye. 'This all happened at the Carillon roof park at, what, mid-fifteens?'

'Yes, Madam.'

'There's a report of a malfunction in the caretaking system. The gardener, a saccule named Blue, found signs of vandalism and made a report at sixteens-ten. More than an hour later.' Aleen paused, raising one eyebrow, the one over her flesh eye.

Vida said nothing, merely clasped her hands between her knees and waited. Sé Hivel leaned forward.

'Vida, come on,' he said, and his voice was gentle. 'Tell us what really happened, okay?'

Vida looked down at the floor. In her mind she could see the Lep's sleeve falling back and the barrel of a weapon.

'Vida,' Sé Hivel went on. 'That Lep was trying to kill you. How can we keep you safe if we don't know everything?'

'True, Sé.' Vida looked up. 'All right. There weren't any men. There was a revenant. In the control slab for the bells. His name is Calios. He reprogrammed the Lep's finder. So the Lep would think I'd got out, I mean, and gone somewhere else.'

'And how did you call this rev up, Vida?' Sé Hivel asked. 'Come on, you can tell me. I'm Cyberguild, aren't I?'

'I don't know how. There weren't any icons. I touched the slab; well, I ran my hand over it, so I must have touched a lot of controls. And he appeared. He shone a light into my eyes and started talking about deens, whatever that is.'

Sé Hivel laughed, a short sharp bark, then turned to Aleen.

'Bright red hair,' he said, conversationally. 'And access revenants from the old technology do her favours after they've typed her DNA.'

Aleen nodded, glancing back and forth between Sé Hivel and Vida.

'You've guessed, haven't you, Hi?'

'Have I?' He grinned at her. 'You tell me. A lot of people have red hair. Well, not a lot, but people from all kinds of families.'

'Madam?' Vida could stand it no longer. 'Please? What does he mean?'

'I don't mean to tease you,' Aleen said. 'Vida, what did I tell you about your parents?'

'That my mother was a woman over in Service Sect, and she had an illegal pregnancy. After the Protectors arrested her, the courts gave me to you to raise as an Unauthorized.'

'True. What did I tell you about your father?'

'Nothing, Madam.'

'True.' Aleen glanced away, as if she were thinking. 'He was Orin L'Var.'

Sé Hivel made a little cackling noise.

'Thought so,' he said. 'But how do you know?'

'None of your business.' Aleen gave him a look that would have silenced the First Citizen himself. 'I have my sources.' She turned back to Vida. 'You're a L'Var, all right, the last of them. The last person alive of an entire family.'

'But I can't be!' Vida clenched her hands in her lap. 'They were traitors!' She turned to Sé Hivel. 'I can't be.'

'Yeah, kid? Well, I'll tell you something. There's a lot of people on Palace who have their doubts about that traitor business.' He smiled briefly. 'I wouldn't lose sleep about it, if I were you.'

Vida could only stare at Aleen as if she were begging for help. Aleen ignored her. Sé Hivel held up his left hand and let the sleeve of his robe slide back. Vida nearly yelped – his whole left arm shone with metal, gleaming circuits and jack studs, embedded into the flesh and bone. He rested his arm on the arm of the datachair, wiggled it a bit until one of the jacks clicked in, then glanced away. Half of his mind seemed gone somewhere far away even as the other half looked out across the room. All at once he smiled, but it was a bitter twist of his mouth.

'What have you found?' Aleen said.

'A murder during the festival. The Protectors found a young monk dead in an alley. His robes were stolen. Nothing else. Brother Lennos was his name.'

Vida yelped and crammed a hand over her mouth. Sé Hivel freed himself from the datachair and pulled his sleeve down over the cyberarm.

'Out with it,' Aleen snapped at Vida.

'I talked with him. He gave me an Eye and blessed me.'

'Too bad he couldn't bless himself,' Sé Hivel said. 'Kata must have been right behind the girl, Aleen. She's damn lucky.'

'It wasn't just luck. The revenant helped me.'

'That's true. And very interesting.'

'You won't hurt him, will you?'

'Vida!' Sé Hivel laughed, but gently. 'You can't hurt a revenant. They're not real.'

Vida felt herself blush.

'But they can look like it, yeah, and be very convincing,' Sé Hivel went on. 'Don't be embarrassed. Why did you think I'd hurt him?'

Vida hesitated, torn, but Sé Hivel was right. Calios was only a visual embodiment of data coupled with an audio through-put and sensor capacity, just as her textbooks said, not a young man with jet-dark skin and a charming smile.

'He said someone was chasing him. That's why.'

'Did he? Did he use the words tracking program or tracker?'

'Yeah, he did.'

When Sé Hivel turned to the madam and raised an eyebrow, Aleen took his cue; she stood up and gestured at Vida.

'Come into my office for a moment, Vida. I want to show you the legal certificates about your birth. Then I'll seal off this room so you can wait here, while I do some hard thinking.'

'Wait, Madam?'

'Sé Hivel is providing us with a bodyguard for you.'

'A bodyguard? I don't need – well, yeah, I guess I do.'

'You learn fast,' Sé Hivel said.

'Thank you, Sé. And thank you for the bodyguard, too.' As Vida followed Aleen into the dim fastness of her office, she found herself remembering the festival day behind her. For the first time in her life she hated her eidetic memory. Try as she might, she could not banish the image of Brother Lennos, smiling at her.

As soon as Aleen shut the door behind her, Arno walked out of the washroom. The flesh side of his face was grinning.

'A L'Var,' Arno said. 'A real live L'Var! Famous genotype and all.'

'Yeah, yeah, but don't get carried away. A lot of what you hear about the L'Var genotype is just plain crap.'

'Ah come on, Dad. Are you trying to tell me that they didn't have mysterious secret powers?'

'A race of cybersorcerers? No. I actually heard them called that once on the newsfeed.'

'But their genes were engineered to do something. They were the original cybers, weren't they?'

'Sure were. That was a long time ago though. Who knows now?' Hi shrugged. 'It's interesting, yeah. I'm not sure how significant she is.'

'Significant enough for Riva to want to kill her.'

'True.' Hi mimicked Aleen's crisp tone. 'True, Sé Arno. What do you think about the revenant?'

'There are plenty of records of just that kind of rev. They set up Map access for citizens, helped people make comm connections, all the things a Maprunner does now. Nothing out of the ordinary.'

'None of them has functioned since the Schism Wars. I checked while I was jacked in. Their access sockets were sabotaged.'

'What? Why?'

'One of the factions saw them as an insult to God the Creator. They looked like sapients, they spoke, they seemed to think like sapients – blasphemy, is what they called it.'

'What a load.' Arno shrugged. 'So at least one survived, huh? We should look into this.'

'I intend to as soon as I can. But what counts now is getting you hidden.'

'I'd better be out of sight when Nju Tok gets here, that's for sure.'

'I wish to God that the Garang would lie! Just once in a while, just every now and then – like now. But you might as well try to drain the damn swamps as get them to.'

'Well, if I headed for the Spaceport with a Garang bodyguard, I might as well buy time on the screens and advertise. Or walk along shouting my name.'

They headed for the lift booth in silence, spoke no more on the way down to the third floor, a warren of tiny rooms for saccules and other servants. The room where Arno would hide stood down at the end of a hall and round a corner. A pallet on the floor with shabby blankets, a washstand – but Aleen had dug up a portable jack from somewhere and a box of what looked like odd spare parts. Hi slipped the blackbox out of his pocket: it was working just fine. Arno knelt down and began poking through the box of tri-stil and metal oddments.

'You know, I think I can actually piece together some kind of access from this stuff,' Arno said. 'Amazing. I can get into the areas I need, anyway. I don't want to just use Aleen's listed Mapstation to get myself a false name and a ticket off planet.'

'Yeah, don't,' Hi said. 'And remember, give me a few days before you hit the street. Let's let the Protectors earn their salaries.'

'That's true, but the longer I stay here, the more likely it is that he'll find me.'

'If he's been arrested he won't be finding anyone.'

'Well, yeah, but –'

'Look, patience has never been one of your virtues. We both know that. How about giving it a try this time?'

'Sure, Dad. Don't worry. Besides, maybe even if they don't arrest him, they can keep him busy while I get off planet.'

'Good thought. So it's come to this, has it? I'm sorry, son, really sorry. I never thought I'd be sending you into exile.'

Arno shrugged and got up to glance round the shabby room. It was all an adventure to him, Hi supposed, whether tracking a rogue cybermaster on the Map or pretending to be a drug addict, living in the steamy corners of Pleasure Sect while all the time he was a secret agent for the Cyberguild – and now this, running for his life under an assumed name and a new identity. Hi sighed, remembering what it felt like to be young and believe yourself immortal.

'Where are you going? Or should I even ask?'

'Souk. I don't want to say more than that, but they always need cybers on Souk.'

'Good. Sell out the whole guild if you need to.'

Arno laughed, aiming a fake punch at his father's shoulder.

'Thanks, Dad. A parting gift, huh? Look, you'd better get out of here. Remember what I said about Rico, okay? He's the only cybe we've got who can do what I can do.'

'His mother would kill me if I sent him underground.'

'Don't, then. Going underground didn't do me a damn bit of good, did it? Why waste your time? They'll only be looking for it again. Hide him in plain sight, and Riva will look somewhere else for your agent.'

'Yeah. Yeah, that's true.' Hi hesitated, glancing at a tiny window. Outside, the festival noise swept down the street like a river. 'Well, look. I'll get back here tomorrow. You can give me the details on what you found then. Okay?'

'Okay. I'm not going anywhere tonight, that's for sure.'

Hi opened the door and stepped out, but he stood for a moment with his hand on the edge of it and looked back.

'Hey, Dad?' Arno said, still grinning. 'Wish me luck.'

'Luck,' Hi whispered. 'Lots of it.'

Hi closed the door behind him and strode off, heading for the lift booth. How could he do this? How could he let his own son go off into exile, let him run the risks he'd run already? It was for the sake of the Map, he reminded himself. At the moment he could trust no-one but his own son. The Map was what he'd sworn to protect at any and all costs, the Map that kept Palace – hell, that kept the entire Pinch – up and running. Without the Map all the technology and knowledge that made the citizens of the Pinch civilized would disappear like a display from a dying screen. Since the colonial days, they'd lost too much knowledge already, thanks to wars and other disasters. They couldn't afford to lose any more.

And now some rogue cyber, someone who had to be a master at his craft, was subverting the Map, just a detail here and there. So far. Hi had no idea of what this dangerous idiot hoped to accomplish. Finding out what was part of his job; searching him out and stopping him cold was the rest. Tangled up with the hunt was another problem: Riva, who'd been using the Map illegally for years now despite the guild's efforts to catch and identify her. This time she's gone too far, Hi thought. I can bring in all kinds of police agencies now, if she's using guided revs to hire murderers.

The lift booth delivered him straight to the kitchen, where two Stinkers scrubbed pans while a cleaning bot scrubbed walls. Hi found himself wondering if the Colonizers had needed slaves with flesh and blood hands to clean up after them. He doubted it. As he stepped into the hall, he could hear laughter and music from the gardens of the Pause. All these people depended on the Cyberguild – they depended on him – to keep their lives safe and decent. He did his best to remember that always. At the entrance to the Pause he glanced out and saw Rico, sitting on the grass with Lera. Lying on the grass in front of him was an enormous plate of food, which Rico was eating his way through while she chattered at him. Rico looked a little shell-shocked, but he'd recover. Grinning, Hi walked on.

'Sé Hivel!' Tia came trotting down the hall. 'Sé Hivel, wait!'

Hi stopped, still smiling a little, and let the panting Tia catch up to him.

'There's two Garang at the front door,' she said. 'They insist you summoned them.'

'I sure did. Thanks.'

Out on the gravelled walk Nju Tok, dressed in the midnight blue uniform of the Cyberguild's employees, stood waiting, his arms crossed over his chest while he scowled at the elaborate architecture of The Close. With him, also scowling, stood a taller, thinner version of Nju, but this Garang was wearing a nondescript green pullover and a pair of grey trousers. In the artificial light their golden fur gleamed like metal.

'Jak.' Nju jerked a thumb at his brother.

'Pleased to meet you, Jak.' Hi shook hands briefly. 'We'll have to get you a uniform. The Cyberguild will be paying for this temporary job.'

'Sé Hivel!' Nju interrupted before his brother could speak. 'Have you repented of your earlier foolishness?'

'Yes, Nju. I've repented mightily.'

'Good. The next time you come here to waste your time upon unmanly activities, will I accompany you?'

'Yeah, you sure will.'

'Good. Then let us enter and see the child of whom you told me.'

They found Vida up in Aleen's public bedroom. Curled up in the formfit, she was watching the news on a vidscreen that had appeared among the icy wastes of Tableau. The two Garang nodded in her direction, then stood staring at holo images from the day's Centre Council meeting while Vida sat up straight and stared at them. She looked remarkably self-possessed, Hi decided, for what she'd just been through. The girl had guts, but then, all the L'Vars had, when there still had been L'Vars.

'Where's Aleen?'

'In her office making a closed comm link. She said she wanted to call Cardinal Roha.'

'Roha? *The* Cardinal Roha?'

'Sé Hivel,' Nju said. 'There can only be one such personage.'

'Yeah, I know, I know. Did she say anything else, Vida?'

'No, Sé Hivel. There's a lot of stuff I just don't understand.'

'Yeah, I'll bet.' Cardinal Roha? Why would a madam be calling the highest-ranking prelate on the planet? Why, for God's sake, would he be taking her call? 'Well, she'll tell us what she wants us to know and not one thing more.'

'Exactly right.' Aleen walked out of the holo of the garden. 'So. This is Nju Tok's brother?'

Both Garang swirled round and bowed to her, a gesture she acknowledged with a nod. When she flicked her hand in Vida's direction, the girl rose and mimicked her nod.

'So,' Nju said. 'This is Sé Vida?'

'Yeah, it sure is,' Hi said. 'Jak, her life is very important to a lot of people.'

Jak stood between Hi and Vida, glancing this way and that in confusion, until Nju spoke a few words in their language. Then he smiled, if you could call the thin twitch of a Garang mouth a smile, and knelt at Hi's feet. Hi put his right hand on Jak's softly-furred head.

'There shall be a contract between us,' Hi said. 'The guild pledges your wages and support for as long as Sé Vida needs you.'

'And I in turn pledge my life. Should an enemy get past me and harm this girl, and I still live, then I will live only a short while longer.'

'I witness,' Nju said. 'Madama Aleen?'

'I witness as well.' Aleen turned to Vida. 'You must never leave your room without Jak. Do you understand me?'

'Yes, Madam. I do.'

Vida stood looking at her temporary guard with an expression Hi couldn't read – bewilderment, certainly, at the events of this day, but some tougher feeling as well lay in her eyes. As he studied her, the red hair of course, but also the shape of her finely modelled jaw, her wide-set green eyes, and her small, tightly set ears, he wondered why he hadn't realized a long time ago that she was a L'Var. That genotype had been one of the best-maintained in the Pinch, and it seemed to breed true in all aspects. He hadn't realized it because it had never crossed his mind that such a thing was possible, he supposed. From now on, he'd better keep reminding himself that in this dangerous game he and the rogue cybermaster were playing, nothing was too improbable to be true.

By the time Uncle Hi came to fetch him from the Pause, Rico was lying on the grass, half-asleep and yawning, with his head in Lera's naked lap. He had never felt so good in his life, he decided, as he felt right then. Not even the sight of a scowling Nju Tok could ruin his mood. How the Garang Japat could think that sex was something unmanly lay beyond his reckoning. He sat up, gave Lera a last kiss, then got to his feet and stretched.

'Hail, Nju!' he said. 'So you caught up with us, huh?'

'Your uncle caught up with his senses, Sé Rico. Shall we leave this place of foolishness?'

'Sure,' Hi said. 'I hope we'll be able to get a cab back to the hotel. It's not a short walk for these old bones.'

'If Sé Hivel is weary, then I shall carry him.'

'No, no, no, not that weary. Besides, I need you to keep your eyes open. We may have an enemy in Pleasure.'

Nju smiled and flexed his long fingers. Steel claws slid from hidden implant sheaths, ready.

For a long while the three of them stood at the gates of The Close with one of the uniformed guards, while the other hovered on the kerb outside, flicking the switch on his hand-held call box. In ordinary times a robocab would have made its way to them in minutes, but not tonight, not during festival. Rico took the chance to walk down to the end of the wall and look up – sure enough, someone had already scrubbed away the racist graffiti. UJU. What did the acronym mean, anyway? No-one knew.

Rico walked back and stood watching the flow of celebrating sapients clogging the streets, humans, Leps, the occasional Hirrel, most of them laughing in whatever way their race had of showing mirth, some singing or dancing down the street to music only they could hear. Every once in a while, though, Rico saw a sapient, usually human, taking out a mean drunk on a saccule servant with their hands or a vinyl strap while the Stinker cowered and squealed. Rico would have liked to have intervened, but he knew from growing up on Palace that such compassion would only mean a worse beating for the saccule later.

Once a cab finally arrived, the ride seemed interminable, since the unit had to practically inch its way through the mobbed streets. By the time they reached the hotel Rico drowsed. Yawning, rubbing his eyes, he followed his uncle blindly into the vast echoing lobby, all inlaid tile and marble, dimly lit here so close to dawn. Over a vast floral display a vidscreen hung, glowing with a collage of images from the festival. Hi hiked up his robes and began searching his trouser pockets for their lift booth keycard.

'Ah, a pleasant surprise!' Nju said. 'Sé Barra is here, awaiting us.'

This 'pleasant surprise' brought Rico wide awake in a hurry. Sure enough, there was his mother, rising from an upholstered armchair and scowling their way. Since she was wearing midnight blue coveralls with digital readouts down the sleeves, he could assume that she'd come looking for them straight from work. Hi groaned under his breath as she came striding over, a tall woman with waist-length black hair, bound neatly in a long braid to leave the chip slots at the base of her skull unobstructed. Although she was beautiful in a strong sort of way, and no-one would have called Hi handsome, they shared a certain look, the same intense black eyes and sharp profile. Golden numbers flickered up her sleeves, changing endlessly. Apparently, she was still transmit-linked to that job. In their family, Barra was the hardware expert, though she could walk the Map with the best of them when she needed to.

'Well, hello there, Sis,' Hi said. 'Come for the festival?'

She ignored him and looked Rico over. He could feel his face burning as she sighed and looked away again.

'Let's go up to your room,' Barra said. 'Nju, hail.'

'Hail to you, Sé Barra. Do you have luggage or some case that I might carry for you?'

'None, thanks. I won't be staying long.'

This promise got Rico through the silent ride up in the lift booth. No-one spoke as they all trooped down the long hall to the suite Hi had rented for this festival night. Once they were inside, Nju sat down with his back to the closed entry door. He would sleep there, too, curled up on his sleep mat. The rest of them went into the spacious main room, carpeted in pale pink, draped in tan silk, scattered with soft brocade furniture. Two big vidscreens hung on the longest wall; one ran the Centre Council report while the other showed tower graphs of the popularity rating garnered by each politician for the day's votes. The graphs rose and fell in a kind of dance as each vote changed the constituents' opinion of their representatives. Barra sat down in the middle of the sofa, while Hi headed straight for the small liquor cabinet.

'Something to drink, Sis?'

'No. I've got something important to tell you, by the way.'

Hi grinned and pulled the blackbox card out of his shirt pocket. The edges glowed red.

'Where did you get that?' Barra said.

'Don't ask.' Hi put the card onto an end table, then opened the cabinet. 'I'm just looking for bottled water, or soda, something like that. The water you get in Pleasure tastes like swamp to me. Rico? You want something?'

'No thanks.'

Rico headed for a slender wooden desk on the far side of the room. It held the antique frame he'd discovered that afternoon, a flat black screen embossed with a couple of archaic access points of the sort he'd studied only in history classes. Hi set a carafe of pinkish soda down on the low table in front of the sofa, then pulled off his robes and dumped them onto a chair.

'Damn things are so hot,' he remarked, then returned to pouring his drink. 'I've got something important to say, too, but you go first. Why didn't you just send me a packet, anyway?'

'I didn't want this over the lines just yet, though I suppose the wretched grids will find out soon enough. Rico, what are you doing over there?'

'Just fooling around, Mom. You should come take a look at this. It's really old hardware.'

Barra did join him, leaning over the desk with one hand on the back of his chair. She smelled clean, of soap and the wipe chemicals she used on circuits, not like the women in The Close. He felt himself blushing.

'Rico, it's all right,' she said. 'Everyone does it.'

'Well, I thought you –'

'Look.' Barra considered him for a moment. 'It's the people in Pleasure that bother me. Penned up like criminals, trapped here forever whether they like it or not. It's not what they do. It's the way we treat them.'

Rico felt all his good times run away like spilled water. He'd never really thought of that, never really let himself think about it. Barra leaned over and flipped up a narrow panel on the desktop.

Underneath lay a row of tiny disks like coins in a wrapper.

'You can load those,' she remarked. 'Yeah, in those slots there. Someone's modified this link to the usual Map sockets for Pleasure Sect, but you're right. This is a very old frame. I'm surprised it still works.'

'I'm surprised it ended up in a hotel,' Rico said.

'Oh, those loads are probably games or something. And it's a nice-looking piece of furniture.' Barra turned back to her brother. 'Is that pink stuff drinkable?'

'Better than the water. I'll pour you some.'

Rico heard the sofa creak as she sat down again. He powered on the frame and found the icons that had so puzzled him earlier in the day. Most were standard – little circles each marked with an access glyph for different agents and utilities, room service, commcalls, banking access, and so on. One area of the holoscreen showed a set of five icons, though, that he'd never seen before, and one that should have been there was missing, a general route out to the Map at large. Every sect Map contained a pipe to whatever artificial intelligence coordinated the sect, which would then supply the out-route. But this frame showed nothing to mark the pipe, unless Pleasure used a glyph he couldn't recognize? On a frame this old the glyphs might well mark subordinated access areas, too. Since the frame had no jacks, he was limited to finger-tapping icons like any tourist – irritating enough to make him stubborn about it.

He began expanding the icons, one at a time, into new clusters, each linked by colour, but he found nothing recognizable as a pipe. Activating the sub-icons brought him air conditioning controls, a commcall directory, some rather startling holos of various sapients having sex in unusual ways, and other end-user objects. Loading in the coin-like objects brought him games and more pornography. The frame's structure and sockets stayed stubbornly closed until he realized that he had a repair utility in hidden files, just sitting waiting to be unpacked. It took him a bare few minutes to break the passwords and bring the utilities up. Now! He could add a pipe out, easy as easy – well, easy for someone like him.

As he worked, he could hear Hi and Barra chatting, teasing each other. All at once something caught his attention.

'Been asked to take a team up to Orbital,' his mother was saying. 'I'll be leaving pretty soon.'

Rico sloughed round in his chair to listen. Hi was sitting at one end of the sofa, a glass in his hand, and Barra was at the other end.

'Orbital?' Hi said. '*Orbital*? Isn't that dangerous as hell?'

'Not any more. They've finally got the radiation levels down. It's only taken what . . . fourteen years to clean the place up? Well, it's not spotless, no, but I'm not going to be having any more children. My genes and I will be safe enough.'

'Ah.' Hi paused for a sip of his soda. 'Well, well, well. We're finally going to get hands-on access to the Nimue AI.'

'It's about time, huh? Think I'll have any better luck than you did?'

'I never got to go up to Orbital. The Lep had just exploded their pulse bomb, remember, when their flagship suicided. The place was hot enough to cook your dinner. What examination I did had to be through the Map, and the Map out there was a mess. It'll be great to start getting things untangled.'

'If we can. After fourteen years of floating out there with nothing but radiation soakers and clean-up bots, who knows what's left?'

'Well, you can always count on my help through the Map.'

Barra grimaced. 'I may have limited clearance. The Council's putting one of Karlo's officers in command, some Captain Niko, some name like that.'

'What? The guild won't stand for that!'

'That's what I told him. We need to lodge a formal protest. If you hadn't been gone today –'

'Yeah, I know, I know. First thing in the morning I'll take care of this. I don't understand why the military's even involved.'

'Well, Nimue *is* a defence installation. And it was disabled as an act of war. But mostly, it's the new way of doing things.' Barra grimaced again. 'The Peronida way.'

Hi nodded and looked balefully into his glass.

'This soda's terrible,' he remarked, then set the glass on the table. 'Think you'll find any new evidence of the L'Var treason?'

'Why would I? I thought you'd found plenty.'

'I delivered it to the courts under formal protest, if you'll remember.' Hi hesitated, frowning, glancing Rico's way. 'It was a standard record holotape, fuzzy as hell from the disruption but readable, tagged with full routing code coming from the L'Var family compound out in the swamps. There were other bits and pieces of code that looked like a shut-off order and an override, or there could have been one before the pulse bomb went off, I mean. There were images, in various conditions, but some were pretty clear. And there were voice fragments left – Kella L'Var's voice, all right, logging in. The judges ate the tape up. It wasn't the only evidence, thank God. But it executed Kella L'Var and her two brothers.'

'What was wrong with it?' Rico said. 'Something must have been.'

'Smart boy.' Hi flashed a grin. 'Nothing was wrong with it. But it wasn't right, either. For one thing, it was so damn convenient that it would survive. The pulse bomb scrambled packets, blew codes, fused sockets – you name it. But this nice convenient record of the traitor's act just somehow survived, all chewed up, maybe, but it did.'

'Well, something as important as a shut-down order gets routed right into the safe box,' Barra objected. 'It wasn't just some list of icon counts.'

'Yeah, yeah, but still.' Hi leaned back, considering. 'I kept having the feeling that Nimue was trying to tell me something, the whole time I was jacked in. Call it cyber's intuition. The AI was practically junked – shut down first, then hit by that pulse wave – but she was trying to reach me. I could just feel it. And she tried the hardest to reach me when I was finding the evidence that killed the L'Vars.'

Barra frankly stared. Hi grinned at her.

'It sounds crazy, I know,' he said. 'What do you think, Rico? Think your patron's losing a few databanks with age?'

'No,' Rico said. 'I know that kind of feeling.'

Hi raised an eyebrow.

'Yeah? We'll have to talk about this some more.' Hi turned to Barra. 'Huh. I wonder if Karlo's putting one of his men in charge to make sure that you do find some new evidence. A lot of people grumbled about what happened to the L'Vars. Some of them are still grumbling. Karlo would love to produce more proof, just to lock down the crematorium door one more time.'

'But Uncle Hi?' Rico said. 'If it wasn't the L'Vars, then who was it?'

'Good question, kid, a very good question. I don't know. There wasn't one shred of evidence on the Map that pointed to anyone but the L'Vars. That's why I finally turned the tape over to the courts. And by then the Makeesa had a lot of hard evidence that the L'Vars had been bargaining with the Leps. Witnesses, that kind of thing.'

'Witnesses can be bought,' Barra said. 'I wouldn't trust Vanna Makeesa with a six-bit coin, much less someone's life.'

'It's a hard world,' Hi said, grinning. 'And Vanna's one of those sapients who makes it just a little bit harder for us all. She saw her chance to get her claws into the L'Var property, if you ask me, and took it.'

'She'd kill someone for money?' Rico broke in. 'That's really loath.'

'Not just money,' Barra said. 'Hatred first. Then money.'

Rico considered, leaning over the back of his chair. This conversation was giving him different data than the history downloads he'd been assigned on the School Map. Hi was watching him, he realized, as if waiting for some reaction.

'Well,' Rico said. 'What if Karlo wanted Nimue down so he could save the day with his Fleet? It sure made him a hero, and that made him First Citizen.'

Hi laughed and pointed at the blackbox on the table.

'Never say that without one of these around, Rico, but you know something? A lot of people have wondered the same thing.'

'Too simple,' Barra said. 'Karlo had already seen one planet destroyed by the Lep invaders. He's not a monster. I don't see him risking it happening again. All of his ships were Kephalon ships. Every man and woman onboard had just lost their families, their homes – everything. I think they wanted to kill Leps first and worry about politics later.'

'Yeah.' Hi nodded. 'And we're all damn lucky that Karlo was bringing his bunch of orphans our way.'

Rico felt a cold stripe run down his back. The history downloads had made that part clear enough, that without the Kephalon navy, Palace would have been destroyed once the defence grid went down. Palace had always trusted in its AIs, had never built a navy of fighting ships. With Nimue off-line, the planet floated in space as helpless and fragile as a bubbleflare. No wonder, he supposed, that public opinion had cheered Vanna Makeesa when she rooted out the traitors – or at least, the family that most people considered traitors.

'You don't think that tape was real?' Rico said.

'I *think* it was real,' Hi answered. 'I *feel* that it was a plant, a fake, a send-up, whatever you want to call it. The courts aren't interested in feelings.'

'Huh. Could I get onto that part of the Map?'

'What?' Barra broke in. 'Hell, no! Don't you go trying to breach the firewalls, either. Rico, we're talking about military secrets and legal matters here. Planetary security matters. Do you understand me?'

'I was just curious.'

'I know what your "just curious" means.' Barra was glaring at him. 'Don't you remember what I said the last time you got into an unauthorized area? I will not bail you out of trouble again, young man. I mean that. You may be my own blood and genotype, but the guild comes first.'

'Ah, Mum! Don't worry! Come on! I don't have any of the metas. It's way above my level, I bet.'

'Don't bet,' Barra snapped. 'You'll only take that for a challenge.'

Rico tried smiling at her, but she merely glowered in return. When he realized that Hi was watching, he did his best to look contrite.

'Well, I promise you, then,' Rico said. 'No poking around the Nimue gate.'

Barra relaxed. It was a cheap promise, Rico decided. He was certain that security routines of many different kinds had locked the gate to Nimue and the defence grid far beyond his ability to reach it, much less pass through it. The readout down Barra's sleeves winked and changed. She frowned and punched a couple of transmit buttons, waited, frowned again.

'I've got to go,' she announced. 'The re-route carrier's hit some kind of snag. What's your news?'

'Oh, nothing much.' Hi got up, yawning, offering her a hand to help her out of the sofa. 'I'm just going to make Rico my heir, that's all.'

Barra stared, then slowly got to her feet.

'Well, my God,' she said at last. 'Why?'

'Why do you think?' Hi stared down at the carpet. 'I need someone to leave my collection of crap to, don't I?' He looked up, towards his nephew with eyes brimming sadness. 'What do you think, Rico?'

'I think we should find Arno, that's what, and –'

'Rico.' Barra's voice sounded soft, quiet, which meant that she was dangerously furious. 'You don't know what you're saying.'

'Mom, Uncle Hi told me about the drugs.'

'Oh.' She glanced at her brother, who nodded, then back to her son. 'Did Hi tell you how those drugs leave someone's mind?'

Rico started to say that he didn't care, but the quiet ache in her voice stopped him.

'Rico,' Barra went on. 'You've got to start thinking of Arno as dead. The Arno you knew is dead. All his memories, his skills, everything that makes a person a sapient – they're gone now.'

In his mind Rico could see Arno staggering away, could remember how he smelled, too, and how long it had taken him to recognize his father's voice. Hi was staring at the carpet hard enough to be counting tufts.

'Okay,' Rico said. 'I'm sorry.'

Hi looked up.

'Well, that's a first,' he said. 'We'll hold the ceremony in a couple of days, then. We'll make a big deal out of it, let the gridjockeys in, the whole parade. We've got to do it fast if your mother's heading starside soon.'

'That's true.' Barra was still looking at Rico. 'Do you know what this means? Do you realize what your uncle's giving you?'

Rico certainly did, whether or not he wanted to take it – to take it away from Arno, as he could not stop thinking of it.

To be the heir of a man like his uncle, who was both a family's chief patron and the master of a guild, did a lot more than just make you rich. It brought favours to dispense, access to allow, data to trade off, a presence to display on the newsgrid screens: power, in short, all those things that meant power on the world of Palace. Just being a Jons on his mother's side would have brought him some influence, and being in the Cyberguild, some position, but to be Hi's personal heir?

'Do you?' Barra repeated.

'Oh yeah.' Rico got up, turning to his uncle. 'You sure we can't do anything for Arno?'

'Real sure, kid. I wish I could say otherwise.'

'Okay, then. Thank you.'

Although the festival of Calios had started out as a secular celebration, nearly a thousand years ago now, the Church of the Eye saw no reason why the occasion shouldn't taste of holiness as well as strong drink. All day Cardinal Roha had presided over events: private religious services for the Lifegiver order at dawn, a luncheon for the heads of the great families, public services in the afternoon, a tour around Pleasure Sect in the tenwheel owned by his order, more public services in the evening, and finally a dinner of bishops and abbots to honour the new Itinerant, a papal legate from the holy planet of Retreat. Now, late on festival night, he wanted nothing more than to sleep, but etiquette demanded that the Itinerant be privately entertained. She seemed to be the tireless sort, this Sister Romero. Roha was profoundly afraid that she would prove to be tiresome as well.

Roha's rank brought him a suite in the Chapter House, a building within Government House. In his private sitting room, decorated in pale blues and golds for the sky and the sun, he sat with several important guests, but old Bishop Faru slept, snoring in an overstuffed chair, and the younger, leaner Bishop Pol seemed to envy him the state and said little. Sister Romero, however, sat bolt upright in an armless formfit, declined an offer of wine, and seemed ready to talk all night.

A tall woman, with sharp features and wary dark eyes, she wore her wave of jet-black hair bound back in a black headband, studded in the centre with a single white gem. In the pleasantly dim light of the sitting room, the gem glowed, flickering. Although the cardinal and the two bishops wore their elaborate ceremonial robes, Romero wore only a simple sunsilk shift of black embroidered with stars.

'So,' Roha said. 'I trust you won't find our city too damp for you. It's very grey, Palace, I'm afraid.'

'Grey but interesting.'

'How kind of you! You've travelled to so many worlds, of course. After the beauty of Belie, Palace must seem bleak.'

'Oh, I wouldn't say that.' Romero paused for a smile. 'It's not a garden spot, no, but the city has, what shall I call it, a presence, a personality, really. I'm hoping to find some time from my regular duties to explore a little.'

Roha smiled, but he felt his stomach clench. Itinerants always acted as spies as much as ambassadors; such was a given. The question lay with what she'd come here to find.

'The city itself is a fascinating place,' Roha said. 'The architecture can practically provide you with a history of the Pinch, style by style. I do believe it was the first human settlement of any size.'

'So I've learned, yes. I've been doing some background study, of course, to prepare for this assignment.'

No doubt, Roha thought, no doubt. Just how much did the Pope suspect, anyway? What had he been told? Bishop Pol roused himself briefly.

'Now, if you're interested in the blueglass,' Pol said, 'I've made quite a study of it. Palace has the finest collection of it in the Pinch, you see. Be glad to show you around.'

'Thank you.' Romero inclined her head his way. 'I'd love to be able to do that. Maybe once the research station's open.'

'Going to be a lot of work, that,' Roha said. 'Those stations haven't been used in a very long time, and for a doomed enterprise like this, it seems –'

'Doomed enterprise?' Romero interrupted, smiling. 'I see Your Eminence has already made up his mind.'

'Well, my dear Itinerant, when you've lived with the saccules as long as we all have, you really come to see that they're clever animals and nothing more.'

Romero glanced at Pol, who shrugged.

'Don't know, myself,' the bishop said. 'Every now and then you see them figuring things out in a pretty amazing way. But symbol use?' He shrugged again. 'Never seen one master even a simple glyph. Can't be sapient without symbolic capacity, eh?'

'Very true,' Romero said. 'But they do seem to understand sapient speech.'

'Mere conditioned response.' Roha waved one hand as if batting the argument away. 'Training them takes a very long time, I'm told, and a great deal of patience.'

'Um.' Romero smiled pleasantly. 'Well, a proper study will tell us, sooner or later.'

From another chamber came the sound of a commcall, sharp and insistent. Roha cocked his head to listen. Yes, his factor had answered.

'My priority line,' Roha said, rising. 'One of the friars – a grand old man, one of our best researchers – at the abbey is very ill. I promised to come myself for the last rites, you see. It seemed to mean much to him.'

Romero nodded; Bishop Pol sighed. Roha made a half-bow and hurried out of the room, only to meet his burly factor in the short hall.

'It's not the abbey,' Brother Dav whispered. 'A woman. She said to tell you it was an old ghost calling.'

For a moment Roha could only stare at him.

'Is it a prank, Your Eminence?' Dav turned beet red. 'I thought it might be, but she was so insistent, and she did have the private code, and –'

'It's all right, it's all right. Just surprised.' Roha cleared his throat. 'Make sure no-one interrupts us.'

In his private office, a spartan place of dark walls, a few pieces of dark furniture, and a bare wood floor, the wall screen glowed with Aleen Raal's face, as sharp and grim as Sister Romero's despite her emerald-coloured hair. When the cardinal stepped into sensor range, she smiled, very briefly.

'My apologies, Your Eminence. But someone tried to cancel our contract once and for all today.'

'May the Eye protect!' Nothing like a little fear to wake one up, Roha thought. 'I take it that the document in question is still safe?'

'It is, yes, but I don't know how long I can keep it that way.'

'Um, of course. Was it the um . . .' Roha paused, searching for the right word in their agreed-upon code to indicate Vanna Makeesa. 'Was the person who tried to cancel the usual lawyer, the one who's given us such bad legal advice in the past?'

'I don't know, but I doubt it very much. That particular lawyer would have simply gone to the police for a subpoena or some kind of writ of confiscation.'

'Quite so, quite so. Do you have any idea who else –'

'Well, when the original business went bankrupt, it left a lot of creditors behind. Any one of them might be trying to cash in, illegally now, since the court order failed them.'

'Mph. Have you reported this to the Protectors?'

'What if their report caught someone's eye, someone who'd take it to our hostile lawyer?'

'Well, yes. Let me think.'

Aleen nodded. Orin L'Var had had enemies, all right, those 'creditors' of their code, but he'd also had friends. Roha could remember him so well, laughing over some obscure joke, striding along with his easy walk, one of the most important men on planet, certainly, but never too busy for his old friend from university, that awkward young monk who didn't even know what fork to use at a formal dinner. Roha had learned a lot from Orin L'Var; even at this lapse of years he missed him still. If he hadn't already hated Vanna Makeesa for a thousand reasons, he would have hated her for Orin's death alone.

'Well,' he said at last. 'What counts is getting the documents to some safe place on the Map, somewhere with proper security systems and so on. It's time we thought about the long-term future, if we're going to re-open the business or not. If it weren't for all these old creditors, you could have started it up safely yourself in Pleasure Sect, not that it's exactly the site I would have chosen, of course, but it's a respectable one in its way, I know, my dear. I don't mean to insult you.'

Aleen's image smiled, but she seemed suddenly weary.

'It's too bad about that lawyer,' she said. 'Government House is the safest place in the Pinch, if it wasn't for her.'

'Yes, I could bring the documents here and store them with my entourage's belongings. Wait a moment! We could store it here, among the archives of the Lifegivers.'

For a brief moment Aleen's image boggled; then she laughed.

'I fail to see why this idea is so amusing, my dear.'

'I'm sorry, Your Eminence. I was just thinking of the contrast. It's a long walk from Pleasure to the Chapter House.'

'True, true. But I'm sure I can smooth things over, since the contract hasn't been sealed yet and signed over to someone else. Now, do you have some protection against this thief?'

'I've sent for a Garang bodyguard.'

'Splendid! That will do while I arrange a proper safe deposit for the papers. And do be careful yourself.'

'Don't worry about that, Your Eminence.'

'Good. We'd best get off-line. I never know what might be overheard around here if I give them a long call to work with.'

Sure enough, once he'd terminated the call Roha found a message on his screen from the scrambler utility – a failed attempt at intercept and interpret. Dukayn's work, no doubt. Roha was heartily sick of Dukayn, Karlo's so-called factor and head of security – his head of a secret police force would be more accurate. Roha had to admit, though, that with Dukayn in charge, Government House had become what Aleen called it, the safest place in the Pinch. Could he find a place for young Vida that would be as safe from Vanna Makeesa as Vanna was from her enemies?

When he returned to the sitting room, he found Faru awake and Pol standing, obviously ready to leave.

'My apologies, my apologies, my dear friends.' Roha bobbed and bowed all round. 'Not our friar, but another grave matter.'

At that Romero rose as well – one good thing about this mess, Roha thought. A wave of polite farewells washed the guests out the door, leaving the cardinal alone to think of ancient promises and of how he might carry this one out.

*   *   *

Karlo Peronida had never slept much, not even as a boy. He'd always been proud of the natural gift that gave him extra time every night when he could work and study to gain an edge over the slower men around him. Now, when he stood on the verge of gaining more than he'd ever thought he'd have out of life, the irony bit deep. Extra hours, extra life – all the extra life he'd ever have! Often late at night the irony drove him out of bed, as it had this night, to stand at the window of his office and look out on the silver skies of Palace.

Down below in a roof garden, perched on one of the many buildings of Government House, tall spear trees stood in rows among a scatter of flowering shrubs. When he opened the window he could smell perfume and wet earth, the cool air tinged with the perpetual rot of this city among swamps. Why the hell had the Colonizers built a capital here? By accident of course – he did remember reading about it once, that what had been planned as a simple research nexus grew inordinately when the settlements on Nox failed. He didn't particularly care about ancient history. What did matter was the future, and his was going to be short. Although he'd known the truth now for some ten years, it never ceased to eat at him.

The Colonizers had brought life-extension with them to the Pinch. The drugs were actually a disease engineered with nanotech, a retrovirus that selectively modified a person's DNA, or repaired it, really, to prevent all those small changes that led inevitably to death. In time, every individual developed an immunity to this virus; a second round of treatment, maybe a third, could overcome the body's unthinking traitor, its own immune system, but in time, with time, time always won, though after a long time, in the run of things that the Pinch considered normal. Some people, however, were born immune to the life-extension retrovirus. Karlo was one of them.

Every now and then, like now, standing in a darkened room and smelling the rot of swamp on the wind, it made him laugh, that he of all people, the street fighter, the soldier, the officer who'd fought his way up from the ranks, and finally the admiral – he of all people, who'd lived through war, who'd lived to see his home planet wiped out by war, who'd lived to get his revenge on the enemies that had destroyed her – he of all people would never win this one last battle. The best medical technology had failed him again and again. His immunity to life-extension was hardwired and deep and irreversible, at least by the science left in the Pinch. The Colonizers, no doubt, had solved that problem as they'd solved so many others, for all the good that would do him. Their solution was lost, along with a lot of solutions to other problems.

Karlo was sixty years old, practically a Not-child still in the eyes of the Palace citizenry. He would die at an age that they would consider still young, for an adult. At times he hated them all.

Behind him he heard a noise or felt perhaps a presence and swung round, to find one of his Garang bodyguards stepping into the office.

'Sir? I have a message from Cardinal Roha. He wondered if perhaps you waked.'

'He's starting to know me well.'

The message lay on an old-fashioned writing tablet, self-contained and thus free from the spy utilities that various people had placed in Government House's internal Map over the years.

'Are you still up?' it read. 'If so, will you do me the honour of joining me in my suite?'

Roha never would have sent a message like that for a trifle. Karlo was always aware that he needed the support of the Lifegivers if his long-term plans were going to succeed. He glanced at the Garang, standing stiff and straight in his grey uniform.

'Call him and say just this and only this: the First Citizen agrees. I'll get dressed, and we'll go.'

When Karlo arrived, he found the cardinal wrapped in a black dressing gown and sitting in an overstuffed chair in his blue and gold sitting room. He was a tall man, the cardinal, with a sharp, thin face under a very high forehead; curly grey hair clung to the back of his skull. On a small marble table sat a silver tray with fluted glasses and a decanter of pale green liqueur.

'A drink, First Citizen?'

'No thanks, Your Eminence.'

Roha poured himself a flute of the poisonous-looking stuff and settled back into his chair.

'My apologies, my dear sir, for dragging you over here in the middle of the night. There's no doubt, though, that the middle of the night often seems the safest time for a chat.'

Karlo allowed himself a smile. He sat down and stretched his long legs out in front of him.

'Oddly enough,' Roha went on, 'I wanted to talk with you about your wife.'

'Ah.'

Roha stared into the narrow glass and swirled it round, sending a wave of liqueur up the side. The odour of sweet spices wafted like a saccule's smile.

'This is very awkward,' the cardinal said at last. 'You know that I have the greatest respect for the Second Citizen.'

'Of course.'

'But she's been known to, shall we say, have a long memory for unpleasant matters.'

Karlo laughed.

'Hold a grudge, you mean? Oh yes. She'll tell you that herself, Your Eminence. Proudly. She's a fine hater.'

Roha sighed and sipped from his glass.

'I've been approached by an old friend about giving her young ward a position in the church, perhaps in my own entourage. The girl's an orphan, but very bright, and she'd do well with the courses of study being a Lifegiver demands. But you know how things are on Palace. She has no real family to speak for her. She'd never be allowed into the order in the normal course of things.'

'Oh yes, I know.' Karlo heard his voice tighten. 'Our best citizens wouldn't allow it, the bunch of self-important bastards, snobs, all of them, the whole fungi-sucking pack.'

'Well, er, my dear First Citizen. There are reasons.'

'Of course. There are always reasons for snobbery, aren't there? In this case, it's breeding your offspring like dogs.'

'My dear First Citizen!'

'Sorry, Your Eminence. But you can't imagine how peculiar it seems to someone from off planet, that you people – well – it's like breeds of dogs, let's face it. The best genotype for this, that and the other. And if you're a mutt like me, it's stay in the alley where you belong.'

Roha winced.

'Sorry,' Karlo said again.

'Perhaps if one put things less adamantly –' Roha held up a long ringed hand to fend protest. 'I agree. Things are difficult for those without the right genotypes. Now, if I take the girl under my personal protection and bring her here, we can work around all those difficulties.'

'Ah.' Karlo allowed himself a smile. 'But you're worried about Vanna's reaction? Who is it that my charming wife hates? The girl herself? Her foster mother? She's got so many grudges going that I can't keep them straight any more, myself.'

Roha attempted to smile at the joke and failed.

'Let me be honest,' the cardinal said at last. 'I'm rather afraid to tell you.'

Karlo considered the problem. If he sheltered one of her enemies, Vanna would be furious. On the other hand, there was no doubt that her constant hatreds and intrigues were undermining his plans. He wanted to consolidate their power over the government, not start a revolution against them. Getting her to make a show of clemency would be a good step.

'Well, Your Eminence, if you declare that the girl has your personal protection, and I back it up, then she should be safe enough. Vanna likes to keep things legal, you know, and get the laws to do her killing for her.'

Roha winced.

'Oh my God!' Karlo snapped. 'This girl's not a L'Var, is she?'

Roha answered by turning dead pale.

'Well, no wonder you're worried,' Karlo said. 'That's a nice little problem you've got on your hands.'

'Oh yes, oh yes. I'm not going to tell you who or where this child is, by the way.'

'Good. It's best I don't know.'

'Yes, yes indeed. But you see the problem. Once she enters the church, she'll no longer be a L'Var. She'll have to renounce her name, her worldly goods, her family, all of that, swear the oath, and be . . . um . . . well, rendered unable to have children. Once she chooses her simple novitiate's name, as far as the rest of Palace is concerned, the last L'Var will be dead all over again. But will that satisfy the Second Citizen?'

'Huh. Good question.'

'There's the matter of the L'Var holdings, you see. After the executions, the courts confiscated them, and they became government property. However, the standard form of that decree makes some provision for what's termed "innocent issue", minor children unimplicated in any wrongdoing. I've been doing some research tonight, as you can tell. If this girl turns up, a provable L'Var, a mere infant at the time of the trials, all that property will be hers.'

'For about three days – until the church gets its paws on it.'

Roha pursed his mouth and looked severe.

'It is traditional, First Citizen, for personal property to be given over to one's new order when one joins the church.'

'Oh yes, very traditional. As the last L'Var she must have quite a lot of property to give over.'

'A good-sized fortune, I'd say. Or rather, the whole of it comes to a fortune. Some of the properties have been tied up in lawsuits ever since the government confiscated the L'Var holdings. There are some collateral cousins – they have absolutely no claim on the family name, of course, because their genotypes are far too deviant. But they may have a right to some of the property.'

'Ah. I think Vanna did mention that. She's in court so much that I can't keep her lawsuits straight, either.'

The cardinal allowed himself a sickly smile.

'Your wife won't want to part with her control over the confiscation. As head of the Council, you see, she's been overseeing the holdings.'

Overseeing. A nice polite word, that, for skimming profits.

'Well, that makes things dangerous, Your Eminence.'

'So I feared. I should hate to see this child harmed, First Citizen.' Roha leaned forward. 'As your spiritual counsellor, I'll beg you to never say a word of this to Vanna.'

'You can rest easy. I've got nothing to gain by telling her.'

'Thank you.' Roha allowed himself a smile. 'It's a pity you've nothing to gain by helping this girl.'

'Yes, I –' All at once Karlo saw something so obvious yet so brazen that he laughed aloud. 'Oh, I don't know about that, Your Eminence. I don't know about that at all.'

Roha finished the rest of the liqueur in one gulp.

'Consider this,' Karlo went on. 'My son. His marriage. The problems with that marriage. Your good advice on the subject's been invaluable, of course, but there's no way around the obstacles. What kind of offers have I been able to arrange? It's humiliating, seeing these rotten snobs, these dogs and bitches, turn their ugly noses up at my son. Son! As if they wouldn't have been fried like the swines they are in the war, without my Fleet, my risks, my losses. Sometimes I think I should have stood off and let the rotten Leps bomb this God-forsaken place into oblivion!'

'First Citizen, please.'

Karlo realized that he had been shouting. He took a long breath and let it out as slowly as he could manage.

'I'm sorry, Your Eminence.'

'Well.' Roha dabbed at his lips with a small lace handkerchief. 'You have justification, yes.'

'Damn right I do. Look at what I've managed to get for Wan! Look at the terms those mincing le-Yonestillas offered me! And I had to take them, didn't I? Concessions and all. Damned if I'll bargain away half a million in mining rights if I don't have to, not for a little slut like Anja le-Yonestilla. Betrothal contracts have been broken before.'

Roha stared for a long moment, then leaned forward and poured himself another drink.

'I think,' Karlo said, 'that you begin to see what I'm driving at.'

'Oh yes. But what will Vanna say?'

Karlo shrugged.

'A lot of words not fit for a churchman's ears, that's what. I'd like to bluster and say something like, oh just leave her to me, but I've not got this far by being out of touch with reality.'

Roha laughed, lifting his glass with a shaking hand.

'Don't worry,' Karlo went on. 'I won't put the girl in the slightest bit of danger. She's too valuable for me to risk her.'

'Good, er ah, splendid. Well, I doubt if she had much spiritual vocation anyway. Inducting her into holy orders was merely the best I could do for her.'

'Just so, yes.' Karlo rose, still smiling. 'Well, I think I may be able to offer her something a little different. Not a word of this, Your Eminence, till I've spoken with my wife.'

'Of course, of course. You may rest assured of that.'

It was some hours after sunrise before Karlo got his chance for a private word with Vanna. For breakfast he put on the dress uniform of a Kephalon admiral crossed with an honour sash bearing the glyphs of the city-state of Palace and took an airhopper to a fashionable hotel, where he was addressing a merchant council of some type – Karlo gave so many of these speeches that he could never quite remember the names of all the groups. That was, after all, his factor's job.

In the vast dining room the gridjockeys swarmed round the edge of the seated guests. Karlo smiled, bowed, stood still for transmit snaps and moved gracefully for holo ops while the pix and the intakes pointed their hands, muttered under their breaths, and bobbed their heads to activate various chips. After a cold, greasy breakfast, Karlo gave a speech on the necessity of interplanetary security for the growth of trade and trotted out his standard slogan,

'Continuity in government means safety in a changing world'. The assembled guests applauded, but what would really count, of course, was the popular response to the recorded version that would play later over the interactive news. As he was leaving, surrounded by bodyguards, he caught a glimpse of himself on one of the lobby's vidscreens; in this shot he was opening a new canal – when had that been? Yesterday? Day before? It didn't really matter, he supposed. He did notice that he looked tired, a little too tired for a man who had to project calm strength and trustworthiness. He'd have to do something about those bags under his eyes.

Back to Government House and his staff, all talking at once as he strode down the long blue hall to his private suite. He handed them all over to Dukayn to sort out and bolted through the door – for the few minutes he could spare for privacy. In a khaki fatigue uniform Vanna sat waiting on the white silk sofa, lounging back with her red and blue hair hanging free over her shoulders. When he sat down next to her, she allowed him to kiss her tattooed cheek.

'How was the speech?'

'It seemed to go well. I'm not sure when they'll broadcast it. It wasn't a high-priority event.'

Vanna nodded, then spasmed, her head flinging itself back, then forward. She sighed and reached up to lay shaking hands on either side of her face.

'I've got to go for a med treatment soon,' she said, and her voice sounded far too high. 'What did you want to see me about?'

'A little bargain, my love. I've been thinking about those datablocks, the ones I confiscated after the genocide trials. The ones you want to turn over to that Interstellar Guild research team. Remember?'

All attention, Vanna leaned forward.

'Of course I remember them,' she said. 'I thought you would have destroyed them by now.'

'I probably should have. I don't know why I didn't. I'm a good citizen of the Pinch, I guess. Destroying knowledge – even knowledge like this –' He paused, shaking his head as if he could shake off the pain of remembering. 'It's murderous stuff. It murdered an entire planet. It murdered my home.'

Vanna laid a hand on his arm, a comforting sort of warning.

'Don't dwell on it,' she said. 'That's not the part we're even interested in, over at the guild. I don't have one goddamn scruple about wiping every piece of data about that plague off the blocks.

I'd do it myself if I knew how. It's the other files we want, the Lep research into the human genome. Ri Paha Tura was a monster, but she was a brilliant one. All the minds on her team were.'

He looked away, staring at nothing, remembering the faces on the vidscreens of his ship, when the Fleet had made contact with Kephalon at last. Horrible, horrible faces, swollen and bloated, softening, bleeding, rotting off the skulls of living human beings who felt the agony of flesh that pulped like rotten fruit, who could smell the stench of their own death creeping up on them an inch at a time. They'd lifted rotting hands, too, into sensor range to show him. He could still hear their voices, screams from dying throats, rasped whispers and sobs.

'Karlo!' Vanna's voice cut through memory. Her hands clutched his arm. 'Karlo. Please. Don't get lost in it. It's over.'

He shook his head again and wished that he could weep, just once. He never had, not in the fourteen years since he'd blasted the Lep fleet into oblivion just beyond Palace's orbit. He'd laughed, then, when he and his ships had chased the surviving vessels down and blown them to bits, laughed and laughed every time they found an escape pod or lifeboat and killed again, no matter who screamed for mercy. He'd saved Palace, but he'd done the killing for Kephalon's sake.

'Karlo!'

'Yes, right. Sorry.' He sighed, once and sharply. 'About Tura's datablocks. I know Interstellar wants them. Why?'

'Not for the plague.'

'I know that. I've never thought you were all fools and murderers. But you must have some reason for wanting them.'

'You don't need to know.'

'The hell I don't. The data on those blocks killed one whole world. It could kill another. Yeah, I know there's supposed to be a cure now, and inoculations – '

'Supposed to be? Of course there is.'

'But still. It preys on me, Vanna. You weren't there. You can't know.'

'No, that's true.' She rubbed his arm with long strokes, like soothing a dog. 'I told you we'd wipe that off the moment we got them. Have I ever lied to you, Karlo, outright lied, face to face? Have I ever gone back on my sworn word?'

'No, no, you haven't. That's true.'

'Well, then. I give you my sworn word that Interstellar's

researchers will destroy every trace of plague data they can find and make no record of it, either.' She leaned forward. 'If you turned them over to Biotech, they wouldn't do that. They'd want the data kept. Good citizens of the Pinch, just like you said.'

'You really want these, don't you?'

'Damn right. Look, my love. Have you ever considered that there might be something in this for you? What did that plague do? Made its victims die by inches, speeded up necrosis and cellular changes beyond their bodies' ability to self-repair. What if someone found out how to do the opposite? It might lead to a life-extension virus that you're not immune to.'

Karlo swung round to look at her.

'If the Lifegivers get their hands on that data,' Vanna went on, 'they'll wipe the lot. The last thing they want is a life-extension process they don't control. They must think that some of the data on those blocks could lead to a new process, too. That's why you've got the only copies of those blocks, isn't it? Why else would they have tried to destroy them? I know they succeeded in getting the Map storage wiped away.'

'Oh yes. I had a stiff talk with the cardinal about that at the time.' He paused, considering. 'But there's no guarantee that Interstellar has the tech it needs to decipher the research. You people don't have labs and the right kind of people to run them. Or do you?'

Cradled between her hands her smile flashed, still a lovely smile, he thought.

'Do you really think I'm going to tell you that?' she said.

'No.' He had to smile in return. 'Not in a thousand years. But back to our bargain, my love. You want the datablocks. We've established that now.'

'You're going to make me pay high for them, aren't you?'

'As high as I can, yeah. You'd be disappointed in me if I just gave in. Admit it.'

She started to laugh, then twitched with a shudder of her narrow shoulders.

'I would have brought this up later,' Karlo said. 'But it's something that has to be decided right away.'

'It's all right. I'm getting used to this tremor, damn it. There's nothing they can do, nothing that'll really cure it, so I'd better, I suppose. So, very well. You'll give me my datablocks, then, if I do what?'

'Well, actually, it's more like if you don't do something, a non-action.'

'Sounds good so far. And what is it I'm not supposed to do?'

'Kill one of your old enemies or, I should say, just don't bother to have this sapient removed. A simple act of mercy. You've got so many grudges, my love. Surely you can spend one of them to buy Interstellar the blocks.'

Vanna turned sour in an uncontrollable flutter of eyelids.

'You could get a couple of points of up ratings from it, too,' Karlo went on. 'There's nothing like public compassion to bring up a rating. We can't risk another vote of confidence before we get the Fleet appropriations pushed through.'

'Who is it?'

'I'm not going to tell you yet. I can't risk your going after this person. Come on – you've got to admit that's fair.'

'I suppose I do.' She lowered her hands from her face and considered him so steadily that he knew he'd enraged her.

Adrenaline always helped control the spasming.

'We can let the matter lie till after your treatment,' he said.

'No. If it's someone I hate that much I want this settled so I can relax.' She made an attempt to smile, but the tattoos were standing out sharply against pale skin. 'Damn you anyway.'

'You've never even met this sapient.'

Vanna started to speak, then paused, reaching up a trembling hand to push a red wisp of hair back from one cheek. Her dark blue eyes considered him, probing his face for some clue.

'Then why,' she said at last, 'are you so worried about me killing it? We'll say "it", all right? so you don't give anything away.'

'All right.' He smiled and leaned a little closer. 'Well, you do have an old reason to want it dead, and probably a couple of other sapients along with it, the ones who've been hiding it from you.'

Although he thought that he was giving her a clue, she looked so honestly puzzled that he remembered his remark to the cardinal. Perhaps she could no longer keep all her grudges straight, either. And perhaps she was thinking something similar? She looked away, abruptly sad.

'Well, I wonder if it even matters,' she said. 'Tell me something, Karlo. Do I hate it for something that happened a long time ago?'

'Yeah, I'd say it was.'

'Damn. I really want that data. I suppose I'm going to be furious with you when I find out the truth.'

'Not as furious about this as you would be about some other things.' He decided to keep the matter of the L'Var property to himself, if she didn't raise it. 'I'm not talking about Jolo Emmen, for instance.'

'Good. You know damn well I'd give up half of everything I own to see that fat bastard dead.' The rage was back, dancing in her eyes. 'He'll pay for that one of these days, making fun of me on the vids, pretending to spasm, mocking my voice, and then claiming he was just a comic. Art, he said. Parody. One of these days! And I'll get that goddamn judge with him, slapping down my suit.'

'Hush.' Karlo grabbed her wrist. 'Don't upset yourself.'

'Oh shut up!' Vanna pulled her hand free. 'But you're right. This person, this it – it can't be as bad as that. You'll swear about the datablocks? You'll give them to me?'

'I'll swear it on the Eye of God.'

Vanna considered. Ever since the spasming had started, she'd been growing more concerned with God and his Eye.

'What about you?' Karlo said.

'I'll swear it on the Holy Eye as well. Your it and its little helpers are safe from me.' She raised her hands and pressed her thumbs and forefingers together to form the Eye. 'Its life is in your hands, not mine, and so are theirs.'

'Very good.' He made the same gesture. 'And you'll have your datablocks today. I'll fetch them for you after your treatment. Dukayn's been hiding them.'

'Of course. I could guess that much.' She leaned over and kissed him on the mouth. 'Promises. True promises.' Smiling a little, she rose. 'Well, come on, Karlo. Who is this it?'

Karlo got up, using his height and standing over her.

'A child,' he said. 'A girl of about seventeen, still a child. Her name's Vida.'

'All right. I've never heard that name before, no. Why do you think I'll hate her?'

Karlo took a deep breath.

'Because she's a L'Var. The last of them.'

Vanna went still, dead-still. The tattoos bulged out, royal blue against dead-white skin.

'You bastard,' she hissed. 'You slimy, filthy bastard!'

'Oh for God's sake! She was an infant during the war, barely two years old when it ended. What harm could she have done –'

'That's not the point.' Her voice stayed steady. 'It isn't her! Yes, of course, she's just a child. How could I have anything against her? It's the people who hid her from me. Oh, you're very smart, Karlo my love, including them in my promise. Very, very smart.'

'One of them's Cardinal Roha.'

That brought her round. She tossed her head in a ripple of red and blue.

'There's not much I could do about that officious little bigot anyway.'

'Exactly. And the people who actually hid the girl are nobodies, complete nobodies. They were just doing Roha a favour, or taking his orders is more like it.'

'Most likely, yeah. Damn you anyway!'

'Damn me all you want. There's the little matter of your solemn promise.'

'Oh I know, I know. But these datablocks had better be worth it, Karlo. And this child had better watch her step around me. What are you doing with her, anyway? Why bring her out of hiding like this?'

'Because she's going to marry Wan, and the le-Yonestillas and their precious Anja can swallow their dirt-cheap contract offer, one clause at a time.'

Vanna stared for a long long moment, then began to laugh, a pleasant sort of chuckle.

'Every now and then I remember why I married you,' she said at last. 'I've got to get to the clinic. We'll talk more later.'

She swept out, slamming the door behind her. Karlo smiled and let out a long sigh of relief. Later, of course, she'd remember the confiscated property, but he had a gut feeling that the worst was over.

A dark and vertical place, Tech Sect – the lowering grey sky of Palace turned it to a kingdom of black giants. Sunrise brought a weak dance of maroon-coloured light to wash the buildings with reflections that seemed to come from the flames of a dying fire. Clustered in little parks, glass towers and plastostone shafts rose from the straggly turquoise-blue boostergrass and unpruned fern trees, dripping long sprays of purple and black flowers. Even the dwells for lower-class techs and their families stood high in long pink blocks, all soot-streaked. The headquarters of the Cyberguild, a huge grey cube of a building topped with a gold dome, occupied one entire side of the sect's main plaza. Crews of saccules, roped to the pinnacle, worked round the clock to keep that dome shining.

Slinging his rucksack over one shoulder, Rico got off the transect wiretrain at the Eldo Canal stop. He could see the dome at some distance, with the saccules little moving dots upon its surface. He felt good, that morning, and in no hurry to get to the guild as he strolled along the southern bank of the Eldo. Autobarges chugged by, laden high with nets full of fruit and produce from South Hort Sect. Saccules swarmed over the mossy decks and worked at some mysterious job as the robotically controlled barges followed their programmed paths up the canal. Rico could hear the saccules singing as they passed, their booms carrying across the water like the beat of giant drums. The plaza already bustled. Pedestrians in the midnight blue of Cyber or the green of Biotech Guild rushed across the grey tiles and dodged the robocabs that kept pulling up to one entrance or another. Hanging from the gold double helix that arched over the headquarters of Biotech, a clock flashed the time and rang six long notes.

Since he could tap his uncle's credit line with the crypchip embedded in his jack, Rico bought a sweet roll from a vendor out on the Plaza and walked slowly, eating in big bites. His footsteps crunched. Green spores, blown in from the swamps, blanketed the stones and piled up in wind-drifts against every wall and obstruction. The crews from Service Sect would be bringing the clean-up bots in as soon as the wind slacked. On the far side of the plaza, a pair of Protectors had stopped a Lep man for some reason – to ask for papers. They let him go, then stopped another Lep, a woman this time. Apparently they were doing a sweep, looking for someone Lep. Rico shrugged; none of his business.

With a chatter and a chirr of bright green wings, a flock of flying lizards settled round his feet. He tossed them the last crumbs of the roll and watched for a moment as they snapped and fought. He couldn't help but think of his fellow apprentices. When he laughed out loud, the jadewings flew with a burst of colour like bubbleflares at festival.

The Guildhall swarmed with apprentices coming in early, like him no doubt angling for points with their masters or the teaching journeymen. As he walked up the steps, Rico made a point of nodding to or smiling at everyone he recognized; they in turn made a show of smiling at him. The apprentices learned early to save their battles for the Map. In the echoing confusion of the marble foyer, sapients rushed by, some in the midnight blue robes of guild-masters, others in business clothes or coveralls with read-out sleeves – Hirrel as well as human, though the Hirrel wore long skirts of midnight blue that left their torsos and the all-important breathing slits uncovered. He saw not a single Lep. After the war of fourteen years ago, Leps were officially barred from the Cyberguild, even loyal Palace citizens. Every year Hi tried to get the ruling reversed; every year he was defeated.

In front of the lift tubes, Rico saw Pukosu, a gawky young woman with brown eyes that would have been beautiful if they'd ever showed anything but suspicion. The brightest star among the apprentices, now that Arno had gone, she headed the line waiting for promotion to full journeyman. Rumour said she'd get assigned to the Alpha project, too, the century-old effort to write a new AI.

'Sé Rico,' she murmured.

'Sé Pukosu.'

'I wonder, if you please, would you honour me with a moment of your valuable time?'

'Sure. What do you want?'

'It is such a trifle, hardly worthy of your attention . . .'

'What?'

'There is, oh you will laugh to hear it, the most absurd rumour.'

Rico rolled his eyes.

'Get to the point, will you, Pukosu?'

He had the distinct pleasure of seeing her blush.

'Yes. Well. There is a rumour that Master Hivel has named you as his heir, to replace the . . . eh . . . unfortunate Arno.'

She smiled when she said Arno's name, just barely, but she did. At that moment Rico hated her.

'Where'd you get such a stupid idea?'

'Mm.' Pukosu considered him, then shrugged. 'Oh, who knows where these foolish rumours come from? I believe I might have seen a graffito on a wall in the Map.'

'Right. Well, I've got to go.'

'Of course, Sé Rico.' She started to turn, then looked back, just as if a sudden thought had occurred to her. 'Ah, if such a happy event did come to pass, however, you would certainly wish to share the news with the other master-tracks?'

'Oh yeah, right, of course.'

Her lips quirked a bit.

'Look, I gotta go,' Rico snapped. 'I've got a project burning.'

'Yes, naturally. My apologies for detaining you.' She nodded slightly to him, then moved on.

Rico turned and headed for the rank of lift booths across the lobby. At the door to a booth he glanced back once to find Pukosu still watching him. She wasn't even the worst of the lot. He stomped into the booth and shoved his thumb against the ID plate so hard that the unit beeped in protest. He let up on the pressure.

'Apprentice Rico Hernanes y Jons cleared for station access.'

'Good. Floor seventy.'

The lift shot up, then bobbled to a stop. The doors opened with a snap, releasing him into a long grey corridor, lined with doors. No-one else was here, thankfully. He wasn't even sure if his cubicle would be unlocked this early, but when he pressed his thumb to the ID plate, the door slid back. He walked in, shut it again, locked it, and sat down at his work unit, an older station, fitted with only a pair of cybernodes and a big flat screen instead of a holobox. The guild handicapped apprentices, doling out upgrades as rewards when they mastered some new technique.

For a moment he merely sat, staring at his reflection in the dead black and thinking about Arno. Although the official story had never mentioned drugs, his cousin had been expelled from the guild six months ago and committed to the special hospital the guild kept for its failures. Somehow or other Arno had escaped, and now he'd shown up again in Pleasure, the one place on planet where he could find cyberdrugs illegally – or at least, some compound that mimicked their effects. It all seemed to fit together, that Arno was just another regrettable casualty of the drugs, a tragedy, but not unheard of.

'I don't believe it. I just don't.'

Rico knew all about cyberdrugs, though he'd yet to take any. Every apprentice studied them, had it drilled into them just how dangerous they could be if you didn't follow the guild rules. Arno had always told Rico that the guild was right, too – odd of him, since Arno held most of the guild's rules in utter contempt. Rico had never seen his cousin abuse anything, not even anything legal, like alcohol. Arno was on the strange side, maybe. Cybes who volunteered for that many implants always were more than a little strange. But a drug addict? Rico grimaced. Would *he* end up like that, burned out and left to rot somewhere? He shuddered with a toss of his head, then leaned forward in his chair.

'Unit on.'

The screen came glowing to life with green icons bright as jadewings. Rico took the vizor from the drawer and put it on, then tilted his chair back and scooted forward, sliding half-under the desk. His left hand rested comfortably on a sculpted pad.

'Jack.'

The jack-staple rose, slid forward, lowered and connected to his implant with the familiar jolt of electricity up his arm.

'Transmit.'

The vizor darkened his view briefly, then cleared into a gateway that allowed Rico to step inside the screen, or so he perceived it – stepping inside a suddenly three-dee space. The icons, many-coloured now, hung in opalescent air before him.

'Load personal icon.'

Through the jack he could feel the flicker of power that meant the command had been obeyed, but nothing changed on the screen. As he travelled through the Map, however, others would see the humanoid shape that represented him and be able to interact with him. He as well could now interact with the icons that he came across, whether they represented other Map walkers or mere objects. Mail always came first. When he touched the blue, winged icon, it opened like a flower and spread, listing out the items in clusters of words. When he saw a message marked with official guild glyphs, he flipped it open immediately. They'd put him on the list for an expanded work space, a holobox, and a larger cubicle. He'd been cleared as well for his second jack. His apprenticeship was nearly over. But were they doing this because he'd earned it, or because he was about to become Hivel Jons's heir?

Heir or no, he had a scutwork group waiting to be read, the results of boring database searches left for him to route, then fresh orders from masters and study assignments from teachers. Migel had Rico down for sanitation work on the Map, and Hondro wanted him to test a collection of error-checkers. Next to these hung his manifests for completed projects, each tagged with master critiques. He ran his hand down the tags, flipping them over and reading the comments. 'Acceptable work', 'successfully concluded', and finally a 'publish this in the Library'. Rico grinned. He'd been getting a lot of this sort of praise lately. The last tag, though, carried Hi's route marks. He could count on that one being a scathing critique of all the flaws that the other masters had missed, and he left it for later.

Personal messages next: Rico skimmed them fast, but he found no note from Jodi Sanchis, a girl in Bio that he'd been corresponding with. Thinking about Jodi made him remember Darla. He felt himself blush, so hot that for a moment he slipped out of the screen. If he could – and with Jodi? He forced his mind back to the icons and stepped inside, closing his mailbox with a sweep of one virtual hand. He could open docks for those scutwork projects later.

His own projects clustered under an icon he'd designed, a human skull with red flowers growing out of the eye sockets. Although Hi laughed at him for what he called its 'drama', Rico insisted on keeping it. When he expanded the dock, though, a set of more conventional icons, glyphs on disks, appeared. They led to hook-ups with the only AI unit that apprentices were allowed to access, Caliostro. 'Poor old Caliostro', the masters called him, a once-powerful AI who'd been damaged first by the neutrino wave that had wreaked havoc on all the Pinch's AIs, and then again later, during the Schism Wars. Mere apprentices never learned the details of Caliostro's crippling, though of course everyone had a theory. The guild had cannibalized and reconfigured the AI dozens of times over the years, until nowadays it functioned mostly as a virtual chamberlain utility for Government House.

The masters had, however, kept part of its function space as a training ground for the guild, a safe area where apprentices were supposed to stay. Of course, being apprentices, they never did, and there was a kind of unspoken tolerance for those apprentices bold enough to push the limits, provided they didn't push too far. If you strayed into a high security area and got caught at it, the masters broke you back down to a neophyte. Getting caught more than once meant automatic expulsion. Being unguilded put you at the economic level of saccules. You'd need a lot of luck to so much as get a work permit over in Service Sect to collect the garbage that the street cleaning bots missed.

Rico had heard the lectures a hundred times. He'd seen a couple of apprentices publicly stripped of their blues and turned out into the street. But he kept thinking of Arno, mumbling about metas and the Son of the Morning.

'Time?'

The numbers appeared in the nacreous haze around him. Twenty into the sevens. His supervisor, Dian Wynn, tended to run late. Probably, he had a good hour of free walking before she jacked into tandem with him. He slipped off his vizor and shook his head, relaxing his neck muscles, then lay back in his chair and flipped up the leg rest. When he was plugged in, he saw the world as if he stood within the screen, but his body was always present, nagging him about comfort. Only the cyberdrugs could set your mind truly free from physical reminders, but Rico knew a trick or two.

Once he was settled, he put the vizor back on, but this time he plugged in the earpiece as well. When he went back into the screen he could hear the low tone of audio going functional. Caliostro's icon hovered above him. When he touched the glyph, a blood-red wand, it turned hot and disappeared. The gate opened before him like the petals of a silver flower.

Rico stepped through into the apprentices' meeting room, which he saw as the interior of a green sphere pimpled with doors, each labelled with a Master's gene-glyph. Although each guild drew on many families, each family tended to belong to a single guild, apprenticing out their young people to uncles or aunts over the generations. The Jons and the Hernanes clans had fallen into this pattern for nearly a thousand years. Yet as large a clan as each was, they never could have supplied the guild with enough sapients to fill it.

That morning Rico recognized none of the other apprentices – or rather, their iconic bodies – who travelled in the sphere, some hanging upside down from his point of view or walking across the ceiling. When a female form floated past, upside down and at a sharp angle to the vertical of his own icon, he felt himself twisting automatically to match her, then caught himself. The visual conventions of Mapspace took a long time to master. While he could see everyone else's icon, for instance, he could see nothing of his own. He was aware of reaching and touching various icons, but he never saw a hand when he did so. The sensations of reach and touch were only neuronic conventions, his brain's way of symbolizing the manipulations of objects in the ancient stylizations of the Map.

Rico used his personal meta to unlock the Jons family's access door. He floated through and found himself hovering over what seemed to be an immense wheel with hundreds of narrow gates, shaped like longtubes, spoking up from the rim. The entrance to the gate leading to his personal work space, a simple arch enclosing dead black, carried no meta-lock; apprentices had to earn that much privacy. For a moment, though, he hovered in the wheel room and looked out over the portals to other clan work spaces, research virtualities, and storage areas. Somewhere here, too, hidden from any outsider that might drift this way, lay the Jons clan's jealously guarded secret, the Chameleon Gate, an ancient artifact brought online at least a thousand years ago, maybe more, so long ago that no-one even knew why or how it had fit into the original schemata of the Map.

Accessing the Map by all the known and legal means – and this definition covered the vast majority of possible means – left routing marks and ID codes visible to anyone but the rawest apprentice. If Rico tried hunting for Arno from his own work space, he might as well send mail about it to Hi and every other master around. But if he used the Chameleon Gate, he would leave no trace at all. At his level he wasn't even supposed to know how to access it, but Arno had taught him a shortcut. Of course, he really should just go into his work space, finish that icon-stacker, and forget all about the encounter with Arno in Pleasure Sect. Hadn't Uncle Hi ordered just that? And Hi was his family patron and guildmaster both. But he found himself remembering Arno, his filthy clothes, his desperate voice, his tendrilled eyes, glancing this way and that, tearing in the bright sun.

No-one else flew or hovered in the clan Mapspace.

'Open sesame,' Rico said.

Arno's shortcut program began to run.

In the Mapspace an icon formed, thin and pale at first, then turning solid: Arno himself as he'd looked when he'd written this routine – his face all flesh, smooth and clear, grinning at the risk he was running, blue eyes snapping – yet since the icon only showed his head and shoulders, he was disembodied, a floating portrait in the pale Mapstuff. The routine chugged on, cloning the icon exponentially, flashing the clones like sparks through the clan space until an Arno hovered before every portal.

'Doorbreaker,' Rico said.

The submeta clicked in, searching for the right unlock routine for every single portal in the clan space. Since the Chameleon Gate only mimicked a portal, its image alone would be left, an imitation of a locked portal, once the meta finished its work. Rico hovered, waiting, watching the monitor numbers flickering in his peripheral vision as the meta found and stored the lock code. At any minute a clan member – even Hi or his mother – might casually enter the space. He would have only a bare moment to shut the meta down before they would see what was going on. He heard a faint bell as the meta announced it had completed the search; now it had to copy code so that it could lock the doors again before any master or professor noticed them open. Rico had written this part of the meta for Arno; he cursed himself for not doing a more elegant job. The numbers built up slowly, it seemed, painfully slowly. Another bell sounded. Now!

'Open!'

In the centre of the clan space, a ripple of colour appeared like a waving curtain. The doors sprang open, hung that way for a heartbeat, then slammed shut. Along with them the crowd of Arno-icons vanished, all but one, standing before the open portal to the Chameleon Gate. Rico rushed forward and flung himself through the portal. Behind him the Arno-icon ran a verbal component.

'Good luck!'

Then it vanished as well, and the door shut with a spray of rainbow like a breaking wave. Rico found himself floating through an ice-blue mist. He could see nothing, hear nothing, but he could feel. It seemed that invisible hands moved in the mist and wrapped his entire body with thin sheets of pure cold. When something much like a membrane of cold settled over his face, he felt as if he were suffocating and lifted his hands to claw at it. The wrap of cold remained, fused to the seeming-skin. Needles of lightning played over his entire body, making him writhe until he could steady his form by sheer will. His real body was getting all the air it needed, back in its chair in his cube. His station and the jack in that body's hand were only translating his psychodynamic contact with the Chameleon Gate. He knew all that. He knew that the Map only mimicked bodily sensations. The sensations were just more data. He knew that, he knew it all, he could repeat his textbook definitions over and over, but still he felt as if he drowned in a sea of ice. He gulped and shook and repeated all the definitions once more; the sensations never vanished.

As if it had lost patience, waiting for him to enter location coordinates, the Gate began to move, slowly at first, swinging back and forth in a lazy arc, then a little faster, back and forth, around and around like a pendulum. Rico, still choking, felt his stomach turn over and threaten to empty. He gasped for words.

'Stabilize.'

Nothing happened. If his body threw up, lying on its back, he could be in real trouble.

'Oh no! By God's Eye!'

The Gate stopped swinging, then began to move straight up,

faster and faster, rushing upward into blackness like a lift booth gone mad. Rico could barely think, much less try commands, as it careened into the Interstice, a black-seeming coruscation that buffered the Map construct from the end-user station interfaces. It was only another illusion, the blackness, but as he gasped for breath and shivered, wrapped in the freezing membrane, Rico found it real enough. He could not see, could not hear. What had Arno told him – he couldn't remember – he'd been a real *dim*, a dead chip, to think he knew enough to use the Gate.

All at once Rico heard a sound like beeping clocks. The Gate burst out of the blackness into pale blue and stopped, floating. Rico looked down on what seemed to be Palace itself, the whole planet turning under him but stripped of its cloud cover. He looked up and saw Tableau, glittering with ice, hanging a seeming few feet away, and Souk, too, pale green and a couple of yards beyond. Trailing off in a long spiral hung all the worlds of the Pinch, or rather, their Maps, including a dead-black cinder of a sphere that had to be Kephalon. He was hanging in the Hypermap. He was seeing the entire Pinch.

Rico turned slowly round, smiling, staring, almost laughing, looking at this panoply of worlds that dangled in a pale sky without stars. Somehow he'd never realized that it would be so beautiful, the Hypermap, that it would seem so *whole*, so elegant. All he'd ever known before was the Map of Palace, a thing as cluttered, swarming, patched, and tattered as the city-state it represented. But out here, for instance, hung the Nimue Archipelago, a sphere defined by blueglass moons. In the physical world, they orbited Palace's star beyond the orbit of its farthest planet, but here they constellated a perfect form. As he studied the planetary Maps, Rico noticed faint lines of golden light that webbed each world round. Each planetary web sent out tendrils that touched and knotted between the worlds, and from each knot grew more golden lines, fusing the webs into one vast whole. Rico had seen diagrams of these webs in school material, the hyperwave carriers for messages, the crucial lines of communication that kept Pinch civilization functioning. They followed the pattern of the interstellar microshunts; indeed, this construct of lines had been the original 'map', a simple analogue of the microshunts for navigation purposes. All of these elaborate worlds and their cross-connections had come later, laboriously built by the first cybermasters of the Pinch. Rico wanted to stay there for hours, staring at the splendid sights of the Map, but always he remembered Arno. He looked down and concentrated on Palace.

'Magnify.'

The Gate dropped – that was how he felt it – dropped down and suddenly. His skin seemed so cold that Rico felt he might shatter, his body as brittle as ice, but all at once the Gate stopped, floating over the planet, which now filled his entire view. He was at the analogue of an orbit suitable for a communications satellite, he figured. Below him he could see the vast swamps of the northern continent, Nox, a thing of temporary islands and drowned lands, taken by the sea only some fifteen hundred years ago.

'Show Palace city.'

A voice sounded, thin and electric.

'Error correction.'

'The city of Palace.'

'Error correction.'

Damn you, he thought.

'Throw ambiguity switch. Find: correction terminology for the city-state that occupies the coast of the continent known as Lux.'

A moment's pause, then the voice.

'Polis. The city.'

The lightning cold seemed to play down his spine. You knew that, kind of, Rico told himself. You read about it in ancient history class. How old was the Gate, then? Had it been made by the Colonizers? And why hadn't Uncle Hi or some other member of the clan found and solved this terminology glitch already? No time now to wonder.

'Enter permanent term amplification. Polis equals Palace.'

'Done.'

'Show Palace.'

This time the Gate stayed steady while the Map turned beneath him, then stopped. The view below centred round the famous twin towers of blueglass in the midst of Government House. From this high vantage, Rico could clearly see that the towers formed the central points of an enormous ellipse, marked out by the dot pattern of fusion power nodes as well as by hundreds of Mappoints, the blueglass structures that functioned as work stations for those who knew how to use them. Over this basic pattern ran and tangled thousands of developments, or devs, marked out as lines of so dark a blue they were almost black. They lay like lace over another kind of map, that of Palace's streets and buildings, drawn and stippled in red and maroon.

'Show Tech Sect.'

'Error correction.'

Damn! Some words in Gen it understood perfectly; others only glitched its databanks. Since Arno had been working with the Gate, he must have amplified – added additional meanings to – some of its commands but not others, or so Rico could suppose, anyway. Probably Arno had entered standard guild metas to save time and memory.

'Arco daz dev.'

In answer, the Gate swooped down. Rico felt the membrane of cold tighten, digging into his skin like a thousand needles, as the Gate turned and swung like a meteor close over the surface of the Map. At first, scattered Mappoints whipped by, dots of blue, and isolated devs snaked under him. As they flew round toward Palace, the points and the devs increased, clustered, tangled together into a massive snarl over Government House and the twin towers, only to loosen somewhat as they slid past Centre Sect and glided, more slowly now, over Tech.

Without the close packed dwells and warehouses, without the webwork of canals and barges, and the thousands of small shops and other structures that had no analogue on the Map, Tech Sect sprawled thin as a skeleton. What remained were a welter of low-level accesses and perhaps two dozen blueglass Mappoints, the most heavily guarded structures in the Pinch. Rico had no intention of meddling with them. The Gate might be able to get him undetected onto the Map, but getting anyone past the array of sensors and security devices that protected the perimeters of those Mappoints lay far beyond its function level.

'Arco trez dev.'

The Gate hesitated, then dropped a little lower, fastening on to the development line and gliding along it like a highway. On this level of citizen access stations, Rico saw plenty of light pulses that meant a robotic grab tool, bringing information about shopping or banking to someone's home screen. He also saw iconic bodies shaped like humans and Hirrel – the Maprunners, whom ordinary citizens could hire to do more complicated jobs for them. A lot of Cyberguild members never progressed beyond the runner level. Every now and then Rico saw an icon marked by a Lep crest, but the crest only meant, under the new post-war dispensation, that some human Maprunner had taken a job for a Lep who needed business done.

The Arco trez dev led Rico and the Gate into the heart of one of the strangest areas on the Palace Map, a place of shanties and shacks in the real world and their equivalent on the Map. Over the past thousands of years various sapients had built these Mappoints out of cannibalized blueglass and odd bits of equipment, then linked them up to a section of the Map that had been badly damaged at the closing of the macroshunt, when a neutrino shock wave had swept over through the Pinch, blowing out the nearer AIs and damaging most of the distant ones. Though Palace had suffered less than most worlds, even so here and there lay areas like this one, where isolated functions and utilities still worked or agents still ran, but in such a broken form that they were of no use to the real masters of the Map. Every now and then, though, one of these fly-by-night operations made good, against all odds, only to find themselves stuck with their Map location now that all their customers and suppliers knew it.

It was a good place to hide a message drop, and Arno and Rico had built theirs by adding a bit of Mapspace onto one of those recently legitimate enterprises, Pansect Media, where no-one would ever check dimensions. In return, like good guests, they'd built the company a scrubber submeta to improve its transmission quality. As the Gate ran to the end of the meta and slid into the message drop, which they'd visualized as a hut, Rico felt a change in his body's simulated interface. Although the lightning had stopped crackling along his skin, he felt even colder than before, as if half-frozen he stood in a freezing wind.

Inside the dim walls, vaguely marked to resemble wood planks, lines of scintillating colour shot back and forth, the secured narrow-band transmissions of the Pansect operation. These Rico and Arno had always left strictly alone. They had a band and niche of their own.

'Furious green,' Rico said.

On the floor an illusion of planks vanished, revealing another illusion, a metal trap door. In the air around him icons of jadewings appeared, all safely green – red would have meant someone had been tampering with their cache. Rico knelt down, but he hesitated before he opened the panel. He'd been checking it regularly ever since Arno's disappearance only to find nothing. What made him think there would be something now? He remembered Arno's voice, shaky but urgent, telling him a submeta, and the way he'd reached out a shaking hand to meld jacks. It wasn't just some accident, meeting him there in the festival.

Rico opened the panel, swung his feet over the edge, and climbed downstairs. Waiting at the bottom lay a cave, an image from a holovid they'd both loved as boys. Grim grey stone walls lowered round a pool of water, and greenish stalactites gleamed with phosphorescence. From a ledge they'd hung shields, painted with clan devices, and representations of something called laser guns – symbols from the primitive tribes in the holovid, who had taken to the caves to defend their sacred places from evil Lep invaders. Just how the guns were supposed to work in a culture that lit their rooms with fire was one of the holovid's many lapses, but no matter – they'd loved the story anyway.

Inside the pool lay a sealed box. Rico pulled it out, sat down cross-legged, and lifted the lid with trembling hands to find a revchip, a frozen figurine of a jadewing. Rico picked it up and held it in the palm of his hand, but thanks to the wrap of ice the Gate had placed round him, he could barely feel it. He was aware, though, that the cold had deepened. All at once it occurred to him to wonder just how long you could use the Gate safely.

'Time is running out.'

Although Rico said the words, he felt as if some other sapient had somehow placed them into his mouth. They seemed to come from the inside out, as if the Gate had borrowed his consciousness to make them heard. He'd had other experiences like this on the Map, when it seemed as if the Map itself was whispering to him. Arno had always teased him about it, too, but now Rico could consider Uncle Hi, saying that dead Nimue had once tried to reach him. It was real enough, then. Time was running out. He held up the figurine.

'Open and run.'

The revchip melted in Rico's palm and turned to a glowing green puddle, leaking between his fingers to the cavern floor. He flung the last of it down and jumped to his feet as the liquid swelled and grew like a tree-trunk, a shaft of green that first turned grey, then shaped itself into a saccule, but one with a human smile. When it spoke, even its voice sounded nothing like Arno.

'Greetings, user,' the rev said. 'If you're who I think you are, you can tell me who the ice cube with eyes is.'

'Pukosu.' Rico laughed – they'd called her that a hundred times.

The saccule revenant rippled, then solidified. When it grinned, it wore Arno's smile, and the voice had changed, too, into his cousin's. Yet its eyes became empty holes through which Rico could see faint sparks of colour.

'I have to make this quick, pal, so you'll have to figure out some of this stuff yourself later. But let me tell you something right now.' The revenant leaned forward with its hands propped on either thigh, a gesture that only Arno could have programmed in. 'I never abused drugs. When I saw you at the Pleasure Sect this morning, it broke my heart. I don't care what the Man says, you deserve to know that I didn't turn into a head and leave you behind just for the fun of it.'

'The Man? Do you mean Hi?'

The revenant froze briefly. So, Arno hadn't had time to program in an interact function. Damn!

'This rev,' it went on, 'is nil-heuristic and self-erasing, so listen close. I've been undercover for months. I can't tell you why, but don't worry, the Man will tell you everything when he gets back from where you saw me last. Here's what you need to know. There's a girl coming out of Pleasure Sect. She's got hair the colour of that rev we found on your birthday.'

It took Rico a moment to remember the peculiar russet-red cow they'd found that day, wandering the Map on its own, someone's idea of a joke.

'Can't risk telling you her name, but you'll know her when you see her. She's very important. The Man and some other people will be watching her, but I want you to keep an eye on her, too. I have a feeling about her, pal. Someone's trying to kill her. Keep her safe, okay? Last thing. Big thing. I gave you an all-meta when I saw you. Remember?'

Rico had to grin at that – as if he would have forgotten.

'Don't use it unless you absolutely have to, but if you're in trouble, don't hesitate. It's a fine thing, pal, and I wish I could be there to see your face when you run it. You're going to be amazed.

'Anyway, I've got to go. Chances are, you won't be seeing or hearing from me again for a very long time. Whoever's trying to kill the girl is trying to kill me, too. You know me, though, I can be pretty quick when I have to. Keep the faith, pal. Be careful. Keep your eyes open. Test the limits. And don't let the Man run your life. The Map moves, buddy.'

The saccule raised a stubby hand, then winked out. On the floor the last traces of the green puddle dried up and vanished. That rev would never play again.

'Time is running out.'

The voice sounded as thin and cold as a line of the same ice that wrapped him round. Rico turned, heading for the stairs, just as the cavern exploded all around him. A roar, a blast of fire and fiery air lifted him up and out, threw him on a hot wind and a huge billow of black smoke. He could see chunks and pieces of the message hut – hell, of the entire Pansect Media construct – whirling through the air around him and with him. Charging through the smoke and heading straight at him was a towering pillar of flame, so white-hot that he had to look away.

'Arco sec attack.'

Out of the wreckage the security drones flew up. They buzzed round, firing bolts of energy at the thing, the candle, Rico thought of it, a huge white candle blazing in Mapspace. The energy bolts – a visualized form of erase and delete utilities – bounced off the white wax, but the candle hesitated just long enough.

'Arco daz dev home reverse now.'

Wrapped in ice the Gate blasted free of the wreckage and flew up in a trail of smoke. When he glanced back, Rico saw the Candle dimming itself to a blood-red, then peeling off a spray of energy. All hundred of his carefully crafted defenders burst into flames. No rev, no iconized utility, nothing at all should have been able to do that! The Gate was swooping up, rushing away, but the Candle began to move, slowly at first, sucking up energy from the shattered icons until it glowed as white-hot as an arc weld. As it moved, as it glowed, it gained speed, rose up and arrowed after Rico and the Gate. Its heat, its immense glowing heat, reached out long fingers ahead of it and clawed through to Rico's bones.

Faster, faster, it was gaining on them even as they raced and dipped over Tech Sect, heading for the Map terminals clustered round guild headquarters. The membrane of ice round Rico stabilized itself at last, then grew colder still, until the Candle's heat seem no more than the touch of the sun on a cloud-free day. Still it gained, and to his horror Rico saw it dimming back down, glowing first yellow, then orange, then red. Rico kept seeing the defenders, bursting into flames. He was next, most likely. He thought of the all-meta – was this the ultimate danger? Had Arno known about this Candle thing?

With the chime of a hundred clocks, the Gate swooped into the

Interstice and released him, spun him off like a thrown ball into the darkness, where he fell, down and down. No more ice around his skin, he could breathe, but still he fell, could barely think to call out his station number. At last he caught himself, steadied himself in the darkness, and found that he hovered over his own black arch entrance to clan space. He turned and looked back to see the Gate as a thin web of icy-blue lines, flickering through the Interstice, twisting this way and that, heading back up to the Map. Behind it raged the Candle, burning white again as it turned its energy inward for the chase.

In a desperate fear for the Gate's safety, Rico started after, flinging himself through Mapspace, but at that moment the Gate and the Candle both disappeared, diving through some hidden barrier. He could see nothing, he could do nothing, he could never follow. Once he was back at his station, though, he'd be able to run searches, and see if the Gate had survived or even try summoning the Gate with Arno's shortcut.

Rico slid down his access into clan space, floating all quiet and orderly with its rim of gates. What would happen if the Candle ever moved through here? He would have to tell his uncle, have to warn the guild – how? Tell them he'd been illegally using the Chameleon Gate, admit that he'd messed around in forbidden areas, confess that he'd directly disobeyed his guildmaster's orders about forgetting Arno? For a moment he couldn't breathe, clutched by a worse cold than any the Gate had built around him. As he glanced around he saw other icon bodies hurrying through, and among them were several marked with the gold of masters.

'Oh my God! Time?'

Nine of the eights. Bad, real bad – Wynn was never this late. What had she done when she jacked in and discovered that he was off Map? Sure enough, he was just heading for the hub and the egress from clan space when Wynn appeared in her tall iconic body, swirling with gold and the simulacrum of blue cloth.

'Rico!' she snapped. 'Didn't you hear your call-alarm? You're supposed to be in the guildmaster's office. You better get over there. Sé Hivel implied that this was a very important matter.'

'Yes, Professor. I'd uh forgotten.'

'Well, from now on don't forget! He wants you there physically, so get off the Map now.'

'Yes, Sé.' Rico had never been so glad to obey an order.

He hurried out of clan space, raced across the access hall, and slid into the chute numbered for his station. All at once he saw himself standing in the screen with mail icons floating around him. Off to one side lay an exit panel; he touched it and felt as if he dropped from a height into sand, with a crunching kind of thud, a groan, and the abrupt sensation of weight, of gravity, of his flesh body lying in a chair, of clothing, soaked through with sweat.

'Shit.'

Rico sat up, running his hands through sweaty hair. The backs of his hands stung, he realized, and it wasn't just the usual pins and needles of returning circulation. His skin was bright red, as if he'd lain under a sunlamp for hours. When he glanced at himself in the monitor, his reflection showed the same burn blazing across his face.

For his private, inner office Hi kept a cube not much bigger than an apprentice's, though it did have a dark green carpet on the floor and a programmable leather chair, standing in front of the state-of-the-art Mapstation. Powered down, the Mapscreen looked like a mirror in a chrome frame and nothing more. When Rico walked in, Hi noticed him glance at himself in the mirror and wince.

'What have you done?' Hi said. 'Fried yourself under a sunlamp down at the gym?'

'Yeah, 'fraid so. I fell asleep. Guess I'm still tired from yesterday.'

'Probably so, yeah.'

Hi hesitated, considering him. Ten to one Rico was lying, judging from his nervous eyes, but why? And about what? At the moment it seemed too unimportant to bother with.

'I've got a job for you. Think you're too tired to do some climbing? Not stairs. Up a lattice-work on the side of a tower.'

'A what?'

'Back in Pleasure Sect.'

Rico grinned.

'Not that we'll have any time for non-business activities. Your mother wanted you home this afternoon, remember?'

The grin vanished.

'Well, yeah,' Rico said with a sigh. 'If she's shipping out to Orbital soon, then there's a lot of stuff about the house I've got to know.'

'Right. Let's get out of here and up to the roof. Nju's waiting with an aircar.'

Not just Nju, but another Garang bodyguard and a driver went along with them that morning. As they circled up from Centre, Hi looked down through green-tinted glass at dark streets and found himself thinking about Arno. Hi had spent a lot of time that morning lighting a fire under the Protectors about Vi-Kata. He also had a couple of connections in the Special Services branch of the Military Guild who would be more than glad to know about the assassin's presence on Palace. With a lurch the aircar steadied out, then leapt forward at top power. Klaxons howled as other 'hoppers and 'cars scattered before them. The Garang drove as they lived – full speed ahead.

Rico turned in his seat and seemed to be looking out the window, but from the way he held one hand to his mouth, as if he were going to chew on it, Hi wondered if the boy was quite simply hiding something. He'd never seen Rico this troubled before, not open, honest Rico, a little naive, yeah, as Aleen had called him, but as clean and true as a Colonial gold coin.

'Something on your mind, Rico?'

'No, Sé.' Rico glanced at him with a parody of his usual smile, then looked away fast.

'Yeah?' Hi hesitated, considering. If they'd been alone, instead of in a small car with three Garang, he might have probed, but as it was, he didn't want Rico confessing something in front of sapients who couldn't be bribed to forget it. 'Well, let me tell you what we're up to.'

As they headed toward Pleasure Sect and the Carillon roof park, Hi told Rico about Vida's revenant and the suddenly active Mapstation. To this Rico listened with his usual serious attention, asking, here and there, an intelligent question or two.

'So you see,' Hi finished up. 'that station is so old that the tower's been sealed off. I dug around in a couple of archives this morning. There used to be another tower on the roof, one with a lift booth in it, and a bridge between the two. The first one had to be torn down before it fell down, about twenty years ago now, and what with one thing and another, and then the war, it's never been replaced. I tried to access the station through the Map, of course, but it was sealed off as non-functioning a long, long time ago, just about the time of the Schism Wars.'

'That long?' Rico said. 'But can't you get in from above, from the Hypermap?'

Hi sloughed round in his seat and considered Rico, who blushed even redder than his lamp burn.

'Just what do you know about that, kid? I didn't think you were that far along in the training.'

'Well, just what it says in the manuals.' Rico was suddenly all puzzled innocence. 'You can always reach any point on the Map from the Hypermap, unless a master cybe's blocked it with an umbrella, I think they called it.'

'Yeah, that's right. And there was an umbrella over this Map-station. I don't want to close it up just yet, because I want to know who put it there.'

Rico nodded, considering this with genuine innocence. Hi figured that he'd found the reason for Rico's earlier unease. He'd been poking around and found the keys to some higher level manuals. Apprentices always did, or at least the ones who were worth anything. A sin like that could be safely ignored.

The aircar suddenly changed its whine, hovered briefly, then lowered itself fast enough to turn Hi's stomach over.

'Nju!' he yelled. 'Tell that driver to take it easy!'

For an answer he got a bump, a scrape, and a jarring sort of thud.

'We have arrived, Sé Hivel,' Nju called out. 'Quite safely, too, I might add.'

The roof park stood deserted except for one saccule gardener, who leaned onto his rake and stared at them as they got out of the car. When Hi tossed him a small coin, he honked twice, slipped the coin into the pocket of his baggy grey coveralls, and turned away to get on with his work.

'I thought saccules didn't understand money,' Rico said.

'Yeah, that's what we're told, all right. Hey, for all I know he might like coins just because they're shiny.' Hi glanced round, taking another look, assuring himself that they were indeed alone except for the gardener. 'There's the tower, and there's the lattice of vines and grillwork. Think you can get up there and down again?'

'Sure. Do you have a comm link on you?'

'You bet.' Hi reached into his pocket and brought out a trans-ceiver combo, a long sliver of blue metal. 'Clip that onto your shirt, and head on up.'

Although the climb looked easy enough for someone young and in good shape, Hi watched in a state of nerves until Rico successfully scrambled into the bell tower. If the kid fell, Barra would have Hi's head on a platter, and he knew it. In his matching transceiver clip, he could see a tiny picture of the inside of the tower and the black slab that Vida had described. Rico's voice transmitted shrilly but clearly.

'Okay, I'm running my hand over the slab, like the girl said. Hey, here he is.'

Hi could see something like a revenant form over the slab, but the transmit of a hologram was always muddy, and this was no exception. Hi could, however, hear the artificial voice quite clearly.

'Greetings, user. I'm sorry, but your deen is a nonpriority. Please give access request that I may triage.'

'Calios,' Rico said.

'You are not authorized for that password.'

The revenant disappeared.

'Damn!' Hi said, and simultaneously heard his nephew say the same.

The Eye of God that Brother Lennos had given her was a simple thing, a wooden disk strung on a leather thong, no fancy holo here, just an inscribed eye rubbed with black paint. The monks and nuns made dozens of these to hand out to children at festivals. When Vida turned it over, she found a small mark scratched on the back – Lennos's own mark, maybe, or his monastery's.

'I still feel so terrible,' Vida said, 'thinking he was killed for my sake.'

'It's a terrible thing,' Jak said, nodding, 'to kill a poor Lifegiver for his robes.'

They were sitting in Vida's bedroom, Vida in the chair by her Maplink screen, Jak on the small blue rug with his back propped against the door. My bodyguard, Vida thought, and the thought made her stomach turn cold. She slipped the Eye on its thong round her neck.

'I still can't believe that someone wanted to kill me,' she said.

'Why not? God has obviously marked you for great things, Sé Vida.'

'What? Oh, come on! Not me!'

'Why else would someone try to kill you? No-one hires famous assassins to kill some unimportant little person.'

Circular though it was, the argument rang true. Vida glanced at her screen, where her lesson menu hung in the opalescence. Studying was impossible. She was just reaching over to shut the link down when her call code sounded.

'Answer,' Vida said.

The school menu dissolved, and in the resulting swirl of colour a face appeared, a slender young man with ebony dark skin and silver hair.

'Calios!' Vida said.

'Greetings, Veelivar.' He was grinning at her. 'Someone is trying to forge your password and access me.'

'Who?' Vida went cold, thinking of assassins.

'A member of a clan whose genotype is not on my priority list. He refuses to identify himself beyond repeating your password.'

'Is he a Lep?'

'He is a human.'

'Well, that's something, anyway.'

'I cannot parse your input, Veelivar.'

'I mean, it's good that he's human, but still, this kind of scares me. Please deny any information about me to anyone who asks.'

'Input accepted. Running cancel utility now. I have already umbrella'd my own access. You may be certain that the cancel utility run will be successful.'

'Good. Thanks.'

The image on the screen disappeared. Slowly the school menu reappeared, a line at a time. Jak was frankly staring.

'Never, Sé Vida, have I seen such a thing, a revenant such as that, I mean.'

'Well, neither have I. I suppose the really important people get to use them, the Cyberguild people and the people in Government House, I mean.'

'Now that may well be true, indeed.'

'At least now I know what he means when he says Veelivar. That's me. Vida L'Var y . . .' She paused, thinking back to the legal form Aleen had shown her the night before, and the name of the woman who had been her mother. 'Vida L'Var y Smid.'

'Smid? I don't know that clan name, Sé Vida.'

'I don't think it is a clan, exactly. I wonder what happened to my mother. She would have spent three years in the work camp, Aleen told me. But what about after that?'

Jak shrugged.

'Perhaps there is a public record?'

Although the school Map was strictly limited, Vida could access some public records from its menus – some, but not the correct ones. In an hour of running the few public utilities open to non-adults, she learned nothing but the knowledge that there were thousands of Smids in Palace.

'It sure is a common name,' she said to Jak. 'I'll never be able to ask them all.'

'If they would even admit such a thing, Sé Vida. To spend years in the work camps is not an honourable activity.'

Someone knocked. Jak sprang to his feet and opened the door a bare inch.

'Ah,' he said. 'Madama Tia.'

'Vida, Aleen's sent for you. She's in her office.'

'Her office? Oh God. That means trouble.'

With Jak marching behind her, Vida left her room and headed down the hall to the lift booth station. As they stepped in, Vida remembered that she'd never even combed her hair. Aleen hated mess. She ran trembling hands through it and pushed it back from her face.

'Office.'

The booth slid up fast, making her gulp for breath – no, that was the nerves. When the booth stopped, it took Vida a moment to force herself out. If Jak hadn't been standing right behind her, a reassuring presence, she might have lingered in the foyer for a long time. Apparently the tri-stil door into Aleen's office had been programmed to expect her; it slid open as she approached and let her into the oval room, filled with a cool blue light.

A hundred niches, filled with holo art large and small, dissolved the walls into a web of images. The huge dome of the ceiling displayed fractals, moving, melding, changing in time to the sweet trilling music of *pa'ali*, gill-pipes invented by Hirrel musicians. Next to an enormous crystal globe of Palace, Aleen sat in a chair modified to allow simultaneous comm and data work. She said nothing until Vida sat down opposite in an armless formfit. Jak took his usual place at the door.

For a long time the madam considered her from over arched fingers, while Vida shivered. At last Aleen leaned back in her chair and glanced away, glanced up at the patterns swirling, forming, dying on the ceiling dome.

'Something very strange has happened, Vida. An arrangement's been made for you that's rather different than anything I'd ever expected.'

Vida tried to answer, instead licked nervous lips.

Aleen brushed a sensor on the armrest of her chair and the music shifted into something slow, sombre – a funeral dirge of the saccules, a twined thing of harmonies and variations. The fractals became shifting shards of black glass. Without thinking, Vida laid her hand on the wooden Eye hanging from its thong. When Aleen held out her hand, Vida slipped the Eye over her head and gave it to her. Aleen looked at it for a long moment.

'What do you know about the Eye of God, Vida?' Aleen's voice had changed into her familiar lecturer's tone.

'I . . . the Lifegivers say that the Eye watches over all of us, sees our sins and good deeds and when we die, if we've been good, God sends us into the sky to become stars, the lesser eyes of God.'

'And if we're sinful?'

Vida squirmed in her formfit; the chair squeaked, then reconfigured itself under her.

'Then we're sent back to live again as some low animal, like a ver or a saccule, until we earn the right to become human again and try to become true stars.'

'Very good. You also know that a thousand years ago, the Church of the Eye split into four different Schisms, that each Schism had a different definition for 'sapient' and 'animal'. How many sapients died in the wars that followed?'

'Over a million, most of them on Belie.'

'Correct. It's something I want you to think about.'

'What, Madam? I mean, why?'

'You'll understand why if you think about it long enough.'

Utterly baffled, Vida stared at her until Aleen laughed.

'Here's a clue, Vida. When you read about the old days on the Rim, you can see how we're losing our diversity, out here in the Pinch. The Hirrel are a dying race, and so are the Garang Japat. The humans and the Leps breed so fast that none of the others have a chance, compared to us. What do you think about that?'

'I don't know, Madam.'

'What about this, then? We all look back to the Colonizers, all of us, from some half-educated scavenger in Service Sect up to the cardinal himself. No-one looks forward, not out here in the Pinch. We're a colony full of archivists, struggling to regain what we think we've lost. Don't you think that's dangerous?'

'Well, uh, I guess. It's never seemed like anything I should worry about. I mean, there's nothing I can do about it.'

'No?' Aleen smiled, just briefly. 'You're going to be in a position to do a great deal about a great many different things, Vida.'

'Me, Madam?'

'Yes, you. You're going to sign a marriage contract with Wan Peronida, heir to the First Citizen. He's asking for fifteen years.'

All Vida could do was stare. She was going to marry Wan Peronida? Ridiculous! But if she did, she'd be free, out of Pleasure forever. Never Marked – free . . . From his place at the door Jak laughed.

'Great things, Sé Vida,' he said. 'Great things.'

'No, not me.' Vida found her voice at last. 'Madam, how, I mean, what –'

'Karlo Peronida has taken an interest in you,' Aleen said. 'I thought he'd be your enemy, but it seems he thinks he can use you. Which is lucky for you, very lucky.'

'What do you mean?'

'You were hidden from Vanna. You know how she hated your family. Everyone – I – assumed Karlo would take on her feud when he made a contract with her. But he hasn't. None of the great families want to marry a daughter off to his son, you see, except on the most limited terms. When he found out that you exist, that a *L'Var* exists, he saw his chance.'

'But I'm nobody.'

'Not any more, Vida. You're going to inherit the L'Var property. You'll be rich. The L'Var traced their bloodlines all the way back to the Colonizers. Your genotype stands three cuts above the Peronidas, and Karlo knows it. So will everyone else in Government House.'

Vida sat, barely thinking, for what seemed to her a long time. The music whispered and sobbed around them.

'There's an obvious question,' Aleen snapped. 'Think! What is it?'

'Do I have to marry this Wan? What if I say no?'

'Very good. If you say no, no-one can force you. But you'll have to stay in Pleasure Sect. I can't really protect you any more, not from somebody who's powerful enough to hire an assassin, but at least you'll have a chance here.'

'A chance, Madam?'

'At staying alive for a little while longer.'

Vida went cold all over. In her mind she could see Brother Lennos, smiling at her.

'The security in Government House is amazing, from what I hear.' Aleen glanced at Jak.

'This is very true, Madama Aleen. We Garang make it our business to know these things. Sé Vida, if you become the Peronida's lawdaughter, you'll have the best protection in the Pinch. Nobody will dare threaten you.'

'But I don't want to leave!' Vida blurted out. 'This is my home.'

Aleen leaned back in her chair and stroked a sensor, dropping the lights down to an azure mist. In the glowy dark the saccule dirge hummed and boomed. Her voice came from the shadows like a memory of sound.

'The Pleasure Sect is no-one's home. We're all culls, dumped here, adopted out. It's a holding pen, not a home. Vida, think! In Centre Sect you'll have freedom, you can do great things, you can be a somebody in this world if you marry the Peronida heir. Don't fail me, Vida.'

'Fail you? What do you mean?'

No answer, only the music, wailing in the dark.

'When . . . when do I have to leave?'

'Today.'

'Today!'

'I've already spoken to Cardinal Roha.' Aleen turned her flesh eye Vida's way. 'He's sending Lifegivers, his best men, to bring you to Government House. They'll arrive late this afternoon. There's no need to pack. You won't be taking anything of Pleasure with you. Dukayn specifically told me that.'

'Who, Madam?'

'The head of security in Government House – among other things. Vida, there's just so much I haven't told you yet. I'm sorry, but what I've had time for will have to do.'

'Can Jak come with me?'

'I'm afraid not, but don't worry. The cardinal's men are highly trained. They're not the usual run of monk.'

Vida twisted round to look at Jak, who nodded confirmation.

'But –'

'Hush!' Aleen snapped. 'There's no time for me to tell you everything you need to know. Maybe it's better if you figure things out on your own. But remember everything I taught you. You know how to be charming from being raised here, so charm them all. Trust no-one. Vanna Makeesa's your most dangerous enemy, but there will be others, a lot of others. In particular, keep an eye on the cardinal.'

'The cardinal? I thought he was helping us.'

'At the moment.'

'Oh. Oh, I see. He could change.'

'He most likely will change. Government House does that to people.'

Vida hesitated, framing one last question.

'It's getting late,' Aleen said. 'You'd better leave.'

'Madam, what happened to my mother? Where is she now?'

'You may leave.' When Aleen leaned back to watch the play of darkness across the dome, shadows fell like a pool of blood on her face.

Vida stood and started to walk out, but at the door she hesitated, while Jak hovered in the foyer. Aleen had raised her, protected her, taught her, and now she was surrendering her as easily as if Vida were some pet jadewing she'd been boarding. Vida fought back tears. Aleen would only despise tears.

'Goodbye, Madam. I'll miss you.'

She waited a moment and then a long moment more, but Aleen said nothing. The saccule dirge grew in volume until it shook the air. Swallowing hard, Vida left without looking back.

After Vida left, Hi entered Aleen's office from a listening niche, hidden behind a holosculpture of a woman riding some six-legged creature. He'd come straight to The Close after sending Rico back to Tech Sect on the wiretrain. As if she hadn't noticed him, Aleen lay back in her chair, her eyes closed. Hi sat down opposite her in the chair Vida had just vacated. He could smell the girl still, or rather, a flowery cheap perfume and her sweat. She'd been terrified, Hi supposed, and rightly so. Abruptly Aleen opened her eyes, then sat up, tossing her green hair back from her face. With a small whine the chair followed, curving round her back. She swept her hands over its controls, silencing the thunder of the dirge, brightening the light in the room.

'So,' Aleen said. 'What do you think of her?'

'Bright. Quick thinking. Naive about everything outside this sect. You're very fond of her, aren't you?'

'Of course. The Protectors brought her to me when she was three days old, a smelly little pink thing wriggling in a blanket.'

Aleen smiled at the memory. 'I never thought I was the sentimental type, but she was so goddamn helpless.'

'Three days old? They found her mother fast, then.'

'The poor little slut needed medical help after the birth. I don't know why those women risk it, having illegal babies. They usually get caught.'

'Maybe they're the sentimental type?'

Aleen shrugged and rose in a shimmer of long emerald hair. Hi found himself remembering the first time he'd met her, sixteen years ago now. He'd just won election to the mastership of the Cyberguild and come to Pleasure to celebrate with the most beautiful courtesan he could find. Instead, Aleen had caught his attention – good-looking, yes, but far from the most beautiful woman in the Sect. She'd been vital, instead, and strong, a woman going places, as far as she could go, anyway, trapped in Pleasure.

'What are you thinking about?' she said.

'The first night between us. Bet you don't even remember.'

'Yeah? You'd lose the bet.' She smiled, briefly. 'It stood out.'

She walked over to a polished dark wood cabinet and took out a green bottle, an asymmetric swirl of glass. When she raised an eyebrow, Hi nodded. The drink was swamp wine, one of the few decent trade items – besides neuters – offered by the free gendered saccules outside the human cities. While she poured it into green glasses, her hair slipped forward, framing her face. The red sun tattooed on her forehead seemed to gleam, as livid as a tumour. Barra's right, he thought. Pleasure Sect's turned into something ugly and corrupt. His sister had got those subversive ideas from Vida's father, as he thought about it. Orin L'Var had been something of a crusader.

Most citizens on Palace never learned that along with the tattooed sun came a brain bomb, lurking inside a Marked person's skull. How could Pleasure function as a repository for culls, all those individuals Palace society scorned for one or more of a hundred reasons, if the culls could simply walk away from it? The laws of the Lifegivers declared that the Unauthorized and Undesirable – and any offspring as well – must never be allowed to mingle with the population at large. With someone as powerful as the cardinal on her side, releasing unMarked Vida was easy. If Aleen ever tried to leave, a Lifegiver would transmit a pulse after her, and she would die, no matter who was on her side.

'What's wrong?' She handed him a glass. 'You look like death.'

'Do I?' He saluted her with the glass. 'I'm feeling old.'

'Don't.' She smiled and sat down opposite him. 'You're not.'

Hi took a cautious sip. Swamp wine always tasted cold, even when it wasn't, and deceptively mild. Aleen cradled her glass in both hands and waited.

'All right,' he said at last. 'How come I didn't know about the girl?'

'I would have told you, in time.'

'Sure. Right. Why in hell did you let the cardinal in on this?'

'You're asking the wrong way round. It's the cardinal who's known about Vida from the beginning. He approached me when he found out where the Lifegivers had placed the baby.'

'What? Why did he protect her from Vanna?'

'I don't really know. To preserve the L'Var line, I suppose. He's a great believer in maintaining the purity of the genome.'

'Yeah, that's for sure. A little too worried about it, if you ask me. But why did he leave her here?'

'What choice did he have? She was an Unauthorized birth, wasn't she? Roha was only a priest, then. He didn't have the connections he does now.'

'Well, that's true, yeah. What I really don't understand is how Roha talked Vanna around.'

'He didn't even try. He talked Karlo around, and the First Citizen made Vanna swallow it. I'm sure it didn't taste very good going down.' Aleen paused for an unpleasant smile. 'His Eminence told me that Karlo wanted a rich marriage partner for his son, and no other family in Palace was going to give him one, not on good terms.'

'Karlo never much liked the le-Yonestilla match Vanna arranged. That's no secret.'

Aleen nodded and took a long drink of her wine. For a moment they sat, regarding each other like a pair of chess masters over an unstarted game. Hi could guess what she wanted from him; he merely wanted to see what she'd offer in return. After a moment Aleen turned blunt.

'Vida will need protection in Government House.'

'You think so?' Hi had guessed right. 'The cardinal will take care of her, won't he?'

'Maybe. Maybe not. If Vida becomes a political liability, who knows? And Vanna is right there.'

'I see your point. But why would I want to risk angering the Second Citizen by taking an interest in the girl?'

'Who said I was asking you to?'

Hi laughed – she'd won that round. She merely sat and watched him.

'Well,' Hi said at last. 'Her genotype is valuable, I suppose. Don't you go believing that legend, though, about the L'Vars having some kind of magic built-in power over AIs.'

'She's the *last* of the L'Vars, Hi,' Aleen said. 'She'll inherit their confiscated property.'

'Yeah, so? I've got plenty of rich allies already.'

'Maybe you *are* growing old. Don't you understand? The L'Vars aren't just any old house. They're one of the First Families, one of the automatically enfranchised families. Vida will be confirmed as their chief patron. She's it, the last of them. As soon as she's old enough, she'll inherit their seat on Centre Council.'

'But that'll be years from now. She'll have to be thirty-five at least.'

'No, not if Karlo and Roha decide to force the matter. There's an emergency provision to allow the oldest Not-child in a family to take that seat if no-one else is available. I looked it up. She'll be a Not-child in five more months.'

'God!' Hi had another sip of wine. 'Yeah, you're right. I'm practically senile, missing that. If she were inclined to favour the Cyberguild . . .'

Aleen smiled, very gently.

'Yeah, yeah.' He grinned and swallowed the entire contents of his glass. 'Don't worry. I'll make sure she survives. You can count on it.'

He hadn't expected her to thank him, and she didn't. He rose, setting his glass down on her desk.

'I'll be in touch later,' he said. 'I've got to talk with Arno. About all the things you don't need to hear.'

'Of course. I just hope he doesn't blow out the power grid for the whole damn Sect, with the stuff he's put together in that room.'

By the time that the wiretrain let him off at his stop, Rico's burns ached and stung, especially along the backs of his hands, where climbing up the vine-covered grillwork had scraped the skin. He was tired, too, and decided that if he was going to be a rich man's heir, he might as well start acting like it. Out in front of the station stood a queue of bright red robocabs. He took the first one and sank into the soft cushions of the back seat.

'Riovizza District, Tech Sect,' he said. 'Long Street, Block seventy-four, rear complex.'

'Submit authorization for entrance to Riovizza.'

'Oh, right, sorry.' Rico leaned forward and pressed his thumb onto the ID plate.

'Cleared. Please sit back.'

Rico did, watching the towering glass and marbalite buildings flash by as the cab darted and squealed through the streets. At the big stone gates the robocab paused just long enough to transmit its passenger's thumbprint to the guard mechs, then zipped through into the quieter air and long lawns of Riovizza. Even the shops and service booths clustered near the entrance stood among native fern trees and plantings of pale turquoise grass from Belie. Purple flowers hung in huge sprays from the languid branches of pole trees; roses bloomed red and yellow amid statuary and stone benches. As the cab ran deeper in, the shops disappeared, the turquoise lawns grew longer, and the dark green trees grew thicker, hiding the houses set well back from the street inside security walls. Private cars purred past, every now and then; once a big open truck, carrying a squad of Garang Japat, dressed in the black and red uniforms of the le-Yonestilla family, sailed slowly past, heading to the compound of their clan. Rico stared after them, golden-pale with their long narrow faces and prominent green eyes. Tufted with gold hair, their clawed hands clutched stunsticks, the only weapon private citizens were allowed.

The Jons clan compound, which sheltered its employees and retainers as well as the family, stood on a rise overlooking the River Algol. From his bedroom window, in fact, Rico could see the river, if he leaned out just right to catch the view between the trees. From the street, though, where the robocab deposited him, he could see nothing but trees and the white walls of his family's compound and the one across the street that belonged to the Sanchis family. Rico pressed his thumb on the ID plate next to the wrought-plasto gates and started to punch the key for the pedestrian gate, but the pain in his hand stabbed at him. He spoke to the gatepost.

'Send a passenger cart down.'

'Voice recognized. Will do.'

The fog swirled overhead, and sunlight poured through. Rico leaned against the pillar and basked in the unfamiliar warmth until he heard the cart whooshing through the gravel. When he clambered onto the front bench, the cart sensed his weight and trundled off up the glittering white drive. Around him fern trees swayed; he heard the soft calls of the tiny songflies, all jewel bright colours and dappled wings, that lived in the gardens in Palace. The house itself loomed pale lavender and white at the top of the rise, a bent spiral of wings and corridors, all leading to the big central meeting hall. One of the family saccules was washing fungal spores off the front steps with a powermop and a hose. When Rico drove up, the neuter sniffed the air, then wheezed out a greeting from its side throat-sacs – a more respectful sound than the full boom from the front sac.

'Hi, Gran,' Rico said. 'Is my mother home?'

The saccule let loose a scent like overripe fruit, and hissed a sound quite close to a human yes.

'Thanks.'

Rico let himself in by a side door, avoiding the meeting hall, and went to his mother's wing. Although he took the servants' stairs up to the second floor and walked as quietly as he could, Barra still caught him, coming out of her bedroom door just as he was reaching his. She wore a pair of loose blue slacks and a flowered shirt, and her dark hair flowed over her shoulders – she would have just got up after her night's work.

'Rico! What have you been doing? You're filthy.'

'I bet. I've been climbing up this tower in Pleasure Sect, trying to run the antique Mapstation inside it.'

Barra blinked several times, rapidly.

'No, honest, Mom. Ask Uncle Hi. It was his idea. The station's in the Carillon Tower, and the stairs were torn down or something a long time ago.'

'I *do* know the one you mean, yeah. Is the station still functional?'

'Kind of. It's erratic, and someone's put an umbrella over it. But you can raise a rev from it.'

'I want to hear about that, but you look like you could use a shower. Why don't you clean up and meet me in the gather?'

Taking a hot shower, Rico found, made the skin on his face and hands peel. By the time he dried off, his reddish-brown skin was so badly streaked with beige that he looked like a victim of one of Palace's many fungal infections. While he dressed, he stared at himself in the bathroom mirror and tried to figure out what he was going to tell his mother. Suddenly he realized that he was planning on lying to her, just as he'd lied to his uncle and guildmaster, when all the time the Candle was burning somewhere on the Map. He felt as cold and breathless as he had in the grip of the Chameleon Gate when he saw what lay ahead of him, his unguilding and a life of shame and poverty, but how could he go on lying when the Map was in danger?

Someone could get killed, he told himself. Just like you nearly were. The cold deepened until he shook. What if someone already had, and just because he'd never said a word to Hi this morning, when he had his chance?

The gather lay at the head of the stairs, a semi-circle of a room with two heavy wood doors on the flat wall; one led to Hi's office, the other to the dining area. In the curve, soft furniture covered in pale koro hide stood before polarized windows giving onto a long view of the river, running through turquoise lawn. Along the walls, in recessed niches, stood small bronze statues and fine examples of glazed pottery from the various planets of the Pinch. Most of these hid interference field generators and other anti-snoop devices. Rico sank into a chair and watched Barra, pacing back and forth. Already the brief sunlight had faded, and the sky beyond the windows hung low and grey.

'Something wrong?' he said.

'Yes, but there's not much I can do about it. It's this trip to Orbital. I do not want one of Karlo Peronida's officers there, breathing down my neck and asking dumb questions.' With a sigh she sat on the long sofa opposite him. 'I just got a commcall from your uncle. He's been invited to meet with the Peronida this evening. He says he'll raise the subject then. Oh, and don't forget – you're supposed to go to that formal reception with him tonight.'

'I can't. I just can't.'

'What? Rico, you've got to. It's a very important thing, this invitation. Do you understand? The Peronidas had your name put on the invitation, too. Dukayn must have heard that you're going to be Hi's heir.'

Rico nodded, but he could barely hear her. The cold had gathered in his stomach and turned into a spiked blade. Barra tilted her head to one side and considered him.

'What's wrong?' she snapped. 'Rico –'

'Uh well, you're going to have to disown me. When they unguild me, I mean.'

'What? Oh Rico, damn you! You went messing around the Nimue gate, didn't you? And after you promised –'

He shook his head no. His tongue seemed frozen to his mouth. Barra leaned forward, her hands on her knees.

'Rico.' Her voice was very soft. 'Tell me. You went somewhere forbidden, didn't you?'

'Yeah.' He forced himself to look at her. 'And I ran into some trouble.'

'A supervisor recorded your route mark.'

'No, jeez, I wish. Far as I know no-one knew I was there. But I saw this unregulated object. It was, well, I don't know what it was. But it was destroying things, burning parts of the Map. There was a crash today, wasn't there, at Pansect Media?'

'Yes. How do you know?'

'I saw it happen. This – this thing blew up their transmission routing centre.'

Barra sat quietly, very quietly, for a long moment while Rico sank deeper into his cushions and wished he could die, right there and then, and save her the trouble of reporting him to the guild.

'Pansect Media's in a public area,' she said at last. 'No-one's going to unguild you for going there.'

Hope. He sat up straight and winced when his hands dragged on the chair cushions. Barra leaned forward, puzzled.

'Why are you saying I'll have to disown you?'

'Well, I didn't log in exactly.'

She sighed, a long hiss of breath.

'You commandeered the Chameleon Gate.'

'Yeah. 'Fraid so.'

'Well, no-one's going to unguild you for that, either.' All at once she laughed, but it was a sickly sort of sound. 'The Jons family has never bothered to tell the rest of the guild about it, has it? Hi's not going to be yelling at you in public about it now.'

Rico started to smile, but the skin around his mouth cracked. Barra leaned forward for a good look at his face.

'You shouldn't use sunlamps when you're tired,' she snapped. 'It's too hard to stay awake.'

'I didn't get this from a sunlamp. I got it from the unregulated object. It burns like some kind of huge candle and explodes constructs with icons that look like fire. When I left Mapspace I was burned like this.'

Barra stared at him, her mouth slack.

'I don't see how that's possible,' she said at last. 'But that doesn't mean it isn't. Come into the bathroom and let me get rid of that mess. A couple of squirts of ReGen spray should do it. And then you're going to tell me every detail you can remember. No-one's going to be asking me awkward questions when I report this to Hi. The Gate leaves no records. For all anyone knows, I used it just because I was in the mood for a little jaunt.'

Rico felt as if the planet had just wrenched in its orbit.

'You're going to lie for me?' he whispered.

'Why wouldn't I? You had the guts to tell me, didn't you? Even when you thought it was going to cost you your place in the guild?'

'Well, yeah. But someone could be killed by that thing. I couldn't just not say anything.'

'You didn't consider just keeping your mouth shut and hoping that a master would track it down from the Pansect disaster?'

'Well, no.' Rico felt profoundly embarrassed. 'That never occurred to me.'

Barra grinned. He could remember once before, seeing his mother smiling that way, when he'd won the first position in his year's crop of guild apprentices and entered the program with full honours. As she had then, too, she suddenly turned away and wiped her eyes on the back of her hand.

'It never even occurred to you,' she repeated.

'Well, no. I guess that was kind of dumb of me.'

Barra looked at him with the grin back in place.

'No, it wasn't dumb,' she said. 'Know something? I think your father would have been proud of you.'

Rico looked away fast with tears threatening. His father had been killed so long ago that he barely remembered him, but he did remember how loss felt and the pain of watching his mother cry.

'Sorry,' Barra said. 'Well, come on, I want to spray something on that burn. You've got to look decent for the reception.'

'I can't go. I mean, what am I going to say to Hi, knowing that you're well, uh . . .'

Barra considered, letting her smile fade into a genuine sadness.

'Know something, Rico?' she said. 'I raised you to be honest because I never thought you'd have a public life. Arno was so brilliant. It was obvious from the time he learned to talk that he was going to succeed Hi and take over the guild. You always loved to be alone, figuring things out, working puzzles, fiddling around with frames the minute you were old enough to kneel on a chair and reach one. A researcher, I thought. Maybe my little boy's going to be the person who figures out how to build a new AI – something grand like that. I never dreamed things would work out like this.'

'Well, yeah, Mom. Neither did I. But –'

She held up one hand for silence.

'You've got to learn to lie, Rico. If you can't lie, you won't last two minutes in the guild. And you can start tonight.'

Rico stared. Barra forced out a small laugh, but her eyes stayed sad.

'You're going to go to this reception, and you're going to be the life of the party,' she said at last.

'What? I can't do that!'

'Well, then, you're going to go and be miserable, but either way, you're going. Hi will figure out that something's up, knowing him. Fine. Just don't tell him what it is. Tell him he's got to talk to me first. You got that? Look him in the face and lie.'

'Well.' Rico considered for a long moment. 'Yeah, I do get it. I don't like it much.'

'Neither do I. Why do you think I've always stayed in tech support instead of angling for power in the guild? Now let's go get rid of that mess on your face. And you can start telling me about this candle.'

Rage was always an enemy. Rage meant haste, impulse, and failure.

Vi-Kata sprawled in the dirt underneath a frond-tree beside the Boulain. All round him in white and red heaps lay litter from the festival. Yellow-green scavenger flies whined around him. Jadewings rooted through the garbage nearby. He merely sat, dressed in rags; he'd sprung his long beaky mouth at the jaw, as Leps could do, and now he drooled helplessly down the filthy remains of his wrap jacket. Every now and then workers from Service Sect trotted by, guiding their clean-up bots down the actual street. It would take them all day to get around to sweeping up among the trees. No-one noticed him, this single sapient casualty among the many that drifted through Pleasure Sect.

Through the trees he could see the back of The Close. Inside, hid the girl who'd beaten him, the filthy little human, barely more than a hatchling. Somehow or other, she'd managed to slip out of that bell tower and then lose him on the streets. The finder he'd been using had tracked her to the tower, then suddenly lost her, only to pick her up some blocks away. It could well be, he supposed, that the tower contained a hidden, pulse-shielded stairway. Whatever the case, he'd never caught up with her again.

He breathed out, long and slow, and visualized his rage flowing out, thinning out, vanishing like a mist hit by strong sun. He would take her yet, slit through her throat perhaps with one long claw and see the bright red human blood run. The thought cheered him and dissolved the last of his rage. Sooner or later, she would leave The Close again. When she did, she would be his.

Once he'd eliminated the girl, he could turn his attention to the second kill, this Arno Jons y Perres, who had managed to disappear on him – but only temporarily, Kata reminded himself, only for a little while. The easy camaraderie at the bottom of society among the trash addicts and other sapient refuse, had already given Kata plenty of information about this Arno, who was, as he was, only pretending to belong here.

From overhead came the stuttering roar of an airhopper, circling over Pleasure, dropping lower, heading toward The Close. Even from this distance Kata could see the Eye glyph of the Lifegivers on the 'hopper's side. What were celibate monks doing, heading for a brothel in the middle of the day? The Close seemed to be an important sort of place. Some hours earlier, Kata had watched an aircar glyph-marked to the Cyberguild lift off, carrying some important person away. From its trajectory, this airhopper would land out in front, he realized, on the opposite side of the building from his lair among the garbage.

Out in the middle of the Boulain a pair of red-armoured Protectors came hurrying along, swinging their stunsticks. Kata went very still, willing himself to blend in with the garbage and the shadows, until they'd moved out of sight. This was the third pair he'd seen this morning – odd, since the festival had left the Sect too exhausted for trouble. He got up, making a great show of moaning and staggering in case someone might watch, then shuffled along, head bent as if he were looking for edible scraps in the litter, until he reached the cross-street that would lead him round to the front of The Close. Even then he walked slowly, talking to himself in Gen, drooling down his front and waving his hands randomly in the air. The people he passed either looked away or moved away fast; no-one would be able to describe him, if they should be asked.

By the time Kata reached the front of The Close, children had gathered round the sleek silver airhopper. He hung back across the street, found a doorway with raised steps, and hunkered down at the top to watch. While he waited, he memorized the airhopper's markings and registration numbers, just in case he needed to find out where it had come from and where it might be going.

'Are you looking forward to seeing Centre?' Tia said.

'Oh yes.' Vida felt as if her body had become a bubbleflare, floating higher and higher, aching to burst into coloured light. 'But I won't forget you. I'll call you, and as soon as I can. I'll call everyone.'

'Well, I think you might have a little trouble finding the time for long talks on the comm screens.'

'Maybe so. But I promise to write to you about everything. And then you can download the letter and pass it around.'

Tia merely smiled in a weary sort of way. They were waiting for the Lifegivers in a small blue room near the front doors of The Close. Although Vida was wearing her best green dress, she carried nothing else, not even a belt pouch.

'I don't know,' Tia said at last. 'It might be best to keep your past separate for a while.'

'Yeah, I suppose so. Tia, you want to know something strange? I don't know who I am any more. You and Madam call me the last of the L'Vars, but that name doesn't mean anything to me, except that they were all a bunch of traitors. I'm Vida of The Close. I always will be.'

Tia reached up to put her arm around Vida's shoulders.

'Inside, in your heart. But you've got to learn how to act like a chief patron. One of these days, Wan Peronida might be ruling Palace.'

'Well, maybe. I –'

The outer door opened, and a saccule servant bustled in, bowing, nodding, exuding an anxiety-scent like spilled alcohol. Behind it strode two tall men, draped in the star-scattered cloaks and cowls of the Lifegivers. The faces that peered out were pale, the bleached features of men who spent most of their lives in the cathedrals of the Eye. One of them carried a flat black case, which he put down on an end table.

'Madam Aleen?' He had a pleasant enough voice, though he sounded bored.

'No, I'm Tia, her business manager.'

'This is the girl?'

'Yes.' Tia held out a datastrip. 'Her papers.'

The Lifegiver flipped open the case. The strip went into a reader, where he could study it, rubbing his chin with the back of a long hand.

'Come here, girl,' he said. 'I want a bit of your hair – just one strand will do.'

Vida separated one hair and broke it off, then handed him the fragment to put into a portable gene scanner. When he smiled, nodding, the second Lifegiver knelt on the floor in front of a startled Vida. What was she supposed to do? Bow to the man? He fumbled with a belt pouch and brought out a small metal device halfway between a pair of tongs and a transmit cylinder.

'Hold out your wrist, child.'

'What are you going to do? What's that?'

'It's not going to hurt. It's a gene-specific releaser.'

'Do what he says, Vida,' Tia said.

Two soft touches on her wrist and the wrist-tel fell into his open hand. He smashed it with the releaser, which broke from the impact, and for good measure he stamped both into fragments with his boot.

'Have your servant clean that up,' he snarled at Tia.

She looked at him for a long moment, seemed to be about to speak, then snapped her fingers for a saccule. Vida stared with wonder at the unblemished band of skin around her wrist, as if she'd painted it with white light. Free. She really was free.

Crying a little, Tia gave her one last hug. Vida could no longer hold back her own tears.

'I wish I could say goodbye to Aleen.'

'It's better this way.'

Tia turned with a wave to the servant. The two of them walked through the inner door, which slid shut behind them with a crisp hiss.

'Come along,' the Lifegiver said. 'We can't keep Government House waiting.'

Out on the Boulain, surrounded by curious children, sat the sleek silver airhopper with its egg-shaped body, flanked by big windows and swept-back wings. Just aft of the passenger cabin a transponder/transmit disk rose like an unfurled umbrella. When they saw the Lifegivers, the children scattered fast. One Lifegiver opened the hatch and handed Vida into the blue formfit seat. Before the hatch closed, Tia ran out to her with something bunched in her hands.

She pressed it into Vida's lap, kissed her on the cheek, and ran back into The Close.

As the airhopper rose, Vida looked at what Tia had given her. It was Aleen's green shimmercloak, rippling in her hands like a tree in the wind. Had Aleen relented, then, and sent her a parting gift? Or had generous Tia just found the first gift at hand and figured on paying for it out of her salary? The latter, Vida assumed. Most likely Aleen didn't even care that she was gone.

Vida turned in her seat to stare out the window at the city below. Since it was the first time in her life that she'd ever been so high, the sight of Pleasure Sect from above made her feel both light-headed and sombre. The Sect spread out in a roughly circular area, some few thousand acres jumbled with gold and silver buildings, nestled like a jewel in the spider trap of wiretrains and powerlines that spread out from it in every direction. All round its huge wall she could see filigree of pulse transmitters that kept Marked citizens in their place. With a start, Vida recognized the Straight bisecting the Hub and the serpentine length of the Boulain that snaked lazily over most of the Sect. Off to one side stood Carillon Tower and its roof park. The sprinklers sprayed a fine mist, casting rainbows in the morning air.

The airhopper continued to rise, until Pleasure Sect shrank to the size of a fist covered with jewelled rings. With a whine from the engine, they began skimming south over other sects: Tech, a geometrically precise arrangement of canals and hugely tall buildings; Import with its warehouses, clustered round landing fields for gigantic airtrucks; Power, hidden under sheets of tri-stil, sending out tendrils to every other sect from its dozen fusion reactors; the Hort Sects, angular squares of orchards and farms, growing speciality foods and flowers for the luxury trade. In between lay smaller sects, jumbled together and unrecognizable. In and among all of them ran the blue network of canals, draining off the ground water and rain that constantly threatened to pull the city down.

Vida pressed her face against the glass of the airhopper's passenger window and watched, smiling. Every beat of her heart brought something new: the pink dome of a structure so tall that it dwarfed its Sect; a flight of birds flashing in the silvery light like coins flung into water; a ziggurat with thousands of people swarming over its steps; a barren crater like a hole in the world, surrounded by roboguards, black and needled with strange weapons; and in every interstice, the web of wiretrain tracks, silver crosshatching arching over sect and open field.

'Sé Vida?' asked one of the Lifegivers.

Vida started. She'd forgotten they were there, forgotten where she was, even who she was.

'We're approaching Centre.' He pointed to a curve of light ahead of them.

Centre spread out in a strange amalgam of the ancient and the modern. The histories said that Palace had been built as a scientific colony over two thousand years ago, located where Centre was now. Lost technology had built an infrastructure that showed no signs of wear after two millennia of hard use, though wars, floods, and other disasters – including the explosion of a fusion reactor – had left scars. From her vantage, Vida could see the bones of that original colony, the strange blueglass metal that ran through Centre like a skeleton. In the rest of the Sect rose every imaginable structure, all jammed in together, from ancient moss-encrusted bridge-homes across the patchwork of canals in the north of the Sect to the hypermodern flailtowns in the south – immense tapered needles with enormous faceted spheres hanging from their tips like drops of water on the end of a bent blade of grass. Bright geometries of colour, the window shades of the people who lived there, faceted each sphere. Through the Sect ran wiretrains and robocabs, while above flitted hundreds of flying vehicles of every kind, like a swarm of songflies over flowers. Among turquoise lawns stood a huge lavender hemisphere, or rather, it seemed to float above the ground. From above, Vida could see nothing supporting it.

'What's that?' she called out.

'The Floating Amphitheatre.' The Lifegiver leaned over to shout above the engine noise. 'A war memorial. For the dead from the Schism Wars.'

In the centre of Centre lay the collection of buildings and bureaucracies known as Government House, completely surrounded by a long blue wall topped with the web-like filaments of a sensor bank. From the jumble of what looked like squat office buildings and power stations Vida could pick out a columned white building with a peaked roof that she knew from school holos, the Chambers of Justice. She saw gardens tucked here and there, and long lawns bordering a narrow river. Just beyond the lawns sat a walled compound of squarish buildings with green-glazed roofs and pale tan walls, arranged round a circular plaza. The monk gestured at them.

'Those buildings making up the eye are the headquarters of my order and an abbey for researchers. Lovely, yes?'

'Very.'

Now that he'd clued her, she could see how the outer edges of the buildings were indeed staggered to form the shape of a huge eye. Just behind them rose the gold dome of the Cathedral of the Eye, a structure that she'd seen many times in pictures and holos, lying like half a sun with its protruding rays and sculpted corona.

The 'hopper slid past and began dropping down toward an enormous compound. Although it stretched over an area as large as the entire hub of Pleasure Sect, it shone like a pool of water, built entirely of blueglass. Out of the lower storeys rose two gigantic fluted pillars joined by a half dozen hollow bridges – longtubes, Vida suddenly realized. The tops of the two pillars lay green and billowy, covered by elaborate roof parks, though on the pillar to her right she spotted a small landing field.

'Those towers?' she called out.

'Parts of the colony ship, Sé Vida. The ancients brought it down in pieces when they realized that the macroshunt had sealed over for good. In that one there,' he pointed to the westward tower, 'are the meeting rooms and offices and chambers for the Centre Council. In the other,' he paused for a smile, 'lies the brain of Government House. And the residence of the First Citizen.'

Somewhere in there, the Peronida and the Makeesa families lived and essentially ran the world. And she was to join them? For a moment she knew beyond doubt that she was really back in Pleasure, lost in some new interactive holonovel she'd forgotten buying. The airhopper spun about its axis and drifted into a flight lane, while dozens of other airhoppers scrambled out of its way. She felt so nauseated that her fantasy about the holonovel vanished.

'Nearly there,' the Lifegiver said cheerfully. 'We've been given priority.'

They plunged through green trees, caught, and hovered, then landed delicately on the small strip. Vida let out her breath in a gasp.

'Welcome,' said the Lifegiver. 'Welcome to Government House, Sé L'Var.'

Through drooping frond-trees, heavy with pale blue fruit, the

Lifegivers led her toward a blueglass penthouse guarded by armed soldiers in grey uniforms. Vida moved in a daze, clutching Aleen's green shimmercloak to her chest as if it were a shield. The flowered scents of the roof park overwhelmed her, made her skin tingle and her nose itch with confusion. Most of the species here she'd never seen. At the glittering pale doors leading inside, the pair of guards raised long silver cylinders in salute. What the tubes were Vida didn't know.

Inside, the chamber gleamed with ranks of metal boxes, blueglass plates, glowing screens, and beeping regulators. One Lifegiver paused near the doors out; the other started toward a large obsidian table on a raised dais in the middle of the room. The tall Lifegiver smiled.

'Well, Sé Vida. There's a small welcome planned for you.'

When he placed a hand on the black table, it flared with light. A revenant – a balding man with angular features and a thin little smile – appeared in the centre of the table. He wore the robes of a Lifegiver, but these glowed with rich crimson. The headband that circled his balding head contained sigils that Vida had never seen before.

'Greetings, Sé Vida L'Var.' So – not a revenant after all, but a directed holo of a human being somewhere in Centre. 'Welcome to your new home.'

'I . . .' Vida's voice cracked; she knew she was blushing. 'Hello. Who're you?'

'I am Roha. I have the honour of serving the citizens of Palace as their cardinal. I hope that we will be friends. Please join the First Citizen and me at your earliest convenience.'

'Uh well, sure.' All at once, she felt like an utter fool. 'I mean, thank you, Your Eminence, for all your concern.'

She bowed and brought her thumbs together in the gesture of respect she had seen Aleen use on so many occasions.

'Ah, interesting.' The cardinal's smile turned sharper still. 'A student of the Schisms, then? We shall have many fascinating talks, I'm sure.'

'Thank you, Your Eminence.'

'I have requested a friend of mine to help you in your first few days here. You'll need to be shown around, introduced to people, that sort of thing. She should be – ah, here she comes.'

The inner doors slid open for a young woman, short and square-shouldered, her black hair piled in braids round her head. She wore a severe grey dress with a large white collar. She glanced Vida's way, then bowed to the directed hologram.

'My apologies, Your Eminence,' she said. 'I know I'm late.'

'No harm done,' the cardinal's holo said. 'My dear, this is Vida L'Var. Vida, may I present Samante Dinisa y Gossales?'

When Samante bowed to her, Vida held out her hand. Samante hesitated, then took it.

'You honour me,' she murmured, as they shook hands. 'My thanks, Sé L'Var.'

Vida wondered if she'd made some sort of gaffe, but she kept smiling. She could hear Aleen's voice in her mind. *You know how to be charming. Use it.*

'No, you honour me, Sé Dinisa. I can't tell you how much I appreciate your taking the time to welcome me.'

Samante glanced at the cardinal's image.

'I shall actually see you both in a moment,' the holo said. 'For now, farewell.'

The directed holo vanished.

'Sé Vida?' The tall Lifegiver caught her attention. 'We've got to log you into the defence grid. I'm sorry. This will take some time. For a start, we'll register your genotype.'

'Of course. I quite understand.'

'May I have that cloak?' He held out a hand. 'Dinisa, are there new clothes waiting for Sé Vida?'

'Oh yes, the cardinal had one of the guest suites readied for her. I've provided some things that she can wear this afternoon.'

'Excellent.' The Lifegiver glanced at Vida. 'Once you've changed, send that dress to me.'

'Well, sure, but why?' Vida handed him the cloak.

'It'll have to be destroyed, just like this will.'

'What? No! I mean, that cloak was a present from someone.'

'I'm sorry.' He looked nothing of the sort. 'But we've been informed that you have a dangerous enemy. We can't risk any kind of tracker.'

'I don't understand.'

'Government House has the best security system this world has ever seen, but I wouldn't bet your life on it being foolproof. What if this enemy of yours had a contact in, well, let us just say, in your former location?' The Lifegiver raised a scornful lip. 'Sapients come and go through there all the time. If something we can't find has been planted in your clothes –'

Samante nodded agreement.

'He's right, you know. I'll have a servant bring that dress to him as soon as we've got you changed. There's some lovely things waiting for you, Sé L'Var. The cardinal told me to spare no expense.'

'Well.' Vida caught her breath. 'Well, that was wonderful of him. Thank you.'

The Lifegiver smiled, then bundled the cloak and tossed it into a metal bin. As she followed him toward the bank of equipment, Vida realized, with a cold clutch round her heart, that she'd traded one prison for another.

'I should have been consulted!' Vanna spoke much too loudly for the small room. 'Why wasn't I?'

'There was no time, Second Citizen.' Cardinal Roha stepped back out of reach. 'We weren't even able to find Wan –'

'Then you should have waited to bring that damn whore here.'

'Madam, she's not a prostitute. And I couldn't leave her where she was.'

Karlo turned from the window and looked at them, merely looked, but they fell silent. In her pale blue Interstellar uniform Vanna stood in the middle of the crystalline blue reception chamber, facing off with Roha, while young Damo slumped miserably in a corner, as if he were trying to blend into the holostar-scape behind him.

'Stand up straight!' Karlo snapped at the boy, who did so fast. 'Now. Our Vida will be here any minute. Let's get a few things settled. Your Eminence, who's going to be attending her?'

'Samante Dinisa, First Citizen.' Roha's voice turned smooth, ingratiating. 'She's a licensed Interpreter, to begin with. And her family is absolutely loyal to the Peronidas.'

'Are you sure of that?' Vanna snapped.

'Of course, Second Citizen.'

The cardinal bowed in a sweep and rustle of scarlet robes. Karlo considered his wife. Her head was nodding like a heavy flower in a wind.

'I don't like secrets, Roha,' Vanna went on. 'You should have told me about this girl years ago.'

The cardinal said nothing – what, after all, could he say to this ridiculous statement? Karlo decided to intervene.

'My dear marriage partner! The past is past. You made me some promises, remember?' He waited for her to nod sulky agreement. 'And, my dear Second Citizen, think of the propaganda value. The L'Vars had plenty of supporters. There's been grumbling –'

'But everyone thinks they were traitors,' Damo put in. 'I don't understand. Everyone's going to hate her.'

'Damo, don't interrupt,' Karlo said. 'Or you'll be sent away.'

'The boy's got a point.' Vanna smiled, a thin twitch of her lips that sent a tic spasming across her left cheek. 'I wouldn't call the L'Var name a valuable political commodity.'

'The trials were thirteen years ago. People – the little people – they forget these things. We'll spread her picture across the vid-screens, the poor orphan child saved by the cardinal's generosity. It's a good story, Roha.'

The cardinal bowed. Vanna considered.

'And as for the people that matter,' Karlo went on. 'Well, some of them had a different opinion of the L'Vars than our Second Citizen does. This will shut them up. And then, of course, there's the Cyberguild.'

'Ah, yes.' Vanna nodded, agreeing. 'That's true, isn't it? We need the Cyberguild.'

'We need them all.' Karlo shot her a smile. 'The cybermasters are going to be very pleased to have their precious L'Var genotype back again.'

'Have you told them yet, First Citizen?' the cardinal said.

'Come off it, Roha!' Vanna snapped. 'I'm sure they knew all about this before I did.'

The cardinal forced a smile.

'I'll tell them officially later tonight,' Karlo went on. 'I invited the guildmaster to the public reception, and I'll have a few words with him privately, too.'

The cardinal nodded, Vanna smiled. Damo started to speak, then gulped the words back.

'What is it?' Karlo said. 'Don't mumble.'

'Yes, Sé. Uh, well, it wasn't anything much.'

'You must have had something to say. Out with it.'

The boy bit his lip hard and stared at the floor. Karlo was about to order him to speak up, when the door slid open for a saccule servant, sashed shoulder-to-hip in maroon, carrying a silver tray and little cups, all marked with the L'Var crest, which it placed upon a low table at the back of the room. At the sight of the Stinker the cardinal gathered his robes like an old woman and stepped back out of its way. Ostentatiously, he swept a handkerchief from a pocket and held it to his nose with a strong waft of flowered scent. The cardinal's disgust with all things non-human had served Karlo well, so far, but Karlo couldn't help wondering if in the long run it would prove as dangerous as Vanna's hatred of the L'Vars. To her he turned, smiling.

'So tell me, my love,' he said. 'Didn't you agree about the marriage?'

'I see your reasons. That's not the same thing as agreeing. But I don't suppose I have any choice about it, anyway.'

'Please don't be difficult.'

'Why shouldn't I be difficult? You and the cardinal dig up this little whore from Pleasure and – '

'Madam, please!' The cardinal stepped forward. 'She's unmarked. She never was a prostitute.'

'This little cull, then. This bit of genetic trash.'

'Vanna.' Karlo did his best to sound soothing. 'You agreed two minutes ago that – '

Vanna snarled. The sound was sharp, unmistakably animal. The saccule whimpered, shrinking back; Damo winced and went ashy, moving away from his lawmother. Karlo dismissed the servant with a point toward the door and laid a reassuring hand on the boy's shoulder. Vanna sighed sharply, fighting the tremors that took over her hands as she raised them, claw-like, to push her hair back from her face.

'I'm sorry,' she whispered at last. 'Yes, of course I agreed. Yes, of course you're right.'

'Vanna?' Karlo said. 'Should we call for a med tech?'

'No.' By sheer force of will she lifted her head smoothly, held it steady, seemed to be forcing the tremors down into her hands, which shook and fluttered like birds trapped in nets. 'I do want to see this girl, this resurrected L'Var of yours.'

'All right, then. Damn it all, where is she? And more to the point, where's Wan?'

'He was out hunting, sir,' Damo said. 'With Pero. They had to be called on the transmit. They're back in Government House now though. I do know that.'

'Good. I'm glad someone knows something around this place. Go see what's holding him up.'

'Yes sir.' Damo glanced around, then started across the room to the comm unit built into the wall.

'Don't trace him, go find him!' Karlo snapped. 'Find him and bring him back here. Right now.'

Damo skittered out of the room fast. Karlo waited until the door slid closed behind the boy, then crossed the room in two swift strides. He grabbed Vanna's forearms and dragged her close to stare into her eyes.

'Listen to me. You promised me that you wouldn't harm this girl. Remember?'

'Of course I do. Let me go!'

'We need the heirs.' Karlo tightened his grip. 'We need heirs from one of the big families on planet. Remember that?'

'Yes, Karlo.' She was stammering slightly. 'I promised you, damn it. Now let me go.'

'Promises have a way of getting forgotten on this God-forsaken world. If Vida dies in some strange accident, I'm coming straight to you.'

She hesitated, words dying on her lips. He let her go, then took her chin in one hand and kissed her.

'Bastard.' She slapped him across the face so hard his eyes stung, but when he wiped them clear he could see that she was fighting back a smile. The adrenaline of rage had worked its temporary magic once again.

The cardinal dabbed his face with the perfumed handkerchief and sighed. For a moment the three of them stood watching each other, Vanna rubbing her forearms as if they ached, the cardinal tucking the handkerchief away, Karlo merely watching. They needed each other, if they were going to realize their dream, their grand dream of a human-dominated empire controlling the entire Pinch. If Karlo could make Palace his and elevate the office of First Citizen above the petty politics of the moment by making it hereditary, Palace was rich enough to maintain the Fleet he needed to conquer the rest. But to establish a dynasty he'd need heirs fit to rule.

To the sound of laughter and the ringing of boots on crystalline floor, Wan and Pero strode in, dressed in blood-streaked hunting clothes, all camouflage cloth and pockets. Both of them stank of swamp mud. Pero, the elder by a good ten years, stood tall and slender, though his broad hands showed his strength and long muscles. As homely as swamp mud, too, my Pero, Karlo thought. His lack of looks would matter for the vidscreens, those all-important public screens that functioned as entertainment, education, and governmental regulators all in one – not that Palace would ever allow Pero, an Unauthorized birth in their eyes, a chance at any public office.

Wan had the looks and the birth papers that the populace would accept; tall, broad-shouldered, he stood like a leader and smiled like one too, a tight-lipped grin of command. In his dark face his green eyes glittered, so bright and wide that they seemed more like gems than natural flesh. Behind them came Damo, slipping in silently, regaining his corner out of everyone's way.

'Welcome home, Sé Wan,' the cardinal murmured with one of his perennial bows. 'I trust the hunting was good?'

'Very, Your Eminence.' Wan glanced round and nodded briskly. 'Father, Second Citizen.'

Pero was watching the cardinal with a tight set of his mouth. He hated being ignored, hated being unimportant. Although Karlo admired him for it, he knew it was past time to move his eldest son out of Government House. Out of temptation's path, he thought, off planet would be best.

'Where have you been?' snapped Vanna.

'Dressing our kills, lawmother.' Wan turned to her, all smiles and charm. 'Just like you taught us. The man who kills it, cleans it and then eats it. Your advice.'

Vanna snorted in pretend disgust and started to speak, but Karlo got in before her.

'There's no time now for your little jokes. Wan, what did they tell you over the transmit?'

'To come straight home.' The smile widened. 'They said you had a marriage contract for me. Where's Anja?'

'I have a partner for you, yes, but it's not le-Yonestilla. This girl's a L'Var, the last of them. She's at Government House now, and I expect she'll be here any minute. There's going to be a formal reception tonight to announce the marriage agreement.'

Wan went dead-still, then blushed, started to speak, thrust his hands into his trouser pockets and glared at Karlo for a long, long moment, while the room turned cold and still around them.

'Yeah?' Wan said at last. 'What if I say no?'

The cardinal gasped; Karlo heard a rustle and smelled the scent of that damned handkerchief being brought into use, but he refused to look away from his son's face. The green eyes glared back at him.

'You can't say no.'

'Is that right?' Wan's handsome features tangled with rage.

'I take it back. You can say no. Of course, if you do, I'll kick your ass out of Government House right now. Myself. Think you'll live long on the streets, unguilded and without one goddamn credit in your access?'

Wan took a step toward his father, fists clenched. Karlo merely stared back, waiting, smiling a little. Wan let his breath out in a long sigh and turned away. The cardinal stepped forward and mopped his sweaty face.

'My dear Wan,' the cardinal said. 'We must all make sacrifices, mustn't we? If the Peronidas are to rule as a dynasty, then marriage contracts must become weapons.'

'What's that supposed to mean, old man?' Wan snapped.

'Hush!' Vanna grabbed his arm. 'Don't speak that way to a Lifegiver.'

'My apologies, Your Eminence. I forgot myself.'

The cardinal bowed, Wan bowed. Pero watched with a curled lip.

'Wan?' Karlo said. 'You're going to marry this woman.'

Wan hesitated, but briefly.

'As the First Citizen commands, then.' Again the hesitation. 'Since I have no choice.'

Karlo's retort was interrupted by the door. A pair of saccule servants bustled in, carrying food and drink, followed by a group of some twenty human officials – among them Karlo's appointment secretary, the head butler of Government House, some Council members – and two young women. Karlo recognized Samante Dinisa immediately: she'd done some translating for him at a meeting with Hirrel leaders. Walking beside her came a much taller girl, slender and lovely, with red hair tumbling down her back – the L'Var colouring, all right, and Karlo noticed Vanna grimace at the sight of it. She was wearing a dark green slithergown with soft sleeves that fluttered halfway down her arms. Karlo found himself thinking that Wan would have to be crazy to complain about marrying a woman this lovely.

Everyone stared: the cardinal with his little fixed smile, Vanna in undisguised rage, Pero with a sly grin of assessment, and Wan with eyes that showed nothing at all. The servants and officials parted, fluttering like birds to either side of the chamber. Samante stepped back, leaving Vida standing alone, looking at her future husband with eyes whose colour matched his. 'What?' Wan snapped. 'She's just a child. I can't marry this.'

The silence broke – servants gasping, officials murmuring, drawing back, stepping forward again in a rustle of cloth and shimmercloaks. Karlo restrained himself from stepping forward and slapping Wan across the face. Gossip like this would be all over Government House in an hour and all over the city in a day to undermine the official story. Samante stepped forward and laid a protective hand on the girl's shoulder. Apologize, goddamn you, Karlo thought to Wan – never had he wished for a touch of mindspeak more. Wan merely crossed his arms over his chest and looked out at nothing. The cardinal stepped forward in a wave of scent.

'Youth brings a fortunate bounty of innocence, my dear Wan.' The cardinal caught the girl's hand and bowed over it. 'Welcome to Centre, Vida.'

'Thank you.' Vida had a pleasant voice, low for someone her age. 'Your Eminence is too kind.'

'Allow me to introduce you to our First Citizen,' Roha went on, unruffled, 'and his family.'

'Thank you, Your Eminence.'

'Yes,' Vanna drawled. 'Let's get a good look at her. Here, child. I imagine Centre's very different from the kind of places you're used to.'

Vida turned to Vanna and smiled.

'Why no, Second Citizen. I'd say they have a lot in common.'

Everyone laughed in a burst and gabble, hastily stifled. Vanna's face went rigid except for the tic on her temple, twitching in time to some unheard music pounding in her adulterated blood. The adrenaline was wearing off, Karlo supposed.

'I think,' Karlo said slowly, 'that I'm going to like my new law-daughter. Vida, welcome to Government House.'

'And welcome from me, too.' Pero stepped forward, grinning, bowing. 'May I call you sister?'

'Me, too.' Damo hurried forward. 'Hello.'

Pero flung an arm round the younger boy's shoulders.

'Good kid,' he said. 'You know, Vida, the Lifegivers say that without family, the stars are only light without a soul. Isn't that true, Your Eminence?'

'Indeed,' said Roha. 'Very well put, too.'

Vida smiled, Pero smiled, Damo stood awkwardly, glancing

round the crowded chamber. Bowing, the butler strode forward to serve drinks; the officials gathered round Vanna and began talking of official things. Samante made some pleasantry to the cardinal, and the noise picked up – at last – into some semblance of a normal reception.

Karlo crossed his arms across his chest and glared at Wan, who glared right back. Karlo tried to remind himself that this temporary trouble would pass, that it was only a small sour note in the vast symphony of his plans. The girl would give him heirs with the L'Var name, and thereby a legitimate seat on the Centre Council, along with the near majority he controlled through proxies and alliances. Then he and the cardinal would turn the office of First Citizen into something hereditary, into, one fine day, the overlordship of the entire Pinch. And as for you, Wan, Karlo thought, we will have a little talk over this, and I'll bet you don't like it much. Wan suddenly looked away, a fearful expression on his face, as if indeed his father's thoughts had reached him.

But Wan had only noticed the door opening. Another group of guests floated through on a wave of talk, among them the Papal Itinerant, Sister Romero, dressed in severe black except for her headband with its glowing jewel. Karlo turned to greet them just as his factor, Dukayn, entered, as slender and dark as an obsidian dagger, and about as deadly, too, one of only a handful of humans ever allowed to train on the Garang Japat homeworld. His dark eyes, almost all pupil, gleamed from an angular face, a sculptor's bronze of a face with exaggerated shadows and sharp planes of jaw and cheekbone.

'First Citizen?'

'What is it, Factor?' Karlo strolled over to meet him.

'Hivel Jons, the Master of the Cyberguild, is here on your request.'

'About time. Very well. Have a servant take him to my office. I'll be there presently.'

Dukayn subvocalized the order into some chip or other while he glanced around the reception room. People were talking normally now, laughing and gossiping, sidling up to Vida to pay their respects to this girl who was so suddenly rich and powerful. Vida herself seemed all charm, smiling at a council member, making a gracious nod to the round little Countess of Motta, who as always had managed to wangle herself an invitation, then accepting her introduction to Sister Romero with just the right degree of awe.

'The girl looks good,' Dukayn said, quietly. 'I don't mean her pretty face, either.'

'Yeah, I think she'll do.'

Dukayn hesitated, glancing around.

'Something you want to tell me?' Karlo lowered his voice.

In mutual unspoken agreement they drifted out into the long corridor, with its pale marble floor and blueglass walls. Dukayn turned round in a slow circle; he had implants at the base of his skull, including a couple to pick up sound or the traces of either photonic or electronic surveillance. Although he worked for Karlo, he was far more than a servant. They'd been together since Karlo's street-fighting days on Kephalon. If Karlo had trusted any one, it would have been Dukayn.

'It's about Tableau,' Dukayn said at last.

'Shit.'

Tableau meant Susannah, Pero's mother. Although they'd never had a binding marriage contract by Palace law, by Kephalon's she had a very big claim on him indeed. He'd spent plenty to buy her off. She'd taken the money and bought herself a high-living style worthy of Pleasure Sect, from what Dukayn's spies told him.

'How important is it?' Karlo said. 'I've got that arrogant bastard of a guildsman to deal with.'

Dukayn considered.

'The news could wait,' he said at last. 'I don't know if I'd call Jons arrogant.'

'What would you call him then?'

'A man people never cross. There's a big difference.'

'You've got a point. Maybe it's just his manner that gets on my nerves. Yeah yeah and tech slang and isn't he the man of the people, the ordinary guy. Makes me sick.'

'Ah, I see. Wan's trying to eavesdrop, by the way.'

Although Dukayn had his back to the door into the reception room, Karlo didn't doubt him for a minute.

'We'll talk later, then,' Karlo said. 'Keep an eye on Vida for me.'

Dukayn nodded and turned to walk into the reception room. Karlo noticed him speak to someone just inside the door; a sheepish Wan followed the factor back to the chattering guests clustered round Vida and Cardinal Roha. Karlo strode off down the hall.

As chief patron of the Cyberguild, Hi visited the First Citizen's office every now and then, but he always found it impressive. Anyone entering from the public door had to walk a long way over soft beige carpet to reach the massive desk, which was made of the rare metal icelight, imported from Tableau. Blueglass mottled with ancient patterns panelled the two long walls. Behind the desk hung a holo of Palace, taken from lunar orbit. On the dark face of the planet thin lines and sprawls of artificial light glittered, tracing out, down near the equator, the coastline of Lux, the small continent where the vast majority of the population lived. The biggest clot of light marked the city of Palace itself, halfway up the west coast and some miles inland, while thin lines of gold light traced out its major highways and boundaried its Sects. Government House shone a red dot in the midst of a galaxy of white.

In front of the desk stood two soft brown chairs, ready for visitors. Hi stood next to the nearer and considered it. He had no doubt that those chairs contained enough recorders and monitors to bug a normal-sized house, and that all of them fed directly back to that blade of malice, Dukayn. Since he'd come representing the guild, Hi wore his full ceremonial robes, cross-sashed in gold. Woven into the sash were various smart threads, some to record the First Citizen's speech, others to feed data from the functioning portions of Caliostro directly to Hi's implants.

When Hi laid his left hand on the top sash of the pair, a casual gesture, he could feel his palm jack vibrate. Everything was online. Good. No doubt Dukayn's security programs knew all about this sash, but so far at least they'd found no way to disable it. They would, however, expect him to try to circumvent them. A certain amount of predictability in these matters went a long way to establishing trust, or so Hi always thought. He laid his other hand on the back of a chair, felt power flow back and forth between the two jacks – between two different subroutines of the damaged AI. Hi sent Caliostro a kill message for the datachair, waited till he felt it die, then sat, smoothing his robes decorously under him.

A small door behind the hologram opened, so that the First Citizen seemed to stride out of the stars. Peronida looked every inch the commander with his tall build and Fleet uniform, bristling with gold braid and medals. His hands, though, made a strange contrast – all veined and sinewed, calloused and pitted as if they'd never forget his long years of poverty on a primitive world. Karlo smiled, very briefly, and sat down in the high-backed leather chair behind the desk.

'I'll be blunt,' Karlo said. 'I called you here to tell me what your guild thinks of this L'Var girl.'
'Very little, actually, since we've never met her.'
Karlo lifted an eyebrow but didn't challenge him.
'Well, you will at the public reception. I take it you can stay? Good, good. But you know what I mean, Jons. What about that genotype? The one you people have been moaning about publicly all these years.'
'Does she have it? It's a dominant gene, sure, but it's not automatic. There were plenty of L'Vars who lacked it.'
'Cardinal Roha's office found her medical records, including a blood scan. She has it, all right. I've seen her myself. The coding you want is gene-linked to the L'Var red hair, and now that I've seen her, I can tell you that she's got the hair.'
Hi leaned back in his chair, put his fingertips together, and considered Karlo for a moment.
'Interesting,' Hi said at last. 'I wonder if she'll pass it on? It's not automatic, you know.'
'Yes, so you've said. But I can't worry about that. Who knows what the future will bring, eh?'
'Some people do their damnedest to have the future bring them exactly what they want.'
'Well of course, that's only natural.'
'Of course, First Citizen. Perfectly natural.'
Karlo smiled; Hi waited.
'There's one other matter,' Karlo said. 'A minor thing.'
'Yeah?'
'Your sister, Barra Jons y Macconnel. I hear she's been appointed to the Nimue project.'
'Yeah, she sure has.'
'I'm very pleased, of course. My factor tells me that she's the best person on planet for the job.'
'Well, I'd jack into any station she reconfigured, that's for sure.'
Karlo blinked several times, as if he were translating this bit of tech speak, then went on.
'But I also understand that the military presence on the team is insisting on holding the command.'
'So I've heard. You'd know more about that than I do. He comes from your Fleet.'
'Yes, he does.'
Karlo leaned back in his chair and waited. Hi folded both hands

on his sash. The chair was trying to turn itself back on – he sent another kill order.

'Um, well,' Karlo said. 'I'm in a position, of course, to give the command to whomever I choose.'

'You sure are, First Citizen. I can't imagine that anyone would try to countermand you.'

'Just so. Overriding the military CO on this would cause some friction, of course.'

'Of course. It's not the kind of thing you'd do, right? Unless there was a good reason.'

'Just so.' Karlo hesitated, then shrugged. 'Well, no use playing around about it. I want my son Damo assigned to that project.'

'What? First Citizen, I'm sorry, but first of all, he's just a boy, and second, he's not a member of the Cyberguild. We can't let him anywhere near guild work.'

'I know you have your rules . . .'

'Rules and principles. Hell, any guild would hold to the same: of the guild, by the guild, but for the World.'

Briefly Karlo looked sour, then shrugged again.

'You've probably heard all the gossip about the boy being a genius. I'll give you my personal word that it's true.'

Since the guild had accessed the school map for Government House long ago, Hi already knew a great deal about this strange genetic anomaly – an undoubted genius born from a woman better known for her breasts than her brains. Not that anyone would have ever called Karlo stupid, of course, but still, Damo's intelligence was an outstanding example of the kind of surprise that unregulated breeding gave you.

'It's a damn shame,' Hi said at last, 'but –'

Karlo leaned forward and rested his large fists on the smooth and silvery top of his icelight desk.

'Record him as an observer. Induct him as an apprentice. Adopt him into the guild. There are a thousand ways to get around the rules. You people do it all the time.'

'Damo isn't a full citizen of Palace.'

'Don't give me that. His mother was a citizen. He was born here.'

'Born here illegally in most people's eyes.'

Karlo went still, dangerously still, his huge hands clenched on the desktop. Hi was amazed all over again by the effrontery of the man, daring the Lawgivers to take his second son away, daring them to enforce the laws at the expense of the Saviour of Palace.

'Screw most people,' Karlo said at last.

'Yeah? You owe them a lot. It was their votes in the polls that kept Damo out of Pleasure Sect.'

Karlo made a sound deep in his throat, then leaned back in his chair and shut his eyes. For a moment Hi felt utterly baffled, then realized that the man was trying to calm himself, that this exchange was running close to the edge of physical violence. The savage from Kephalon – what a lot of Palace citizens called Karlo behind his back – was trying not to live up to his reputation. Briefly Hi wondered if he himself were frightened, or should be. Karlo's eyes snapped open, and he leaned forward, openhanded, onto his desk.

'Don't you ever say that to me again.' Karlo's voice rasped, steel on steel. 'Do you understand me?'

'Perfectly well. I suggest you never give me any reason to.'

Again that dangerous stillness. Hi considered, weighing risks, decided against speaking, even something conciliatory. At last Karlo sat back in his chair.

'First Citizen,' Hi said. 'The Cyberguild was created to *serve* the average citizen. We maintain the Map. The Map is the real body of this world, and information is its blood. Think. Do you remember six years ago when Imports had that grid crash? Remember the chaos? And the panic?'

Karlo nodded.

'That's why the guild's important,' Hi went on. 'That's why it has to be trusted and trustworthy. A good newsgrid image isn't enough.'

'That panic was . . . impressive.' Karlo made the admission slowly. 'There was a Map on Kephalon, of course. We had full access, we used it. But it was nothing like I see here.'

'Kephalon was a very different place, yeah. The Map there was limited, with only one AI on planet, and besides, the government didn't run on it. When no-one votes, having everyone online isn't as important. But here –'

Karlo raised one eyebrow, as if daring Hi to go on.

'That crash,' Hi said instead. 'It turned out to be the work of saboteurs, unguilded people, working with a former cybermaster. Extortion was their game. You know what happened.'

'They were all hanged on Exiles' Square. The vidscreens broadcast it all over the planet.'

'Yeah. It's an archaic way of executing someone, but it makes a good object lesson. The ratings were real high. Just like for the L'Vars.'

The insult drifted between them for a long long moment.

'Go on,' Karlo said.

'The guildmaster tightened the nooses around those nine necks.' Hi lifted his hands from the arms of his chair and spread them. He still saw the eyes of those people in his nightmares. '*I* am the guildmaster. I'm ultimately responsible for my guild and for any damage to the Map. I can't break the rules for a personal favour.'

'Personal favour? Does the guild really want its team on Nimue to be working under military command?'

'No. But we can live with it if we have to.'

Karlo considered, drumming his fingers on the arm of his chair. He knew, it seemed, how easily the guild could circumvent most military controls, because he made an effort to smile.

'Well, guildmaster, seems to me I've heard of exceptions to the rule. Isn't there an old tradition among the First Families of fostering promising children across guilds?'

'The First Citizen's been doing his research. The pages, yeah. A strange term, isn't it?'

'I think of it as an apprentice factor. Foster Damo to Barra, and I think we can bypass the guild difficulties. Look, let me be blunt again. I know you're afraid I'm sending a spy, but he's just a child. If he were Barra's page, he couldn't do one damn thing without her knowing it.'

'That's true.' Hi hesitated. 'First Citizen, may I ask why this is so important to you?'

'It should be obvious. He's my son, isn't he? And so I want what's best for him. Everyone tells me that he belongs in Cyber. He talks about the damn Map all the time, he spends every minute he can fiddling around with his terminal. It's my fault, damn it, not his, that I didn't get that second licence. Why should he pay for it?'

Hi nearly gaped from the shock of realizing that the man was perfectly sincere. He wanted Damo in the guild because the boy wanted it and because he'd do well there. That was all. Nothing more.

'Look.' Karlo leaned forward a little more and smiled, as ingratiating as a swamp worm chasing prey. 'I know that Palace is overpopulated as well as anybody. But –'

'First Citizen.' Hi held a hand up flat for silence.

Karlo stopped and sat back in his chair.

'First Citizen, you're right. This is a pretty unusual case. Why don't I bring it up with Barra for you? I can't force her to take the boy on, you know, but I can see what she thinks about it.'

'Of course. But I'm willing to bet that she'll think she'd like to be free of military command.'

'Well, you know, I think that's a pretty safe bet. The real question is what the Cyberguild will think of it.'

'Huh.' Karlo raised one eyebrow. 'Didn't you just finish telling me what it means to be guildmaster?'

Hi waited.

'Come on, Jons! What do you want? There's something I can do for you, isn't there? There always is.'

At that, Hi had to laugh. He found Karlo's famous 'blunt and simple soldierman' routine engaging in spite of himself.

'Well, yeah, now that you mention it. Back in the old days, the master of the Cyberguild used to operate directly out of Government House. We had our own offices and newsgrid feed, Map point, aircar, the works. It'd be a real status coup for me to get that back for the guild.'

'Is that all?' Karlo said.

'Well, it's going to run to considerable expense.'

It was Karlo's turn for the expansive laugh.

'I don't think that's going to matter to me from now on,' Karlo said. 'Let's just consider it the cost of my son's education.'

'Fair enough. I'll start the fostering process tomorrow. Barra will treat the kid well, I promise.'

'Good. Thank you.'

For a long moment they merely sat, considering each other. Behind the First Citizen the holo gleamed as the image of Palace turned in its rotation. On the glowing terminator, caught in a stripe of dawn, lay drowned Nox.

'Well,' Karlo said at last. 'I wanted to ask you about the Pansect Media crash.'

'Ah yes. We have that under investigation. I started a team of three masters and their journeymen working before I came here.'

'Good. Glad to hear it.'

Karlo smiled, Hi smiled. Hi crossed his hands on his chest again. The chair sat dead under him, but Caliostro flashed a fragment of the East Tower's floor plan behind his eyes: movement out in the hall, someone approaching. Hi stood up, and Karlo joined him.

'Well, First Citizen,' Hi said. 'I shouldn't be taking up more of your time.'

'Nor I yours. Have your factor transmit mine a list of what the guild needs for those offices, all right? And you'll be at the public reception, of course.'

'Of course. May the marriage be a good one, for the girl's sake as much as anything.'

'I'll make sure she's well-treated. You don't need to worry about that.'

'Good. Thanks.' Hi paused, still smiling. 'I'll bet you're looking forward to grandchildren.'

Karlo's smile froze, then thawed into something twisted.

'Of course. I grew up on a world where the people valued their posterity.'

'Yes, of course.' You fired the hidden switch that time, Hi told himself, or poked the hidden bruise. 'Of course, First Citizen. May the Eye see you well.'

'And you, Master Jons.'

As he was leaving the office, Hi met in the hall another guild-master, Wilso from Power, a skinny, grey little man lost in his scarlet robes. When Hi saluted him with a vague wave, Wilso reached out a bony finger and tapped him on the sleeve.

'Having a little chat with the First Citizen, eh? No doubt you're ecstatic about the L'Var girl, eh?'

'I'm glad to see one of them survived, yeah. It doesn't mean much to us yet. She'd have to be trained to be any good, you know.'

'Certainly, certainly, but still, I'll warrant you're glad to have the bloodlines back, eh? Can't underestimate the importance of good genes, eh? I'm certainly pleased that the First Citizen takes an interest in such matters.'

'If you ask me, Karlo's interested in putting a lid on the grumbling. The L'Vars had a lot of friends.'

'Certainly, certainly, of course. But we've got the gene bank to think of, eh?'

'We do?' Hi performed a pantomime of peering at Wilso's robes. 'Funny. These look red to me, not green. When did you switch over to Biotech?'

'Come on, Jons, you know perfectly well what I mean!' Wilso glanced round the hall and dropped his voice. 'We're outnumbered out here. We must keep that in mind always, eh? Mustn't let a good human trait fall by the wayside.'

'Oh, I dunno. I can think of a few traits we'd all be better off without. Eh?'

Wilso started to answer, then stopped, his mouth half-open.

'Better go on in,' Hi said. 'Can't keep the First Citizen waiting. He likes his tea stirred to the left.'

Wilso glared at him, then scurried into the office without another word.

'You did well,' Samante remarked. 'His Eminence was impressed.'

'Thank you,' Vida said. 'I'm glad you think so.'

'I'm glad we've got this time to get away, though. We need to practise what you're going to say to the gridjockeys. I've been thinking about it all day, and I've got some notes. You've got to get the official story down so well that you believe it.'

Vida tried to smile and failed. They were sitting in her guest suite, three large rooms that seemed even larger thanks to their expanses of sleek white walls. Round the ceiling ran a dark blue and silver moulding; on the floor lay dark blue and green striped carpets. The furniture – a pair of chairs, a sofa, a scatter of small tables out here in the gather – was stark white and chrome. The only decoration on the walls were a pair of vidscreens, each a good six feet square. One showed only pale grey static; the other ran constantly changing tower graphs in lurid colours, tallying votes or opinions on this issue or that. Vida lay back in her armchair and stared out the bank of windows at a view of green gardens under a grey sky.

'Is that a holo?'

'No, it's real.'

'That's nice. I'm glad something is round here.'

'Well, um. This must be hard on you.'

Vida stared at her for a long moment. Hard on me? She wanted to laugh or maybe even scream at the understatement. She lifted a hand to brush her hair back from her face and found it shaking.

'Vida, Vida, do try to control yourself.' Samante's voice sounded vague and indifferent. 'Yes, Wan acted like a piece of swamp filth. Do you think that's the worst insult you'll have to face around here? Think of what you're gaining in life.'

'Oh come on.' Vida tried to speak quietly, but tears were running down her face. She dropped her face into her hands and sobbed.

'Sé Vida,' Samante murmured. 'Please.'

'Shut up!'

'I will not shut up. You're in Centre now, and people here are going to judge you, seeing how strong or how weak you are. If they think you're weak, they'll take advantage of you. Now do come on and stop that noise.'

Vida raised her head and glared through tears. 'You weren't the one Vanna was looking at that way. I thought she was going to walk over and slap me or something.'

'Well, that's true. The Second Citizen was not at her best today.'

'Not at her best!' Vida wiped her face on her sleeve. 'I wish I could go home. I want to so bad.'

She looked up to find Samante staring at her in something like stunned disbelief.

'Oh, I know what all you snotty suck-ups think of us, but Pleasure was my home, and people were good to me there. At least we're honest, aren't we? Maybe we're culls, but we know what we're selling, and we don't pretend to be giving it away for free.' Vida paused for effect. 'Can you say the same?'

'Just what do you mean by that?' Samante turned bright red.

'I saw how the Peronida treated you. Like a pet dog. And you had to take it and fawn on him for more.'

Samante got up and stalked across the room to stare out of the window.

'Sé Vida.' Samante had pressed her voice as calm as a dead flower. 'We need to get ready for the public reception.'

'Do we? I'm glad you're going to change that dress. It's boring.'

'It's suitable for someone in my position.' Samante spun round and glared at her. 'It's part of an interpreter's job, being invisible.'

Vida hesitated. She could think of a thousand insults that would make Samante drop her carefully gathered calm – but why was she even thinking this way? She needed Samante, who was after all only looking after her as a favour to the cardinal. She took a deep breath.

'I'm sorry, Samante. I'm just all to pieces. Everything's happened too fast.'

'Yes, yes, I suppose that's very true.' Samante cocked her head to one side and considered her for a long moment. 'And I'm the only person you can take it out on.'

Vida felt herself blushing.

'Look,' Samante said. 'I'm sorry, too. When His Eminence told me about you, I really didn't know what to expect. May I be blunt, Vida?'

'Sure. Why not?'

'Well, I've never been to Pleasure Sect. For all I knew you were going to be some coarse little thing with a mouth like a sewer.'

Vida laughed.

'There are lots of girls like that, but not in Madam Aleen's houses.'

'So I see. I've heard of Aleen Raal, oddly enough. A lot of information seems to change hands in her . . . um . . . establishment.'

'Yeah, probably so. All the best people come to The Close.'

'I was afraid – well, it doesn't matter.'

'You were afraid you'd have to tell me not to grab my food with my fingers?'

'Something like that.' Samante allowed herself a brief smile. 'I hope you like the clothing I bought you. Madam Raal transmitted your size data to a very nice shop.'

'It's all fine, yeah. What kind of thing did you bring for the reception? Let me guess.' Vida grinned at her. 'Something black with a real high neckline and it's baggy.'

Samante grimaced in wordless acknowledgement.

Vida got up from her chair and rubbed her face with both hands. Although she felt that she would weep for hours, if she should let herself start again, she knew that Samante was right, that she'd have to keep a Garang's watch over her feelings from now on. Aleen would say the same thing, she told herself, and with the telling she saw a truth. Aleen raised me for this, didn't she? She knew it would happen, sooner or later.

'What's wrong?' Samante said. 'You look so strange.'

'Nothing. Just thinking about something.' Vida took a deep breath. *Don't fail me, Vida.* 'Just remembering something my guardian said to me, once.'

Samante was waiting, puzzled. Vida arranged her best bright smile.

'You're right. We'd better get changed for the reception. Look, why don't I help you pick out a really sharp dress? There's lots. Something short on me will be evening length on you.'

'Well, I –'

'Oh come on, Samante! And we can get your hair out of that mousy braid, too. I know lots of ways to fix someone's hair for them. It'll be fun.'

The interpreter hesitated, glancing away. Vida followed her glance and found her looking at the vidscreen, where a tower graph was building up in blue and magenta as the public gave its opinion about appropriating more money for Karlo's Fleet. It was going to be a close call, apparently, with nearly as many cons as pros.

'Well, all right,' Samante said at last. 'I imagine you would know a lot about being stylish.'

'Oh yeah. I've been trained.'

Samante laughed, a dry little sound but sincere enough.

'So have I, Sé Vida. So have I, just for something very different. Now. What colour dress do you think I should wear?'

'That red one, of course. It'll look beautiful with your black hair. I can't wear red.'

'Oh, I couldn't either. That's much too bright.'

'No, it's not. You'll see once you try it on. I'm going to try that white satin one. Do we have to hurry? When is the reception?'

'Soon, but we'll wait here until Brother Dav sends us a commcall.'

'Who's he?'

'The cardinal's factor. He's orchestrating your entrance. We don't dare arrive on time.'

'Why not?'

'Because you're the one who's being presented. There's no use in presenting you to a half-empty room, and all the best people will only be late, anyway, so they don't look too eager.'

Sure enough, by the time that Brother Dav summoned them, the reception hall teemed with hundreds of people. Vida and Samante stood in a secret room behind and halfway above the hall and looked out through a security window while the stout and red-faced Dav, a comm unit clipped to his Lifegivers' cowl, talked urgently with his security people down on the main floor.

Vida had never seen a room so large or one so shiny, either. Everywhere she looked, she saw shattered light, reflecting and glaring off surfaces or jewels. Burnished silverwood, set here and there with gold lighting fixtures, panelled the walls of the enormous oval hall, except for the eastern end of the oval, where ten floor to ceiling windows gave out onto a view of Palace's shrouded sky, a darker silver now, dappled with gold and pink from the lights of the vast city below. Despite the crowds of guests, a welter of bright colours in guild robes and gowns, Vida could see enough of the floor to realize that it glistened with jadium, pale green, dark green, and rose, inlaid in a pattern of concentric rings. Along the outermost ring stood oases of dark green and onyx furniture, formfit chairs and little tables, each oasis enclosed by a gold isolation torus of pure energy. Although a sapient could walk through the force-fields, they would stop sound waves or transmit beams.

'Look at all the saccules,' Vida said. 'I've never seen so many servants, and they're all dressed up, too. I guess the guests brought their own, huh?'

'Oh no,' Samante said. 'They all belong to Government House.'

Out in the centre of the hall stood a huge three-step dais made of some strangely nacreous substance – whether it was metal or some sort of artificial material, Vida couldn't say. Among chairs and floral arrangements the Peronidas and the cardinal waited for her there, as far as she could see from her height. She could certainly pick out a small crowd of people in the white and pale blue dress uniforms of the Military Guild, which these days meant the Kephalon Fleet more than the traditional land and sea militia of Palace itself. Halfway up the steps on each side stood pairs of Garang guards, uniformed in white.

'Now remember,' Samante whispered. 'The whole point of this is the testing. The public has to see your genotype confirmed, or they'll never believe the truth. So do your best to act natural for the grids, all right? There's going to be a lot of them.'

Vida's mouth went suddenly dry. She turned from the window to look at Samante.

'I'll do my best,' Vida said.

'Good. That's all anyone can – oh, look at that!'

Vida swirled round and followed her point. On the back wall of the security booth hung the usual pair of vidscreens. On one of them glowed a holo of a young woman with russet-red hair tumbling down past her shoulders. She's pretty, Vida thought – oh my God, that's me! All round her holo the screen windowed into display units – blocks of text, other holos, Vanna, the cardinal, Karlo, people she didn't know – THE LAST L'VAR? GIRL FOUND IN PLEASURE SECT! END OF LONG SEARCH? CYBERGUILD HEAD ADMITS ELATION OVER DISCOVERY!

'Good,' Samante said. 'I wonder how long it'll take to tabulate the first poll? The initial reaction won't mean much if it's bad, though, so don't worry. Once we get you a newsgrid presence, people will stop caring about ancient history.'

Vida barely heard her. On the vidscreen her own holo was beginning to morph. As she watched, her hair shrank and shortened, her jaw turned strong, her shoulders broadened, the clothes in the picture changed from her old green slither to a military uniform.

A man's face looked out at her, but the eyes were hers, the set of the ear, the cropped off russet-red hair. ORIN L'VAR – TRAITOR'S LAST LEGACY?

'That's my father,' Vida whispered.

'Oh yes,' Samante said. 'And no-one will ever doubt it, seeing that morph.'

Vida stared at the screen as the holo began to change back, softening, narrowing, turning into her own face again. WILL PUBLIC ACCEPT LAST OF THE CYBERSORCERERS?

'Good question,' Samante said. 'But there's no use in worrying about your ratings yet. Brother Dav?'

Wiping sweat from his face, the burly monk turned from his control panel.

'Yes, it's time you two went down. Nikolaides is on his way up to fetch his lawsister.'

'Who?' Vida said.

'Pero,' Samante put in. 'On Kephalon, children took their mother's family's name. Pero Nikolaides, Karlo's son, was the Kephalon idea of a full formal name.'

Vida nodded, still watching the vidscreen. The holo of her face was fading now to a dark grey featureless head, turning slowly in a pale blue void. GIRL'S MOTHER STILL UNKNOWN – COURT RECORDS SEALED. Sealed records or not, the newsgrid intakes would be chasing her down, Vida knew. If they succeeded, would she get to meet her? Would she want to meet her? Up in one of the corner windows Orin L'Var's holo reappeared. My father, Vida thought. But a traitor.

At the door, a knock; Pero strode in without waiting for an answer. He bowed to Vida, then glanced at Samante and grinned with a lazy flick of his wide mouth.

'A lovely dress, Interpreter Dinisa,' he said.

'Thank you, Captain Nikolaides.' Samante sounded cool, distant. 'The uniform becomes you as well.'

'Nothing becomes me, Interpreter.' Pero turned to Vida. 'Sister, you look lovely tonight. White, hum? Well, you're about to contract into the Military Guild, all right. May I have the honour?'

Vida was glad to have his arm to lean upon, just as she was glad to have Samante there, walking right behind. From the security booth a lift brought them down to the main floor, where Brother Dav's people, dressed in Lifegiver black, were waiting to clear them a straight path to the dais. As the guests realized who was entering the hall, a ripple of silence spread. Vida was remembering every posture lesson Tia and Aleen had ever given her – walk tall, walk gracefully, walk as if you wore a thousand-credit dress like this every day of your life. On either side the open path, behind the casually placed security guards, stood guildmasters, aristocrats, high-ranked officers, and priests, and they were all watching her silently, coldly, with nothing on their faces but hard assessment.

Vida concentrated on looking straight ahead, but there, waiting for her on the dais, stood Vanna, glaring at her with eyes of ice, shuddering abruptly, twitching an arm, bobbing her head, but always steadying herself to glare once more. She wore a sheer smartgown of pale blue that set off the royal blue of the tattoos scrawled around her muscular arms, face, and neck. Vida could see the shadows of even more tattoos under the gown on every curve of breast or hip, each one a mark binding her to the Interstellar Guild and one of its grades. Behind her stood the Peronida men, all of them wearing the same uniform as Pero, even Damo, knee-length smocks of shimmering silver and blue over high white boots. Karlo and Wan each wore the headband forbidden to Pero, though, engraved with the Peronida glyph – a sine curve of grey bisected by a blue bar to show that their genotype had yet to be registered. At the sight of her Karlo smiled with a nod her way, but Wan stood impassive, his eyes focused on the wall far behind her. Off to one side she saw the cardinal, wearing the full regalia of an officer of the church, including the gold gloves of a Witness and a black mesh veil that fell to the middle of his chest. His crimson robes, embroidered with stars of every spectral type, pooled around his feet like a bowl of magma.

Standing in ranks around the mother of pearl dais were easily a hundred human pix, camera hands pointing, swinging in arcs, focusing down on new targets, pointing again while the intakes among them subvocalized data to their implants. As if at a signal they all swung toward Vida. Light fell on her in a column of gold and blinded her utterly. *Don't fail me, Vida.* Vida smiled with a toss of her head that made her hair ripple around her shoulders.

'This is so lovely,' she called out. 'I'm so happy to be here.'

The pix sighed and pushed forward, a happy crush, calling out, 'Look this way, turn right, straight forward, can you wave a little, that's it, smile now smile smile smile . . .' Vida turned and smiled and waved and smiled and turned again.

'That's enough!' Karlo's voice boomed out. 'Turn that spot off, will you?'

The column of gold flickered and disappeared. Her eyes full of sudden tears, Vida blindly turned Karlo's way. Pero caught her arm again and gave it a comforting squeeze.

'Good job, little sister,' he whispered. 'Now we're going to go up the steps. Count 'em – one, two, three.'

At the top she could see again. Karlo stood, one hand outstretched, smiling at her while Vanna watched him with poison in her eyes.

'Father,' Vida said. 'May I call you father?'

'Of course, child,' Karlo said.

While Vida made him a formal bow, she caught Vanna's expression, a good bit less poisonous now. Vanna turned to whisper to Wan, who scowled, then stepped forward to take Vida's arm.

'No poaching on my preserve, brother,' he said to Pero.

His voice rang false as a hologram's smile, but the gridjockeys loved it, clustering close, pointing and murmuring, always pointing even as they shoved each other for the best positions. Wan made a show of clasping his hand over Vida's, of kissing her forehead chastely while Pero made faces at him behind his back. A family moment. Human interest. It would be all over the vidscreens by the morning, Vida knew. She looked up at Wan and smiled the smile she'd practised against the day when she would take her place among the Marked women of The Close and greet her first customer. All at once, out in the hall, someone clapped, another pair of hands joined in, then more and more – a cascade of approval rang round the enormous hall.

Laughing, Karlo raised both hands and turned slowly round in a circle, calling for silence, while Vanna began whispering stage directions – Vida and Wan to sit on a small divan directly behind Karlo, Pero and Damo to hurry off to the side, while she herself sat in a gilded chair next to the cardinal's. Once they were settled, Karlo stepped to a small podium, a black pillar, truncated at an angle, with rainbow colours flickering over its surface. Vida noticed a small transmit clipped to the wide collar of his uniform.

'Citizens of Palace, I'm pleased to be able to introduce Sé Vida L'Var. Yes, we all remember the treason her family committed, but she was only an infant, an innocent little child, at the time. Now that my son has found her, I think it's time to heal that old wound. The L'Vars were a noble family once and will be again. When my son, Wan, came to me and told me just who he'd fallen in love with, I was furious at first, but he talked me round.'

Wan pasted on a smile.

'So,' Karlo went on. 'I can understand that you, too, must be wondering how anyone could consider raising a family that had fallen so far. But look at this child! Is she really stained with her family's treason? All I'm asking is this: give the girl a chance to be herself, in the here and now. Give her a chance to redeem her family name, not be dragged under by it.' He paused, looking round the crowd, making careful eye contact with various individuals that, Vida assumed, he'd salted there earlier. 'Can we do this? Can we put the past aside and let the L'Var family live again?'

The salts in the crowd began to cheer and clap. Caught up in the moment the guests began to join them, a few here and there at first, then more and more until the metallic hall seemed to buzz like a warplane with applause. When Vida smiled at Wan, he looked away and slumped a little on the divan, his full mouth set in a sulk. Oh how loath! she thought. He's five years old or something! A beaming Karlo held up both hands again for silence.

'Thank you, my friends,' Karlo went on. 'Thank you, my fellow citizens. I know that you're all wondering about the genetic marker that set the L'Var clan apart. Well, she's already had a gene scan, and the marker is there, but I think you all deserve to see for yourself, to prove her family line . . . Cardinal?'

Roha rose, bowing rather randomly – it would be hard to see through that veil, Vida thought. Carefully he shuffled the few steps to the front of the dais and laid a hand lightly on the podium-like black pillar. Since the pix still swarmed around, he flung back his veil in a dramatic gesture and held the pose for a few moments before speaking in his booming dark voice, well-suited for the cathedrals of the Eye.

'Citizens of Centre, Palace, and the Great Pinch itself, I have come before you this day as a Witness for God.' The cardinal raised his gold-gloved hands and the crowd hushed. 'Today, we celebrate a great healing. Sé Wan Peronida, the son and heir of our beloved First Citizen, has found the last of the L'Vars, and she has won his heart. The Eye of God, who sees all, has decreed that the suffering of the L'Vars must end. But first we must prove without any trace of doubt the heritage of this girl.'

Roha gestured to a woman standing at the foot of the dais –

Sister Romero, Vida recognized, wearing a sunsilk shift of black embroidered with stars. She clasped her heavily veined hands at her waist and looked down as she strode up the steps. The cardinal held out one hand in acknowledgement.

'My fellow citizens,' he went on, 'this is Sister Romero from the holy world of Retreat. Many of you know her as the Pope's Eye. She came to Palace for many reasons, but now she's taken on an additional task. She's graciously agreed to test Sé Vida and, with the permission of the Family Peronida, to approve the marriage contract.'

He paused, letting the crowd murmur among itself for a few minutes. The people nearer to the dais, the ones Vida could see, were nodding to each other in approval. The entire Pinch trusted the Pope of Retreat and his direct messengers, the Itinerants. The cardinal motioned to Vida to stand, then bowed to Sister Romero.

'Shall we proceed?' he said.

Sister Romero turned her dark gaze on Vida, then summoned her with the curl of one hand. As Vida walked over, she was only aware of Romero's eyes, judging her, probing her so intensely that Vida wondered if she were actually a cyberdroid instead of the flesh and blood she seemed.

'Stand there,' Romero said, and her voice seemed oddly soft compared to those dark eyes. 'Yes, just by the console.'

Vida stood. With flicks of her bony fingers, Romero activated the holo function of the panel. A revenant appeared, about the size of Vida's forearm, and bowed to the Itinerant. All round the dais the gridjockeys pressed in, subvocalizing to increase the power to the audio pickups they wore in their headbands. Romero waited until this insect-buzz died away.

'Meta: Romero One,' she said. 'My name is Romero. Identify yourself.'

'Geno-deen ident unit.'

'Have you been accessed before this moment?'

'No. First access under Romero-One meta nine seconds previously.'

'Are you prepared to conduct a genetic DNA test and cross-match the result to the database of human DNA compiled and stored by Retreat?'

'Yes.'

Romero offered her palm to Vida, who placed her hand in the Itinerant's dry and gentle grip. Romero turned her hand over and laid it palm-down upon the console. Vida gasped as a glass fang pricked her index finger. On the console a small black circle turned a sudden red, filled with her blood. When Romero released her hand, Vida sucked the tip of her finger. Camera hands swung her way to record the gesture.

'Analyse,' Romero said.

After a few seconds, the rev spoke. 'Genetic code sequencing complete.'

'Search the sample for the following peptide chain: AGT AGC TCG GTA . . .' Romero reeled off a string of codons from memory while the pix swung her way, recording.

'Found,' the rev answered immediately. 'Linked pair, allele positive, peptide unique. The subject is unquestionably a L'Var Prime. Family traits follow. Female line: ambidextrous, red hair –'.

'Stop.' The cardinal stepped forward, and at his command the rev paused.

When Roha nodded slightly to the Pope's Eye, Romero ignored him. He hesitated for a moment, then went on.

'Palace is grateful to you for your service, Sister Romero. But I really don't believe that we need a complete listing of all L'Var genetic traits. These two children would be too old to enjoy their marriage.'

The audience dutifully laughed. Romero seemed to be studying the cardinal's elaborate robes. Finally, she shrugged and turned to the rev.

'Lock database. End meta: Romero One.'

The rev vanished. Smiling, raising his hands in benediction, the cardinal stepped forward again.

'Gentlefolk, we have our final proof. This innocent child is the last of the L'Vars.'

People began to clap, first a scatter, then a swell of applause, booming and slapping on the polished walls of the hall, on and on, louder and louder. Just as it seemed sure to fade, Karlo strode forward and flung up one hand for silence. The other he clamped onto Vida's shoulder and squeezed in what he must have thought was a reassuring manner. Vida winced.

'Please welcome her,' Karlo said, 'an innocent child saved from being Marked to Pleasure Sect so she could bring happiness to Centre and joy to the Peronidas.' He looked down at the swarm of pix and intakes. 'We've set aside one of the side rooms for you people. She'll answer your questions there.'

Vida saw Brother Dav and two of his security guards pushing their way toward her. Behind her she could hear Samante whispering to Wan, and while she couldn't make out the words, the interpreter's tone stung like a goad – which Wan needed, apparently. When he joined her, he looked down on her as if she were a burden of inexpressible weight. Vida remembered Aleen, smiled brilliantly, and allowed herself to be led away. The gridjockeys trailed after, like a long ragged cloud chasing a storm.

The wood-panelled room stank of humans and spilled drink, barley beer and fermented fruit in equal measure. In the dim shadows that flickered from the vidscreen on the wall, human men crowded around one long table while Leps sat at the other. Dice rattled above the whisper of the vidscreen, which the Lep bartender had silenced at his patrons' request.

Vi-Kata didn't need to hear the audio. He sat alone, nursing a glass of bright red liqueur, and watched Vida's triumph with rage building in his heart. Government House. They had taken her to Government House, the one place on this stinking mouldy planet that he could never reach. Kata had become the great assassin he was by knowing his own limits. For him to try some elaborate ruse to get past Dukayn's defence system would mean a wasted suicide. Sooner or later, though, the little human bitch would have to come out. She would be guarded, of course, but guards were not Government House.

He finished his drink in one swallow and stood up, smoothing down his most recent change of clothes, a long tunic and a wrap kilt, shabby but respectable enough. With this suit he could wear the amber pendant openly, though he'd transferred it to a cheap, strong chain. He tossed the Lep bartender a coin.

'Toilet back there?' Kata jerked his thumb in the direction of the back of the bar.

'Yes, Sé. Down that hall. It's the blue door.'

Kata had just reached the entrance to the narrow hallway when the front door of the bar banged open. He took two quick strides into shadows, then glanced back to see Protectors, red armour flickering like fire in the moving light, trotting into the room, stunsticks at the ready.

'Hey, what?' the bartender shouted. 'Nothing wrong going on in here!'

'Then you don't have to worry, do you?' One of the Protectors glanced around. 'All right, all of you, up against the wall! You – down there in the hall – get out here!'

Kata opened not the blue but the unpainted door Riva's message had told him about and stepped through. He could hear the Protector shouting as he shot the bolt that locked it – a thin thing, and they'd break through in seconds. With one hand he found his pendant and pulled it free of his shirt. It gleamed in the darkness of the storage room to show a gate was near. When he whispered the activation code, a portal appeared on the far wall.

'Open up!' A voice from the hall, and then a heavy body slammed hard into the wooden door behind him. 'Open up now!'

Kata strode across the room and stepped through the transmit gate. Although the icy feel of non-existent fingers made him as nauseated as ever, he could feel his crest lift as he imagined the look on the Protectors' faces when they burst through to find the room empty. Behind him the door disappeared, leaving him in the usual pale grey cubicle. He could hear, as always, the throb that might have been heavy machinery. With a heavy sigh he leaned against a wall to wait. Those Protectors – were they a routine police sweep, or had someone realized that he was on planet, his brother perhaps?

Far up on the opposite wall a point of light appeared, spread, then transformed itself not into the directed hologram he was expecting, but the image of a vidscreen. In the upper right corner Riva appeared like a news presenter, smiling her peculiarly human smile. The rest of the screen windowed into images of Vida and Wan Peronida, some from the front, some the side, long shots, close-ups, all patterned into a mosaic of gesture and movement – somehow or other Riva had accessed the raw feed from one of the news centres on the Map. The pair was sitting in a pale gold room, it seemed, and although there was no sound, from the way that one or the other of them would speak briefly, then wait before speaking again, Kata could guess the presence of intakes, just out of camera range.

'Riva! Can you hear me?'

'Of course, Vi-Kata, of course. This is just a little show for your amusement.'

'I know that I have failed.' Kata's head felt far too heavy; it seemed to sink toward his chest of its own will. 'Let my ancestors know of my shame. The girl still lives.'

'My enemies moved much faster than I thought they could. I

never even considered this. Don't berate yourself, my friend.'

'How can I not? I swear to you, she will die. She can't live her whole life shut up in Government House. Once she leaves, my knife will be her destiny.'

'What? Do you really think you could kill her in public and then escape?'

'No, not and escape. But the honour of my house –'

'Stop! Listen to me! Think! If you kill the girl, then make some spectacular public death, won't there be an investigation? Look at her there on the screen. Isn't she beautiful by human standards? Beautiful, young, suddenly rich? My archives tell me that humans adore these things. Kill her now and the whole city will be howling for vengeance.'

'True, but –'

'There is no other side to this question. Do you hear me, Kata? You must not risk a public death for the girl. If the Protectors ever learned of me, our plans would fail. Do you understand that? Your shame is nothing, nothing at all, compared to what we can accomplish for the Lep race.'

Kata considered for a long moment. Riva had said nothing against a private, untraceable death for the girl.

'Do you understand me?' Riva snapped.

'I understand you, yes. And of course I'll follow your orders.'

'Good. Together we shall light a fire that will warm our people's hearts.'

Kata raised his crest, but he found himself wondering about her peculiar, stilted language – had she learned her Gen from cheap drama shows? The image of the newsfeed screen suddenly went blank, then brightened again. Riva sat in a green websling, her coils of knotted silk wound round her – an onscreen holo, not a revenant.

'You have other game to hunt. I have information about Arno.'

'Excellent.' Kata's crest raised. 'I know where he's hiding.'

'Good. I have information that tonight he's making his run for the Spaceport. He's booked passage under a false name on a cargo ship to Souk leaving early in the fives. I suggest you see to it that his berth stays empty.'

After an exact hour of questions, Dukayn flung back the door of the interview room. He said nothing, merely stood just to one side of the door with his arms crossed over his chest, but the gridjockeys, human and Lep both, all got up and began filing out.

'He has them well-trained,' Wan muttered.

'I'm glad. Aren't you?' Vida said. 'You must be as tired of questions as I am.'

Wan looked at her for a moment, then rose, stretching his arms over his head. When Vida got up to join him, he turned his back on her.

'Wan?' she said. 'They didn't give me any choice about this, you know. It wasn't my idea any more than it was yours. We're kind of in this together, aren't we?'

He glanced at her, then walked off down the by now empty room. Although Vida hurried after, at the door a pair of young men were waiting for him. One, tall and pale-haired, wore the Fleet uniform crossed with a factor's brown sash. He carried a portable scribing tablet. The other, short and dark, began talking to Wan in Helane, the language of Kephalon. The three of them huddled, leaving Vida hovering on the outside. Dukayn touched her arm lightly.

'Sé Vida?' he murmured. 'Come with me. We'll find you a suitable escort.'

'Thank you. I suppose I should meet my husband's factor?'

'Not right now. He's drunk. Of course, Leni's usually drunk. We'll have to arrange a breakfast meeting.'

Vida managed a smile and let him lead her into a reception hall all changed and gone magical. The burnished silverwood walls glowed with a thousand colours that fell in almost palpable shafts from the vaulted ceiling hundreds of feet above. When Vida looked up, she saw that a tech crew had transformed it into a vast display of vidscreens, showing landscape holos from the worlds of the Pinch.

A satellite flash of Centre at night made the sect look like a black lake filled with burning eyes of many colours, the Lake of Fallen Stars, Vida thought, with a shudder, the final hell of those who failed to be reborn into the night beside God. Another screen showed time lapse vids of Palace's cloud of orbital satellites, each trailing on the film a long tendril of light so that the planet seemed webbed round by them. Grey-blue Souk with its delicate stalk-cities and vast archipelagoes spun in the middle of yet another panel. Icy Tableau reflected light as bright as a small sun while verdant Belie revolved with a stately elegance, its surface features a mystery under a swirl of emerald atmosphere. They were all human worlds, Vida noticed. She wondered why they didn't show Indang, the Garang Japat homeworld, or the Lep systems, or the Hirrel Nomadia.

Far up, under the highest dome of the ceiling, a bank of hologrammatic clouds appeared, swirling like a summer storm. Distant thunder murmured through the hall and the sound of a high wind, while flashes of sheet lightning strobed over the guests, gathered far below. It seemed to rain – silvery holograms flickered and splashed so convincingly that Vida couldn't stop herself from touching her hair to see if it were wet. Laughing and calling out, most of the guests were doing the same. The thunder died away, the rain stopped, and slowly the clouds cleared from the dome to reveal an image of the sun, shining at the apex. A flood of hologram butterflies exploded throughout the room and fluttered in the brightening light. Among them fell pale green and gold bubble-flares, bursting with scent. The applause boomed out as loud as the artificial thunder.

'Ah, there's Nikolaides and the interpreter,' Dukayn said abruptly. 'Good.'

Vida suddenly realized that the factor had paid not the least bit of attention to the show. Dukayn raised one hand and made an imperious sort of wave. Out in the crowd, shadowed now in a hundred shifting lights, someone in a white uniform waved back and began making a slow way toward them. Vida recognized Samante's red dress, then Samante, as they came closer.

'Sé Vida?' Dukayn said. 'The Peronida asked me to watch out for you. If anyone gives you the slightest trouble, anyone, you summon me. My number on the commgrid is 0000. Easy to remember.'

'Yes, it is. Thank you so much.' Vida turned her best smile on him and received the barest twitch of one in return – but from Dukayn, that was a triumph. 'By the Peronida, do you mean Wan or Karlo?'

'Karlo, of course. Wan – well, huh. Ah, here they are. Nikolaides, your brother seems to have been called away on business. His factor showed up looking for him, anyway.'

'Business.' Pero rolled his eyes toward the ceiling. 'But you'd like me to tour my charming sister around?'

'Just that.' Dukayn turned serious. 'She's to have a good time.'

'Yes sir!' Pero snapped off a perfect salute. 'Interpreter Dinisa, will you join us on this grave mission?'

'Gladly, Captain, if Sé Vida allows?'

'Of course,' Vida said. 'Samante, I'm so hungry. Is there anything to eat?'

'I think we might say so,' Samante said. 'There's a buffet. Over there.'

When Vida looked to the far wall, she saw a crowd of sapients gathered around something that she assumed must be this buffet. Reaching it took them some while. It seemed that everyone wanted to meet her, all the people that two days before would have recognized her existence with a wrinkle of their noses, if they had recognized it at all. Vida smiled and bowed and waved and exchanged 'sé' with people in expensive clothes, but all the while she was aware of her memory, clicking like a pix's hand, filing names with faces, faces with scraps of information. Ah, you come from Hort Sect; oh, I met your husband just a moment ago, from the university, right? Some she recognized as clients, regulars at The Close, a master from the Biotech Guild, a journeyman from Archives. She'd even brought them drinks for the tips. Now they bowed over her hand and announced, maybe a little too loudly, how pleased they were to finally get to meet her. She was glad when Pero caught her arm to lead her onward.

'Slow work, getting anywhere in here,' Pero grumbled. 'Ah, look, there's a lane opening up.'

'Not that way,' Samante hissed. 'Look who's standing right there.'

'Oops. You're right. This way, lawsister.'

'What?' Vida snapped.

Pero and Samante were looking toward two tall men, both bald, both wearing the charcoal grey robes, sashed in red, of the Industrial Guild – brothers, obviously, from the similarity of their wide, dark eyes and long noses. Next to them stood a girl who'd inherited their eyes and height – she would have towered over Vida – but not, fortunately, the nose. Muscled and lithe, she stood like an athlete, one hand on the hip of her severe black dress. In the other she held the biggest glass of swamp wine that Vida had ever seen. The only decoration she wore was her own hair, a hip-length fall of it, honey-blonde and gleaming.

'Lis and Reel le-Yonestilla,' Pero whispered. 'The girl's Anja.'

'Vida doesn't know.' Samante leaned close, murmuring. 'She and Wan were supposed to marry. Karlo voided the contract this morning.'

'Damo told me it was quite a scene,' Pero said, grinning. 'I'm surprised they showed up.'

'Politics is politics,' Samante said. 'Now let's get out of here.'

Vida followed, letting Pero bring up the rear.

'Samante?' she said. 'Is that why Wan hates me? He wanted to marry someone else, someone he really loved.'

'I don't think Wan is capable of loving anyone, but he wanted Anja.'

'Well, they can always have an affair or something. I won't mind.'

Samante stopped and swung round, one eyebrow raised. Vida merely looked back, puzzled.

'Well, I won't,' Vida went on. 'Why would I? Don't believe the publicity. It's not like I love him.'

'I think you're going to do well at this.' Pero joined them. 'But Anja would mind. No second place for a girl like her.'

'Well, that's too bad.'

As they snaked their way through the crowd, Vida noticed that mostly humans gathered in the reception hall, though here and there stood groups of Hirrel, dressed in ceremonial long skirts and the odd little vests, open at the sides, that showed off the fluttering of the gills inside their pale red slits. Off in the curve of a wall stood a few Lep, too, clustered together, richly dressed in slashed kilts of purple brocade, their scales oiled to a high sheen.

'See that scaly guy over there?' Pero said abruptly. 'The one with the triple honour sashes and then the blue and black spiral pattern in his scales? That's Sar Wik Benar, Chief Minister of Finance and head of Lep Sect.'

'Pero!' Samante broke in. 'It's properly referred to as Finance Sect.'

'Yeah, sure.' Pero smiled, his wide slash of mouth drawn even wider. 'Face facts, Sammi! My father and Roha have built a fence round those people. Call it what you want, it's still a pen.'

When Samante made a face at him, he laughed, reaching one hand toward her, drawing it back, and as if her hand were tied to his by an invisible string, she reached out toward him, then stopped, glancing round. Lovers, Vida thought.

After another determined guest or two, including Samante's law-uncle, Wilso from Power Sect, had been met and smiled upon, they reached the buffet. On the wall behind the tables hung vidscreens, displaying the backs of the saccule servers and the food itself: a long spread of fruit, vegetables, salads, confections, platters of cheese, bowls of mushrooms, pitchers of sauces, heaps of little cakes, baskets of breads, and in the centre of the table, an entire side, front and back haunches both, of some huge animal – real meat, a fortune's worth. Vida stood gawking until a saccule, cross-sashed in Fleet white and blue over a silver shift, hurried up to her, honking and gesturing.

'Sé Vida will please have a seat,' Pero said. 'You will be waited upon as the luminary you are. How about including your poor weary lawbrother in this invite?'

Laughing, Vida began to point, honking back at the saccule, who exuded a flower-scented smile. Bowing and whistling, it escorted the three of them to a round table among the isolation tori, then scurried off to fill their orders. Vida glanced at Samante and forgot the trivial remark she'd been about to make.

'What's so wrong?' Vida said.

'Sé Vida, you shouldn't be making noises at saccules. It's undignified.'

'What? I wasn't just making noises. That's how you talk to them. You should know that. You're the interpreter.'

'Saccules have no proper language, merely a system of call and response codes.'

'Well, then, I called and it responded, if that's the way you want it. Look! It's bringing us everything we asked for, isn't it?'

Their original waiter came trotting over, laden with plates, followed by another sashed saccule carrying drinks on a tray.

'They understand better if you speak a little of their language,' Vida went on. 'See?'

Samante opened her mouth and shut it again, suddenly troubled. Honking in a drifting scent of flowers, the two saccules spread out the feast, bowed, then trotted off. Samante raised a hand and waved it randomly in front of her face, as if she were clearing off the scent, while Pero watched her, one eyebrow raised.

'Oh, do let's eat,' Samante said suddenly. 'I'm hungry, too.'

Vida had taken no more than three bites when she was interrupted yet again. She heard someone calling out, then laughter, then a kind of hooting and shouting back and forth, and looked up to see a handful of guests chasing each other around the polished floor. One of the men had grabbed a tray of drinks from a saccule waiter; he held it balanced precariously over his head on one hand as he fended off a pair of young women. Not one of them wore formal clothes, though some were cleaner than others. Blue trousers, white shirts, here and there a stained work tunic or smock – clothes didn't much matter to someone so heavily tattooed, Vida supposed. Hands and faces, arms and what she could see of their chests – every inch of skin sported long curves and blue lines.

'Interstellar people?' Vida said.

'Oh yes,' Samante said. 'Oh God! They're coming our way!'

Laughing and hooting, the fellow with the tray came dancing up with a ragged line rushing after him.

'Watch that thing!' Samante snapped. 'Don't you dare spill –'

'Me? Spill expensive booze? You do me grave insult, lady.' Grinning with a flash of gold tooth, he lowered the tray, only to be swarmed by snatching friends. With the drinks all safely stowed in Interstellar hands, he glanced round, saw a saccule, and sailed it the tray. With a mournful honk and sigh, it grabbed it from midair and hurried off. The guildsman made Vida a long bow.

'Sé Vida,' he said. 'You have enough of this formal shit yet? Come dance with us! We're the slickest jammers in the Pinch, no lie. We'll show you shunts that've never been mapped. Eye's Truth!'

'You've been to an unmapped shunt? Really?'

The fellow opened his mouth, then shut it again, while the troop roared with laughter and pointed. A woman with a laugh like stones rolling down metal slapped him on the back.

'Called your bluff, eh Ket?' Grinning, she tapped Vida on the forehead. 'Think, sweetling, wouldn't've you heard 'bout a new shunt on all the screens?'

'Well, I guess so, yeah. Hey, I'd settle for seeing a mapped one.'

'Not a lot to see.' The woman went on. 'But you can feel it when you're riding one down, honey. You bet you can.'

'Oh, I'd love to know that feeling.'

Ket leaned forward, smiling, and laid a blue rippled hand on Vida's arm. 'Damn, but you're my kinda woman. I can see it in your eyes. You're a jammer born. You ever need a berth in a shuntjammer, ask for *Ket's Ribbon*, the sleekest slake that ever slid the micros. Maybe you and me'll wriggle a new micro one'a these days, eh?'

'You'll have to win her from Wan first,' Pero said, and coolly, '*Sé* Ket.'

Ket let go her arm and stood, glancing back and forth at the other jammers. With a smooth gliding step, they closed in behind him. No-one said a word, merely waited, watching Pero, watching Ket. The woman with the jarring laugh looked Pero over, her mouth a little twisted.

'And how is Susannah, Pero?' she said at last. 'Your *dear* mother?'

'Very well, Purser Jale.' Pero spoke smoothly, calmly. 'You

should say hello to her next time you jam to Tableau.'

'Unlikely.' Jale paused for a sip of her drink. 'Vanna's looking fit, eh?' She glanced Vida's way. 'She's my sister, honey. You know that?'

'No, I didn't. I uh –' Vida froze. This was Vanna's guild, Vanna's kin – did they all hate her the way Vanna did?

'I know her better than anyone in the Pinch,' Jale went on. 'A word to the wise, honey. Keep an eye on your back around her.'

Ket rapped out a string of words in some guttural and glottal tongue that Vida had never heard. Jale laughed, very briefly, then buried her nose in her drink when Ket swung her way, one hand raised. The other jammers turned on their heels like a dance troupe and swept Jale off. Ket lingered, leaning over to whisper.

'Don't worry it, sweetling.' He squeezed her arm, then hurried after his crew.

With an elaborate sigh, Pero leaned back in his chair. Samante was studying her half-eaten plate of food. Vida picked up her fork.

'Well, I knew that about Vanna,' she said. 'And I'm still hungry.'

'Good.' Pero raised his glass in salute. 'So am I.'

They were still eating when Vida, glancing over the crowd, saw Sé Hivel, looking somehow taller in his long robes, walking in through a nearby door. With him was a tall young man in the midnight blue smock of a cyber apprentice – a good-looking boy, she thought, with his untidy mane of dark hair and firm, striding walk. All at once she remembered Sé Hivel's nephew, the first-timer. Maybe that was Rico? She felt herself blushing and grabbed a napkin to wave it around her face.

'It's so hot in here,' she said – casually, she hoped.

'It's all the warm bodies, crammed in together.' Pero glanced in the direction that she'd been looking. 'Aha, Sammi! Our humble reception is honoured indeed. Sé Hivel approaches, and I believe his nephew?'

'Oh yes, the one who's going to be invested as his heir,' Samante said. 'That gossip's been all over. Vida, that's the head of the Cyber-guild, and never fool yourself. The guildmasters are the real rulers of Palace, no matter what your new lawfather thinks.'

Vida nodded, not quite trusting her voice. What was she supposed to do? Pretend she'd never met Sé Hivel? Probably so. Certainly he was looking at her pleasantly enough, but with the mild anticipation of someone about to be introduced, not to greet a friend.

'You stinking whore!' The voice came hissing from behind her, like a knife through taut cloth. 'So this is the stinking whore, is it?'

Vida twisted round in her chair and ducked just in time as an openhanded slap struck at her face. She saw a black dress, long legs, another flying hand just as someone grabbed her hair and pulled hard. Caught seated as she was, she could only yelp and flail, but Pero was already moving and grabbing.

'Let go, Anji darling, or I'll break your lovely arm.'

The grip on Vida's hair went limp and fell away. She leapt up, shoving the chair to the floor. Anja writhed and kicked, but Pero had her arm twisted behind her back. She was crying, long ugly sobs that twisted her mouth and left coloured streaks of mascara down her face.

'I hate you, you rotten little cull!' She screamed so loudly that Vida stepped back. 'I hate your ugly guts. Whore! Traitor! Stinking L'Var traitor!'

Sé Hivel stepped forward and laid one large hand over Anja's mouth. All at once Vida realized that the reception hall had fallen silent, that everyone had turned, that everyone was staring, shocked and staring.

'Dinisa!' Hivel snapped. 'Get Sé Vida out of here. Nikolaides and I will deal with the madwoman.'

Samante grabbed Vida's arm hard and started walking, giving Vida no choice but to follow. She drew herself up to full height and walked fast but smoothly, nodding every now and then to anyone who looked familiar. They stared back, silent and unyielding. I'm going to hear this again and again, she thought. Whore and traitor. That's me, the cull. I might as well learn to stare them all down. Behind them she heard a crash and glanced back to see Anja free of Pero's grip and kicking over furniture. Rico grabbed her by the shoulders and thrust her back into Nikolaides' arms. Vida looked away and smiled at the Countess de la Motta, who waved back in feeble surprise. The guests around the countess merely stared.

Halfway across the hall, Brother Dav and his black-robed security people met them. Vida let out her breath in a long sigh.

'It's a good thing we'd finished eating,' she said to Samante. 'I'm afraid Sé Anja's spilled our table.'

Samante was grinning, open-mouthed and admiring. Vida made herself remember Aleen.

'I'd like some air. Is there some way we could get outside?'

'Oh yes, Sé,' Dav said. 'The roof garden. Just follow me, and I take it you won't mind if my security people join you?'

Vida followed him to the lift booth with Samante trailing after. Once the door slid shut, she could allow herself to cry.

It took both Rico and Pero to wrestle the screaming Anja out of the reception hall. Hi followed them into the corridor, then laid his cyberarm over the smart threads in his gold sash and subvocalized Caliostro's call code. As soon as the AI responded, Hi sent an order to summon a medic. Out in a side corridor, just beyond the reception hall, they found a blue plush divan sitting against a mirrored wall. Pero unceremoniously threw Anja face down onto it and sat next to her, holding her down by the shoulders, but by then she was weeping too hard to fight. Blood ran down Pero's face and dripped onto his dress uniform.

'You've got a nasty little bite, Anji,' Pero said, but he sounded halfway amused. 'Rico, you okay?'

'Just scratched.' Rico was looking at his hand and arm. 'Well, a couple of times.'

'Oh shit!' Pero said. 'She's going to throw up.'

Anja did, repeatedly and noisily, leaning over the end of the divan. Hi sent another order to Caliostro for a saccule with a mop while Pero found a handkerchief in his smock pocket and began wiping her mouth. She sat as miserably as a wet child and let him.

'Uncle Hi?' Rico said. 'The girl with the red hair? That's Vida?'

'Sure is, kid. What do you think?'

'She's lovely.' Rico was whispering. 'I've never seen a girl like that. I mean, I did see her, once, at the festival, you know? Just on the street. But I never thought I'd see her again. God, she's so beautiful.'

Hi gladly left Anja to Pero and turned to look at his nephew. Besotted, he thought. Just what we need now!

'Look, kid,' he said. 'She's just been raised a couple of cuts above you. And then there's her husband to think about. Wan and little Anji here would have been a good match. They have a lot in common.'

'He doesn't love Vida.' Rico shook his stubborn head. 'You could see it on the screens. When we were watching that interview, you know? He doesn't love her at all.'

It was true enough, but Hi was saved from having to answer by the medic, trotting down the hall with Anja's father, Lis, who was muttering to himself in fury. By then Anja was sitting up, leaning against Pero and gasping for breath. Greenish vomit streaked the hair round her face. Lis grabbed her arm.

'What in hell did you think you were doing? Disgracing our family this way? Are you crazy? What kind of marriage contract am I going to get for you now, you stupid little –'

'Lis, Lis, hey.' Hi laid a friendly hand on his shoulder. 'The kid's sick as a dog, okay? Can't you berate her later?'

Lis let out his breath in a long sigh and looked at his weeping daughter.

'Anji, I'm sorry. Hi's right. We'll talk later.'

The medic began fussing over Pero's wound, the saccule arrived with the mop, and Hi took the chance to make his escape.

'Come on, Rico,' he muttered. 'I need to work the crowd at this affair. There's some people here you've got to meet, too.'

'Yes, Sé. Do you think Vida will come back?'

'Not if she's smart, and I think she is. But after we run the see-and-be-seen utility, we're going to have a talk. Something's on your mind, kid. I want to know what it is.'

'Mom says you've got to talk to her first. It's important, yeah. She's got something to tell you about that Pansect Media crash.'

'Oh.' Hi considered – Rico was hiding something, but if Barra knew, then it could wait. 'All right. We'll take it up with her when we get home. There are two people here I need to talk with, Military Guild people. When I find them, you go help yourself to the buffet, okay?'

'Sure. I don't mind disappearing when there's food involved.'

Hi laughed and clapped his nephew on the shoulder.

'That's a good attitude. So let's go be social.'

'I'm so glad she didn't actually hurt you,' Samante said.

'So am I,' Vida said. 'I felt so dumb, just sitting there and squealing, but I couldn't get out of that stupid chair.'

'Well, fortunately Pero was right there.'

'Fortunately, yeah.'

With Brother Dav's security guards trailing a respectful distance behind, Vida and Samante were walking through the roof park atop the East Tower of Government House. Although the sky above hung thick and silver with fog, and the air felt cold, the walkways sported strip heating along the ground as well as amber lights hanging like flowers themselves from slender poles. Here and there among the dense plantings certain flowers answered the lamps with phosphorescence, like mirrored stars caught among the shadows. Although the roof park overall stretched for acres, tall hedges cut it up into separate gardens, giving the illusion of privacy.

'Shall we sit down?' Samante said. 'There are benches all over. And they're cushioned.'

'Maybe in a minute? I'm just so restless.'

Samante sighed. Vida was about to give in and stop for a rest when she heard a rustle, just ahead, behind a cluster of shrubs. Could it be the assassin, come to finish his job? She froze, listening, slowly raising one hand to beckon the guards closer. When she glanced back she saw them drawing stunsticks from the holders at their belts. The rustling ahead sounded louder. A cloaked figure rounded the bend, heading toward them. From the hip-sprung walk and broad shoulders he had to be a Lep.

'Get down, Samante!' Vida yelled. 'Guards!'

Samante screamed. The guards darted forward. The Lep chuckled, said something sibilant in his own language, and spread spindly arms wide.

Samante laughed, shaking a little, and answered him.

'What?' Vida snapped. 'Oh no, have I done something dumb again? How loath!'

When the Lep flipped down the hood of his cloak, the amber light washed over him, shining on polished scales, so that it seemed he was bathed in liquid gold. Down his arms ran a pattern of stripes and dots completely unlike the scale markings of the assassin – though of course, he might have dyed them.

'I merely reminded Sé Dinisa that I'm lame and not terribly adept at chasing women. I flatter myself that I have been the subject of a chase or two, however, from the women of my own kind.' The Lep's voice lisped slightly on the sibilants, but otherwise he spoke perfect Gen. 'I am Ri Tal Molos. I am pleased to cross your present, Vida. You will forgive me if I sit down uninvited.'

Molos limped past them and settled himself on one of the cushioned benches. Vida turned and waved to the guards, who sheathed their stunsticks. With a little sigh Molos began searching through the inner pockets of his cloak. At last his crest lifted, and he brought out something in a closed hand.

'I'm a friend of your guardian, Aleen Raal,' he said. 'Here. She sent you this to prove it.'

When Vida held out her hand he dropped onto her palm a

wooden Eye of God medallion on a leather thong. She turned it over, held it up to an amber light to read the mark. Yes, it was the amulet that Brother Lennos had given her during the festival. 'Aleen inadvertently kept it this morning, or so she told me,' Molos went on. 'She said you'd come to her office? Ah, I see by your nod that this is so.'

'If you're a friend of Aleen's, then I'm pleased to meet you, Sé.'

Samante laughed under her breath.

'What's so funny?' Vida snapped.

'Oh, nothing. It's just rather amusing, that you'd think Aleen so important that you'd judge Molos by her, not the other way around.'

'Oh yeah? I won't have you sneering at Aleen.'

Samante stepped back.

'Well, then, I'm sorry,' Samante said. 'But you obviously don't know who this is. Allow me to present Ri Tal Molos, one of the greatest cybermasters in the Pinch. He spent years on Souk, negotiating the settlement that saved the Leps on Palace from deportation. While he was there, Souk's Map nearly crashed, but he saved it. On top of that, he –'

'Enough, Sé Dinisa, enough.' The Lep raised a clawed hand that glittered with strange rings. 'I'm not an ambassador any longer. I'm back on Palace, just an aging Lep who can't keep his snout out of politics. Normally, I'd enjoy a bit of verbal fencing, but these are not normal times, and we've met by chance in a place where we may speak freely. This is not an opportunity to be wasted.'

'By chance?' Vida smiled at him. 'Oh come on. You've been waiting for us.'

'Perhaps so.' Molos's crest waved pleasantly. 'Now tell me, last of the L'Vars, what do you make of Government House?'

'I'm scared of it. I think I'm going to hate this place.'

'Ah, an honest answer. Perhaps then you might be interested in making as many allies as possible, such as my humble self.'

'Allies? Why should a Lep want to be friends with a L'Var? Don't you think I know what my father's crime did to your people?'

'You might as well ask why a reputable sapient would wish to be acquainted with a member of the despised Tal line. Both of us, my dear Vida, come from a clutch raised in *sraa*.'

'I beg your pardon? In what?'

'*Sraa*. I believe in Gen the word would be treachery?' He glanced at Samante.

'Not exactly,' the interpreter said. 'It's an allomorph, after all.

Vida, it can mean the betrayal of an innocent nest mate, or the tricking of an innocent into a betrayal, depending on the conditioning.'

The silence hung as cold as the fog above. Molos reached into an inner pocket of his cloak and brought out a pinch of some black substance that he rubbed, slowly, into a discoloured section of his throat.

'Molos!' Samante snapped. 'And at your age!'

'It is my one vice, Samante.' He waggled a claw at her. 'Don't lecture.'

'What is it?' Vida asked.

'A derivative of Geriose, the life-enhancement treatment,' Samante said. 'It's a highly addictive drug used by Leps who ought to know better.'

'Peace, Samante, peace.' Molos kept his crest raised. 'We have more important things to talk about than my weaknesses. Vida, please, I need some information from you. Aleen told me about the assassin. Can you describe him for me?'

'Sure.'

Vida closed her eyes and called up her memory pictures of that other roof park and the assassin. As she talked, describing every detail she saw in her images, Molos would occasionally ask her a brief question, but mostly he said little until she was finished.

'You have an extraordinary memory, Sé Vida.'

'Well, that's what everyone always says.'

'I believe it's an inherited trait. Our genes bring us many strange things and, unfortunately, tie us to some strange people as well.'

Vida turned back to stare at him. His crest hung languidly.

'I suppose you mean the L'Vars,' she said at last. 'Is the eidetic memory a L'Var trait?'

'So I always heard, yes.' Molos rubbed a finger along the discoloured patch on his throat, as if to grind the drug a little more deeply in. 'And I also mean the line of Tal, my own family, though that word truly doesn't fit our Lep arrangements very well. Vida, I know who chased you. And you are very fortunate to be alive. Aleen told me she sent you to Government House for your protection. A wise move, but then, Aleen makes no foolish ones. This assassin goes by the name of the Outcast.'

Samante yelped, then covered her mouth with one hand.

'A famous sapient in his way,' Molos said, fluttering his crest. 'And I'm afraid I know him much too – well, who's this?'

Vida spun round to see Dukayn stepping onto the path out of the foliage. Her guards, caught by surprise, all began talking at once.

'Shut up,' Dukayn said. 'And I'm reporting you all to Dav. Sé Vida? I'm not so sure it's safe up here.' He glanced at Molos, then away again. 'And it's late.'

'Dukayn, we're fine,' Samante broke in. 'I thought that Sé Vida would like to stroll through the roof park. It's been a long and trying day for her.'

Samante's expression reminded Vida of Tia, smiling while she spoke to some client she detested. Molos leaned back on his bench and gazed up at the night sky. Dukayn glanced at Samante as briefly as common courtesy would allow.

'Will you do me the honour of accompanying me back inside, Sé Vida?' Dukayn said. 'I'm sure your fiancé is worried about you.'

'Really?' Vida said.

'Well, Karlo is. And Dinisa's right. You must be exhausted.'

Vida doubted very much if he was truly concerned with how tired she might be. Putting her back in her cage like an exotic animal, on the other hand – no doubt he was concerned about that.

'Well, I *am* tired. Samante, shall we go back in?'

The interpreter nodded, stifling a yawn with one hand. Vida bowed to Molos.

'I hope we can talk some more later, Sé.'

Dukayn turned on her with ice-sharp eyes.

'Let's go,' he snapped. 'Now.'

Molos raised his crest and imitated a human wink, then rose, shuffling off with his limp down the direction he'd come. Dukayn waited until the Lep had disappeared among the shrubbery.

'Don't let the cardinal see you associating with sapes like that,' he said. 'Now let's go. Dinisa, your uncle's looking for you. Wilso.'

'He's only my law-uncle,' Samante snapped. 'And he can call me if he wants to make an appointment.'

'None of my business. I'm sure Brother Dav's people will be glad to walk you home.'

In a flash of fear that caught her by surprise, Vida turned toward Samante, the only person she felt she knew, here in this new life of hers.

'It's all right,' Samante said. 'I'll see you in the morning. Let's have breakfast?'

'Yes, sure, I mean, thank you. I never sleep real late. What about at half of the nines?'

'That's fine. I'll see you then. Sleep well.'

By the time Dukayn led her to the door of her guest suite, Vida felt as if she could sleep forever, but once she was alone, standing in the utter quiet of an unfamiliar room, she found herself restless. She flipped on the panel lighting, turning the stark white walls to a soft gold. On the poll screen the tower graphs were building to show the public's opinion of new canal construction. When she turned on the vidscreen proper, she saw pictures of herself, walking down the length of the reception hall.

'Change.'

Onscreen, a talking head – the Chief Master of the Protectors' Guild.

'And so we ask all Lep citizens to keep an eye out for any suspicious activity: any newcomer whose story doesn't quite ring true, say, and in particular someone whose scale patterning looks like it might have been altered. Please call us immediately, and don't try to take any action yourselves. The fellow we're searching for is dangerous.'

Vida suddenly realized that he was talking about the Outcast.

'Change! Search for landscapes and music.'

A moment's grey; a panorama of the sparse and wind-torn grasslands of Belie's polar continent filled the screen, while stringed instruments played in quarter tones. Vida left the screen on and wandered into the bedroom, flipped on the golden lights there as well, and stood glancing around. The bed, covered in blue satin, stretched long and wide, filling a good half of the room, while in the other half stood a white dresser and a strange narrow cabinet, about waist-high. When Vida tried to touch it, she realized that the cabinet was only a holo, hiding something.

'Image off.'

The cabinet winked out of existence, revealing a black pillar, angled at the top, much like the pillar in the Carillon. So these rooms each had a Map terminal – made sense, she supposed. Unlike the one in the bell tower, though, this pillar sported icons she could read. She pressed Access.

'Meta one,' she said, imitating Romero. 'Calios.'

The revenant sprang to life, grinning at her.

'Hello, Veelivar. How may I help you tonight?'
'Well, I don't know, exactly. I just wanted to see if I could call you up from this pillar.'
'I don't understand your words.'
'Um, well, datapoint: may I access you from all Map terminals within Government House?'
'Yes, you may now.'
'Now? Explain word choice, now.'
'Formerly I was confined to the Map segment once designated Quarantine, now known as Pleasure Sect. Just recently, however, some cybertech has implemented a new pipe allowing access to the non-segmented over-configuration of the Map.'
Vida had no idea of what this meant.
'Can you display data on the vidscreen in the other room?'
'I can access any vidscreen in Government House now.'
'Good.'
All at once the revenant disappeared. When the music from the other room stopped, Vida returned to find Calios grinning at her like a news presenter from the corner of the screen.
'There you are,' she said.
'Here I am. What shall I do for you?'
'Please search for, access, and display titles of archival files, subject: Orin L'Var.'
'How many levels of database shall I access?'
'I don't know. Please display the levels available.'
As it turned out, only one level displayed on the screen in a pitifully short list for an important public figure.
'That's all?' Vida said.
'Yes. Many public records were locked by court order after his trial.'
'I see.' Vida hesitated, considering. Although she wanted to know, and badly, what her father had been like, she was afraid she already knew: a traitor, a criminal, hanged in Public Square while the entire planet watched on the vidscreens.
'What shall I display, Veelivar?' Calios said. 'Level One is open to you.'
'I don't want to see any of them right now. Clear screen.'
The panorama of pale grass returned, dappled here and there with tiny white wildflowers. The music picked up, whining and howling like the wind she could only see.
'Calios?' Vida said.

He didn't answer. Her command must have returned him to the database, she supposed, but when she went back into the bedroom, he was waiting, hovering over the pillar in another set of bizarrely antique clothes: a pair of pale blue, tight-fitting trousers, a short-sleeved white pullover shirt with writing upon it in a language she couldn't read. She realized that she'd merely been out of sensor range when she'd spoken. He's not real, she reminded herself. You can't make that mistake. He's not real.

'What may I do for you now, Veelivar?'

'I'm not sure. Please wait.'

On the word 'wait' he froze and turned faint, a hologram put on 'pause.' Vida turned away and stared at herself in the long mirror above the dresser. Her hair was slipping down in strands from its rhinestone clasps; her white satin dress was losing its cummerbund; down one side of the skirt she found a faint spatter of green – spilled wine from somewhere. She pulled the clasps out and threw them on the dresser top, then touched the smart thread at the neck of her dress.

'Open.'

The dress split like a cut fruit. She peeled it off and threw it onto the floor, then stripped off her gauzy shift and underwear to throw them after it. In the mirror a frightened woman, her red hair a tangled mess, stood looking back at her. She spun around.

'Activate.'

Calios reappeared full-strength with a little toss of his head. His hair was still silver-coloured but curly, now, cropped close to his dark skull.

'What may I do for you, Veelivar?' he said.

Vida sat down on the edge of the bed.

'Can you tell me a story?'

'Explain, please.'

'Tell me a story. Do you have entertainment programs?'

'Entertainment base opened. Searching on keywords.' A pause; then he smiled. 'Why, yes, Veelivar. I have accessed files containing stories.'

Vida threw back the satin blanket and lay down. The pillow sighed briefly, then conformed to her head.

'Which story would you like, Veelivar? Shall I list available titles?'

'No. Just pick one.'

'Very well. I shall collate data about your situation and do a search on themes.'

Vida pulled up the blanket, which began to warm. Calios struck a strange pose, with one hand stretched out, palm up, the other set upon his jutted hip.

'Once upon a time, and a very good time it was, a poor repair tech had a shop on a planet called Earth. He lived in a tiny dwell on the edge of town and got by on small jobs that the Cyberguild gave him. He did have, however, one treasure, a daughter, and he named her Beauty . . .'

Vida fell asleep to his voice, telling her of a rich master of the Military Guild, who had been morphed into the body of an ugly beast after he'd mocked a passing Lifegiver.

With Nju driving, the ride home from Government House turned out smoother if less exciting than their morning's jaunt. Rico stared out of the window at Palace passing below, a spilled jewel box of lights under its silver sky, and wondered if his mother really would be able to hide his crimes from her older brother. Rico had never been able to hide anything from Arno, after all, and he assumed that being a younger sister would be much the same as being a younger cousin. They landed on the roof pad on the top of the Jons compound, which sported a penthouse as well as this private landing facility. Rico followed Hi downstairs while the Garang stowed the aircar in its hangar. In the top floor vestibule, a drowsy saccule, old Gran, nodded in its chair.

'Go to bed, Gran,' Hi said, then hissed out of the side of his mouth.

Gran honked, nodding, and got up to stretch.

Barra was waiting in the gather, sitting in a pool of soft light and reading a magazine. When Hi and Rico came in, she tossed the thin screen onto an end table and yawned at them both. Hi took off his robes, let them fall to the floor, then flopped into an armchair opposite hers. Rico sank onto the couch. He was glad that he was too tired to be frightened at the conversation ahead. His mother smiled at him, the bland smile she used to cover secrets.

'It's good to be home,' Hi said. 'I've been running all over the city today.'

'So Jevon told me when she got home tonight,' Barra said. 'I called your office earlier, but you'd already left for Government House.'

'Yeah. I checked in with her after I talked to Karlo – oh, yeah, I've got something to discuss with you about that, too. Don't let me forget. Sorry I'm back so late. At that reception I got buttonholed by a couple of masters from the Media Guild.'

'About the Pansect crash?'

'Just that. It was spectacular, huh? I haven't seen a real report on it yet. Rico here tells me you know something.'

'It wasn't just an ordinary crash. It was vandalism or most likely more of the sabotage we've been running into.'

Hi swore with a shake of his head.

'I was afraid of that. What's the evidence?'

'A delete and scramble icon shaped like a huge burning candle. It exploded the Map construct for Pansect's narrow-band transmission by radiating icons that appeared as waves of fire. The worst thing is that it must have an independent power source – somehow. It would discharge a wave of iconic fire, then seem to dim down. A few seconds later, it would draw power from somewhere and explode more constructs.'

Hi swore again, then considered, staring out into space.

'I need to get right on that,' he said at last.

'Hi,' Barra snapped. 'You're too tired and you know it.'

He merely shrugged.

'If you end up with a stroke,' Barra went on, 'who's going to track this thing down? Don't tell me that there are plenty of other masters in the guild. Sure there are, but which one of them are you going to trust?'

'You have a point, Sis. I'm willing to bet that most of the guild is one hundred per cent loyal to their oaths. Most. But who's the traitor, huh? I just can't figure out what he's going to get out of this. Or she. The last time it was extortion – they wanted lots of money, a little revenge, a ride off planet. I just can't believe that anyone would be that stupid again.'

'Neither can I,' she agreed. 'The money's not worth the risk of being hanged.'

'So it's got to be some bigger goal. But what? What in hell would drive someone to start ripping up the Map? What can they hope to get out of it?'

It was Barra's turn for the shrug. Rico had heard his mother and uncle chew over the problem a hundred times. They never got any farther than 'someone in the guild must have gone crazy'.

'Well,' Hi said at last. 'You're right. I need to get some sleep, and first thing in the morning I'll read over the report. Who saw the candle-like object?'

Rico felt his stomach clench.

'I did,' Barra said. 'From the Chameleon Gate. So there's no record of my route in the day's log.'

'What were you doing in the Gate? Not that I mind or anything. Just curious.'

Rico had to sit up. It seemed that every muscle in his body was going to spasm unless he moved. When Hi glanced his way, Rico found he couldn't look at him.

'Yeah, yeah, I get it.' Hi sounded amused in a weary sort of way. 'That's what's been eating you all day, isn't it, Rico? Don't worry. I'm not going to turn you over to the Discipline Committee.'

Rico felt his face burn worse than the candle had made it burn. He heard Barra laugh, just softly, and managed to look at her.

'Your uncle's sharp,' she said. 'That's why he's the head of the guild, and I'm just a lowly repair tech.'

'Lowly?' Hi snorted profoundly.

Rico gulped once for air, then steadied himself.

'Well, this is better, anyway,' Rico said. 'This way I can tell you everything I saw. If it saves the Map I don't much care what you do to me.'

'Yeah? Okay. Let me rephrase that question. Rico, what were *you* doing in the Gate? Joyriding?'

'Not exactly.' With all his will Rico forced himself to look at Hi. 'I wanted to see if Arno had left me a message in this drop we had. But I didn't want to leave a route record.'

'So you thought you'd try the Gate. Figures.' Hi sighed, briefly sad. 'You heard Arno talk about it, I'll bet. But then you saw this candle?'

'Yes, Sé, and I saw it blow up the Pansect construct. I had to tell someone, I mean that thing could kill somebody, maybe, and so I told Mom. And she said –'

'She'd lie for you,' Hi broke in. 'What do you think is going to happen to you?'

'Well, you'll probably kick me out of the guild.'

'I probably should, yeah, but I'm not going to. You know why?'

'No, Sé.'

'Because I can trust you, that's why. Remember what your mom and I were just talking about? Rico, something really big's going on with the guild. One of us, maybe more, is destroying everything the guild stands for. One of us is trying to crash the Map. Do you realize what it would mean if they succeed?'

Rico tried to agree but found he couldn't speak. The room had suddenly turned enormous and very, very silent. Hi and Barra looked at him, then at each other, then back to him.

'Disaster, of course,' Barra answered for him. 'Palace has the best Map in the Pinch – the most complete, the most heavily used. It survived the neutrino wave when a lot of other systems went down. We lost some of it in the Schism Wars, but not as much as other planets lost of theirs.'

'We have a lot of AIs left, is what it boils down to,' Hi said. 'There's Dee over on Nox. His scientific functions are in pretty good shape, and I doubt if he was ever configured for more than the research he's doing, anyway. Then there's Nimue, and I still have hopes your mom can bring her back online. There's what's left of Caliostro. And then Magnus, out in the swamps. He's another limited AI, of course, but what's left of him functions well. Damn good thing, when you think of how important those pumps are.'

'Compared to the other settled worlds,' Barra put in, 'we're rich. If the Palace Map goes down beyond repair, the whole Pinch will feel it.'

'Feel it?' Hi said. 'Hell, the whole Pinch will crash with it.'

The pool of lamplight seemed to have shrunk around them. When Rico looked away, he felt himself shiver.

PART TWO

When the alarm clock implant in the back of Hi's skull went off, it did nothing so crude as stimulate his neurons to 'hear' a noise. Rather, it induced neo-serotonin to flood the receptors in his cortex, so that he was not only awake, but wide awake and alert. He sat up in bed and listened for a brief moment to the dark silence of the compound. The house's autonomic functions – heat, humidity control, fungicide release, lights, fresh air intake – all transmitted information to another neural chip, this one in his cyberarm, so that he, the oldest member on planet of the Jons family, the master of this house in the most literal way possible, really could seem to hear it breathing around him.

On the wall just above his nightstand a comm screen blinked red with urgent code. His clock had picked up the transmission.

'On,' he said aloud.

The code cleared off to reveal Aleen. Her emerald hair hung in tangled curls round her face, utterly free of cosmetics. The flash of fear and the ripple of adrenaline that Hi felt had nothing to do with neural chips.

'What is it?' Hi said.

'Bad news.' Her voice sounded oddly tentative. 'Hi, I just got a call from my tame Protector. The one who released,' a long pause 'your son to me.'

'Yeah?' Hi knew, then, but he could pretend for a few more seconds that he didn't.

'Hi, they found Arno's body about an hour ago. Not far from the Spaceport gates. He'd been, well, murdered.'

There it was, the truth. No use pretending now.

'I take it he'd left The Close?'

'Yes. I tried to talk him into staying a couple more days. He wouldn't.'

'He just couldn't wait any longer, huh?' Hi got out of bed and stood looking at the blank wall rather than the screen. 'Well. Shit.'

'Hi, I can see you shaking. There's nothing wrong with crying.'

He turned dry eyes her way.

'Where's his body? I'll get dressed and go right down.'

Aleen sighed. On the screen her face seemed a little grey, more than a little exhausted.

'In the morgue at the Security Admin building. The one in Centre Sect.'

'Ah. Okay. I'll wake up Nju, then.'

'Yeah, don't go alone. Hi, uh, well, the Protector said it was pretty bad.'

Hi tried to speak and failed.

'I'll be in all day,' Aleen went on. 'If you want to drop by.'

'I can't think of anything I want more. Trouble is, I can't do it. Today's my nephew's investiture, and we've got a real problem on the Map. And now I've got to make, well, arrangements.'

'Oh. But Hi, I worry about you.'

It was an admission that would have pleased him at any other time. As it was, he stared at the wall and tried to think of nothing. When he looked back at the screen, Aleen had hung up.

He put a call through to Nju, then dressed and wiped his face down with depilatory. He let himself think of nothing but the Map, of the Candle on the Map, made himself rehearse every detail that Rico had told him the night before. The recital lasted him through the trip up to the landing pad on the roof. In the chilly silver light that did Palace for dawn, Nju was standing beside the aircar. With him, carrying her black sling-sack of scribing tablets and comm units, stood Jevon, dressed in a pale grey suit that matched her narrow grey eyes. Her long black hair hung perfectly, set in its tringlets and braids, studded here and there with a glass bead.

'What are you doing up?' Hi said to her.

'Nju woke me.' Her voice was soft, controlled. 'He said we had an emergency on our hands.'

From the waist Nju bowed to Hi.

'How could I deny her rightful place at your side?'

Jevon glanced back and forth between them with eyes that revealed nothing.

'Yeah, well, hell, I'm glad you're both here.' Hi paused and looked off at the brightening horizon, where he could see the lights of Tech Sect dimming down and winking out. 'We're going to Centre, Nju. Security Admin building.' He paused and took a deep breath. 'The morgue. Arno's dead. Someone killed him last night.'

Nju hissed, open-mouthed and feral, then threw back his head and wailed. Jevon never moved nor spoke, but tears welled in her eyes and ran.

'Yeah, I know,' Hi said. 'You don't have to come if you don't want to.'

'There will be forms and affidavits and things like that.' Her voice had gone very small, like a child's. 'Nju's right. It's my job.'

Yet once they'd reached the morgue, once they were walking down an echoing grey corridor on their way to identify the corpse, Hi regretted bringing his factor along. She walked in small steps, clutching her sling-sack in her arms, and looked only at the floor, counting tiles, he supposed, to keep from thinking. With them walked a chatty Protector in a brown office uniform, talking away while Nju glared at his back as if he were thinking of silencing the man with a knife.

'Brought him in at the ringing of the fours, Sé Jons. Too bad, isn't it, I'm real sorry, but well, you must have said goodbye to your son a long time ago, huh? When he took to the drugs, a real tragedy, but anyway they found him in an alley behind the parking structure at the Port. He'd been dumped there, not killed there, yeah, we're sure of that. Well, here we are, and maybe the lady would like to wait outside?'

They stopped before a pale green glass door, lettered with official glyphs and a sign, 'No Admittance Unaccompanied by an Officer'.

'I'll go in,' Jevon said, but her voice was almost too soft to hear.

'No,' Hi said. 'Leave it to me and Nju. Officer? Is there a chair?'

'I'll stay out here with her. The coroner's waiting for you inside, Sé Jons.'

The coroner, a tall woman with wound braids of grey hair, stood at a counter at the near end of an echoing white gymnasium of a room, cold enough to make Hi shiver and Nju's fur rise and fluff. She herself wore a white lab coat over a bulky sweater, bright red and sticking out at the sleeves and neck.

'Sé Jons?' she said. 'Well, first of all, let me offer my sympathy. Identifying the body is always hard on the family. But this time – well, prepare yourself. I think it must be some kind of drug-related killing. That's the only thing that'll explain it, gang rivalry, maybe, and they wanted to make an object lesson out of him. I'm very sorry.'

Hi and Nju followed her down the long room to a wall covered with drawers, a huge cabinet with each ID plate flickering with red readout. The coroner opened a drawer at about waist-height and pulled it out with the waft and reek of heavy chemicals. A long white cloth covered something roughly man-shaped. The coroner glanced at Hi and picked up a corner of the cloth.

'Are you ready?'

'Yeah, Sé. Go ahead.'

With a twitch of a practised hand the coroner flicked back just enough of the cloth to reveal a head, a face, Arno's face, but gone all pale and bluish – a mouth, twisted in frozen agony; a long thin slash down each cheek, crusted with black blood; and the eyes. Hi nearly gagged. The killer had pulled out his implants, then gouged out his flesh eye, leaving sockets filled only with blood, dry now and congealed. He was alive when they did that to him, Hi thought, and with the thought, he noticed one thing more and felt as if he'd turned as cold as the corpse. Arno's head was not attached to the body underneath the cloth.

'That's my son, all right,' he growled. 'What did they do to him?'

'You don't need to see more, Sé Jons.'

'What else did they do to him?'

'His whole body's been cut. Slashed like those cuts on his face. He bled to death, actually.'

Hi could only stare at the thing on the slab and wonder just how long it had taken Arno to die. Had the killer, had Vi-Kata, made one cut at a time and taunted him before he made the next? The coroner flipped the cloth back and released him.

'Just unofficially,' she said, 'those cuts look like Lep work. The retractile claws, you know. They tell me your son was a drug addict. A couple of the biggest dealers in Pleasure Sect are Leps. But this has to stay off the record – I'm just speculating.'

Nju began to chant under his breath, a few words repeated over and over. Hi could guess what they meant: vengeance. The coroner touched Hi's arm and made him look away.

'So you agree with our DNA scan identification of this body? Arno Jons y Perres?'

'Yeah.' Hi was surprised to find that he still had a voice. 'Yeah, I'm afraid I do. How soon can I – well – can I take him away?'

'That's for the investigating officer to decide, I'm afraid. Not long, though, a day or two.'

'Okay. My factor will be in touch.'

Nodding, the coroner slid the drawer shut. Nju threw his head back and howled, one long high note that echoed down the enormous room.

* * *

In the small grey room where he met with Riva, Vi-Kata sat cross-legged on the floor and waited as Riva always made him wait. Kata focused his concentration on the *li-iyi* in his lap – a braided silver rope, coiled in a complex pattern so that all of the hundreds of knots were visible. With one claw he touched each knot and murmured the Moment that it represented. That he did this and not a grandmother of his line meant sacrilege, but who else survived to perform the prayer? No-one but his coward of a brother and him.

'Vi-Kata.'

He opened his eyes to see Riva, or rather her revenant, sitting on a little stool in the corner of the room.

'Forgive my intrusion into your meditation.'

'I'm the one who should beg forgiveness.' He rested his hands on the coil to let his ancestors hear his shame. 'The girl's still alive.'

'I do not want the girl to trouble your soul. Let us concern ourselves with your victory. I've heard that the meddling cyber-master is dead.'

'He is.' Kata's crest lifted and rustled. 'I caught him on the streets at fifteen of the ones and took him to a place I'd prepared nearby. He didn't die till just past the fours. At the end he screamed, begging for death to set him free of his long dying.'

'You what?' For a moment the revenant froze and seemed to thin. 'Could anyone hear him?'

'Of course not. I'd chosen this place because it was soundproof. Let me tell you how I made the first cut. He could still see, then, though in a while I blinded him, so he'd have to face death in the utter dark of his own blood. I –'

'Enough!' The revenant flickered back to full life. 'Let me make sure I understand you. There were three hours when someone might have found you, three hours when he was still alive.'

'Well, yes, but we were well-hidden. I –'

'I don't want to hear excuses. This must never happen again. Do you understand me? It's too dangerous.'

Kata got up and stood, wrapping the *li-iyi* around his waist.

'Do you understand me, Kata?' Riva looked up at him with narrow eyes.

'I understand, and I obey, as I've always obeyed you.'

'Good. There's too much at risk for you to amuse yourself by playing with your kills.'

Kata's head snapped up. Riva sat on her stool and stroked her coils of knotted silk as calmly as a grandmother sitting in the hot sun of the home planet. Didn't she realize what she'd just said to him? Obviously not, and what an interesting thing that was! From far away, through the floor, he felt as much as heard the low throbbing sound change, as if a massive gear had ground.

'Have you been receiving your payments?' Riva said.

'I have, and thank you for your generosity. The Protectors have been looking for me, by the by, but they're clumsy fools. I'll stay hidden, safe enough. I'm ready for whatever job you have next.'

'Good, good. You know, of course, about this UJU movement among the humans.'

Vi-Kata pantomimed spitting on the floor.

'Just so,' Riva said, nodding. 'Most Leps here on Palace refuse to take it seriously. The Protectors will keep those bigots in line, they say. This is a civilized world, we'll be safe – I hear that constantly, and it sickens me. We must defend ourselves against this growing threat. What if UJU sends armed gangs into our sects and our streets? Will we be safe then?'

'Not in the least, no. Do you think that could happen?'

'I have very good information that UJU is considering just such a move, very good indeed. We must organize against them. We must convince our people that we need to organize against them and now, before it becomes too late.'

'Very true, but I'm not much of a public speaker.'

The revenant laughed, a low rumble of Lep laughter.

'I didn't bring you here for talk, no. I have other agents for that. Tell me something, Kata. Does rain ever fall from a clear sky?'

'No.'

'Do people hate without a cause?'

'No.'

'And have you ever drunk the pale yellow wine of Ri?'

'I have, many times.'

'Can you make this wine without crushing the ma'ill-ik fruit?'

'Of course not. What –'

The grandmother revenant held up one clawed hand for silence.

'If our people refuse to arm themselves,' she said, 'until after the human UJU scum have armed themselves, the streets will run with Lep blood. We must give the Lep cause to hate those who hate them.'

'Huh! The Peronida's laws should have done that already.'

'Yes, indeed, and I don't understand why they haven't. I think it's because the laws have only affected the few, not the many. Yes, there are no more Leps in the Cyberguild. There were five hundred and six to begin with. No Lep may receive a security clearance above a certain level, and so nine Leps lost their high-level passes. There are twenty other laws, but they all share one thing. With one exception they only affect the few, not the many.'

'The exception is the Tech Sect regulations, then?'

'Exactly. No Lep may own property in Tech Sect nor live there without a special clearance. Thousands upon thousands of Leps were forced to sell their homes at below value and move elsewhere. There isn't a Lep on planet who hasn't been affected or had a friend affected. And of all the regulations that's the one that still makes our people mutter and curse. We need other regulations to fire their blood, other chains so they may feel their weight.'

'But there's not going to be any. The war's been over for a long time. There are a few humans who have a sense of decency. They've put Peronida on a leash.'

'Then we need to let him off again. What if something stirred up the old hatreds? What if the human citizens of Palace began clamouring for Lep blood?'

Kata raised his crest and shook it.

'Riva! You're saying we need an outrage done.'

'Yes. Peronida's iron fist will slap us all down then. Once our people are furious, once they are frightened, then those of my grandsons who have tongues of gold will be listened to at last.'

There it was again. Where *had* she learned Gen, anyway? Aloud, Kata said, 'I understand, yes. I've met good men, here and there, while I've been living in the dark places of Palace, but except for young Sar Elen they lack passion. They lack hate.'

'Just so. Can you give them hate?'

'Oh yes.' Kata's crest rose. 'I can do it. But it's going to need a lot of thought.'

'Return to me tomorrow, at the twenty-twos, say, with ideas.'

'All right. I'm going to need help to carry out our plans. I suggest Sar Elen.'

'I agree.' She reached out one long hand and pointed. 'Your door is open.'

Sure enough, a black portal had appeared on the far wall. When Kata turned back to her, the revenant had disappeared.

That morning Kata walked the foggy streets for hours. Since the

Protectors were sweeping through Pleasure Sect, he risked taking a wiretrain to Service, where a good many of the displaced Leps lived. Although he saw plenty of Protectors there as well, he could keep moving and keep ahead of them; in walled Pleasure it was too easy to run a fugitive into a dead-end. Only once did he have to show his false papers, and they passed the quick archive check, all that this particular pair could muster with their portable unit.

As he walked, Kata thought of Riva and her flare of anger. Amuse yourself by playing with your kills! Why didn't she recognize the ritual, the death of the slow cuts that custom assigned to any enemy of long-standing? Why had she refused to listen to the proper recounting of the ritual? He was beginning to suspect that Riva had been born and raised on Palace in one of the decadent enclaves that aped human ways. Perhaps she wasn't even female, but had chosen that persona as a further disguise. Surely a real grandmother would know about the slow cuts.

But why, if she'd been raised on Palace, was her Gen so stilted? Whoever Riva really was, she'd never been properly educated in true Lep ways. That much was clear. Kata realized that he'd have to keep his plans for the L'Var girl strictly secret. He'd been hoping that Riva would eventually relent, knowing how much Vida's death would mean to him, how shaming it would be for him to leave her alive. But a person who could dismiss the death of the slow cuts? No.

Every now and then as he walked he passed vidscreens, flickering silver with news, or public posting screens, where cheap adverts scrolled by announcing used goods for sale, the grand openings of shops, public health warnings, that sort of thing. Finally, as he turned down an alleyway, one poster caught his eye. On Eighteen Gust, just eight days away, UJU was going to hold a public rally with speakers, musical entertainment, and free literature. How many humans would they draw? Thousands, probably, all packed together in an open-air amphitheatre. Kata stood in front of the poster for a long time, his crest waving in delight.

Breakfast in a guest suite at Government House meant a parade of saccule waiters, bearing white linen and porcelain dishes, fruit juices and herbed drinks, protein blocks sliced and textured under rich green sauces, breads plain or stuffed with soy cheese, seed cakes and little pastries, twisted into knots and glazed to a high sheen. Vida and Samante sat opposite each other at the table by the window and looked out on the garden, green and rustling in the rising morning breeze. In the cold light Samante's black hair, back in its business-like braids, shone with bluish highlights.

'So you've been busy?' Samante said.

'You bet. When I got up this morning, I accessed the public databanks. You know what? You can reach a lot more of them here than you could in Pleasure, an awful lot more.'

'Well, yes, I should think so. You found the search utilities, then.'

'Yeah.' Vida smiled, thinking of Calios, who had discovered a good many interesting things. 'I hadn't realized how big the L'Var holdings were – are, really. It's strange, but it's the lawsuits that have kept them safe. They'd have been broken up a long time ago if it weren't for all those suits against Vanna.'

'I gather there are a lot of L'Var cousins. The ones who weren't culpable or genotype matches, I mean.'

'Oh yeah. I imagine they're all going to hate me, because of the money. If Vanna's forced to turn it over to anyone, it's going to be me, now. But at least she'll have to pay their legal fees. And it's not like I'll actually have it, not to spend it or something. It'll end up tied up in trusts, and I'll only get the interest in some kind of allowance. It should be plenty to let me have a proper suite and stuff like that, though. I figure that I'm supposed to put on a kind of a show with the way I live, like aristocrats do.'

Samante was listening with an odd expression on her face, a small pleasant smile undermined by a certain bewilderment in her eyes.

'What's wrong?' Vida said. 'Have I got it all backwards?'

'Not at all. This is exactly what the cardinal told me yesterday, when he asked me to help you get settled. I'm just surprised that you've worked it out like this. Because you're so young, I mean.'

'Oh huh. Because I'm just a cheap cull from Pleasure, you mean.'

Samante winced and laid a half-eaten pastry down on her plate.

'Sé Vida, please. I do not think of you that way, not in the least.'

'Well, okay, I'm sorry. But that's what most people think, isn't it? You saw the way they looked at me last night.'

'Thanks to that little beast Anja.'

'I'll bet Vanna's gloating, too.'

Samante glanced round and laid a finger over her lips.

'Oh, right,' Vida said. 'I'm sorry. But I can't see how she'd have any illusions about me. About the way I feel about her, I mean.'

'She may think you're stupid. If so, good. Let her underestimate you.' Samante twisted in her chair and looked at the vidscreens, where a flowery landscape from some unnamed planet bloomed next to the inevitable tower graphs. 'You don't have the news on. We should be checking for your ratings.'

'My ratings?'

'Of course.' Samante got up and pitched her voice to reach the screen's sensors. 'Search on terms: Vida and L'Var, Wan and Peronida.'

The screen dimmed, but only briefly. A new graph began building: a small tower of yellow completely overshadowed by a rise of blue. Samante laughed as she sat down.

'Look at those!' she crowed. 'Vida, the public loved you last night! These are from your entrance into the reception hall. Look – now they're tipping in the interview ratings, too. The big green stack favours you, and that small orange slice doesn't.'

Vida stared, open-mouthed, as those towers faded and a new set appeared: Wan's unimpressive ratings of the morning before compared to the much higher blue stack of this day's.

'That's really something,' Vida said. 'Maybe it'll make him like me better. I mean, if he can see how useful this is.'

'Oh, that's so sad! You thinking of your first marriage contract as, well, only useful.'

'Samante!' Vida turned back and grinned at her. 'You're a romantic at heart.'

'Well, maybe so. But –'

'But what? What else would I have had? You know what I was going to do for my living. At least there's only one of him.'

Samante blushed scarlet.

'I'm sorry,' Vida said. 'Maybe I am just a cheap whore from Pleasure.'

'No, you're not. Never think of yourself that way, please. After all, there are plenty of people who are going to do it for you.' Samante paused for a sip of pale blue juice. 'I don't suppose you've had a chance to talk with Wan yet?'

'No. I've got a commcall in to his factor. I found the comm codes when I was looking around. So I put a call in to Leni, but I haven't heard back yet. From what Dukayn said last night, I probably won't till later and he sobers up.'

'Probably not. At some point Cardinal Roha will want to talk with you, but it's up to Brother Dav to set that appointment up. You're going to need to hire staff, and very soon.'

'Really? But what am I going to pay them with?'

'Well, Roha told me yesterday that he'd take care of things until the trust fund got straightened out. The order has funds from somewhere, he said, for this kind of thing. It'll be an interest-free loan.'

'That's great! I'll have to thank him. He's sure been awfully kind to me. I wonder why?'

'All I know is that your father was a friend of his.'

Her father. There he was again, Vida thought, the mysterious figure of Orin L'Var, who was simultaneously a traitor and a friend of priests. She would have to look at those files, sooner or later. There would be vidclips of her father, audio of his public speeches. She could see and hear him. Eventually.

'What are you going to do this morning?' Samante said.

'Well, I don't know. Study the databases, I suppose. There's an awful lot of stuff about Government House that I don't know.'

'The more you do know, the safer you'll be.' Samante helped herself to a roll flecked with bright red seeds. 'I hope I'm not stuffing myself too much?'

'What? Of course not.'

'Thank you. I'm supposed to have lunch with Uncle Wilso today, and that means a pretty meagre spread. He pinches every credit he earns, at least twice.'

'Why is he inviting you, then?'

'I don't know. Something unpleasant, I'll bet. If you'd like, I'll stop by here afterwards.'

'I would, yes, and thank you. But I must be keeping you away from your work.'

'I'm between jobs. When you start out as an interpreter, it takes you a while to find a good place. You get hired for all kinds of temporary jobs at first. You know how it goes on Palace. Being a Not-child's all very well, but until you're at least fifty . . .' She shrugged. 'The guildmasters have all the secure posts, not a journeyman like me.'

And that, Vida supposed, explained why a meagre lunch made a difference to Samante, and why she'd brought an old dress for the reception.

Wilso apparently offered Samante not just a cheap lunch but a short one as well. Vida spent the morning sitting cross-legged in a white silk chair and studying screens of data, memorizing as she went – first the L'Var holdings, down to the last credit that was a matter of public record; then the inheritance laws; finally the records of the entire thirteen years of legal proceedings against Vanna and her counter-suits in turn. Once Vida had those safely stowed in her memory, she took a plateful of leftover breakfast rolls, balanced it in her lap, and called up another important batch of files that Calios had discovered, an informal list and description of the sapients living in Government House in general and in particular the twin towers.

She was assuming that she'd have several hours before Samante returned, but she'd just started the profiles of the Peronidas when the door alarm buzzed, and a tiny image of Samante appeared in one corner of the screen. The interpreter's face was flushed, and her eyes seemed swollen. Vida gulped down her mouthful of bread.

'Open!'

The door slid back to let Samante enter, arranging as she did so a bright, tense smile.

'What's wrong?' Vida said. 'The lunch must have been awful.'

'The lunch was one glass of wine and a few crackers.' Samante threw her sling-sack onto the divan so hard that cushions flew. 'Why did Aunt Halla have to marry him? I hate him so much, I don't even care who's snooping to hear it!' She flopped into a chair near Vida's. 'He had a permanent position for me, he said.'

'And it was something loath?' Vida held out the plate of breads.

'Thank you.' Samante took a large fruit roll, but she only held it. 'I have been reassigned to you as your factor.'

'Really? But, that's great! I mean, well isn't it?'

'I'm an interpreter, damn it all! Vida, it's not you. Do please understand that. But I've trained all my life to be a bridge between languages, to understand the thoughts under the words, to find common ground between sapients. I even thought once . . . I thought, maybe I'd be the one to find a new sapient race and learn their language. And now what? I'm to be your factor. Your glorified secretary, keeping your appointments, making dinner reservations, answering interview requests, buying clothes.'

'I'm sorry, I really am. You don't have to be my factor, do you? I'll understand if you just tell him no.'

'I can't just tell him no.' Samante laughed, but it was a bitter, cracked little sound.

'Because of the money?'

'Mostly, yes. I have none of my own. The Dinisa clan never had money, only brains and a grand old genotype. Then my aunt married that beastly little bigot. What choice do I have about my posting? I'm not a chief patron like Wilso is. I'm not even an heir. My mother died in a wiretrain accident, and my father never had any grasp of finances. If not for my dear law-uncle Wilso – well, I wouldn't have even been allowed to train as an interpreter, let alone get a posting to Government House. He spent all last night at the reception getting this appointment for me – calling in favours, making political promises, that kind of thing. If I turn it down now, he might ship me off to some empty Ag Sect to teach a patron's children how to sound cultured, or make me a translator at the saccule market – anything.'

'There's one thing I don't get. Why does he want you to take this job?'

'For the influence, Vida. Come along – think! You're going to be rich. You're going to be the First Citizen's lawdaughter. Cardinal Roha himself is taking an interest in you. If I'm your factor, then the Dinisa clan has something to bargain with – access to you.'

'Oh.' Vida felt her stomach twist, but for her own sake, not Samante's. 'And if I told Wilso that I didn't want you?'

'It would be worse. He might even unguild me. I told you that I was well-trained, didn't I? You told me that I was like a pet dog, didn't you? Why do you think I was so irked by that? Well, now I have to do what my master says.'

Samante remembered her fruit roll and bit into it savagely. When pastry flakes scattered she let them fall. Vida glanced at the screen-full of profiles.

'Clear. Resume landscape programming.'

Both women stared at a night view of the phosphorescent seas of equatorial Souk. In the background Hirrel sang like limpid flutes.

'All right,' Vida said at last. 'So, you're going to be my factor, whether you want to or not. Or, rather, you're going to do all the things a factor does – for now. You're really my interpreter. I mean, the Chief Interpreter of the L'Var clan.'

Samante smiled, but only briefly, and went on eating.

'No, really!' Vida went on. 'I've been reading stuff all morning. The L'Vars were a noble house, once, and we come from the first settlers. They always had an interpreter on their staff, because they received guests from all over the Pinch, and they did business on Souk. One of these days, Samante, we'll be great again, and then I'll have a new factor, and you'll have a staff of experts under you.'

Samante brushed crumbs from her lap, then looked up with a fixed smile.

'Is that a promise, Sé Vida?'

'Of course it is, Chief Interpreter.'

'Then thank you, and I'll accept the post with your family and house. Oh God, I'm afraid to laugh – I'll start crying if I do.'

'Don't laugh. I'm serious. I had a Garang bodyguard once who told me that I was destined for great things. They always say Garang can tell.'

'Well, that's true, so they do. Very well. Thank you, Sé Vida. I'd best start filling in, then, until you can hire that real factor.' She sighed, got up, and looked at the mess round her chair. 'And the first thing I'd better do is get us a servant. And a proper suite. You'll have to tell me how much I can spend for it.'

'Okay. I've got that all figured out, actually. I went on studying while you were gone. I was raised to be good with money, you know.'

'Yes? Well, yes, I suppose you were.' Samante brushed a few more crumbs from her plain grey dress. 'You know what the worst thing was, Vida?'

'No, what?'

'Wilso told me he was doing this for my own good.' Samante looked up on the edge of a snarl. 'So I didn't have to deal with all those aliens, he said. He just couldn't stand to have his lawniece being forced to associate with Leps. *Forced* to! I hope he – I hope he gets Kephalon Plague and rots!'

Every master of the Map could access it without being physically at guild headquarters, and for Hi it was easier than most. After he'd left the Security Admin building, he'd realized that he simply could not face people he knew without some time to himself. Since Jevon had set up Rico's investiture ceremony for later that day, there would be guests, a lot of guests and all of them important. He returned to the compound, told Barra the news – Rico was still asleep – then went to his office, a small but soundproof room down a corridor just off the gather.

For a moment he stood in the middle of the room and tried to remember what he was doing there. All around him were his familiar things: his desk, made of black wood shipped all the way from Belie; a scatter of brightly coloured rugs on the tile floor; a pair of tinted engravings hanging on one wall. On the desk stood a set of holocubes displaying pictures of Arno and Rico at various young ages, a two-foot high brass statuette of a severely stylized

Garang warrior, and a scatter of storage cubes, filled with guild business. The statuette, ancient and fabulously expensive, had been a parting gift from Arno's mother, Celise, when their contract had expired. He couldn't remember what he'd given her in return.

Celise. He would have to tell her about their son. He picked up the statuette, cold and hard in his hands, heavy, too, with the heft of real metal. Since Celise lived on Belie, the public news would take weeks to reach her, if indeed a small item like the death of another drug addict even made it onto one of the interplanetary news services. He could contact her through the Hypermap much faster, reach her himself and tell her as gently as possible. Not just yet. Not right now. He set the statuette down again and turned away.

Guild business. The Pansect crash. Of course – that was what he was doing in his office. He sat down in his Mapstation chair and powered the unit on. Fortunately, he'd not eaten that morning. This particular jaunt on the Map was going to require drugs, and a full stomach would only be a liability. Or should he just do a quick reconnaissance?

'Time?'

Behind his eyes the clock chip flashed numbers: just half of the nines. And the investiture was when? He couldn't remember. He glanced at the screen on the wall.

'Daily schedule. Search on investiture and plans.'

Jevon's image appeared, smiling, dressed in the blue dress she'd worn the day before. In the corner of the screen a spiral icon whirled, marking the image as a recording.

'Patron Jons, I've set the time of the investiture at the twelves. The refreshments will be served at the thirteens. Afterward, there will be a newsgrid interview for you and Rico, but I've yet to choose a bid from the competing stations. After –'

'Stop. Clear.'

So, the thing started at the twelves; he'd better be ready before that. Details, there were always details. So what kind of time did he have now? For some reason this minor decision, this everyday judgment, seemed impossibly difficult. Did he have enough time to tank himself up on cyberdrugs or not? Come on, Jons, he told himself. What's so wrong?

And then, of course, he remembered. His only child lay not merely dead but mutilated. He made himself think of Arno's face – if he was going to cry, he'd better get it over with. For months he'd been acting out an elaborate charade about Arno, that he was as good as dead, that he was disowned, gone, out of his father's life forever. He would need to keep the act up now. In the monitor he could see a ghost of his own face, slack-mouthed, the hair rumpled in six directions. He'd never combed it, he assumed. But no tears, no feeling of tears. Shock. He was in shock. That had to be it.

There remained the Map and the Candle. No drugs, not now. If he was in shock, he couldn't handle them. That decision at least he could make. He leaned back, pulling up his shirt-sleeve, and laid his cyberarm over the connector plates on the chair with the familiar tremor of electricity through his system. All at once it seemed that he had many eyes and many fields of vision, many ears and many voices to hear, each perfectly meaningful and clear.

When he shut his physical eyes, it seemed he floated on this sea of data, all red and yellow, silver and black, fields of numbers, lists of words, readout and input from twenty different regulators on the Map. After so many years, his brain had adapted to the Map, had perhaps even become part of the Map, but at the least had grown the pathways it needed to integrate all his chips and implants into itself. The cyberdrugs contained various synthetic hormones that encouraged the growth of axions and neurons within the brain, allowing it to develop new pathways in response to new functions. After all, what was the brain but patterning and relationship, a constantly adapting field of memory and sensory input? Like all masters, Hi now had a consciousness different than that of any normal human being. His brain had adapted to new senses and built the delicate webs of memory it needed to operate them.

Route marks, for instance – he only needed to subvocalize 'route marks' to see them, long lists and trails, words and diagrams not so much side by side as co-mingled. He received sensory impressions that were both words and diagrams at the same time in a way that something as linear as speech could never describe. The numbers, though, were different, listing down a field in his brain beside the word-diagram constructs. By subvocalizing he could change the field to read back in time, back to the day before – early, when Rico was heading toward Pansect Media. He could also move the field in space to centre around Pansect's Map address. Route marks and routes appeared, heading to and from, bypassing, but always the number code contained Pansect's three-digit ID. The Chameleon Gate had left no trace; neither had anyone else but Pansect employees – unless of course this rogue master had managed to disguise himself as a Pansect employee. Those cheaper operations could get pretty lax about security.

Hi moved the field up a level on the Map, until behind his eyes he saw the same map that Rico had seen, speeding over Tech Sect with its rivers of blue development lines and dots for stations. Pansect's area had turned into one big black spot, as charred as burnt paper. Again, he found not a single trace of route markings beyond the completely expected and normal ones. What if this rogue master controlled an artifact like the Chameleon Gate? A frightening possibility, that. As Hi watched, a slither of new route markings appeared, but all included the ID of the Cyberguild, 666. Someone had told him once that this ID, the three sixes, contained an ancient joke, but Hi had forgotten what it was.

Dian Wynn's code, and two journeymen – she was starting the repair job for Pansect, placing construct on the Map as fast as the two journeymen could create the code back at their waking-mind terminals in guild headquarters. For a few minutes Hi floated above, wondering what he was doing there. Someone else had already done all the preliminary work. Another master had compiled a full report. It would be sitting in his mail box, waiting for him. Once he got around to reading it, he could see if any of the information there jibed with the data from Arno about the mysterious tip and the dump at the Caliostro firewall. Arno.

'Time?'

The numbers flashed in green: forty after the tens. Time ran fast when you were on the Map. Undrugged, his body began to impinge on his thinking – part of him felt numb, part ached. In his mind the fields of numbers were receding, growing faint; the words faded. Hi no longer needed elaborate constructs and gates to leave the Map. He opened his eyes, sat up, wiggled the cyberarm free, and saw on his screen code for an incoming call from Media Guild headquarters, from the master of the guild himself. He could guess what that was about. Some apprentice intake, stuck with the bottom-level job of hanging round the morgue, had learned of Arno's murder.

Hi let the screen blink unanswered and stood up. He needed to comb his hair, needed to dress in full ceremonial robes, needed maybe to eat, even, though his stomach never growled or complained. He stood for a moment rubbing his face with both hands, then decided that what he really needed was to get out of this office and into the open air.

Out behind the compound lay a formal garden, filled now with caterers and workers. In the middle of the turquoise lawn some Leps were snapping together a temporary stage while human men stood by with dark blue and gold drop cloths; up on the garden wall behind the stage, two human women were hanging a comm system. Caterers in spotless white coats set up trestle tables in the spotty shade of fern trees. In the midst of it all stood Jevon, her scriber tucked in one arm. When she saw Hi, she came hurrying over. Although normally she wore little make-up, her eyes were heavily darkened – to hide the crying she'd done, he supposed.

'Master Jons, I have the investiture invitation list for you, your speech is queued on the podium, and the follow-up interview has been granted to Tarick Avon.'

'From Pansect? Good. That will put them in a better mood about the Cyberguild.'

'Theirs wasn't the highest bid, but I wrung a couple of concessions out of them. I marked a couple of family subjects off-limits, and they agreed.'

'Great! Sounds like you did your usual top job.'

Normally she would have acknowledged the praise, but now she merely glanced away, making him remember that he'd never bothered to smooth over the unpleasantness about his trip to Pleasure.

'Look, I was out of line that night, the festival of Calios, I mean. You were right: I had no business running around without a bodyguard. And I sure had no right to shoot my mouth off at you. I know you were only doing your job.'

'You're the chief patron. I'm only your factor. I shouldn't have argued with you.'

'Yes, you should have. Look, any time I make an ass of myself, it's part of your job to tell me.'

At that she looked at him with the beginning of a smile.

'The day before the festival, weren't we talking about a raise?' Hi went on. 'Jump yourself a pay grade.'

'A whole – well, thank you, Sé!' She did smile, then, only to freeze, to look away and let the smile fade fast.

'What's wrong?' Hi said.

'Nothing. I mean. Well. What's happened.'

'Oh. Yeah, that. Well, that's going to be with us for a long time.' The act, he reminded himself. For God's sake, don't forget how you're supposed to act. 'I'm sorry, too, Jevon, but I mourned him a long time ago, when he checked himself out of that hospital and hit the streets.'

Jevon seemed to be watching the caterers, who had begun to cover the tables with seal-on sheeting from a big blue roll.

'Well,' Hi said. 'There wasn't anything else I could do.'

'If you say so, Sé Hivel.'

'Now hey, wait a minute! It's not like I didn't try to get him to clean up.'

'I know, Sé. It's not my place to be discussing this with you. If you have no more orders, I need to tend to things out here.'

Hi found himself wondering why he could think of nothing more to say about Arno, whether true or false. Shock. The word was acquiring a certain magic.

'One more thing,' Hi said. 'Tomorrow Rico and I will be moving to Government House. We'll need transports and lift bots, things like that. You'll be coming with us, of course, and Nju and a few of the other staff members.'

Jevon stared, her mouth gaping.

'Keep it quiet for now,' Hi went on. 'But I want it all over the screens tomorrow, okay? I'll brief you tonight, but the gist is that the Cyberguild's finally won back some old privileges.'

'Of course, Sé, of course. I can start the arrangements during the ceremony.'

'You don't want to sit down for a minute and watch? You'll need the rest.'

'No, Sé.' Her voice shook and badly. 'I don't want to watch.'

Before he could say another word, Jevon turned and marched off, clutching her scriber. All at once a hundred small things fell into place, a hundred memories of Jevon smiling when Arno came into a room, of Arno perched on the corner of her desk, telling her with a grin some long involved story while she smiled up at him. Hi was too stunned even to swear, that he would never have noticed their affair until now, when it was too late to signal his lack of censure. For a moment he watched her, standing straight and proud in a suit as grey as the turgid sky; then he turned and went back into the house to look for Rico.

Hi found his nephew up in the boy's bedroom, where Rico was being helped into his dress clothes by a pair of saccules, wearing midnight blue sashes over their usual grey shifts. Today Rico would become a journeyman as well as the heir to his clan. No more apprentice's smock for him – he wore trousers and a tight-fitting jacket, all in guild blue, with the details of collar and sleeve picked out in gold piping.

'Hey, kid,' Hi said. 'You look great.'

'Yeah?' Rico turned round, and his face looked as Hi's must have – dead pale, blank eyed, rigid with the stress of carrying on with the day. 'Mom says I look like a scarecrow. I don't even know what that is.'

'Some kind of agricultural gadget.' Hi glanced at the saccules, who were leaning against each other and smelling sour with anxiety. 'Leave us alone, guys. Go get something to eat.'

Squeaking and honking, they scurried out. When the door shut behind them Hi sat down on the edge of Rico's narrow bed. He meant only to yawn, but the sound came out sounding more like a moan. Rico caught his breath in a sob, but when Hi looked, he found his nephew dry-eyed.

'I can't cry either,' Hi said. 'It's the shock.'

Too late he realized that he'd let the act slip. Rico sat down on the chair of his school desk, which stood at right angles to the bed. The top lay empty of cartridges and printout; a dust cloth covered the small Mapstation; the desk and chair both looked much too small for him.

'I mean, uh, I had to think of Arno as dead a long time ago,' Hi said. 'But it's still a shock.'

'You don't have to lie to me,' Rico said. 'Arno left me a message, telling me the truth. Uncle Hi? Remember the festival day, when I got so mad at you? I'm sorry. I didn't understand then, about his working undercover.'

'He – you?' Hi turned furious – briefly. 'Well, hell, doesn't matter now.'

'Yeah. Guess not. Do we have to go on pretending? Not about what he was doing – about . . . about how we feel.'

'I do. You don't. Everyone knows how close you and Arno were.'

'Okay. I don't mind lying about the work he was doing, but I just can't lie about . . .' Rico let his voice trail away.

'Well, yeah.'

From outside drifted music. Jevon had apparently picked re-creations of ancient music for the day's event, and they listened together to the sound of harps and flutes, some small percussion instrument, some instrument with many metal strings. Kephalon music. Hi placed it at last. Music from a dead planet for a dead son. It seemed appropriate.

'Uncle Hi?' Rico said at last. 'Someone needs to keep on with what he was doing.'

'Yeah, so they do. One of the last things he told me was that he figured you were the only one good enough to pick up where he left off.'

Rico almost wept – Hi could see it in the slackness of his mouth, the pain in his eyes – but the boy choked it back.

'But you're going to do it openly,' Hi went on. 'No more elaborate dodges. We've got to move fast, for one thing. The attacks on the Map are a lot worse than when he started looking into the problem.'

'I figured that.'

'By the Eye, we need help! Two of us aren't enough. There's one cybermaster in particular that I really want to bring into this. Him I know I could trust. But I can't use him, thanks to the goddamned new laws. He's a Lep. Ri Tal Molos. Ever heard of him, kid?'

'The Molos Utilities?'

'That's the one, yeah. Goddamn laws! I've worked my butt off, trying to get them repealed, but there's always some goddamn group like this lousy UJU movement to keep the newsgrids stirred up.' Hi was surprised at how suddenly good it felt to be angry. 'Now there's a group that could use a little suppressing, if you ask me. Why the hell should they go hiding behind the free speech laws when they won't let other groups speak freely? Them and their damned vandalism! No-one even knows what their lousy name stands for. Round them all up, that's what the Peronida ought to do, round them all up and send them to the education camps!'

'Sé Hivel?' Jevon was standing in the doorway. 'Sé Barra asked me to tell you that it's time for you to dress.'

'Right, yeah. Sorry.' Hi got up and paused to lay a hand on Rico's shoulder. 'I'll see you in a while.'

'Sure.' Rico glanced at Jevon. 'Tell my mom I'll be right down, will you? I've just got to think for a minute.'

Much to his horror, Hi found the gather filled with guests, and the only convenient route to his wing of the compound lay through it. Muttering apologies, calling out greetings, he walked in, kept walking, kept muttering, until he reached the far door and came face-to-face with Dian Wynn, Rico's teacher, stout and impressive in her master's robes. She touched his arm with two fingers.

'Jons, you don't have to apologize for being late. We've all heard the awful news by now. I'm just surprised you didn't cancel this get-together.'

'Oh, well, that wouldn't have been fair to Rico.' Hi forced the muscles of his mouth to relax into the semblance of detachment. 'As for Arno, hell, he was dead to me months ago. And now that's the end of that. Too bad. Arno could've been a good cybe, if he hadn't taken to the drugs like a jadewing to the air.'

Wynn nodded, sadly but in agreement. When Hi glanced round, he saw the same or very similar expressions on the faces of the other guests. Only Barra, standing by the window, watched him with one eyebrow raised. She didn't believe a word of it, he knew, and of course, she was right.

'Well, I'd better get dressed,' Hi said. 'It's time to invest a new heir. The old one's dead and gone, right? Life goes on.'

They nodded, sighed, murmured condolences. One more obstacle stood between Hi and the safety of the door, Ymel Rethe, a cybermaster who liked to fancy himself the second-in-command of the guild. He had the years of experience, yes, and he had the skills, but at times Hi found himself wondering if this were the Map vandal, this pale and muscular man who dyed his beard and moustache in a brindle of azure and turquoise. He had no proof, unless you could count Rethe's taste for petty malice proof, but Hi's intuition went off like an alarm every time he saw the man.

'So sorry, Jons,' Ymel said. His dark voice rumbled like distant thunder. 'Damn! This is a bad day for the guild.'

'Yeah, sure is.'

Ymel glanced around and whispered.

'Interesting choice you made, to replace Arno, I mean.'

'Yeah? I see this as a family matter, not a guild matter.'

Ymel raised one turquoise eyebrow.

'Scuze,' Hi snapped. 'I've got to get dressed.'

Hi stepped round him and dodged through the door into his private hallway. He found himself thinking of Rico more than of Arno and felt his throat tighten over tears. It was time to bring another child into the line of fire.

Rico would always remember the investiture as one of the worst moments of his life. At least he could grieve, unlike his uncle, but still, he was forced to smear his cousin's memory with lies. When he walked into the gather, Gran handed him a drink, fruit juice heavily laced with alcohol, which normally Rico left alone. That afternoon he needed it. It seemed that every guildmaster there had to wag a solemn finger in his face and warn him about the terrible evils of abusing cyberdrugs. Each time Rico would have to agree and shake his head sadly, that his brilliant cousin had fallen so low.

The ceremony itself was mercifully brief. Hi simply announced that he'd jettisoned his prepared speech to save Rico the agony of sitting on a stage when he was in mourning, and the assembled guests all clapped, solemnly but with one eye on the refreshment tables under the fern trees.

'You all know why we're here,' Hi went on. 'I publicly acknowledge Rico Hernanes y Jons, my sister's son, as my full heir. All the legal forms have been transmitted and registered. You can always look them up if you don't believe me.'

A few guests managed a chuckle at this attempt at a joke.

'So, well, one thing I'll say about Arno. He loved a party. Why don't you all remember him by making this event a good one? He would have liked that.'

The guests clapped. Hi left the podium and gestured to Jevon, who started the music again. The ceremony was over.

Rico considered another drink, but his head throbbed from the last one. He'd never eaten breakfast, faced as he had been with Barra's news when he'd woken. When one of the caterer's trained saccules passed with a tray of bright purple ices, he grabbed one, then let it melt in its paper cup until he could sip the sugary result. Guests came and went, stopping to congratulate or commiserate, while he stood on the turquoise lawn by the white garden wall with a fixed smile on his face.

The worst was Pukosu, flouncing up to him in her blue apprentice's smock. She made a great show of stroking the sleeve of his jacket while her big brown eyes, as hard as ever, judged his reaction.

'Oh, I'm so looking forward to getting one of these of my own,' she said. 'The journeyman's coat, I mean. You're so lucky, Rico.'

The stress on the word, lucky, was faint but unmistakable.

'I wouldn't call it luck,' he snapped. 'I'd give anything to have Arno here instead of me.'

'You probably would, yes. You're that type.'

Before he could think of a suitably nasty answer, she smiled and trotted off to join Ymel Rethe, her mentor in the guild.

After a while everyone ignored Rico and began to chew over the week's gossip with their plates of refreshments – the last of the

L'Vars found, and wasn't he a clever one, that Peronida, wasting no time in marrying her off to his son?

'It's the money, of course,' ran the assembled opinion. 'And a chance to show Vanna that he can be his own master if he wants to.'

No-one mentioned Wan, Rico noticed, only Karlo. Finally he asked Dian Wynn about it, when she swept up to him to offer her congratulations. She'd done her auburn hair into a tower of curls for the occasion and brought with her a youngish blond man wearing the green journeyman's coat, piped with brown, of the Biotech Guild. She introduced him as Payder.

'I don't get this,' Rico said. 'You'd think Vida was marrying Karlo.'

'Well, my dear Rico,' Wynn said with a wink in Payder's direction. 'Everyone knows that Karlo writes the code and Wan just runs it. I'm afraid he inherited his dear mother's brains as well as her looks.'

Rico stared, puzzled.

'You – a decent young fellow, aren't you?' Wynn was smiling at him. 'I was being catty, dear. His mother's a holostar. Brains are not part of her resumé.'

Rico dutifully laughed. He'd learned to do dutiful laughs during the years he'd spent under Wynn's tutelage. He noticed that Payder laughed, too, but a little louder.

'Well, anyway,' Rico said. 'I hope Wan's got the brains to appreciate what he's getting.'

'Doesn't take brains for that,' Payder broke in, grinning. 'She's a sexy little number, isn't she? And one of those girls from Pleasure.'

'She wasn't ever Marked,' Rico snapped.

'Oh yeah, but I bet she knows all there is to know already.' Payder went on grinning. 'They train their girls with VR, you know. They're technically virgins, sure, but. Heh. I'd like to run a few tapes with her, myself.'

Rico's hand tightened on his fortunately empty paper cup and collapsed it. Payder stepped back sharply, the grin gone.

'I think, Payder dear,' Wynn said, 'that Rico has made the acquaintance of Sé L'Var in some social way.'

'Oh well, hey, yeah, sorry. Didn't mean to insult a friend of yours. You know?'

'Sure.' Rico let out his breath in a long sigh. 'Just keep in mind that she's not what you think. Okay?'

Payder forced out a watery smile, muttered something about getting another drink, and dashed. Wynn raised one orange eyebrow in Rico's direction. When he merely looked at her, she laughed.

'My last little lesson for you, Rico,' she said. 'Learn to hide these things better. Nothing a man like Payder says is going to harm your friend, not one bit. She could buy and sell twenty of him. What none of them says matters. Do you understand that?'

'Yes, Sé. And thanks.'

With a little nod Wynn moved off, gliding like a tower through the chattering guests. Rico looked at the smashed cup in his hand and wondered if this was what love felt like.

Out of respect for the family's mourning, the guests left early, fading out on a long wave of condolences until by the fifteens only the caterers remained in the garden. Hi was just escorting Ymel to the door in order to savour the pleasure of having him gone when Jevon marched up to him.

'Tarick Avon in ten minutes, Sé,' she announced.

'Can't we just put him off?'

'No. If you do, we'll be swarmed by gridjockeys. I made it one of the terms of his exclusive – he keeps the rest of the pack off our lawn. He said he'd bring Garang with him.'

'You know something, kid? You're brilliant. Okay. Where's Rico?'

'Sé Barra's fetching him. Oh, and Patron Jons? There's a lot of food left. The caterer wants to know if he should pack it for storage.'

'Tell him no. Get our servants out here and let them gorge themselves. You know how saccules love to eat. And hey, his guys can join in, if he'll let them.'

'Oh, I'm sure he will. I'll tell him.'

Ymel had been listening to all of this with his usual bemused expression, one raised eyebrow over the glitter of his simtil left eye.

'Something wrong?' Hi said.

'Oh no. I was just thinking that someone else could always take over this part of your job – the interviews I mean – if you don't care for them.'

'This interview's about the family matter, too.'

'Ah.'

For a moment they considered each other, Ymel smiling a little through his brindled beard. Hi believed him, all right, about his being ready to take over as much of the guildmaster's job as Hi would let him sink his fangs into. For a moment he wondered if he really should go through with the move to Government House – but saving the Map meant a great deal more than guarding his position in the guild.

'Well, good to see you,' Hi said. 'Gotta run.'

'Of course. See you at the next guild meeting.'

Hi lingered in the hallway for a moment watching old Gran show Ymel out. What if, just for instance, just as a speculation, what if Ymel thought he could cause a limited crash on the Map and then step in to save the day, the only master who could repair that mysterious damage? You don't have any proof, Hi told himself. Not yet anyway. With a shake of his head he turned away, then hurried to the gather for his interview.

Tarick Avon was slender and not particularly tall, but under the rainbow-striped robes of a master of the Media Guild, he was lean and muscled, and even sitting still in one of the big beige chairs he gave the impression of a man of immense physical energy. Although he had the usual cluster of audio pickup and transmit chips visible in the back of his skull – he was going quite heavily bald for a man so young, not even sixty yet – Avon had brought along a pix, a young Lep woman wearing the long striped kilt of a journeyman, who said nothing during the entire proceedings, merely paced around, pointing her camera hand.

At first the interview went smoothly. Avon got things started with some general talk about the possibility of reprogramming the Magnus AI, which gave Hi the welcome chance to heap scorn upon the idea. Turning more personal, Avon asked Rico questions about his apprenticeship and Hi some very tactfully phrased questions about Arno, so tactful that Hi knew the reporter was planning on springing something on them.

Sure enough, just as it seemed the interview was winding down, Avon turned to Hi with his charming smile.

'This Pansect transmission crash,' he said. 'It's part of the larger problems afflicting the Map these days, isn't it?'

Hi thought something foul. Aloud he said, 'It depends on what you mean by the larger problems. We've run into what we call a maintenance cluster. We all know that the Map is an ancient artifact, and just because it's so old we tend to think of it as uniform, that it was all built back in the mists of time. Well, of course that's not true. The Colonizers built it up piece by piece over a long time. At various points they'd patch in whole new areas. Now, the constructs that were patched at the same time tend to wear out together. It's fairly normal to hit these clusters. A real nuisance when they happen, of course.'

'I see.' Avon hesitated, half-convinced. 'They've happened before?'

'Oh yes. Let's see, I was just finishing my apprenticeship when the last big one occurred. I remember that within eighteen months we had five major dev lines go down and a number of station crashes. It was pretty frightening, but in the end, the guildmasters got everything up and functioning again. I'm sure you can find the details in the archives.'

'I'm sure I can, yes. Patron Jons, there's something our audience wants to know.' He paused, making sure the pix had his face in her point. 'During our morning call-in, we let you, our audience members, vote on which question you most wanted Hivel Jons, master of the Cyberguild, to answer for us today. So here it comes. What about this L'Var girl? Is she really a cybersorcerer?'

Hi forced himself to smile at a question grown tedious.

'No,' Hi said. 'The L'Var genotype produces an aptitude for cyberskills, not mysterious built-in powers.'

Avon looked disappointed. No doubt his audience shared the feeling. 'Not even a well, a kind of empathy for AI units?' he said.

'There's no such thing. AI units are not living creatures. They merely mimic the behaviour of living minds.' Hi smiled into the camera. 'If any of you would like more information on this subject, the Cyberguild has a series of download pamphlets, part of our ongoing effort to keep the people of Palace informed. Just go to Public Service Area Twelve, Confederated Guilds, and press the Cyberguild outreach icon.'

'Well, thank you, Patron Jons. I'm afraid, folks, that our time is up. This is Tarick Avon, signing off for Pansect Syndication Services. You all have a bright night!'

The camera sighed and snapped her outsized fingers once to turn her unit off. Avon stood, subvocalizing to his chips, but Hi decided that trusting him to keep them dead would be a mistake. He himself got up, leaving Rico sprawled miserably on the sofa, and began to stroll toward the vestibule, giving Avon no choice but to follow.

'My condolences on your loss, Patron,' Avon said. 'Your factor warned me that if I tried to dig for private data on that subject during our interview, I'd never get near you again.'

'Did she? Good.'

Avon flashed him a smile of near-convincing sincerity.

'But there's just one thing I'd really like to ask you, Sé, off the record, of course. The Protectors have been making public service spots on all the grids, asking for tips about some mysterious Lep from off planet. I can't help wondering if there's some connection between that and this sad event.'

'Yeah?' It took all of Hi's will to keep him from throwing the man out there and then. 'That's for the Protectors to say, not me.'

'Well, of course.' Avon hesitated for a long moment. 'I've had tips that the Outcast is back on planet.'

'No kidding? Hey, sounds like a big story for you, if it's true.'

'You don't have any thoughts on the matter?'

'I'm not a member of the Protectors' Guild.'

'Of course. Of course, Patron Jons. Well, thank you very much for your time. And if you ever need something fed onto the grid, you can count on me.'

Hi had Gran show Avon out, then returned to the gather. Long legs akimbo, Rico still sat slumped on the couch. Hi pulled off his robes and stood dangling them in one hand.

'It's over,' Hi said. 'Thank the Holy Eye.'

'Yeah.' Rico tipped his head back to look up at him.

'Uncle Hi? When you told the intake that AIs aren't alive, that you can't have any empathy for an AI, is that true?'

'Officially it's true. That's what it says in all the manuals and all the faqs. That's what you'd better say during your exams, if anyone asks you.'

'Yeah, I know all that. But is it?'

'No.'

Rico smiled for the first time all day.

'I didn't think it was,' the boy said. 'Is that why we can't make a new AI out here? We don't know how to make them come alive? The way the Colonizers did, I mean.'

'That's my guess, yeah. Hey, I'm glad to see that someone else agrees with my private theory.'

'Well, I asked Arno once, and he thought I was crazy.'

'He said I was, too. I can't support the theory with hard facts, so I keep my mouth shut about it. I suggest you do the same, but I'm real glad to find someone who shares my intuitions.'

'Okay, but I wonder.' Rico thought, chewing on his lower lip, for a moment. 'There's got to be evidence somewhere. If we can't deduce it from the way the AIs work, maybe there's an uncatalogued archive file somewhere.'

'With the mess the wars left things in, maybe we'll find one someday, but don't bet your allowance on it. I haven't had a lot of time lately to come up with new places to look, either. But hey, that's right, something I need to tell you. Maybe it's time to start looking for that evidence. We're moving into Government House tomorrow, you and me, Jevon, Nju, and maybe a couple more staff members. It's time for me to do a little work on Caliostro.'

'Government House?' Rico practically bounced off the couch. He was grinning on the edge of laughter. 'We're moving into Government House? We're going to live there?'

'Yeah, we sure are. Hey, I didn't think you'd be so excited. What is this? Ancient architecture's a hobby of yours?'

'Huh? Uh, no, no.' Rico wiped the grin away. 'Just uh well, it'll be a change.'

'Oh right. The L'Var girl.'

Rico blushed scarlet. Hi sighed with a shake of his head. One minute the kid was showing his brilliance; the next he was – was what? Acting like a normal man of twenty, that's what.

'Hey, it's all right, Rico. If I were eighty years younger, I might be giving you a little competition. She's some girl, huh?'

'Yeah.' Rico smiled in a grateful kind of way. 'But look, I know she's going to marry someone else. Okay?'

'Okay.' Hi felt his mind ticking over like a subroutine counting files. Vida brought with her a hell of a lot of influence, and he'd promised Aleen, after all, that he'd put himself in a position to look after her. 'Well, I shouldn't be saying this, but her marriage contract's a political one. In that situation, both partners have a lot of freedom, and well, arrangements get made. But a word to the wise; showing Wan up publicly would be a good way to die young. Government House is full of snoops who've got nothing better to do with their time than gossip.'

Rico stared, then nodded down at the carpet. 'Yeah,' he said at last. 'Yeah. I get you.'

They exchanged a smile. Arno's right, Hi thought. This kid is brilliant, figuring things out in his own quiet way, like about the AIs, and here I never noticed. Arno.

'Uncle Hi?' Rico grabbed his arm. 'You all right?'

'No.' Hi sank down and perched on the edge of a chair. 'No.'

And at last he could weep, in short convulsive sobs, while Rico stood by and wept with him.

* * *

The afternoon came and went, but no word from Leni. While Samante started hunting for a suitable suite in Government House, Vida stayed in her guest rooms and studied files. She kept checking the time, and at the fourteens put in a second call to her husband-to-be's factor. Still no answer. By the eighteens, Vida had had enough. She knew the address of Wan's suite; Calios found her a map file. Once she had the location memorized, she went into her bedroom and considered what to wear, finally settling on a business-like pair of black pants and a flowing black shirt. She was in no mood to look girlish.

Vida took a moment to record a message for Samante, then left, following the map in her mind. As she strode down the hall, her eyes moved constantly, taking in every detail: the strip-cameras whose lenses extended the length of every corridor; the strange intaglio designs on the blueglass walls, stamped by some ancient tool, long lost and forgotten; the elaborate floor tiles, blue, grey, and green, that formed spirals and mazes underfoot. After a hundred yards or so she noticed that while the floor pattern followed a regular repeat of six units, the abstract decorative units on the blueglass did not. Every now and then an entire brick did repeat, but always in a different context. The Colonizers had generated the patterns randomly, she supposed. From her school work she remembered that they'd been fond of the visual arts, but the course of study that Aleen had set up for her had spent little time on such amenities as art history.

Wan's suite stood on the same floor as her guest rooms, but on the other side of the tower. Walking there gave Vida a visceral understanding of the scale of the towers that not even her airhopper ride could supply. She could begin to imagine the size of the original colony ship, scavenged for these buildings. On each of its journeys from the Rim to this new world, over a hundred thousand people had travelled inside, though most had been stored in cryonic boxes to save air and water. She wondered about her guest rooms. Had they been a fancy cabin for important Colonists, or had the walls been installed a hundred years later, when everyone had given up all hope of ever returning to the Rim? Perhaps Calios would know, or at the least, perhaps he could find her some history archives.

The dark blue door to Wan's suite, like all doors in Government House, had an icon tablet inlay. Vida pressed 'Announce' and turned toward the sensor. For a long moment she waited, wondering if Leni would offer her the ultimate insult and refuse her entry.

She was just about to leave when the door slid open to reveal a human man, barely a Not-child from the look of him, all long dark hair and muscles and wearing nothing but a pair of tight grey trousers. He stared at her through the scent of hard alcohol.

'Who are you?' Vida snapped.

'Uh, Dan. Lord Dan of Motta. Uh, sorry.'

When he stepped back, she marched in, brushing past him before he could think to object. She found herself in a huge white room. Weapons racks were the only furniture she saw, each holding a different category: ancient rifles, antique laser guns, swords, clubs, and so on. Each piece sported a catalogue tag. On the far wall hung row after row of animal heads, creatures from every planet on the Pinch, each mounted on plastocrete plaques. In the centre hung a six-foot-long horn from a crested swamp worm, the most dangerous predator on planet.

'Well,' Vida said. 'At least my fiancé's well-organized.'

The countess' son merely stared at her, bewildered.

Through the open door to the next room came shouts and laughter. With young Motta trailing after, Vida walked through a side door and found a room even bigger than the last. Scattered round stood soft furniture in gaudy reds and oranges. Scattered on the furniture were young men and women, drinking, laughing, while saccules hurried through, serving drinks and food. Some of the guests Vida recognized from the reception of the night before – very young, all of them, and some of them not even of patron track rank.

No-one noticed Vida and Dan; they were all watching an impromptu sports-ring that had been set up in the middle of the room – a white carpet isolated by a long red ribbon strung from armless chairs. In the middle stood dark Wan and blonde, pale Leni, each dressed in casual dark trousers and white tunics, each wearing a heavy white vest that seemed to provide protection of a sort. They were fencing with the jarak-ar, a long grey stick with a metal ball at one end, the Garang Japat's idea of a parlour game.

Game or not, Vida saw immediately that Wan Peronida was a gifted athlete and a ferocious fighter. Leni fought well, for a game; he moved fast and gracefully, ducked in, feinted, danced back. Wan matched his feints, then snarled and moved in hard, thrusting from the side, slashing toward the back, always thrusting, driving, forcing Leni to move round and round the ring while he parried and dodged, more and more desperately, his grace and style forgotten.

The crowd began to jeer him, laughing out insults, waving empty glasses. Leni hesitated just long enough. Wan leapt forward and slammed his left fist down on Leni's weapon arm, then thrust with the jarak, slicing across his opponent's unprotected neck.

Leni screamed as the electrified ball flashed and crackled, then staggered once and fell to his knees. The smell of burnt flesh drifted in the air. Laughing out loud, Wan stepped back, raising his weapon above his head while his guests shrieked and howled and clapped so hard you would have thought that he'd vanquished a whole regiment of Garang. Wan lowered the jarak, flicked its power switch to off, then tossed it on the floor next to Leni. A saccule hurried forward with an icy glass on a tray. Wan took the drink, saluted the crowd, and drank half of it off. He glanced round, saw Vida, and went still, glaring at her over the rim of his drink.

'Well,' Wan said at last. 'If it isn't the little whore from Pleasure. Want to show us some tricks?'

Vida couldn't move, couldn't think.

'Hey, Peronida,' Dan said. 'That's loath, man.'

'Oh yeah?' Wan turned his beautiful green eyes, as hard as emeralds, his way. 'Shut up, Motta. Go eat mushroom manure.'

The guests all laughed, snickering in Vida's direction, as Dan shrugged and took a few steps back. Out in the ring Leni had managed to get to his feet. Wincing and swearing, he staggered a few steps, caught the ribbon and tripped, sending chairs smashing to the floor. Everyone laughed again and began yelling for more drinks.

'You know something, Peronida?' Vida snapped. 'You remind me of a bargecrawler, the kind who buys unbonded streetwalkers. You're not good enough for a real whore from Pleasure.'

The crowd roared, laughing and clapping, yelling out, 'She's right, Wan, she's right.' Wan flushed scarlet, then swung round, whipping out one hand and grabbing Leni hard by the collar of his tunic. Leni staggered, still dazed. Vida could see the black and red flash-burn on his neck.

'All right,' Wan snarled. 'You lost the jarak, so you've got to screw her. Lemme know if she's any good, okay? I've got to marry this cull, but I don't have to fuck her.'

Oddly enough, no-one laughed. Suddenly sober, Leni gulped and tried to pull away, but Wan held on.

'You fucking little coward,' Wan hissed. 'What's wrong with you?'

Leni made a strangled sort of noise. His eyes had gone wide with fear, Vida realized, and he was staring at something behind her.

'Good evening, Sé Wan,' said a cool voice.

Wan's face drained an ashy grey under the brown. The room went deadly silent. Vida spun round to see Dukayn, standing in the doorway. Dukayn's eyes moved around the room, pausing on each guest in turn. Some began to put down drinks and get out of chairs, but all in the cold silence.

'May I speak to you privately, Sé Wan?'

The remainder of the crowd rose, gabbling apologies, dropping things, kicking over drinks, stampeding for the door. Dan Motta touched Vida's arm.

'Sorry,' he muttered. 'You're pretty flash, know that?'

When Dukayn turned his limpid gaze Dan's way, the young lord bolted for the door like the rest of the party. Wan and Leni ended up alone out in the middle of their smashed gaming ring. Behind them the two saccule servants cowered against the wall and let out a stench of fear like vomit. Leni started to speak, thought better of it, then turned to Wan with a look that seemed to wish that Wan had killed him in the fight.

'Sé Lenobai?' Dukayn purred. 'Will you excuse us?'

Leni nodded vigorously, stepped over the ribbons, then dashed out of the room, still in his white vest.

'Well.' Wan finally found his voice. 'What do you want, Dukayn?'

'Your factor called me.' Dukayn turned to Vida. 'She got the message you left. I don't think it's wise for you to go running around alone.'

Vida nodded.

'As for you,' Dukayn returned to his leisurely study of Wan. 'I've just spoken to your father. He was wondering how you were getting along with your fiancée.'

Wan's green eyes flicked over Vida, then away.

'Oh, did he? Why doesn't he just screw her himself, if he's so damn desperate for heirs?'

Dukayn moved. All at once he was across the room and grabbing Wan by the throat. Vida gasped aloud. So fast! She had never seen anyone move so quickly, not even her self-defence teacher. When the two saccules rushed forward, Dukayn let go of Wan, then sent them howling with a pair of well-placed kicks. Wan feinted in, then tried to land a punch on Dukayn's face. Dukayn swept it aside with one hand and grabbed with the other, caught Wan's throat a second time and slammed him back against the wall. For a few minutes Wan tried to break his grip, but his face was turning a dangerous dark red. He began choking, flailing as he struggled to breathe.

Dukayn let him go and stepped back, crossing his arms over his chest. It was Wan's turn to fall to his knees, gasping and coughing, drooling down his protective vest while he rubbed his throat, which began to swell, purple with bruises.

'All right,' Dukayn said. 'You will never speak of your father in that tone in my presence again. Is that understood, boy?'

Wan could only nod, eyes down.

'Good.' Dukayn turned mild eyes Vida's way. 'Now. What are you doing here, Sé Vida?'

'I wanted to talk with Wan, that's all.'

'Ah. I'll wait outside.'

Dukayn turned and strolled out, as casually as if he walked in a garden. Gasping, panting, Wan got to his feet. Reeking of the vomit-smell, the two saccules rushed forward to help him, but he waved them away and leaned against the wall.

'All right,' he croaked. 'What was it you wanted to say?'

Vida considered for a long moment.

'Go on, whore!' he snarled. 'Or are you enjoying the show too much to talk?'

'No, I'm not enjoying it at all.'

He caught his breath at last and straightened up.

'Maybe not,' he said. 'So, go on. What did you come here to say?'

'Only that this is a political marriage, Sé Wan. They happen all the time. We should try to make the best of it.'

'The *best* of it?'

In two quick steps he crossed the room and swung, slapping at her face. Vida spun out of the way, spun back, and kicked him as hard as she could across the kneecap. Even drunk, his reflexes amazed her. He slid to one side just in time to avoid being crippled, but still the blow caught him. He winced, swore, and then swung again, grabbing her hair, pulling her close. Vida yelped with the pain, but her lessons had become reflex, over the years. She brought her knee up hard and caught him between the legs. The protective vest had a crotch strap that saved him the worst, but he did let her go. She moved back against the wall and dropped to a fighting stance. Wan relaxed, smiling, just a small twist of his mouth, but a sincere one.

'I'll be damned,' Wan said. 'Not bad.'

'Is that the only thing that can get through to you? Violence?'

'Oh come off it, Vida! Don't preach like a fucking Lifegiver! I'd forgotten, but yeah, someone told me that the girls in Pleasure all know self-defence. You want to make sure the customers pay for it, huh?'

'Know something, Wan? I'd rather marry a Stinker neuter than you.' Vida spat on the floor in front of him. 'The sex would be better.'

She turned on her heel and marched out to the sound of his laughter. Dukayn was leaning against the wall of the outside corridor, his eyes distant, his mouth a little slack – he was accepting download from his neural chips, she supposed.

'Sé Dukayn?'

'Yes?' Immediately he was all attention, glancing round, bowing to her.

'I'd like to speak to the Peronida himself, and right now, please.'

'What? You're joking.'

Vida looked the factor right in the eye. It was one of the hardest things she'd ever done.

'No, I'm not. This isn't going to work. You saw him. I'm going back to Pleasure. I'd like the First Citizen to arrange it. Immediately.'

'Don't be ridiculous, girl. You aren't going anywhere.'

'Sé Dukayn.' Vida put every bit of steel she had ever learned from Aleen into her voice. 'You can either tell Karlo, or I will. Either way, this is not your decision. It's mine.'

Dukayn considered, caught between amusement and anger. The amusement won.

'Very well, Sé Vida. I'll inform the First Citizen of Palace of your decision. I'm sure he'll drop everything to come down here and discuss it with you.'

'Good!'

Vida strode off down the hall.

'Sé Vida?' Dukayn called out. 'Do you have a key to your guest rooms with you?'

Vida stopped walking. She could feel herself burning in rage and embarrassment both as Dukayn strolled up. He handed her a small silver disk.

'Your factor gave me this to give to you. She noticed you'd gone off without it.'

'Thank you.'

'And will you be able to find your way back?'

'That's one thing I can promise you. You don't need to worry about that.'

Still, he trailed her all the way across the tower. Vida had the satisfaction, once she reached her rooms, of looking over her shoulder to see an amazed Dukayn watching at the intersection of the corridor.

Earlier Kata had left Sar Elen a message, suggesting they meet to discuss 'something interesting.' As he walked through Finance Sect, he was wondering if the youngling would appear. Displays of spirit came cheap; following the spirit into danger cost a great deal more. On the bridge over Golden Canal Kata paused to wait, leaning onto the railing. In the glow of the streetlights he could see fungi, hanging in orange and purple clusters from the steep sides of the canal. In the curves and twists of the wrought plasto railing itself he found sulphurous yellow masses of life – whether fungi or moulds, he wasn't sure. When he idly flicked one with a clawed finger, the mass let out a smell like excrement and puffed up twice its original size. Kata stepped back fast and moved a couple of yards down the railing. This time he confined himself to watching the water ripple.

Kata had just about given up hope when he saw young Sar Elen striding along, dressed in grey and shabby clothes, just as Kata had suggested. The youngling put his back to the railing and raised his crest. Kata answered with a rustle of his own.

'I take it you got my message,' Kata said.

'Yes, I certainly did. I'm honoured that you'd let me join you.'

'Well, it's a nice evening for a stroll. Let's keep moving, and I'll tell you about an errand we might run. It has to do with this UJU rally.'

It was close to the twenty-twos by the time Karlo finally appeared at Vida's door. Vida and Samante were sitting in front of the vidscreen, studying floor plans of the various available suites, when the Announce buzzer sounded, and Karlo's image appeared, laid over a blueprint.

'Open!' Vida called out, then stood to face the door.

Just as Samante joined her, Karlo strode in, followed by Dukayn and Cardinal Roha, dressed in his everyday robes of plain black. Vida could hear Samante gasp, and her own heart began to pound.

'First Citizen, thank you for coming.' Vida heard her voice squeak. 'Your Eminence.'

The cardinal answered her bow with a nod of his head, but Karlo merely stood, his hands on his hips, and looked her over. He was trembling, she realized, just ever so slightly, like an aircar set on idle, ready to leap to the sky at any moment.

'Sé Vida.' Karlo's voice rasped tight and hard. 'Dukayn tells me that you have some ridiculous idea about not marrying my son.'

'Did Dukayn tell you why?'

'The drunken party? Oh yes. That won't be happening again. I give you the word of an old soldier on that.'

'Wan also hit me. It's a good thing I know how to defend myself, or he would have really hurt me. Sé Karlo, your son's a fool and a drunk. He's not worth being your heir.'

Samante made a little chirring noise like a jadewing. Dukayn gaped; the cardinal grabbed his scented handkerchief from his sleeve and clutched it. Vida kept her eyes on Karlo, who stared back, as tense as steel, his hands shoved deep in the pockets of his grey trousers. All at once the First Citizen laughed, a long rumble of cold mirth. It was the cardinal's turn for the gasp and the nervous chirring. Vida was dimly aware of Samante sitting down again, and rather quickly.

'You're right, Vida,' Karlo said, glancing at Dukayn. 'Do you know anyone else on this planet of cowards who'd say it to my face?'

'No, Sé,' Dukayn said.

'Well, then,' Vida snapped. 'That's why I can't marry him.'

'Oh, but you're going to.' Grinning, Karlo glanced round, took his hands out of his pockets at last, and gestured at the remaining chair. 'Sit down, Vida. That divan will do for the rest of us.'

Although the cardinal and Dukayn both sat, and Vida took her chair next to Samante's, Karlo stayed standing, pacing back and forth, all coiled muscle on the edge of rage.

'I know what Wan's like,' Karlo said at last. 'I'll tell you about my mistake. I left him with his mother while I went back to Kephalon, just before the war, and then of course I couldn't get back till it was over. I should have taken him with me on shipboard, and then he'd have been raised right. She treated him like a pet dog, spoiled him rotten – when she remembered he existed, anyway. Brainless bitch!' He paused, glancing at Dukayn. 'Have I ever told anyone else this?'

'No, Sé.'

Vida wondered why he thought Dukayn's corroborations would be convincing. Aloud she said, 'I'm honoured, Sé Karlo, that you'd tell me about it.'

'Good.' Karlo hunkered down directly in front of her. 'It's Wan's children that concern me. They'll be born Palace citizens, they'll be Peronida y L'Var, and this time I'll have the raising of them. Does this shock you, Vida? That I want to raise my own grandchildren and not leave it to the servants? You're Palace born and bred, after all. But I'll say it anyway. It's not only your DNA that matters when you're trying to raise a child fit to hold command. I'm sick and tired of hearing about people's genes! Sapients aren't your goddamn Mapstations, programmed from birth!'

The cardinal made a very small mutter of protest. Karlo ignored him.

'Sé Karlo,' Vida said. 'I understand what you're saying. My guardian raised me to be something, too, something worthy of my L'Var genotype, yeah, but even if I lived in Pleasure all my life, I still could have been somebody. But that's why I won't marry Wan. I'd rather be a madam and run The Close than that.'

Karlo laughed with a toss of his head. When Vida glanced at Samante, she found her factor dead-pale.

'I can't say I blame you,' the First Citizen said. 'But what about that assassin?'

Vida flinched. She'd forgotten the Outcast, here in the safety of Government House. The cardinal leaned forward in a rustle of black robes.

'Sé Vida.' Roha's voice purred. 'It's only a political marriage. Once the First Citizen has his heirs, I'm sure you'll have a great deal of freedom.'

'Hell, yes,' Karlo snapped. 'You can have a lot now, for that matter. Look, we've established that Wan's a slimy little son-of-a-bitch. There's no reason you couldn't make some other arrangement on the side, with a man more to your taste, I mean. Just so long as the children are Wan's, and I know damn well that Palace women have plenty of ways to ensure that kind of thing.'

The cardinal shot him a look that would have curdled milk. Karlo laughed, winking at Vida.

'Sé Vida, let us think of higher things.' Roha clasped his hands in front of him. 'You'll soon be confirmed as the chief patron of your family. You'll have the power to bring that proud name back to honour.'

'Well, Your Eminence, I don't care about the L'Var name. My real family's in Pleasure Sect.'

'Ah, but what about your hereditary seat on the Council?' Roha went on. 'In just a few more months, you'll be a Not-child, and the First Citizen and I can invoke the emergency ruling to get you seated. And what about the goodwill trips throughout the Pinch? And the enormous –'

'Trips?' Vida's heart raced. 'Trips off planet?'

Karlo grinned like a trap closing.

'Okay, Vida.' The Peronida stood up, dusting off the knees of his uniform trousers. 'Give me those grandchildren, and I'll give you your own shuntjammer.' He looked down into Vida's eyes. 'How's that for a bargain?'

'Well, uh.' Vida had trouble speaking. She was aware of Samante, too, gone tense with hope now instead of her former fear. 'It's tempting, sure, but there's still Wan.'

'I'll take him in hand.' Karlo's voice was flat, casual. 'Dukayn and I will take him in hand.'

Dukayn allowed himself a slight smile at the prospect.

'Two grandchildren,' Karlo went on. 'Your licensed allotment and then Wan's. Two authorized heirs – sons, daughters, I don't give a damn which. But I raise them.'

Never in her life back at Pleasure had Vida ever considered that she'd have a child. She'd never even seen a pregnant woman, not that she could recall. She'd be trading away very little, to her way of thinking, in return for more freedom than she'd ever dreamt possible.

'Well, after all,' Vida said at last. 'If I'd been Marked, you know? Every now and then you get customers like Wan – really drunk, I mean, and brutal – and I would have had to put up with them.'

Karlo winced in a sincere sympathy. The cardinal raised his handkerchief to his face and looked away. Vida ignored them, her mind full of the stars.

'All right, Sé Karlo,' she said. 'I'll stay. I'll marry Wan.'

'Good.' He turned on her a smile so charming that she suddenly understood why his beautiful holostar had signed his contract. 'Can I trust your word?'

'Of course.' Vida stood up and offered him her hand. 'And everyone on Palace knows that you keep yours.'

Karlo engulfed her small pale hand with his huge dark one. The cardinal rose, smiling all round.

'The Eye of God will witness this bargain,' Roha said. 'And I shall have Brother Dav see to the drawing up of a marriage contract. If you allow me to take a hand in this, that is, Vida.'

'Your Eminence, you're too kind.' Vida turned to him. 'I owe you all kinds of thanks.'

Roha's expression turned very odd – as if he were so happy that he was fighting back tears.

'No matter what heretical opinions our First Citizen holds,' Roha said in a shaking voice, 'you're very like your father, Vida.'

Holding his handkerchief to his face, the cardinal swept toward the door, which opened to let him hurry out into the corridor. Karlo bowed to Vida.

'You're worth a dozen of Wan,' he said. 'I'll promise you something more, Vida. Your children will be giants on this planet.'

With Dukayn in tow, he followed the cardinal out. After the door closed behind them all, Vida sat down and looked at a pale and trembling Samante.

'Hey, it's okay,' Vida said. 'You know something, Samante? You might get to discover that new language after all.'

Samante managed a brief smile.

'I was afraid I was going to have to compose your funeral oration,' the factor said. 'I've never seen anyone talk to Karlo like that.'

'Maybe you should try it. He seems to like it. Besides, he couldn't kill me. I've been all over the screens now.'

Together they turned toward the tower graphs, building up a high blue stack of sheer political power, welcoming the new L'Var home.

Cardinal Roha left Vida's apartments in a strange state of mind. Vida reminded him so much of Orin, wilfulness and rebelliousness and all, that he felt as if his friend's ghost had returned to him. Even as he walked down the long corridor with a silent Karlo and Dukayn, he was remembering Orin. All those long nights at university, when they'd sat up talking till dawn, or the wonderful weekends when Orin had taken him, a poverty-stricken scholarship student in molecular biology, out to the L'Var estates – it had been a perfect friendship, and it had outlasted their college days as well.

Even after Roha had given up his family name and taken the final vows as a Lifegiver, and Orin had gone to the Military Guild, they had stayed in touch, sharing their triumphs and setbacks. Every man and woman should have a friendship like that, Roha thought. At least one – pure and unsullied by either lust or ambition. They'd only ever argued over one thing, Roha's growing conviction that human beings alone should hold power in the Pinch, and even there, they'd eventually agreed to disagree.

'Something wrong, Your Eminence?' Karlo said.

'No, no, just thinking about the L'Var girl. She certainly has a mind of her own.'

'Yeah, she sure does.' Karlo smiled briefly. 'I like that in a person. She reminds me of my old street-fighting days.'

Dukayn nodded silent agreement.

At the lift booth pillar they parted, Karlo and Dukayn to return to the First Citizen's quarters, Roha to take a booth down to the private transport station in the basement of the tower, where waiting for him was the sleek black bullet train that ran from the twin towers to the Cloister of the Eye, the library and research laboratories of the Lifegiver order. While the train whipped through darkness, Roha was considering how to best keep his headstrong little Vida safe. He could feel his hatred of Vanna Makeesa well up and burn. More fed that fire than Orin's death and the threat to his only child.

Like most members of Interstellar, Vanna considered aliens no different than human beings. She admired the Hirrel so extravagantly, in fact, that she often said they were better than human beings. Roha saw her as an obstacle to his plans and to those of the entire Lifegiver order – or rather, of the direction that Roha was planning for the order to take, once Karlo's post of First Citizen became hereditary. As soon as the popular polls could no longer unseat the Peronida, Roha would be confirmed as the abbot of the entire order. Then we'll see, Roha thought to himself. Then we'll just see who dares to argue theological biology with me! But in the meantime, there was no doubt that she would do Vida harm if she could – nothing so crude as physical harm, of course, but harm nonetheless.

Before returning to his quarters, Roha went to the Cathedral of the Eye. As he walked up the long path, he felt a clutch at his heart for the sight of the flood-lit Cathedral. According to historical holos, the cathedrals of the Rim had been meagre structures; the religion of the Lifegivers had been only one of thousands of faiths practised by dozens of sapient races, after all. In the Pinch, however, the True Faith, as Roha thought of it, had won out and alone survived.

Shaped like a sun with stylized corona and prominences jutting out from the circular nave, the Palace Cathedral stood two hundred feet high, a glitter of gold-coloured plastocrete. Around its circumference lay 'sunspots', actually portals into the Gaze, which stood open night and day. Inside, dim light played in the immense round room. The scent of old incense seemed to ooze out of the white walls and the wooden benches standing under the high dome of the ceiling, which glittered with a hologram that Roha had commissioned upon his assumption of the cardinal's robes.

As he did nightly, Roha sat down on a bench to lean back and contemplate his artificial sky. All the close stars and nebulae shone in their correct places, but the view centred on the streak of light that represented the edge of the galaxy, the fabled Rim. While the settled worlds of the Rim did indeed lie far-off, some thousands of light years away, the artist had portrayed the galactic edge as if it lay a million lys away, where it would seem a mere lambent wisp, an unreachable promise of better times and holy things, an apt symbol for the doctrines Roha preached. He was a firm believer in the doctrine of Perfect Separation, that is, the belief that the closing of the macroshunt had been part of a divine plan. Here, separated from the hordes of unbelievers in the Rim, the Lifegivers could clarify their teaching and hone their faith for the eventual reuniting with the Rim, where they would become holy prophets in the church of the Eye of God.

Of course, Roha had added a few new twists to this ancient belief, twists that lesser minds might term heresies. And was that why the Papal Itinerant was favouring him with a visit? With a little shudder at the thought of Sister Romero, Roha got up and strode out.

Behind the cathedral stood the Chapter House, a square building of plain tan stuccocrete. On the ground floor lay the offices of the diocese, while on the floors above were various residences, a library, and the central Mapstations and storage archives of the order. The cardinal's quarters occupied the top floor, behind a triple series of specially configured autogates. At the outer office, Roha paused for a word with Dav, who was studying a report from the laboratories.

'It's getting late,' Roha said. 'You can leave any time you'd like.'

'Thank you, Your Eminence, but I wanted to get through this.' He waved a fleshy hand at the vidscreen of his Mapstation. 'Test results from the novitiates. This is a pretty weak batch when it comes to microgenetics, I'm afraid.'

'If you have to flunk the lot, do it. They have all the time in the world to repeat the course, after all.'

Dav grinned.

'Hold all my incoming calls here, will you?' Roha said. 'I'll answer them tomorrow.'

The cardinal's inner office was spartan, with a simple desk positioned before a wall that consisted of a small, flattened version of the hologrammatic sky of the Gaze. Waiting on his vidscreen hung a long queue of details requiring his attention and approval – every new parish proposal, complex genetic alteration requests, each budget submission from every Gaze of Palace, invitations to important social events, and even a few letters from children from all over Palace. When he had the time, Roha enjoyed clarifying difficult questions of theology for young people. He could remember back to his childhood when he'd written a letter himself to the Pope on Retreat. Getting a real answer had been the highlight of his young life. Perhaps it had even set him on the path he now walked.

After an hour or so of work, Roha caught himself yawning. Nothing left on the queue had to be dealt with immediately, he reminded himself. The morning would be time enough. He was just getting up to leave when an obsidian disk on his desktop chimed, turning pale blue.

'Blast you, Dav! I told you to hold my calls.'

A hologram of Sister Romero's unsmiling face formed upon the disk.

'I'm afraid I pulled rank on your factor,' the holo said. 'I apologize for the intrusion, Your Eminence.'

Roha felt himself sweating. Damn the woman!

'Oh, Sister Romero, it's always a pleasure –'

When the holo raised one dark eyebrow, Roha ran out of words.

'Let me get right to the point,' she said. 'I promised you that I'd let you know as soon as I heard from the Papal Offices about my posting here.'

'Ah, yes.'

'His Holiness has ordered me to remain on Palace for some time, as much as several years if necessary. He found certain aspects of my report worthy of a little further study.'

'Well, um, yes, no doubt.'

'The main focus of my work, of course, will be the saccule

study. Apparently he's received a number of independent reports about them, reports that indicate grounds for classifying them sapient.'

'You must be joking! Reports from whom?'

'Well, there was one from me, for starters.' Romero smiled in an unpleasantly mirthless way. 'And then several independent scientists from the Lep community have filed briefs.'

'Leps? Oh, well, then, that doesn't amount to much. No doubt they're only trying to stir up trouble, you see, to get back at us for the Peronida's new laws. They're a vengeful people, you know, very much so, and –'

Suddenly Roha realized that Romero might be recording this conversation.

'– and no doubt they really do have serious grounds for their grievances,' he went on. 'I'm afraid that Peronida is as vengeful as they are. No-one could council him toward moderation, not even his current marriage partner, though certainly she tried, just as I did.'

'I see,' Romero said. 'Well, I'll bring that point to His Holiness's attention in my next report.'

Yes, damn her, she was recording, then!

'Thank you, yes,' he said aloud. 'And of course, we always must differentiate between the gendered saccules and their genetic aberrations, the neuters. There's no doubt in my mind that the neuters are particularly lacking in sapient traits. Since I've never spent any time out in the swamps, the gendered individuals might be different, for all I know, but the neuters are most definitely mere animals.'

Romero's hologram floated silently, her dark eyes considering – whether him or his opinions, he couldn't tell.

'By the way,' she said at last, 'I understand that you've waived the L'Var girl's full genetic screen. Why?'

'Well, it seemed unnecessary in light of the circum'

'A full genetic screen is mandatory before marriage, Cardinal. By the laws of our own Order. With your permission, I'll take care of it. We already have the blood sample.'

'Uh, of course, Sister. But you're so busy, wouldn't it be better –'

'Oh, please don't bother to concern yourself with my workload, Cardinal, not when you're so busy with your own. I'll expect the girl in my office tomorrow at the tens to discuss the results.'

'I'll have Dav notify her, unless your factor would –'

'Thiralo will handle that, yes. One last thing before I power off.

Several citizens have mentioned to me that you've been preaching the theology of Perfect Separation.'

'I have, yes. Why not? It's not standard doctrine, but it certainly doesn't fall under the heading of heresy.'

'No, that's true. Not in its usual form.'

Roha hesitated, wondering just what she'd been told. Romero's image merely watched him and waited.

'Ah well,' Roha said at last. 'Have any objections been raised to my use of the doctrine?'

'I wouldn't call the comments objections.'

'Indeed? May I ask who put these comments forward?'

'Merely some of your parishioners who considered your emphasis on *human* perfectibility a little . . . shall we say, shrill.'

'It's a pity they didn't come to me with their doubts. I tend to use human examples and analogies in my sermons, yes, but that's because there are so few aliens in my congregation.'

'Indeed? Perhaps our Lep and Hirrel brethren feel less than fully welcome in the Gaze.'

'Well, if so, then I'll certainly devote some attention to the matter. The Holy Church teaches that all are equal in the sight of God.'

'Yes, exactly. I'm sure you know the origins of the doctrine of Perfect Separation as well as I do. Some would say it was an adjunct to one of the Schismatic heresies.'

'The belief that the separation is God's way of testing the various races, you mean? To see which will be given the rulership over the others? Heavens! That was declared heretical centuries ago. A very outmoded set of beliefs.'

'Precisely.' She paused for her brief, cold smile. 'I'd merely like to ask you to be very careful with ideas of separation and purity. His Holiness agrees that they can be very dangerous.'

'As indeed, I agree. I've been giving my little talks only to well-educated congregations, you see, and only when I can be sure they won't reach the general vidscreens.'

'No doubt a wise policy for any number of reasons. Let's see, I have on my schedule that we dine together tomorrow?'

'At the nineteens, yes.'

'Splendid. We can have a nice long talk then.'

Romero blanked off without a word of farewell.

Well, now you know, Roha told himself. Yes, the Pope is displeased with your activities, and yes, she's his little spy. Weary and unsettled, the cardinal powered off his vidscreen and locked his desk. Walking through the wall holo brought him to the autogate, self-contained and buffered from the Map, that led to his apartments. Roha had had it installed after word came of that customs gate crash, all those long days ago now. No-one must ever be able to break into his private apartments. No-one must be allowed in for any reason without his being there as well. No-one.

His pale blue and gold sitting room stood ready for him in softly shadowed light. Quiet music played. By his favourite armchair, the small marble table held a silver tray with an array of glass fingertubes, filled with aromatic liqueurs, green and gold and the darkest red. The cardinal stripped off his heavy black robes and tossed them onto a watered silk divan, then kicked off his shoes. Dressed only in a plain grey tunic he sank into the chair and let his long fingers hover over the liqueurs. Souk amaranth tonight, he decided, and picked up a red tube to drain it straight off.

'Sweetie!'

A saccule wearing a little smock of pink lace and sheer silk came out of a back room. For a moment it hovered uncertainly, then darted toward the robes on the divan. As it moved, it squeaked, a sound much like a wordless human chatter, and let out a series of smells, musky and spiced. Roha's perfumed handkerchief lay out of reach, shoved into a pocket of the robes. I should be strong, he told himself, I should resist this temptation. Damn Romero anyway! It's her meddling that's made me so tired, too tired, and that smell! So tired I forgot my handkerchief. All her fault.

'Come here, Sweetie. Put the robes down.'

Chattering, the saccule dropped the robes on the floor and edged closer. With every breath Roha drew, the musk scent set fire to his blood. He reached out and stroked the saccule's big front sacs.

'I know what you want when you make that smell,' he murmured. Sweetie rubbed itself against his hand and stared up at him through slitted eyes. An animal, no more, with an animal's lust. How could anyone think this creature sapient?

The cardinal's breath came fast and short, but he pulled away and gulped down the contents of two more fingertubes. Mustn't give in to the temptation too soon. Forcing himself to wait made the pleasure better, but it was very hard. He giggled to himself. Yes, very hard indeed.

'Strip, Sweetie.'

The saccule let out a soft moan and did as it was told.

* * *

Every week Dukayn presented Karlo with something the factor liked to call an 'internal security report.' Karlo called it 'gossip,' but gossip was a useful commodity on a world where popular opinion controlled the government. All elected officials and the most important civil servants lived in the East Tower, stewing each other's juices – or so Karlo thought of it. What went on socially in East Tower, therefore, furnished important clues and omens about key votes in the Councils and temporary alliances between factions and personalities.

After he left Vida's rooms, Karlo returned to his private office, where he called up the weekly report on his secured vidscreen: feuds and love-affairs, backbiting and social climbing – the usual sort of notes that Dukayn thought worth making. One entry stood out: *Ket's Ribbon* had left Spacedock. The captain's filed itinerary included the Belie system as well as Souk, his ultimate destination. Why had Dukayn found this interesting? The factor never commented on the news he collected; he would have considered doing so an insult to Karlo's intelligence. Karlo could think of one good reason for the entry. He powered off the screen and went to look for Vanna.

He found her in the black marble spa adjoining their bedroom. The spa room sported black tiles, too, though all the fixtures were picked out with gold. In the bubbling cauldron of mineralized water Vanna lounged like some exotic lizard; the blue tattoos stood out all over her body, as shiny and mottled as scales. The steam smelled of roses and musk. When he came in, she smiled at him and stretched out a lazy arm.

'Come join me,' she said.

'Good idea.'

Karlo ran his hand down the front of his shirt, which obligingly opened. While he stripped, tossing his clothes on top of hers on a marble bench, she watched him, her eyes heavy-lidded. He stepped into the spa and eased himself into the water, then sat on the underwater bench opposite her. She stretched out one leg and twined her ankle with his.

'You look tired,' she remarked. 'Were you working late?'

'Oh, I was just finishing up some details. How was your day?'

'Busy. I'm bringing up the Fleet appropriation in Council later this week.'

'Good, good. I suppose it's too early to tell how that's going to go?'

'I wouldn't be forcing it out of committee if I didn't think we had a good chance. But you never know with these things. We can't wait much longer if we're going to disburse the monies on time.'

'That's true. I just worry. If this thing doesn't pass, we'll have to drydock half the Fleet.'

'I know. Believe me, I know.'

They both sighed, leaning back, letting the water bubble around them.

'Speaking of fleets,' Karlo remarked, 'I noticed that *Ket's Ribbon* left orbit today.'

'Um? That's right, yes. Jale called me yesterday after they shuttled up. Just to say goodbye.'

'Just?' Karlo raised an eyebrow at her.

Vanna smiled and cupped scented water in one hand.

'I was wondering,' he went on, 'if those datablocks went with him. The plague blocks, I mean.'

Vanna considered, scooping water and dribbling it again like a child.

'Yes,' she said at last. 'No reason you shouldn't know. You could send the whole Fleet after them, but they'd never catch Ket.'

'Probably not, no. I'm mostly curious, anyway. I said they were yours, and they are.'

'Still worried about the plague data?'

'A little, but I know it's not rational. It's just after what I saw –'

'Don't.' She leaned forward, all sudden attention. 'Karlo, don't let yourself drift.'

He made himself concentrate on the feel of the water, the warmth and the caress of bubbles, and on her body, too, so close to his. Perfumed steam beaded on her breasts and slid down over her nipples.

'That's better.' She was smiling at him. 'Ket's got the blocks safe, off planet where we wanted them, so I'll tell you something. There's a copy of the human genome map on them.'

'What? The whole damn thing?'

'It's compressed and it's stylized, but it's better than the partials that the Lifegivers dole out. I don't know how the Lep research team got it, but they did. And now it's ours.'

'What in hell does Interstellar want with a genome map?'

'That I'm not going to tell you.' She laughed, lounging back. 'Did you really think I would?'

'No, not really.' He slid round on the bench. 'At the moment I don't care, either.'

With another laugh she turned into his arms and kissed him.

'They're sending you out fast, huh?' Hi said.

'I'm glad of it,' Barra said. 'I've been dying to get my hands on Nimue for years.'

With the lighting turned down to glow setting and the windows polarized for maximum visibility, they were sitting in the gather and looking out in the direction of Centre Sect. The lights of the vast city caught the cloud cover and turned it to a magical canopy of gold streaked with pink and silver. At times Hi was aware of how he loved this city – like bloodkin. He'd been born here, spent his hundred and five years here, and had never felt the least desire to go anywhere else. There were whole sects of Palace that he hadn't explored yet. Why waste time elsewhere? Barra had always felt differently.

'I haven't been off planet in years,' she remarked between yawns. 'I'm actually as excited as a kid about this trip, especially since we've got rid of the military escort. But, well, the timing could have been better. I hate leaving you and Rico right now.'

'Rico could use your being here, all right.'

'And you couldn't?'

'Yeah, yeah, well. But it can't be helped.' Hi tried to steady his voice, but he could hear himself failing. 'After all, it's not like this came as a surprise. Trash addicts never live long lives.'

'Save that for the newsjockeys.'

He looked at her, studied her face, saw only concern, not any knowledge of the truth.

'Hi, for God's sake, I'm your sister. I know you better than anyone else ever will. You can't fool me into thinking you don't care about Arno.'

Never had he wanted to tell her the truth more; never had he been more aware that he could never tell her, not when her son was going to take over Arno's work.

'You're right,' Hi said instead. 'It's tearing me up inside. I should have done more for him. When he left the hospital, I shouldn't have been so goddamn stubborn about searching for him. That's what's really eating me now.'

'Ah. I figured. But the doctors agreed. Hi, you can't help someone who refuses to be helped. You really can't.'

Hi stared out the window at the silver-streaked sky. Jewelled with red and gold safety lights, airhoppers flitted under the high fog.

'He was so young, that's what I keep thinking,' Barra said. 'All that wasted life ahead of him, a hundred years or more of life, and now it's gone, just thrown away.'

Hi nodded, not trusting his voice. The silence built between them and threatened tears.

'I wouldn't push on you if I wasn't leaving in a few days,' Barra said at last.

'I know. I just haven't taken it in yet, that's all. It's just not real, and so I don't know what I want to say.'

She merely looked at him.

'Well, hell,' Hi went on. 'It's not like I don't have anything else on my mind.'

'That's true, but – '

'But what? We've got some goddamned object on the Map that can delete locked executives and burn virtual circuits like paper. We don't know who put it there. Wynn and our best team have been trying to track it down and can't. I can't trust anyone in the guild and so I'm going to have to go after it myself. Isn't that enough to keep a man busy?'

'Sure. Especially when he's determined to stay that way.'

'Damn it, Barra!'

'All right, all right.' She hesitated a moment. 'What about his funeral?'

'I've transmitted my instructions to the morgue already. A standard cremation. They'll do it tomorrow, first thing in the morning, and it'll be over with. No fuss, no service. Hell, if we gave a public funeral, the whole guild would show up, pretending they cared, trying to suck up to me. Arno hated crap like that.'

'That's true. He did.' With a long sigh she stood up, hesitated for a minute, running her hands through her long dark hair and pushing it back. 'I'm going to go see if Rico's still awake.'

'Good idea.'

'But I – well, you know I'm always available if you want to talk.'

'I do know. And thanks. I just don't know when, is all. We're moving into Government House tomorrow, too.'

'Tomorrow? That's fast!'

'We don't have a lot of time to lose. I want to be pretty much in charge of Caliostro, I want to know him like I know this house before you reach Nimue. Then, when we team up on the Hypermap, we'll be in a position to really throw the photons around.'

'And make 'em stick, yeah.' She smiled, just briefly, her eyes brimming tears. 'Okay. But call me tomorrow?'

'Sure. And go check on Rico. I'll bet he's still awake.'

For a long time, after Barra left, Hi sat at the window and thought of very little. When he finally went to bed, he realized that he ached all over, as if he'd rolled down a flight of stairs.

Although her eyes were stinging from sheer exhaustion, Jevon stayed in her office after the rest of the Jons y Hernanes compound had gone to bed. The large, airy room, decorated in blues and greys, had windows that opened out onto the gardens. On the waft of damp night air, soothing in itself, she could smell flowers, a mutated form of the ancient honeysuckle and the little blood-red vines indigenous to Palace. She leaned back precariously in her chair and stared at the Mapscreen on the wall, where the day's mail listed out in a triple column display. She'd already answered all the business letters and deleted all the advertisements from the queue. With the transmit ring on her index finger, she was tagging the remaining headers on the list and separating them into two groups: condolence letters that would have to be answered and those that did not. A great many people, most of the important people of four different species here on Palace, had seen fit to have their factors drop Sé Hivel a few lines of sympathy upon his son's death.

No matter how little it meant to him.

With the letters tagged, Jevon got up and walked to the windows. The high sill was just the right height for her to lean upon it and look out into the shadows. A strange diffuse light fell from the cloudy sky above – a glow of city lights, just bright enough for her to make out the dark outlines of the garden walls, the fern trees nodding in the wind, the dim shapes of the flowering vines, clustered on trellises. It was about this time of night that Arno would show up in this office or come knocking at the door to her private suite across the hall.

Never again. His father had let him die out on the street like a dog hit by a fivewheel.

You should quit. Her friends kept telling her so, and she believed them. She told it to herself every night, but every night she thought of her high wages, the extra money that meant so much to her family, and of her suite, so beautifully, so generously appointed, and of Barra, who had spent hours letting Jevon cry in her company, rather than alone, when Arno escaped from the drug hospital and Hi refused to scour the streets for him. Still, how much was the money worth? She could get almost as much elsewhere. Barra would make sure that Sé Hivel gave her a splendid recommendation.

She went back to her desk and sat down, cleared the mail list from the screen with a voice command, brought up the house utilities instead. No-one was awake, or at least out of bed, besides her.

'Write.'

The screen changed to an eye-soothing green, and an oblong note pad appeared.

'Dear Sé Jons. I cannot remain in your employment any longer. No, erase. I'm very sorry to tell you that I have to leave your no, erase.'

On the screen her one finished line hung, Dear Sé Jons.

'Close write. No save.'

The screen glowed an opalescent blue. The readout from the house utilities returned. She was too tired to struggle with a resignation letter, she realized. Better to leave it to the morning, if she could even bring herself to write it then. She was just about to shut down her Mapstation when the comm terminal rang. Two beats, two pulses, then silence. She waited – was this just a wrong number or was it the signal? On the schematic of the house status report, she could see that all the multiple defences – the scrambler utilities, the pulse code generators, the electronic alarms and the Map firewalls that permeated the compound were fully online. If it was the signal, she would be able to talk safely.

The comm pulsed again. She let it ring twice, then said aloud, 'Pick up.'

On the screen formed the scrambled image of the person she knew only as UJU Prime, a glittering blue humanoid shape. The voice, too, ran through some sort of distort utility; it sounded rumbling-deep yet syrupy at the same time.

'Good evening, UJU Quarz. We will reign in what?'

'Splendour and the light of God's Eye. When will the time of splendour be?'

'At the opening of the return.'

'Then we understand each other. Good evening, UJU Prime.'

The humanoid shape had no real face, only darkly shadowed areas where features would be. These moved, but what they might be expressing, she had no hint.

'I've heard from UJU Trey,' the figure said, 'that you're thinking of leaving Sé Jons' employment.'

'Well, yes, I am. It's for sheerly personal reasons.'

'You have no personal reasons any more. UJU requires you to stay.'

Jevon felt her hands clench, her nails bite into her palms.

'Your work there is invaluable,' Prime continued. 'We need to know what the Cyberguild is at all times doing and thinking. You will stay.'

'Very well.' She felt as if she were dragging the words out, one at a time, from a great distance within. 'If you need me here, then I'll stay.'

'I don't need you. There is no I in UJU. The cause needs you. You are one of those preparing for the glory of the return, when the long exile ends, and the chosen people go home.'

'May the end of exile come swiftly, but always it is His will, not mine.'

The screen went blank. The comm buzzed and whistled to signal the connection's ending. For a long time Jevon stared into the opalescent blue of the screen. It was only when she reached out to punch in a manual shut-down confirmation on the Map terminal that she realized her palms were bleeding.

In the cold grey light of a Palace dawn Vida woke, sitting straight up in bed. Although the blue blanket lay warm around her waist, the room itself seemed cold, stark with shadows on white walls.

'Close drapes.'

In a rustle of brocade the dark blue drapes slid down their tracks and darkened the room. For a while Vida lay still, thinking about her dreams, hoping to get back to sleep. No luck. She'd been dreaming about her father's image morphing on a black screen, back and forth between his face and that of some screaming demon. She got out of bed, yawning while she considered the Mapstation pillar. When she touched Access, Calios appeared.

'Good morning, Veelivar.'

'Good morning, Calios. Do I have any messages?'

'You do, including a priority code message from the First Citizen.'

'Oh now what? Summarize.'

The revenant blinked twice.

'Summary of priority mail communication,' he said. 'From: Karlo Peronida. To: Vida L'Var y Smid. Subject: Wedding date. Summary: Sé Peronida puts forth his reasons for deciding today when you will sign the marriage contract his son has proposed to you. His suggested date is the Seventeen of Gust.'

'That's next week!'

'Six days from now, to be precise, but within the definition of the word, week.'

Vida ran both hands through her hair, lifted up the heavy mass, let it fall again. Six days? Only six days? She picked up her black pants from the floor and stood holding them while Calios seemed to watch her.

'I can't do this, I just can't!'

'Do what?' Calios said. 'How may I be of assistance to you?'

'There's no way you can help. I mean: I don't want to sign Wan's contract, I don't want to have his children, I want to go home.'

'I could arrange for transport from this complex to Pleasure Sect.'

'It's not that simple. It just isn't.'

'Summoning personal transportation is a very simple action.'

'I know that. Cancel request.'

She put on the pants, then went to the window to look out at the far view, where the blueglass wall sealed Government House away from the rest of the city. Out there somewhere an assassin roamed, waiting to kill her.

'Shall I display the full message from Karlo Peronida?' Calios said.

'No. I'm going into the other room. On the screen there, display the stored files on keywords Orin and L'Var.'

Vida sat cross-legged in her favourite armchair. The list of files, black lettering on pale green ground, snapped into existence, hanging above the three-dimensional holospace on her vidscreen. Calios appeared in his default window at the top.

'Shall I open a file?'

'No. I feel too panicked.'

'Please explain term panicked.'

'Well, look. I'm a L'Var, right? So that means I have the L'Var genotype, and my children will, too.'

'Correct.'

'So I want to know what my father was like. If I have his genotype, then I'm going to be like him.'

'Yes, this follows the general theory of genetics.'

'All right. But he was a traitor, a criminal. Am I going to end up like he did, hanged for something?'

The revenant went still, its holo eyes moving as it searched some database.

'Veelivar, your father supplied only half of your genetic material.'

'That's true, yeah, but my mother was a criminal, too. She had an unauthorized child. Me.'

'I am considering the implications of this new data. I am arriving at my conclusion now. Even so, the possibility of your being a criminal as well is still low. Reason: you did not spend your childhood under the influence of your mother and father. The creation of a criminal mind requires environmental factors as well as genotypical predisposition.'

'Really? They told us the opposite in school.'

'School data is notoriously incomplete. I have accessed three different databases of a high level. All agree.'

'Then if I have a child, it won't be a criminal either?'

'The probability is equally low.'

Vida laughed aloud in sheer relief, but a sudden thought turned her quiet again.

'But what would have made my father a traitor, then? He grew up in one of the best families.'

'Best family is a term that connotes genetic, not environmental, factors. Furthermore, not all of my databanks agree that your father was a traitor. I have accessed a court brief filed by one Hivel Jons expressing grave doubt about the validity of certain pieces of key evidence.'

'That's right. Sé Hivel did tell me that.' Vida got up. 'I'm going to finish getting dressed.'

'This is advisable, Veelivar, since you have an appointment with the Papal Itinerant.'

'That too, yeah. But Calios, in those displayed files onscreen? Do any contain vid of my father being hanged?'

'Yes, Veelivar. One file is a twenty-two minute capture of the live event.'

'Please remove that file from the display. I do not want to see it, not ever.'

'Very well. I shall tag it permanently unavailable.'

'But I think – well, I think maybe I'll look at one of the other ones, that one of vidclips from his early career.'

'Define early.'

'Until he reached oh um what? Fifty-nine years of age.'

'Very well, Veelivar. It will be waiting for you after you've performed the function, dress.'

Romero leaned back in her chair and rubbed her neck while she considered peptide chains, protocols, and genealogical abstracts. For the last several hours she'd been studying Thiralo's analysis of the L'Var restoration and found everything in order. Even the girl's genotype had proved dull, her L'Var-ness an unquestionable fact, her traits perfectly normal – for the L'Vars, anyway. Romero would have liked to have seen a few unusual base pairs, or at least a rare recessive. But no, Vida was a perfect candidate for marriage to Wan Peronida. Romero could think of no valid reason to prevent the contract, though she wished she could. This whole scheme stank of politics as raw as sewage.

'Thiralo.'

Propped on her desk like a mirror stood a simple two-dee screen that operated on transmit beams, free of the Map and thus of Dukayn's spying, or so at least she could hope. Her factor's thin face appeared, sallow above the cowl of his Lifegiver's robes.

'Do you have the information I asked for?'

'No, Sister. I haven't been able to trace her mother at all. The court records were of course sealed – it's a standard procedure in these cases. They don't want the birth mother tracking her child down once she's out of the camps.'

'What? Surely the police wouldn't keep the information from a papal representative.'

'They didn't, no. They gave me all the records they had of the arrest and trial. Lin Smid, gardener and lawn specialist, was arrested at a hospital where she was undergoing emergency treatment for haemorrhage. The placenta from her illegal pregnancy failed to separate cleanly after the birth.'

'Poor woman! She must have been terrified. I'm glad she didn't just stay home and die. That's happened on Palace, you know. Where did she meet Orin L'Var, anyway? I've been wondering about that.'

'Very simple, Sister. He hired her to oversee work on the lawns at his family compound. The police report says that they had a drainage problem.'

'Ah. I see. So – the usual affair, and she decided to get pregnant. We know how that ended: she was arrested and the child given to the Raal woman. And then?'

'Smid served three years in an education camp, as demanded by law, then disappeared.'

'Disappeared?'

'Just that. Since she'd served her sentence, the police had no reason to keep track of her. Her own mother had died before her arrest, and she had no siblings, no family to speak of.'

'Well, but the police must have done a genetic scan.'

'If they did, there's no record of it.'

'No record?' Romero tapped the top of her desk, thinking hard. 'Well, isn't that interesting?'

'I thought so too, Sister. And somehow the police failed to record a number of small details, such as the address of the dwell she lived in before the arrest. They recorded the drainage problem, but not her address? I rather doubt –' Thiralo hesitated, listening to some sound that Romero couldn't hear. 'I think the L'Var girl's arrived.'

'Good. Send her in. As for the mother, keep looking. Someone's been tampering with the records, if you ask me.'

'Do you think it's the cardinal?'

'No, oddly enough, I don't. We'll talk later.'

'Very good, Sister.'

'One more thing. I've decided to visit the saccule training pens, but I want to arrange it so that no-one knows I'm coming.'

'Very good, Sister. A surprise visit, then?'

'Yes, so look into the situation there. Pick a good time and see when you can fit it into my schedule.'

'Very good. Ah, yes, here's Sé L'Var.'

The small screen blanked, then filled with a still holo of the domed and many-spired Cathedral of the Eye on Retreat. Thiralo in the flesh opened her office door.

'Sé Vida L'Var.'

Vida walked in, hesitated, then at Romero's beckon walked down the long room to the desk. She wore a flowing turquoise wrap-shirt over a pair of sand-coloured narrow trousers, a suitable costume, Romero noted, but then one would expect a girl from Pleasure Sect to understand dressing for effect. She'd braided her mane of red hair into controlled little tringlets and wrapped it round with a headband etched with the L'Var gene-glyph. On each cheek lay a modest stripe of turquoise face colour, a nod to the fashion of the moment but not a surrender.

'Sit down, Vida.'

'Thank you, Sister Romero.' Vida took the chair set ready for her, then folded her hands in her lap and waited, her eyes wary.

'Now, then,' Romero said. 'Do you know why you're here?'

'Well, not exactly. My factor said you needed to look at my gene scan or something.'

Briefly Romero felt annoyed. Didn't this child realize what magnificent treatment she was getting – having a Papal Itinerant doing the work of a birth clerk for her? Then she remembered that a girl from Pleasure would have no idea of how a marriage contract was arranged.

'I'll explain the procedure to you,' Romero said. 'This is a gene counsel, yes, but it's also a guidance session. You're in a very unusual situation. Usually, I would have consulted with your patron about this matter, but in this case, you *are* the patron.'

'That's true, yeah.'

'Fine. Do you *want* children, Vida?'

'Well, I –' The girl hesitated, caught by surprise. 'I guess so.'

'You guess?' Romero leaned forward, hands linked on the desk before her. 'The Lifegivers receive thousands, millions, of birth permit requests every year. We deny most of them. It's the price we pay, out in the Pinch, for living such long lives.'

'I understand that.'

'Do you? I wonder.'

'I'll bet I understand it better than anyone else in Government House.' Vida put a snap in her voice. 'Why else was I stuck in Pleasure Sect whether I wanted to be there or not? Because my mother had a baby without a permit.'

'Vida, I'm sorry. I forgot what you've been through.'

'I didn't mean to speak out of turn, but –'

'You didn't, really. Now I'm going to ask you some questions. It's part of the regular procedure. All right?'

'All right, sure.'

'Have you considered when you will have your children?'

'As soon as possible. I want to restore the L'Var genotype. After all, I'm the chief patron now. I have to consider the family.'

'That's true, but is that really the reason? Or is it that the First Citizen demands his heirs?'

Vida blushed.

'I thought so,' Romero said, smiling. 'Nevertheless, you *are* the chief patron of the L'Vars. Do you believe that a match to Wan Peronida is in the best interest of your family?'

Vida looked away, biting her lower lip.

'Answer me.' For a moment Romero felt as if she were back teaching chemistry to the girls at the convent school, a part of her past that she disliked remembering. 'Is Wan a fit father for your children, Sé Vida?'

The girl said nothing.

'Is he? Come along, speak up.'

'Sister.' Vida's voice had gone soft and small. 'You're forgetting something, aren't you? I don't have any choice about this.'

Romero sighed sharply.

'No, no, I don't suppose you do. Vida, I only want what's best for you and your children. The Lifegivers have always blessed the births of children, even before we were trapped in the Pinch. The Eye of God sees every choice we make.'

'I know. I don't mean to be disrespectful, really I don't. And I want to make the right choice. I just don't have a lot of – well, a lot of things to choose from.'

'I can see that. Let me tell you something about myself. I come from Arim. Do you know about that world?'

'The mines? Where everyone lives underground?'

'That's it. Underground in tunnels, and the only lights you see are artificial. The one way out of there for me was the church. I was a bright child, a precocious child, even, but my parents were dirt-poor. There wouldn't have been any university for the likes of me if the order hadn't accepted me. Fortunately, I believe in God with all my heart and soul. I wanted nothing more than to live under the gaze of the Holy Eye. But what if I'd been a doubter, mocking God in my heart?'

'Would you have lied?'

'Yes,' Romero said. 'Lied, and quite cheerfully, too.'

For a long moment Vida considered, then smiled with a charm so spontaneous-seeming that Romero was sure she'd practised that smile for years.

'Do we understand each other?' Romero said.

'Sure. I kind of think we do.'

'Good. Now let's consider our procedure. Normally, the counselling process can take anywhere from six months to years. Don't look so upset.' Romero held up one hand. 'This can work to your advantage. It won't be good for you to find yourself rushed into motherhood before you're ready for it.'

'All right. Is it hard to do or something?'

'Yes. Not the simple physical birth, but the rest of it. It can be very hard to do right. I keep forgetting how much you don't know, Vida. Didn't the Protectors saddle your guardian with other Unauthorized children to raise, and you have to help?'

'I was the youngest, the last one. She filled her quota with me.'

'Ah. I see. Well, I'd like you to have some time to learn what having children entails, at the very least.' Romero tapped an icon on her Mapstation, then swung the terminal around so that Vida could see the checklist. 'We won't need to evaluate the children's position in the hierarchies of possible open guilds. I suspect that the Peronida will see to it that they join Military, and he'll provide a career track, training, and observers for them. Who will be the child's uncle? You have no brothers.'

'Uh. I don't know. Pero?'

'He's probably the best of them.' Romero paused, struck by a sudden thought. 'Have you had much chance to talk with little Damo?'

'No, I haven't. He's kind of strange, isn't he?'

'Very strange. A good example of what happens when an unauthorized child ends up raised by unorthodox methods. Surely you don't want that to happen to your children?'

Vida stared at her in utter incomprehension.

'Well, we can discuss this later. Vida, I'll be blunt. I'll approve your marriage contract, but the birth permit will have to wait.'

'Oh no! But –'

'There isn't any but. You're not suited to motherhood at the moment. You just quite simply don't have the information you need to understand the implications of your choice. By the nebulae! Do you even know what being pregnant means?'

'Well of course!' Vida drew herself up, suddenly haughty. 'I passed my first level in biology.'

Romero glanced heavenward for a little help.

'Does the first level tell you that you may have to rush to the toilet all the time? What about breast feeding? We're all still mammals, you know, no matter how far we've come from the home planet.'

Again the uncomprehending stare.

'I see the first level course left a few things out. You know, on poor planets women sometimes die in childbirth. That would never happen here, of course, but I mention it to show you that having a child isn't as easy as buying a new dress. You have some learning to do, Vida, chief patron or not.'

'Well, I learn really fast, Sister, really I do.'

'Good. We'll see. I want to spend a little time with you, to see how you deal with the world of Government House. Will that be all right?'

'Sure.' Vida hesitated, then blurted. 'But I don't see why you'd bother. There's not even anything I can do for you.'

'Believe it or not, sometimes people do things just because they're right.' Romero suddenly laughed. 'I can see that my stay here's going to be interesting. I'm not like the cardinal, you know. I don't believe that children are pawns for politicians. They are precious, all of them. They're the living stars of God.'

'Of course, Sister. How long before you'll issue the permit?'

'At least six months after your marriage. At least.'

'Standard months or Palace months?'

'Standard.'

'Well, at least that'll be a little shorter.'

'Quite a lot shorter, actually. But I'm not making you a promise, mind. If it takes years for you to grow into your position, then you'll wait years. Standard and Palace.'

Vida pressed her lips together tightly – choking back anger or tears?

'One last thing,' Romero said. 'Your implant. It must be standard procedure for girls in Pleasure Sect, getting their anti-conception implants. I just wanted to make sure you've had yours.'

'Yes. My guardian made sure of that, as soon as I started my periods.'

'Good. Some women have tried to take them out themselves. I don't care how good a scalpel you use, it's dangerous and it leaves scars.'

Reflexively Vida clamped a hand over her left side at her waist – the standard location for birth control implants.

'I'd never do that, Sister!'

'Good. The wound can go septic, and then you're faced with telling a med technician what you've done.'

'I won't do it. I promise.'

'Good. You can go now, Vida.'

'Thank you, Sister.' Vida rose with a small bob that leaned toward a bow. 'You're right, you know. I hadn't thought about any of this.'

'Well, now's the time to start.'

Vida trotted down the long room, but at the door, she turned back to Romero. 'Why doesn't anyone care about the children in Pleasure Sect, Sister? Why aren't we precious?'

Without waiting for an answer, Vida left. Romero spent a long time afterward considering both what she'd said and the sort of person she must be to say it.

'Renting the suite went very smoothly.' Samante patted her shoulder sack. 'I've got a printout of the lease. But what happened with Sister Romero?'

Vida considered the question while she chopped a chunk of melon into bits. The two women were having breakfast in a restaurant in East Tower, on a level known as the Mercado, where little shops and restaurants clustered around tiled courtyards or lined curving alleys, deliberately narrow and shadowed to ape the mysterious bazaars of Souk. From their blue plush window seat they could look down at the roofs and gardens of Centre Sect, stripes and squares of grey or green far below.

'Well,' Samante said after a moment. 'Something must have happened. You looked really troubled when you came out.'

'Did I?' Vida said. 'Do you know anyone who's pregnant?'

'What? Well, let me think. I do, yes, a woman I made friends with on my last job.'

'Can I meet her?'

Samante frankly stared.

'I want to ask her how she feels,' Vida went on. 'Talking with Sister Romero – well, I feel so ignorant. It's really loath.'

'Ah. I see. Romero's pretty intimidating.'

'No, it wasn't her. Not exactly.' Vida considered the mangled fruit on her plate. 'What else do I have to do today?'

'Lots,' Samante said. 'First, we need to make a start on choosing your entourage.'

'What? Why do I need an entourage?'

'To take care of the administration of your estates and deal with the grids and the bureaucracy. Once you're seated on Centre Council, you'll need a political secretary, too.'

Vida sighed and leaned back against the plush, looking around while she chewed on a bread-hook, a bit of baked dough dipped in a spicy candy coating, then touched with salt. She was aware of the flow of traffic in the restaurant: customers, mostly human, heading for their tables or strolling out; waiters, mostly Leps in starched white kilts, trotting back and forth to serve them. Whenever this eddying river of activity flowed near their table, it slowed. The customers seemed to find some reason – a coat button, a dropped sling-sack – to linger near Vida, to glance at her sideways or even straight on. The waiters swung out a little further, as if they wished to distance themselves from this L'Var, this newly-hatched member of the family whose treachery had swept their people up in grief.

'Let's go,' Vida said abruptly. 'I can't stand this.'

'All right. We need to get a start on the entourage, anyway. You have a formal dinner tonight with the Peronidas.'

'Oh no! I can't face Vanna again so soon.'

'You have to. It's a holo op. I can see the grid coverage now: Palace's first family dines out.'

'Oh all right, then. And that reminds me. I got a message from Karlo this morning. He wants me to sign Wan's contract next week.'

'Next week? That's way too soon. You need to deliberate over the offer.'

Vida felt herself sigh in sharp relief.

'That's what I mean about the staff,' Samante went on. 'You need a lawyer, and I think we'll hire one today.'

The head waiter himself brought the check, which Vida accepted by pressing her thumb on a sensitized square. As they made their way through the crowded tables, Vida was aware of more stares, more whispers, more heads turning to watch them leave. Just beyond the heavy glass doors stood a fountain made of emerald green tiles; in the centre rose an enormous bronze flower, its tiered petals overflowing with water. Hiding behind it, it turned out, was a pix, a human male in a striped smock. As soon as Vida walked out, he leapt forward, pointing and clicking.

'Stop it!' Samante swung her shoulder bag up like a shield and stepped in front of Vida to block the shot. 'Go away!'

The pix dodged to one side, still shooting.

'Come on!' Vida snarled. 'He's too stupid to listen.'

She took off, walking as fast as she could, making Samante trot to keep up. The pix followed, saying nothing, not even pleading with her, but she could hear the constant click of his implants, as if he hoped she'd turn around. At the lift booths they finally lost him. Vida hurried into a car down and kept the door open for Samante, who ducked in just as Vida hit the 'close' icon hard. With a hiss the booth shut and moved, leaving their pursuer behind.

'What a nuisance!' Samante said.

'Yeah, and I bet there's going to be more of them.'

Thankfully no pix were waiting when they left the lift booth at their floor, but as they were walking back to the guest rooms, Vida kept a sharp watch. Down an intersecting corridor she did see a commotion of sorts. Over Samante's complaint she drifted that way to take a look.

Out in the middle of the hall stood a neatly-dressed woman, her black hair tied in tringlets much like Vida's own, though she wore no headband. In one hand she held a tablet, in the other a scriber, which she kept jabbing in the direction of a pair of human men who wore the green jumpsuits of Peronida staff.

'Are you ignorant as well as stupid?' the woman was saying. 'This is guildmaster Hivel Jons y Macconnel. You can't expect him to work in a shabby little hovel like this!'

Since the door to the suite stood open, Vida could see dozens of foamstil boxes on autoforks, piled just inside, and beyond them a stretch of pale pink rooms. Sé Hivel himself trotted out, waving a roll of what seemed to be floor plans. Right behind him came Rico, dressed in his journeyman's piped trousers and a pale blue shirt, open at the neck, the sleeves rolled up halfway. She'd not noticed at the reception what an attractive colour his skin was, a light brown verging on copper. Vida stopped across the corridor to rubberneck.

'Jevon, hey, we can make do,' Sé Hivel was saying.

'Sé Hivel!' Jevon snapped. 'There's no reason for you to have to make do.'

The two staff men ambled as slowly as possible into the suite, with Jevon following, berating them all the while. Hi hurried after her, but Rico stayed, hesitating in the doorway, looking Vida's way.

'Vida,' Samante said. 'We've got so much to do.'

'Oh, I know. But – but I want to have a word with Sé Hivel.'

'What about?'

'Hiring a bodyguard. No, that isn't as dumb as it sounds. I'll explain later, if you just want to go on ahead.'

Muttering to herself about schedules, Samante did just that. Vida walked halfway across the corridor before her confidence deserted her. For a long moment she stood watching Rico watch her, until all at once he smiled and stepped forward.

'We've never been introduced,' he said. 'But I'm Rico Hernanes y Jons.'

'How do you do?' Vida automatically held out her hand. 'Vida L'Var y Smid.'

They shook hands, and she liked his grip, decisive and firm but not some exaggerated strongman act. For a moment he let his hand linger on hers. When he let it slip away, she felt disappointment so sharp that she could think of nothing to say. Neither could he, apparently. They stood in the middle of the hall, lost in the sight of each other, until Hi's sudden voice brought them back to the moment.

'Well, good morning, Sé L'Var.'

'Sé Hivel.' Vida felt as if she should shake herself awake. 'Uh, I just stopped by to ask you something.'

'Ask away.'

'The bodyguard you got for me? Jak? Is he still available? To hire, I mean?'

'I think so, yeah. I'll just ask his brother. He's around here somewhere.'

'Good. I'm feeling like I need my own bodyguard, not just someone who works for the Peronidas.'

'Smart move.' Sé Hivel turned away, glancing into the suite. 'Let me just see if Nju's still in here. He might have gone out through the other door.'

Vida and Rico followed him for a few steps, then paused, lingering near the wall out of the way of the passers-by in the corridor. Yet Vida was always aware of being noticed, looked at, whispered about. Rico seemed aware of it, too; he stood completely tongue-tied, glancing every now and then at someone walking past, but always his gaze returned to her.

'Uh well,' Vida said at last. 'Looks like your uncle's factor is a little upset.'

Rico grinned, and the smile made her feel as warm as a rare shaft of sunlight, falling through Palace's clouds.

'Yeah, Jevon can be fierce when she thinks Uncle Hi isn't getting the proper respect.' Rico hesitated. 'Uh, so, you're going to be living here in the East Tower now?'

'Yeah, I guess so.'

'You don't sound too happy about it.'

'Well, I wasn't given much choice.'

'Yeah, that's true. Neither was I. Uncle Hi kind of commandeered me for this new Caliostro project, and we need to live here to work on it.'

'Oh.' Vida suddenly laughed. 'Well, you know, this is dumb of me, but here I was thinking that someone who didn't live in Pleasure Sect could do anything they wanted, any time they felt like it. I didn't even know I was thinking it, I mean, till just now.'

'Huh, I only wish! Once you're apprenticed to a guild, you do what the guild wants. Period. No arguing.'

'Yeah? Well, I can see that.'

She smiled, he smiled, the silence fell between them again. All at once Rico shoved both hands into his trouser pockets, turned slightly and looked away, troubled.

'Something I need to ask you,' he said. 'Did you know my cousin?'

'What? What's his name? Or is it a her?'

'Uh, well, he was a he.'

'Oh! I saw the news – that cousin?'

Rico nodded, staring down at the floor. Vida laid her hand on his arm.

'I'm so sorry. It must be horrible, losing him to drugs and now this.'

Slowly, very slowly, Rico took his opposite hand out of his pocket, looked at her, then just as slowly laid it over hers, still resting on his arm. She could feel him trembling.

'Yeah,' he said. 'It was.'

Out of the corner of her eye Vida saw someone striding up to them, someone military, carrying a tablet. She broke away from Rico's touch and turned to smile at Dukayn.

'They're waiting for you inside,' she said. 'Good morning.'

'Morning to you, Sé Vida.' Dukayn ran his cold-steel glance down Rico and up again. 'You are?'

'Rico Hernanes y Jons, journeyman of the Cyberguild.' Rico seemed to be surveying him from some great height. 'I take it you're the factor responsible for this mix-up?'

Dukayn stared, only briefly but long enough to award Rico the point.

'I usually get blamed for everything around here, yeah,' Dukayn said. 'Where's your uncle?'

'I'll take you to him.' Rico glanced her way. 'Vida, maybe later –'

'Yes, of course, and do thank your uncle for me. I appreciate his help about that bodyguard.'

Before Dukayn could turn his attention her way, Vida strode off. By the time she dared to glance back, Rico had led the factor inside.

The pix caught her again at the turning of the hall, two of them this time, clicking, pointing, cajoling her in soft voices. 'Please Sé Vida, just turn this way, please, just look at us, just for a moment.' Vida dodged round them and ran all the rest of the way back, but she could hear them running after, hard boots on the shiny floor, voices loud now, begging and whining. She slammed her hand onto the doorplate and burst through the door, whirled round and slammed it shut manually just in time.

'You were right to start asking about bodyguards,' Samante said.

Vida nodded, panting for breath. Samante was standing in the middle of the little gather, her hands on her hips, glaring at an empty grey vidscreen.

'What's wrong?' Vida said.

'Listen to this.' Samante pitched her voice to the screen. 'Replay message.'

Vanna appeared, dressed in her full Fleet uniform, sitting casually in a leather chair worth a week's average salary on Palace. Her smile dripped enough acid to etch glass.

'I'm sending you a little gift, Vida dear,' Vanna's image said. 'Most likely you need someone to clean up after you.'

The image froze, then faded.

'Bitch!' Vida snapped. 'What kind of gift? Bet it's poisoned.'

'Not exactly, and it's already here.' Samante glanced at the door into the bedroom. 'Greenie!'

Out of the inner room came a young saccule neuter, wearing a dirty grey shift. In a cloud of horrible stink, it took two steps toward Vida, then stopped, cowering back, raising its webbed hands to its face. All its communication sacs hung flaccid and empty.

'What's wrong with the poor thing?' Vida said.

'It's fresh out of the pens,' Samante said. 'Barely trained at all. Look at those cuts. That's where they put the microtracker and the teacher.'

On each side of its head lay bright pink scars, freshly healed over.

'Teacher?' Vida said. 'What's a teacher?'

The saccule whimpered as if it understood the word.

'It's this little thing they implant. It gives them pleasure when they obey and a shock when they don't.'

Greenie hissed air into a sac and let it out again in a moan.

'Are you hungry?' Vida said. 'Food?'

The little creature whined and raised its eyes to her. Vida reached into her shoulder bag and pulled out a bundle wrapped in a napkin.

'What's that?' Samante said.

'The extra bread-hooks from breakfast. I didn't see any reason to waste them.'

'Oh Vida! How cheap! You've got to learn to act like a chief patron.'

Vida ignored her and unwrapped the bread-hooks. Apparently the saccule could smell them; its eating mouth twitched and it crept a cautious step closer. Vida held the food out with one hand.

'Come here, Greenie,' she said, as softly as she could manage. 'It's all right. This food is for you. It's all right.'

Another step, then another – at last it could snatch the food with trembling hands. It stuffed the bread in, smacking and gulping, and matched the candy-scent with an effusion.

'It's starving, the poor little thing!' Vida snapped.

At the anger in her voice Greenie skittered backward and let out a smell of rank decay. It sucked air fast into a pair of sacs.

'Shorry shorry shorry,' it hissed, then began to tremble.

'Oh my lord!' Samante said. 'This won't do. We'll have to send it back. Vanna can just howl all she wants.'

Greenie whimpered and crumpled, sinking to the ground with breadcrumbs stuck all over its face. Smelly air hissed as it tried to fill its sacs.

'No,' Vida said. 'Greenie, you'll stay here. You're safe now. Understand?'

The saccule looked up, looked back and forth between the two women while Samante sighed as loudly as a saccule herself.

'Vida, you can't let pity get in the way of choosing good servants. You've got a position to maintain and appearances to keep up. This neuter's obviously the runt of its litter. We'll have to send it back and buy another one ourselves.'

Greenie began to moan and move its head from side to side. Vida turned to the vidscreen. Just in time she stopped herself from summoning Calios and called up the clumsy search utilities instead.

'Find: saccules and purchasing. Find: rules and regulations. Now: answer query. What happens to a saccule who is first bought, then returned?'

The utility answered briskly in a light mechanical voice.

'A saccule that is returned is considered untrainable. Untrainable saccule neuters are killed.'

Greenie shrieked in a skirl of compressed air. Samante whirled round and glared at the screen.

'That can't be right,' Samante snarled.

'Cross-checking secondary databanks,' the utility said. 'Information is correct. Untrainable neuters are terminated by lethal injection. This procedure is fast and virtually painless. The drug used is –'

'Stop!' Vida snapped.

Samante turned from the screen and stared at Greenie with one hand over her mouth.

'I knew you wouldn't believe me,' Vida said. 'That's why I called that data up.'

Very slowly Samante lowered her hand.

'It understood the word killed,' Samante said. 'I know they don't train them to that particular word as a conditioned response. It picked it up somehow, on its own.'

'Yeah, so?' Vida was briefly puzzled. 'Oh! I see what you're driving at.'

'Yes, I imagine you do. It can learn words – symbols.' Samante turned back to Greenie. 'It's all right, Greenie. You're going to stay with me and Sé Vida. You must do everything Sé Vida says, but first we'll get you some more food.'

Greenie smelled like ripe fruit. For a long time Samante stood staring in its general direction.

'What's wrong?' Vida said at last.

'I'm just surprised, is all.' Samante turned away and looked vaguely out of the windows. 'At how blind we can be when we want to. When there's a good reason to stay blind.'

'Yeah,' Vida said. 'I kind of know that, growing up in Pleasure like I did.'

'I suppose so. Oh my lord, this past couple of days! I feel like I hardly know who I am any more.'

'Huh? Why not?'

'Well, I – I don't even know why I said that.' Samante shuddered with a little toss of her head. 'Let me just call Service and get some proper food sent up for Greenie. Then we've got to start hiring the rest of the staff so I can get some furniture into our suite.'

The first thing Hi had installed in his new suite in East Tower was a transmit link. It allowed him to splice the Map terminal that came with the rooms into the photonics of guild headquarters. Since no furniture had arrived yet, he stood in the room that was going to be his office and called up onscreen Dian Wynn's report on the damage to Pansect Media. While her team had found plenty of traces of the mysterious candle's destructive path, they'd failed at tracking it to an origin point. Whoever had created the candle must have had some powerful utilities at their disposal, the sort that would only run on the Map itself. Besides, the thing had obviously been drawing power from some on Map socket. Yet as far as Wynn could tell, the candle had been written off Map and its icon then dumped right into the middle of it.

Hi shook his head and swore. Why? All the questions kept coming back to that. Why would anyone be writing objects to damage the Map? If he could find the answer to that, he would have some idea of the psychology of the vandals, which in turn would tip him off to their way of working.

'Sé Hivel?' Nju leaned round the doorjamb. His voice boomed in the empty room. 'Jak has arrived.'

'Good!' Hi said. 'I've been thinking that maybe the guild should just go on paying his wages, as a favour to the new patron of the L'Vars.'

'That would be an excellent gift.' Nju walked in and looked round the echoing white room, set with floor to ceiling windows on one wall. He paused to glance up at the inlaid and painted ceiling that hung a good eighteen feet above the marble floor. 'These quarters seem quite satisfactory. Will we be accepting them?'

'If you think they're defensible.' Hi powered off the Mapscreen with a few quick commands. 'Been meaning to ask you about that.'

'Oh yes. I like this arrangement with the single public door. That other suite – it had too many ways to get in that didn't require an entrance code.'

'Which is why Dukayn tried to foist it off on us. He must be dying to do a little snooping.'

'Sé Dukayn dying is, I trust, a mere metaphor.' Nju smiled and showed fang. 'I also trust that I will not need to make it a reality.'

'So do I. Let's take Jak to Sé Vida's rooms. That way I can make my offer.'

The Cyberguild's new installation at Government House stood two floors above the guest room level in the East Tower. Flanked by two unspeaking Garang, Hi took the lift booth down and headed for Vida's rooms. As they passed the corridor where the first suite offered them stood, Nju glanced down, then muttered a laugh.

'Hah! Workmen are leaving. They seem to be carrying some sort of equipment out with them. It drips wires.'

'I think we can guess that the place was pretty thoroughly bugged, yeah,' Hi said, grinning. 'So was the one we have now. I ran a blow-out and fry utility on it as soon as I got the transmit link set up. We were meant to demand a new suite, Nju. They were hoping we'd accept the new one as a spur of the moment choice and not look too closely at the photonics.'

'Amazing!' Nju turned to Jak. 'Consider how Sé Hivel is always thinking. You should aspire to the same.'

Dressed still in his cyber blue, dark against his golden fur, Jak allowed himself a curt nod. Even for a Garang, Hi decided, he was a dour soul.

Warned by a call from Jevon, Vida and her factor were waiting for them in the white and blue living area of the guest rooms. Hi was preparing to make some pleasant remarks and then lead up to his offer, but Jak forestalled the courtesies. When he saw Vida, crowned with her gene-glyph, elegant in her silk clothing, the Garang spread out both enormous hands in her direction, palms up.

'Jak!' Vida said. 'I'm so glad to see you. I asked Sé Hivel for you specifically, you know.'

'Did you, Sé Vida?' His voice growled with some deep emotion. 'Did I not tell you that you were meant for great things?'

'You sure did. Now I'll have to live up to that. You'll have to help me make it come true.'

Vida was smiling a little, speaking casually, but with a supple twist Jak flung himself down and knelt at Vida's feet. She flinched, then held steady, the smile gone.

'Your life is of value. Mine is of no value,' Jak rumbled. 'I will spend my life freely to preserve your life.'

Standing next to Hi, Nju nodded in satisfaction.

'My blood will pour out to preserve your blood.' Jak flicked one long golden hand.

All at once, he was holding a steel-bladed dagger, which he proffered to Vida hilt-first. When Hi made a hasty pantomime, Vida took the dagger and held it steady. Jak darted his head forward and kissed it so hard that his lip split against the blade's edge. Dark brown blood welled and oozed into the golden fur on his chin. Vida yelped and without thinking leaned forward to wipe the drops off with her free hand. Damn! Hi thought. I should have coached her! Nju winced, then shrugged.

Jak was looking up at Vida in a spasm of devotion as, still reflexively, she licked the blood from her finger.

'I shall serve you till I die,' he whispered. 'May the gods be kind! May my last sight as death gelds my eyes be your face.'

When Vida offered him her hand, he took it in both of his and kissed it with bloody lips. She stared down into his golden eyes as if she were looking into the deep of interstellar space.

'So much for a temporary job,' Hi muttered. 'This is going to cost the Cyberguild plenty.'

'Destiny,' Nju said. 'It must be destiny. And none of us, Sé Hivel, can argue with that.'

Samante had watched all this with one hand over her mouth. When Hi glanced at her with a questioning eyebrow raised, she lowered the hand.

'Sé Hivel?' Samante said. 'There's one thing I don't understand. How did Jak get that dagger into Government House?'

'Madama Samante.' Nju spread his hands and bowed to her. 'Most beautiful Madama Samante. It was not a dagger when it entered.'

'Then the assassin could –'

'No. But what if he did?' Nju gestured toward his brother.

All three of them turned toward Vida, who still allowed the kneeling Jak to clasp her hand. He stared back at her in a rapture close to sexual as the blood welled from his wound and ran. Nju called out a few words in his own language. At that, Jak bowed his head, let go Vida's hand, and rose, nodding to his elder brother.

'Well, we've all witnessed your vow,' Nju said in an oddly conversational tone of voice. 'May you never regret it. Now let's find a heal-strip to put on that cut.'

Gaining journeyman status in the Cyberguild meant cyberdrugs. Without them, the farther reaches of the Map lay beyond the range that an unsedated body would allow a consciousness to travel. Journeymen who either could not tolerate the drugs or preferred to live drug-free could make a decent living Maprunning or performing lower level guild work, but anyone who aspired to master rank had to learn to use them. Adjusting to their effects took time; it could make you sick for days; it could kill a human with a weak heart or a Hirrel whose renal filter-glands were too small. Rico had heard all the strictures, over and over ever since he'd been accepted as an apprentice at twelve.

'If you're scared,' Barra said, 'you're not going to tell me anyway, so I won't ask.'

Rico laughed. They were sitting in the gather at the Jons compound, where he'd gone to pick up a few things from his old room on his way to his first drug-testing appointment. The things – download cubes and some clothing – lay near his feet in a synthskin travelling sack, gleaming pale brown in a stripe of watery sunlight. Outside, beyond the polarized windows, the afternoon sun tried to fight its way through fog.

'Not scared exactly,' he said. 'Nervous, sure. But I don't have any doubts. The Chameleon Gate showed me what the Hypermap looks like, just that one glimpse. I want to go back there by myself, so I can look around.'

'You got the Gate to take you up? How?'

'I think I said the meta by mistake. I was scared, and I remember saying "Eye of God" out loud.'

It was Barra's turn for the laugh.

'That's it, all right. An old joke – when you're on the Hypermap, you see with the Eye of God.' She turned serious, considering him. 'I was wondering how the idea of the drugs would strike you. Because of Arno.'

For the first time Rico realized that his mother believed Arno's cover story, that Hi had never let her into the secret of Arno's work for the guild. He hesitated, wondering if he should tell her now that Arno lay dead and beyond all danger. But would she guess that he'd taken up the job?

'You look troubled,' Barra went on. 'I don't blame you.'

'Well, yeah, if the drugs could take him over –'

'You're a different sort of man than Arno. He could never admit that he was wrong, you know, or that he'd got himself in trouble. Sometimes I wondered if the idea that he might be wrong ever occurred to him.'

'Well, yeah, that's true, isn't it?'

'Unfortunately. Look, you'd better run. You don't want to be late for your appointment.'

'And you've got to pack, too. When do you meet this kid they saddled you with?'

'Damo? I already have. He's a very strange child.'

Barra got up, glancing out of the window with a frown. Automatically Rico rose as well, grabbing his travelling sack. Together they drifted toward the door out.

'Is he as smart as they say he is?' Rico said.

'Oh yes, no doubt about it. He took some tests for me, the ones from the apprenticeship folder – they're open to everyone, after all. And then I squeezed the rules a little and let him try some puzzles from the next round. He solved them instantly, Rico. He read the questions and told me the answers. Even Arno had to think about them, and he was a couple of years older when he took those tests.'

'Yeah? Hey, that's really something. Everyone keeps talking about his mother, how dumb she was.'

'Huh. Well, there's dumb when it gets you what you want and dumb when it gets in your way. Magla falls into the first category. She's a Makeesa, did you know that? Vanna's first cousin. That's how Karlo met Vanna, in fact, through Magla.'

'Yeah? Fascinating.'

'Don't bother to lie, dearest son of mine. I know gossip bores you. But if you're going to be in Government House, you have to pay attention to gossip.'

'Uncle Hi says the same thing.'

'Good. Listen to him. I keep wondering something. Why didn't they get a birth licence for Damo? The Lifegivers never would have denied an extra permit to Karlo, Saviour of Palace, would they? One of his two children wasn't even a Palace citizen.'

Rico did become interested.

'No, of course not,' he said. 'But why then –'

'Why, indeed? Do me a favour, will you? If you hear anything about this, let me know, okay?'

'Sure. I don't suppose I'd better ask outright.'

'I wouldn't recommend it, no. And you'd better get down to guild HQ right now.'

'You bet. I'm on my way.'

The medical centre in the Guildhall took up the entire seventh floor. Directly opposite the lift booths lay a reception area, carpeted in peaceful blue, with chairs and the much shorter Hirrel-sized rest bars scattered round. On the far wall stood a closed door. Behind a curved desk a human woman in blue coveralls with readout sleeves sat frowning at a screen. Half her face glowed with circuit plate, but flesh eyes looked up at him.

'Journeyman Hernanes y Jons,' Rico said. 'I've got an appointment at the sixteens.'

'Right. The doctor will be with you in a minute.'

Rico found a chair, sat down, and wished that the test guidelines hadn't insisted he fast all day. He could hear his stomach growling loud enough to be embarrassing. The medical tech laid her hand on her terminal with a flash of metal fingers – two of them, as far as he could tell, were full replacements.

'All right.' She looked up with a glow of circuitry and half a smile. 'I've accessed your records, and they tell me you passed all your pre-tests.' She sat for a moment, staring at nothing, so slack, so motionless, that he wondered if perhaps she were merely a rev. She smelled, however, of perfume and freshly washed flesh. 'You did sign the disclaimer?'

'Oh yes. And I gave a blood smear for the DNA confirmation.'

Her eyes moved as she accessed some inner screen.

'Here it is!' She glanced his way. 'Sorry. Someone linked it to the wrong socket. All right, Hernanes. You're cleared. Ah. Here's the doctor now.'

The inner door slid open to reveal a smiling human man, on the stout side, with brown eyes and dark brown skin. His white suit smelled faintly of disinfectants.

'Rico? I'm Dr. Sisky,' he said. 'Come on in. Now, you've heard the lecture about the drug tests, right?'

'Right. They measure tolerance. I didn't eat anything this morning.'

'Good. I was going to ask you that next. Some people cheat, and it can get pretty messy.' Sisky flashed a grin. 'Now, if you do feel nauseated, tell me, and I'll give you a shot to settle your stomach. Once the drug takes hold, I'll give you a piece of equipment to wear, and we'll see how you work under suppressants.'

'Okay, sure.'

The test chair looked to be an ordinary med tech recliner with built-in pressure jacks at the base of his skull and paste-on electrodes for the nerve bundles on the backs of his hands. Once Rico got himself settled, lying back just right to align with the jacks, the doctor switched on a ceiling display. A beach appeared in warm sun beside an ocean, the water a turquoise-blue streaked with purple.

'That's from the equatorial region on Souk,' Sisky said. 'The purple stuff's algae. I understand that they harvest it for food. Sounds pretty tasty, huh?'

Since he was obviously expected to smile, Rico did. Sisky opened a white cabinet and took out a bulbous helmet-like thing made of shiny white plasto. Transmit spines stuck out of the top like a cluster of long hairs.

'This is the equipment. When you put it on, it covers your eyes and ears. In a crude way it reproduces jacking in. You'll see the test once you're wearing it.'

'Okay. Sounds interesting.'

'Good. Now just relax.'

Sisky was so deft with his needles, so smooth with his patter, that Rico barely felt the hypo slide into his arm and drive the chemicals deep.

'Remember, this is the maximum dose. You'll be using a tenth of this from now on, so the needles won't be necessary, just a pressure skin pump.' Sisky withdrew the needle and tossed the unit into a receptacle. 'Now, it'll take a few minutes to take effect. Remember – you tell me if you feel nauseated. You won't be able to throw up, and we don't want you choking.'

Sisky stood frowning at the pressure jack readouts while Rico stared at the long purple waves, rolling up onto the white sand of the beach. Looking at the scene made him smile, or rather, it might have done so if he could have felt his face. His face was gone. So were his hands, his legs, all of him – nothing there any longer, just mind, just thought, just the images of the beach on Souk, the purple waves and the white sand. He was not floating; he was not numb. He simply was not there. He made himself remember Vida and the touch of her hand on his arm. He could see her image as clearly as if she stood in the room with him, but he felt nothing, not the usual stab of desire that her memory invoked.

Sisky's voice was a separate creature, handing him words.

'How are you doing, Rico?'

'Okay.' He spoke, but he did not feel his lips move, did not feel his chest move. 'Not sick at all.'

'Wonderful!' The words dropped into his brain, one at a time. 'Let's try the helmet now.'

The view changed. For a moment he saw silver darkness, the inside of the helmet; then he saw a glow, the program being loaded. All at once he existed in a pale blue light. He did not float; there was no up and down; he merely existed, but he was himself, too, still Rico Hernanes y Jons, perfectly aware that he was being tested for drug tolerance. A voice dropped words like ripples in the pale light.

'Rico? How do you feel?'

'Just fine, doctor.' He laughed at the perfect ease with which his words came into being. 'Start the test whenever you want to.'

In a ripple of darkness the helmet floated away from his head.

He saw Dr. Sisky, grinning at him, holding the helmet, setting it down onto the side table.

'Well, Rico, that was the test.'

'What? Did I fail already?

'No, oh no. You passed the whole thing. The medical readouts are all fine. But what counts the most is the way you accepted your complete lack of any propriorperceptive sensation. A lot of people start screaming the minute that helmet covers their face.' He picked up another hypo. 'Let me just give you the antidote now. No use you hanging around for another hour when you could be bragging to your patron.'

Rico wanted to yell at him to stop, to keep the damn antidote in the tube where it belonged, to let him float there in the light forever, free, for the first time in his life free. Instinct stopped him. If he admitted how much he liked this stuff, they'd never let him have it again.

'Sure. I've got a lot of work to finish tonight.'

By the time Vida finally chose a dress for dinner, every piece of clothing she owned lay, tried and rejected, strewn across the bed. Since she had only costume jewellery, she decided to follow Anja's example from the disastrous reception and picked a short sleeveless dress of pale smartsilk – a few voice commands, and the fabric colour began cycling in a subtle range, from dusty pale green to blue to green again. She unbraided her hair and found it nicely curly from its day's confinement – a hard session of brushing and she had a mane of wavy red hair that would simply have to do instead of jewels.

'What do you think, Greenie?'

The saccule let out the scent of flowers, but she doubted if it had understood the question. More likely the poor thing was responding to a kind tone of voice. Some commands, though, it did know.

'Hang up all those dresses and the other clothes. Can you do that?'

Honking and hissing, it picked up a dress in one hand and a padded hanger in the other. At least Vanna had sent her a saccule that had started its training as a lady's maid. Idly Vida wondered if they kept records on individual saccules at the pens. Sister Romero would know, she supposed.

From the other room she heard the door alarm buzzing, and

Samante's voice. Vida slipped on a pair of silver sandals, grabbed a bluish-grey velvet stole, and hurried out. Wan was waiting for her, his hands shoved into the pockets of his grey Fleet uniform jacket. He looked so perfect, with his beautiful eyes and ramrod posture, that Vida found herself thinking of him as a recruiting holo, designed by experts to lure young people into the navy. Her heart thudded in her throat; somehow she'd been hoping for Pero or even a servant. Samante stood at the other end of the room, as if perhaps she'd moved as far away from him as she could.

'You look lovely, Vida,' Wan said. 'Only a girl as beautiful as you could get away with dressing like that.'

Vida stared. Was this the same man who'd grabbed her by the hair and tried to hit her? She had the brief fantasy that Karlo had replaced him with an android, but around Wan's neck, just barely visible above the high collar of his white shirt, lay the marks of the bruises that Dukayn had given him.

'Uh, well, thank you.' Vida swallowed heavily. 'Samante, would you just hand me that evening bag? Thanks. I'll see you tomorrow.'

'All right.' Samante handed over the silver reticule. 'Have a lovely dinner.'

Wan gallantly offered Vida his arm. As she took it, she found herself wondering just what Karlo and Dukayn had done to him. The pain he'd caused her was still fresh enough to keep her from feeling any sympathy. The door slid open, and they walked out into a mob scene. Reporters, cameras, assistants holding up light bars – they crowded round, called out incomprehensible questions, pressed forward. Vida took a step back and found the wall behind her. Only Jak, still in his Cyberguild blues, stood in the mob's way, but his presence seemed protection enough. Under his breath he was growling, and the mob stayed back.

'Ah shit!' Wan whispered. Louder, he said, 'I'm so glad you've got that bodyguard, darling. Obviously you need him.'

'Well, yes,' Vida said. 'Jak, come with us, will you? Keep them back?'

Jak nodded and growled a little louder. When he raised his hands, implant claws flashed in the camera lights. Some of the noise dimmed.

'The family and more guards are waiting up on the top floor,' Wan whispered. 'If we can make it to the lift booth –' They started walking; the mob crammed itself forward; Jak took one perfectly aimed swipe at the nearest pix's face. Although he made sure to miss, the message went through. Shoving backwards, cursing, elbowing and kicking, the mob slid to the other side of the hall. With Jak bringing up the rear, Wan and Vida trotted rather than walked to the lift booth. All three rushed into a booth, and Jak slammed the door shut manually.

'I am sorry, Sé Vida,' Jak said. 'That I had not returned to your room in time to precede you out of it.'

'Well, you were there when it counted,' Vida said. 'Jak, I don't think that one of you is going to be enough.'

'I doubt this myself, Sé Vida.' Jak cast a calm eye Wan's way. 'Perhaps your affianced can be of some assistance?'

'Of course,' Wan said. 'Jak, do you want another Garang or a pair of humans? If it's the humans, I can supply a military guard whenever Vida wants to go somewhere.'

Jak considered.

'The military guard would be best, Sé Peronida. We can set up a three-point formation that way.'

'All right,' Wan said. 'Vida, after this, if you want to leave this tower for any reason, have Jak contact Dukayn first.'

Vida nodded, suddenly miserable and for no reason she could name. The lift booth stopped. When the door opened, Jak punched a button to keep it that way and stepped out, glancing around. 'Let me just go down this corridor and make sure that no pix are lurking.'

'Fine,' Wan said. 'Good idea.'

As soon as Jak walked off, Wan turned to Vida.

'I owe you an apology,' he muttered. 'I was drunk. I'm sorry.'

He sounded like a child, blurting out an imposed speech. It was better than nothing, Vida supposed.

'Well, okay then,' she said. 'Do you get drunk a lot?'

He shrugged, staring at the floor, scuffing the carpet in the lift booth with the polished toe of a black boot.

'Wan, what did they say to you? Your father and Dukayn, I mean.'

He stared unmoving at the floor. Vida waited, waited some more, thought she might speak, then hesitated, searching for words until she saw her bodyguard returning.

'Oh good, here's Jak.'

Wan looked up at last, his face wiped clean of any trace of feeling.

'Then let's go,' Wan said. 'And I hope to God that my law-mother's in a good mood tonight.'

'So do I.'

Wan actually laughed, a little mutter like a Garang. 'Yeah, I bet you do,' he said. 'I just bet you do.'

The UJU rally would be held in Algol Park over in Centre Sect, according to the posters Kata had seen. To reconnoitre the site, he and Elen rode the wiretrain, blending in with the evening crowds. As they were gliding down on the long escalator from the train platform, Kata could hear yelling in the street below and see a crowd forming at the intersection. He could pick out a line of Protectors in their red helmets, holding the crowd back behind yellow-flashing barriers. He could also see that the barriers extended for at least several blocks in each direction.

'A strange time of night to hold a parade.' The speaker rode the step just in front of him – a Lep man, dressed in a rich velvet jacket and matching kilt.

'I'd say so,' Kata said.

'It's not a parade,' Elen chimed in. 'It's the damned Peronidas, going someplace fancy, I'll bet.'

All three of them ritually spat.

By the time Kata reached the ground, the Peronida's long grey limousine was gliding past on its cushion of compressed air. 'Why the hell didn't they use an airhopper?' Elen muttered. 'Why cause all this trouble for everyone?'

'It's safer on the ground,' Kata said. 'It's a lot harder for some bribed mechanic to arrange a fatal accident, and they don't have to worry about their bodyguards getting separated from them.'

One flat truck of Garang guards glided just ahead of the limo, and another came right behind it. In a special turret on the limo's roof rode three more, and these carried pulse rifles. The crowd watched, silent and glaring, as the procession reached a ramp some blocks down and slid up to rejoin the elevated roadway.

'All right, folks, the show's over.' One of the Protectors held up a control wand. When he flicked it, all the barriers vanished at once with a small hiss and crackle. 'Go about your business.'

The crowd pushed across the intersection, then eased out and spread on their different routes. As Kata and Elen crossed the wide avenue, Kata was wondering if Vida were in that car. He had the strange intuitive feeling that she was.

In the cold night Algol Park stretched desolate beside the river. Here and there a tall street lamp stood in the midst of a silver sphere of light that seemed to swirl as the fog drifted through it.

Wrapped in cloaks Kata and Sar Elen tramped over the wet grass of a playing field, marked out with white chalk lines for some human game.

'They'll be setting up the refreshment booths here in this area,' Elen said. 'And then over there, toward the road, the permit stated that they were going to put the portable toilets.'

Kata looked where he was pointing and saw the dark shape of a thick stand of trees, growing low to the ground and providing a suitable camouflage for this necessity.

'And the actual rally?' Kata said. 'Are they going to put up one of those snap-together stages?'

'No. They're renting the Floating Amphitheatre.'

Kata felt his crest lift.

'Let's go take a look at it, youngling. If I'm remembering it correctly, we're in luck.'

Over the lawn by the river hung the Memorial Theatre, two-thirds of a lavender globe, like an enormous fruit with a wedge cut out. Although everyone on Palace referred to it as 'floating,' in actuality it rested on what appeared to be a single huge column, shaped like a tree-trunk with branches that wrapped around the base of the globe and clutched it. Around this tree coiled vines, bronze-coloured power cables, while inside ran lift booths, grouped around a solid steel core. The whole structure stood a good fifty yards in diameter, but compared to the globe above, it appeared as graceful as a flower's stalk.

Lit from within, the pale purple bowl gleamed in the foggy night. On the ground below, Kata and Elen walked slowly around the energy fence that kept the curious and potentially vandalism-minded away from the tree-trunk structure when the amphitheatre was closed. Although the massive steel gates stood locked shut, they found, near a ticket stall, a complete plan of the interior posted on a white plastocrete slab, helpfully illuminated by an embedded light strip.

'See this area here?' Kata extended a claw and pointed. 'The stage lies right at the bottom of the bowl, where the bowl comes to rest on the steel pillar. I'm betting that the electric and photonic cables all run down through a conduit from that point.'

'We can find the plans easily enough. They're in the open library files on the Civic Map. That's where they display all the public permits.'

'How wonderfully trusting the Palace government is.'

'Well, people have a right to know. It's our tax money.' Elen spoke casually, his mind elsewhere as he stared up at the enormous bowl that seemed to hang from the sky.

'You're a true citizen of Palace, aren't you, youngling? Things are very different on the homeworld, let me tell you.'

Elen swung his head around, puzzled.

'It doesn't matter,' Kata said. 'We'd better move on before the damned Protectors come by.'

They walked off, heading back to Finance and the warmth of Sar Elen's apartment. Kata was considering the amphitheatre. If he remembered correctly, a force-field generator amounting to an approximation of anti-gravitic technology actually kept the globe upright. Steel or no steel, the pillar alone would never have supported its mass and weight. When he used Elen's Map terminal to open the public files, Kata found that he was right. A relic of Colonial days, the force-field generator had braked the sections of starship coming down from orbit to form the twin towers of Government House. Now it was being wasted – or so Kata thought of it – on this entertainment complex.

'Look,' he said, pointing at the Mapscreen. 'The generator's right here, just two floors below ground level. It's not very large, either, and the fools haven't even armoured it! Suppose an explosion disabled it?'

'Well, even if the globe crashed to the ground,' Elen said. 'It wouldn't be destroyed.'

'It doesn't need to be destroyed. It'll be full of people, and none of them are going to be strapped into their seats, are they? All it has to do is fall. Fall hard and tip.'

In the limousine Vida and Wan had taken the rear seat, with Karlo and Vanna riding ahead of them. Up front, separated from the passengers by a pane of smartglass, Jak sat next to the driver, another Garang. The limousine's interior was all grey and silver – grey koro hide upholstery, silverwood panelling. Since Wan sat slumped, his arms crossed over his chest, and never said a word, she had plenty of time to play with the car. Built into each armrest was a control bar for fresh air and a reading light. She flipped each on and off, sent the window up and down, talked to the smartglass in the window and had it darken and lighten, until finally Karlo turned in his seat to laugh at her.

'If you like gadgets so much, lawdaughter,' he said. 'We should prentice you for an engineer.'

'I'd like that,' Vida said. 'But I know you're just teasing me.'

Without answering Karlo turned back to his marriage partner. Vida could just see Vanna's elaborate hairdo, a shining swirl of red and blue held with a diamond clasp, above the padded back of the seat. The thought of facing her at dinner knotted Vida's stomach. With a hiss of air the limousine settled to the ground in front of the restaurant's marble façade. When Vida started to slide toward the door, Wan reached over and caught her arm.

'Wait,' he said. 'The Garang have to deploy before we get out.'

'What?'

'Well, we're in Lep Sector. They don't exactly love the Peronidas, and then there's that assassin of yours, too.'

Vida felt suddenly sick and a little cold. Wan let his hand lie on her arm, but the gesture held no affection.

'If they hate us here,' she said, 'why did we come?'

'To show them we can go any damn place on Palace we want to,' Wan snapped. 'No-one makes a Peronida feel like a prisoner. We go where we want to.'

Vida stared out the window and watched squads of uniformed Garang trotting into the restaurant while others formed a cordon along the sidewalk. Up in the front seat Jak was talking in the Japat language through a comm unit; he stopped, nodding, and turned to glance at Karlo.

'First Citizen, the roof squad's in place.'

'Fine,' Karlo said, grinning. 'Let's go have dinner. I'm starving.'

Jak slid out, then hurried to open the door for Vida and Wan. With a toss of her hair she stepped out onto the sidewalk and had just time to read the restaurant's name, The Sapphire Moon, before a flood of light switched on and blinded her.

'Damn it!' Karlo was shouting. 'Turn those off! You'll get your holo ops later. Turn them off now!'

The lights died. Blinking and dazed, Vida clung to Jak's furred arm and tried to see.

'Pix, Sé Vida,' he whispered. 'Like moulds, they occur throughout the city.'

'I was so scared. I don't know, I thought it was the assassin.'

'There will be no assassin.' He patted her hand. 'Sé Peronida's advance guard has been here since early afternoon.'

With a last dance of purple the retinal fatigue wore off. Wan stood by the car and gave orders to a Garang officer while the squad members pushed gridjockeys away from the entrance to the restaurant. Up on the roof someone was being arrested; Vida could hear him shouting about his civil rights as guards dragged him off.

'Let us go in,' Jak said. 'The restaurant itself has been swept and secured. Ah, here is your affianced.'

With so many pix watching, Wan took her hand, bowed over it, and kissed it. Vida gave him her best smile and reminded herself that in a way, she was paying for her dinner.

Under the restaurant's striped green and silver awning Vanna and Karlo stood watching her. Vanna was wearing a long blue velvet gown, tight in the waist, low-cut at the bodice to show off the enormous diamond pendant that nestled between her tattooed breasts. She wore diamond earrings, as well, that matched the clasp in her hair. Yet when the party walked into the green depths of the crowded restaurant, Vida realized that no-one was looking at Vanna, that everyone was looking at her, in her simple little frock and evening sandals. Vida's strategy had paid off. Vida remembered Aleen saying, 'always learn at least one thing from each enemy.' Vanna turned to her and smiled, a curve of full and glossy lips while her eyes stayed narrow with hatred. There's a lot I can learn from you, isn't there? Vida thought. And I'd better learn it fast.

Late that evening, sitting on the floor of the tiny room that was going to be his, once some furniture got there, Rico brought the interactive news onscreen and saw a thirty second segment on the Peronidas, dining at some fabulously expensive restaurant in Finance Sect. Watching Wan fawn over Vida for the pix made him realize that in the right circumstances at least, he was capable of committing murder. He consoled himself by sending his transmit in favour of her but against Wan when the pop rating approval targets appeared onscreen. When they showed the final tower graphs, it was obvious that he wasn't the only one voting that way, but still, Wan's ratings stood a little higher than they ever had before.

Over the next few days, Rico saw Vida on the vidscreens during the 'Life and Living' segments of the interactive news. He watched her go shopping for a dress to wear when she would sign Wan's contract; he saw her entering the Cathedral of the Gaze in the company of the Papal Itinerant, Sister Romero herself; he watched her sitting in court with a lawyer beside her as they looked at documents relating to the L'Var lawsuits appearing on the courtroom vidscreens. When her new suite – the suite she and Wan would share – was furnished, she graciously allowed Tarick Avon of Pansect Media to arrange a 'Visit with the People of Palace', as it got itself billed in the listings. For twenty minutes Rico watched her pointing out antique chairs or original wall holos and listened while Avon made much of the distinctive colour scheme, ivory white with accents of dark green and maroon, the traditional colours of the L'Var family.

While Rico knew that Vida had to give these interviews to maintain her position, he was shocked at Avon, whose specialty was trapping government functionaries into damaging admissions. Rico kept waiting, kept hoping that the intake would suddenly force Vida to admit that she didn't love Wan in the least, but instead Avon grinned and bowed and gushed over everything Vida said or did.

'Well, she's made a conquest there,' Uncle Hi said. 'I don't think the way he's acting is just part of the grid contract.'

'Yeah? Then he's got an ion cloud where his brains ought to be.'

When Hi raised a questioning eyebrow, Rico got up, slammed out of the suite's little gather, and into his bedroom.

Now that he was living in Government House, Rico had trouble sleeping. He'd always had strange dreams, ever since he could remember, but here they'd turned ominous. He'd find himself on a wiretrain in orbit above Palace, and sitting opposite him would be Arno, or rather, his mutilated corpse. Or he'd dream of Vida, a dream that would start out pleasantly erotic but end with her lying dead in front of him on some sort of altar. Every time he would wake with a cry to find himself alone and sweating in his narrow bed.

The evening of her interview he dreamt of following Vida through her suite while she kept pointing out incomprehensible objects on the walls. He was just about to catch up with her when a Lep jumped from the shadows and stabbed her to the heart.

Again, his own cry woke him. He sat up in bed, shoving sweaty hair back from his face with both hands.

'Time.' His voice echoed oddly in the dark.

A few minutes to the fives. The glowing green numbers, flashed by an implant, faded after a few seconds. He shucked off his clammy sleep gown, balling it up and throwing it as hard as he could into a corner. He got out of bed, pulled his trousers on without bothering with underwear or with fastening them, and walked to the window. When he murmured a command, the curtain lifted.

Outside, pink fingers of dawn reached up from behind the haze of clouds. Puffs of green filled the air, the morning sporefall through a windless sky. Rico looked down on the northern arc of Centre Sect, criss-crossed with the glowing geometry of wiretrain tracks and the starry sparkle of the windows of family compounds and warehouses – there were a lot of sapients up with the dawn, guild-masters trying to win an edge, maybe, or apprentices hoping to impress their masters with their diligence. What did all those people out there really want out of life? What did he want? Rico suddenly felt like one of those green spores, tossed through the air without will or purpose, doomed to die, unremembered, unfulfilled. Slowly the dawn faded and the sky clamped down, relentlessly silver.

On his narrow desk his Mapstation chimed: a commcall. Rico spun round – no-one had his number but Hi.

'Accept.'

Vida's image appeared, grinning at him. Uncombed and wild, her hair tumbled round her face, streaked with the remains of make-up. She was wearing a crumpled green shirt.

'I just got in from an awful party,' Vida said. 'So I thought I'd wake you up.'

'Well, you didn't. I was already awake.' He sat down in his desk chair in front of the station. 'A party, huh?'

'Yeah. Are you working? I can power off.'

'No, no, I was just – well, hell, I was just thinking about you.'

'Yeah?'

'Yeah.'

When she smiled, he felt as if the entire world had turned soft and warm around him. On her side of the comm link Vida seemed to be studying his image; all at once her grin turned wicked.

'You really should have zipped those pants up,' she said.

Rico swore, grabbed a shirt from the floor, and dumped it over his lap. Vida laughed, but there was no meanness in it, not even any teasing, really, just a good-humoured joke. He found himself wanting her more than he'd ever thought it possible to want a woman.

'Uh well, hey,' he said. 'I don't suppose I could take you out to breakfast? Since we're both uh well awake and all?'

Her smiled faded fast.

'I don't know,' she said. 'The damn gridjockeys follow me everywhere.'

'Ah come on, they're not going to be prowling the halls at this time in the morning.'

'But I'll bet they're up in the Mercado. Eating, probably; keeping their strength up so they can chase me around some more.'

'Hey, I know! What about the Kaft Museum?'

'Oh yeah, I'm sure that's going to be open! Rico, the time's only just hit the fives.'

'Doesn't matter. Have you been there? It's got this entrance or porch thing, and no-one's going to see us if we're inside it.'

'What? You're crazy.'

'Oh yeah? Meet me there and I'll show you.'

She hesitated, then grinned, a slow spread of mischief.

'Okay, I will. It's on Floor Ten, right?'

'Right. Fifteen minutes.'

Rico rushed around, found a reasonably clean shirt, put it on, went to tuck it in and remembered how Vida had looked at him. Blushing, cursing, he banged around the room and finally got himself dressed and into the suite's gather, where Nju, unfortunately, sat at Jevon's reception desk, his feet up while he watched the early news.

'You are dressed. Where are you going? I have no appointment for this time listed on your itinerary.'

From bitter past experience, Rico knew that Nju could smell a lie a week away.

'I'm going to meet a girl. I'd like to go alone.'

'Ah.' Nju held up his transmit ring and switched the screen from the news to a plan of the East Tower. 'Where?'

'I don't want to tell you that.'

'Why not? I'd never betray a plot, unless it was against your uncle.'

Rico realized that he was hearing the Garang idea of a joke.

'Oh okay, the Kaft Museum.'

The Museum appeared on the plans as a glowing dot.

'I'm sorry,' the vidscreen said. 'This institution is not open to the public at this hour.'

'I know that,' Rico snapped. 'I'm just going to meet her in front of it. Nju, I don't want to be late.'

'Very well.' The Garang sighed, doubtless at the folly of human men. 'When is your estimated return time?'

'Uncle Hi will want me at the briefing at the top of the sevens.'

'I know. That's why I asked. Be back by then.'

'Don't you worry. And thanks.'

Once he reached Floor Ten, Rico realized that even this early, a lot of sapients were up and busy on the public floors of East Tower. Service workers shepherded flocks of cleaning bots; security guards prowled; here and there important-looking humans with bodyguards and factors hurried to some meeting or other. Still Rico managed to slip along, stopping to peer into windows or occasionally pretending to check the fastening on his boots, without anyone speaking to him. When he turned down the corridor that housed the museum, he saw no-one there ahead of him.

The current façade of the museum was in fact an installation of its own: an elaborate set of tall steel baffles constructed in long strips and curves. In a programmed pattern, floating power spheres in spectrum calories wandered through the curved grey sheets. Rico thought it was the ugliest piece of art he'd ever seen, but it had its uses. As he walked up, he heard a girl's voice giggling, just softly, from in among the baffles.

'Vida?'

'Over here, yeah. Okay, you win. This is really weird.'

She was sitting on one of the museum's actual steps in among the work of art's many pieces. Since he'd last seen her, she'd washed the ruined cosmetics off her face, and her red hair hung down in waves over the huge collar of the green shirt. Faintly she smelled of exotic liquors and perfume. When he wrinkled his nose, she caught the gesture.

'Sorry,' Vida said. 'One of my fiancé's darling friends spilled his drink, and it got all over my shirt.'

'Wan's friends are kind of famous around here.'

'So I'm learning, yeah. Some of them are okay, though. Well, Dan and TeeKay, maybe.'

'Who?'

'Dan of Motta and Tina Karin Rommoff, his girlfriend.'

'Huh. Running around with the aristocrats. Guess you won't have time for lowly techs like me.'

'Don't be stupid, Rico. Or are you joking?'

'Just joking. Hey, I know who really runs this planet, and it's not the Upper Council.'

They shared a companionable smile, and he found himself inching toward her, settling in with his hip touching hers, warm and close beside him. She looked abruptly away.

'Oh, I need to tell you – my bodyguard's here, too. He's just over there, on the other side of the façade. I hope you don't mind, but I'm kind of scared to go anywhere without him. It's the grid-jockeys.'

'I can see that, yeah.' Rico had to admit to himself that he was more than a little disappointed. Still, what had he expected? That she'd fall right into his arms? 'Can I ask you how you got my call number? It's supposed to be private.'

'Really?' Vida gave him a sly grin. 'My search utility brought it right up.'

'Oh come on! I don't believe that. You'd need a special search and retrieve to get into the comm banks. A ferret is what they're called.'

'Well, maybe it is kind of special. I have a meta.'

'A meta?' Rico frowned. 'But you don't have that kind of access to the Map, or the training. And a ferret is one of the hardest metas . . . someone must have made it for you. Who else do you know in the Cyberguild?'

'No-one. Well, your uncle, but I mean –'

'Yeah, Hi would never give you a ferret. Hey, you know, you never answered my question about Arno. My cousin.'

'Didn't I? Oh. No, I didn't know him. Why? He didn't give me the ferret, if that's what you mean.' Suddenly her voice edged with ice. 'Or did you think he'd been to The Close? A customer, maybe?'

'No, no, nothing like that. Vida, I'm sorry. I didn't mean to insult you. I never thought that.'

She shrugged and looked away. When he risked touching her arm, she pulled it away.

'I'm sorry,' Rico said again.

'Oh, it's not even you! I just feel so caught, you know? Everyone's kissing up to me now, but you can practically hear them thinking, the little whore from Pleasure Sect, the little cull.'

'I never think of you that way. Never.'

'Really?' She studied his face for a long silent moment. 'Well, thank you.' She sighed and looked away again. 'I'm not Vida any more, the girl who's going to be Marked. But I sure don't feel like a L'Var either. I've watched vids of my father, but I never knew him. And my mother – well, all I know about her is her name.'

'Aren't there police records?'

'Oh, they wouldn't show me. I asked, and they read me off a ton of laws and told me to forget about ever asking again. So I went to Sister Romero. She's handling my marriage contract, you know, and I figured she'd have the police files. She did, but she told me the records were incomplete. She thinks someone's destroyed part of them. So now I'll never know.'

'Oh yeah? Once something's been on the Map, you'd have to be a master of the guild to really wipe it away. You can deny access, scramble it, or move it, but it's still going to be there.'

'So?'

Rico merely grinned. In a moment she caught his meaning.

'You couldn't find those records, could you?' Vida said. 'Or wait, that's horrible of me. I never should have asked you. You could get into real trouble, hacking into police files.'

'Not if they don't catch me.'

'This is really selfish of me, but I'm not going to say no.'

They laughed together, and this time when he let his hand touch hers, she let it rest there.

'Well, tell you what,' she said. 'If you look for those records for me, I'll show you my ferret.'

'Okay. That's a bargain. I'll have to get a little time alone on the Map, without Uncle Hi hanging around, I mean, but it should be pretty easy to find the files and then track down what happened to the missing data.'

'That would be really great. You can't imagine how loath this is, wondering what your own mother's like, wondering where she is. For all I know, she's dead.'

'But you don't know, and so you'll always wonder till you do know.'

'Exactly. You really do know how I feel, don't you?'

'Well, I can guess. I lost my own father.'

'Oh! I didn't know that. I'm sorry.'

'He was in an accident, a dumb stupid accident, and the med techs couldn't bring him back. I don't want to talk about it.'

'All right. But I'd be glad to listen.'

Vida was looking at him solemnly, so lovely, so kind, that he leaned forward, hesitated, saw her smile, and bent his head to reach for a kiss. From above them came the sharp and ominous sound of a Garang Japat clearing his throat. Rico let go her hand fast and looked up to find Nju's brother Jak standing on the step above, his arms folded across his chest.

'Sé Vida,' Jak said. 'You have been up all night. You lack necessary sleep. Doubtless this is clouding your better judgment.'

'Well, maybe so.' Vida scrambled to her feet. 'Jak, I don't want anyone to know that I met Rico here.'

'Of course, Sé Vida.' Jak turned golden eyes Rico's way.

Rico got up, feeling a little sick at how indiscreet they'd been.

'If anyone asks where Sé Vida was at this hour,' Jak went on, 'we will say that she lost a scarf, and I suspected you of finding it.'

Rico could only stare. If the Garang would lie for Vida, he must have bonded himself to her in the blood-ritual. You heard about Garang doing so from time to time, but it was an ancient thing and rare.

'A scarf,' Rico said at last. 'Okay, what colour?'

'Green will do,' Jak said. 'You had best hurry, Sé Rico. My brother will be worrying over your return, no doubt.'

'Yeah, he sure will.' Rico hesitated, glancing at Vida. 'I'd like to see you again.'

'Of course.' She grinned at him. 'We've got a bargain.'

Vida's new suite had a Map terminal – every living space in East Tower did – set into an alcove off her bedroom. To those who weren't coded for it, the alcove stood hidden behind a solid-seeming section of wall, but if the retinal scanner recognized certain segments of your DNA, you could walk right through. When she wanted to evoke Calios, Vida used an extra curtain screen utility as well to insure that Samante, who was coded for the station, would know she was handling private business.

As soon as she returned from the Kaft Museum, Vida called the revenant up. With his usual smile he appeared on the obsidian pillar.

'Good morning, Veelivar.'

'Good morning, Calios. Did anyone access my comm while I was gone?'

'No, Veelivar. However, someone tried to access me just a few minutes ago. The tracer came from a known call number, the one belonging to Rico Hernanes y Jons.'

'Hah! I'm not surprised. Was he successful?'

'No, he was not. I have isolated myself from the internal systems of Government House with a membrane.'

'A membrane? What's that?'

'A technical term, Veelivar. A membrane allows the agent instituting it, me in this case, to pass freely out. No other agents, routines, or utilities may pass in.'

'Good. I don't want Rico learning anything about you till I'm ready to tell him.'

'I have been operating on your earlier instructions, given from your station in The Close, in which you said that you wanted no-one to access your data or my executing files. I have installed membranes between this station and the Caliostro AI as well as between this station and the public areas of the Map. I have found your school, medical, and other such records and wrapped them in membranes as well. Finally, I have searched out and destroyed all the data-gathering devices implanted in this suite.'

'What? You mean snoops and bugs?'

'Those are the vernacular terms, yes. I sent a large surge of electric current through them. The vernacular term for the result is "fried".'

'That's great. Well, if there's no mail, I should just go to bed.' She paused, struck by a sudden thought. 'Calios, do you remember the first time I accessed you?'

'When you established my meta. Yes.'

'You called me Veelivar.'

'This is true.'

'But I didn't even know then that I'm a L'Var.'

'True.'

'But you knew I was?'

'I did.'

'How did you know?'

'I do not understand your question.'

'How did you know that I was a L'Var and that my first name begins with V?'

'I do not understand your question.'

'What? This is weird. You shone a light in my eyes. Why?'

'To ascertain your deen type.'

'After you ascertained the type, you called me Veelivar.'

'Yes.'

'What told you to call me that? No, wait, that's not clear. From where did you get the name, Veelivar?'

'From ascertaining your deen type.'

'I know that. But there must have been something more.'

'I do not understand your question.'

'Was there a list of names of people who have that deen type?'

'Yes.'

'Where was the list?'

'I do not understand the word, where, in this context.'

All at once Vida yawned, gulping air. No wonder this conversation doesn't make sense, she thought. I'm so tired.

'I've got to go to bed. Please fill the bedroom with white sound and darken the windows.'

Vida got only a few hours' sleep, though, before Samante woke her, creeping into the dark room in a cloud of apologies. Yawning, stretching, shoving her tangled mass of hair back with both hands, Vida at first had trouble understanding her.

'Who's here?' she said finally. 'I missed that part.'

'Molos,' Samante repeated. 'Don't you remember meeting him? Ri Tal Molos, and he has a message from your guardian, Raal.'

Aleen's name snapped Vida wide awake.

'I'll grab some clothes and come right out.'

When Vida, still carrying a hairbrush, hurried into the gather, she found Molos, dressed in a pale grey wrap jacket and blue slashed kilt, waiting for her with his crest uplifted. He stood in the curve of windows, draped in maroon and green flowered silk, that looked down to the gardens of Centre Sect far below. A nervous Greenie, sucking air into and squeezing it out of various sacs, was laying cups of steaming tea and a plate of breads onto the table in front of the long ivory-coloured couch. The Lep bowed to Vida with a flutter of his crest.

'Good morning, Sé Molos,' Vida said, smiling in return. 'Do come sit down.'

'Thank you, my dear.' He limped over to a broad armless chair that Vida had bought especially for Lep visitors. 'Your hospitality is already legendary, do you know that?'

'Really? No, I didn't. But after all, if there was one thing I was taught it was how to make people feel welcome.'

'A charming trait, and one curiously lacking in most of Government House.'

'Greenie, you may go.' Vida tossed the saccule her hairbrush. 'Samante said you had a message from Aleen?'

'Yes indeed.'

Molos waited till the saccule had left, then reached into an inner pocket of his jacket and pulled out a thick sheaf of folded papers, which he solemnly traded for a cup of tea. Vida glanced at the top page and realized that Aleen had written the entire thing with a pen; her round, firm handwriting was unmistakable.

'Oh, this is wonderful!' Vida said. 'Thank you so much!'

'I hope you continue to find it wonderful. It seems to be a critique.'

Later, when Vida had a chance to read all fourteen pages, a critique was exactly what she found. Aleen had been taking notes on the vidscreen footage of all of Vida's public appearances. Her hair, her clothes, the way she walked, the way she offered her hand to be shaken, the way she bent down to speak with a child – no detail was too small to escape Aleen's sharp eyes. Every now and then, while she read, Vida would wince or even talk back to the pages, but she knew that Aleen was always right. Yes, that shirt was too vivid a colour for the cameras, and yes, that dress too tight to wear to a religious ceremony. No, she shouldn't have spoken that loudly here or whispered so coquettishly there.

At the end ran a few lines of praise, and those Vida read over and over. 'In general you're doing very well, however. I have some reasons to be proud of you. Remember one crucial thing: you'll never win over the best families. To them you'll always be that little cull from Pleasure. But the ordinary people vote the screens, too, and there are more of them. A lot more. With my regards, Aleen Raal.'

She has some reasons to be proud of me, Vida thought. She found herself smiling as if she just might never stop.

Just about every public building in Palace had a rank of citizen access Map terminals, each isolated from the others by a bright red hood. In a grocery store in Service Sect, Kata found a convenient set and took the one farthest away from the noisy crowds of waiting customers. Since he couldn't use a fingerprint ID to activate payment, with cash he'd bought the credit tags that activated public services like these. Here and there over the past few days, Kata had been spending the tags searching for information on Riva. He'd started with the list of the Lep cybermasters and Maprunners who'd been publicly banned from the Map by the Peronida's laws. One at a time he'd tracked other listings down in public records and compiled what data he could find. He knew now who had left the planet and who had compromised themselves and stayed.

The richest data-trove, though not completely reliable, he found in the back files of Pansect Media. Before the war, Lep-owned Pansect had catered to the Lep community; the Peronidas had confiscated it, claiming planetary security, and handed it over to human owners, but its archives reflected its old focus of gossip-mongering about the lives of the rich and eminent Leps on planet. Since Pansect had started life as a scratched together shanty-Map operation, its storage site lay at some distance from its other Map addresses and thus had escaped damage during the peculiar crash that had bedevilled the company the week before. Kata was looking for scraps of information indicating a master who would particularly resent having her career ruined by injustice but who would have good reason for remaining on Palace nonetheless. Speaking Gen as her third or fourth language would be another good indicator – if of course the master was even really female, Kata reminded himself.

While he worked, Kata kept close track of the time, but even so, Sar Elen, arriving a few minutes early, caught him at his research. The youngling let his crest droop as Kata powered out of a report, with video, of a banquet given by the Benar family.

'That's an odd thing to be listening to,' Elen remarked; he was using the Lep language and speaking it very quietly.

'I've got my reasons.' Kata answered him in the same.

'Of course.' Elen lifted his head reflexively to expose throat. 'I'm not questioning, only wondering.'

Kata grunted and pulled out his tag. The Map terminal sighed once and went dead.

'I was just looking for pictures of the Floating Amphitheatre,' Kata said. 'You can see the details of a place on these old newsfeeds.'

Elen's crest lifted.

'Every bit of data helps,' Kata went on. 'So. Has our leader told you where we're going?'

'Yes. A courier brought me the message this morning. It's not far.'

They left the grocery store and walked out into a chilly afternoon. In the fog the passers-by, mostly Leps here in Service Sect, walked fast with their jackets wrapped tight around them. Kata and Elen strode along in the crowd, then turned down a side-street. Just as they crossed to the other sidewalk, Kata saw a flash of a familiar colour and swung his head around fast. A slender human girl, her hair a long mane of russet-red, was walking in the opposite direction. He stopped, stared, and realized that it wasn't Vida, just some other red-haired girl. What an odd coincidence – he'd never seen a redheaded human before, and now he'd seen two.

With a shrug he followed Elen into an alley between two white dwells. Above, narrow bridges crossed, binding the two buildings together. At street level bright red doors led into small shops – food stores, mostly, with signs in their windows stating that they could carry no more credit. 'Pay on receipt' was a new policy for a race renowned for honouring its debts.

The alley debouched into a square courtyard with a cracked fountain, filled with litter, standing in the middle. A few hatchlings crouched on the dirty pavement and played with toy shuntjammers. On the far side, in a shabby low building, another red door led into a tiny store crammed with used furniture. Heaps of cushions leaned against every wall; rolled webbings lay on top of storage chests woven from thin wooden slats. Huge brass jugs, most of them scratched and tarnished, stood crammed together. In the centre of this clutter stood a black plasto Map desk, heaped with little straw boxes and tiny slings, wrapped round trinkets. A grandfather, his neck bowed from the weight of his gold chains, stood behind it.

'We've come to talk with Zir,' Elen said.

The old man considered, exposing his brown and cracking teeth, then jerked a thumb in the direction of a door in the back wall. Kata followed Elen through into a brightly-lit room heaped with photonics and electronics: old Mapscreens, hunks of terminals, interface boards, transmits, comm units, output stations. Some lay stacked on a counter that ran three-quarters of the way round the room; others sat in boxes that trailed power cords like spilled guts. On the far wall stood a closed door. Perched on a sling, halfway up a side wall, sat a young Lep woman, wearing a dirty grey smock over a long flowered kilt. Jewelled studs gleamed in piercings at the corners of her mouth.

'Elen,' she said. 'Have you brought me a customer?'

'I have, the fellow you were told about. The one who wants to talk about output stations.'

'For multiple copies?' Her crest lifted slightly when she looked at Kata. She had eyes of the finest scarlet, set at a pronounced slant; she narrowed them provocatively and looked at him sideways.

'Practically a hatch of them,' Kata answered. 'For a mailing.'

At this exchange of code words, she lifted her crest a little higher and swung down from the webbing, dropping gracefully to the floor with a swirl of skirt. Kata wondering if his throat were reddening; it had been a long time since he'd met a woman capable of catching his attention the way this one had.

'Zir,' Kata bowed to her, head held low. 'I'm honoured that our presents have crossed.'

'May our futures cross as well,' she said gravely. 'And I'm hoping that you'll let me share your past. I've heard so much about you. I'd love to hear you talk about your triumphs.'

'I'm sorry, but no. I never talk about my jobs, not even to someone as beautiful as you.'

She hissed at him, wide-mouthed and sexy, then let her crest rustle. When Kata glanced at Elen, he found the youngling pretending to study a chart of fonts on the wall, but he stood easily, perfectly relaxed.

'I have your new papers for you,' Zir said. 'Elen, what's this about you becoming a street sweeper? You've finally found your true calling in life, have you?'

'Watch your mouth, hatchmate.' But Elen waved his crest. 'We need to keep a low profile, that's all. The Protectors won't be interested in a pair of cleaners if they stop us for some reason.'

'That's true. *She* thinks of everything, doesn't she?' Zir nodded Kata's way. 'We're so lucky to serve her.'

'Oh, I couldn't agree more.'

'She's told me about you,' Zir paused, then looked him full in the face. 'But then, even humans have heard about you, Vi-Kata. They're afraid of you, aren't they? Good.'

Kata ducked his head modestly and hoped his throat was behaving itself. For a woman to stare boldly at a man could mean only one thing, even here on Palace with its debased ways.

'I'll get the papers.' Zir turned away.

She hurried through the door on the far wall and closed it tightly behind her. Kata realized that Elen was watching him with a rustling crest.

'She's one of my hatching mates,' the youngling said. 'Too bad, because by God's Eye, how she's grown!'

Kata lifted his crest in answer. Even now that he knew his ally could never covet her, did he dare take this female up on their mutual interest? It was dangerous to get attached to anyone, no matter how casually, in his line of work. Yet when she returned, moving with a graceful swing of broad hips, he knew that refusing her offer would give him long nights of lost sleep. When she stared into his eyes, he raised his head and exposed his throat in surrender.

'Let's see what you've got for us.' Elen was pretending not to notice. 'I need to start looking for our new jobs as soon as possible.'

Zir laid on the counter two sets of identification papers, the best forgeries that Kata had ever seen, down to the last crisp detail of the printing.

'Riva transmitted these to a secret mail drop I have,' Zir said. 'I printed them out here.'

'An excellent job,' Kata said.

Her crest lifted at his praise. Elen scooped up his set and put them in the inner pocket of his wrap jacket.

'Kata, I'll meet you down at the Labour Exchange at the fifteens,' the youngling said. 'Zir, my best to your grandmother.'

'Thank you, Elen.' Her voice was soft and grave. 'She remembers you in her meditations.'

With a quick nod, Elen let himself out the near door, which Zir locked behind him. Kata heard him saying a few words to the grandfather at the desk; then the shop fell silent. Her crest upraised, Zir stood watching him. In two quick steps Kata crossed to her and caught her by the shoulders to spin her around. With a gentle jaw he caught the back of her neck in his teeth. She sighed, deep with longing.

'Come upstairs to my rooms,' she whispered. 'No-one will bother us there.'

'Gladly.' He ran his teeth ever so lightly along her neck scales, and she shuddered in his grasp. 'Gladly.'

In his private office, Karlo sat at his desk and read through the latest set of speeches that his writing team had prepared for him. When he found something he wanted removed or reworked, he talked his changes into the mark-up utility, but he never put the screen into finalizing mode. If he was going to pay specialists, he always figured, he'd be better off letting them earn their salary rather than overriding their decisions without giving them a chance to change his mind.

Down the side of his vidscreen ran a message window, where notes from his staff scrolled in a continuous loop, waiting for him to freeze them and answer. Although most he would ignore till later, he kept glancing at the scroll, waiting for a particular bit of news. Finally it came: popular vote on the Fleet appropriations would start running at thirty past the elevens.

'Time?'

'Forty-five into the tens,' the screen answered.

'Message mode. Locate Wan and Pero. Tell them to come to the gather in my living quarters right away.'

Pero showed up some ten minutes later, striding in grim-faced to join his father. Since he was still serving under active commission, though on permanent assignment to Government House, he wore grey Fleet fatigues. They went into the gather, a huge pale room with floor to ceiling windows always closed against the fog. Chrome glittered from the picture frames and light fixtures.

'Think the bill will pass?' Pero said.

'I don't know. The lower Council's already cut our appropriations request to the bone.'

'Gratitude usually is short-lived.'

'I can't say I'm surprised.' Karlo shrugged. 'It was always the same at home, people grumbling about how much the Fleet cost them. If the Cyberguild gets Nimue back online, Palace will get even more miserly.'

'It's too bad there's no way we can stop that, then.'

'Who says there isn't? I've been thinking about the problem.'

When Pero raised a questioning eyebrow, Karlo shook his head.

'You'll find out later,' Karlo said. 'Maybe. I'm not going to worry about it unless it looks like the guild can actually repair the thing. Sé Barra warned me that there's a good chance they can't.'

The two men sat down on the white silk sofa in front of the vidscreen, which was running a loop of the pro and con spokesapients, each with their two-minute opinion summary. Karlo muted the sound. Onscreen Vanna stood before a podium, mouthing her arguments for giving the Fleet full funding. Pero stretched his long legs out in front of him and glanced round.

'Where's Wan?'

'Oh, who the hell knows?' Karlo snapped. 'I told him to get over here, but he probably won't bother.'

Pero looked his father's way with an expression stripped of feeling. Karlo found it hard to look him in the eye.

Wan never did appear during the four-hour voting block. Once the process got fully underway, Dukayn joined them, ushering in a pair of saccules bringing drinks and food. Damo slipped in as well to sit on the floor at his father's feet. As every Mapscreen in every home and work place automatically tuned itself to ballot mode, graphs – blue pro, red con, and purple undecided – took over both the big vidscreens. In small windows around the edges ran maps and numbers: votes in, votes tallied as all over Palace, Sects and sub-Sects reporting.

Karlo cast his vote as soon as the screen allowed. Vanna would cast hers over in the Council Hall. In a fit of annoyance he wondered if Wan would even bother to vote, while Pero of course wasn't a citizen. There was nothing more for Karlo to do but watch and swear when the con tower built ahead of the pro or sigh when the negative swing reversed itself. At least the undecided vote held low. And at least a funding matter needed only a simple majority to pass. He'd been dreading seeing the entire matter remanded back to the Councils for further debate. Reworking a bill usually meant lost funds.

'It's going to be close,' Dukayn said at one point. 'We're three hours in.'

Karlo nodded. The blue tower stood a sliver higher than the red, with the purple lurking down at the bottom of the screens. Three and a half hours in – red made a surge, and Karlo heard himself using street language he thought he'd forgotten.

'Blue's rallying,' Pero said abruptly.

'You bet,' Dukayn said. 'There it goes.'

Karlo sank back in his seat and let out a sigh of relief. A side window announced that tallies from Tech Sect were coming in. Maintaining a Fleet meant money for Tech Sect. Blue surged. Although red made a feeble rally toward the end, the gains held. All four of them, even Damo, cheered when the gongs rang out, three long electronic pulses signalling the end of the voting block.

'She did it!' Pero raised his glass to the screens. 'Here's to Vanna!'

'Damn right,' Karlo said. 'Without her this bill would still be stuck in some damned committee somewhere.'

Damo clambered up, stretched, and looked longingly at the last of the ultrajuice on the refreshments table.

'Go ahead,' Karlo said.

'Thank you, Sé.'

Karlo watched while the boy flipped the top of the carafe back and poured the pale pink soda into his glass. He did everything with concentration, Damo, as if the fate of the Pinch depended on his filling his glass just so, neither spilling a drop nor leaving more than a drop behind.

'Hey,' Pero said to him. 'Looking forward to going out to Orbital?'

'Yes Sé.' Damo never looked away from his task.

'Have you met your new patron yet? Sé Barra, I mean?'

'Yes Sé.'

'Like her?'

For an answer Damo grinned, then put the carafe down and wiped his hands on a napkin. When he was done, he smoothed the napkin out, folded it precisely in half, and laid it down on a tray. Karlo turned to Dukayn, who was staring absently at the air while he took download from his chips. When he noticed Karlo glancing his way, he sat up straight, all attention.

'Know where Wan is?' Karlo said.

'No. I was just trying to find out.'

'Damn him! I wonder if he even got my message.'

'I can mount an all-out search.'

Pero was listening to this exchange with his arms crossed over his chest and a fixed smile on his face. When he caught Karlo watching him, he made an attempt to relax.

'I don't think that's necessary,' Karlo said to Dukayn. 'But if you can find him fast, do it.'

'The grids are going to want footage of you.' Dukayn got up, stretching, reaching for his perpetual tablet and scriber.

'Yeah, I've got a speech all ready for them. My gratitude to the citizens of Palace.'

'Sounds good, Sé. I'll just head to the briefing room now and see who's there. I'll start a few of my people looking for Wan, too.'

'Good. Call me when the gridjockeys are ready.'

Karlo and Pero both rose, but when Pero started to follow Dukayn out, Karlo gestured to him to stay. On the vidscreen the ballot mode had turned itself off, although the totals lingered in a side window. Presenters chatted back and forth from their separate panels, analysing the vote, while pictures of warships filled the main screen and captions floated in overlay. THE LEP THREAT: STILL WITH US? INTERSTELLAR GUILD WARNS OF DANGERS TO SHUNT NEXI. Damo sat cross-legged on the floor and stared at the screen while he ate precisely cut squares of cake.

'Come into my office a minute,' Karlo said to Pero.

The two men stood at the window and looked down to the roof garden below, where workers were scraping bulbous green fungi off the walks and benches. At times the spores drifting in from the swamps managed to take hold and grow, and always in the most unlikely places.

'They grow so damn fast,' Pero echoed his thought. 'Once they hit, you can practically see the cells dividing. If you let them get established, their rhizomorphs break things up.'

'Their what?'

'Roots. Well, their equivalent of roots. They can get into a crack in a slab of concrete and split it open if you let them.'

'Where the hell did you learn that?'

'I asked a cleaner.'

'Yeah? Why?'

'I was curious, that's all.'

For a moment they watched the maintenance people, who wore white masks over their mouths and noses. One worker would slice a growth away from its perch with a thin, flat blade while others stood ready to catch and seal it inside plastic bags.

'They explode once they're big enough,' Pero said. 'They release more spores that way.'

'Yeah?' Karlo said. 'The damnedest things interest you.'

Pero shrugged and said nothing.

'Anyway,' Karlo went on. 'I wanted a word with you. You've been on Palace for about a Standard year now, attached to staff. How does that sit with you?'

Automatically Pero fell into parade rest, clasping his hands behind his back and straightening up while he considered the question – considered it for a long while, as if he knew that answering held its dangers.

'It's all right,' Pero said at last. 'It has its compensations, ground duty.'

'I've been thinking that it was time for you to move on to a new assignment.'

'As the Fleet commands, Sé.'

'Of course. But I want to know how that would sit with you. I'm not talking about endless patrols or hanging around a shunt gate, waiting for pirates. There are places out there where someone I trusted could build up some elite units.'

'Oh.' Pero allowed himself a brief smile. 'I see.'

'The day is going to come when we won't have to grovel in front of civilian councils for operating expenses. I intend to be ready for it.'

Pero nodded.

'I'm not sure of the details yet,' Karlo went on. 'Let me think about it. I'll be glad of input from you, too, Captain Nikolaides.'

'Yes Sé. I'll put some work into it.'

On the screen the commcall buzzed, and Dukayn's image appeared.

'Be right there,' Karlo said to him. 'Pero, we'll talk about this later.'

'Huh,' Rico said. 'Are you sure Vida isn't a cybersorcerer after all?'

'What?' Hi said. 'What are you talking about?'

Rico leaned back in his desk chair and considered his uncle, who was standing in the doorway to Rico's room. Hi carried a schedplate – a specialized writing tablet for guild work – tucked under his arm.

'And what are you doing?' Hi went on. 'What's that on your Mapscreen?'

'Old code, Sé, the oldest I know. I'm trying to break through a membrane, but I didn't want to jack in right now.'

'We've got official work to do, yeah. But what membrane, and what's it got to do with the L'Var girl?'

'She's got a ferret, that's what. I tried to get a look at it, but her Mapstation's sealed off by a membrane. It's built in some weird old code, just like that umbrella over the Calios station in Pleasure.'

Hi frowned at the lines of symbols.

'That language you're using isn't very old at all,' Hi said at last. 'Not compared to Calios. You'll have to go back about a thousand year's worth of modifications to talk to him on his own terms. He's probably the ferret, by the way, just like he's probably the one who installed the umbrella.'

'What makes you say that?'

'Those old-style "citizen's assistance" metas did a lot of things routinely that it takes a trained Maprunner to do now. Keeping private data private was part of their job.'

'You know what? I found membranes around all kinds of things belonging to Vida – her school records, her database, even her medical history.'

'And what were you doing, hacking into her records?'

Rico felt himself blush.

'Ah, it's love!' Hi winked at him. 'Let me give you a tip, kid. Never read a girl's medical records. They blight the romance real fast.'

'Sounds like you're saying that from personal experience.'

'Bitter personal experience. Anyway, I sure would like to get a look at Calios. Wonder if Vida would let us play around with him?'

'I'm working on that.'

'Yeah? Don't tell me how. I'm willing to bet I don't want to know. Now wipe that code off your screen and pay attention. We've got a lot of work ahead of us.'

'Yes, Sé. I found those old records you asked for, the Caliostro repair sheets. They go back about six hundred years.'

'Standard or Palace?'

'Standard.'

'Ah. Well, that's still a lot of data. I want to plot the rate of deterioration and see if it's holding steady or getting worse. Did you find anything like a schematic?'

'Lots of them, including one that's only fifty years old. It's really complete – all the damage marked and noted, in Gen as well as code.'

'Great! Then we'll use that as our starting point. I've got an errand for you first, though. Have you ever actually seen Caliostro? His box, I mean.'

'No, Sé.'

'Here.' Hi handed over the tablet. 'I want you to take a look at him. Here's the last set of photonics diagrams made, back about fifty years ago, same time as that schematic. See how it checks out.'

'I'll do it right now, if you like.'

'I would, yeah. I'll be gone till evening, so this will keep you out of trouble. That reminds me – how are you doing with the drug training?'

'Fine. It sure is easier to get work done when you use them.'

Hi considered him, his dark eyes so shrewd that Rico felt like a box full of faulty photonics himself.

'How do the drugs feel to you?' Hi said at last.

'Okay.' Rico shrugged. 'I'm pretty much used to them. I'm sure glad you can use a pressure injector, though, and not one of those needles like the medic had.'

'You've adapted real fast, you know.'

'Uh, have I? Didn't know that.'

'Real fast. Rico, listen to me. We both know that the addiction was just Arno's cover story. But that doesn't mean the damn drugs aren't dangerous.'

'Well, yes, Sé, sure. Hey, I passed the readiness course.'

Rico found himself wondering about his voice – had he snapped at his uncle? He was surprised at his own sudden discomfort.

'Good,' Hi went on. 'Then you know what I'm talking about. Remember what you learned.'

'I will. I promise.'

'Okay. Let's meet back here at the eighteens. We'll have dinner, and you can give me a quick report.'

That was all: no more help, no more instructions, not even a clear goal. He was a journeyman now, all right, not an apprentice.

Caliostro lay deep inside the underground areas of West Tower in what had originally been the engine rooms of the colony ship. Getting there from the suite in East required going down seven levels, taking a movebelt through a longtube to the other tower, and riding a maintenance lift booth down even further. Once Rico finally found the correct booth, he had to wait while workers in Peronida green loaded cleaning bots. He glanced idly around and out of the corner of his eye saw a girl with short cropped red hair. His heart pounding, he spun around – but she wasn't Vida, just some other redhead. Weird, he thought. Vida's the first girl with red hair I ever saw, and now here's another one.

'Bots are all loaded, fella,' someone called out.

When Rico elbowed his way in after, the maintenance people paid him no attention. He slid his heavy toolkit off its shoulder strap and set it beside him. In a corner near the controls stood a man wearing the grey coveralls of the Industrial Guild.

'Level?' he said; he was a tall silver-haired fellow, his skull studded with chips. 'Hey, kid, I'm talking to you. What level? These old tubes don't respond to voice.'

'Yeah? That's weird.'

'Nah, just old.' He grinned. 'But hell, it's a job. What level?'

Rico consulted the plate.

'Minus Seventy Four, sector Q-O. Please.'

The man grunted and keyed in the coordinates. With a lurch and a groan, the tube slid downward. Rico leaned back against the wall and studied his schedplate. The mechanics got out a few floors later. In silence Rico and the liftjockey rode down, and down, a long way down, Rico suddenly realized. He glanced up at the read-out over the door and watched numbers slipping by.

'Don't usually get anyone going down this far,' the operator said. 'You're Cyberguild, huh?'

'Sure am.'

'You must be heading for a look at Caliostro.'

'Yeah, that's right.'

'When you want to come back up, there's a command plate by the door. Hit the emergency alarm. Don't panic, but it'll take someone a while to get down to pick you up. You're not claustrophobic, are you?'

'Why?'

'You'll see.'

Rico did see when the lift booth finally reached his floor – hit bottom, really, or so the operator informed him. The doors opened into a narrow grey corridor of some twenty feet with a swing-hatch at either end. Rico brought up the map programmed into his schedplate and took the north hatch, which led into a tunnel, strung with bundled cables in blue and red and just barely high enough for him to stand upright. The only light came from the flashlight in his toolkit, but the little gold dot on his map beeped cheerfully and led him along. They travelled straight for some yards, then turned down another tunnel, then another, until Rico realized that if anything happened to that schedplate, he might never get out of there again. For a moment he found it hard to breathe, then remembered that his guild coveralls had a built-in alarm and tracer. He'd always wondered why. Now he knew.

After they'd spent about ten minutes threading the maze, the map brought him to a red door. Inlaid about level with his eyes gleamed a black sign with lighted lettering.

'No Admittance without Cyberguild Clearance.'

Rico swore. He'd forgotten – he should have known – he'd never got himself a clear-code token, and now he was going to have to go all the way up to the surface and probably down to guild headquarters, too, if Uncle Hi had already left the suite. He wasn't looking forward to hearing what Hi was going to say about his oversight, either. He knelt and searched through his toolkit, but as he expected, none of the code tokens in the standard issue set led to anywhere as important as an AI housing. He straightened up and considered the door. On an impulse he spoke aloud the all-meta Arno had given him.

'Morning light.'

The doors hissed and slid back. Beyond them pale white light panels flickered into life on a ceiling some twenty feet above. Feeling suddenly cold and for no reason he could name, Rico stepped inside.

The room stretched about twenty yards long but narrow, lined from grey floor to glowing high ceiling with alternating panels of metal plate and blueglass bricks. The metal plates flickered with readouts and inserts while reflections splattered the blueglass. Rico walked a few yards in, then stood looking around, turning slowly in this tall box of light.

'Caliostro.' Somehow it seemed appropriate to greet the intelligence who lived here. 'Caliostro, son of the morning.'

Later he'd convince himself that it was only a fantasy on his part, but it seemed to him that the lights dimmed slightly, then brightened again. For a moment, for the briefest of moments, he thought he heard not so much a voice as the echo of a voice, fading from a long time ago, answering him.

'The kid's got guts, all right,' Hi said. 'You trained her well.'

Aleen allowed herself a small smile.

'Before I left for Souk, Aleen consulted me about Vida's education,' Molos said. 'I venture to say that since the child survived Aleen's training, she will doubtless be able to survive anything.'

Hi laughed. The three of them were sitting in a small parlour on the second floor of The Close. Amid real flowers as well as the floral holos filling the corners of the room, they lounged on green velvet chairs around a low table, where Hi's blackbox card glowed among the remains of lunch. Aleen's hair had turned to pale gold since the last time Hi had seen her, and she wore a dress of the same colour, set off by a flower pinned to the wide collar. The blood-red bloom echoed the tattooed sun of her Mark.

'Well,' Aleen said. 'Once I learned who her father was, I knew I'd been handed something useful. I was hoping that sooner or later, Palace society would want their L'Var back.'

'Useful for what, though, my dear Aleen?' Molos said with a rustle of his crest. 'Can you believe it, Hivel? She's never told me, not during all these years.'

'Oh, I believe it, yeah.'

Both men looked at Aleen, who leaned forward, picked a crumb off the green table cloth, and flicked it onto her flowered plate.

'What worries me now,' Aleen said at last, 'is keeping Vida safe. I'm beginning to wonder why we pay taxes. The Protectors are worthless, it seems.'

'No,' Molos said. 'It's merely that my brother is very clever.'

'Unfortunately that's true,' Hi put in. 'I'll have another word with my contact in Military Intelligence, but she warned me that they'd have to wait before coming in on this. Can't go poaching on the Protectors' territory, not right away, anyway.'

'What?' Aleen tossed her head with a ripple of gold. 'We have to wait until he kills someone else?'

'My dear, it must seem that way, but Hivel's right. There are protocols in this sort of thing.'

'Stuff the protocols!'

'Now, now, my dear Aleen. It's only been what? Six days, seven? Since my despicable brother made his attempt on Vida.'

'Yeah, six,' Hi said. 'It happened on Eight Gust. It's Fourteen now.'

'With all the kickbacks I give the Protectors, that should be time enough.' She glared at them impartially. 'Hi?'

'Yeah, yeah, you're right. It probably will take another death.'

'It had better not be Vida's.'

'Now that I doubt very much.' Molos leaned forward earnestly. 'The Peronida's taking every precaution –'

'Like driving her right into Finance Sect for dinner? What is wrong with those people? Don't they think?'

'When it suits them,' Hi said. 'The rest of the time they depend on armed guards. Karlo took half a regiment with him for that little drive.'

'Oh. Well, that's better.' Aleen sat back in her chair. 'But I don't like this, Hi, and I know neither of you do either, having Vi-Kata prowling the streets after –' She paused, glancing Hi's way. 'After what happened.'

Hi picked up the napkin from his lap, tossed it in the air, caught it again. Not an hour passed without his thinking of Arno. If only he'd stayed in The Close, if only I'd made him wait longer – he blamed himself even though he knew that Arno never would have listened to him. Molos was watching, his crest flattened in sympathy.

'So,' Molos said. 'Let us review. We know that Riva has hired my less than beloved brother. We also know that Riva must be a cybermaster of great skill. How else could a Lep gain access to the Map these days? Other than these pitifully few datapoints, we know nothing. What does Riva want? The name translates as "unblemished scales", but the actual meaning is closer to "racial purity". I suspect that she leads a group that sees itself as an answer to UJU. I hear things, now and again, when I'm dining out in Finance Sect, about such a group. The rumour is that the membership is growing. The Benars are worried, very worried. They would have a great deal to lose if violence should give the Peronida an excuse for further actions against our people.'

'Violence?' Hi said. 'What about crashing the Map?'

Molos hissed like a hundred cats.

'My apologies, my dear Aleen,' he stammered. 'And at table, too! I must be getting senile!'

'No, no, it's all right. I understand.'

Hi felt his mind ticking over. Of course – it was obvious – why hadn't he seen it before, that the vandalism on the Map might well be related to the racial tensions in the city? 'Well, look,' Hi said aloud. 'I've been thinking that we had two separate problems, Riva and then the vandal, the rogue cybermaster. What if we only have one?'

'Hah!' Molos stopped himself from hissing again. 'It makes sense. Damage to the Map would be the ultimate act of terrorism. And that's why Arno would be a danger to Riva, a serious danger. By tracing the vandals, he was tracing her.'

'You bet. And this latest round of vandalism started about twelve years ago, right after Karlo passed his damned laws.'

'That's significant, yes.' Molos's voice turned dry. 'I remember my own feelings at the time, and here I was given special privileges, thanks to my dear friends.' He paused for a nod Hi's way. 'Others who were not so fortunate were outraged.'

'I don't blame them.' Hi held up one hand with his thumb tucked behind his fingers. 'There were only four Lep masters who had the skill to do what Riva's doing. Two of them left the planet after the ban, and the third one's you.'

'And the last, Var En Ha'i, is very old and very ill,' Molos said. 'Besides, I can't imagine him damaging his beloved Map. No, I really can't. As for the other two, well, they could access the Palace Map through the Hypermap, but it would be extremely difficult for them to do it secretly. They'd have to be as intelligent as an AI to do so, and while I esteem my former colleagues, they don't qualify for that honour.'

'Yeah, that's true. And if Riva's a woman –'

Molos let his jaw go slack while he thought.

'That narrows our field to nobody, doesn't it?' the Lep said at last. 'I can't think of a single Lep woman master of the requisite skill. Or – wait – there are many Lep masters of lesser grades. What if they were pooling their skills, and our Riva is only their leader?'

'That would make sense, but how the hell are they getting on the Map without a sign-on code?'

Molos considered, sucking a meditative tooth.

'Well, yes,' he said at last. 'But that problem would apply to a human suspect, wouldn't it?'

'Right. It would.'

Aleen was listening, glancing back and forth between them. Every now and then her cybereye flashed, but she would blink the pattern to turn it off.

'Any thoughts?' Hi said to her. 'Sometimes an amateur sees things a pro misses.'

'Just one thing,' Aleen said. 'Do you remember when Arno was telling you about Vi-Kata for the first time? He said that someone tipped him off. Did you ever find out who that was?'

'Not yet.' Hi leaned back with a long sigh. 'Too much has happened, too fast. It's on my agenda. I've got Rico doing a general survey right now, in fact, that will give me the base data I need to make sense out of what Arno told me.'

'I wish Molos could get back on the Map to help you. That's the most useful thing I can think of, but it's impossible.'

'Alas, yes,' the Lep said. 'My special privileges extend only to the lowest possible level of the Map, such as banking tasks that I could do without bothering to jack in at all.'

Hi considered the thought that crouched before him, snarling like an animal. When Molos started to speak, Aleen silenced him with a wave of her hand.

'By the bloodshot Eye,' Hi said at last. 'This is such a damned dangerous idea I can't believe I thought of it. Molos, if anyone ever caught you on the Map, the pair of us would end up in jail.'

'Just so. And in the cells of the condemned at that.'

'Want to risk it?'

Molos extended his crest and waved it in the equivalent of reckless laughter.

'I take it you see a way to smuggle me on?'

'I sure do. But oh my God, it's risky.'

Aleen was watching him with her face utterly expressionless, and her hands lay quietly in her lap.

'I'm not going to talk about this in front of you,' Hi said. 'I don't want you to know one thing more. Forget what you've already heard, okay?'

'Okay.' Her voice shook, just barely. 'I keep having the urge to disgrace myself. You know, by saying stupid things like "be careful".'

'A useful warning, actually,' Molos said. 'But I agree, Hivel. We shall meet elsewhere and soon?'

'Very soon. I don't want to see Kata make another kill any more than Aleen does.'

'No more do I,' Molos said, then glanced at Aleen. 'Lep cybermasters have our own code, different than the human and Hirrel systems. The Ancestors developed it before the various maps in the Pinch were merged to become *the* Map. Hivel knows it, of course, just as I know the other two systems, but I think I'm safe in saying that he's somewhat slower in that mode, just as I am with the human.'

'It's one thing to know an alien code,' Hi took over. 'It's another to be able to think in it. But what really counts is the way you know the Lep community. I'm probably missing a lot of clues that might lead you to one of the vandals.'

'I was thinking the same thing. And Riva's a greater danger than my brother.'

'We'll let the Protectors go after him while we go after whoever hired him.'

'It sounds like an excellent plan – if we can manage to put it into action. Have your factor call me –'

'No.' Hi shook his head hard. 'I'll call you myself. I don't want anyone else implicated in this. Hell! I'll have to tell Rico something. Maybe. I'll think about it. But I'll call you myself. I don't want anyone on my staff to go down with me if it turns out that we go down.'

'Excellent! I shall follow the same policy, not that I have much of a staff these days.' Molos rose, bowing to Aleen. 'My thanks for the marvellous lunch, my dear. I shall be off. No doubt you have other matters to discuss with Hivel, and I have some thinking to do.'

In a swirl of pale gold skirt Aleen rose to see him out. At the door she turned, glancing back at Hi.

'Can you stay for a while?' she said.

'I shouldn't, but I wrestled some time out of my damned schedule.'

'Why don't you wait for me upstairs, then? Make yourself comfortable.'

'Good idea. I will.'

Aleen smiled, just briefly, then walked out after Molos. Hi felt his desire for her welling up like warm water. Maybe it could, for a little while, wash his grief away.

'Come in, my dear, come in,' Cardinal Roha said. 'Brother Dav, you'll make sure we're not disturbed?'

'Of course, Your Eminence,' the burly monk said. 'Sé Vida, your bodyguard can wait out here with me.'

'No.' Jak crossed his arms over his chest. 'I would prefer to accompany Sé Vida.'

Imposing in his new green uniform, Jak glared down at Dav, who despite his muscles stood a head shorter than the Garang. Vida glanced at the cardinal, standing in the doorway to his inner room.

'Jak is really trustworthy, Your Eminence,' she said. 'He won't repeat anything he hears.'

'Very well, then,' Roha said. 'Both of you come in.'

'Thank you, we will.'

With a scowling Dav holding the door for her, Vida walked into Roha's private office. She glanced around at the small, white room, bare except for a desk, a vidscreen, and against the far wall a hologram of the night sky. Roha sat in a hard-looking chair, though a black formfit stood nearby. Jak shut the door, then took up his usual position with his back to it.

'Do sit down, Vida,' Roha said. 'I'm so glad our factors could finally arrange this little meeting.'

'So am I, Your Eminence.' Vida sat, smoothing her modest green dress under her. 'I'm sorry I've been so busy.'

'Oh, I understand. Getting established here in Government House is quite a job. Have you been enjoying the experience?'

'Enjoying it? I don't know if I'd call it that. It's been exciting, maybe, but not exactly fun.'

'I see you've inherited your father's bluntness.' Roha seemed genuinely pleased. 'He had the same direct way of putting things.'

'Well, the woman who raised me never wasted any words, either, when she had something to say.'

'No doubt, but genes will tell, Vida; our genes will always tell. At any rate, I asked you to come here to discuss several important points. The first is the matter of your suit to regain control of the L'Var properties from the Makeesa. I see that Samante has engaged a very good lawyer, and the first reports I've heard are quite encouraging.'

'They are, yes. Since the courts have been holding the property in trust, anyway, it mostly seems to be a question of transferring the executorship to someone new. I can't control it myself until I'm thirty-five, of course.'

'Of course. Which brings us to the matter of your seat on the Council. You'll be a Not-child very soon, and the First Citizen and I are planning our campaign to invoke the emergency law. We don't want you waiting all those years to claim your vote.'

'Thank you, Your Eminence. May I ask you something? I can't help thinking that the lawsuits would go a lot faster if I had that Council seat. And they'd be more likely to go in my favour, too.'

'Ah, you're learning about Government House, I see.' Roha smiled briefly. 'Yes, indeed. No doubt they would.'

'I'm glad you think I'm learning, Your Eminence. I've been trying.'

'Good, good. You know, Vida, one very important thing to learn is how to make the right sort of friends. There should always be room in our lives for a real friendship, such as I had with your father. Real friends demand nothing from us but a decent delight in their presence, and yet we feel like offering them a great deal.'

'Well, yeah, I can see that.'

'Good. But then we can also, if we're not careful, make the wrong sort of friend, someone who will lead us astray on the pretence of friendship. Such people are traps and snares.'

Vida hesitated, caught by a sudden flash of anger. If he meant Rico, he could save this sermon for the cathedral! Roha leaned back in his chair and arched his hands with the fingertips together.

'Your father was a very open-minded man,' Roha said absently. 'Have you listened to any of his Council speeches? Everything that happens in Council is recorded and stored.'

'Yes, I have, Your Eminence.'

'Perhaps you have seen him speaking just before the Lep War? There was a period when it seemed that conflict might be averted, and he spoke several times in favour of seeking negotiation from Souk.'

'I did see those, yeah. I thought he was splendid.'

'Oh yes. He was also wrong.' Roha peered at her over the arch of his fingers. 'I do not for a moment think that Orin was a traitor. I'm certain that he was unfairly accused and unjustly convicted. I said so then and I'd say so now if anyone should ask me. But his kind words about the Ty Onar Lep came back to haunt him during the trial. Enemy sympathizer. That's what his enemies – that's what Vanna Makeesa – called him.'

'Well, they were lying.'

'Oh yes, but the jury believed them. Why? Because he was known to consort with Leps. One must be very careful about the company one keeps here in Government House.'

Vida stared, puzzled, more than a little uneasy. Roha leaned forward, his long bony face all earnestness.

'Ri Tal Molos is not fit company for you, Vida,' the cardinal said. 'I'm distressed to hear reports that you receive him socially.'

'But Molos is a friend of my guardian's, Your Eminence. He's been nothing but kind to me.'

'No doubt. You have a great deal to offer such as him, while he, of course, has nothing to offer in return.'

Vida felt as if her mouth had gone numb, leaving her speechless. After a moment the cardinal sighed and leaned back in his chair.

'A word to the wise, my dear,' Roha said. 'That's all. Just a word to the wise.'

'Well, thank you, Your Eminence, but –'

Roha held up a thin hand for silence.

'Let us not discuss it further at the moment,' he said. 'I wish us to be friends, and a friendship should never start with a quarrel.'

'All right, of course.'

Roha smiled, nodding, glancing away. Vida felt like an utter coward for not defending Molos, but Roha was, after all, the cardinal of Palace and she, only a child and a newcomer. While she groped for something to say, the silence grew poisoned.

'Um, well,' Vida said at last. 'Samante's negotiating the wedding date with Wan's factor. Had you heard that?'

'No, I didn't.' Roha looked back her way and smiled. 'Will it be soon?'

'Real soon, Your Eminence. Karlo wanted it to be on the tenth, but I'm trying to get it put off till some time in Timber. We'll probably end up compromising on Twenty Gust.'

He laughed, a good facsimile of a kindly chuckle.

'Putting it *off*? You look very nervous, my dear. Tell me, are you regretting your decision to marry Wan?'

'What? No, of course not.'

The cardinal raised one eyebrow.

'Well, it's not like I can get out of it now, anyway.'

'Perhaps not, no. I doubt very much if we can seat you early on the Council if for some reason we should lose the support of the First Citizen. And if we can't, well, I can't speak for the courts, but your properties might be in danger.' Roha's smile gleamed like a knife. 'You do need to remember that, my dear.'

'I will.' Vida laid a hand at her throat. 'I kind of thought that might be the case.'

Although Rico was expecting that he and his uncle would go out for dinner, Hi had a meal sent in. Once the various dishes were laid onto the table in the eating area of their suite, Hi tipped the saccule servants and sent them off. Jevon was dining elsewhere, but Nju helped himself from various plastofoam containers, then started to carry his plate out to the gather.

'Oh, Nju?' Hi said. 'Don't let anyone in without warning me first. No-one. I don't care if the place is on fire.'

'Very well, Sé Hivel. I shall ensure it.'

After Nju left, Hi laid the blackbox card down on the table, then sat and watched Rico eat.

'Aren't you hungry?' Rico said at last. 'This pseudomeat is really good.'

'No thanks. I had a late lunch.' Hi got up and walked across the room, then walked back. 'How did Caliostro check out?'

'Weirdest thing.' Rico swallowed hastily. 'That schematic I found? There has to be a more recent one.'

'Yeah? Why?'

'Well, it charted one area as damaged that wasn't. It's been repaired, I mean.'

'Oh. Go on eating, kid.' Hi flopped into his chair. 'If that schematic isn't current, your report can wait. Sorry about the wasted errand, though.'

'It was worth the trip, just getting to see Caliostro. Now that's a *box*.'

'Yeah, it sure is. Wait a minute. Did you find any report of that repair?'

'None, no.' Again Rico had to gulp down a mouthful. 'That's what's weird. It was an internal repair, using a daemon to re-install some damaged code. It wasn't a lot of work and all it did was bring a side-route cage back online, but the tech still should have filed a report.'

'Damn right. Caliostro is what keeps the towers running and the rest of Government House, too. Anyone who touches his systems had better log in.' Hi picked up a roll and took an absent-minded bite while he thought something over. 'If the photonics diagrams date from only fifty years ago, I should know the person who made them. What's the name on the report?'

'There isn't one.'

'What?'

'Well, maybe I just didn't notice.'

While Rico hurriedly shovelled in the rest of his meal, Hi scrolled through the entire schedplate. By the end of it he was swearing under his breath. Rico washed down the last bite with a gulp of water.

'What's wrong?'

'You're right, that's what,' Hi said. 'There's no name, no code ID number, no guild ranking, no nothing. I never noticed it when I transferred the data to this plate. What about that schematic you found? Any name on that?'

'Not that I remember.'

'Let's check it out.'

As soon as Rico brought the schematic up on his Mapscreen, they could see the utterly blank header where all the tech's personal data belonged.

'I found these reports right where they should have been,' Rico said. 'Right in the repair log directories. There's some old utilities in there, too: diagnostics, a compare and clean daemon, that kind of thing, and then a bunch of old logs.'

'We must be looking at backup copies,' Hi's voice sounded uncertain. 'But why they survived and not the final registers is beyond me.'

'But I thought you said that there hasn't even been any vandalism on the Caliostro system. That all the damage is old stuff.'

'Damn! You're right. Unless wiping off the originals of these documents is the first bit of vandalism we've caught.'

'Why would someone do that and not wipe off the backups, too?'

'Beats me.'

For a moment they stared at each other, then turned back to the screen.

'I've got an idea, a real strange idea,' Hi said after a moment. 'It's based on something Arno told me, right before – well. Anyway, it's possible that we've got an ally on the Map, someone who tipped Arno off to danger, and maybe for all I know someone who's doing a little repair work in secret.'

'But why wouldn't they tell you who they are?'

'That's a good question, kid, a very good question. I don't have a clue. But tomorrow, first thing, we're going to jack in, both of us, and we're going to work in tandem to match this schematic to Caliostro's Map. If nothing else, we'll both know him real well by the time we're done.'

'All right, Sé. It sounds like a good place to start.'

'Yeah. I'll tell Jevon to cancel any appointments.' Hi glanced round. 'Oh, right. She asked for the evening off. Well, remind me to ask her in the morning.'

In some ways working in Government House made attending meetings easier, Jevon supposed. She certainly had a shorter distance to travel now that she lived within the blueglass walls of the precinct. On the other hand, because she was becoming well-known there as guildmaster Jons's factor, she also risked running across someone who recognized her. Since this particular night hung cold with fog, she wore a heavy sweater with a cowl that she pulled up around her face, a perfectly reasonable garment for the weather, and walked briskly. The few other sapients she saw out and about also seemed in a hurry to get inside and warm. Still, every noise behind her sounded like a stalking footstep, a Protector or security guard who might suddenly demand her reasons for being out at night alone. She kept turning round, but no-one ever followed. By the time she reached the Cathedral of the Eye, she was shivering from fear more than the fog. She'd also walked so fast that she was in danger of reaching the meeting far too early.

As always the doors stood open to all who would enter, promising warmth and a place to sit down. Jevon ducked inside and felt her breath returning, her fear ebb. All around the rim of the Gaze stood tiny side-chapels, set aside for meditation and prayer, each dominated by a floor-to-ceiling holo of a particular work from God's hand – a nebula, glowing in subtle calories, or a giant planet, striped and speckled, surrounded with rings, or some other such glory of Creation.

Jevon wandered into the Chapel of the Home Planet and sat down on the little wooden bench to gaze at the image hanging in a floor to ceiling niche across the tiny room. Against a stylized backdrop of stars hung a blue world, slowly turning to display green and brown landmasses, roughly triangular, and white icecaps at either pole. Somewhere back toward Galactic Centre, farther away even than the Rim, this planet circled a small yellow star. Its children out on the richer worlds of the Rim kept it as a shrine and a wilderness preserve – or at least, they'd been doing so two thousand years ago, and they still did as far as any one knew. Once every Standard year, each priest of the Eye out here in the Pinch preached a sermon about the Home Planet, a remembrance of the humble origins of something so grand as the human race.

Which, Jevon reminded herself, she'd sworn to serve. She got up and glanced out the chapel door. Although no-one was out in the Gaze, still she lingered, wondering as she always wondered if she were doing the right thing. When she'd first been recruited to join UJU, it had been exciting, a secret that she could treasure during the dull routine of organizing Sé Hivel's life. Just because she could organize events and lives so well, she'd moved up in the hierarchy almost without realizing how. At times like this, gazing at the serenity of the Cathedral, she wondered if the God who had created humanity would really approve of UJU. If she stayed here wondering much longer, she'd be late. She shook the feeling off and hurried out.

They held meetings in a small upstairs room of a library belonging to the Power Guild – the sort of place that no-one would ever suspect of harbouring something interesting. Jevon walked through the big reading room past ranks of Map terminals where sleepy apprentices stared at screens full of engineering diagrams. A lift booth took her up to the top floor and the plain grey room, dominated by a vidscreen-sized Mapscreen. Of the three members of the Second Step, Wilso or UJU-Quinze had already arrived and sat on one of the chairs arranged in front of the screen. He wore an ordinary pair of grey slacks and a blue shirt; beside him lay a shabby jacket.

'Hello, UJU-Quarz,' he remarked, smiling. 'Come sit down.'

'Thanks.' Jevon smiled as briefly as possible, then sat as far as possible, too, at the other end of the row.

'That sweater becomes you, I must say.' He was looking at her breasts. 'Cold out tonight, eh?'

'Very, yes.' Jevon crossed her arms over her chest. 'And how's your wife?'

'Oh, um, quite well, yes, thanks.'

'That's nice. Do you know what time it is? UJU-Trey should be here soon.'

'Well, yes, so he should, eh?' Wilso glanced at the cyberclock implanted in his wrist. 'Yes, really, any minute. I don't suppose UJU-Prime will start the meeting without him.'

'That's true. Funny – Prime always seems to know when we're all here.'

'Just so, just so. Eh?'

Both of them glanced at the screen, where in a brief while the scrambled image of their leader would appear. At times the other member of the First Step, UJU-Deuce, would join them as a guided revenant in the form of an old man with a stylized face and a body reduced to a column of black. No member of the Second Step – Trey, Quarz, and Quinze – knew who either Prime or Deuce was, though Jevon was willing to bet that they all had their theories.

Jevon heard the door opening and turned her head to look. Dressed in black trousers and a black tunic, studded up one sleeve with steel, Dukayn walked in, nodding to each of them.

'I hope I'm not late?' he said.

'No, no.' Wilso glanced at his implant again. 'Just on time.'

Dukayn sat down between the two of them and folded his hands in his lap. All three watched the wall, and sure enough, in a bare couple of seconds a light brightened, an image formed. On the vidscreen hung the bright and crystalline scramble of UJU-Prime.

'Good evening,' he remarked in his syrupy voice. 'We shall reign in what?'

'Splendour and the light of God's Eye,' they chorused.

'When will the time of splendour be?' said Dukayn, as senior member present.

'At the opening of the return. I declare this meeting of the Second Step open. I have two things to lay before you. We must continue to discuss the rally, of course, that our public front will be holding soon. But first, a warning. My sources in Finance Sect tell me that a few Leps have begun arming themselves.'

'Oh, have they?' Dukayn snapped. 'A sweep through –'

'No, no, no, UJU-Trey,' Prime broke in. 'You must do nothing that can be traced to you and through you to UJU. If a regiment of Garang appear in Lep Sect to search for weapons, will not everyone know who ordered them there? From who it's but a short distance to why.'

'Well, true enough, Sé. Still, I have a few good men that I can put on guard.'

'A few for a few, yes, that will be well. Remember, we've only received a tip. It may not even be true.' Prime turned his shadow-face Wilso's way. 'Are you still resolved to speak at the rally?'

'Unless you forbid it, of course,' Wilso said. 'But my views on the subject are already well-known. No-one will be surprised to see me there.'

'That's very true,' Dukayn put in. 'They'd wonder if you stayed away.'

'All right, then,' Prime said. 'UJU-Quarz, you are the contact between the Outer Committee and the Second Step. How are the committee's plans proceeding?'

'Very well, Sé,' Jevon said. 'They've finally got the public assembly permit approved and put it on file with the Recreational Events Committee. I was beginning to worry, with time getting so short. After all, we've already advertised. If we hadn't been given the permit, we would have shot our credibility. Now all that's left is polishing the last few details.'

The meeting settled down to those details of UJU's first public event, the rally in Algol Park with music, speakers, free refreshments, and a fine air of moderation all on the programme. Yet no matter how temperate the speeches, the rally would deliver a message, that on Palace there were plenty of humans who were sick and tired of seeing alien needs getting special treatment and alien species living on human turf.

'After all, we pay our taxes, too, and we all vote,' Jevon remarked at one point. 'Remember, that's the note we want to strike. Peaceful change through the interactives and our elected officials. We all vote.'

'That's right, eh?' Wilso said. 'That's exactly the point I'm going to emphasize in my opening remarks. We have a government on this planet, and we live under the rule of law. It's lasted for over a thousand years, our government, which goes to show how well worth respecting it is.'

Dukayn smiled, glancing away, so remote that Jevon felt a flash of fear run down her spine. Just what was he thinking, that he would smile like a hunter seeing his prey?

Slender and delicate, TeeKay Rommoff stood just over five feet tall. Her hair, blonde at the moment, tumbled round her heart-shaped face in carefully randomized curls. Her eyes were blue and deep-set, her mouth delicate. When she arrived at Vida's suite, she was wearing a shirt of white lace, her favourite fabric, tucked decorously into well-cut blue slacks.

'Dan isn't here yet?' she said. 'Shit!'

'That's your favourite word, isn't it?' Vida said.

'It suits my life, let's face it.' TeeKay flopped onto the divan and flung an arm over a pillow. 'Aren't you going to offer me a drink?'

'Well, if you mean alcohol, I don't think we've got any.'

Greenie shook its head and let out a long sigh from a cheek sac.

'For an ex-whore from Pleasure, you're really stuffy, y'know?'

Vida laughed. This business of the ex-whore had become their joke, a way of defusing potential hurt.

'Oh well,' TeeKay went on. 'There will be drink a-plenty where we're going. I can't imagine Wan making reservations at somewhere lacking in that department. You look great tonight, by the way. I like that dress. It shows just the right amount of tit.'

'Thanks.'

'It'll be wasted on your dumb-ass fiancé, I suppose. Well, sorry, I shouldn't call him that, not that I hear you rushing to defend him.'

Vida shrugged and sat down in an armchair, then gestured at Greenie to leave. Humming and hissing, the saccule bustled out.

'We all do what we have to, huh?' TeeKay said after a moment. 'But why don't you have a liquor cabinet?'

'I never thought of it. I don't even know what to put in one.'

'Then we'll go shopping, and I'll tell you. God, Vida! A babe in the wilderness, that's you.'

'Back at The Close the bartender always took care of that.'

'That makes sense.' TeeKay hesitated briefly. 'Tell me to shut up if I'm out of line, but I was curious about something. Do you ever feel like you'd like to go back to The Close?'

'I'd like to see my friends there, sure. I'll never miss the rotten life, but I really miss Tia and Aleen. They were my family.'

'That's amazing! Wanting to see your family, I mean. I'm always so pumped when I can get the money to get away from mine. Living in Government House sure beats the ancestral home and all that shit.'

'You don't have an allowance?'

'I do, but it's minuscule.' TeeKay rolled her eyes. 'My father is so cheap he'd charge for his farts if he could. Thank God I've got relatives I can blackmail, or I'd be living like a Lifegiver in some crummy room in Service Sect. Or worse yet, living in the ancestral muck out in the swamps. Do you know why there are aristocrats on Palace, Vida?'

'Well, uh, no. I never gave it any thought.'

'Because no-one would have been stupid enough to go live in those stenchy swamps and grow the food for this God-forsaken planet, that's why, if they hadn't been bribed up the ass. I mean, it's obvious. The Colonists weren't dumb. No-one would have gone out there because they just absolutely *loved* hydroponics.'

Vida had to laugh, and TeeKay grinned companionably.

'But that's not what my father will tell you,' TeeKay went on. 'He loves to talk about ancestral genotypes and quality. Quality will out, he says. In mushrooms as well as men. By God's little tear ducts! If my genotype is so superior why doesn't he give me a decent allowance? That's what I want to know.'

'He's not like Dan's mother, then.'

'No. Spoiled rotten, that's what Dan is. Oh well, it means I can always pry credits out of him when I need some. I am thankful for life's small blessings when they come my way.'

The blessing in question arrived a few minutes later, dressed in a narrow-cut red velvet suit. He'd pulled back his long dark hair into a gold clasp and carried a gallant armload of blue and white flowers, a gift for Vida. The saccule bustled in after him.

'Greenie,' Dan said. 'These go in water. Put the water in vases. Know what those are? Good. Then put the flowers in the water, but don't cram them in too tightly.'

Greenie pantomimed a spreading motion with both hands, then took the flowers and bustled out.

'God only knows what the poor creature's going to do with them,' TeeKay said.

'Eat a few, probably.' Dan sank down into the sofa next to her. 'But there's lots.'

'When's Wan due here?' TeeKay said.

'In five minutes,' Vida said. 'But what'll you bet he'll be late?'

'Huh,' Dan snorted. 'I never bet on sure things.'

Half an hour passed in small talk, another half in playing cards, which left the three of them hungry and irritable. When Vida put a commcall through to Wan's suite, no-one answered. They waited twenty minutes more in case he was on the way.

'Let's just go,' Vida snapped. 'I don't have to put up with this.'

'A good point,' TeeKay said. 'Shit, I bet we've lost our reservations.'

'It's so late it won't matter. Jak!'

The Garang stepped through what had appeared to be a portion of wall. TeeKay yelped.

'Were you there all this time?'

'Of course, Sé Tina Karin.' Jak bowed to her. 'I gather, Sé Vida, that you would like me to summon the military escort? We are still going to the same restaurant? I shall call ahead to alert security.'

'Yes, that'll be fine. And leave a message telling Wan where we are, in case he deigns to show up. The restaurant's right here in East Tower. Even someone like him should be able to find it.'

'Ooh,' TeeKay said. 'You've got nice sharp claws tonight.'

Calling the military escort turned out to be a good move. As soon as the party left the lift booth on the Mercado level, pix and intakes appeared like a swarm of flies. Thanks to the pair of Marines, armed with stunsticks, they hovered a decent distance away, but nothing could stop them from taking pictures or from yelling.

'Sé Vida, Sé Vida, where's Sé Wan? Where's your fiancé? When's the contract signing? Sé Vida, Sé Vida! Is something wrong between you and the Peronida?'

Her head held high, Vida swept in ahead of her guests. Since the small lobby opened directly into the corridor, she hoped they wouldn't have to wait for a table right in view of the pix, but in the event, the restaurant had been more than willing to hold its best table for Sé L'Var and her friends. The owner himself, a fat Lep with painted claws and glitter-decorated scales, seated them. When Vida insisted that Jak sit at their table to round out the party, he sent a waiter to the kitchen to slice raw meat as an appetizer for the Garang to match those that appeared, instantly and unordered, for the humans.

'This is all lovely, Sé Ki Ki,' Vida pronounced. 'My friends would like drinks as well.'

'Of course, Sé Vida, of course.' He bowed and rubbed his hands together. 'We have a well-stocked bar, if I do say so myself.'

'Oh come on, Vida,' TeeKay said. 'You have to have one, too.'

'I've got to stay sober so I can chew Wan out when he gets here.'

'You bet,' Dan said. 'TeeKay, lay off her.'

'Oh okay! I just like to see everyone have a good time.'

If drinks could have given her one, Vida thought, then she'd have drunk herself blind. All through the evening – the elaborate meal, the stage show, TeeKay's jokes and Dan's stolid version of banter – Vida fumed, turning constantly in her chair to glance at the door, where Wan never appeared. Finally Jak leaned over to whisper.

'Sé Vida, you are distressing yourself.'

'I know. It's the insult, damn him. It's not like I enjoy his company or anything.'

'I shall discuss this matter with Dukayn. For now, why do we not leave and put an end to this humiliation?'

'You're right.' Vida turned to TeeKay and Dan. 'What do you say we call this an evening?'

'Yeah, good idea,' Dan said. 'Jeez. I don't know what gets into Wan, sometimes. He can be really loath.'

'So I've noticed. I hope there aren't any more pix waiting. I can see it now. This is going to be all over the screens: Where was Wan? Wan and Vida have a tiff.'

'Maybe so. Well, we'll get you home.' Dan paused, staring over her head. 'That's weird. Look, there's another woman with red hair! She's, like, the third one I've seen today. Jeez, Vida, I thought it was rare.'

Surreptitiously Vida glanced around and saw, indeed, an older woman with thick red hair, done in matronly braids.

'It's dyed,' TeeKay whispered. 'All of them. You see redheads all over the place. They want to look like Vida. You're fashion, Vee.'

'Oh come on! Me?'

'Of course, you.' TeeKay rolled her eyes heavenward. 'You'll see what I mean. Let's go to that party, for starters, the one up at Mara's. I'll bet Mara herself's gone red.'

'I can't,' Vida said. 'I've got to look good for the newsjockeys tomorrow. It's a big press conference.'

'Vida! Don't be so stuffy.'

TeeKay argued the case while Vida was signing the chit, then shut up when Dan told her, only to resume arguing outside. This late at night the Mercado levels stood empty and dimly lit, so silent that their voices rang against the mosaic walls. When TeeKay stopped talking, Vida could hear the splash of water in the many fountains scattered through many courts. All at once Jak raised one hand and turned, listening hard. The two human Marines went on alert, watching him, waiting for his superior hearing and sense of smell to give them the data they needed to act.

'Footsteps,' Jak said. 'Ten humans, coming fast.'
'Newsjocks,' Vida groaned. 'Oh no.'
Jak and the Marines strode to positions that placed Vida and her guests in the middle of a triangle. By then she could hear the footsteps, too, and in a sudden swirl of black their makers strode around the corner.
'Priests!' TeeKay said. 'Ugh.'
'Shut up!' Dan hissed.
Apparently some of the local clergy had been taking Sister Romero out to dinner in some plainer establishment farther down in the Mercado. In a companionable crowd, priests, factors, and a couple of monks were walking along, talking to one another and nodding seriously over points of theology while Sister Romero merely listened. She was the only one who noticed Vida and her guards standing at the side of the corridor. As she passed, she raised one hand in a frozen wave and smiled when Vida waved back. 'My factor gave me your message, Sister,' Vida called out. 'I'll be glad to help.'
Romero laid a cautious finger to her lips and glanced at the other church officials with her. Fortunately they were paying no attention; the rules of the Lifegiver order held no strictures against alcohol consumed in moderation, and moderation was a flexible term. TeeKay waited until they'd disappeared into the lift booths.
'Do you know the Papal Itinerant?' TeeKay said.
'A little bit, yeah. I like her.'
'Like her?' TeeKay rolled her eyes. 'She scares me shitless. Though she scares my father, too, which makes her heroic in my baby blue eyes.'
'What?' Dan said. 'What's he worried about?'
'The Stinkers, of course. He thinks the Pope wants to free the Stinkers, and then he'd have to pay his servants, and you know how cheap he is.'
'Oh come on!' Dan snapped. 'No-one would do that. They're just animals.'
Both of them glanced at Vida, as if for support.
'What are you guys thinking?' Vida said. 'That the Pope lets me in on his secrets? You'd better go to your party. I'm awfully tired.'
When Vida returned to her suite, she checked the delivery status of the message Jak had left for Wan. It still hung in his queue, unread.

* * *

On the big vidscreen in the gather of Karlo's suite, stars shone inside the three apparent dimensions of a virtual cube. Among them, grossly out of scale, blinked small red points, each marking the disposition of one squadron of the Fleet, while thread-thin gold lines designated the microshunts near them. In a deep armchair of silver brocade, Karlo sat in front of the screen with his feet on a glass coffee-table and a transmit wand in one hand. Occasionally he would target a squadron, magnify its red point into a status readout, then minimize it again. The men and women who commanded these units had fought through the entire war; after Kephalon's death, they had pledged to Karlo the loyalty that they once had given to their home planet. No matter how badly he wanted a new commission for Pero, Karlo refused to demote a single one of them.

Reassigning a ship or two from each command to form a new unit seemed possible, if Karlo could find the reasons that would convince his chiefs of staff. He hadn't kept the loyalty of this orphaned Fleet by making arbitrary decisions, after all. When he turned a ring on the wand, the scale changed, and the Fleet disappeared. A view of the entire Pinch glittered within the virtual box of stars, or rather, a schematic of the Pinch. Real distance between two points meant nothing; what counted were the microshunts. Two planets lying at either end of a shunt could be tens of thousands of light years apart yet still hang close together in the navigable sky, while a pair off the shunt system, though separated by a mere five hundred, were for all practical purposes lost to one another.

Here in the Pinch the shunts formed an almost symmetrical pattern, rather like an abstract diagram of a skewed crystal. Old navigation maps of the Rim survived, and there the shunts stretched out in what the human eye saw as a random scatter, although mathematicians postulated that chaotic equations underlay their placement. The Pinch, however, divided itself neatly. Ri, the main Lep world, lay on a corner facet of the crystal with Palace almost diametrically opposite. Souk stood in the middle at a nexus of six different shunts. The other habitable worlds hung at regular intervals at other nexi. The pattern broke down at the edges, where shunts led to empty space. One of these false trails had once ended in the macroshunt and the Rim.

In a corner of the vidscreen a red alarm blinked.

'Display,' Karlo said.

In the centre of the stars an iris opened, forming a round window controlled by the security camera, which had caught Vanna and Dukayn walking in the front door of the suite. In her grey business suit, Vanna looked sweaty and exhausted. In between her tattoos her skin seemed dead-pale.

'Alarm off.'

The Pinch schematic returned. Karlo laid down the transmit wand and rose just as the pair entered.

'I'm sorry I'm so late, darling,' Vanna said. 'I had to stick around for the victory party. My staff worked itself to the bone for this vote, and I wanted to thank them all.'

'Of course. Come sit down. Have you eaten?'

'There was a buffet at the party.' Vanna kicked off her shoes and sank into the sofa. He could see her hands trembling, out of control. 'I'd like a drink, though.'

With a nod Dukayn went to summon a servant. Karlo sat down next to her and kissed her on the forehead.

'Thanks,' he said. 'The whole Fleet will be drinking a toast to you for this.'

'Huh. As long as they're prepared to return the favour someday.' Vanna glanced at the vidscreen. 'Making plans?'

'Trying to figure out where to put Pero. It's not doing his temper any good, getting to see what an incompetent fool his younger brother is.'

'Ah. Dukayn told me that Wan didn't show up for the vote.'

'Yeah. The gridjockeys who dropped by for quotes weren't impressed by his absence, I'll tell you.'

Vanna leaned back against the pillows of the sofa and shut her eyes. Her hands began clenching and opening again of their own accord. When Karlo caught them between his, they quieted.

'Maybe Wan's off with his little Vida.' Vanna opened her eyes.

'Maybe so. You know, my love, I don't understand why you hate that girl so much.'

Vanna pulled her hands free and sat up, turning a little away from him.

'Well, hell,' Karlo said. 'Sorry I said anything.'

Vanna ignored him with a toss of her red and blue hair. While Karlo was still considering what to say, Dukayn returned, leading a saccule who carried an icy glass on a silver tray. Vanna snatched the drink and took a long swallow. Dukayn sent the servant away and sat down on the edge of the armchair.

'Did you ever find Wan?' Karlo asked him.

'Yes and no, Sé. I never did find out what he was doing all morning, but he and Leni left Government House just after the sixteens. My informants thought they were going to Pleasure Sect.'

'Huh,' Vanna muttered. 'One whore isn't enough for him, huh?'

'Please!' Karlo snapped.

With a slight smile she considered the ice cubes floating in her drink. Karlo turned to Dukayn.

'If Wan comes back at any kind of reasonable hour, I want to see him. If not, first thing in the morning.'

'All right, Sé. I've got a tracer on him. The minute he or Leni puts a thumb on an access plate for East Tower, I'll know.'

'Damn him anyway,' Karlo went on. 'I wish to the Eye of God that he'd been born on Kephalon and Pero born here! If Pero had Wan's goddamn birth papers or if Wan had half of Pero's brains, we'd be in fine shape. As it is . . .' He let his voice trail away into a growl.

Dukayn nodded.

'They say the Colonizers could transfer one person's mind into another's body,' Vanna put in, still smiling. 'It's just a myth, most likely.'

'Too bad,' Karlo said. 'We could just switch them over.'

'You're sure it can't be done?' Dukayn leaned forward, all seriousness. 'There's usually some core of truth in these old myths.'

'I only wish,' Karlo said. 'No, no, it's only the kind of crank theory that shows up on the late-night vids. You know those shows, a lot of crap about the magical mysteries of our ancient past. Magla narrated one once.'

'She's got a beautiful voice for that kind of thing,' Vanna said. 'And a perfect delivery.'

It struck Karlo as bizarre that Vanna had never been in the least jealous of his ex-wife but would hold a grudge against a girl she barely knew. There were times when he despaired of ever understanding how Palace people saw life.

'So,' Zir said. 'The job hunting went well?'

'Very well,' Kata said. 'In a couple of days your hatchmate Elen and I will be working for the D and B Cleaning Service. They hold the main contract for Algol Park. If anyone sees Elen and me walking around the amphitheatre in D and B uniforms, they won't think twice about it.'

Zir let her crest lift high and hissed for good measure. They were sitting in her repair shop, Zir on a high stool as she bent over the counter, Kata comfortably cross-legged on a floor cushion. For a moment he merely watched her while she removed the delicate mechanism of an output station and laid it on an anti-mag pad. She had beautiful hands, long and slender, glistening with pale green scales and delicate claws, unsheathed at the moment to let her use them as tools for her work.

'Riva said you have another set of papers for me,' he said at last.

'Yes, I certainly do. This one identifies you as a photonics technician. But there's something I need to tell you.' She sat back on the stool. 'It's stamped for access to the force-field generator. That stamp takes a special kind of vinyl ground. I couldn't find the current formula on the black market, so I used the mix from last year. As long as no-one runs it under an analysis beam, they won't be able to tell the difference. But I wanted to warn you.'

'Thanks. I'll work out some story to cover it.'

'Good. Riva told me not to worry now that you're in charge.'

'Well, you're pretty impressive yourself. I never would have known about that vinyl mix.'

'I try to live up to Riva.'

'Yes, and so should we all. I'm amazed by what she can gain access to. These passes, our fake IDs – it's incredible how good she is. Palace lost a great cybe when Karlo passed his laws and threw her off the Map.'

'Really,' Zir said, nodding.

'And access codes are nothing to her, either. I'm still marvelling at the way she got me onto this planet. She somehow or other overrode the autogates. Did Elen tell you about that?'

'He did.' Zir allowed her crest to rustle. 'I'd have loved to have seen the faces on the Protectors who figured that one out!'

Kata began to make some pleasantry but paused, struck hard by a sudden thought. Once before some sapient had overridden access codes for an AI, and in the service of the Lep cause at that, only to be thwarted by the unforeseen approach of the Kephalon Fleet.

'What's wrong?' Zir said. 'You look so strange.'

'I just had a strange idea. Who shut down Nimue, Zir? Do you know?'

'What? Of course not. Oh!' Her jaw dropped sharply. 'You don't think it was –'

'Who else?'

Zir hissed at him. 'Shush!' she said. 'We'd best not talk about that.'

'Why not?

'Riva doesn't like it when we talk about her.' Zir hesitated briefly. 'Don't speculate, Kata. It's dangerous.'

'Very well, then. But something just struck me. This repair team that's going out to Nimue? What if they find something that leads them to Riva?'

'I wouldn't worry.' Zir raised her crest. 'I'll bet you she's already thought of that. I'll bet she's got it all planned out, just how to eliminate them if she has to.'

'That's true. If nothing else, she always has me.'

Wan returned to the tower just after Datechange. Although Vanna had long since gone to bed, Karlo was still studying his Fleet schematic when Dukayn marched Wan into the gather. Dressed in baggy civilian clothes, all rumpled, Wan stood staring at the floor. The scent of alcohol hung around him. Karlo flicked the schematic off and rose, laying the wand down.

'I was just wondering,' Karlo said, 'why you didn't bother to show up for the vote this morning. Didn't you get my message?'

'I didn't, no.' Wan looked up, green eyes snapping. 'I wasn't in my rooms all day.'

'Yeah? Where were you?'

'I didn't realize I needed to file an itinerary whenever I go out somewhere.'

Karlo hesitated, caught. Wan seemed to be bracing himself, his feet a little apart, his arms crossed over his chest. His face revealed nothing but a distant hatred. At moments like these Karlo almost liked him.

'No, you don't,' Karlo said at last. 'I should have made it clear earlier that I needed you there.'

Wan neither moved nor spoke, all wariness. Dukayn cleared his throat.

'I got a commcall a little while ago from Sé Vida's bodyguard.' Dukayn turned mild eyes Wan's way. 'They were worried about you at dinner.'

Wan went white about the mouth.

'What's this?' Karlo snapped.

'As I understand it,' Dukayn went on, 'Sé Wan made arrangements to accompany his fiancée to a dinner party, then never showed up.'

'Damn that meddling bastard,' Wan hissed. 'What business of his was it, calling you like that?'

'Jak had his reasons,' Dukayn said. 'I don't feel like explaining them to you.'

'Oh yeah? Maybe I should just get rid of him, then. Get Vida to fire him.'

Dukayn actually laughed. It was the first time that Karlo had heard that particular rusty chuckle in years. Flushing red, Wan took one step forward, froze, and stepped back sharply when Dukayn stopped laughing.

'Sit down, both of you,' Karlo snapped.

They followed orders, Wan slouched on the sofa, Dukayn perched on the edge of the armchair. Karlo shoved his hands in his pockets and began to pace back and forth while he talked.

'Listen, Wan, there's something you don't realize about Vida's bodyguard. He's blood-bonded himself to her. Do you know what that means?'

'I've heard about it,' Wan said. 'So what?'

Dukayn laughed again, a cold mutter under his breath.

'So what?' Karlo snarled. 'Get this through your thick skull. Never try to cause trouble between Vida and her bodyguard. You'll be marrying Vida, sure, and Jak will tolerate that because Vida's agreed to it. But he's going to hate you every goddamn minute that she's your wife. He'd love an excuse to break your neck first and apologize later.'

'Yeah?' Lounging back among the cushions Wan smiled. 'Well, they say those girls in Pleasure will fuck anything.'

Karlo saw Dukayn leap up and move just in time to throw out an arm and stop him. Behind that barrier Dukayn stood trembling, his lips drawn back from his teeth. Slowly, deliberately, Wan got up and stood facing him.

'What's wrong?' Wan said. 'You want her yourself? Go ahead. I don't give a shit.'

'Shut up,' Karlo snapped. 'It's not the insult to Vida that's making him angry.'

'You don't understand the Garang.' Dukayn brought himself under control. 'You don't understand much, boy, but especially not the Garang. Yeah, Jak's devoted to the girl, but it's got nothing to do with raw sex. In his mind she stands for something greater, something fine and pure, something a piece of crap like you couldn't understand if you tried.'

Bewildered, Wan looked back and forth between them. Karlo considered turning Dukayn loose, then dismissed the thought as unworthy.

'Go to bed,' Karlo said to Wan. 'We can talk about this when you're sober. For now, watch what you say about the L'Var girl. Do you understand me? Keep your filthy mouth shut about her.'

Wan hesitated, then turned on his heel and strode out of the room. Karlo waited till the door had hissed closed behind him, then lowered his arm. Dukayn sighed profoundly.

'Sorry, Sé.'

'It's all right. He can be a little shit when he wants to be. But you've got to remember that you're right: he doesn't know much about the Garang. He knows even less about their – about your – religion.'

Dukayn brought both his palms flat together and touched his fingertips to his forehead.

'May She who lights the sky forgive him, then,' Dukayn said. 'I can't, even if he is your son.'

'I don't expect you to.'

'Thanks.'

Dukayn turned to Karlo and looked at him with eyes so full of devotion that Karlo nearly took a step back. You should be used to this by now, he told himself sharply. It had been years now since Dukayn had left to train with the Garang and come back a convert to more than their martial arts style.

'Please don't kneel,' Karlo said.

'As you wish, of course, Ay-lang Japat.'

Ay-lang Japat. My living god, my god in this world, however you wanted to translate it – Karlo swallowed his faint revulsion and said the one thing that would please Dukayn the most.

'My blessing upon you.'

Dukayn smiled, his eyes brimming with tears close to joy. Karlo was never really sure exactly what he felt at these moments, beside embarrassed, of course. Frightened, maybe, and oddly humble both, that any man, that a man like Dukayn, had decided to elevate him to the status of a god.

PART THREE

With a long sigh the wiretrain slid onto the platform at route end. Kata and Elen quit the car to find themselves on a long concrete platform beside a corrugated metal station building, both grey, both stained. Open stairways led down to the ground. Down at the far end of a narrow street they could see docks and a canal, glittering in a shaft of the day's first sunlight. Elen looked around and shivered in the damp dawn wind.

'This is it?' he said.

'Yes,' Kata said. 'I was hoping for a little more traffic, so we wouldn't be so noticeable.'

The sunlight faded as clouds closed. Kata hoisted his heavy websling over one shoulder and led the way down the stairs. A shambling village of sorts huddled around the train depot: a few shops, a few houses, a fuel station, all of them settling so unevenly that windows and doors hung angled. The place looked oddly festive thanks to the fungi in green fronded festoons or sulphur-yellow globes stuck under eaves and protrusions. When Kata glanced up, he saw huge bunches of purple fingers hanging from the underside of the wiretrain platform.

'The swamp is taking it back.'

The voice came from under the stairs behind them. Kata swirled around to find an old human woman sitting on a rusty oil drum. She'd wrapped herself in layers of clothes that were barely more than rags, a dirty medley of red and brown with the odd touch of yellow.

'I saw you looking at the Hands of God,' she said. 'That's what I call 'em, the purple ones, the Hands of God. They soften things up, like, because they ooze this acid, and then they pick things right apart. It's busy busy fingers, plucking here, poking there. The men come and scrape them off, but the swamp sends more right the next day.'

'Well, it's a problem, all right, the fungi.' Elen fished in his websling and found a couple of coins. 'Here, grandmother, buy yourself something to drink.'

'Thank you, youngling, I'll do that. And you remember, when the city comes a-tumbling down, you remember what I told you. The swamp's taking it back.'

'We will, grandmother,' Kata said. 'And a good day to you.'

Heading for the water, they hurried off down the street, past a straggle of houses, listing and cracking, sporting a fine crop of fungi and moulds.

'Living out here would make any sape a little crazy,' Elen remarked. 'The swamp's taking this village back, all right.'

'No-one wants to keep it, that's why. Spread a few gallons of Megatox over these buildings, and the swamp would get its claws out fast enough.'

'Well, there are problems with that stuff.'

'This isn't a problem?'

'You win.'

Their destination lay right on the water: a wooden dock, soaked black in what looked like old-fashioned creosote, with a bait and tackle shop perched on the far end. Since most Leps had a taste for flatties, the grey fish that swarmed at the edge of the swamplands, Kata was expecting no fuss over their renting a boat, but when they walked into the crowded little shop, the first thing he saw was a shiny white notice, taped to the wall:

All Leps must show full ID for any rental transactions.
By Order of the Edge Sect Council.

The brown little human man behind the counter saw him reading it and winced. 'I'm real sorry,' he said. 'That sure wasn't my idea. You people are my best customers, this time of year.'

'Well, can't be helped,' Kata said, reaching into his jacket. 'Here you are.'

His fingers touched the smooth metal of his pulse gun, and he debated – no, a death would leave a trail more obvious than a mere signature. When he laid his false papers onto the counter, the fellow barely glanced at them.

'That's fine,' he said. 'How big a boat will you be wanting, and for how long?'

'A twelve-footer, and just for the day,' Elen said, stepping up. 'What time do you close?'

'Have her back by the twenties.'

Elen sat in the stern and steered while Kata crouched in the bow of the little hydrofloat with a fishing net out and ready for appearances' sake. To the soft purr of the solar-volt motor, they glided away from the dock and turned down a tunnel in the bluish-green frond trees, growing on sand bars to form a canopy over the narrow channel of open water. They passed huge clumps of island-roots, so named because their fleshy olive-green stems tangled so thickly at the water's surface that flying lizards and insects could live on them, and airborne dirt and airborne seeds both collected there to grow into floating gardens, studded with fleshy red flowers and sprays of yellow fungi. As the sun rose higher behind the perpetual fog, the air turned warm and steamy. Kata stripped off his wrap jacket, then took a turn at the motor to let Elen do the same.

'If we were really fishing,' Elen said, 'we'd turn down one of these side channels and anchor.'

'Ah. But as it is, I'd better take a look at Riva's map.'

Elen took over while Kata opened his websling and brought out the map and a receptor for the public satellite locator system. Riva had warned him that the data she could provide might be outdated when it came to the ever-shifting channels and bogs of the swamps. Although there was a chance that someone might pick up their transmit signals to the satellite network, it was small compared to the chance of a fatal accident if they should get lost. Go too deep into the swamps, just for one thing, and the worms would be waiting for you.

'All right,' Kata said. 'When this map was drawn, there was a real island straight ahead at the end of this channel. If it's still there, we turn right around it, but we have to be careful of shallows.'

'In this part of the swamp, you always have to be careful of shallows,' Elen said. 'And it's going to get worse once we reach the old pumping station. How far is it?'

'About fifteen miles. What's that? An hour away?'

'Sure, if we could open full throttle and head straight there. Here, I've set up the motion recorder so we can find our way back. Let's see what we can do.'

In a few minutes they glided out of the channel and its embracing fronds. Ahead stretched green water and brown land commingled into something neither, all heaped and wrinkled like an unmade bed, stretching to a dirty grey horizon. The openness proved an illusion. They managed to travel about a hundred yards at a time, tacking in one direction only to stop and wait while they puzzled out the next leg of their zig-zag. Dead logs, tangled in vines, floated just under the surface; the murky water turned shallow before you could see the bottom; here and there drowned rocks threatened. Insects swarmed round and whined. Although their scales mostly protected the two Leps, their eyes were still vulnerable, and they kept swatting and hissing the things away as they tried to make sense of Riva's map.

'It's so damn strange,' Kata growled. 'She has access to all the data in the world, or so it seems, except a decent map of these shit-ugly swamps.'

'No-one can keep a good map up,' Elen said. 'They're out of date the minute you print them.'

Kata muttered something foul.

Rather than the map, luck helped them out after two hours of this painful progress, when they hit a run of clear water that led them west-north-west, roughly in the direction of the old pumping station, for a good five miles. In time, though, it petered out into a maze of island-roots and real islands, if you could call lumps of mud covered in mushrooms islands. Kata eased back to the middle of the boat, then stood up, looking around them with a pair of binoculars.

'Oh for God's sake!' he muttered. 'We're not far from shore. Have we gone the wrong way?'

'No, there's kind of a peninsula here.' Elen was studying the map. 'Oh, of course! It's the saccule market, where the Stinkers come to sell their neuters off. That's stable land, because it's got pumps. We'll find an open passage out, too.'

'There are people there. I can just make them out. We don't want to go too close.'

'Do we have any choice?'

'No. Let's hope they think we're just a pair of fishermen.'

When the hydrofloat chugged by, no-one on shore seemed to notice. Kata could see various humans and Leps trotting back and forth around a black airtruck parked on the landward side. In the middle of the tiny peninsula stood a herd of neuters, wearing collars and tied to what appeared to be stakes of some kind with crude-looking ropes. The neuters were shrieking and skirling, and the reek of their fear came close to making him vomit himself.

'We're at the channel out,' Elen said, gagging. 'Just in time, too.'

Elen slammed the hydrofloat's gear shift into high. They sped out to the suddenly clean-smelling air of the swamp itself.

* * *

As a souvenir of her childhood in the mines, Sister Romero had trouble sleeping in open spaces. Since she owned almost nothing, she tended to cram her few clothes and toiletries into a dresser drawer and sleep in the closet of whatever room she was inhabiting. Most were long enough for her to make up a bed of blankets and a pillow right on the floor, the only 'mattress' hard enough to mimic the sleepnests of a typical Arim house. The actual bed, therefore, ended up as a table – my research planner, she always called it – where she could lay out handwritten notes and heaps of printout, weight them down with data cubes, and generally pile up in plain sight various kinds of evidence for whatever problem she was working on at the moment. Here in her bedroom in East Tower she'd laid out information about the neuter saccules in a pattern that had great meaning for her but that would have no doubt escaped most people seeing it.

Yawning in the early light, a cup of steaming tea in her hand, Romero stood looking over her pattern. Up at the head of the bed she'd added some tangential evidence: a data cube holding a UJU pamphlet and printout from a screen capture of one of their advertisements for their up-coming public rally. Although UJU members focused their multiple resentments on Leps, Romero saw a connection between using one race for slaves and another for a scapegoat. She doubted very much that the citizens of Palace would ever allow themselves to see the same thing, especially if she added the culls of Pleasure Sect into her pattern. Talking with Vida was making her think that Pleasure belonged in it.

On the wall a pale blue oval chimed.

'Yes?' Romero said.

'Good morning, Sister.' Thiralo's face appeared on the oval. 'Sé L'Var's servant is here with a package for you.'

'Good. Send it in.'

Dressed in a maroon shift and a short green vest, the saccule trotted through the door and bowed so clumsily it dropped the leather case it was carrying. Whistling from its facial pouches, it grabbed the case upside down. Clothes spilled onto the floor, and the saccule moaned and stank of dead animals.

'Shorry shorry shorry,' it hissed from a chest sac.

'It's all right, Greenie, it's all right. Here.' Romero pointed at the case. 'Take that back to Sé Vida.'

Whimpering it clutched the case to its chest and dashed for the door. Romero went to a window and opened it wide to let the smell of saccule embarrassment out. Outside in the brightening light of day, pale green spores fell through the air in long streamers, teased out by the wind.

Although Vida was taller than Romero, the clothes she'd sent fit well enough, a pair of fashionably narrow grey trousers, a plain but expensive blue tunic to go over them, and matching silk brocade shoes and handbag to set them off. For her visit to the pens Romero wanted to look like a prospective customer, not announce to all and sundry that she was not only a Lifegiver but the Papal Itinerant – her headband, therefore, went into a drawer before she left and her hair came down from its usual braid. When Thiralo appeared, he'd procured himself a brown business suit of the sort many factors wore; he carried his scriber and tablet as well.

'We look quite the pair of lay people,' Romero said. 'Good. Are we going by wiretrain?'

'No, Sister. I hired an airhopper. The pens are a good long way away, and we want them to think we're prosperous.'

A long way, indeed – it took the airhopper an hour to fly to the edge of Palace. Romero spent the trip looking out the window at the spread of the city, criss-crossed with its canals and wiretrains. The closer they came to the swamps, the lower the buildings grew, dwindling down to rambling compounds of plastocrete, roofed with peeling pink shingles, or stacked brown housing modules, listing to one side or the other from age and the spongy ground underneath. Rarely she saw a strip of turquoise lawn or a tiny garden. Once, when the airhopper swung around in a turn, they dipped low over a pumping station, a tower of blue-grey metal, quivering from its own machinery, at the junction of three broad canals. Although she'd been hoping for a view of the swamps, they reached the pens while the waterlands still lay at the horizon, a stretch of dirty green shot through with the sparkling silver of ponds and streams. The airhopper abruptly turned and circled, dipping one wing. Romero saw among the shabby buildings an area roofed in black solar panels that stretched a good four square blocks. All around it rose a high fence woven of strands of wire and red cables.

'Electrified?' Romero said.

Thiralo nodded and made a note on his tablet.

In the middle of the compound lay a landing pad big enough for half a dozen airhoppers, but this early in the morning the strip stretched empty. Even so, the pilot landed off to one side and taxied close to the edge.

'Airtrucks land here,' Thiralo remarked. 'Full of supplies, I suppose.'

They stepped out into gusts of wind and the hum of huge fans, mounted up on the black roofs of the adjoining buildings. Even so, the smell of saccule lay heavy in the air, a maelstrom of scents and most of them unpleasant. On three sides of the landing pad stood dark brown walls without windows, though Romero did notice a pair of double doors on one structure. On the fourth side was the front of the saccule market proper, a long low building with a glass front shaded by a red and gold striped awning. Flowering shrubs and pole trees grew around the entrance. When they reached the door it slid back to reveal a skinny human man with thick and untidy bright blue hair.

'Good morning, Sé,' he chirped. 'Come right in. My name's Mil, and I'll be helping you today.'

'Thank you, but I'm just looking,' Romero said. 'I'm weighing getting a pair trained for cleaning against a bot.'

'Ah, well, cleaning bots have really gone up in price. I'm sure we can find you a good bargain.'

Although Romero had been dreading a cross between a zoo and a jail, the long room stretched curiously empty. At one end stood a low dais in front of a pair of closed doors; at the other, a cluster of desks and chairs. In between stretched bright red carpet and nothing more. Romero noticed here and there lines cut into the carpet, forming big squares, as if it had been ineptly patched.

'Come sit down,' Mil said. 'I'll show you what we have in stock on the vidscreen. Give you some idea of the prices.'

'No, I'd like to see the actual saccules,' Romero said. 'I know you have a visitors' area.'

'Sé, normally we're glad to show our customers around, but it's early. I don't think our graduates are looking their best at the moment.'

'I have no time to wait, and I'm not interested in making another trip back here today. If you're not ready to do business, you shouldn't have opened up.'

'Er, well yes of course. Just come this way.'

The tour behind the scenes did live up to Romero's fears. Mil led them through double doors to a long dim corridor, lined with open pens. The so-called graduates lived one to a tiny pen, just barely big enough for a saccule to lie down to sleep. In one corner of each stood a pool of dirty water, where most of the neuters were sitting, slumped over and staring at nothing. Every now and then one would slap the water with the flat of its hand and make a booming noise. Others would slap and call out in turn. Despite the roar of evacuation fans, the combined stench of excrement and saccule despair made Romero feel sick to her stomach by the time they reached the end of the row.

'I've seen enough,' she said. 'Now, do they come with health certificates?'

'Oh yes, Sé. We guarantee both good health and tractability.'

With Mil in the lead, they began walking back toward the doors, which still stood open. In the shaft of light Romero could see the floor of the corridor more clearly. In the middle lay a square panel that seemed to be a sliding hatch of some sort.

'What's that?' she said, pointing.

'Oh uh, nothing, nothing.' Mil threw back his head like a startled animal. 'Uh, um, a repair to the floor.'

'I see. Just curious.'

Thiralo made a small note. As they walked out into the light and air of the showroom, Romero heard a loud whining sound that grew, turned piercing, then swelled to a mechanical roar.

'Airtruck!' Mil yelled. 'It'll land soon.'

With the two men following, Romero headed toward the bank of windows. Hovering on huge rotors the black truck plunged straight down, caught itself with a whine of engines, then settled to the pad. The noise stopped, leaving Romero's ears ringing.

'Well, Sé, come sit down.' Mil hurried to her side. 'Right over here, and we'll look over the price schedules. Just this way.'

Romero said nothing, merely watched as a door hatch swung up on the airtruck's side. A long ramp slid out, and a pair of humans wearing black coveralls trotted down to secure it to the pad.

'Sé, please.' Mil was whining with anxiety. 'Do come sit down. Can we get you something to drink, perhaps? We have a nice vidscreen presentation of the graduates to show you.'

On the far side of the landing pad the double doors into the brown building were sliding open to reveal two more men in black, carrying electric prods. One of the men on the pad was frowning a little as he fussed with the settings on a long control wand of some sort.

'Sé, please.' Mil laid a hand on her elbow.

When Romero swung her head around and glared at him, he

took his hand away and fast. Back at the landing pad, the herder had activated his wand. Glittering walls of yellow barrier ran from the truck to the open doors. Even through the plate glass Romero could hear the whimpering and squealing as saccules poured out of the truck and rushed down the ramp. Several hundred, she estimated, and they were pushing each other, stumbling with bare webbed feet on the unfamiliar footing of first the ramp, then the pad. Now and then a saccule would lumber into the barriers and recoil, screaming in agony, as the force-field snapped out sparks.

Romero found her hand on the door. Before Mil could stop her, she pushed it open and stepped out. A stench like raw vomit made her gag, but she held her ground and watched as the saccules lurched and staggered into the building beyond. She could hear human voices shouting from inside the truck, herding out the last of the new stock. One undersized grey creature tripped on the ramp and went down. She could hear it skirl in terror as the press of its fellows behind poured over it, kicking and trampling.

'Sé!' Blue-haired Mil was standing right behind her. 'Please come in!'

Romero took another couple of steps closer. As the last saccule trotted into the building, with a hiss and flash the barriers went down. The saccule who'd fallen lay moaning and bloody on the ramp. With a wave at Thiralo to follow, Romero hurried over just as the two men in coveralls grabbed it, feet and head, and tossed it onto the concrete pad. It fell with the crack of breaking bones.

'May the wrath of God chill your lungs,' Romero hissed.

Startled, they looked up, then turned to call out to Mil.

'Who the hell's this?'

Mil made a fluttering sort of motion with his hands but kept quiet. Romero knelt on the concrete and laid a hand on the saccule's pouchy face, half-covered in oozing orange blood. It turned dull grey eyes her way and died, spasming once, then falling still with a scent alarmingly like roses in full bloom.

'May the light of God guide you.' Romero put thumbs and forefingers together in the sign of the Eye. 'May you find peace in His heavens.'

Mil and the two workers were staring in something like disbelief. Romero got up and pointed at the nearer of the men in coveralls.

'Why did you kill it?'

'Well, hey, lady, it was all banged up, probably gonna die anyway.

They're not worth the vet bills until they're trained.'

'I see.' Romero glanced at the salesman. 'Is that standard practice around here?'

'None of your business,' Mil snarled. 'Just who are you?'

'My name is Sister Romero, and this is my factor, Thiralo. Perhaps you've seen me on the vidscreens?'

She had never seen a man look as frightened as Mil did then. Dead-white and open-mouthed, he stepped back out of her reach.

'The Papal Itinerant?' the man with the control wand said.

'What are you doing here?'

'You'll find out in the fullness of God's time,' Romero said. 'Thiralo, let's go. I've seen as much as I need to.'

She marched off with Thiralo hurrying to catch up. Once they'd climbed back into the airhopper, the factor slammed the hatch shut and sank into a seat. Romero sat opposite him and buckled on her safety belt. Up in his tiny cabin the pilot started the engine with a roar.

'Blessings to the Holy Eye,' Thiralo called over the noise. 'I was afraid they weren't going to let us leave.'

'They wouldn't have dared harm us.' Romero suddenly smiled. 'But why don't you just tell the pilot to get us into the air?'

Before Thiralo could relay the order, the airhopper shuddered and leapt from the pad, rising straight up, then spinning around and heading out fast. Apparently the pilot shared Thiralo's opinion of the danger. Romero looked down at her borrowed pants, stained a crusting orange and filthy at the knees, and sent up a silent prayer to God, that He might inspire her to see the best path toward justice for His creatures in those pens.

Just at noon Kata and Elen reached the island that held the old pumping station. As they nosed the hydrofloat into shore, Kata could see that ten-yard-wide slabs of concrete had been piled to form the island's skeleton, as it were, and that time and the shifting of wind and tide had deposited soil. Years of rooting plants had done the rest, compacting the mass into something as stable as anything could be, out in the swamps. In the middle of the island stood frond-trees, rustling in the wind, and what looked like a stack of house-high metal cylinders. Pipes stuck out at odd angles only to end in mid-air.

'They must have taken the machinery when they abandoned this place,' Kata said. 'Why did they, anyway?'

'It probably wasn't worth the fuel it took to run the pumps any more,' Elen said. 'Sometimes the swamps win one, you know. They hit springs when they're blasting out channels, and the water just keeps rising, no matter how hard you pump it.'

In his gear Kata had brought a telescoping metal rod designed to keep swamp explorers out of quicksand pockets. As they walked he tested the ground ahead of them for every step.

'No-one's been out here for years,' Kata said. 'I hope the stuff is still good. Riva didn't bother to tell me how she knew it was here, and I hope she wasn't reading some out of date database or something like that.'

'Well, those sheets don't decompose or anything.'

'Yeah? I hope not.'

The ruins of the pumping station sat on a solid bedding of concrete that must have been anchored with pilings, Kata supposed, to stay so stable over the years. Up close he could see rust eating through the empty metal housings – no, not rust. A fine textured life-form covered the silvery metal like velvet.

'I've never seen that before,' Elen remarked. 'Let's not touch it.'

'Don't worry about that.' Kata unrolled the map again. 'Now then. The explosives are supposed to be in the old foreman's shed, according to this. That must be that concrete bunker kind of thing, over there.'

Inside, the doorless bunker sloped down to a pool of slimy water. When Kata ran his metal pole through the slime, half-seen things rose to the surface and snapped. Kata backed out fast.

'Anything left in there fell to pieces long ago.'

'Probably so.' Elen was frowning at the map. 'Wait a minute. Look over there – that square of plastocrete flooring? That looks more like the shape of a shed. I'll bet the walls fell in or something.'

In a collection of muck and fungi they did find decaying slabs of corrugated panelling. Since the boat came equipped with a shovel for digging out small sand bars and the like, Elen went back to fetch it while Kata squatted down and considered the fleshy tangle of life, plant and parasite both, that had taken over this attempt on the part of sapients to extend solid ground. Small silvery tubes with legs crawled through red pulpy strands; sulphurous yellow globes puffed up, ready to stink, when he reached out a tentative claw. He moved away fast, squatted again, and saw, sticking out of something black and decayed, part of a big plastic ring.

'There it is,' he said aloud. 'It makes sense, that they'd store explosives underground.'

Sure enough, when Elen returned with the shovel, they scraped away the thick layer of life to expose a trapdoor made of plastocrete. When Kata tried prying up the edge, it crumbled, falling away to reveal a trench some four feet deep and three on a side. At the bottom, wrapped in long strands of mildews and moulds, lay a cubical shape.

'I think I can bring it up with the shovel,' Kata said. 'Get ready to grab it if it starts to fall back in.'

'If Riva's right, there's enough plastique in that box to blow us and this island to hell and back.'

'That's why you shouldn't let it fall.' Kata lifted his crest. 'Get ready.'

Swearing under his breath, Elen followed orders. Kata slid the shovel under the cube and spooned it out like the inside of an egg, raised it just high enough for Elen to grab it and haul it to solid ground. The white beard of mildew fell and scattered in the wind. Torn, stained steelweave wrap covered what seemed to be a box. Although the lettering was half eaten away, they could make out the red interplanetary sign for danger.

'That's it,' Kata said. 'Riva's done it again, by God! How the hell could she know this stuff had been left out here?'

'Beats me.' Elen was eyeing the box as if it might bite. 'We'd better get this back to the hydrofloat.'

'Right, but we need to stay out long enough to look like we were fishing.'

'Let's fish, then. I'm hungry, and flatties really are best raw. You bite their heads off and just crunch them down. The humans cook them and then complain they're bitter.'

'That's like them, isn't it? Good idea, youngling. I think we'll wait to open this box till I have some proper tools.'

'Vida, I'm dreadfully sorry.' On the comm screen Sister Romero's strong face looked nothing of the sort. 'I'm afraid I've ruined those trousers you lent me. They're stained and not worth trying to clean.'

'Oh please, don't worry about it,' Vida said. 'I've got lots.'

'Thank you for being so generous. I'll send the rest of the things back later. Do we still have our lunch appointment for tomorrow?'

'I'm looking forward to it.'

'All right. Good luck at your news conference today.'

Romero powered out, leaving Vida painfully curious. Just why had the Papal Itinerant borrowed secular clothes, anyway? She left her Map terminal and returned to her bedroom, where Samante stood waiting for her, tablet and scriber in hand. Over the dark coverlet on the wide bed lay most of the clothing she'd referred to, spread out and arranged in outfits.

'Any inspirations?' Vida said.

'I'm leaning toward the grey suit, myself,' Samante said. 'But you know me and my taste in clothes. You need to pick something you'll feel comfortable in, remember. The right image is crucial, but you can't look uncomfortable, either. These press conferences have to be managed just so.'

'So I'm learning. You really do think we should accept this version of Wan's contract offer?'

'I don't see how we'll ever get better. It's extraordinarily generous, and we've got him down to twelve years from fifteen. The Lifegivers won't issue a birth permit for any shorter marriage than that.'

'Okay, then.' Vida considered the clothes on the bed and realized that she was tending toward all black – very much the wrong image. 'Flowered stuff is too giggly girl.'

'I agree. That tailored green outfit?'

'I always wear green in public. It's getting boring. I know. That royal blue dress with the big collar.'

'Yes, perfect! You're catching on to this very nicely.'

'Am I? Thanks.'

On the vidscreen the morning interactive news spread its logo. Samante called up the sound, then sat on the corner of the bed to watch while Greenie began putting away the rejected clothing. Vida paid little attention to the news until the serious political business of the day had been dealt with. Sure enough, the very first entertainment segment featured her dinner party. Not only did the show roll footage shot out in the corridor, but at least one pix must have been concealed in the restaurant itself long enough to take a couple of still holos of the table, with Jak conspicuously in Wan's place. AND WHERE WAS WAN? floated across the screen while the presenter droned on about the Rommoff family.

'Damn him!' Vida burst out. 'I knew it, I just knew it!'

In a side window the interactive opinions began totalling.

Although Vida's pop ratings held steady, Wan's had dropped from the night before.

'Serves him right,' Samante said. 'I'll bet Karlo hears about this.'

'I hope he waits to chew Wan out till after the beastly press conference, though. I don't want him sulking.'

Samante was studying her face so intently that Vida wondered just what she'd given away.

'Don't worry, I'm not going to crack under the strain or anything.'

'I didn't think you were,' Samante said. 'I was only – well, you look so sad.'

'Do I? You know, I keep thinking about my guardian. I really miss her. I wish she could be here for all of this.'

'I suppose you must. She seems to have been very kind to you.'

Vida was remembering Aleen, saying, *Don't fail me.*

'Kind?' she said aloud. 'I guess you could call it that.'

'What?'

'Oh never mind.' Vida snatched the blue dress from the bed. 'I'd better get ready. At least I don't have to actually sign his lousy contract today.'

In the sunny white gather of the Cyberguild suite, Rico sat curled in a formfit chair and glared at the vidscreen, where Vida and Wan's press conference unrolled, announcing that she was accepting his latest contract offer. The couple sat at a table in front of a mound of white and blue flowers while Vida's factor stood at a podium, reading a summary of the clauses. Hatred felt like electricity, Rico decided, like jacking in to a poorly-wired terminal. He felt it crackling through his soul every time he looked at Wan, who sat stone-still in his perfect Fleet uniform with his perfect looks and gazed indifferently away.

At moments he wondered if he hated Vida, too. How could she smile like that? How could she turn and look at Wan and smile like that? For a moment his eyes filled with tears. Damn her for being so beautiful, damn her. Damn her for lying, for pretending she loved Wan Peronida while the pix clustered around, pointing and clicking, while the intakes stood and yammered, desperate to get their questions acknowledged.

'Screen off.' Hi walked into the room. 'You're only making yourself miserable, kid.'

The vid went grey and dead.

'Yeah, guess so.' Rico got up and found to his surprise that his muscles ached. 'How long have I been sitting there?'

'About thirty minutes. Now come on. Caliostro's waiting for us.'

With the cyberdrugs Rico felt his body fall away and leave only mind. He became a cursor, or so he liked to think of it, a travelling point of consciousness who existed only in relation to the Map. What Vida might be doing meant nothing to that consciousness. Once he melded with the Map, he was free. Although most cybes hated being on the Map without a realistic iconic body, Rico had found that he preferred working as an abstract shape. A personal icon existed only for handling object icons, and images of eyes and fingers weren't really necessary to see and touch on the Map.

Working with Hi, however, taught him the limits of this approach. As they floated in clan space above the great wheel of doors, Rico showed off his new iconic form – a slender rhomboidal solid like a jack-knife, bristling with tools.

'Yeah, great, kid. You look like a directory icon, one full of repair utilities.'

'But it's really efficient.'

'Sure. Wait till someone tries to open you.'

'Oh hey!'

'Go back down and activate your old icon. Now. I don't want to forget what I'm working with and reach over for a sort tool.'

By the time Rico returned, a sullen presence in humanoid form, Hi had opened a storage directory and brought out an array of icons that Rico had never seen before. Each circle, seemingly made of blueglass, bore a single symbol in green.

'AI internal access nodes,' Hi said. 'You won't get the password for these for at least ten years. Let's slide over and get to work.'

Checking Caliostro's map against the schematic became boring fast, as it was a matter of Hi calling off coordinates for objects while Rico confirmed their presence or absence on the diagrams. Every now and then they found a new repair, which Hi noted into a log file in some detail. Occasionally the schematic proved so deviant from the actual map that they were forced to pause and redraw a particular nexus or flow chart. Still, they discovered nothing remarkable until they reached Caliostro's interior firewall, built over a thousand years before to seal off the major damage of the Schism Wars from those areas that still functioned. Iconic code represented it as an immense obsidian wall, glittering in cold blue light.

'Remember the meta Arno gave you?' Hi said.

'Yes, Sé. The all-meta, you mean?'

'No. He said he gave you two short runs, too.'

'That's right, yeah.'

'Which one do you think applies here?'

'Son of the morning.'

The wall in front of them dissolved to flow like water, pouring down in a black fall, then parted, as if around a rock, to reveal a gate icon.

'Good choice,' Hi said. 'This is the data dump Arno told us about.'

'It's not on the schematic.'

'No. Its location's been lost for about fifteen hundred years. I'm not even sure now exactly where we are. We can eventually figure it out, but without that meta, we'd never have found this.'

'I don't understand. Why wasn't the location recorded?'

'Because it dates from before the guild system got put into place. Maprunning used to be a business, Rico. There were a lot of competing little firms, and each had a piece of the Map or its own Map. Objects got lost all the time, because firms hid information from one another. If a firm went out of business, its exclusive cache went with it if they wiped their data storage for resale.'

'That doesn't make a lot of sense. Data should belong to everyone.'

'It does out here in the Pinch because it has to. Redundancy means safety, but we learned that lesson a little late. Now, want to see if you can open that gate?'

'Sure. I'll try some old code I picked up.'

Old it may have been, but not old enough. Rico shaped five different sets of archaic commands into icons, not a bad try for a journeyman, but the gate stayed locked until the master took over. On the second attempt, Hi's icon worked. When the gate opened they slid through to find themselves in a virtual room, papered with glowing silver directories. Rico allowed himself to float while he struggled to make sense of the object tagging system, which might have been code but could well have been words in some archaic language.

'Arno called this a garbage dump,' Hi said. 'Maybe it is, but garbage this old can be pretty damn valuable.'

'Do you think there might be information in here about AIs? About how the Colonizers made them come alive, I mean, like we were discussing.'

'I doubt it.' Hi had thrown an analysis icon against one wall and was studying the directories it highlighted. 'None of these are high-level archives. Huh. So far what I've seen looks like business records, some kind of commercial logs, anyway. I can't translate this old code fast, not without reference tables.'

'Oh. Real garbage, then.'

'Not to a certain kind of scholar. I think we're going to copy the lot and pull it into clan space, just in case someone else finds it and decides to wipe it off.'

'But if anyone's snooping they'll find the record of the move.'

'Good point, kid. We can use the Chameleon Gate as a donkey and then store our copies in an off Map backup cube. Your next job is going to be running translate utilities on these files and sorting them out.'

'Yes, Sé.'

'You sound really enthused.'

'Well, uh . . .'

'Yeah, yeah, it's going to be boring as hell. Tell you something, Rico. Eighty per cent of a cybe's work is boring. Details – they're our line of work. Finding details, storing details, sorting details. Boredom comes with the territory.'

'Unless something goes wrong?'

'You got it. And these days there's a little too much excitement to suit me.'

Later that afternoon, working alone at his own terminal, Rico found himself wishing for some of that excitement. He took what seemed to be the oldest of the captured files, in the hopes that it would contain ancient and valuable secrets, and ran it through two sets of translation utilities. While the data was ancient, all right, dating from before the Schism Wars, it turned out to be spreadsheets for a small business. With a randomizer he picked three more files and translated those: they were all business transactions, spreadsheets and inventory lists. When he read through one list, he realized that these businesses had been dealing in saccule neuters.

Why had the shadowy figure who'd tipped Arno off chosen to hide the audio tape in a data dump like this? Did that person for some odd reason want Arno and thus the guild to find these particular files, or did they just assume that no-one would be looking for life-and-death information in such an odd location? He translated a few more files and all at once saw a pattern. In the earliest records, saccule neuters were rare and extremely expensive. As time went on, however, the buys out in the swamps became larger and the price dropped. When Hi came in to see how the work progressed, Rico pointed out the change.

'See?' Hi said. 'I told you historians would find this stuff interesting. That's the kind of thing they look for, meaningful patterns.'

'Okay, I can see that. And I found an embedded note, too, on this file here.' Rico tapped the listing on his Mapscreen. 'After the Schism Wars, the number of available neuters suddenly jumped, and the gendered saccules became really eager to sell them off. The guy who wrote the note doesn't know why.'

'That *is* interesting. Tell you what. When you get these files translated and organized, we'll donate them to the University Map. I'll bet they keep a couple of professors over there happy for years.'

'Sounds good to me.'

'And speaking of happy, you've put in a lot of work today, Rico. Why don't you take the rest of the afternoon off? Get out in the fresh air or something.'

'Hey, thanks! Sure.'

As he powered down his station and saved the translated files to an off Map cube, it occurred to Rico that he had money now. His journeyman's salary wasn't much, but he was getting his room and board for free. He could convert some credits to cash and go to Pleasure Sect, if he wanted. If he dared. And why shouldn't he? No reason, he told himself, no reason at all.

By sheer chance Kata saw the end of Vida's press conference. He and Elen had returned the hydrofloat and were waiting for the wiretrain when the station's vidscreen switched over to the news. For a few minutes he stared at her images, all red hair and smiles. Her youth infuriated him. How had this little human, barely a hatchling, outsmarted him? Even though he reminded himself that hatred, that any personal emotion, was a trap and a danger, all the way back on the train he brooded his hatred the way a Lep mother brooded her eggs.

Although the new laws banned Leps from the Map, they said nothing against a cybe consulting with a Lep. Hi saw no reason why he couldn't invite Molos to his office, but he'd sent Rico off to make sure he wouldn't know about it, and Jevon was gone, too, on her regular day off. On the dining table in the suite's eatery he spread a printout of the updated schematic for Caliostro. He and Molos stood on opposite sides and for a long while merely contemplated the mysterious repairs, marked in red among the black lines of the schematic and labelled in green with code-bursts that summarized the AI's disrupted functions.

'None of these patches are out of the ordinary at all,' Molos said at last. 'Except of course for the extraordinary fact that they exist.'

'You bet. They don't go to the core of Caliostro's dysfunctions, nothing dramatic – just a lot of clean-up work. And I mean a lot. You can see the extent.' Hi paused to lift up one sheet and expose another below. 'Look at those reconstructed external access codes. That must have taken fifty hours to do.'

'Just so. Am I remembering correctly? All of this has been done since the festival of Calios?'

'No, the work started the day before. None of these repairs have route marks, IDs, or log tags attached to them. At first I thought they must have been done by whoever tipped Arno off about the assassin, but he or she would have left marks somewhere.'

Molos extended his claws and sheathed them again, a gesture of bafflement. Hi laid the page down.

'The only explanation I can think of is a self-repair utility,' Molos said at last. 'We know that the Colonizers had some very sophisticated agents at their disposal.'

'Yeah, but why now? If it's an agent, why hasn't it worked in the last thousand years? Who turned it on?'

'An excellent question, if rhetorical. Obviously I have no idea.'

'I'm going to examine each repaired area real carefully, next time I jack in. There's got to be some kind of clue, somewhere.'

'Yes. If we only knew exactly what we were looking for, it would be of considerable help.'

'I've been thinking about that.' Hi ran a finger over a line of green symbols. 'I'd like to compare Caliostro's code with the same functions on another AI. You know, use it as a template. It would work the best if we had an AI that had never been damaged, but as it is –'

'Exactly. As it is, we don't. The idea itself strikes me as excellent, however. Dee and Magnus are perhaps the most complete systems we have, but they're not as complex as Caliostro was.'

'That's true, but their core modules must be pretty much the same.'

'Not necessarily. We know that the various AIs came from different parts of the Rim and that they were brought online over a period of several hundred years.'

'That's true, but it's better than nothing. I've got Rico digging in the archives, looking for the oldest schematics he can find for both AIs. If we're lucky, he'll find something that dates from before the Schism Wars.'

In silence they turned back to the printout. With one claw extended Molos flipped through the pages, back and forth.

'I can't give you a quick answer,' the Lep said at last. 'But I think I see a pattern here.'

'Take the printout if you'd like.'

'I will. At some point soon we should discuss that other matter.'

'I haven't forgotten. In fact, tell you what. Tomorrow night Barra will be leaving for Orbital. After that, I'll be stopping by the compound regularly, just to keep an eye on things while she's gone. Maybe you could join me out there?'

'Why yes.' Molos flipped his crest to full extension. 'I've always been very fond of your gardens.'

'Then sure, come on out, and we'll have a look around.'

They exchanged, each in their various ways, a conspirator's smile.

When Rico returned just after the seventeens, Hi took him straight into his office. He gestured at a chair, then activated his blackbox card.

'Something's up, huh?' Rico said.

'Your uncle's just getting careful in his old age, that's all.' Hi sat down opposite him. 'Let me be blunt, okay? Have you seen much of Vida lately?'

'Uh well no.' Rico turned bright red, perhaps on general principles. 'Why?'

'I'm getting more and more curious about that ferret of hers, that's why. I've got this feeling it's really important.'

'Oh, that!' Rico's colour ebbed to normal. 'We made a bargain, kind of a joke, that if I did something for her, she'd let me look it over.'

'Yeah? What?'

The blush came back.

'Never mind.' Hi held up one hand. 'Why don't you just do what she wants?'

'I haven't had time.'

'Make time. Tell you what – I'll get that report for the guild together on my own. You work on your bargain with Vida. If that ferret of hers is the Calios revenant, and I'm thinking that it's got to be, then we need a look at it soon. Got that?'

'Yes, Sé. I'll be glad to.'

'Bet you will be, yeah.'

Whenever Jevon visited her mother, she took along food: loaves of real grain bread, slices of real meat, sacks of cereals, and a bag of fresh fruit. She and her mother, Mag, kept up the fiction that Jevon was just bringing 'a little something' to go with the meal Mag would put out for Jevon and her third husband, Ben. Since Mag had only been able to qualify for a single birth permit, Jevon had no siblings. Mag and Ben lived in a tiny apartment on the third floor of a bright pink dwell in Service Sect. There was no lift booth, and Jevon puffed up a twisting staircase made of cast metal through a stairwell that always smelled faintly of urine, even though the super of the building was scrupulous about fixing the drains.

When Mag opened the door, Jevon saw at once that something was wrong. Although her mother had put on a clean print dress for the visit, her hair straggled around her thin face, and she wore no cosmetics whatsoever. Mag never allowed herself to look unkempt. Ben, a tall heavy-set man with dark skin and darker hair, appeared immediately to help with the bags of food, instead of allowing Jevon and her mother their usual few minutes of 'girl talk.'

'What's up, Ma?' Jevon said. 'Feeling under the weather?'

'A little. Ben says I should go to the doctor. I don't know about that. I'm just tired, these days.'

From behind Mag Ben mouthed, 'Make her go.'

The apartment had three small rooms arranged in a row, so that you walked right into the kitchen and could see the tiny gather, its vidscreen turned to some drama filmed in a jungle somewhere, through the far door. After he'd put the food down, Ben ostentatiously withdrew to watch the end of his show and leave them alone.

'What is it, Ma?' Jevon repeated. 'Something's wrong.'

'I don't know.' She reached up and tucked one strand of greying brown hair behind her ear. 'I'm just tired.'

'Well, the doctor can give you something for that.'

Mag shrugged and began to open packages.

'I invited your cousin Jay over for later,' she said. 'Real nice of you to bring all this, honey. Jay's lost his job. Did I tell you?'

'No, you didn't. That's too bad. I thought he was working in well there.'

'So did I, but they had a cutback. They have a lot of cutbacks, these days, seems like.'

'It's the damn lizards,' Ben was back, standing in the doorway. 'Between the damn lizards and the Stinkers, there isn't going to be any work for human men pretty soon.'

'Well now,' Mag said. 'The Leps got to do something. They lost some good jobs themselves, didn't they? And they've got families, same as us.'

'So?' Ben snapped. 'Why can't they raise them on their own turf? I don't wish 'em any harm. I just want 'em gone. I know your daughter there agrees with me.'

'I do,' Jevon said. 'They should have been deported, that's all, sent back to their own people.'

'Well now,' Mag said. 'I just don't know. I keep thinking about Ba Ridda, she was so nice to me when you were just born, Jev. She was a real grandmother – to us too, not just to her own family.'

'I'm not saying there aren't any good ones,' Ben broke in. 'I'm just saying they belong with their own kind. And we belong with ours. That's just the way it should work.'

'Well, I don't know.' Mag shook her head. 'Come eat, you two. I found a nice soyloaf at the market, and there's gravy, and then this nice little something Jevon brought us.'

People in Service Sect ate soy in one form or another flavoured with fungi of some species or another for practically every meal of every day. There was always plenty of it – the Palace government let no citizen starve – but it was always soy, no matter how you disguised it. The squishy texture and cool taste of the loaf brought Jevon memories of other meals, crammed into tiny kitchens like this, where her elbow would rest on the window sill beside the narrow table. After the meals she would study at the same tables, bent over to stare at the tiny Mapscreen that the government issued to poor people. Education was the way out of Service Sect, and Jevon had taken it.

'How's your job, honey?' Mag said. 'I saw on the screens that your Sé Jons's boy was killed. That's a sad thing, poor man, losing his son that way.'

Jevon had drilled herself against this moment.

'Very sad,' she said. 'I liked Arno myself. It doesn't seem to bother Sé Jons much. He says it's because of the drug thing, that he had to keep thinking of his son as already dead.'

'Well, that's the way it works.' Ben took another slice of bread. 'I hate to say it, Jev, but he was right about that.'

This Jevon had never expected. She felt her face sealing over like ice freezing.

'Guy I worked with, trucking,' Ben said. 'He got into trash drugs, and there was nothing any of us could do or say. Nothing. It broke his wife's heart. And they had a baby, too, a little boy.'

'They didn't have the money for private hospitals like Sé Jons does.' Jevon forced her voice to measure out each word whole and steady.

'No, they didn't, but I don't think it would have mattered a snowball in hell.'

'Maybe not, then. Ma, want some of this fruit?'

'In a bit, maybe, honey. I'm full already.' Mag turned, glancing at the clock above the tiny white stove. 'Jay should be here soon, anyway.'

When Jay arrived, the evening turned predictable with talk of relatives and worries – worries about jobs, worries about the cousin who desperately wanted a birth permit but probably wouldn't get one, worries about children who wouldn't study hard enough on the School Map, worries about Mag's health, which she refused to discuss whenever the subject came up. It wasn't until Jevon was leaving, and Ben walked her to the wiretrain stop, that Jevon finally got some solid information.

'It's time for her to start the Geriose,' he said. 'God knows we qualify for the subsidy, and she could have it, but she keeps saying she doesn't want it.'

'What? I don't understand! Why wouldn't she want it?'

Ben shrugged, his shoulders hunched, his hands shoved in his jacket pockets. In the flickering light from the street lamps he looked suddenly old.

'She keeps saying she's too tired,' he said at last. 'Keeps saying she's lived long enough.'

Jevon nearly broke down. Only the other people on the street, the curious faces passing them by and glancing at her expensive clothes, kept her from weeping.

'Talk to her, honey?' Ben said. 'I can't get through to her. God knows I've tried.'

'I will. Don't worry about that. I'll call tomorrow. And you can always call me if things get worse.'

'Well, I don't know about that, calling you in Government House. It was one thing, when you worked out at the compound, but Government House is well, it's just different.'

On the ride back to Government House, as Jevon stared out the window and watched the long lawns and parks of Centre Sect whipping by her in the night, she was thinking about doctors, specialists in depression and mental illness. To refuse the life-extension treatments was slow suicide, plain and simple. She knew that Sé Jons would allow her time from her work to shepherd her mother to specialists, if it came to that. He was so generous, Sé Jons. It shocked her just how much she wanted to hate him. The memory of Ben's calm voice ate at her, 'it wouldn't have mattered a snowball in hell'.

If she couldn't blame Sé Jons for Arno's death, there was no-one left to blame but Arno himself. She pressed her face hard against the glass and tried not to think at all for the rest of the ride home.

Even though Hi had told him to do whatever was necessary to gain access to Vida's Calios meta, Rico waited until his uncle went to bed before hacking into the Protectors' databanks. All that evening he worked in his room at his Map terminal, using the open guild records to plan out his strategy. Once or twice Hi walked in to ask him a question, but each time he saw onscreen nothing more dangerous than a condensed Map of all the administrative stations in Centre Sect.

Once both Hi and Nju had retreated to their quarters to sleep, Rico jacked into the Guildhall Map. While he watched fields of icons drift like spores across the pale blue screen, he debated tanking up on cyberdrugs. Although he worked so much better with them, he found himself yawning, and every guild drug manual warned against using them when you were tired. Better not, then. He was surprised at how irritated the decision made him. You're getting lazy, he told himself. Concentrating without them is hard work.

He reminded himself that he was doing the work for Vida and jacked in, logged on in his normal Map body, and hurried over to clan space. Now that he was a journeyman, he could seal off his personal work area. Behind a secured door icon, guarded by green jadewing defenders, his iconic rhomboid hovered waiting for him. He transferred into it, then left his work space by the back exit he'd built the day before. Once back in clan space, he could summon the Chameleon Gate.

When he ran the open sesame meta, the sight of the encircling portraits of Arno made him freeze with grief. For a moment the entire illusion of clan space and doors wavered as his body threatened to assert its right to mourn and drag him back. He could feel the jack plugged into his hand, hear his own breathing. Desperately he concentrated on the wheel of doors. With a ripple of colour the Gate appeared. He threw himself into the enveloping cold of the Gate's membrane and with the motion forgot all about his body.

In his iconic form the clutching feeling of suffocation no longer bothered him, as if having the illusion of a body had programmed his mind to fulfil a body's expectations. This time his brain conceptualized contact with the Gate as a smooth click and a sense of rightness, as if he were the icon for some essential subroutine slipping into its socket. Yet he and the Gate both knew that he commanded their dual operation. As they floated in clan space, all he needed to do was speak the location codes for the Protectors' databanks for the Gate to start moving.

As the Gate sped along the correct devs, Rico realized that he felt no motion; he could merely see the Map unrolling 'beneath' them as the Gate cross-connected to the correct grid points. The Protectors' pages appeared ahead as a vast area of grey shading over the bright colours of Mapspace. A firewall, iconized in glossy black, bounded the special areas set aside for the Protectors by the guild, but several centuries ago, the citizens had voted against giving the police unbreachable security after a scandal about spying on private citizens. Since the guild had built the firewall, Rico could make educated guesses at the sort of code that would breach it. His second attempt produced the image of a gate in the black. Gliding through brought him straight to the root of the data dump's tree.

'Expand listings.'

Bright gold against grey, the long directory structure unrolled. With a hook Rico grappled onto the icon marking closed cases and swung his rhomboidal self inside. The Gate registered his search like a fall, a long tumble through a branched and spiky tree of words, studded with icons instead of leaves. The letter S flashed by – Rico flung another hook and slid through. Another fall brought him to the Smids; hundreds of cases, it looked like. What did Vida come from, a long line of criminals? Since he had no time to sort, Rico flung a copy net around the lot and pulled his copies into storage as fast as they'd transfer. As he closed the cache, he heard a thin wail: somehow an alarm had got itself triggered.

'Run for it.'

Whether he or the Gate had spoken, he didn't know. With a swoop it broke out of the iconic forest and flung itself for the firewall. Running down bright red devs, black guard icons rushed to cut them off. Although Rico could have simply bailed out of Mapspace back into his body – to face a terrible headache but nothing worse – doing so would leave the Gate trapped where the Protectors' Maprunners could examine it.

'Eye of God.'

With a flash of white light it bounded upward like a living being and flew straight for the Hypermap. If there was an umbrella over those files – Rico refused to think about the crash that lay ahead of them. Below them the guard icons dwindled and fell away; ahead lay only blackness, whether only the Interstice or an umbrella he couldn't tell. Up and up, and now the Gate's motion was as smooth as a lift booth and as fast. In a symphony of beeps like a thousand clocks it burst through the blackness and floated, quivering, in the pale blue of the Hypermap. Below him hung Palace, turning cloud-free and crowned at each pole with white ice. Tired as he was, eager as he was to examine his cache, Rico lingered, staring at the icecaps.

'The Map icon for Palace has changed since the last time I saw it. Explain discrepancy.'

'Access occurred in error mode. Icon furnished by historical archive.'

'Error was?'

'Accessed emergency memory area.'

'Why?'

'A state of emergency was diagnosed.'

'Data noted and approved.' Rico hesitated – it made sense that the Gate would read 'emergency' from their flight, but what did that have to do with the Palace icon? He had no time to worry about it just then. 'Return mode. Arco daz dev home reverse.'

Back in his ordinary consciousness, Rico logged off from the guild grid and disengaged his jack from the terminal. Once he had his stolen copies up onscreen, he could eliminate most of them immediately. All but two belonged to other Smids than the mysterious Lin, whose files turned out to be curiously incomplete, just as Vida had reported. Since Rico had netted them in the state of raw data directly from the Map, all their routing marks, download records, and other such tagging had come along with them. If someone had deleted portions, he should have left tracks. Rico was quite sure that his own hasty raid had left plenty; although they'd be untraceable thanks to the Chameleon Gate, not even the Gate could prevent the marks from forming.

But Lin Smid's records showed no such tracks. Legitimate access requests and copy notices decorated their undercode like a palimpsest, but not one mark pointed toward the deletion of so much as a single word.

'This is weird.'

It was also frustrating. Rico had been counting on those tracks to lead him to the dump where the stolen data might still lie. The thief must have been a master cybe to get so clean away. Rico found himself wondering why a master cybe, why anyone had bothered meddling with such selected portions of the records. What were they hiding? Certainly the one big thing about Lin Smid was that she was Vida's mother, and nobody was denying that. Finally he closed the files down and went to bed.

Tired as he was, Rico lay awake for over an hour, running the evidence up and down a mental screen. He could make no sense of it and fell asleep at last, only to wake and find himself sitting upright in bed. A crack of grey light filtered under a partially closed shutter.

'No-one deleted anything. It was never there.'

He got up, pulled on a pair of pants, then sat down at his desk. Inserts. They had to be. It was the only thing that made sense, really, and when he brought the files up onscreen, their smooth self-containment made him more sure than ever. Since he could check his theory in semi-public files, he jacked back onto the Map and headed for the gargantuan database located like a separate township in Centre Sect's Map analogue. For two hours he searched and copied, double-checking through old backups and obscure record bases. On an impulse he turned to the public announcement scroll records and found that like good citizens of Palace, the Maprunners in charge had never thrown one bit of data away. Old advertisements lay rolled on miles of virtual tape, ready for his search routines. By the time he finished with them, he knew that he was right, as bizarre as his theory was.

He left the Map and found himself back in a body that was soaked in sweat and growling hungry. Even so, he hated to leave his screen, where in long columns his evidence stood waiting for his physical eyes to give it one last review.

'Hey, kid?' Uncle Hi's voice, and behind him.

Rico yelped and sloughed round in his chair.

'Sorry. Didn't mean to startle you.'

'It's all right, Sé. I was just looking over data. I've found what I need to find, the thing Vida wanted, I mean.'

'I wondered. I just got a commcall from the Master of the Protectors' Guild. Someone breached their firewall last night.'

Too exhausted to think up a lie, Rico waited for the long and sarcastic diatribe he figured was coming his way.

'I told him,' Hi said instead, 'that I'd get right on to it. Don't do that again, okay? Next time ask me first, and I'll tell you how to disable those guard icons so they can't socket their agents into the Protectors' power supplies.'

Rico tried to speak and then decided against it.

'Well, come on!' Hi snapped. 'What did you find?'

'Nothing.' Rico allowed himself a smile. 'And that's the whole thing, the kernel, the core drive. Nothing.'

It was Hi's turn for the stare. Rico got up, wincing at stiff muscles and a sore back.

'I can't tell you, Sé. I've got to tell Vida first. This is supposed to be a secret. And to tell you the truth, I'm not real sure what it all means.'

'Okay. All I want is a look at Calios. I don't care about anything else.'

'I'll call her right now. Oh, Uncle Hi? Something I wanted to ask you. Did Palace ever have polar ice?'

'Sure did. When the Colonizers landed, they didn't realize that the solarsphere ecology was just entering a warming phase. And the fuel the colonies were burning didn't help the global equilibrium any, either. That's why those settlements on the Nox coast failed. They drowned when the sea level rose. What do you want to know that for?'

'Just curious. The Gate accessed a view of the planet with the polar caps intact, that's all. Said it was an emergency error, but it seemed like a weird kind of error message to choose.'

'Huh. Sometimes I think the Gate has a mind of its own.'

'It's got to, doesn't it? It must be a fragment from one of the AIs to act the way it does.'

Hi tipped his head to one side and considered him for a moment.

'Good point,' Hi said at last. 'I like the way you figure things out, Rico. Now go get breakfast and give Vida a call. I want to see that ferret more than ever.'

'Okay, but don't forget that I've got to go out to the Spaceport later.'

'Jeez, that's right. I'd better give your mother a call while she's got the time to say goodbye.'

'Knowing her, she's been packed and ready to go for days.'

'Probably, yeah. But I want to tell her how the stake-out for those candles is going.'

'How is it going?'

Hi made a sour face.

'Lousy, that's how. Hasn't been one sign of them, anywhere. You'd almost think it knows we're watching for it. Maybe it does know, huh? Or its creator, I mean. There's no way we could have kept this secret from the entire guild.'

When Vida returned to her suite after her lunch with Sister Romero, she found a message waiting from Rico, asking her to meet him 'somewhere outside'. She conferred with Jak, who asked Dukayn. Inside the blueglass walls around Government House lay a small park that Dukayn deemed safe enough for Vida to visit. Even so, two Fleet Marines, her usual extra guards, accompanied her and Jak when she left the towers. Although silver mottled the sky, every now and then brief sunlight fell golden across the turquoise lawn. A little stream wandered into an artificial lake where, under nodding fern trees, Vida found a wooden bench.

'This looks nice,' she said.

'Very well, Sé Vida,' Jak said. 'I'll just deploy the guards.'

With the two Marines behind and to either side of her, a decorous thirty feet or so away, and Jak out on the lawns, Vida sat at the centre of an armed triangle. She'd brought a magazine with her, a prop for her pretence of just getting out for some fresh air, but she laid the tablet down beside her and watched the stream, running over pale sand. Pretence or not, it did feel good to get out of the towers.

In a few minutes Rico in his Cyberguild blues came strolling along the walkway. He and Jak exchanged a casual wave; then Rico made a great show of noticing her on the bench. She waved, smiling, as he trotted over.

'Fancy meeting you here,' he said.

'Yeah, a real surprise. Why don't you sit down and join me?'

'Okay.' He sat down a careful couple of feet along the bench. 'You don't have to worry about someone picking up this conversation with a sound-gun, by the way. I borrowed something from my uncle.'

'All right. Unless someone's spying who can read lips.'

'What?'

'It's just something I found in a holonovel once. The hero thought he was safe from being overheard, but the bad guy could read lips and picked up the secret code that way.'

'Say, you really know how to make a man worry.'

'Yeah?'

When Vida smiled at him, he blushed and spent a few moments smoothing down his jacket. Finally he looked up.

'Remember our bargain?' he said.

'Of course. You find information about my mother, and I'll let you see my ferret.'

'Well, I found something, all right, but it's real strange. Lin Smid doesn't exist. Somebody made her up.'

Vida could only stare.

'They must have been hiding who your real mother was,' Rico went on. 'That's the only thing I can think of, anyway. Look, let me run my theory down for you, okay?'

'All right. This is the last thing I ever thought you'd tell me.'

'I'll bet. Okay, first I, um . . . well er . . . gained access to the Protector files. I managed to get hold of the two pertaining to Lin Smid. No-one's ever deleted anything from them. They were entered into the database in their incomplete state. All the datapoints that are missing are things like her address and her business licence number, stuff that would be easy to check and verify. What's left is a pretty convincing life. She did well on the school Map for techs, she was a gardener in Service Sect, she met your dad on a job, that kind of thing. The court records of her trial look really official, too, with all the right codes and sign-offs. To do that, whoever invented her must have had help from one of the Protectors. Any clerk would do; it wouldn't have to be someone high up on the force, and I'll bet you could bribe some low-paid clerk if you had untraceable cash.'

'Well, yeah. The clerk wouldn't really be doing anything against the law. It's not like they were destroying records. Just the opposite.'

'And there wouldn't have been much chance of getting caught,'

Rico said. 'So, once the records were in place in the Protectors' database, the cybe who was inventing Lin Smid could crack into a couple of other bases and insert records there, too.'

'Like the hospital.'

'Yes, and then the education camp. I didn't try to get into that database, but I'll bet they have another partial file on Lin Smid. Here's how it works: suppose a gridjockey's interviewing a hospital official and asks if they have a file on Smid. The official would look at the directory and say yes. Thousands of people go through the emergency rooms, don't they? A doctor wouldn't even think twice if she couldn't remember Smid personally, especially not after eighteen years.'

Vida nodded.

'But what clinched it,' Rico went on, 'was the gardening. Our cybe had to give her a job and one that would let her meet your father. He couldn't leave that out. Now, if she had a lawn service, she'd have to advertise. She'd have to be in the public directories, too. Well, he inserted her name and a fake access code in the City Comm listings, but he forgot about the business listings, and I never found one ad for her service, not one, in any of the public scrolls. Let's face it, people who get to be cybermasters lose touch after a while with what ordinary people do. That's what Uncle Hi always says, anyway.'

Vida nodded again and stared across the lawns. Jak was sitting down on the grass, as relaxed as any Garang could look, but she knew that he'd coiled himself in such a way that he could spring up at any moment.

'I'm sorry,' Rico said. 'I was hoping I could find her, not lose her, for you.'

'You don't have to be sorry.' She turned back to him and found that he'd laid his arm along the back of the bench and leaned a little toward her. 'I asked you to find out the truth, didn't I? Well, you did. And I've got to have a mother somewhere.' She attempted a smile. 'The laws don't let you grow babies in tanks any more.'

'Yeah, that's true. Maybe she was from another old family, a woman who loved your father but couldn't get a permit.'

'That's a nice thought, but if she was rich and powerful, why couldn't she hide me, maybe take me out to her estate and pass me off as the daughter of one of her servants? That's what happens in the holonovels all the time.'

'Maybe she didn't read as many holonovels as you do.'

Vida made a face at him.

'The thing is,' Rico went on, 'she must have had some reason for hiding you. You were born before the war even started, so it wasn't because of your father's – well, the way he was accused of treason. All I can think of is no birth permit.'

'Me, too. No matter what, I'm still Unauthorized. Just a little cull, that's me.'

'Vida, don't!' Rico laid his hand on her shoulder. 'Don't call yourself that.'

For a moment Vida was afraid that she would weep. She'd built up such a satisfying story about Lin Smid, seen her as a heroine in her way, risking everything to have the child of the man she loved against all odds, only to have the child snatched from her. Lin would have been so happy to have found her daughter again, or at least, to have seen her on the vidscreens and known that she was safe and well. But there was no Lin, no story, no happy reunion ahead.

'Hey,' Rico said, and his voice had turned soft. 'Whoever had this done risked a lot for you. She must have really loved you and been trying to find a way to keep you with her. I guess something went wrong, and she couldn't do it. But she risked a lot to try.'

Vida felt herself turn cold. The very thought of tears vanished, frozen by sudden insight.

'Wait a minute,' she said. 'What do you mean, tried to keep me with her?'

'Well, she must have had some reason to hire a cybe and go to all of this trouble. Unless she was a cybe herself, of course. That's a real possibility.'

'No, it's not. I mean, I think you're right. I think that keeping me is exactly what she was doing.' Vida's heart was pounding. 'Tell me something, Rico. You're Cyberguild. You must know Ri Tal Molos.'

'Well, I know about him, like everyone does – he's a real genius. He's a friend of my uncle's, but I've never met him. He's been on Souk for the last fourteen years or something, hasn't he? What does he have to do with – oh. He's kind of a friend of yours, isn't he?'

'He's gone out of his way to be one, like he had some reason to be interested in me. Do you think he could do what you're talking about? Insert those records?'

'As easy as rustling his crest. Do you think he'll tell you if he did?'

'I bet I can make him tell me.' She felt her voice shaking in her throat. 'Rico, thank you. If you want to see Calios, sure, any time later, but I can't right now. I've got to think about this.'

'Okay, yeah. Can my uncle come too? Vida, this is important.'

'Of course, sure, whatever you want.' She stood and saw Jak springing to his feet in answer. 'Thanks. Have your factor call mine or something.'

Vida strode off, leaving him on the bench behind her. As Jak joined her on the walkway she glanced back to see the two Marines falling into position.

'Sé Vida, what's wrong?' Jak said. 'Has young Rico distressed you?'

'No. He's just done me a favour.' Vida forced out a smile. 'I'm fine, Jak. Really. But I need to get back right now.'

Only after they'd reached East Tower, when they were in the lift booth, in fact, gliding up to her floor, did Vida remember her magazine, lying on the bench. She hoped that Rico would realize what a splendid excuse returning it to her would make, then forgot about it completely. When they reached her suite, Jak lingered in the hall to dismiss the two Marines. Vida rushed inside.

'Samante, Samante!'

'I'm right here.' Samante came hurrying into the gather. 'What's wrong?'

'I need to talk to your friend Molos. As soon as possible. Do you think you can find him?'

'Well, I'll try, certainly. Vida –'

'I'll tell you why later. Okay?'

'Well, of course. Here. You sit down. Vida, you're shaking.'

Vida held out one hand and realized that Samante was right. She took a deep breath and forced herself calm while Samante watched with sincere concern.

'I shouldn't be in too much of hurry,' Vida said. 'It's going to look really strange if I am.'

'Too much of a hurry to do what? Talk with Molos?'

'Yeah. But I – well, look. Why don't you see if you can find him? If you can't, I won't be able to talk with him anyway, and so there's no use in getting upset now.'

While Samante worked at her comm unit, Vida flung herself down on the green brocade sofa. Breathe, she told herself. Remember what you learned in self-defence class. Breathe and slow down, breathe and calm down. She stared up at the featureless expanse of ivory-coloured ceiling and let herself relax, one muscle at a time. By the time she'd stopped trembling, Samante had finished her calls.

'Molos's factor told me he's here in Government House. He'll contact him and ask him to stop by.'

'Thanks.' Vida sat up. 'I'm sorry I was so upset.'

'It's all right. I need to confirm something with you about the wedding. Cardinal Roha called while you were out. He wants you to solemnize the contract in the cathedral. It means a lot of work and fuss, but the gesture would really please him.'

'Of course. After all the help he's given me, it's the least I can do.'

Vida felt her calm petrify to a cold inertia. She really was going to marry Wan, and soon. There was no getting out of it now, not after they'd made the contract public. All at once she brightened.

'If we're going to do the signing in the Cathedral, it'll take time to plan the ceremony, won't it?'

'That's what I was just telling you.' Samante looked briefly severe. 'We've got to reserve a date for the Gaze, for one thing, and then we need to put the media contract out for bids. I'm sure we can sell an exclusive on this easily.'

'All right. Do we have to consult with Wan about this?'

'Yes, unfortunately. Oh by God's Eye! I'm going to have to work with Leni.'

'Just keep him drunk, and he'll agree to anything you say.'

They shared a mirthless laugh.

Molos arrived an hour later. Samante ushered him into the gather, then left on the excuse of supervising Greenie while it put together some refreshments. Molos settled himself on his favourite chair and lifted his crest.

'Kind of you to invite me, my dear,' he said. 'I'm surprised that your most holy benefactor hasn't warned you off me by now.'

Vida winced.

'Ah,' Molos said. 'I see he has.'

'Well, it's not like I listened to him.' Vida hesitated, then realized she had the opening she needed. 'Aleen raised me to treat all sapients as equals, you know. I don't see any reason to change now.'

'Your guardian is an amazing woman, yes.'

'You've been friends with her for years, haven't you? I've been trying to remember, and I think I must have met you when I was just a little kid, before you left for Souk, that is.'

'I do remember that, yes. Once or twice, I believe, Aleen presented you to me.'

'That was sort of odd of her, wasn't it? I mean, I was just a cull dumped on her by the Protectors.'

'Vida, please! Even I remember you as a charming child, and as I'm sure you know, the men of my race have very little interest in anyone's offspring, even our own.' Molos gently waved his crest. 'I think Aleen was sincerely fond of you.'

'I've got some reasons for thinking the same thing, actually.'

For the barest moment Molos tensed.

'Indeed?' His voice stayed level.

'Sé Molos.' Vida leaned forward and put on her best charming smile. 'Everyone knows what a splendid cybermaster you were, before that awful ban got passed, I mean. Rico Hernanes y Jons tells me that you're a genius.'

Molos's mouth opened, and his jaw dropped, on the verge of springing loose in the Lep gesture of utter surprise. He swallowed heavily and snapped it back into place.

'It would have been awfully easy for you to add those files,' Vida went on. 'The ones in the Protectors' database.'

'My dear Vida.' Molos's voice had turned feeble. 'I'm not sure what you're implying, but um . . . well, my dear Vida.'

'Who thought up Lin Smid? You or my mother?'

Molos raised a quick hand and laid it on the underside of his jaw. Vida waited, perched on the edge of the sofa.

'Aleen,' he said at last. 'I'd like to know how you found out.'

'I was only guessing. You just told me.'

Molos's crest snapped up and waved.

'I outsmarted the Peronida's negotiating team on Souk, but you've just got the better of me.' He shook his head. 'You're very much like your mother, Vida.'

'Am I?' Vida rose and walked to the window. Although the view gave out in the general direction of Pleasure, the Sect lay too far away for even the Carillon Tower to be visible over the sea of roofs and trees of Government House. 'I don't want her to know I know. Not yet, anyway. I want to be able to tell her myself some day.' She turned and looked at the Lep. 'Does that make sense?'

'Oh yes. I imagine you need time to assimilate this.'

Vida nodded, remembering her life at The Close. She'd always had her own little room, when most culls shared a dormitory. She'd had the best schooling, too, that the Map could provide, while Aleen had taught her all the other things she needed to know: how to dress, how to charm, how to handle the finances of a big establishment like The Close – or those of an aristocrat.

'Vida?' Molos said. 'She was afraid to tell you, afraid you'd let something slip if you knew. She couldn't bear to lose you.'

'I can see that.' Vida found herself on the edge of tears. 'I'm just remembering how she sent me away.'

'It was the hardest thing she's ever done. She told me that.'

Tears spilled. Irritably Vida wiped them away with the back of her hand.

'I'm sorry,' she said. 'There's no need to cry over this.'

'Very much like your mother.'

'I'm glad.' Vida managed a smile. 'But Molos, you won't tell her I know? Please don't?'

'Of course, my dear. I'll keep your secret.' He waved his crest again. 'I hardly want her knowing how easily you got the better of me.'

Humans were, all in all, a sloppy race of sapients, but Kata was finding those on Palace to be the sloppiest of the lot. First the various guilds went to great expense to clothe their members in distinctive uniforms; then they left those uniforms lying around where anyone could steal them. His first day on the job, Kata was just leaving the Floating Amphitheatre by the employees' entrance when a donkeybot chugged by, its hopper filled with soiled Power Guild coveralls. He glanced around, saw no-one, trotted alongside the bot just long enough to grab a pair in extra large and stuff them into his wrap jacket. On his way back to Zir's, Kata stopped at a launderette and tossed them into a hypersound cleaner. They came out good as new.

The cleaning service issued its employees dark grey coveralls, which they had to keep up themselves, unlike the higher status sapients in Power Guild. After dinner that evening, sitting cross-legged on Zir's floor, Kata turned the grey set inside out, then eased the scarlet pair over them, right-side out. Up in her bedsling Zir rustled her crest at him.

'What are you doing?'

'I'm going to sew the red coveralls onto the grey ones. Very carefully – you have to match the seams for this to work. To change my profession, I simply peel off this ugly human garment, making sure I'm turning it all the way inside out, and then I step into it again. It takes just a few seconds, if you practise, and the cleaner disappears like magic.'

'That's wonderful! And your pass to the generator area will be pinned on the red coveralls, right?'

'Right. So I walk right up to the generator, plant my device, then walk away again. In the lift booth – more magic. The cleaner's back when I step off on the top floor.'

'Perfect! Although . . .' She let her voice die away.

'Although what? Still worrying about that plastique?'

'Do you blame me? Any compound that old is bound to be unstable.'

'It's the best I'm going to find on this planet of herd animals. I can't believe the restrictions these people put up with! This is illegal, and that's illegal; no guns here, no explosives there. Huh! They think one of their damned Protectors with a stunstick is something fierce and frightening.'

Zir merely considered him through slitted red eyes.

'Well, I'm not going to fix a conventional fuse to it,' Kata said at last. 'That will lower the risk considerably.'

'Good.'

'In fact, I have a little job for you. Have you ever heard of a frequency activator? A specified sound opens a circuit and allows a pulse of electricity through its switch?'

'I learned how to put one of those together on the School Map.'

'Splendid! One of the speakers at this rally is Wilso of the Power Guild. He has a pretty distinctive voice, way up in his ugly little human nose. And I've got a recording of one of his other speeches. There's a certain high note that he hits which should work just fine.'

'I like that. One bigot blasting the others into Eternity. It's fitting, somehow.'

Before Rico went out to the Spaceport, he picked up a sheaf of security passes from Dukayn's office. A bored and blonde young woman took his thumbprint, then handed him a set of chits and a picture-badge to wear at all times. Since Barra and her new ward Damo were travelling in the Peronida limousine, Rico took the wiretrain out alone. When he got off at Port Station, he found the first security checkpoint at the doors leading to the movebelt. A chit got him past the long line of passengers at the temporary blockade, all of them fuming and demanding explanations while silent Garang in Peronida uniforms searched their luggage.

He handed over another chit at the far end of the movebelt to another Garang post and gained entry to the shuttle terminal. In the huge domed room, human Protectors armed with stunsticks stood at regular intervals. Up on the mezzanine gleamed more red uniforms. Rico took a lift booth up to the third floor and the Newsgrid Lounge; Garang met him when the doors opened at a marble foyer. Rico surrendered still another chit to the sergeant in charge.

'Expecting trouble?' Rico asked. 'I've never seen security like this.'

'Not expecting it, Sé,' the Garang sergeant said. 'Just prepared in case.'

An ordinary security guard took his final pass at the door. Gridjockeys crammed the lounge itself, a half-round room carpeted and painted in pale blue. On the straight wall stood a tall dais with an interview table. Behind it stood a row of uniformed Garang. Flanked by Damo on one side and Karlo Peronida himself on the other, Barra, dressed in her guild coveralls, sat in a pool of harsh white light and fielded questions from the sea of intakes lapping around the dais. Pix hovered just behind, pointing and clicking as they jostled each other for the best positions.

'Well, we're hoping to repair her, of course,' Barra was saying. 'Reconfiguring Magnus to take Nimue's place would be a real long shot. Maybe we could do it, maybe not. Next question? You.' She pointed, then leaned forward to listen to the mumbling intake who'd caught her attention. 'No, the guild's made no firm decision on Magnus at all. A lot of the members think we should just plain leave him alone. Next?'

Rico glanced around and saw a buffet in the curve of the wall. He made his way through the crowd that stood behind the gridjockeys – a few guild members, port officials, Garang guards, and some civilians that Rico couldn't identify. At the buffet his picture-badge earned him a plate, which he heaped. He stood back against the wall while he ate and listened to the pix shouting questions and his mother's calm voice answering. Looking skinny and pale in his Cyberguild blue smock, Damo sat with his hands folded in front of him and stared out at the pix.

'No, we have no idea how long the repairs will take, if we can even make them,' Barra said. 'Diagnostics come first. How long? Maybe six months. Standard, yes, not Palace. I've been studying the Map schematics in preparation, of course. No, we can't do the repairs from here. The schematics aren't real reliable, that's why. I'll have better answers for you once I get out there.'

On and on they went, some good questions, some meaningless, some stupid enough to make Rico realize why Tarick Avon occupied an exalted position among intakes, just because he could ask such clear questions and such pointed ones. Rico handed his empty plate to a saccule waiter, then began to edge his way forward – not an easy thing to do. He never would have got close to the dais if Karlo Peronida hadn't spotted him. The First Citizen leaned over and whispered something to Barra, who broke out in a grin and looked Rico's way with a wave. Karlo stood up, smiling around at the newsgrids.

'Very well, ladies and gentlemen, time's up,' Karlo said in his dark and booming voice. 'You know the contractual agreements. We've arranged some hospitality for you there on the buffet.'

The white light on the dais went out. The Garang moved from behind the table to form a wall between it and the gridjockeys below. With one last round of clicks and shouts of 'good luck', pix and intakes alike headed for the free food.

In answer to his mother's gesture, Rico climbed the steps up to the dais and followed her through a little door in the wall to an elegant private lounge. On the far pale grey wall hung a huge pair of vidscreens, filled with news clips. Among leather chairs and divans, saccules sashed in Fleet grey drifted through the crowd serving drinks. His mother's staff and what seemed to be half the Peronida household were standing around talking in hushed voices, while Garang stood guard. Barra caught Rico's arm.

'Come be introduced to the First Citizen,' she said, then whispered. 'He's oddly human up close.'

Karlo was standing near the far wall with Pero Nikolaides, also in full Fleet uniform, while behind them stood Dukayn, all in black, frowning at his factor's tablet. Fortunately there was no sign of Wan. On the vidscreens behind Karlo, his images, shot from different angles, were speaking soundlessly.

'Here's Rico,' Pero said. 'We've met, Father, over that unfortunate incident at Vida's reception. You could call us brothers-in-arms.'

'I'm glad to see that bite healed up okay,' Rico said. 'She was something, Anji.'

'The le-Yonestilla girl?' Karlo said, offering a hand. 'Ah yes, I heard about that. Good to meet you, Rico.'

'Thank you, Sé. Good to meet you, too.'

They shook hands; everyone smiled; Dukayn stepped forward.

'First Citizen?' the factor said. 'If you're going to speak at the Centre Council meeting, we need to leave.'

'Of course.' Karlo turned to Barra. 'Thanks again, Sé Jons.' His voice suddenly wavered. 'Take care of my boy for me, okay?'

'I'll do my best,' Barra said. 'Why, First Citizen! I think you're going to miss him.'

'I think you're right.' Karlo cleared his throat twice. 'Well, we'd better be on our way. Pero, stay and do the honours for me?'

'Yes, Sé.'

Pero saluted, Karlo returned it, Dukayn led him firmly away. When a couple of staff people hurried up to Pero, Barra caught Rico's arm again and drew him away to a wall of floor to ceiling polarized windows. Rico looked out at the shuttle, waiting a safe distance from the buildings across a long stretch of black paving. A sleek white bullet with swept back wings, it crouched at the end of the atlatl launch ramp that would help sling it free of the planet. A portable lift booth stood beside it, ready to load passengers. Fuel tankers and luggage loaders trundled back and forth.

'Getting excited?' Rico said.

'I feel like a kid again. I've got a couple of custom diagnostic modules all ready to go, and I figure I'll have plenty of time to work up more on the flight out. It'll be three weeks before we dock at Nimue Station.'

'Will you be off Map all that time?'

'Pretty much. The resources on the in-system ship are strictly limited. I might be able to contact you and Hi, maybe not.'

'Once you're there, though, it'll be different.'

'Once I'm there I'll practically be living on the Map. I'm hoping you'll keep in touch.'

'Oh hey, Mom! As if I wouldn't!'

'Just checking.' She paused, glancing around the room. 'Ah, there's Damo with Nikolaides. You know, I really did think his mother might have shown up to say goodbye.'

'I was wondering about that, yeah. Seems strange that she wouldn't.'

'There is a lot that's strange about it.' Barra dropped her voice to a barely audible murmur. 'I'll tell you from the Map.'

As if he'd felt her attention, Damo came skipping toward them. Although Rico was wondering what to say to the boy, Damo ignored him and skipped past. He pressed his nose and hands to the window and stared at the shuttle.

'That's ours?' he said to Barra.

'Yes. What do you think of her?'

Damo merely shrugged. On the far wall the vidscreens were showing Barra's press conference, edited into smooth dialogue and intercut with graphics and video of Nimue Station.

'Attention, all passengers.' A voice spoke from the ceiling. 'Launch in minus thirty. Please report to Gate Five. The bus to the launch ramp is loading now. Launch in minus thirty.'

'That's ours!' Barra said with a laugh. 'Damo, do you have to use the restroom? We won't be able to go again until after we dock with the in-system ship.'

'Okay.' The boy turned around and stared at Rico as if he'd just noticed him.

Rico felt the same feeling he got from being snapped by a pix, as if Damo were imprinting his image somewhere in his brain.

When he started to speak, Damo darted off, heading for the restrooms at the back of the lounge. Rico gave his mother a rough hug.

'See you on the Map, Mom. Take care of yourself, okay?'

'You bet. Oh, this is going to be fun. The best puzzle in the world.' She held Rico at arm's length. 'And you take care of yourself, too. And take care of your uncle. I don't care what he says, losing Arno is tearing him up inside.'

'Well, yeah.' Rico felt a sudden lump in his throat. 'I'll do that.'

In Vida's suite Samante had her own rooms – a bedroom, a bath, and an office with its own Mapscreen as well as a pair of vidscreens, which she'd programmed to show every scrap of news available at any given time. Since they were waiting, that afternoon, for media bids on the rights to her wedding, Vida went into the office to watch Barra Jons y Macconnel's press conference. She slouched in an armchair while Samante sat at her desk, partly watching, partly studying bids.

'This Nimue project?' Samante said. 'Is it painful for you to hear about it?'

'No. I keep thinking that Sé Barra's going to find some evidence that clears my father. Oh I know – I've been reading too many holonovels again.'

'Maybe not. I don't pretend to understand what happened out there, the cyber part of the evidence I mean. Maybe it's possible that something got overlooked.'

During the conference, Vida found herself waiting for the rare glimpses of the crowd of newsjockeys so she could search for Rico among them. He'd be there, wouldn't he, for his mother's departure? At last, just at the end of the broadcast, she saw him handing a dinner plate to a saccule waiter and heading for the dais. Once the conference had ended, she could pay full attention to Samante and the business side of her contract ceremony.

'Pansect's bid is low,' Samante remarked, 'but Avon is offering a number of concessions. First, he'll be the only intake to speak to either you or Wan. Second, he's not insisting on an interview with either Karlo or Vanna as part of the deal. And finally, you get to choose the pictures for the memorial video they'll be selling afterward. All the other grids are demanding full control over that.'

'Avon knows how to offer. I don't want to give up control over the video.'

'Neither do I. Sometimes they absolutely butcher the tie-ins, and the person's pop rating hits bottom.'

'I'm just surprised that everyone's offering so much.'

'Oh Vida, please! This is the big social event of the year. Of course they want the rights.'

Vida shrugged the praise away. Who would Aleen choose? she thought. Who would my mother choose? The answer seemed obvious.

'Let's go with Pansect. Aleen always said that you have to look at the long term, not just take the cash and run.'

'Good,' Samante said. 'I was hoping you'd see it that way. He's really something, that Avon. He knows that Pansect can't compete with the other grids when it comes to money, so he finds ways to outbid them on other levels.'

'When he did the visit to the suite, you know? He told me then that he intends to build Pansect into a really big player one day.' Vida suddenly laughed. 'I told him that we have a lot in common. We're both starting at the bottom and trying to make ourselves into something, aren't we?'

'I never think of you as being at the bottom of anything.' Samante made a face at her. 'But you've got a point. Let me just draft a couple of transmits. We should give the other grids a chance to match his concessions, but I bet they won't.'

Vida got out of Samante's way while she worked and went back into the gather of the suite. In the silvery light from the windows, the room's ivory walls, the greens and maroons of the furniture and drapes, seemed cold and faded. As she stood looking out of the window, she wondered what it would be like to live where the sunlight was always yellow and warm. She should be doing something, she supposed, not just standing around like this. Aleen would have had her studying one of the optional texts on the School Map rather than just wasting time.

It was at moments like these, when she had no engagements, no appointments, no public appearances, not even an agonizing dinner with the Peronidas ahead, that Vida missed the other women at The Close the most. In her old life there was always someone to talk with, always some gossip to share. She wandered over to the sofa and flopped onto it, wondering if her new life was going to be full of empty afternoons.

'You've got to do something,' she told herself. 'You can't just be the girl who gives the Peronidas good ratings.'

Maybe she could gain acceptance to the University Map and be a biologist like Sister Romero or a tech like Rico's mother? She found herself remembering her lunch with the Papal Itinerant, and Romero's advice. How exactly had the sister phrased it? That she 'needed a public role'. That was it. Going on the University Map wouldn't give her a public role. Well, then, what could she do? What had she been trained for, really?

'To be charming, that's what. That's what Aleen said. You've been taught how to charm, so charm them all.'

To be charming and to please customers, to wait on them, listen to their troubles, bring them drinks, give them sex, send them away happy back to their real lives – to do favours for people, that was all it came down to. If she tried to do favours for people in Government House, if she tried to use her access to the first family as a commodity, they would eat her alive and sneer at her behind her back for it. She didn't need Aleen's advice to see that. If you were going to charm people for your living, you had to make sure you'd get something back for it, like the money if she'd stayed in Pleasure Sect. Here, money was the one thing she didn't need to worry about. What she needed was respect. It was only respect that would give her position on the Centre Council any real power and meaning. She remembered Aleen's remark that the other great families would never respect her.

But the ordinary people would. She sat up straight and considered just what that might mean. In her thoughts, she knew, she had the germ of a good idea, if she could only develop it correctly. When some twenty minutes later Samante came bustling in, her hands full of printout, Vida was still thinking.

'Well, you've been quiet,' Samante said. 'I've got the final bids here.'

'Good. Tell me something, Samante. What do you think of this idea? The people's factor. That's what I'm going to be, once I get that council seat: the people's factor. There are all kinds of things that people need help with, and they can't get anyone to listen to them, because they're not rich. I mean, the Public Assistance Map is good and everything, but sometimes you need a person on your side.'

Samante frankly stared.

'Does it sound too dumb?' Vida said.

'No, it sounds brilliant. But you're letting yourself in for a lot of work. And it could be dangerous if you end up going against the Peronidas.'

'I'll start small. And I'm only going to be married to Wan for twelve years. By the time I'm rid of him and them, I'll know what I'm doing.'

'That's true.' Samante considered for a moment. 'That's very true. Once we get this ceremony planned, we need to do something about hiring you a political secretary. I'll put it on my to do list.'

'Okay. And the bids?'

'Pansect all the way. We were right. The control over the video was the deal-breaker.' Samante wrinkled her nose. 'Now I've got to call Leni. Wish me luck.'

When Rico returned to the suite in East Tower, he found Nju in the gather, watching sky hockey on the vidscreen, and Jevon in her office, sorting out a guild meeting agenda with a comm unit clamped to her ear and her Mapscreen up and running. Since the door to his uncle's office stood partway open, he walked in without knocking only to find Hi jacked in.

Rico closed the door behind him and stood waiting. Hi was lying, three-quarters reclined, in his leather chair, his cyberarm melded with its jack panel. Although his body lay dead-still, his eyes moved, looking up and down at something, and every now and then his hands twitched, or he mouthed soundless words. It was like watching a pet animal dreaming. On the Mapscreen in front of him, bits and pieces of his work flashed by, but the screen and circuits could never keep up with a human brain, properly trained and merged with Map. Broken lists, distorted graphics, half-finished commands, torn directories – only fragments of the access session ever showed onscreen.

Rico was just considering leaving when Hi finished. First the screen went dead; then Hi opened his eyes, shook his head with a yawn, and disengaged his cyberarm. He sat up, glancing at Rico.

'How long have you been back?'

'Just a couple of minutes. Mom sends her love.'

'Yeah? Shuttle lift off okay?'

'Sure did.'

Still yawning, Hi got up and considered the dead screen.

'I was just talking with Dian Wynn. She was showing me how they've set up the stake-out for the candles. None have turned up yet, and I bet none ever will. Tell me something, Rico. You trained with Wynn. Think we can trust her?'

'Yeah, actually, I do.'

'Why?'

Rico thought for a moment before he answered.

'Because she cares about the Map as much as she should, but no more than that – she doesn't care enough to turn bitter. She'll never be master of the guild, and "so what" is her attitude. She's got the job she wants, and she's got enough money, and what she really likes is enjoying life.'

'Sounds good to me,' Hi said. 'I think we can tell Wynn a little more about what's going on. I'll have Jevon call her factor and set up lunch or something. The less honest talk we do over the Map, the better.'

'How could anyone monitor without you knowing it?'

'How could anyone create candle icons that burn holes in the Map and give witnesses sunburns?'

'Oh. Oh, well, yeah.'

'Did you talk with Vida?'

'I did, yeah. She told me that we could take a look at the ferret any time.'

'Good! Call her now.'

Calling Vida so casually, so easily, as if he had every right to pick up his comm and speak her number, made Rico's heart pound. He'd called before, only to find her gone – but she had returned that call, after all. If she were gone, she'd return this one, wouldn't she? Still his pulse thudded in his throat until at last her factor answered.

'Hello, Samante. This is Rico Hernanes y Jons, and I'm calling on Cyberguild business. Is Sé Vida available?'

'I'll ask.' Onscreen Samante looked faintly irritable; then the screen greyed out to 'hold'. Samante's voice resurfaced but not her image. 'I'm switching you over now, Sé Rico.'

Vida's image appeared, smiling at him, her russet hair gleaming in its tumbled waves around her face. For a moment Rico could only smile in return. Behind him Hi cleared his throat loudly.

'Uh, sorry,' Rico blurted. 'Vida, I've got my uncle here, and we were wondering if we could have a look at Calios.'

'Sure. You picked a good time. I don't have anything on my calendar.'

'Great.' To Rico it seemed that God himself must have had a hand in this piece of luck. 'We'll come by.'

Vida herself met them at the door of her suite and ushered them in to the green, ivory, and maroon gather that he'd seen onscreen so many days ago. Rico felt as if he'd walked into a glorious cavern of treasures from some fabulous tale. Every piece of furniture, every work of art on the walls, every passage of stencilled decoration – she'd chosen all of them, she saw them every day, they'd soaked up the magic of her presence.

'Thanks for letting us come over, Vida,' Hi was saying. 'I think your ferret has some important information, you see, data that's been lost for centuries, even, and the guild could use a look at it.'

'Of course, Sé Hivel,' Vida said. 'That's kind of exciting. Lost data of the Cyberguild. It's like a holonovel.' She glanced Rico's way with a slight smile. 'Rico tells me I read too many holonovels.'

Rico felt himself blush for no reason at all. Mercifully Hi chose to ignore it.

'This suite must have a Map terminal, then,' Hi said.

'It does, yeah. Come down this hall, and I'll open it.'

The alcove that housed a standard black access pillar was more of a Mapstation than a simple terminal, Rico realized, but he couldn't tell how much of the equipment – flat panels on a wall, a row of jacks, a capped power strip – would be operational. He'd run across other such set ups in East Tower only to find them long dead.

'All I have to do is power up the pillar.' Vida laid a finger on an icon. 'And then say, meta One: Calios.'

The silver-haired revenant flickered into life over the obsidian pillar. Rico noted the images of archaic clothing: a pair of light blue, tight-fitting trousers and a white pullover shirt with lettering printed across it. Although he could pick out the individual letters, the words meant nothing to him when he mouthed a few.

'That's Inglis,' Hi said. 'The language, I mean. This set of images goes way back.'

Calios was looking Vida's way as if he could see her. Apparently he could – and more.

'Good evening, Veelivar,' the rev said. 'You have company.'

'Yes,' Vida said. 'They want to ask you some questions.'

'Shall I answer them?'

'Answer questions on any subject other than those I asked you to keep secret.'

'Very well.' The image turned on the pillar and looked at Hi. 'You have been given secondary access to my databanks.'

'Thanks,' Hi said. 'My name is Hivel Jons, and I'm the current master of the Cyberguild. Do you know what that means?'

'I do indeed, Master Jons.'

'Good. To answer my questions, access all the following routines and utilities: Boolean, fuzzy, neural connectivity, Ri Karsh Rol associational.'

'My neural connectivity routines have been damaged. May I compensate with the Karsh Rol pathways?'

'You may, yes. Now. Before Vida accessed you, you were dormant. Is this correct?'

'I was dormant until three days before Veelivar accessed me.'

'Who woke you?'

'I do not know.' The rev faded, then blinked its eyes rapidly. 'Accessing full Karsh Rol routines. I have no clues or possibilities-of-statement concerning my awakening. I was able to derive the time, date, and my location from the Map itself.'

The rev returned to full strength, an illusion of flesh and blood above the gleaming black shaft.

'Calios,' Vida broke in. 'Tell them how you got out of Pleasure Sect.'

'Formerly I was confined to the Map segment once designated

Quarantine, now known as Pleasure Sect. Just recently, however, some cybertech implemented a new pipe allowing access to the non-segmented over-configuration of the Map.'

Rico stepped forward.

'Was the pipe implemented on the night of the festival of Calios?'

'It was, yes,' Calios turned virtual eyes his way. 'Who are you?'

'Rico Hernanes y Jons, journeyman of the Cyberguild, and the tech who opened that pipe.'

'You did what?' Hi snarled.

'When we were at the hotel, you know? And I was fiddling with that antique frame? I set up a pipe just to see if I could do it. I only just figured something out. Pleasure doesn't normally have pipes to the over-config, does it?'

'It happens to be against the law, yeah.' Hi paused to swear under his breath. 'No-one wants some amateur cybe in Pleasure messing around with public records and erasing someone's cull status. By God's great weeping Eye! Remind me to make you go close it down when we're done here.'

'Wait a minute,' Vida said. 'I don't want to lose Calios. That's not fair.'

'I have relocated my base of operations to the Government House sub-configuration, Veelivar. I will continue to function normally if Master Jons wishes to enforce the Quarantine Laws.'

'Oh, all right then.' Vida glanced at Hi. 'I'm sorry I interrupted, Sé Hivel.'

'It's all right, Vida. I've got a lot of things to ask Calios, but nothing that should upset you. It's mostly technical stuff. Calios, open a record file under my name.'

As Rico had expected, the first round of questions concerned Calios' abilities which, while amazing by modern standards by no means made him omnipotent. Although he could perform all of the everyday functions that citizens needed – banking, shopping, voting, and so on – his access codes were strictly limited. He could socket into Caliostro, for instance, to ferret data, but the socket was strictly one-way: he could change not one bit of an AI's code or core databanks. All his authority lay in odd jobs.

While Hi and the revenant talked back and forth, Vida leaned against the wall and listened, frowning now and then when the jargon left her behind, but most definitely absorbed in the data.

'Sé Hivel?' she said at one point. 'Let me see if I have this right.

Calios can't access anything that's been marked secret or off-limits by a high-level cybe, right?'

'Right.'

'Then how did he know I was a L'Var before I knew it?' She glanced at Calios. 'You called me Veelivar the first time I accessed you, back in Pleasure.'

Although revs of course had no feelings, Rico could have sworn that Calios looked embarrassed.

'I do not understand your question,' the rev said.

'Oh come on!' Vida snapped. 'You've got to.'

'No, not really. It's all right, Calios,' Hi said. 'Some cybe embedded that data in core consciousness of the old Citizen Assist net while you were still dormant. That's my guess anyway. You woke up knowing without knowing how you know.'

'Master Jons, that explanation seems true, but I can do no more than label it highly probable. I do indeed know without knowing how. This then is not an early sign of malfunction?'

'No, not at all.' Hi frowned, considering. 'Though damned if I know why anyone would do that.'

Rico and Vida exchanged a glance. It was Molos, Rico thought. And I bet she's thinking the same thing. But again: why? Hi shrugged as if dismissing the problem and returned to his questions. These first concerned the limits and locations of the old Citizen Assist net, then moved on to the mysterious repairs that someone or something had made to the Caliostro AI. Calios could tell them little when it came to damage control for an AI system. His own net had provided sealed toolkit utilities, lacking the code to affect the rest of the Map.

'Calios, thank you,' Hi said at last. 'I'll have to study what you've given me before I can ask you more questions. Vida, if I could come back in a few days?'

'Of course, Sé Hivel.'

'Thanks.' Hi glanced at the revenant. 'Calios, you said that your neural connectivity routines had been damaged. Journeyman Hernanes here can fix those for you, if you'd like.'

'Any return to full functioning is desirable, Master Jons.'

'Fine.' Hi turned a perfect poker face to Rico. 'Hernanes, think you can find time to come over here and repair Sé Vida's access revenant?'

'Sure.' Rico lost words, swallowed heavily, found some at least. 'Calios, is that row of jacks operational?'

'It is, Journeyman. If you uncap the photonic power strip, I can test and restore it as well.'

'Fine.' Rico summoned courage and looked at Vida to find her own expression a pleasant mask. 'I'll call your factor and see when it'll be convenient.'

'That'll be fine, yeah.'

They dared not look at each other. Rico knew it in his soul that she felt it as deeply as he did, that there with witnesses they had to turn away and look elsewhere.

'One last thing, Calios,' Rico said. 'Do you know the location of any archives concerning the process of constructing an AI unit?'

'A search on those terms will take several minutes.'

'Start search now.'

The rev turned pale and froze, held that pose for some minutes more, then finally snapped back to full strength.

'I have encountered an anomaly,' Calios announced. 'I have found location coordinates where that data should be housed. When I attempted to access the housings, I found them non-existent. I failed to find any redirection notices giving their current locations.'

'That's probably because they've been destroyed,' Hi put in. 'Please record those addresses, though, for further manual searches.'

'Locations recorded in a note in your new file, Master Jons. File has also been tagged with access for Journeyman Hernanes. Requesting input: why would those records have been destroyed?'

'For religious reasons. During the Schism Wars, several factions believed that any cybernetic approximations of sapient – particularly human – forms and functions were an affront to God. I know as proven data that these religious factions were the sapients who disabled the Citizen Assist network and sent you dormant. Mark as a probability only that the same human sapes destroyed all archival information on AI construction.'

'Done, Master Jons. Requesting input: were these factions responsible for the second disabling of the Caliostro AI?'

'Yes, and for the crippling of the Dee AI.'

Rico caught his breath. So that's what had happened to poor old Caliostro! Hi glanced his way with one eyebrow raised.

'Why keep it secret?' Rico asked. 'What happened to the AIs, I mean.'

'Because the Lifegiver order holds a lot of power in the Pinch these days. They don't like being reminded of past sins.'

'It was the Lifegivers?' Vida sounded shocked.

'Yeah, sure was,' Hi said. 'Though the order's certainly changed over the years. They were new at the time – one of the Schisms. Call it a beta version of the order. You can't call them heretics because they won.'

To settle the last details for the contract ceremony, on the morrow morning, Wan and Leni came to breakfast in Vida's suite. While a nervous Greenie laid plates of sliced fruit onto the table in the eatery, Samante read aloud the various lists that she and Leni had compiled earlier. Much to everyone's surprise, Leni had been sincerely trying to rise to the occasion; he kept it up now, listening carefully, making notes on his tablet or occasionally asking an intelligent question. Wan slouched in his chair and stared out of the window.

The cold grey light flooded his beautiful face and revealed the fine red lines of burst capillaries across his cheeks. Vida reached up and adjusted the polarization on the windows to soften the glare.

'We've got a major decision to make today,' Samante finished up. 'You need to choose the friends who'll stand with you as witnesses. They need to be asked right away so they'll be available for rehearsals.'

'Rehearsals?' Wan spoke without looking away from the window. 'You're kidding.'

'Hey, Wanito,' Leni said. 'This is going to be a big deal. You want things to go right, don't you?'

'I don't want things to go at all.'

Leni winced with a quick glance Vida's way. She slammed both hands flat on the table and leaned forward.

'All right,' Vida snapped. 'Let's call it off. Why don't you just get Karlo on the comm and tell him right now that there's not going to be any contract?'

Wan sloughed around in his chair to face her. Neither Leni nor Samante seemed to be breathing.

'Ah shit,' Wan said. 'I forget that you're not much happier about this than I am.'

'No, I'm not. But if we both put some energy into it, we can make it work. We don't even have to be together all that much.'

'I suppose you're thinking of me like one of your customers.'

'Why shouldn't I? You keep calling me a whore. So okay. You're the john in this deal.'

Wan opened his mouth, considered, then laughed.

'You know something, Vida?' Wan said. 'I think I'm starting to like you.'

Leni let out his breath in a long sigh. Samante picked up her lists and set them down again with a flurry of papers.

'I'm starting to see what the old man means,' Wan went on. 'Everybody else on this fucking scab of a planet sucks up to us. Hey, Leni. If I call her a whore again, tell me to shut up or something.'

'I will, yeah. You can count on it.' Leni took another deep breath. 'Now what about the witnesses? TeeKay and Motta?'

'Whatever Vida wants.' Wan shrugged. 'Vida – no, my darling Vida – you got anything to drink in this place?'

'Yeah, I do. I went shopping with TeeKay. There's a liquor cabinet in the gather now. By the windows.'

Wan got up and slouched out, slamming the eatery door. Leni sloughed around in his chair to stare after him, mouthed a few foul words, then turned back to the table.

'To hell with him,' he announced. 'I hope he drinks himself sick and stays out of the way. We've got to throw it into overdrive here. It's Seventeen Gust today, and we've got the Cathedral reserved for Twenty-two.'

Leni had it right: Wan never returned, not for the planning or the breakfast. When the three of them finished, they went into the gather to find Wan sprawled in the middle of the green sofa, a glass in hand, while he stared rather vaguely at boat races on the vidscreen.

'South Canal team all the way.' Wan gestured at the screen. 'Not a real good race.' He glanced at Leni. 'You guys done?'

'Yeah. Can you walk?'

'Ah shut up.' Wan set the glass on the floor and hauled himself to his feet. 'See you later, darling.'

All at once he grinned, walked over, and caught Vida by the shoulders. Before she could move away, he bent his head and kissed her, his mouth sloppy-warm and smelling of alcohol. Although Vida was expecting to feel revulsion, in actuality she felt nothing at all. The kiss was as meaningless as a lick from a dog.

'Yeah,' she said. 'See you later.'

With a wave he followed Leni out, and Samante shut the door hard behind them.

'Vida, can you really do this? Marry that slime?'

'Why not? Oh, I know what you're thinking.'

'Well, I certainly couldn't stand to sleep with him, no matter how good-looking he is.'

'But I've been taught how to put your mind somewhere else while they're doing it.' Vida picked up the dirty glass and handed it to Greenie. 'This goes in the washer, please.'

Greenie bustled out, carrying the glass carefully in both hands. Vida sat down on the sofa, and in a moment Samante joined her.

'I've been thinking,' Vida said. 'If I'd stayed at The Close, I'd be having my first customer any day now. Do you know what the big deal about your very first customer is?'

'No.' Samante sounded oddly wary. 'Do I want to?'

'You cost more, a lot more, and you get half of the extra. The madam gets the other half, of course. You can take that money and invest it in something, or spend it, which is what a lot of girls and guys do. I'd already decided I didn't want to just fritter mine away.'

'Somehow I'd never thought of anyone in Pleasure investing in anything.'

'Well, there are a lot of shops, restaurants, and stuff like that. Not every cull gets sent to one of the madams. And when you're a whore, you dream of being able to buy into a business like that, so you don't have to work the houses any more.'

Samante sat silently for a long while.

'I see,' she said at last. 'And so that first money's important.'

'You bet. And anyway, the only customers who can afford all that extra cash are usually getting old and wrinkly and stuff. They're not what you'd pick for fun.'

'And so Wan's no worse than that?'

'He might be better, for all I know. Am I embarrassing you, Sammi? You look embarrassed.'

'Well, a little. You look at these things in a really different way than anything I'm used to.'

'You've got to, if you're going to survive in Pleasure. I mean, no-one says it's a wonderful life or anything. Why do you think they stick the culls with it?'

'Well, that's true. And it's awful, actually.'

'Yeah, it is. But no-one's ever going to change it, I'll bet. We're like the Stinkers – too valuable the way we are.'

Vida found herself thinking of her first investment again that morning and of Aleen. Her virginity was going to buy her many things: political support to regain the L'Var seat on the Council, the return of the L'Var name and the L'Var fortune. Aleen had found her a splendid first customer, all in all. Not that Wan would care if he were the first or not; in fact, he probably wouldn't even believe that he was. He'd made that clear enough. It seemed a real shame to waste something of such value on him.

'Vida?' Samante was standing in the doorway. 'There's a commcall from the Cyberguild. The tech said something about repairing your Map terminal?'

'Oh yeah, that's right. I'd nearly forgotten. Can you make him an appointment this afternoon?'

'All right. Leni and I are meeting with the caterer soon, so should I put him on the schedule early or late?'

'How long will you be gone?'

'Probably all afternoon. After the caterer, there's the florist.'

'Then have him get here early, if he can make it. I'll need the terminal if you're going to be out. Are you going to be buying things?'

'Yes.'

'Why not take Jak with you to carry them? I'll be perfectly safe as long as I stay in the tower.'

Samante disappeared back into her office. Vida leaned back on the sofa, tucked her hands behind her head, and considered an important question. What kind of clothes would Rico especially like to see her in, when she first answered the door?

In a swirl of morning mist Hi and Molos walked among the fern trees. The garden smelled of roses and mutant honeysuckle, espaliered along the garden wall. Even wrapped in several layers of jacket, the Lep shivered.

'We can go in if you'd like,' Hi said.

'In a moment. I really do love this garden. It's just that I'm feeling the damp these days, especially in my bad leg.'

'I was surprised when you came back to Palace. On Souk you could have had Map access and better weather both.'

'I came back to keep an eye on Karlo.' Molos paused, contemplating a spray of bloodvine. 'If he were a mindless bigot, he wouldn't frighten me so much. As it is, he has good reason to hate my people. You can educate someone's prejudices. You can't talk the Kephalon plague out of existence.'

'I'm afraid not, yeah. Can I be honest?'

'By all means.'

'I've never been able to reconcile that act with the Leps I know. I cannot imagine any of you doing such a thing.'

'Neither can we.' Molos let his crest rise. 'Neither, I gather, could many people on Ri. The biological warfare project was top secret, of course. There was immense public outrage when the news broke, which is the reason that the government was so obliging about turning over the scientific team as war criminals. Ri is not a democracy, not by any stretch of the imagination, but its warlords know that they won't stay in power without some sort of consent.'

They left the walled garden and stood at the top of the long turquoise lawn that sloped down to the river, a murky gash through the landscape. On the other side an answering lawn sloped up to the grounds of another white walled compound. Molos shaded his eyes with one hand and considered the view while he talked.

'Karlo was dead serious about deporting all the Leps on planet to Tableau,' Molos said. 'The logistics of such a thing! Good God, there are nine million of us! I knew then he was no longer rational on the subject.'

'I'd say so, yeah. The newsgrids did a cost analysis of that proposal. Most people gave up on the idea right then. And of course Vanna Makeesa weighed in to change his mind. I've got to give her credit for that.'

'Vanna can't push the life-extension forever. What will happen when she's gone?'

'That's a good point. I'm hoping that Vida will have some influence over the Peronidas by then.'

'So am I. Fervently.'

They turned and began walking around the edge of the compound's grounds. Neither of them was in any hurry to commit a capital crime, Hi supposed, no matter how irrational the law that made their proposed actions a hanging offence.

'Have you ever figured out why Riva wanted Vida killed?' Molos said.

'No. Any ideas?'

'None.' Molos sighed and looked up at the house, looming white and severe above them. 'I've been doing a lot of thinking about how to search for Riva. I want to start at the beginning, with the crash of the Spaceport autogates. Well, provided I can get on the Map.'

'Oh, you can. I've tested this access out, and it'll work. It's a family secret, something we call the Chameleon Gate. We'll move you over from your bank access point.' Hi smiled, briefly. 'Now's the time for both of us to back down if we're going to.'

They looked at each other.

'A peaceful retirement never appealed to me,' Molos said.

'I'm not ready for retirement yet, but there's a hell of a lot at stake here. I'll risk it.'

'Very well. Let us savour the last few minutes that we are honest men rather than criminals – and then get to work.'

On the big vidscreen in the gather of their suite, Karlo brought up the schematic of the Pinch, then tipped in the Fleet's positions. Tiny red stars bloomed among the white. Vanna leaned forward on the sofa and considered the display with her shaking hands tucked between her thighs.

'I see what you mean,' she said. 'Tableau really is vulnerable.'

Karlo nodded, then telescoped on Tableau's small yellow star until its sector filled the screen. The planetary system hung near the end of a solitary microshunt – isolated by Pinch standards, although its night sky showed a neighbourhood crowded with stars.

'We've got a Kephalon unit at the other end of the microshunt,' Karlo said. 'And then a couple of ships and a support base at Tableau. Their commander wants to retire, and I don't blame her. She's been through a lot.'

'If you reorganize the squadrons to give him a few more ships, it would be a good posting for Pero. He'd be out of the way, and maybe he could do something about his mother.'

'I doubt that. He's not a miracle worker. But I think I can present this to the Military Guild councils as a necessary move. I'd like to appoint him military governor of the planet, if that's possible. There's nothing like an exalted title to soothe egos, and besides, he'd be a damn good governor.'

'There's no doubt in my mind.' Vanna leaned back, still studying the screen. 'It's too bad he's so ugly. We could maybe get him citizenship, but he'd still never get elected to anything.'

Karlo started to snarl, then thought better of it.

'Well, we've had this conversation before.' Vanna had noticed. 'And yeah, I agree. It's stupid and superficial and everything you say, but that's just the way things are on Palace. Everyone's pretty. Everyone's been tweaked to be pretty. And someone who isn't –' She shrugged. 'That's just the way it works.'

'Yeah, I know. Do you think we can pull together enough civilian support to get him the governorship?'

'Probably. In the end. It depends on how much you want to bargain away. I say wait a few months. The Interlocking Councils will be having their session, then, and the memory of the Appropriations Bill will have faded. Centre Council members get real huffy if they feel that all their time's taken up with Fleet affairs.'

Karlo made a small growling noise deep in his throat, but he knew that she was right.

'In a few months,' he said, 'we'll have another ally on the Council anyway. Once Vida's a Not-child, Roha and I can get her seated.'

Even though he knew that Vanna would turn sour at the mention of the L'Var girl, still it irked him to see her lips tighten and her nostrils flicker in disgust.

'Damn it, Vanna!' he burst out. 'Why do you hate the child so much?'

'She's a L'Var. That should be enough reason. I've told you what her family did to mine.'

'Yeah, sure. Over a hundred years ago now, wasn't it? By God's Eye, that's ancient history!'

'I still remember.' Vanna got up. 'I don't want to discuss it.'

'I don't care if you do or not.' Karlo rose to face her. 'I want to work this out. I'm sick and tired of seeing you snarl at her. It's not good for our public image.'

'Oh damn you!' Vanna turned and strode to the windows.

Karlo took one step after her, then stopped. Maybe it wasn't worth it, pushing some kind of forced peace through. Against the backdrop of gauzy white curtains Vanna stood stiff and straight in her grey Fleet fatigues. Beyond the windows hung cold grey light. He saw her suddenly as an image of herself, trembling like pixels on a screen in a memorial video of her career. With a sigh he walked over and laid gentle hands on her shoulders. She spun round. Tears streaked her face.

'I'm sorry,' Karlo said. 'I'm sorry, darling.'

'Oh damn you!' Her voice hissed like a Lep's. 'Why shouldn't I hate her? I'm dying, Karlo. You know that as well as I do. What do I have left? Two years, three years at the most? If I'm lucky I have that much. And there she is, a stinking L'Var, young and beautiful and with all that life ahead of her, all those years, a hundred years, a hundred fifty, and she'll bring her ugly genotype back again, and there's nothing I can do about it, because she's young and I'm dying.'

He wrapped her in his arms and let her cry.

Samante and Jak were both gone, and Greenie curled up in its water-den in the pantry. Vida debated music, decided against it, and walked through the rooms: her bedroom and dressing room, the enormous bedroom she'd share, at least on occasion, with Wan; a room that would be Wan's study should he want one in her suite; the guest rooms; the gather; the eatery; back to the gather again. At every shiny surface she paused to look at her reflection and wonder if the clothes she was wearing were the right ones – a soft wrap dress that would open if someone, if Rico, pulled on the ties at her waist. It was modest, it was flowered, it was what she called 'giggly girl' but which, she supposed, he would see as innocent. Men liked that, Aleen always said, if you looked innocent.

From the vidscreen the doorbell sounded, and Rico's image appeared, windowed in a corner, dressed in his guild coveralls and carrying a toolkit. Vida arranged a smile as she walked to the door, but when she opened it, she felt nothing but solemn. For a long moment Rico merely looked at her, his lips half-parted.

'I really like that dress,' he said.

'Thank you. Come in.'

Rico walked in, glancing around.

'It's sure quiet in here,' he remarked.

'Yeah. Samante's gone. I made sure she had errands to do.'

Rico very nearly dropped his toolkit. He caught it, then knelt beside her and set it on the floor. When Vida stroked his back, she realized that her hand trembled, that he trembled as well at her touch.

'Fixing Calios can wait, can't it?' she said.

'Sure.' He stood up and turned to her. 'If you – well.'

She merely smiled. He caught her by the shoulders, bent his head and kissed her, pulled her close while she wrapped her arms around him and took a kiss in turn. It seemed to her that the entire world had shrunk to this room and to Rico, that nothing else would ever matter, not in her entire life, as much as his kisses did.

'Vida, Vida,' he whispered. 'I love you.'

'I love you too.'

The words had spoken themselves, or so it seemed. She drew

back, looked at him, smiling at her as if no grief could ever touch him again. What, she wondered, had happened to the rational transaction she'd so carefully planned?

'Do you?' he said. 'Do you really?'

'Yeah. I'm kind of surprised, but I really do.'

He laughed, kissed her, caught his arms round her waist to swirl her off her feet while she laughed with him. When he set her down she refused to let him go, kissed him, felt him respond.

'Oh Vida,' he was stammering. 'Please? Can we I mean oh please, come to bed with me?'

'Of course.'

With his arm twined around her she led him down the hall to her bedroom, hesitated, then steered him across the hall instead to the master suite. Wan would never know or care who'd been here before him, and so what if he did? In the dimly-lit room she sat on the green satin quilt that covered the bed and watched Rico strip off his boots, his coveralls. Still wearing an undershirt and a pair of trousers he sat down beside her and drew her into his arms. As she kissed him, she felt his hand at her waist, felt the ties loosen and the dress slide open across her bare skin underneath. That at least was going according to plan.

'I love you,' he said again. 'I love you so much.'

'I love you, too.' Not a surprise, this time, but the words still felt strange and foreign. 'Help me take this dress off?'

He laughed and kissed her, but she felt his hand, running over her shoulder, pulling the cloth down, then lingering at her breast. From that moment on she could think of nothing but him and his body, so warm, so close to hers.

Afterwards, she lay cuddled next to him, her sweaty face resting on his sweaty chest, and luxuriated in the feel of his hand stroking her hair. She could hear his heart beating, steadying out its rhythm, and she smiled. She'd thought to give him a gift, she realized, only to receive one in turn.

'Vida?' he said.

'Yeah?'

'Don't marry Wan.'

She sat up, glaring at him. He lay still and considered her.

'Don't talk about that now,' she said. 'Don't spoil it.'

'I'm going to talk about it. Don't marry him.'

'Rico, I've got to.'

'Why? Are you worried about being sent back to Pleasure? Well, sign a contract with me. They won't be able to touch you if you do that.'

Vida went stone-still. Somehow the thought of being Rico's wife had never occurred to her. He did sit up, then, and grabbed her wrists. His beautiful dark eyes brimmed with tears.

'You can live here in Government House with me, and you'll be safe. I'll keep you safe.'

She shook her head, battled to find words while his grip tightened and his voice turned pleading.

'Vida, please, I can't stand it. I love you, and you say you love me. I can't stand it, thinking of him – well, you know.'

'It's too late,' she whispered. 'We made the announcement and all of that.'

'So what? People break off contracts at this stage all the time.'

'Yeah? They're not with the Peronida family.'

'Oh hell! What's Karlo going to do to you if you've signed with me? We're Cyberguild, Vida. I'm the heir of the man who runs Cyberguild. Don't you realize what that means?'

She did, suddenly, and she realized as well that none of her rational objections to marrying him, none of the reasons she'd thought would put him off without hurting his feelings, were going to work. She looked up and shook her hair back.

'I can't marry you and restore the L'Var family both,' she said. 'I need Karlo's support for that. Yeah, I could sign with you, and I really really want to live with you, but what's going to happen when we get tired of each other? What'll I have then?'

'I'll never get tired of you. I'll love you forever.'

'A hundred and fifty years?'

Rico let her go, turned away, still sitting on the bed, and let the tears run. Vida threw herself across his back and sobbed.

'Don't, Rico, don't. I'm sorry. Oh God, I'm so sorry. I love you, I really do. But I just can't marry you now. I've got to have something of my own, and the Peronidas will help me get it. But I'll never love anyone else, ever. I'll always love you, too.'

He sat like stone, unmoving, dead-silent, his flurry of tears over.

'When my contract with Wan is up, I'll sign one with you.' She rubbed herself against his back like a cat, stroked his shoulders, kissed the back of his neck. 'I promise, Rico.'

At last he sighed and turned toward her.

'Please?' she said. 'Please forgive me?'

'There's nothing to forgive.' He flopped back, lying on the

pillows with his hands tucked under his head. 'You don't want to take my offer, and that's that.'

'Don't be a jerk!'

'I'm not being a jerk!'

'Yes you are. It's not that I don't want to. It's that I can't, I just plain can't. If you can't see the difference, then you're being a jerk.'

'Damn you!'

Vida got to her knees, leaned over and kissed him. Her hair hung over them like a canopy. He tried to ignore her; she sidled over closer, kissed him again, then lay down, half on top of him. As if to push her away he took his hands out from under his head, but when they touched her shoulders they stayed to caress her.

'Oh please, Rico?' Vida whispered. 'Let's do that again. Please?'

She kissed him, felt his hands tighten on her shoulders as he took the kiss open-mouthed and hungry. With a little laugh she slid on top of him and felt his body fit into hers.

Hi returned to the Cyberguild suite in Government House just at the eighteens. The day's work with Molos had been immensely profitable, but he felt his worry as a sick cold in the pit of his stomach – not for himself, but for Rico. He'd realized about halfway through their session that if Molos were using the Gate, Rico would have to know. What if he called the Gate up and found it unavailable? He'd be bound to come running to Hi and raise the alarm, or even take steps to track the interloper down himself.

Hi found Rico sprawled on the couch in the gather and watching the evening interactives on the vidscreen. When Hi glanced at the screen, he noticed that the usual presenter had coloured her hair red.

'Evening,' Hi said. 'You eaten yet?'

'No.' Rico looked up, then pitched his voice to the screen. 'Sound off. You want to go out and get something?'

'Good idea. How was your afternoon? Did you get Calios repaired?'

Rico hesitated, then stood up, visibly thinking hard. Finally he shrugged and seemed to be deciding on the truth.

'No,' he said and smiled.

Hi was about to say more, then realized that he really didn't need to ask one damn thing. Nju strode in briskly from stowing the aircar.

'Sé Rico,' the Garang said. 'Hail.'

'Hail, Nju,' Rico said. 'Want to go out for dinner?'
'I'd be honoured.'
As they all trooped out, heading for El Mercado, Hi felt a quirk of shame. You're practically a pimp, he told himself. He'd just handed his nephew over to a powerful woman in a bid to gain influence. Aleen, he suspected, was going to laugh at him when she heard.
At the restaurant, of course, Hi could say nothing about the Chameleon Gate, and even when they returned to the suite, he put it off. He could think up plenty of jobs that would keep Rico busy without needing the Gate for at least a couple of days. If the guild was going to catch Molos, it would happen fast. Better to wait so that if the worst did happen, he could swear under oath that his nephew knew nothing of his crime.

As the most recently hired members of the D & B clean-up team, Kata and Elen had got stuck with the night shift. With the UJU rally coming the next day, they expected to be assigned to the Floating Amphitheatre, but when they reported to their shift boss, a fat human with bristling brown hair and a moustache to match, they found him unlike his usual tyrannical self.
'Uh well, hey, guys,' he said. 'I'm afraid I can't offer you time off with pay, but if you wanted to take the night off, well, hell, can't say I'd blame you. I'd fix it with the super so it wouldn't go on your records.'
'Uh, thanks, I guess,' Kata said. 'What's going on?'
'Well, the only job lined up for tonight is prepping the bowl for that UJU rally. If you couldn't stomach it –'
'It's all right,' Kata broke in. 'I need the money. But I appreciate the gesture, boss.'
'Me, too,' Elen said. 'Thanks, but I'll take the work.'
The service bussed six full crews over to the amphitheatre and a truck full of cleaning bots as well. With so many sapients hurrying back and forth on various errands, Kata and Elen had no trouble putting their plan into effect. First Kata volunteered for the job that everyone hated – hand-polishing the brass wall decorations that were too delicate to trust to a bot. The job brought with it a work cart, loaded with brushes, rags, and polishes – a perfect place to put his lunch box and the toolkit hidden inside.
His first job lay up in the Floating Amphitheatre itself. The service lift booth took him and his cart up and let them out behind

the stage. Humming under his breath, Kata trundled the cart through a split curtain and walked out into the actual amphitheatre. For a moment he paused, admiring. In front of him the purple bowl, striped with blue plush seats, stippled with brass railings and fixtures, stretched away and curved out and up to the night sky. The force-field surrounding the structure gave it a perfectly transparent roof. When Kata looked up, he could see in the streaming lights rain falling, but when it reached the field the water parted and ran off, defining the invisible sphere it had just touched. What a pity, really, to destroy something so marvellous! It was just like the humans, to waste beautiful tech like this on their stupid bigotry.

The front of the speaker's podium sported a decorative panel of intertwined brass wires, the work of a Lep artist that would have to be sacrificed to serve his people. Kata got out his brass polish, the small brushes, and a handful of rags, set them in front of the art work, then went back to the cart. If by some odd chance anyone should be watching him from the darkness of the farthest seats, they would only see the janitor pick up a different brush, glance at the podium, and scowl at dirt somewhere on the inside. The little transmit unit he'd just palmed would be invisible. Kata strode up to the podium and began scrubbing some non-existent filth away with his rag while with the other hand, he attached the tiny unit, attuned to Wilso's voice, to the underside of the microphone panel. Since cleaning the podium was his job, no-one would bother to look under there again.

At precisely the fours, in the dead of night after Datechange, Elen took a floor cleaning bot down to the generator level, where he would sabotage one of the bot's photonic circuits. Ten minutes later, Kata made a point of speaking to the shift boss and another worker, so that they'd remember him being in the lobby after Elen had gone down. Twenty minutes after that, Kata stashed his work cart in a men's room stall, then took his lunch box and found a lift booth down. While he rode, he switched his coveralls to the red side and lifted the toolkit from the lunch box. Now came the first small danger. He'd equipped his lunch box with a magnet just inside the lid. With a leap, he stuck it on the ceiling of the booth. With luck, no-one would ever notice it there, even if the booth had riders while he was gone.

Kata walked out of the booth and pretended to look puzzled as he glanced around. A security guard strolled over.

'You come about that dead bot?'

'Sure have. Where is it?'

'Go down this hall, turn right, and follow the arrow that says Generator Room.'

'Thanks.'

Elen and the bot were waiting out in the hall in front of the pale grey doors to the force-field generator. Kata made a show of kneeling down and examining the machine, though Elen had already repaired the sabotage. Elen leaned against the wall in a pose like that of any worker glad of a few minutes' idleness.

'The guard's gone,' he whispered. 'I've been timing out his round. You've got about twelve minutes.'

Kata strode across the hall and laid his hand on the entrance panel beside the grey doors. Another miracle – Riva had indeed coded his prints in, and the door slid open. He walked in, looking, listening, smelling the air, too, for the ugly stink of human, then realized that he was alone in an antechamber, equipped with a pair of chairs and a counter. On the wall four Mapscreens flickered in endless readouts of red numbers. Probably the real safety control point lay elsewhere.

He glanced up and looked over the ceiling; sure enough, he saw the two black lenses of dead security cameras. Riva could buy him five minutes, she'd said, before someone noticed the cameras were down.

Across the room, another door, which again slid open at his touch, and more Mapscreens, more dead cameras – and the generator, sitting on an obsidian base against the far wall, an oddly ordinary-looking piece of equipment for something so powerful. He crossed over fast, and already he'd seen what he needed to: a separation of about two inches between the pale grey housing and the wall, where shielded cables climbed like trellised vines to a power route box at the ceiling.

The generator itself stood about four feet high and six long, big enough to throw the bottom of that gulf twixt it and the wall into deep shadow. When Kata laid a hand on it, he felt only the barest trace of vibration. The Colonizers had built solid tech, all right. He knelt, flipped open the toolkit, and slid out his device, a metal oblong no more than an inch wide and six long, four high, but inside, neatly folded like pastry around a battery, lay ten ounces of the plastique from the swamps.

Provided it had remained chemically stable, it would stay safe until the right electric pulse rippled through its molecular structure.

Provided. Kata set the device on the floor, then brought out the tiny fuse and stuck its metal prong into a hole in the case. With one claw he flipped open the fuse cover and pulled out the antenna. Or tried to. The antenna, a fine curl of wire, stuck in place. If he pulled too hard, and if the plastique had turned vicious . . . – He flicked the cover again and again, finally got a claw tip under the wire and pulled. It reeled out with a fine hiss and nothing more.

Kata let out his breath in a puff and slid the device, antenna and all, back behind the generator with the telescoping rod he'd brought in the kit. He got up, replacing the rod, shutting the kit as he did so, and trotted out of the generator room, hurried through the antechamber and stepped out while the cameras were still dead.

Out in the hall Elen stood on guard.

'Got it,' Kata whispered. 'How are we for time?'

'Here he comes now.'

'Okay.' Kata raised his voice to normal. 'That bot should keep running for a while, but it needs a new core chip. We won't be able to patch it together for much longer.'

'Sure,' Elen said. 'I'll tell my boss.'

On his way out, Kata waved at the guard, who waved back, a semi-salute. In the lift booth his lunch box hung where he'd put it. He leapt up and retrieved it, stashed the kit, then changed his coveralls around. He saw no-one until he was wheeling his work cart out of the men's room, and no-one on the crew ever mentioned looking for him and finding him gone.

For the last few hours of his shift, Kata found himself treading lightly whenever he was walking approximately over the generator room, even though he had to laugh at himself for doing so. If the device was going to blow early, a few footsteps would matter not at all. By the time he and Elen checked out, just at dawn, there had been no explosion, nor had anyone else discovered the bomb. As they were walking to the wiretrain station, Elen allowed as how he was relieved.

'If it didn't blow in the first couple of hours,' Kata said, 'the plastique must still be stable. Unless of course it's completely deteriorated and gone inert.'

'What if it has?'

'We'll find some other little amusement, that's all.' Kata shrugged the problem away. 'Well, it's just chiming the eights now. In about six hours, we'll know.'

* * *

Cardinal Roha always began his work day so early that by the tens he needed a rest. As he usually did, that morning he invited Dav into the inner office to share breakfast while they watched the morning news. The feature story covered the UJU rally slated for the afternoon in a remarkably balanced presentation.

'Interesting coverage,' Roha said. 'I'm surprised to find it so impartial.'

'So am I, Your Eminence. It's a loaded subject.'

'I wonder if maybe we – if the order – should take an interest in this group. Perhaps we should find someone trustworthy and have them join it.'

Dav nearly choked on his drink. He put the cup down fast while his face turned an alarming shade of red.

'Are you all right?' Roha said. 'Should I call a medic?'

Dav shook his head and coughed enormously into a napkin. At last he sat back in his chair and took a deep breath. His colour began to ebb toward normal.

'My apologies, Your Eminence,' he murmured. 'Don't know what came over me.'

'I think I do.' Roha had to smile. 'You thought I was already involved with UJU, didn't you?'

'Well, er, ah . . .'

'I've never hidden my views on these subjects from you. You don't need to be embarrassed, Brother Dav! But no, I've avoided having anything to do with these people so far. For all I knew they were going to advocate murdering Leps in the street. We can't risk having the Church associated with anything coarse, after all, and I'm afraid that at my rank, anything I do will represent the Church in most people's eyes.'

'Of course. I'm sorry, I just –'

'A perfectly understandable mistake.' Roha held up one hand. 'Don't mention it again. But I can't help wondering if these people will be useful, somehow.'

'We could send someone to observe the rally.'

'A good suggestion.' Roha considered. 'But I don't know, I think we'd best wait. I'd like to know a little more about them, you see, before we even go that far.'

'Their advertisements said they'd be handing out free literature. I can send a lay brother to get some pamphlets.'

'Now that's an excellent idea. Do that. And we'll want to see if we can find out if this steering committee has someone else behind them. They certainly seem to have money at their disposal.'

'That's for sure. You don't rent the amphitheatre for spare coinage.'

'Precisely.'

On and off throughout the morning, while he worked on the homily he would deliver at Vida's contract ceremony, the cardinal would remember Dav's assumption, which was of course perfectly correct. He took it as a sign that he'd grown too careless in expressing his views on matters racial. With Sister Romero on planet, he needed to tone down his public image. Since he knew Dav well, he could be sure that his stolid factor had believed his little denials, but still, perhaps it would be wise to voice doubts about the public group, while he kept a firm hand on the secret council behind it. Later, after the rally, he would consult with UJU-Prime and discuss what needed to be done.

Jevon had put too much work into the UJU rally to simply stay away. Although she couldn't allow herself to be seen in the amphitheatre, she did arrange to leave the office in Government House around the elevens and run errands that would take her near Algol Park. Seemingly by chance, she wandered across the lawn to investigate the row of booths down by the river. By then the rally had started. Every now and then she could hear a faint cheer or burst of laughter from the Floating Amphitheatre, which dominated the park like a huge purple planet, dwarfing the horizon of its moon. In the pale light the coiled power cables glittered around its support column.

The literature display stood nearly deserted. Under their red and white awnings, various UJU members waited, forlorn and yawning, behind counters spread with piles of shiny pamphlets. Six young Leps, university students from their shabby clothes, stood to one side carrying signs that read, 'A peaceful end to racism is all we ask.' A few humans, maybe thirty at the most, wandered from booth to booth, picking up pamphlets and laying them down again or stopping to argue. She heard one well-dressed man telling an UJU staffer, 'you're crazy, you people' in no uncertain tone of voice.

Jevon stopped at a booth staffed by a woman with bright blue hair and red fingernails long enough to be Lep claws. She brightened at the sight of a possible audience.

'Things seem slow for you folks,' Jevon said.

'Oh, everyone's in the rally now.' The woman gestured at the

Floating Amphitheatre. 'We had a nice crowd this morning, dearie, really we did.'

'Really?' Jevon picked up a pamphlet and pretended to read it. 'What about the rally? Have a lot of people gone in?'

'They're free, dearie, just help yourself. And oh yes, the rally's very well-attended. Why, I heard that the gate's at least five thousand.'

Since the amphitheatre sat seventy thousand, Jevon winced. She could imagine the crowd, all huddled forlornly around the speakers' podium. She laid down the pamphlet and picked up a schedule for the rally, then checked the time. Wilso should just be starting his speech.

'These ideas are very important, dearie. Sure you won't just take a copy home? It's free.'

Jevon started to answer, but the earth heaved and boomed. At first she thought she was fainting; she found herself on her knees. Again the earth rose and fell under her. She heard screams and saw the booths settling, as if they were giant dowagers sinking onto chairs in a rustle of enormous skirts.

'Earthquake!' someone yelled.

She scrambled to her feet and saw the Lep protesters, signs flung away, rushing to help the humans trapped in the booths. She could hear the blue-haired woman swearing in terror but too loudly for her to be hurt.

'I'm right here,' Jevon called. 'I'll help you! I – oh God. Oh God no.'

The Floating Amphitheatre was tilting on its column. The enormous steel support was bending and twisting as it bent, for all the world as if it were a rolled-up piece of washing being wrung out by invisible hands. Slowly, horribly slowly at first, while everyone outside stood frozen and staring, the amphitheatre began to tilt, following the bend of its column downhill toward the river, slowly and then faster, tilting more steeply, a bowl full of screaming as it tipped. With a boom so loud it deafened Jevon, the support column snapped. The purple bowl fell and hit the riverbank. She felt as if someone scooped her up in a giant hand only to slam her down into darkness.

Rico was sitting at his desk and organizing the saccule files from the ancient data dump when he felt the building tremble. Earthquakes were common enough in Palace that he ignored the tremor and went on working. A few minutes later he heard the first sirens, shrieking at some distance away. From overhead came the pounding of airhoppers, rising up from the centre of Government House and speeding off. Rico got up and rushed to the window, opened it wide and hung halfway out to look. The 'hoppers, red emergency vehicles and black police choppers both, were heading in a huge flock toward the park in the middle of Centre Sect. He could see a plume of what looked like smoke unfurling high into the sky, but as he watched, the plume began to settle back toward the ground.

'Dust? What in hell?'

Rico pulled himself back into the room and turned to the vidscreen.

'On. Search: news and local.'

The screen powered up and filled with windows. Ashen-faced presenters held mike feeds to their ears with shaking hands; intakes mouthed soundlessly. Video: the plume of dust rising; the flock of airhoppers; strange heaps of red and white canvas lying on lawns with humans and Leps, some moving, some ominously still, strewn upon or near them; a crater in green lawns, black and gaping; a twisted rod of snapped steel. And a thing, a purple structure, a sphere of some sort – Rico could not make sense of it at first – lay half on the ground, half in a stream, a child's purple ball dropped carelessly, perhaps.

'Oh my God. That's the amphitheatre.'

Hi came running into the room and joined him, staring at the screen. In a blare of sound the presenters got their transmit feed through at last. Sirens, people screaming, ten different intakes all talking at once, police bullhorns – they all went mute to leave a single voice.

'. . . horrible horrible tragedy,' an intake was saying. 'Here at the Floating Amphitheatre, I'm Jo Caro. This is worse than you can imagine back in the studio. The river is damming up. We need volunteers to get these injured people out of here. It's rising fast.'

'Jo, what happened?' the presenter was doing her best to speak calmly. 'Can you tell us what happened to the amphitheatre?'

'Sabotage of some kind.' He swallowed hard. 'This has got to be deliberate sabotage. The force-field generator apparently failed, and the field went down. I spoke to a Protector who told me there was an explosion, an underground explosion.'

Sirens drowned his voice and the thunder of airhoppers followed.

The feed died. The presenter leaned forward, listening to her earpiece while she spoke.

'Citizens, we've established a link with a pix who was covering the rally. The main window will show feed from her – oh my God oh my God.'

The main window irised into three-dee. Over half the screen, blood oozed in a red, clotted river. Images of corpses, twisted, broken, bleeding, filled the other half.

'Screen off!' Hi barked.

Released by the sudden grey, Rico turned and shook his head as if he could physically dislodge the images.

'Jevon.' Hi's face went white. 'She was going down that way. She had a lot of things to pick up, shopping I mean, and she told me she'd be down by Algol Park.'

'By the park doesn't mean she was in it.'

In two strides Hi crossed the room and grabbed the comm unit from Rico's desk. He barked the number of Jevon's carryround unit, then waited, staring at the far wall. Rico realized that he was holding his breath, let it out with a sigh.

'If she was going to answer,' Hi said, 'she'd have done it by now.'

'Well, I dunno. Maybe she's got her hands full, or she's eating lunch or something.'

Hi went on listening to the unit ring. Nju walked into the room and stood watching him. At last Hi swore and flicked the unit off.

'Jevon hasn't returned,' Nju said. 'Was it her you were calling?'

'Yeah, sure was. I'm going down there.'

'No, Sé Jons.' Nju spoke slowly, firmly. 'In the chaos of a disaster like this, you will be at risk. Do you not have enemies? Have they not already hired a killer once? I alone cannot protect you in a great confusion.'

'Well, damn it all!'

'Sé Rico and I will go,' Nju said. 'I shall call Sé Vida and arrange for you to wait with her and my brother.'

Hi glared; Nju glared steadily back; Hi looked away first.

'Oh okay,' he snapped. 'But Rico, you call me the minute you know something.'

Since Karlo had spent most of his life on naval ships, he realized at once that the trembling of East Tower came from no earthquake. Explosions had a feel all their own. He'd already grabbed his comm unit and was calling Dukayn when the airhopper fleet lifted off and headed for the disaster. Dukayn answered immediately.

'Turn on your newsvid, Sé,' Dukayn said. 'There's been some kind of bombing at that UJU rally in Algol Park.'

Karlo kept Dukayn online while he did so, and linked by the comm they watched the newsfeed together. When the dying pix's feed came through, sheeting the screen in the image of blood, Karlo could wait no longer.

'We need fleet Doctors,' he snapped. 'Those people have been thrown together like Marines in the belly of a hit ship. Our people will know how to handle it. Get every Fleet surgeon on planet over there. Bring down whomever you can from orbit. I'll get hold of the duty sergeant for the Garang, and we'll head down to the amphitheatre. The men in that regiment can handle any looters and provide the police with whatever support they need.'

'Yes, Sé. We'll need a command centre here. Nikolaides would be a good man to put in charge.'

'He would, yeah. I'll call him now.'

By the time Nju and Rico reached the disaster site, other volunteers had already moved the victims who'd fallen among the booths. The dammed-up river had spread out behind the amphitheatre and turned Algol Park into a shallow lake, draining down the main avenue on the downhill side. A steel island, the broken support column rose from the water among the floating kelp of red and white canvas. Sirens wailed until Rico's ears rang in sympathy. Choppers and airhoppers swarmed round the purple globe and dangled rescue slings. Rico could see the tiny forms of medics climbing down to the disaster.

'It's the only way into that thing,' Rico called to Nju. 'Now.'

'I'm looking for a command post.' Nju was shading his eyes with one furred hand and staring across the lake. 'I see none.'

'Maybe around the other side?'

They'd only walked a couple of yards before the air split into fragments, or so it seemed, with the sound of military transports. Like giant moths the airtrucks settled onto the broad avenue uphill from the park. Doors clanged open, and Garang trotted out in orderly ranks.

'Good,' Nju grunted. 'Sé Karlo's taken a hand in this.'

By the time they reached the emergency medical station, all the way around to the other side of the fallen amphitheatre, the Garang troops were beginning to organize the situation and unload equipment: inflatable boats, seeming-miles of rope ladders and grapples, crates of medical supplies, and ominous heaps of pale green body bags. Sergeants with comm headsets walked back and forth, yelling orders and transmitting information. Squads were setting up long tents and cots for the injured, who at the moment lay on the grass. Apparently there had been a doctor in the park at the time of the disaster. With the sleeves of her flowered dress spattered with blood, she was kneeling beside a man on the ground while a Marine ripped open a crate of supplies beside her.

'There will be Fleet surgeons on the way,' Nju remarked. 'The First Citizen will think of it.'

Rico tried to speak and found his mouth had gone too dry. As they walked down the line of patients, some moaning, some quiet with near-catatonic exhaustion, some ominously still and pale, he felt his entire mind and body screaming at him to run, to get out of there, to get away from the sight of blood and broken bones and death. He had to find Jevon. That thought kept him walking, kept him looking.

'Here she is!' he called out, then ran down the line.

Jevon lay like a tidy package on someone's coat, spread for her at some point by a volunteer, her legs crossed at the ankles, her arms neatly by her sides. She lay so still that for a terrible moment Rico thought she was dead, but when he dropped to his knees beside her, she opened her eyes. Dry blood smeared her chin from a bitten lip.

'Sé Rico,' she whispered.

'You bet. We came to look for you.'

Tears welled and ran down her face. When she made no move to wipe them away, Rico searched his pockets, found a wad of tissue, and wiped them for her. Nju knelt down at her other side.

'What happened?' he said.

'It was the impact. I got thrown down when it hit. I'm all right. I want to go home.'

Nju laid his hand on her forehead to keep her still.

'Do not move,' he snapped. 'You may be bleeding internally. You may also have broken ribs, and moving suddenly might puncture a lung. Lie still.'

'The others are hurt worse,' Jevon whispered.

'Some, yes. Others not so bad as you. Do not talk.'

'We'll stay here with you, Jev,' Rico said. 'Don't you worry. Nju, you'd better call my uncle. He'll be frantic if we don't let him know she's okay.'

Jevon shut her eyes and began to tremble.

'What is it?' Rico said. 'Does something hurt?'

'Everything hurts.'

'Don't talk!' Nju snarled. 'Sé Rico, shut up! I'll call Sé Hivel now, but do not make her talk again.'

'Okay, sure.'

With so many comm frequencies pre-empted to handle the emergency, it took Nju a long while to contact Government House. The sky above the amphitheatre swarmed with emergency choppers, lowering help down, hauling victims up, lowering them again to the waiting squads. Rico watched while he sat on the grass and held Jevon's small, cold hand between both of his.

All around them Garang trotted back and forth, setting up the field hospital, bringing in the victims to fill it. Doctors, some Fleet surgeons, some civilian volunteers, poured into the site. At first most of the patients that Rico saw passing by on stretchers were alive, some seemingly at least no more injured than Jevon. A few, though, had been thrown against the edge of the stage or the metal-framed seats. One woman screamed repeatedly; she held both hands over her eyes, and blood welled through her fingers. As the parade went on, the injuries grew worse; Garang, joined by human volunteers, carried past broken and bleeding human beings.

When Rico looked around, he saw at some distance away other Garang hauling heavy body bags to a waiting airtruck. For a moment he was afraid that he'd vomit and disgrace himself, but he forced his mind steady, and his stomach followed.

'Hah!' Nju barked. 'I've gotten through. Sé Hivel? We've found her!'

'They've found her!' Hi said. 'She's alive.' He clamped the comm unit back to his ear and frowned, listening hard.

Vida nodded, relieved more for him than for Jevon, whom she barely knew. Beside her on the sofa, Samante sat trembling, mesmerized by the images on the screen. On the floor beside the couch, Jak sat at Vida's feet, as if he could protect her from the horror of the video footage. When the amphitheatre fell, or so the presenters were saying, the impact had thrown human beings around like sticks of wood. People bleeding, people dying, people dead – the pictures went on and on. Hundreds had suffocated at the bottom of the immense heap of victims while they were screaming and struggling to get free. At a close-up of their contorted faces, Samante whimpered.

'Your aunt!' Vida said. 'Wilso was speaking at that thing. Was she there, Sammi?'

'No, thank God and his Holy Eye.' The factor's voice shook, soft and hard to hear. 'She doesn't approve of UJU. But she must be hysterical, worrying about him.'

'Well, then, go to her, if you want.' Vida laid a hand on Samante's arm. 'You could have asked me.'

'I'm not thinking, that's all.' Samante got up and wrenched her gaze away from the screen. 'Thanks, Vida. Thank you so much. I'll try to call her first.'

'You won't be able to get through. Just get a cab and go.'

'All right.'

Samante ran to her office, came back out with a jacket and a carryround comm unit, and headed for the door.

'I'll check in when I can. We've still got the ceremony plans to finish.'

'Don't be silly,' Vida snapped. 'I can't get married in a couple of days. Not in the middle of this. Don't worry about it.'

Done with his commcall, Hi opened the door for Samante, then shut it again. He sat down in an armchair and turned to the screen.

'You know what's the worst damn thing?' Hi said. 'I can't stop watching this stuff. I don't know why. Every picture's horrible, but –'

'I know,' Vida said. 'But we've somehow got to know. I wish there was something I could do.'

'There is. They're bringing the injured to the military hospital here in Government House. Jak, I'm thinking that it would be safe for Sé Vida to go over.'

'Yes indeed, Sé Hivel, if she wished to. They're bringing them here because this is a secure area, after all. There may be witnesses left alive, and they need to stay alive.'

'But what would I do there? I'm not a med tech or anything.'

'You could comfort people,' Hi said. 'Raise morale. Don't you realize how famous you've become? Palace's sweetheart, that's you, Vida. People would love to see you.'

'This isn't any time to joke.'

'I'm not joking. You're somebody now, Vida. Somebodies matter on Palace.'

Jak rose with a bow Hi's way.

'I shall call the hospital,' Jak said. 'Or rather, I shall start trying to reach them. It will take some time. But we can't leave until my brother returns to fetch Sé Hivel anyway.'

'Hey, I'm quite capable of taking care of myself.'

'Sé Hivel, if my brother returns and finds that I have disobeyed him –' Jak let the phrase hang.

'Well, yeah,' Hi said. 'It'll be better for Vida to go later, anyway, when things are more organized.'

While Jak waited, holding the comm unit to one ear, Vida kept watching the news. Many of the images repeated, since the newsgrid only had limited footage, but every now and then they added something new, either holo feed in the main window or supplementary material down the sides. Jak had just managed to call through to the emergency hospital when a presenter appeared on the screen for an announcement.

'We have an interview with Wan Peronida,' she said. 'Jo Caro has him on feed. Come in, Jo.'

'What the hell?' Hi muttered.

Vida felt utterly puzzled herself. What was Wan doing down there? The interview irised onto the main window. In duty fatigues and a black combat jacket an impatient Wan stood glaring into the camera. The intake's voice came from offscreen.

'As you all know, Peronida's a chopper pilot with the Coast Force of our Naval Reserve. He's been flying rescue missions, and he's been kind enough to give us some of his time.'

'Three minutes, Caro,' Wan snapped. 'There are people dying in there, and I need to get back on duty.'

Vida stared. The image looked like Wan, sounded like Wan, but how could it be Wan? He seemed so alive, so much in authority. In quick phrases he explained how the choppers lined up in formation, one after the other to glide in, drop their rescue team, pick up a sling full of victims, and then glide out again to make room for the next round.

'That's dangerous, isn't it?' the intake said. 'With so many machines in such a narrow corridor.'

'Oh yeah.' Wan glanced toward the camera and suddenly smiled, an expression of innocent delight. 'You get used to it.' The smile disappeared. 'Now let's cut this short.'

'Of course.' The intake's image replaced his on the screen. 'We've been talking to Wan Peronida. Jo Caro, signing off from the site.'

Vida turned to Hi.
'Get used to danger?' she said. 'He loves it.'

Watching the video on the news, Sar Elen broke. As long as the dead existed only as figures in a side window or names in a presenter's list, he sat still and proud, but once the pictures started, he writhed. First his hands began to curl and reach in the digging motion that signalled a troubled Lep; then he turned this way and that on his chair. Kata paid as much attention to him as he did to the video. Sure enough, at the sight of the suffocation victims, Elen got up and rushed from the room. Zir half-rose and hissed at his fleeing back.

'Coward!' she called out. 'What's wrong with you?'

Kata caught her arm and drew her back down beside him on the cushions.

'He's throwing up,' Kata said. 'Either he'll get over it, or he'll begin berating himself for having a hand in this. If does that, he'll have to be silenced. Do you understand that? He's one of your nest mates. Can you accept it?'

'Of course I can. We can't have him running to the Protectors.'

'Just so. I'm proud of you.'

In modesty Zir looked down. Kata left the room and went to look for Elen, found him standing at the back door, breathing fresh air.

'You'll feel better in a bit,' Kata said cheerfully. 'It's time for us to make our report to Riva. Let's get our jackets and go. The walk will do you good, youngling.'

'Thank you. My apologies for that act of weakness.' Elen raised his throat. 'I'll make amends, I'll swear it.'

'Good. Let's get out in the fresh air. We can still travel openly, I think, for now. Dealing with the effects of the bombing is going to strain the Protectors' Guild to their limits.'

Elen's hands dug, but he managed to squelch the motion.

During their long walk to the transport gate, Kata kept to side streets and darkened alleys as much as possible. Whenever he had sufficient light to judge Elen's reactions, he would talk, a distracting chatter. At first Elen tried to keep up the same, but slowly he turned inward to brood until at times he missed a question. When they reached South Canal, they scurried across the brightly-lit avenue and dropped down to the access pathway that ran directly beside the water. There in the dark they paused to catch their breaths.

'Come now, youngling,' Kata said. 'Today you've struck a glorious blow for the Lep cause. Riva's going to be proud of you.'

'I know. I just can't stop thinking about those people. They're my fellow citizens, after all.'

Kata flexed claws and swung before Elen even saw him move. The blow landed cleanly on the softer scales just below the ear. Kata felt his claws bite deep into the otio-jugular arteries and the nexi of nerves leading to the secondary spinal column. Impaled, Elen gurgled and arched his back, his mouth gaping in rictus as the thick purple blood oozed.

'I'm sorry,' Kata said. 'I liked you.'

With his other hand he thrust against the youngling's shoulder. In one smooth motion he freed his claws and shoved the half-paralysed youngling into the canal. Elen splashed and sank into the dirty water to drown. Kata knelt, washed out his claws, then retracted them and walked on.

The door to the shabby bar that housed a transport gate stood open. Kata stepped in to find the place full of Leps, mostly male, all staring at the vidscreen behind the bar as the news footage unrolled. As he worked his way along the back wall, he could hear the muttered comments. Much to his disgust, many of them expressed nothing but sympathy for the victims. More promising, though, was the fear he heard in every voice. What was Karlo going to do about this? What kind of laws was that maniac of a First Citizen going to be able to get passed now? He slipped into the corridor, then into the storeroom. When he activated his transceiver crystal, the portal glowed.

Kata stepped into the small grey room and sat down to wait, but Riva appeared almost immediately. Her revenant that night seemed to wear a long knotted gown of flaming orange silk and over her shoulders a webbing of fine silver chains – a celebration dress, indeed.

'Grandson,' she said. 'You have done well.'

'I thank you, grandmother.' He bowed his head before her. 'I am honoured to have served you.'

'Well spoken.' The revenant gave her oddly human smile. 'Now we need to decide your reward.'

'I've been paid already, and the fullness of my heart is reward enough.'

'Very well spoken. But I have been considering the customs of our people. For this act you should have the dal indit dala, the prize of heroes.'

'No, no, I'm not worthy.'
'You are. What shall you have for the dal?'
Kata started to continue his modest noises, then paused, feeling his crest lift at his sudden idea.
'Grandmother,' he said. 'There's something that my heart yearns for, and it's in your power to give.'
'Good, my grandson. Speak to me of it.'
'I want Vida's life. Help me reach her. I've seen you deaden security systems. I've seen you give me access to high security areas. When she signs a contract with the Peronida youngling, I'll have a chance at her. With your help.'
The revenant froze and paled. Apparently the real Riva, wherever she was, had found his request troubling.
'Riva, grandmother,' he went on. 'You hired me to kill the girl, and I failed. I need her blood to wash my honour clean. Come now, you want her dead yourself.'
The revenant flickered back to full life.
'I do not want to lose you, Kata. You are valuable to me and to the Lep cause. I do not have the hands to hold weapons. You do.'
'Well, you won't necessarily lose me, if we work together on this. You got me past the autogate security at the Spaceport. Surely you can get me into Government House.'
'It's possible.' Riva thought for a long moment. 'I cannot reach the system in the two towers. Dukayn has bested me there. But the wider area known as Government House – I can say with a high degree of probability that I can enter that system and affect its scan subroutines.'
Kata had to think about this bit of convoluted language for a moment before he could answer.
'The towers would be too dangerous, anyway. It's too easy to trap someone in a maze of walls like that. But this ceremony. They'll be signing the contract in the Cathedral, and then they'll be posing for holos and other such garbage all afternoon. The place will be swarming with guests and gridjockeys. Get me into Government House. Grandmother. That's all I ask. I can kill her and get back out again, I'm sure of it.'
'I find that I am not as certain of that possibility as you are.'
'Riva, trust me! Besides, even if I die killing her,' he lifted his crest at his own joke, 'every cause needs a martyr.'
'Very well. I have offered the dal indit dala, and you have taken

it. The laws of our people do not allow me to post further objections. So be it. Let us discuss what you wish to do.'

As soon as she'd assimilated the news, Sister Romero joined forces with a pair of local priests and hurried to the emergency hospital in Government House. The dying needed the last rites: an eye marked upon their foreheads in the blessed oil that they might see the rising of the light, a prayer to guide their going.

While she thoroughly abominated UJU and all it stood for, its members were suffering souls, the same as those sapients they affected to despise. In sombre black the group hurried down to the hospital, then stood uncertainly in a long lobby swarming with medical personnel and volunteers until at last a harried military nurse noticed them.

'Bless you for coming,' he said. 'Cardinal Roha's here too. I'll take you to the wards. We've got a lot of near-terminals.'

Near-terminals. It was even uglier than 'dying', Romero thought. Unfortunately the nurse was right enough. Despite the splendid med tech so common on Palace, too many people had lain too long untended while they bled internally, to be saved. The three priests split up, each with a factor to help them and carry the vials of oil and the cloths.

'This is the worst part of our job,' Thiralo murmured. 'God give me strength.'

They needed it before the night was over. Romero had tended the dying before; she was used to grief and terror. She had not expected rage. Or outrage, really – people who had counted on life-extension to live another hundred years were furious to be dying. To their whispered snarls and curses she found little to say except, 'Go with God. Cling to the rising of the light.' She murmured it over and over as if she were repeating a magic spell. Some were soothed; most died angry. One young woman, who had been beautiful until half her face was torn away, would stay in her memory for the rest of her life.

'It's not fair.' She could barely speak. 'It's just not fair.'

'Life itself is never fair, my child.'

'Why not? It should be.'

A bubble of blood broke on what was left of her lips, and her eyes rolled as she fell still for ever. Romero chanted the prayers over her and moved on to the next victim.

Toward the middle of the night the situation, like the victims, stabilized. The city had finally mustered enough resources to give each victim the sort of med tech they all had taken for granted. Some of the dead, the most recently gone and the least injured, were resurrected with impaired brain functioning that, eventually, Palace's medicine would repair. The young woman with half a face stayed beyond help.

Romero and Thiralo found a moment's rest in an alcove at the end of a hallway, where a scatter of chairs formed a semi-circle opposite a small vidscreen. Thiralo produced a handkerchief from the pocket of his cassock and wiped his face. Romero merely sat, her oily hands limp in her lap, and wondered why anyone would expect life to be fair. On the wall the vidscreen displayed endless video of the bomb site, the victims, the hospital, the bomb site again. Romero was about to yell at the thing to turn itself off when the loop stopped, the screen turned briefly grey, and a presenter's ashen-brown face irised into the centre window.

'The Master of the Protectors' Guild has just made an important announcement.' Exhausted as she was, she could no longer control her shaking voice. 'A group has come forward and claimed responsibility for today's bombing of the Floating Amphitheatre. In a closed comm transmission that so far has proved untraceable, a group called Riva announced that they planted the explosive device to protest the leadership of Karlo Peronida. They will continue to commit random acts of violence, the communiqué stated, until the laws forbidding Lep ownership of property in Tech Sect are revoked. The Protectors' Guild has issued a statement that no compromise with terrorists is possible. In a press conference the First Citizen has stated that he will put the matter into tomorrow's interactives to gather citizen input.'

Thiralo shook his head and sighed.

'Well, well, well,' Romero said. 'UJU has called forth its opposite. Sooner or later that always happens, doesn't it? Odd how that sort never seems to realize it.'

'That's because they don't realize they're that sort.'

'Unfortunately, you're quite right.' With a sigh Romero heaved herself to her complaining feet. 'We'd best do one last check of the wards, and then I think God will forgive us if we go home.'

Toward dawn an exhausted Peronida family and their bodyguards, along with Vida and hers, gathered in Karlo and Vanna's suite, except for Wan, who was breakfasting with the personnel of his chopper unit. Sleepy saccules, smelling of flowers, brought drinks and plates of hastily-assembled cold food. Vida sank into an armchair and Jak sat at her feet, while Karlo, Vanna, and Pero took the sofa. No-one spoke at first, merely ate. Vida was annoyed with herself for being insensitive enough to feel hungry after the suffering she'd seen, but she couldn't deny that she was.

'I saw footage of you at the hospital,' Pero said, glancing at Vida. 'Good job.'

'Thank you. I can't believe how glad they were to see me.'

'You handled it just right. You looked appalled, but you never went to pieces. Couldn't have been easy.'

'Thanks. It wasn't.'

For a few moments more they all ate in silence.

'Well, one thing at least,' Karlo said at last. 'This shows what the Leps on planet are capable of.' He was looking pointedly at Vanna. 'I hope you can see that now. Your precious fellow citizens – they're no different than the rest of their kind.'

'Bullshit!' Vanna said. 'It shows what any sapient's capable of, if they feel pushed to the wall.'

'Oh come on, lawmother!' Pero said. 'Nothing the government's done can justify this.'

'No, of course not, that's not what I meant. I mean you can't make people feel hopeless and not expect them to lash out.' She glanced Vida's way with narrow eyes. 'What about you, L'Var? What do you think?'

Vida gathered her courage.

'I agree with you,' she said. 'Besides, we're forgetting something, aren't we? It's not all the Lep citizens who did this. It's that group of extremists, Riva. The news said that the Protectors have been monitoring them, but they sure did a lousy job of it.'

Vanna laughed with a toss of her head.

'Damn right, L'Var.' Vanna turned to Karlo. 'A real lousy job, First Citizen. I suggest you get the Master of the Protectors' Guild over here tomorrow and rake him over the coals.'

'It's already on my agenda.' Karlo abruptly rose. 'We're all too tired to think clearly. Let's get some rest. The city's going to need us all tomorrow.'

With Jak escorting her, Vida returned to her suite. When the door slid back, she realized that a lamp shone, music played, and someone was sitting in the gather. Jak caught her arm.

'I go first.'

She stepped back into the corridor and hovered, her heart pounding in fear, until she heard Jak call out.

'Sé Rico! What are you doing here? I nearly killed you.'

Vida rushed into the gather to find Rico sprawled on her couch and Jak standing over him. Rico was laughing, a cold mutter under his breath, as he stood up, rubbing his arm – where Jak had grabbed him, Vida assumed. She wanted to run to him and throw herself into his arms, but her bodyguard stood in the way, scowling.

'I put the music on to warn you that someone was here,' Rico said. 'I just wanted to see Vida, and I'm too tired to wait in the hall all night.'

'How did you get in?' Vida snapped.

'Locks like these don't mean much to Cyberguild people.' Rico stood up, grinning in a lopsided way. 'I entered my prints into your system.'

Jak growled and raised his eyes heavenward.

'It's all right, Jak,' Vida said. 'You must be tired, too. Why don't you go fix yourself something to eat? There's cold roast in the pantry, I think.'

'My thanks, Sé Vida.' Jak turned a glowering eye on Rico. 'Next time, *Sé*, perhaps you could leave a note on the door?'

'And have Vida's fiancé see it?'

For a brief moment Vida thought Rico might be drunk, just from the defiant way he was smiling, staring at Jak – staring Jak down, she realized, as the Garang shrugged and looked away.

'A good point,' Jak said, his voice utterly mild. 'No doubt you know best when it comes to arranging these,' he hesitated briefly, 'arrangements. Sé Vida, I shall be in the eatery.'

'When you're done eating, just go to bed.'

Jak nodded in bland complicity. As soon as he'd left the room, Rico took three long steps toward her and gathered her into his arms. She clung to him for a long moment, luxuriating in the feel of his chest beneath her cheek, before she could lift her head and let him kiss her.

'I'm so glad you're here,' she whispered. 'But isn't it dangerous?'

'I don't know.' He was smiling at her. 'Do you think Wan would care?'

'Probably not. It's the ratings I'm worried about.'

'Damn the ratings!' Rico let go of her and strode across the room.

'I can't damn them.'

Rico stood in front of the undraped windows, looked out, and said nothing.

'You don't know what it's like, having to depend on the opinions of other people. You'll always be Cyberguild. You'll always be somebody here. I won't unless I work at it.'

He shrugged and continued staring out at the night. Vida caught herself yawning, walked over to join him, risked laying a hand on his shoulder.

'Let's not fight? Let's not waste the time.'

Rico turned to her at last.

'Yeah,' he said. 'I'm sorry. We're both exhausted, aren't we? But I want to hold you. I just want to lie down and hold you. I want to stop thinking about all the stuff I've seen today.'

'You know something? So do I.' She leaned into his embrace. 'If you weren't here I'd be crying.'

A few minutes past dawn Molos showed up in the Cyberguild suite. Hi had set his neural alarm to respond to Molos' ID code at the door. The moment it flashed he woke and rose, telling the door to open, then grabbing clothes from the floor. Half-dressed, he met Molos in the gather.

'Was this Kata's work?' Hi said.

'Whose else would it be? Besides, explosives are a specialty of his.' Molos sounded exhausted, and his yellow eyes were laced with purple capillaries. 'I've been up all night, following down those leads we found two days ago. I can no longer think, and so I came over to ask you to pick up where I was forced to leave off.'

'You bet. Come into my office.'

While Hi powered up the Mapstation, Molos sank into the visitor's chair and levered up the back rest to support his head. He reached into his jacket and pulled out a sheaf of notes, written on paper.

'I didn't dare trust this to a Map file,' the Lep said.

'All right.' Hi took the sheaf and glanced through it, saw a string of Map addresses, and swore. 'Riva's been using the old Citizen Assist net.'

'Some of it. Only some of it, but somehow she managed to commandeer those resources and reserve them for her exclusive use.' Molos paused for effect. 'That's where her revenant originates.'

'Then we can shut it down. It won't stop her, but it'll do some damage.'

'Ah, but shouldn't we let her stay in a place where we can trap her?'

'You're right, I'm wrong. We'll have to figure out a way to monitor without her knowing it. Not easy, but we can try, and this time, the whole damned guild won't be hearing about it. What was the tip that led you there?'

'Some of the data the Calios revenant gave you. He knew the parameters of the old net. Most of it was accounted for by later use, but not this one healthy slice. Oddly enough, I left examining it till last night. It seemed too obvious.'

'Riva may be getting a little arrogant and a little careless. Good.' Hi glanced up. 'Say, speaking of Calios, there's something I want to ask you before I forget again. Why did you enter Vida in the L'Var clan's roster?'

'You *are* clever, Hivel. Did Vida tell you about my um intervention?'

'No, Rico figured it out. Look.' Hi held one hand up flat. 'I don't want to know who her mother is. Let her keep her secret, okay? I just want to know why you entered Veelivar on the clan genealogy.'

'Because I admired Orin L'Var more than any man I've ever met, Lep or human. When he was murdered – and that's what it was, murder, as far as I'm concerned – I couldn't bear thinking that his line of descent had ended forever. So I put his daughter in her rightful place. All those files were legally locked, and I figured that no-one would ever see her name there. I had no idea that listings for those old families were cross-linked to Citizen Assist at a level no lock could affect.' Molos suddenly hissed. 'Do you think that's where Riva learned of her?'

Hi went cold all over.

'I think your sentimental notion backfired, yeah,' Hi said at last. 'But I'm not blaming you.'

'I'm blaming myself more than you ever could.' Molos shook, and his hands dug at the formfit. 'I'll have to take steps to right this wrong. At the very least I should grovel at her feet.'

'With your bad leg?'

'Hivel! I know your motives are sound, but please don't try to joke me out of it. I have an obligation to Vida now, and that's all there is to say about that.'

'All right. Before you go, get me up to speed here. Your analysis of the autogate failure looks like a good place to start.'

'Yes, indeed. When you jack into the Map, go straight to the document listing the day's activity at that gate. That fellow who was thrown to his death that day? His demise gave me a positive time to work with. About three minutes afterwards, one of the autogates recorded a strange pulse from some sort of photonic token. While the signal wasn't strong enough to scramble the gate, it may have activated some function. I was just starting to analyse the raw data when I realized that I was so tired I was making apprentice-level mistakes.'

'I'll pick up there, then. Your brother's always had a tendency to leave corpses lying around the landscape. This one just might come back from the grave to haunt him.'

After a couple of hours of sleep, Karlo returned to the emergency command centre that Pero had set up the night before in the First Citizen's public office. Tables and Map terminals covered the long expanse of beige carpet; in the brightened lighting the hologram of Palace on the far wall showed dull and faint. At the terminals military personnel sat working, talking back and forth in Helane while a couple of officers wandered from desk to desk, relaying orders. Pero himself stood beside the massive icelight desk, watching readout on the Map terminal set into the desktop. When Karlo walked in, everyone paused, saluted, and went right back to work.

'Morning, Sé,' Pero said. 'Things are well under control.'

'Good. How long will we need this centre?'

'Another twelve hours, no more. Here's what we will need: a routing station to make sure the right medical personnel go where they're needed most and then an intelligence liaison. From what I've seen, it would be best if the First Citizen functioned as a link between the Protectors' Guild, the intelligence wing of the Military Guild, and our people. They all hate each other. I can give you more details.'

'That's fine for now. Okay. Work up a procedure for disbanding this office, choose an officer to put in charge of the medical station, and do some research on the liaison idea. You should bring Dukayn into that.'

Karlo sat down in his usual chair just as saccule servants trotted in with trays of food. Karlo grabbed a sandwich and a cup of grain drink as they went by and settled in to read reports. During the night even the Military Intelligence people had found nothing, since the original explosion had destroyed its own evidence. They were in the process of questioning the security guards who'd been on duty there over the past week – the ones who'd survived, that is. Dukayn appeared some twenty minutes later, bringing with him another problem, this one merely irritating rather than dangerous.

'It's about your son's contract ceremony,' Dukayn said. 'Sé Vida wants to postpone it out of respect for the dead and their families.'

'Of course,' Karlo said. 'So?'

'Tarick Avon of Pansect Media is throwing shit around. He stands to lose money if the coverage doesn't hit the grids as announced.'

'Screw the man! What's he going to do? Sue her?'

'Yes. And Wan, too.'

Karlo relieved his feelings with a string of oaths in Helane and Gen both.

'Get him on the comm, and – no, wait. Get him over here. If he's going to act like an asshole, he can waste his time doing it in person. Set up a meeting between him, me, and Vida. If you can find Wan easily, do it. Otherwise, don't worry about him.'

Karlo spent the rest of that day organizing the liaison procedures and reviewing reports of the hunting of Vi-Kata as they came in. Military Intelligence had managed to collect sightings of a Lep that could only be the Outcast, but they all dated from before the bombing. The Lep community had turned suddenly cooperative, Karlo was pleased to note. Since a police force that rarely saw fatal violence was dealing with a highly-skilled professional, the Protectors' reports generally fell into the category of 'useless.' They did, however, discover that a young Lep found dead in South Canal had worked for D&B Janitorial. He'd been at the Floating Amphitheatre on the night before the disaster. A witness, or maybe a confederate – it didn't much matter, Karlo supposed, since he was unable to tell anyone anything.

At the fifteens Dukayn arrived with Tarick Avon and the news that Sé Vida was on her way. For the occasion Avon wore the guild robes of a full master, but to Karlo the multi-coloured stripes of Media Guild made the man look like a clown. He took him into the small private office behind the hologram, sat him down in a formfit, and stayed standing, walking back and forth with his hands stuffed into his pockets. Avon wasted no time.

'First Citizen, I know you're thinking that I'm a money-grubbing little bastard. You don't understand just how much lost revenue's at stake. Pansect's had to pay an indemnity to the carrying grid.

We'll forfeit if we can't provide the promised feature.'

'Oh? How much?'

'A million credits. That's only the indemnity. Lost time, rescheduling, kill fees to the holders of the spin-off rights – there's another four hundred thousand.'

Karlo opened his mouth and shut it again.

'That's a lot of money,' Avon said. 'Well, isn't it?'

'More than I expected, yes. But still, we've got an issue of basic decency here. Over two thousand people are dead, more may still die, the injuries of most of the remaining victims are major.' Out of the corner of his eye Karlo saw the office door opening. 'What kind of audience do you think you're going to get, anyway, for something as frivolous as a contract ceremony?'

'An enormous one. People get sick of the horrifying, you know. They want something to lift them up, a happy distraction. After four days of those ghastly holos and all the morbid commentary, I'll bet every vidscreen on Palace gets tuned to Vida and Wan's ceremony. Here, you're a soldier. We're talking about the public morale.'

Vida stepped into the office. Right behind her came Jak, who shut the door behind them. She wore black pants with a modest black shirt, and she'd bound her flamboyant hair back in a single braid. At the sight of her Avon flinched. Jak took up a position behind him, crossed his arms over his chest, and scowled at the intake's bald scalp.

'Tarick,' Vida said. 'You're really being loath. I can't believe you'd threaten to sue me.'

'I'm sorry,' Avon was close to stammering. 'It's the grid indemnity money.'

'How much money will you lose if I have my factor put your outfit on my "no access" list? There's an awful lot of society people who'll do the same thing just because I did. I won't even have to ask.'

Avon swore under his breath. Karlo perched on the edge of the desk and left him to Vida.

'Listen to me,' she said. 'I might consent to the ceremony going on like we planned – I might, I said, only might – if you make me a promise right now. You won't repeat anything you hear in this room until I tell you it's okay.'

As he scented big news breaking beyond his reach, Avon's wide blue eyes rolled in agony. Vida waited in silence.

'All right,' he said at last. 'I promise.'

'Good.' Vida glanced at Karlo. 'He's right about the morale, Sé. I know that I can't stand to see any more of that video. All those poor people!'

'I hadn't thought of that, yeah,' Karlo said. 'Go on.'

'I've been thinking. You're pretty sure it's Vi-Kata who made the bomb, aren't you?'

'Everything points to him, yes.'

'And from what Sé Hivel's been telling me, he could hide out in Palace forever, and the police will only find him if they're really lucky.'

'I hate to say it, but Jons is probably right. This city is enormous, and Kata knows what he's doing. Military Intelligence can give him a run for his money, but it's not going to be easy, digging him out of his hole.'

'I don't understand that,' Avon broke in. 'No-one else does, either. It's a question that the First Citizen might want to address on the public vids, in fact.'

'The police can't find him because he's utterly unpredictable,' Karlo said. 'All terrorists are, at least in the beginning. They strike out of nowhere, and no-one has any idea of what their target will be until they've hit. Think about it. If someone's selling illegal drugs, the police can figure out where his customers are likely to be and wait for him there. I don't know where Kata's getting his explosives, but if he has more, he could blow up any building anywhere. How can any of the police forces involved predict the next one?'

'I can see that,' Avon said. 'But the people deserve to know this, too. It'll put them on their guard. You've got millions of pairs of eyes and ears out there, First Citizen. Use them.'

Karlo caught himself on the edge of a dismissive remark.

'You're right, aren't you? All right. You can quote me on that after all. *If* I see the quote in advance.'

'You got my word on that.' Avon reached up and touched one of the chips in the back of his skull. 'It's recorded, and I'll get Dukayn printout.'

Reflexively both men turned toward Vida to see her reaction. 'Then I was right, and my idea might work,' Vida said. 'You know that he tried to kill me, right? Well, then, that's one thing we can predict. Let's go ahead with the ceremony. You can use me as bait.'

Jak threw his head back and made a noise halfway between

a growl and a shriek. Karlo felt like echoing the sentiment.

'Vida!' Avon turned dead-white. 'You could get killed.'

'No. Not with everyone ready and waiting for Kata. I was just talking with Sé Ri Tal Molos, and he told me that Kata would rather die than fail to make a kill. He'll risk dying himself to get at me. Molos is Kata's brother. He knows him better than anyone.'

'I suppose he does.' Karlo considered for a long moment. 'I'm not going to approve this idea, though, until we work out the security. I'll put Dukayn in charge, of course. But unless he can promise me on his word of honour that you'll be safe – no deal.'

'Well, there's always going to be some risk.' Vida's voice was perfectly level. 'And if you don't get Kata, he's going to kill a lot more people.'

'First Citizen.' Avon stood up. 'Pansect's crews are at your disposal. We can add surveillance chips to the array our pix wear and link them to whatever kind of central control you want.'

'Good thought,' Karlo said. 'Very well, I'll include you in this. For starters, we need you to make it very clear on the news that Sé Vida is going ahead with the ceremony only to raise the city's morale.'

'Oh, I'll go you one better,' Avon said. 'We'll make this our question of the day. Should Vida and Wan go ahead and sign their contract? I'm so sure that people will vote yes that I'll start running it on the interactives tonight.'

When Kata woke, just at sunset, the first thing he did was turn on the news. He lay in the sleep web of Zir's upstairs bedroom and watched, switching from grid to grid to make sure that no scrap of news about the Protectors' plans escaped him. The officials were being cautious, of course, and keeping their plans to themselves, but even the locations of the various interviews that the Protectors granted gave him information. As he flipped through the grids, a familiar name stopped him at Pansect Media's evening interactives. He rather wanted to know the answer to that question of the day. Would the citizens approve if Vida went through with her ceremony on schedule?

The screen split into windows. Among holos of Vida walking through the emergency hospital the usual tower graphs built up. The people of Palace, it seemed, overwhelmingly wanted to see her sign her contract. The reasons splayed out into a pie chart. Most of them wanted to see something that made them feel good about Palace for a change. If he'd been outside, Kata would have spat.

'You're awake?' Zir's voice came from the doorway.

'I am, yes.' He shut off the screen, then swung himself down from the web. 'I need to be gone, my love.'

'I know that. I've got a new set of passes and ID cards from Riva for you.'

'Any messages?'

'One. She told me to tell you exactly this: it has been done.'

'Good. That's what I've been waiting for.'

'Will you come back here afterwards?'

'No. It'll put you in too much danger.'

'I don't care about that.'

'I do. The Lep cause needs you.' Kata laid his hand on the back of her neck and gently rubbed. 'I'll miss you, but forget you ever knew me.'

Zir stepped away and stared at the far wall. Briefly her hands dug.

'I'll try,' she said at last. 'But I can't promise.'

It was time to run, and running was one of the things Kata did best. With a shoulder sack and a websling full of supplies, he headed off into the night. Before he could disappear, he needed to make a quick foray into Government House – now, in the night, before the enormous security effort that was bound to surround Vida's contract ceremony got itself put into place. In his sack he had the three pieces of a break-down pulse rifle. Riva could tamper with the scanners all she wanted to, but even the most basic of physical searches would find the weapon. He had several places in mind to hide it until he was ready to pick it up on the morrow.

'What the hell?' Hi stood scowling at the message window on the vidscreen. 'That's all I need right now, a summons from His Highness the goddamn First Citizen.'

Rico looked up from his reading and saw an image of Dukayn looping in the message window.

'The Peronida wants to see you to discuss some matters of increased security precautions. Please call me for an immediate appointment.'

'Off!' Hi snarled.

Dukayn's image froze, then vanished. Hi rubbed his face with both hands and stood for a moment, staring at the floor.

'Are you okay?' Rico said.

'Just tired. Come into my office. While I'm gone, I've got some work I need done. It concerns that autogate crash, the one that let Kata on planet in the first place.'

Since Hi had already brought down the data that Rico would be working with, Rico decided against jacking into the Map itself. He was looking for the autogate function triggered by the mysterious pulse that had allowed Kata through planetary security. From the enormous amounts of information and useless noise recorded by the gate, Hi had spent the afternoon recovering the peculiar artifact that the pulse had delivered: a photonic waveform, an incredibly archaic and thus advanced form of an iconic command cluster – if indeed the thing even was a command cluster.

By special dispensation of Port Security, they had the entire autogate system database to consult. Rico ran various search utilities and translation routines, set up some ID analysis runs and tried those, but the waveform stayed unreadable. Although – he'd seen something like this recently – of course, in the data dump archive of the saccule trade! When he found the cluster of photonic waveform recordings in the archive, he also found notes written in Inglis, which his routines could translate. The waveforms recorded the genetic patterning of typical saccule neuters for further study.

'DNA signatures.' Rico spoke aloud without realizing it. 'This thing might have been a deen sig.'

It made perfect sense. The authorities had long ago entered Kata's deen sig into the databanks of every security system on planet, but the autogate had passed him right through. What had the command cluster done? Overwritten his deen sig with a false one, maybe, or simply deleted it from the records. Deleting would be dangerous; while it wasn't likely, it was possible that someone might want a copy of the sig and find it missing. A false record made sense, and with a couple of the saccule deen sigs to work with, he could run a compare and match. What they encrypted wouldn't matter to the raw code analysis, which went by sheer patterning. Sure enough, the agent chugged once and spat the answer onscreen. The middle of the autogate waveform fell into the same category as the two records from the saccule archives. At the beginning and end of the autogate waveform were two short bursts from a different category.

'Got it!'

Commands at either end, mostly likely, and a deen sig in the middle for sure. Clever Riva, to wait until the last possible moment to corrupt the data! By giving Kata the token that would send the pulse, she'd made sure that no-one could discover that his scan had been changed and restore it before he could get through. Now that Rico knew what he was looking for, finding the list of DNA typing for known criminals in the autogate banks proved easy. Kata's entry still sat there, marked with the highest priority alarm command. How could he tell if it were accurate? He needed a clean copy, but if Riva could corrupt the autogates, the most secure system on planet, surely she could hack into every other security database.

Since he couldn't read the actual encoded information in the waveform, how was he going to compare it with other files he might find? Rico jacked in and began hunting. He swore aloud at how easy it was to access the outer defences of Government House, since Dukayn had no jurisdiction over the public gates. The deen sig registered for Kata matched the one he'd taken from the autogate bank. Since he already knew how to breach the Protectors' firewall, he slipped in there as well and copied their version of Kata's file: another match. Either they were all correct or all corrupted – and who knew if they matched the waveform's data?

Rico left the Map, brought his finds up onscreen, and leaned back to consider them. Even if he managed to gain access to every scan of Kata's on the Map, and even if he found one deen sig different than all the others, he would never be certain if the mismatch was a file that Riva had overlooked or a corruption from some other cause. Unfortunately, Kata wasn't going to come forward and offer him a drop of blood or shed scale to put through a medical scanner. He had better assume the worst and get moving on how to correct it.

Vida's life might depend on how well he solved this problem, how well and how soon. He couldn't afford the luxury of trying to solve it on his own just for pride's sake. Rico copied a few key files to the cube, dropped the cube into his shirt pocket, then grabbed his guild jacket from a chair and ran from the suite. The First Citizen's public office lay several floors up and on the far side of the tower. By the time Rico reached it, he was panting for breath. The door stood half open, and he walked in to find Pero Nikolaides, supervising a military tech at a Map terminal. One other Map work place, deserted at the moment, stood off by a side wall.

'Rico!' Pero said with a wave. 'What are you doing here?'

'I thought there was some kind of meeting going on. My uncle's there, and I've got important data for him. He needs to present it to the First Citizen.'

'They're back in the private office. Come with me.'

Beside the hologram of the planet stood a narrow door. When Pero pressed his thumb on the ID plate, Dukayn's voice crackled through a speaker.

'What is it, Nikolaides?'

'Rico Hernanes is here with priority Cyberguild data.'

A moment's pause; then Dukayn's voice again, sounding surprised: 'Send him in.'

Rico walked through to find his uncle, the First Citizen, and Dukayn sitting around a desk with a flat Mapscreen embedded in its top. Onscreen he could see plans for the Cathedral of the Eye.

'Sé.' Rico nodded at Karlo. 'I'm sorry to interrupt, but I've figured out how Kata got through the Spaceport autogate, and it has a direct bearing on the security of Government House.'

'Then I think I'll forgive you for the interruption.' Karlo waved at an empty chair. 'Sit down and tell us.'

On the way over Rico had organized the data in his mind, and he managed to present his findings clearly. When he laid the corroborating cube on the table, everyone leaned forward and stared at it as if they could read its molecular coding right through the crystalline surface.

'So if Riva's managed to raid the databanks for Government House security,' Rico finished up, 'she could get in anywhere.'

'She sure could,' Hi said. 'Well done, kid. Very well done.'

'Thanks.' Rico could barely speak. His uncle's 'well done' amounted to another man's fulsome praise.

'Let me see if I've got this straight,' Dukayn said. 'The deen sig recorded all over the Map for Kata is probably wrong. That means he can walk through any security system on planet.'

'That's it, yeah,' Hi said.

'If we can't get Kata's correct data back into the banks,' the factor went on, 'I can't guarantee Sé Vida's safety for the ceremony. Come to think of it, I can't guarantee it unless she stays shut up in East Tower for the rest of her life. Government House is just too big. There are too many ways he could get at her.'

A cold hand clutched at Rico's heart. Think, damn it! he told himself.

'Damn Leps,' Karlo muttered.

'Wait a minute,' Rico broke in. 'That's right, he is a Lep. And he has a brother on planet, right?'

Hi leaned back in his chair and nodded Rico's way ever so slightly, as if telling him to push on with this line of thought.

'Lep brothers come from the same clutch of eggs,' Rico went on. 'They hold over ninety per cent of their DNA coding in common. All I need is a scan from one of his scales or a drop of blood, and I can construct a fuzzy logic ID. It'll trigger the alarm if anyone from the Tal family crosses the scanners. It doesn't have to match Kata's scan exactly.'

'I'm sure we can find out if there are any other members of that family in Palace,' Karlo said. 'Sounds good.'

'First Citizen?' Hi leaned forward. 'There are only two members of the Tal clan left. The rest were purged by the Ri government a long time ago.'

'Good,' Dukayn said. 'Makes the job easier.'

'One thing, though,' Karlo said. 'Hernanes, what if Riva figures out what you've done and corrupts the files again?'

'I can loop it, First Citizen. This will guard against him having another one of those tokens, too. The icon will activate every second and re-enter the correct deen sig. Riva can keep wiping it off if she wants. Keep her real busy.'

'If she tries, we can trace her.' Hi was gazing absently at empty air. 'I'm getting some ideas about that.'

'Sounds good to me.' Dukayn allowed himself a brief smile. 'Huh. Looks like Molos is going to be good for something for a change.'

At about the same time as the security meeting in the First Citizen's office was breaking up, Kata walked out of Government House as easily as he'd walked in, using one of the four public access roads through the blueglass walls. On the day of Vida's ceremony Dukayn would probably close three of them, Kata figured; he certainly would, if he were Dukayn. The wiretrain stations would be temporarily closed as well, most likely, and no doubt an umbrella of police aircars and military choppers would cover the sky. Kata could only guess as to which road would be left open for the ceremony guests, gridjockeys, caterers and the like, as well as all the ordinary sapients who worked in Government House. He'd hidden the rifle parts close to the east gate, the narrowest of the four and thus the easiest to blockade with checkpoints.

Not that it mattered, really, since Riva had pulled off one of her miracles again. Two days from now, on the day of Vida's ceremony, he'd walk through whatever gate Dukayn left open, and judging from this night's work, no-one would know a thing.

The medical staff insisted that Jevon stay in the hospital far longer than she wanted. They'd taped electronic bone stimulators over her rib cage to heal the broken ribs and put her on an IV drip of bioactive calcium as well. By the morning of Twenty-one Gust, three days after the bombing, they pronounced the ribs healed and released her to Sé Hivel and Nju.

'Remember to take it easy for a couple of days,' was the doctor's parting shot.

Jevon nodded and agreed, but her mind was already turning to the work that must have piled up in her absence. She needed to work, she absolutely had to work. Work was the one thing that would fill her mind and crowd out the images from the vidscreens that tormented her memory. Sé Hivel, unfortunately, had heard the doctor's remark.

'You're taking as much time off as you need,' he said cheerfully. 'We've got your room all fixed up. Sé Vida sent flowers.'

'Did she? How kind of her.' Jevon felt like crying. I don't deserve it, she wanted to say – no, she wanted to scream it out: I helped kill those people. I helped send them to the rally. 'I mean, she hardly knows me.'

When they reached East Tower, Nju insisted on carrying her to the lift booth and then again to the Cyberguild suite. Wrapped in his arms she felt as small as a child and oddly safe. For the first time it occurred to her to wonder why she'd never hated the Garang the way she hated Leps. A number of painful ideas had been occurring to her, when she'd been forced to lie alone in a hospital bed with only the chattering vidscreens for company.

Yellow flowers heaped the dresser in her room, a match for the flowered drapes and bedspread she'd brought there an eternity ago, it seemed, when Sé Hivel had transferred to quarters in Government House. Nju set her down in her armchair by the window.

'I had thought to procure you a plush animal toy,' he said. 'It seems customary in these circumstances, but Sé Hivel told me that it would not be suitable.'

'It isn't, no, Nju. But thank you for the thought.'

At last they all went away and left her alone. Through the door at first she heard their voices, discussing their plans for the afternoon; then there was silence. She got up, gingerly, took off her jacket and hung it in the closet, then stripped off her dirty clothes and tossed them into a hamper, even though she knew she could never stand to wear those clothes again, the ones she had been wearing when so many UJU members died. Her closet hung crammed with clothing; she took an old robe and slipped it on, then stood looking around her room just for the comfort of her familiar things. On the end table lay a box of her favourite chocolates and two holonovel tapes, presents from her employer. Sé Hivel had been generous again, so damned generous, so gallantly and constantly generous, once again making it clear that he had everything to give while she had nothing.

'Arno,' she whispered. 'Oh, Arno.'

On the vidscreen on the far wall the door unit buzzed. Dukayn's image appeared in the corner.

'Let me in, Jevon. I know you're there.'

Jevon sat down hard on the edge of her bed and gasped for air. The unit buzzed again. Dukayn's hard-edged face showed no feeling at all.

'Jevon, come on. You don't want a public fuss, do you?'

She could not speak, could not find the air to speak, but she did reach out and pick up the transmit from the end table by the head of her bed. At the third buzz she flicked the door switch and let him in. She got up and opened her bedroom door just as he came into the hall from the gather.

'I wanted to see how you were doing,' Dukayn said. 'You don't look well.'

She shook her head and clutched at the doorjamb to steady herself as he strode down, dressed in his usual black with steel studs gleaming down one sleeve. For a moment they stood facing each other over the threshold; when he took a step forward, she was forced to move back and let him in. He glanced around her room, then stood, watching her, between her and the chair. She nearly collapsed onto the edge of the bed.

'I'm sorry,' Dukayn said. 'I didn't think you'd still be ill.' He turned and shut the door behind him. 'Or are you just frightened?'

'Damn you,' Jevon whispered. 'How can you be so calm after what's happened?'

'I didn't set that bomb. Neither did you.' Casually he sat down next to her on the bed. 'I figured you'd be agonizing over this, and that I'd better check up on you. You're blaming yourself, aren't you? You're blaming UJU. That's not the right place to lay the blame.'

'Rationally I know that.'

'Ah, but you keep seeing the images, right? From the vids.'

She nodded.

'And you're thinking about trying to leave UJU.' Dukayn's voice stayed level, almost warm. 'Aren't you?'

She could not look at him. He grabbed her by the shoulders and wrenched her around to face him. She felt trembling start around her mouth and spread like plague until she was shaking in his hands.

'What were you going to do?' Dukayn's voice turned soft. 'Tell Sé Hivel everything? Throw yourself on his mercy? Beg him to protect you?'

When she tried to speak, the shaking overwhelmed her voice. How had he known? How could he have known? He stared into her eyes.

'No, Jevon.' He was whispering. 'No. You can't leave. We need you, and you know a great deal – you know as much as any of us. If you try to leave I'll kill you. I'll find a way, no matter how many Garang your employer hires. You know I will. I'm the one who set up the security system here, aren't I? I'm the one who knows how to circumvent it.'

She could only stare at him and shake. He tightened his grip on her shoulders until the pain made her whimper.

'Am I hurting you?' He smiled a little. 'UJU-Prime wanted you killed right away. He knew you'd break. I talked him out of it. Do you understand? You owe me, Jevon. You owe me your life.'

For a moment she thought that she would faint, tossed her head back and saw the ceiling spin. Dukayn loosed his grip a slight degree. When she looked at him, his smile sickened her.

'Terrified?' he whispered. 'Good.'

He bent his head and kissed her, forced her slack mouth open with his and kissed her again. For a moment she could neither think nor move, trapped by her terror. He shifted his weight against her, flung her down across the bed, and laughed when she started to struggle. She tried to twist free, but he threw one leg across her and pinned her down.

'Don't scream,' he whispered. 'You won't like what'll happen if you do.'

All her will broke. She fell back against the bed and felt herself tremble in cold sweat. With one hand he pinned her hands above her head; with the other he pulled back her robe and opened his trousers. The act itself was mercifully brief. He was so aroused by her terror that he'd barely entered her when he came. When he released her, she rolled away from him and wondered why she couldn't cry. She had never wanted to weep more in her life, but the tears refused to fall. Dukayn grabbed her by the shoulder and hauled her back to face him.

'I'll probably never do that again,' he said. 'Don't worry about it.'

He got up, fastened his trousers, and strode out of the room.

Jevon lay on her bed and stared at the ceiling. She felt like a heap of old rags thrown to the floor, filthy and too limp to move. She could kill herself. She only had one way out that she could see: suicide. And what would that do to her mother? All at once she sobbed, rolled over on her stomach and began to weep in great convulsions of sobs. There was no way out at all.

Two hours later, Karlo Peronida, First Citizen, with the full support of Centre Council and a slight majority of support on the interactives, declared martial law. His regiment of Garang Marines were placed 'at the disposal' of the Protectors' Guild with Captain Nikolaides sworn in as a temporary deputy to head them up. The captain's first action was to establish a curfew for Leps at the twenty-twos with the proviso that those Leps working night jobs could be deen typed and apply for exemptions. The curfew, of course, would protect Lep citizens. Hadn't a Lep been found dead in South Canal, murdered by one of the terrorists? Not that there was any proof of the link, Kata thought bitterly. But Nikolaides knew a point to make when he saw one. He had to hand it to the dung-sucking little human.

Kata had learned all of this in snatches of news from the public vidscreens in Pleasure Sect, while he staggered around dressed in filthy clothes and carrying a pair of equally filthy canvas shopping bags. He sang little snatches of pop songs to himself, and every now and then he drooled. Whenever he saw a brightly coloured piece of litter, he would stoop and pick it up, examine it carefully, then tuck it into one of the bags, which held his websling and shoulder sack under the decorations. No-one ever stopped and questioned him, neither the Protectors nor the one pair of Garang soldiers that he saw.

Toward sunset he began ambling in the direction of the Carillon Tower. A couple of times he turned out of the direct way and wandered down side streets, still singing, still drooling, but he kept one eye on the fading light. He needed find some kind of shelter before the curfew cracked down. Why not satisfy his curiosity at the same time? This time he approached the tower from the street and walked up the public stairs rather than using Vida's longtube route. At the base of the tower he walked round and round, looking for a hidden exit. He found nothing.

By then twilight lay heavy and grey over the gardens. Kata crouched in the shadows, dumped his day's take of litter, and stuffed the canvas bags back into the shoulder sack. He put on the websling, slung the sack over his back, and waited. At any moment the outdoor lighting would turn on, but he needed the twilight as thick as possible before he risked the climb up. Finally he could bear to wait no longer. Under the clinging vines he found the trellis that had served Vida as a ladder and climbed, fast and easily, up to the bell tower. He swung himself over the edge and behind the covering wall just as the lights snapped on.

There was no way out. He sat on the floor and stared at the black obsidian pillar, the floor, the encircling wall. No lift booth, no stairs – nothing! How could she have escaped?

'It hardly matters,' he said aloud. 'Tomorrow she'll be dead, and I won't have to worry about her any more.'

Kata had brought with him a meat stick, a bottle of water, and a detailed map of Government House. After he'd eaten, he studied the plans with a tiny penlight. The Cathedral itself would be heavily guarded, of course, but the warren of Government House, its buildings and monuments, wooded areas and canals, would shelter him after he picked up his pulse rifle. He could see any number of lanes of movement that would bring him close to the Cathedral – close enough for the long-range gun. Sooner or later she would have to come out, and when she did, he would kill her.

He put his map away, pillowed his head on his shoulder sack, and slept, buried in the shadows of the Carillon Tower while overhead the police choppers thudded through the air.

In the dark silence of Datechange Rico followed Dukayn through East Tower's roof garden. Fog hung low; it dripped from the vine arbours and transformed the gleam of phosphorescent blooms into eyes, peering through the night. Lit from within, the blueglass surveillance centre glowed in the middle of frond-trees. Beyond it he could see a landing pad, luminescent in silver. At the door Dukayn laid a hand on an ident plate. The door slid open.

'I've brought the cybertech.'

The entire room glittered with top-rank photonics: a full Mapstation, surveillance screens, comm taps, tracer circuits, scanners of every kind. Two men with the robes of Lifegivers but the stance of soldiers waited by a long control panel.

'All right, Hernanes, let's get that loop of yours up and running,' Dukayn said. 'I'll need it piped into every security system in Government House.'

'Okay, that won't be a problem.'

'What about this? Can you get the alarm to transmit directly to one of my chips?'

'Probably.' Rico hesitated, struck by a sudden thought. 'Can I use that Mapstation to play around a little? I just might be able to go you one better. If we set up triangulations from long-range scanners and channel that to your neural input, you might be able to trace him directly. We could mark his course on a map, but what I'm hoping is that the chip will flash in the corner of your vision. When you get near him, the flashes would come closer together, so you'd know you were zeroing in. But I'll need chip access for that, if I can even do it.'

Dukayn hesitated, torn.

'You can replace that chip or encrypt it again after Kata's caught,' the taller Lifegiver said. 'What Hernanes is offering sounds pretty damn good to me.'

'Right, Brother Thom.' Dukayn nodded briskly. 'Okay, cybertech. Let's get to work.'

Linking Dukayn's neural chip into the scanner system proved possible, but it took Rico half the night to do it. By the time they were certain the tracer would work, the fives were just chiming. Dukayn offered him a cot in the duty room just off the surveillance centre and the chance to get a few hours' sleep.

'We'll need you here later,' Dukayn said. 'Just in case something goes wrong.'

'All right,' Rico said. 'Glad I can help.'

Rico took off his boots, then lay down on the narrow cot fully-dressed. As he was drifting off to sleep, he was thinking about Wan Peronida and how much he hated him.

* * *

'Well, it's here,' Vida said. 'The day I sign Wan's contract. I can't get out of it now.'

'I wish it was only the signing,' Samante said. 'I hope to God that I don't end up wearing black for you, too.'

They were sitting in the eatery, sharing breakfast. From the undraped windows a pale shaft of watery sunlight fell across the table. Vida laid her hands into the brief warmth.

'I was thinking,' Vida said. 'If this were a holonovel, you know? The assassin would get into Government House, then outwit everybody until the last minute. He'd burst into the Cathedral in the middle of the ceremony, and just as he was about to kill me, Wan would save me. It would be awfully romantic, wouldn't it? And then I wouldn't mind marrying him.'

'This isn't one of your beastly holonovels.'

'Oh, I know. It'll probably be Jak.'

'That's not what I mean. I'm just afraid that –'

'That no-one will save me? Well, yeah. I thought of that too. But there's going to be guards everywhere.'

'I'm frightened, Vida, really really frightened. Palace always seemed so safe, and now I feel like anything could happen.'

'Really? It never seemed safe to me, not in Pleasure Sect.'

'No? Well, no, I don't suppose it did.'

Samante picked up a fruit roll and tried a bite, then put it back down.

'There's one thing I wanted to tell you,' Vida said abruptly. 'With your law-uncle gone, you could leave this job if you wanted. I know you're wasting yourself here, with all your interpreter's training, I mean, and I know you never wanted to be anyone's factor. My feelings won't be hurt if you leave.'

For a moment Vida was afraid that Samante would cry.

'That's awfully kind of you,' Samante said at last. 'But you promised me that job as the L'Var Chief Interpreter, remember? A position like that's worth waiting for, so I think I'll just stay on.'

They looked at each other and smiled. Vida was groping for something to say that wouldn't come out sentimental when from the kitchen rang the crash and ping of breaking glass. Samante shrieked and clamped one hand over her mouth. Vida leapt to her feet and yelled.

'Greenie!'

Moaning and stinking, the saccule appeared in the doorway with the remains of a flower vase in its hands just as Jak came barrelling in from the gather. Although Samante laughed, the sound edged toward hysteria.

'Oh by the Eye!' Samante said. 'I don't know what I thought that was.'

'The assassin, of course.' Jak scowled at Greenie. 'Wretched animal! Go clean that up!'

With a skirl from a chest sac Greenie skittered off. Growling under his breath Jak turned and stalked away.

'We're all going to be nervous wrecks till this is over, let's face it.' Vida sat back down. 'TeeKay and Dan said they'd go through with it, by the way. Being witnesses, I mean.'

'Did they really?'

'Oh yeah. TeeKay said: shit, this is the first exciting thing that's ever happened to me. You can't cut me out of it now.'

This time Samante's laugh sounded normal.

'Well, then, at least I don't have to worry about finding you last-minute witnesses. That's something, I suppose.'

Out on the Map, Hi borrowed Rico's rhomboidal personal icon, which Riva would most likely identify as a directory and ignore. He reached the frame page location of Rico's deen sig insertion device, placed the rhomboid in a row of similar icons, and settled in to wait.

The contract ceremony would begin at the thirteens. Just at the twelves Kata reached the east gate of Government House. He was wearing his Power Guild coveralls, stripped of the janitorial greys, with new Power Guild ID pinned to a breast pocket, and carrying his toolkit. On the far side of the broad avenue, at the corner of a cross-street, he stopped and considered the situation. In front of the only functional entrance to Government House traffic snarled and backed up for at least two blocks: robocabs, private cars, service trucks, the occasional public bus. Just inside the entrance itself, a two-lane gap in the blueglass walls, he could see checkpoints. He'd expected no less. With Riva working behind the scenes, they weren't going to matter.

Swinging his toolkit in one hand, his false papers ready in the other, Kata crossed the street. A side walk led to the pedestrian lane off to one side, where a long line of servants, technicians, and government workers, more than a few of them Leps, waited with papers in hand. As the line inched along, Kata yawned every now and then, glanced around, kept checking the time implant in his wrist. Other sapients were doing the same, but he was doubtless the only one timing the circuits of the surveillance choppers overhead. When the line made a turn, he could see ahead a guard kiosk and beyond it a pair of Garang Marines. Those he hadn't expected, although as he thought about it the precaution seemed reasonable enough.

His turn came at last. At the wide window in the kiosk he laid his papers down, then slung his toolkit up next to them for inspection. He knew that his hands were crossing an invisible scanner beam, but he moved no faster than any sapient would. A human woman took the kit and began going through it while a clerk inspected the papers.

'Slow going, huh?' he said.

'Yeah,' the clerk said. 'Here's your papers back. I've stamped them. Just show the stamp when you're stopped again, and believe me, buddy, you will be.'

'All right, good.'

The guard looked up sharply.

'Hey,' Kata said. 'Do you think I want to see another tragedy? I'd rather wait in line half a day than that.'

'That's a good attitude to have. Wish more people shared it.'

With a smile the woman returned his kit. Kata raised his crest politely and walked on.

'He's here,' Dukayn said. 'There goes the alarm. Code red, Brother Thom.'

The Lifegiver turned to the control panel and hit a preprogrammed switch. Rico let out his breath in a long sigh. All morning he'd brooded the fear that his fix-up would fail.

'Hernanes, stay here and watch.' Dukayn gestured at the vid-screen, windowed with surveillance feeds. 'Just in case.'

'Damn right I will.'

With a quick wave Dukayn strode out. Rico settled into a chair in front of the screen. He had a brief moment of wishing that he could hunt with Dukayn's pack. He wanted to get hold of a weapon and run Kata down, or maybe even kill him for Vida's sake. You're as bad as she is, he told himself. Holonovels! He looked at his hands, his long slender fingers, bred for the fine work that he could do so well. In a way, in the way that would count, he already had them around Kata's neck.

* * *

Kata had nearly reached his hidden rifle when all his instincts started screaming that something was wrong. Behind him the traffic began thinning out, as if the entrance had been suddenly closed. All around him lay the office buildings that did the real work of Government House, but the normal noise of the day had turned hushed, as if somewhere at the perimeter of his vision police were clearing pedestrians out of harm's way.

Kata darted off the sidewalk, ran across a lawn, and reached the stand of heavy frond-trees planted between two windowless power stations. He squatted in the shadows among the trees and began to dig through the fallen fronds and soft dirt, pulpy with mushrooms. When his fingers touched cold plastosheet, his crest waved. He pulled out the sack holding his rifle, slid off the plastosheet covering, and retrieved the pieces. First the ceramic barrel, then the battery pack snapped into the housing. He was armed. He got up, leaving the sack and the toolkit where they lay.

Kata had planned on carrying the rifle, in pieces and inside his shoulder sack, as he walked openly toward the Cathedral, which was bordered on one side by the cloisters of the Eye but on the other by a heavily planted park that would have provided shelter. No hope for that now – he slunk through the corridor of frond-trees and surveyed the terrain around him. Overhead, he could hear the choppers gathering, sweeping in wide circles. Would they be projecting scanner beams? What had gone wrong? Somehow or other Riva had failed to hide him. That was all he needed to know.

Off to the north beyond the power stations lay open lawns and two tall office buildings – no cover there. He turned and looked down the corridor of frond-trees toward the south. Their shelter ran for about half a block more; beyond it he could see a spread of low buildings and narrower streets that, he knew from studying his maps, housed shops and restaurants. He'd hoped to avoid them. Cursing under his breath, moving from tree to tree, the pulse rifle ready, he headed south, then paused in the shadows at the end of his safe corridor.

A lone Protector, unarmoured, was trotting down the sidewalk and talking into a comm unit as he went. Kata stepped out behind him and fired. The silent pulse struck the Protector in the middle of his back; he spasmed as his heart locked, then fell forward, hitting the sidewalk hard. Kata raced forward and grabbed the comm unit, then ran across the street. Far behind him someone shouted. In the middle of a turquoise lawn stood a grotesque white structure of huge pillars and statues – some sort of monument. Kata darted in among them. For a few seconds the shiny white stone would confuse tracer beams. He clamped the comm unit to his ear and heard a calm, dark voice – Dukayn, most likely.

'He's heading toward the shopping village. Red Four, swing around on Tay Avenue. Gold Seven's coming up to reinforce. Shit! We have a casualty. Kata's armed.'

They were tracking him down as easily as they'd find a Lep at an UJU rally. Hostages! Kata turned and ran for the shopping village. In his ear, the voice kept talking, disposing units of Garang Marines in a deadly circle. Overhead the choppers swung lower and pounded the air. The circle was drawing in smaller, tighter. Kata ducked down a service alley, turned to a flimsy back door, kicked it open, and burst through into a fruit market. Orange, red, and blue: the merchandise lay in bright, tidy rows on counters in the utterly empty store – not a clerk, not a customer, no-one. Dukayn must have cleared the entire area.

'So. This is the day I die. Very well, we'll see who goes with me.'

Kata ran to the front door and looked out into a deserted street, glanced each way and saw Marines charging from both ends. He ducked back into the market, swirled around and saw a human man, dressed in black and carrying a long black tube, standing in the back door. Kata swung up his rifle, but the fellow fired first. Some sort of energy weapon – Kata suddenly realized that he was still alive, still thinking. He'd been hit by some sort of stun beam. He could not move. His legs were collapsing under him. With an effort of will he tried to fire the rifle, but his hands spasmed and flung it to the floor. He managed one step, lurched, hit a bin, and fell in a long spray of tumbling red plums, smashing like drops of blood on the floor around him. He tried to speak, failed, and realized that his entire body had gone numb. The man in black laughed.

'I'm Dukayn,' he said. 'You're not going die, Kata, not just yet. I'm going to enjoy watching your execution on the vids.' He raised his voice. 'All right, men. Good job. Let's get this bastard into custody.'

Up in the blueglass security centre, Rico and Brother Thom both leapt from their seats and yelled, one sharp bark of victory, then watched the Garang Marines snap a control collar around Kata's neck. Two of them hauled him up by the arms and began dragging him away.

'I can't believe my fix-up worked so well,' Rico said.

'Don't sell yourself short, Hernanes. If you ever had a yen to do security work, Dukayn would take you on in a minute.'

'Yeah? Thanks, but no thanks.' Rico called up his time implant: just shy of the thirteens. 'Well, I'll be getting on my way.'

'You could stay and watch the ceremony if you wanted. It'll be starting any moment. You'll get to see it from all angles up here, that's for sure. Or are you one of the lucky ones with an invitation?'

'No. Thanks anyway, but I think I'm going to go get some sleep.'

Rico turned and strode out, walking fast without really watching where he was going. Any moment. Any moment now the music would start, the cardinal would walk out into the Gaze and call the congregation assembled there to witness the signing of the contract. Rico collided with a wooden bench, clutched the back in both hands, and stood shaking in the chilly light.

'Vida,' he whispered. 'Don't, Vida, don't.'

He looked up at flowering trees, nodding in the wind. Tired as he was, he would never sleep. All at once he wanted to get out of Government House, go home to the family compound, maybe. Anywhere would do but here, so close to Vida, so unreachably far away.

'You mean it's over?' TeeKay wailed. 'Nothing's going to happen? Oh –' She glanced around the small robing room, decorated with symbols of the Eye. 'Oh how loath.'

'Sé Tina, you are the only sapient in this building who could say such a thing.' Jak was holding a comm unit to his ear. 'The duty sergeant with Dukayn tells me that they have captured the Outcast alive, Sé Vida. He will be incarcerated in the high security facility in Centre Sect. You need worry about nothing.'

'May God be praised.' Cardinal Roha raised his hands to heaven. 'Let us thank the Holy Eye.'

During the prayer Vida barely listened, looked instead at the wedding party assembled around her: TeeKay in demure lace, Dan in green velvet, Wan and Karlo in their Fleet dress uniforms, Sister Romero in a black cassock with a white stola draped round her neck. The Papal Itinerant would be standing in her mother's place for the ceremony. It was an immense honour, of course, but Vida would have given half the L'Var fortune to have Aleen there instead.

Aleen would watch her daughter's first marriage contract on the vidscreens, as no doubt everyone in The Close would watch, relishing the sight of one of theirs who had got out to a better life and freedom. I'm no different than the rest of you, Vida thought to them. Wan looked at her with a slight smile and one eyebrow raised. She'd seen him drinking half the morning, and she hoped he wouldn't drop the pen or something equally embarrassing. Tonight she'd have to sleep with him, would have to start paying in advance for the Peronida support she needed to keep this new and better life.

The cardinal finished the prayer. In the silence Vida could hear music filtering into the robing room and the sound of voices from the crowded Gaze outside.

'Very well,' Roha said, smiling all around. 'When I give the signal, you all file in.'

Vida felt dread clutch her stomach. How can I do this? she asked herself. Because she wanted to be a L'Var. Because she wanted a seat on Centre Council. Because she wanted to stay a somebody on Palace, not merely be some cull who was lucky enough to contract into the Cyberguild. To the swelling of the music the cardinal strode out of the room.

If this were one of her holonovels, she would suddenly announce that she couldn't go through with it, that she was going to sign a contract with Rico Hernanes y Jons and so they could all go hang. She could see herself, sweeping out of the room in her long green gown, rushing into the Gaze to make her announcement to everyone seated there, waiting. She would look up and there would be Rico, standing in the back of the Cathedral. She would run down the aisle and throw herself into his arms, and –

'There's the signal,' TeeKay said. 'Shall we?'

'Yeah,' Vida said. 'Let's get it over with.'

Somewhere around the fourteens Hi realized that Riva was never going to make an attempt to destroy Rico's deen sig loop. Through his cyberarm's grid link he received the news that Kata was safely captured and Vida safely married. Riva had no reason left to wander into his trap. Since the cyberdrugs were wearing off, he could feel his body aching and complaining. He left the Map, disengaged his cyberarm from its jacks, and stood up, stretching, to find Molos waiting in the doorway. The Lep had dressed himself in the dirty grey rags that meant mourning to his people.

'How long have you been there?' Hi said. 'You could have taken that other chair.'

'I just arrived.' Molos limped in and sat down with a long hiss. 'I've come to ask a favour, Hivel. I called the prison. They won't let me see my brother. They think I represent a threat to security.'

'I'll get hold of Dukayn.'

'Thank you.' Molos leaned back in the chair. 'I'm very tired. I never thought that this particular present would turn into a past, that Kata – that Nalet, I can use his real name again – would ever really be caught. Now he has no future.'

'Yeah, sure doesn't.' Hi gestured at the mourning clothes. 'He's the last bloodkin you have left, isn't he?'

'Yes. These rags are for the line of Tal, not for him.'

'For their sake, I'm sorry.'

'Thank you. But for your son's sake, I'm glad Nalet is going to die.'

They shared a silence.

'You've probably guessed this already,' Hi said at last. 'Riva never showed up to try to protect him.'

'Yes, I assumed that you'd be celebrating a victory if you'd tagged her. Things look grim on that front. I logged on using the Gate just at the twelves, as we'd planned. I went to her protected area in the old Citizen Assist net and found it destroyed.'

'What?'

'Wiped clean away. The revenant data is gone, completely gone, not a routing mark, not a trace, nothing. I didn't want to contact you on the Map, of course, and spoil your trap.'

'It didn't matter. We've lost her.'

'Not forever. Do you really think she'll be able to stay off the Map?'

'Oh no. She's too damn clever for that.'

'Not clever enough. We'll be on our guard now.'

'Yeah, yeah, but how the hell did she figure out we've been spying on her?'

'She couldn't. There is no way that she could have known without us knowing she knew. She must have panicked when she discovered Rico's looping input icon. That was very clever of your nephew, by the way.'

'I thought so, yeah.' Hi found himself thinking of Arno. He shoved the thought away. 'Where is Rico, anyway? Did you see him when you came in?'

'No. I thought he'd be at the contract ceremony.'
'Not likely.'
'Are you going to Vida's reception? I assume you've been invited. She invited me, but I won't bring my mourning into her happiness.'
'She did, but I'll see her at the guild dinner instead. Let's see what Dukayn can do for you. I'll just give him a call.'

Rico couldn't remember exactly when he'd decided to go to Pleasure Sect. He went to the compound first, showered, and changed his coveralls for some of the non-guild clothes hanging in his old closet. The house seemed so empty that he left almost immediately. At the wiretrain station the E train bound for Pleasure Sect slid in first, and without thinking, as if he'd planned it all along, he boarded.

In a drizzling fog he walked down the Boulain until he found the square where he'd first seen Vida, talking to a Lifegiver at the festival. Two weeks ago – had it only been two weeks? In the near-rain the square stood deserted, but when he looked up he saw Vida or rather images of Vida looming above him on the enormous public vidscreens. In her flowing green gown she stood smiling next to Wan, posed with pen in hand at the special table for signing the contract, handed flowers to a small girl in the congregation, wagged a coy finger at her new husband, posed with Sister Romero. In the centre window her portrait gleamed, maybe twenty feet on a side, smiling down at the world. Her red hair hung unbound and free, and he found himself remembering the way it stuck to her face with sweat when he made love to her.

With an inarticulate mutter of pain, Rico turned away and started walking. He thought of going to The Close, but he realized that it held too many memories of her. They'd be talking about her, all the girls, envying her. Maybe the boys would, too. He was willing to bet that Wan Peronida was the kind of guy who'd appeal to that kind of boy. The thought gave him a great deal of satisfaction.

'Hey buddy, looking for some fun?'

She stood shivering in a doorway, a skinny girl dressed in a black skirt above her knees, a black loose shirt hanging half-open. She was pretty, but only in the way that all women on Palace were pretty, bland except for her red hair, cropped short like a boy's, the same colour as her Mark. Dyed, probably, but it caught him, that soft coppery gleam.

'I can get you drugs, too,' she said. 'Whatever you want.'

'I don't want drugs. How much?'

'Depends on what you want me to do.' She was smiling now, stepping out of her doorway, still shivering in the damp air. 'I can do a whole lot of things. Any way you want it.'

'Let's see some of them. A hundred?'

'Sure.' She brightened and slipped her arm through his. 'I work just down here. Let's get out of this rain.'

Down here turned out to be a cheap hotel sandwiched between a bar and an empty shop front. In a faded gold lobby a clerk wearing a grubby grey shirt sat behind a counter. When he saw the girl, he grunted once and returned to his vidscreen. He was watching Vida's reception after the ceremony, or rather some condensed version of it on the evening interactives, and he seemed totally absorbed in the images. Rich people danced in beautiful clothes inside a dimly-lit hall with an inlaid jadium floor.

When the red-haired girl tugged on his arm, Rico was glad to follow. They took a smelly lift booth up a floor and walked down a narrow hall to her room. She lived there, Rico realized, rather than just working out of it. He could tell by the cheap knick-knacks on the dresser, the clothes hung neatly in the closet, the landscape holo in a cheap frame on the wall, the blue and purple coverlet laid over the hotel blankets on the bed. Out of the window he could see the street, slick with a real rain, now, as the streetlights glimmered on.

'I'm so cold.' She sat down on the bed and curled her arms around her knees. 'At least it's warm in here tonight. They're so fucking cheap with the heat, usually. What's your name?'

'Rico. What's yours?'

'Betta. Come on and warm me up, Rico. You're awfully cute.'

'Think so?' Rico took off his damp jacket and tossed it onto the dirty blue armchair.

For an answer she pulled her shirt over her head and threw it onto the floor. When he sat down beside her she turned, half-naked into his arms.

At her reception Vida danced with everyone but Wan. For the entire afternoon, her new marriage partner sat and drank, or stood and drank, or walked around holding a drink. In the evening, at the formal dinner, sponsored by the Conjoint Guild Council of the city, he did eat a decent meal. Since they were sitting together at the head of the banquet table, she could see that he was making some effort to sober up, refusing a second glass of wine, asking for water instead of an afterdinner drink. The long banqueting room with its sealed windows grew hot, the air thick with the smell of food and excited saccule waiters. Sweat beaded on Wan's face and ran, dampening the collar of his Fleet smock. What with the conversations of two hundred people and the music, the noise stabbed at her ears and threatened a headache. She knew that she had to stay or disappoint the very people whose high opinions would cement her career.

There were speeches. Wan began drinking again. Vida gobbled ice cream like a child and tried to remember Aleen's advice about customers. If they were really loathsome you were supposed to concentrate on how funny they looked, panting and sweating while you didn't really care. But Wan was in his way beautiful. She should concentrate on that, she supposed, and remember the way he looked on the day of disaster, so much in command, so much in love with danger. Her mind insisted on drifting to Rico.

The speeches ended. When Wan went to put his glass down on the table, he missed the edge and dropped it. In the general confusion, with people getting up, calling for coats, talking and laughing, no-one noticed. Leni appeared, also red-faced and sweating, to steady Wan when he got up.

'Vida,' Leni said. 'You go on ahead, okay? Wanito, we're going to the men's room. I'm gonna run your head under the cold water.'

Wan muttered something in Helane. From the way Leni winced, Vida was glad she understood none of it. As they walked, more or less steadily, out the door, Rico's uncle came up beside her.

'May I escort you home, Vida?'

'Thank you, Sé Hivel. I'd appreciate that.'

When they left the room, Jak fell in behind them a respectful distance away; he wore a comm set that linked him with Tower Security. Even with the ranks of lift booths that East Tower sported, the size of the crowd forced a long wait. Vida let Hi lead her down a side corridor to wait in a welcome draught of air from the cooling system. Jak waited at the juncture with the main hall. The silence soothed her, and she yawned.

'I'm sorry,' she said. 'It's been an awfully long day.'

'You bet, kid. You must be ready to drop.'

'I am, yeah, but at least I'm still alive. You don't think Kata's going to escape, do you?'

Although Vida was expecting the usual joke about her taste in fiction, Hi considered the problem seriously.

'No,' he said at last. 'Central Detention is the best planned prison in the Pinch. I helped install the cyberlocks, and they modelled the surveillance on Dukayn's system here. And beyond the fancy stuff, it's got damned thick walls.'

'Okay. Oh, I want to ask you – Dukayn said something to me this afternoon, just when I saw him at the reception, and I didn't really hear all of it. He said Rico saved my life.'

'That's about it, yeah.' Hi smiled briefly. 'Well, he wasn't the only one, but he figured out how to track Kata down before he could get too far in.'

Vida turned away and felt her pulse pounding in her throat like a trapped bird. Why wasn't Rico here? She wanted to bury herself into the shelter of his arms, stammer out her thanks and tell him she loved him.

'Hey, what's wrong?' Hi was speaking softly. 'You afraid he won't love you any more? That's the last thing you need to worry about.'

Vida felt tears well and spill. She rubbed them away, felt her make-up smear along with them, and realized that Hi was holding out a wad of tissue.

'Thanks.' She took them and wiped tears and make-up both away. 'Why do you Cyberguild people always have pockets full of tissue? Rico's the same.'

'For wiping input jacks. They generate a static field, and dust sticks to them.'

'That makes sense.' She glanced around, saw no receptacle, dropped the tissues for a cleaning bot to devour when the crews came through. 'Thank you. I mean, for – well, just thanks.'

'Sure.' Hi was looking down the corridor. 'The crowd's thinned out. We can go down now.'

At the door of her suite Vida wished that she could invite him in and keep him talking, knew it was impossible, and began wishing instead that Wan would forget where he was supposed to sleep that night. When she walked in, she found the high boots from his dress uniform lying in the middle of the gather floor. The narrow trousers were hanging over the arm of the sofa. Down the hall a light glowed from the master bedroom.

'Wan?'

No answer. She found the smock of his uniform, medals and all, lying in the hall, his underwear on the floor of the bedroom. Wan himself sprawled naked on his stomach across the bed. He'd thrown the covers onto the floor, apparently, and then fallen asleep clutching a pillow. His damp hair curled around his neck. Seeing Wan abstractly in the strong modelling of a bedside lamp, she had to admire how beautifully built he was, tall and lean, muscled like the athlete he was at heart. Just as she allowed herself to hope that he'd passed out and wouldn't wake till morning, he roused, pulling the pillow under his chest to prop himself up and yawning.

'Sorry,' he said.

'It's okay. It's been a long day.'

'Yeah.'

Vida took off her jewellery and laid it on a dresser top, tapped the smart thread at the neck of her gown and let it open and fall. Underneath she was wearing a long slip of the same green. In the mirror panel above the dresser she could see Wan watching her with an utterly unreadable expression. She picked up the gown and tossed it onto a chair, then pulled off the slip with a toss of her head to free her hair. She dropped it on top of the gown and walked over to the bed. Obligingly he rolled to one side so she could lie down next to him. He smelled of sweat mingled with the sweetness of half-metabolized drink. First customer, she thought. Rico was something different.

Thinking of him that way she could smile and cuddle close to him, run her fingers down his sweaty chest, mottled with dark hair. He laid one hand along her face and kissed her, made a small appreciative noise and kissed her again, then slid his hand down and found her breasts. She closed her eyes and thought of dancing, of going through the motions of a dance with a partner that she didn't know, who didn't matter. She was aware of every caress he gave her, rough but not brutal, and of every kiss; she could arch her back and murmur in pretended enjoyment; but all the while she wondered what was taking him so long. A few kisses more, and she reached down to fondle him. He was still soft.

At her touch he tensed and moved away. She opened her eyes to find him staring at her, his face set like stone.

'Wan, you've been drinking all damn day,' she said. 'That's all it means. We can wait, you know.'

With a wrench he pulled away from her and flopped onto his stomach again, his arms wrapped around the pillow. He looked so miserable that she reached out and stroked his hair.

'I'll bet you're just awfully tired.' She made her voice sound as soothing as she could muster. 'It happens to a lot of guys.'

'Shut up, will you?'

'I was just trying to –'

'Shut up!'

Vida sat up and found the other pillow lying on the floor. She fetched it and lay down again, tucking it under her head. Wan went on staring at the headboard as if he were memorizing the pattern in the synthiwood.

'Do you want to just go to sleep?' she said.

He glanced her way, then got up and turned his back on her. Lying down, lying still felt too good for her to argue when he picked up his underwear from the floor and put it on. Through half-closed eyes she watched him walk out, saw him stoop to pick up his smock and disappear into the gather. She could hear him pulling on clothes, though, she supposed, he wouldn't be able to get the boots back on without help. In a few minutes she heard the suite door opening, then sliding shut.

'I'll have to figure something out,' she said aloud. 'He's supposed to get me pregnant.'

She sat up, running her hands down her arms. The smell of his sweat clung to her. Briefly she thought of taking a shower, then pulled the sheet and blankets up and lay down again. She fell asleep before she could remember to tell the lamp to turn itself off.

The stun beam wore off some hours into the evening, as far as Kata could tell. His cell lay underground. It contained a bunk with no sheets or blankets, a toilet with no lid, three smooth green walls, a smooth grey floor, and in one corner at the high ceiling, the black eye of a surveillance camera. A forceshield made up the fourth wall. Through the transparent shield Kata saw a broad grey hallway and another wall, blue in this case. To wear they gave him a coverall in a fluorescent white that would show purple in certain kinds of light and the control collar, a smooth light bit of fabric embedded with circuits. It was so lightweight, so humane, that he could forget he was wearing it. Any jailor with the right transmit could make him spasm and writhe upon the floor. That they did not let him forget.

They gave him food. They had a medic examine him to make sure the stun beam had caused him no permanent injury. They told him that first thing on the morrow morning a court-appointed attorney would come to defend him. They told him he had rights;

they read off the list of them while he listened, his heart pounding in hatred. Then at last they left him alone. He lay upon the bunk with his arms crossed over his chest and hated. By that point he hated no particular person or species. He merely hated. He was hate, he breathed hate, hate became his blood and bone.

At some point he slept. He woke suddenly at the sound of sapients walking down the hall and sat up, swinging his legs over the side of the bunk. Two human guards appeared, striding fast. They stopped just at the far side of his cell. Behind them limped his brother, draped in grey mourning rags. Kata got up and walked over to the force-field just as a second pair of guards took up a place at the other side. He could hear quite clearly, though sounds and voices seemed distorted to a higher pitch.

'Well, Molos,' he said in Lepir. 'I see you still have that limp I gave you.'

'Speak to me in Gen,' Molos said in that language. 'That's the bargain I made with your jailers.'

One of the guards raised his hand to show Kata the transmit he was holding. Kata spoke Gen.

'I'm surprised you'd come to see me.'

'So am I.' Molos let his crest lift. 'As for my unfortunate leg, yes, the med tech on Souk regenerated the bone, but the nerves presented a very difficult set of problems. You were quite thorough.'

'Not thorough enough. I wanted to kill you. I wish I had.'

'That was obvious at the time. I'd need to be rather obtuse to have missed your intentions. Let me see, how did that go? First you ran me over with a fivewheel, then you threw me into a lake to drown. I have trouble remembering the actual incident.'

Kata said nothing, remembering that ugly afternoon on Souk. Sheer bad luck, that was all – sheer bad luck that someone had come along to pull Molos out of the lake again.

'But that's neither here nor there,' Molos continued. 'I've come on a fool's errand. I'm asking you to turn state's evidence.'

Kata let his crest rustle in answer.

'I'm asking you for the good of our people,' Molos went on. 'Nothing you do will save your own life.'

'Yeah? They're going to have to prove the charges against me.'

'No. There are quite a lot of old ones that will do very nicely. I heard from the Ri embassy as soon as your capture hit the vids. They want to extradite. You'd have an easier time of dying here.'

'It'd be faster here, that's for sure. What do you want? Information about Riva?'

'Exactly. Nalet, think! If this group goes on committing acts of terrorism, the Peronida will never lift martial law. Bit by bit, every guild, every sect, every other race on this planet will turn against us. Millions of Leps who want nothing more than peace are going to suffer because –'

'Let them,' Kata broke in. 'Can't you see? Until they suffer they'll never fight. They'll never take back what's theirs. And if they don't take it back, no-one's going to give it to them. You're the one who needs to think. You know what's happened here this past week? Riva's lit a fire, a beacon, and it's blazing in our people's hearts and souls. What do you think I'm going to do? Piss on it and put it out?'

Molos spread out his hands and bowed his head. His crest hung flaccid.

'No,' Molos said at last. 'No, I didn't really think you'd do anything at all. But I had to ask. I had to give you that chance.'

Kata spat into the force-field. It crackled silver and hissed. Molos stood his ground.

'What do you think is going to happen when they kill you?' Molos said. 'You'll be a martyr? A hero to the Lep cause? A real Lep at last? That's always been the core, hasn't it, Nalet? I feel it too. I've come to terms with it, but I know what it means to be caught between two worlds, two cultures, two races. You've never felt that we, that you, belong to our own people. Well, you still don't. Why do you think they call you the Outcast?'

'Stop it! I don't want to hear it.'

'No, I won't stop. No more diplomat. This is brother to brother. Yes, it was stupid of our mother to do what she did, stupid of her to raise us herself, to pretend that we were human children and fuss over us the way her human friends fussed over their children. She was a shallow little thing, yes, and yes, she was only doing it to be fashionable. She kept us out of the nests, kept us away from the *mahtis*, turned us both into outcasts among our own people. Don't you think I know how it hurt? The other boys spat on me as much as they spat on you. But at the end, when our house fell out of favour, she sent us away to safety, and she chose to remain on Ri and die with our father. It was a brave thing on both accounts.'

'Stop it!' Kata screamed it out. 'Shut your filthy mouth! I will not listen to this!'

When the guard raised his transmit, Molos turned to him.

'That won't be necessary. The force field's all the protection I need.'

Kata began to shake. His hands dug the air beyond his power to stop them. It was the ultimate humiliation, that his brother was in the position to spare him humiliation. For a long moment Molos considered him.

'I'm wearing these rags for her,' Molos said. 'Just in case you wondered. That's why you wanted to kill me, isn't it, Nalet? Because I know. I know how we were set apart, and I know how you hated it, being set apart.'

As slowly as he could manage, Kata turned away. He walked, also slowly, with his head held high and his traitor hands clasped to stop their digging, to the bunk and lay down. He rolled over with his back to Molos and stared at the wall until at last, he heard them all leave.

Just at dawn Rico staggered into the Cyberguild suite to find Nju awake and sitting in the gather. The Garang leapt to his feet and called out.

'Sé Hivel! He's back.'

Rico supposed that he was about to get the lecture of his life. At the moment he felt too sick to care, nauseated, shaky, and his head throbbed with pain. He walked to a window and threw it open for the fresh air. Outside in a pink dawn green spores fell like rain.

'Are you ill?' Nju said.

'Sort of. Not really.'

'You smell of some peculiar beverage.'

'That's why I'm ill, okay?'

Nju raised plumed eyebrows to the heavens and walked out of the gather. Rico heard him speaking to Hi in the hall; then his uncle strode in.

'Where the hell have you been?' Hi snarled.

'You really want to know? I picked up a cheap whore, and about Datechange I bought her a bottle of something, I don't remember what, and we both drank it, on and off all night. I don't think I ate anything all night. I don't remember. And now I feel like hell. Okay? That enough details?'

Hi sighed in a long exhalation of disgust.

'What have I done?' Rico snapped. 'Broken guild discipline?'

'No. I was worried about you.'

'Why?'

'Because it's dangerous out there on the streets at night.'

'Yeah? You're the one who runs around without your bodyguard.'

'I'm the one who used to. Think, kid! This bombing – these terrorists. You'd make a pretty good hostage. The guild would spend a lot to get you back.'

Rico sat down on the sofa and sprawled, stretching his legs out in front of him. The pain in his head was centring itself in the middle of his forehead.

'We can talk about it later,' Hi said. 'You need to sleep all day. But Palace is never going to be the same, you know. Kata's going to die, but Riva's won this round. People are never going to feel safe again. And you know something? They shouldn't.'

Under the dome of her private office Aleen stood next to the crystal globe of Palace and rested one hand upon it. Vida paused just inside the door and looked around at the holosculptures in their niches. She'd loved this room as a child, with all the treasures displayed on its walls and the programmable dome. When she glanced up, she saw images of blue sky, just touched here and there with clouds.

'So you've come back?' Aleen said. 'It's good to see you, but I'm rather surprised.'

'Well, it's safe now,' Vida said. 'I wanted to see everyone. I wanted to see you.'

Aleen allowed herself a small smile.

'You look good,' she announced. 'I like that suit. It's an excellent cut for your figure.'

'Thanks.'

Vida realized that for the first time in her life, she'd forgotten something. She'd written a little speech that morning, but the words had disappeared from her mind. Aleen gestured at a formfit, then sat in her datachair and smoothed her long blue dress over her lap. Vida sat opposite her and tried to remember exactly how that clever opening had gone, while Aleen considered her, neither coldly nor fondly. Finally Vida could stand the silence no longer.

'Mama, did you love my father?'

Aleen opened her mouth and made a startled little noise – not exactly a gasp, more a stifled curse.

'How the hell did you find out?' she said at last.

'Well, a friend of mine is Cyberguild – Sé Hivel's nephew, Rico. And he found out that someone had put those false files in the Protectors' databanks. I figured out that it was Molos.'

Aleen laughed with a rueful shake of her head.

'I always knew you were bright,' Aleen said. 'Not bad, sweetheart. Not bad at all. I couldn't tell you. Do you realize that? I would have told you if I could have, but you were just a child, and you might have blurted something out at the wrong time. Sure, maybe no-one would have cared if a cull had a little cull of her own, but I couldn't risk it.'

'I do understand, yeah. You were right, weren't you? As soon as someone did find out, I was in big trouble. That's one reason I wanted to come here now, to tell you that.'

Aleen leaned back in her chair and considered the far wall.

'As for your question, no, I didn't love Orin L'Var.' She was back to the self Vida knew: business-like and self-contained. 'I admired him, though. In fact, it was almost hero-worship. He affected people that way. He wasn't a saint or anything, but he was such a good man, so concerned, so decent, so determined to change Palace for the better. He wanted to abolish the laws that keep people in Pleasure Sect, Vida. He wanted to set us all free. He knew he could never abolish the Sect itself, mind. I don't suppose he even wanted to. That's what I mean about him. He had a hard-nosed practical side. He just wanted people to be able to choose to stay or go.'

'That's all we'd ask, isn't it?'

'Yes. And that's why I had his child when he asked me to. You were going to be a kind of – oh, how to put it? One day, when he had the votes he needed, he was going to bring you forward and say, see, this is my daughter. She was born in Pleasure, and I love her no less for it. And he was betting that the people in Palace would vote to let us all go.'

Vida's eyes filled with tears. Aleen pulled a handkerchief from her skirt pocket and tossed it over.

'Actually,' Aleen went on. 'It was pretty damn cold of him, if you think about it, raising a child like some kind of sacrificial animal. That's what I mean. I couldn't love him. He wasn't the kind of man you did love.'

'But did Roha know why my father wanted me?'

'Of course not! And don't you ever let it slip! I tried to warn you about Roha. Don't get too close to him. Now you know why.'

'All right. I won't.'

'Good. You can trust Hi Jons, though.'

'I kind of thought so. He's been awfully nice to me.'

'I'm glad to hear that. I'll have to thank him.' Aleen looked away again. 'He's the only man I've ever given a damn about. If I were ever stupid enough to actually fall in love with anyone, I'd have to say it was him.'

'But you'd never be that stupid, right?'

'Don't get smart with me, Vida. No matter what else, I'm still your –' All at once Aleen smiled. 'I'm still your mother.'

It was close to the eighteens when Vida returned to Government House and the East Tower. When she walked into her suite, she found Samante gone on her day off and a message from Leni waiting on the view screen. She started it playing, took off her jacket, then stood staring at the screen with the jacket dangling forgotten from her hand.

'Vida, I'm sorry,' Leni's image said. 'Wan asked me to call and let you know that he's going out to the swamps. It's a hunting trip. We'll be back in three days.' Leni glanced furtively over his shoulder, as if he'd been leaving the message when Wan was out of the room. 'I'll make damn sure it isn't any longer than that. He didn't tell me why we were going. I guess he's just being – ah well, see you soon.'

The message ended. Vida turned and hurled the jacket onto the sofa.

'You coward, Wan!' she snapped. 'Yeah, go off and kill something! Maybe it'll make you feel better.'

She could call Rico, if she dared. What if Sé Hivel was wrong, what if Rico wanted nothing more to do with her? It took her a long five minutes before she got up the courage to call him, and while she waited, watching the screen pulse, she felt cold all over. At last the comm flashed a 'received' message, and Rico's face appeared on the screen.

'Oh, it's you,' he said. 'What do you want?'

Vida sank into a chair. She could say nothing, merely stared at him while he stared back. With shaking hands she switched the comm off and laid the unit back in its slot.

'I couldn't have signed your contract,' she whispered. 'I guess you can't see why.'

Outside the window the fog swirled grey and dark. She watched it, unmoving, until the door alarm beeped. She heard Jak answering it, heard his voice, heard Rico's voice in turn and twisted round in her chair just as Rico strode into the gather. Jak turned bland eyes Vida's way, then retreated back to the eatery. Rico waited until he heard the door close.

'I'm sorry I hurt you,' he blurted. 'Forgive me?'

'Sure.' She stood up and held out her hand. 'Of course.'

He crossed to her, caught her hand in both of his, and drew her close for a kiss. She slipped her arms around his neck and felt him trembling against her.

'Wan's gone,' she said. 'For three days.'

His arms went slack around her waist. Vida leaned back and looked at him, suddenly distant, suddenly cold.

'Oh stop it!' she snapped. 'I'll bet you haven't been faithful to me, either.'

'So what?' Rico let her go and stepped back.

'What do you mean so what? Or is that supposed to be different?'

'Well, no, but –'

'Oh besides! Last night, you know? He couldn't even do it.'

'You're just saying that to make me feel better.'

'Am not. He'd been drinking all day, and he couldn't.'

Rico grinned, a slow spread of sheer malicious delight.

'But Rico? I'm going to have to, sooner or later. The whole point of this is to restore the L'Vars. I'm going to have to have a child, and that means –'

'Yeah, sure. But I'm not going to have to know about it. Last night – I mean – oh forget about it.'

'Okay. I still love you. Do you still love me?'

'Yeah.' He caught her face between his hands. 'Vida, maybe you're right about that hundred and fifty years, but I'll never love anyone again the way I love you.'

When he kissed her, the passion in that kiss convinced her that he spoke the simple truth.

'Then I'll never love anyone the way I love you,' she said. 'I promise.'

EPILOGUE

After a brief legal challenge by the government of Ri, the Palace courts set Vi-Kata's execution date for Nineteen Timber. Bidding for the rights went too high for Pansect Media. Once the eventual winner, Grid TransPalace, scheduled the execution for the prime evening hours, Kata's attorney filed an appeal on the method of death. The structure of the Lep neck made hanging such a hideously inhumane death that the courts had ordered a lethal injection. Kata wished to die by the ritual of the slow cuts, as befitted a man and a warrior. The courts rejected the appeal.

Zir forced herself to watch. Crouched in her upstairs room she clutched a pillow in her lap and let her claws shred it as her hands dug. She'd been thinking that guards would march Kata out to some sort of ceremony, but to her horror they wheeled him into a room that looked like an infirmary upon a bed that looked like a hospital gurney. He was strapped down, and he raged, throwing himself against the straps, struggling and fighting, screaming at them in Lepir.

'Not this coward's death!' Over and over he shouted it aloud. 'Kill me like a man!'

Zir felt her back arch in shared agony, and she moaned. Two human doctors stepped forward, each with a syringe. Only one held the drug; the other, merely distilled water, so that the cowards would never know which one of them had killed him.

'Kill him like a man,' she whispered.

She turned her head away at the last moment and dug her claws deep into the cushion. When she could force herself to look at the vidscreen again, Kata was already dead, limp under the straps.

'Oh my love,' she said aloud. 'I'll keep fighting. I'll keep the flames burning. I'll do it for the sake of our people, but I'll do it in your name.'